THE MAN
WITH THE
IRON HEART

HARRY TURTLEDOVE

THE MAN WITH THE IRON HEART

DEL
REY

BALLANTINE BOOKS
NEW YORK

Published in the United States by Del Rey Books, an imprint of The Random House Publishing Group, a division of Random House, Inc., New York.

DEL REY is a registered trademark and the Del Rey colophon is a trademark of Random House, Inc.

LIBRARY OF CONGRESS CATALOGING-IN-PUBLICATION DATA
Turtledove, Harry.
The man with the iron heart / Harry Turtledove.
p.   cm.
ISBN 978-0-345-50434-0 (acid-free paper)
1. Heydrich, Reinhard, 1904–1942—Fiction. I. Title.
PS3570.U76M36 2008
813'.54—dc22   2008011463

Printed in the United States of America on acid-free paper

www.delreybooks.com

2 4 6 8 9 7 5 3 1

First Edition

Book design by Karin Batten

THE MAN
WITH THE
IRON HEART

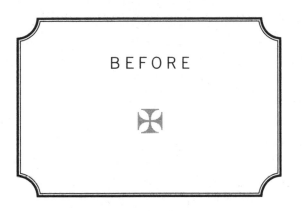

BEFORE

29 MAY, 1942—OUTSKIRTS OF PRAGUE

The big green Mercedes convertible bore a number plate of stark sim-
plicity: SS3. The *Reichsprotektor* of Bohemia and Moravia sped from
his country estate toward the Castle of Prague. German soldiers in
field gray and Czech guards in tobacco brown would salute him when
he arrived. Czech President Hacha also had his offices in the castle,
but his will was as nothing when set against the *Reichsprotektor*'s.
Everyone knew it—including Hacha.

Reinhard Heydrich glanced at his watch. "Step on it, Klein," he
said irritably. "We're running late."

"Right, sir," *Oberscharführer* Johannes Klein answered with a
silent sigh. If they were late, the senior noncom knew it wasn't more
than thirty seconds. Heydrich didn't tolerate tardiness . . . or much of
anything else.

Klein checked his own wrist. Not even half past ten yet. Like a lot
of big wheels, Heydrich bitched for the sake of bitching. He might
look like the perfect Aryan—tall and lean, blond and handsome. He
might be a first-class fencer and pilot and violinist. He had some little
old lady in him all the same.

They came to a corner a minute later. "Slow down," Heydrich said. "The trolley's pulling up."

"I see it, *Herr Reichsprotektor*." Klein sighed out loud this time. You couldn't win. "I see those worthless layabouts who've been hanging around the stop the past couple of days, too. Bums." To him, all Czechs were bums till proved otherwise.

"They look like men with jobs," Heydrich said. "That's a new overcoat the one of them has on."

"What's he doing with it?" Klein asked. The Czech fumbled with something in an inside pocket.

He got hold of it and pulled it out: a submachine gun, an ugly, brutally effective British Sten. He aimed it at Heydrich's chest and pulled the trigger.

However effective Stens usually were, this particular tin Tommy gun jammed. The Czech looked horrified. He jerked at the cocking handle and yelled something inflammatory in his own language.

"Jesus Christ!" Heydrich yelled, and then, "Halt!" He stood up in the passenger side of the car and drew the pistol he wore on his belt. The hammer clicked uselessly—the Luger wasn't loaded. Heydrich said something that had to be worse than what came out of the Czech's mouth.

Oberscharführer Klein had to fight not to piss himself—and not to giggle like a schoolgirl. Nobody's weapon wanted to work! Was this a fight to the death or a low farce?

Then, perhaps with the instincts he'd picked up flying a 109 on the Eastern Front, Heydrich thought to check six. When he looked behind him, he saw the other Czech who'd been hanging around this corner sneaking up on the car. "Gun it, Hans!" Heydrich shouted.

Klein's big booted foot mashed down on the accelerator. The Mercedes was heavy, but it leaped ahead as if somebody'd goosed it. The second Czech threw something. A bomb of some sort—it had to be.

It burst a few meters behind the hurtling auto. Heydrich yelped and swore and jerked his left hand. Blood ran down his palm and dripped from his fingers to the Mercedes' rubber floor mat. He tried to make a fist, then yelped again and thought better of it. Only after Klein flung the car around a couple of corners did the *Reichsprotektor* think to ask, "Are you all right?"

The driver reached up to touch his left ear. His gloved hand came away red. "Just a scratch." He paused a few seconds. "I think we've got away from the stinking bastards."

"*Ja* . . . if more of them aren't lying in wait for us." Again, Heydrich needed a moment to add, "You did well."

"Uh, thanks." Klein sounded a little shaky. Heydrich supposed he did, too. Anybody who suddenly got dropped into combat was liable to. The driver went on, "How's your hand? Shall I get you to a hospital?"

Heydrich was already wrapping a handkerchief around the wound. "No, don't bother. I'll live," he said. "Take me on to the Castle. A doctor'll be on duty there, or we can send for one. And then—" He stopped in grim anticipation.

"Then what, sir?" Klein asked.

"Then we peel this pesthole of a town—this pesthole of a country—to catch the assassins," Heydrich answered. "We don't overlook wrongs from Czechs—never, any more than we let Jews get away with anything inside the *Reich*."

"We don't let anybody get away with anything," Klein said—a good enough rule for the way Germany ruled.

Heydrich nodded. He tried to close his hand again. No luck. It hurt too much. Blood was soaking through the handkerchief. "No. We don't," he agreed. "And when somebody tries, we make him pay."

5 FEBRUARY 1943 — BERLIN

The Reich was in mourning after the fall of Stalingrad. Taverns, theaters, movie houses all closed, at the *Führer's* order. Funereal music played on every radio station. Reinhard Heydrich thought he'd kick in a receiver if he heard *"Ich Hatt' Ein Kamerad"* one more time.

Oberscharführer Klein pulled up in front of SS headquarters. "Here you go, sir," he said.

"Right." Heydrich got out of the Mercedes convertible. Not a trace of the damage from the assassination attempt remained visible on the car. The Czech repairmen who'd worked on the Mercedes would have answered with their necks if any had.

Guards stiffened to attention as Heydrich approached. In SS *Obergruppenführer's* uniform, with the SD patch on his lower left sleeve, his slim, athletic figure was one to conjure with. "State your name and business, sir." The young officer who made the demand knew damn well who—and what—Heydrich was. His voice wouldn't have wobbled if he hadn't.

After naming himself, Heydrich paused a moment for effect before continuing, "I am here for an appointment with the *Reichsführer-SS.*"

"Yes, sir," the youngster said, and his voice wobbled again. If *he'd* had an appointment with Heinrich Himmler, he would have been in more trouble than he could imagine. A parish priest was an honorable part of the Catholic Church, but that didn't mean he expected to get an audience with the Pope. Gathering himself, the officer told off two of his men to escort Heydrich to Himmler's office.

Somebody inside headquarters had a radio on. Sure as hell, it was playing *"Ich Hatt' Ein Kamerad."* Heydrich fumed. He couldn't do anything more, not when one of the black-uniformed men walking with him said, "Terrible thing, what happened in the east."

"Yes," Heydrich said. "Terrible." And it was. The whole Sixth Army . . . gone. Germany was in plenty of trouble in the rest of southern Russia, too. Heydrich was still sick of that goddamn song.

Hastily, the trooper added, "But we'll lick 'em anyway, won't we, sir?" You could get in trouble for showing defeatism. In these nervous times, you could get in trouble for almost anything.

More guards stood in front of the door to the *Reichsführer*'s sanctum. Heydrich's escorts handed him off to them, then went back toward the entrance with every sign of relief. "You're right on time, *Herr Obergruppenführer,*" one of Himmler's guards said.

"I should hope so." Heydrich was affronted. If he was ever late, he made whoever caused the lateness sorry. That he might be late through no fault of anyone else's never crossed his mind.

The guards brought him into Himmler's office. At a nod from their chief, they disappeared. "Good day, Reinhard," Himmler said. "How are you?" He used the familiar pronoun.

"Well enough, sir, thanks. And you?" Heydrich used the formal pronoun. He always had with Himmler, even if they'd worked hand in glove for years. He expected he always would.

It was a funny business. Heydrich knew he could tear Himmler to pieces if he wanted to. Himmler was on the pudgy side. He'd never been very hard physically. The round, almost chinless face behind the pince-nez could have belonged to a chicken farmer or a schoolmaster. To the man who led the outfit that vied with Beria's NKVD for deadliness? It seemed unlikely.

But it was true. And therein lay the rub. Himmler might not look like anything much. When he spoke, though, people listened. Having listened, they obeyed. If they didn't, they quickly departed the land of the living. Himmler, the mild-mannered bureaucrat, had even bureaucratized death. And, because he had, he could intimidate an outwardly tougher man like Heydrich.

And Himmler had another hold on the *Reichsprotektor*. There were rumors of Jews in Heydrich's family tree. Heydrich's father's mother's second husband had been named Süss. He'd even looked Jewish, though he hadn't been. A private genealogist had confirmed that, and the SS had accepted it. Further back, though, there was an unexplained Birnbaum. If Himmler decided that what had been accepted should be rejected . . .

A bead of sweat trickled down Heydrich's back. It seemed to burn like acid. He deliberately slowed his breathing. To his relief, his heart stopped fluttering. He couldn't let Himmler intimidate him, not today. His mission was too important; not for himself but for the Reich.

The Reich. *Think of the Reich, not of yourself.* As long as that was his lodestone, he'd be all right. He hoped.

Himmler steepled his fingers. "Well, Reinhard, what brings you up from Prague today?" His voice was fussy and precise, like a schoolmaster's.

One more deep breath. Forcing his voice to steadiness, Heydrich asked, "*Herr Reichsführer,* what do you think of Germany's war prospects in the light of recent developments?"

Himmler's right eyebrow twitched—only a couple of millimeters, but enough to notice. Whatever he might have expected, that wasn't it. He usually chose his words with care. He seemed especially careful now, answering, "In view of our, ah, misfortune at Stalingrad, this may not be the best time to ask."

"It isn't just Stalingrad, *Herr Reichsführer,*" Heydrich said.

Himmler's eyebrow twitched again. He also hadn't expected Himmler to persist. But the *Reichsprotektor* of Bohemia and Moravia did: "The Russians are taking big bites out of our positions in the east."

"That will stop. The *Führer* has personally assured me of it," Himmler said.

"Yes, sir." Heydrich's agreement was more devastating than any argument could have been. After letting it hang in the air, he continued, "Our allies aren't worth the paper they're printed on. Hungary? Romania? Italy?" He snapped his fingers in vast contempt. "The Finns can fight, but there aren't enough of them."

"What are you driving at, Reinhard?" Himmler's tone went silky with danger. "Are you saying the war is lost? Do you dare say that?"

"Yes, sir," Heydrich repeated. This time, Himmler's eyebrow didn't just twitch. It leaped. Heydrich had put his life—not only his career, but his life—in the *Reichsführer*'s hands. Having done so, he explained why: "The east is coming undone. Maybe we can patch it up, but I don't think so. And even if we can . . . The English and Americans are going to drive us out of Africa. We can't supply our troops there— that's been plain for a long time. And after they do, Sicily's one short hop away. Italy is one more. Can you tell me I'm wrong?"

"Is the castle in Prague haunted? You talk like a man who's seen a ghost," Himmler said.

"I wish it were, *Herr Reichsführer*. I wish I had," Heydrich said. "Instead, I've spent too damned much time looking at maps." He paused, then added, "The bombing's getting worse, too, isn't it?"

"And how do you know that?" Himmler asked quietly.

"Because now we have to talk about it in the papers and on the radio," Heydrich answered. "We can't pretend it isn't happening any more. Everybody knows it is. We'd only look like idiots if we ignored it."

"Dr. Goebbels is many things. An idiot he is not." Himmler spoke with a certain regret. The great lords of Party and State were rivals as well as colleagues.

Heydrich nodded. "I know. And so, *Herr Reichsführer*, I ask you again: what do you think of our war prospects?"

The leader of the SS didn't answer directly. Instead, he said, "We can't lose this war. We mustn't. If we do, it will make what we went through in 1918 look like a kiss on the cheek. Bolshevik hordes storming into Germany . . ." He shuddered at the idea. "And I don't imagine we could get terms before the enemy crossed our western border, either, the way we did last time."

"No, sir. I wouldn't think so," Heydrich agreed. "And if we are invaded, if we are occupied—what do we do then?"

"I think I'd rather take poison than live to see the day," Himmler said.

Heydrich looked at—looked through—him. He seldom held a moral advantage over the *Reichsführer*-SS, but he did now. "Sir, wouldn't it be better to fight? To keep on fighting, I mean? Even if the armed forces get ground down—"

"I don't believe it. I won't believe it," Himmler broke in.

"Devil of a lot of Ivans. Devil of a lot of Americans, too," Heydrich said. "And the Amis can bomb us, and we can't bomb them. Too damned many Englishmen with them. And all the Jews in Washington and Moscow and London will want revenge on the *Reich* and the *Führer*. You know what was decided at Wannsee a year ago."

No one at that conference had come right out and said Germany aimed to get rid of all the Jews in the territory she held. Nobody'd needed to. The high functionaries had understood what was what. So did Himmler, of course.

"Can you imagine the circus they'd have if they took the *Führer* alive?" Heydrich asked softly.

That turned out to be a keen shot, keener than he'd expected. Imagining, Himmler looked almost physically ill. "It must not happen!" he choked out. Maybe he was also imagining the circus the Allies would have if they took him alive. And maybe—no, certainly—he had reason to. Heydrich had had imaginings like that more often than he liked since the Czechs almost assassinated him.

"I hope it doesn't. I pray it doesn't," he said now. "But this is war—war to the finish, war to the knife. Shouldn't we be ready for anything, even the possibility of the worst?"

"What exactly have you got in mind?" the Reichsführer asked. Himmler's voice was almost back to normal. Almost, but not quite.

"You'll know, sir, probably better than I do, how much trouble the Russian partisans have given the *Wehrmacht*," Heydrich said.

"And the *Waffen*-SS," Himmler put in. "Several of our formations are in action behind the lines against those devils."

"Yes, sir. And the *Waffen*-SS," Heydrich agreed. "And the Soviets improvised those bands on the spur of the moment after the war broke out against them a year and a half ago. How much grief could we give enemy occupiers if we started preparing now, this instant, setting aside weapons and training men to fight as partisans if the worst comes? The more we did in advance, the more ready we'd be if, God forbid, they had to do what we'd trained them for."

Himmler didn't answer for some little while. He plucked at his lower lip with thumb and forefinger. That lip was oddly full, oddly sensuous, for the hard-boiled leader of an even more hard-boiled outfit. At last, he said, "This is not a plan I can deliver to *the Führer*. He remains unshakably convinced we shall emerge victorious in spite of everything."

"I hope he's right." Heydrich knew he couldn't very well say anything else.

"So do I. Of course." By the way Himmler said it, he wasn't optimistic no matter what he hoped.

"But don't you think it's something that needs doing?" Heydrich persisted. "It might not be something we could manage to scrape together at the last minute, with everything going to the devil around us. If we'd taken Moscow the first autumn and hanged Stalin in front of the Kremlin, what would the Soviet partisan movement be worth now?"

Himmler plucked at his red lower lip again. He let it spring back into place with a soft, liquid *plop*. After another pause, he said, "If we were to go forward with these preparations, it would be an SS undertaking."

"*Aber natürlich, Herr Reichsführer!*" Heydrich exclaimed. "This is the SS's proper business. The *Wehrmacht* fights ordinary battles in ordinary ways. We need to be able to do that, too, but we also need to be able to do whatever else the State may require of us."

"*Jaaaa.*" Himmler let the word stretch. Seen through the pince-nez, his stare didn't seem too dangerous—if you didn't know him. Unfortunately, Heydrich did. The *Reichsführer*-SS said, "Since you propose this project, do you expect to head it?"

"Yes, sir," Heydrich answered without the least hesitation. "I've been thinking about it for some time—since things, ah, first went wrong last fall at Stalingrad and in North Africa. Even if worse comes to worst, it would give us the chance to do the enemy a great deal of harm. In the end, it might save the *Reich* despite what would ordinarily be reckoned a defeat."

"Do you think so?" Himmler looked and sounded unconvinced.

But Heydrich nodded. "I do. Especially in the west, the enemy is basically soft. How much stomach will he have for occupying a country where his soldiers aren't safe outside their barracks—or inside them, either, if we can smuggle in a bomb with a time fuse?"

"Hmm," Himmler murmured. He plucked once more. *Plop*—the lip snapped back. Heydrich thought the mannerism disgusting, but couldn't very well say so. Pluck. Plop. Finally, the *Reichsführer* said, "Well, you've given me a good deal to think about. I can hardly deny that. We'll see what comes of it."

"The longer we wait, the more trouble we'll have doing it properly," Heydrich warned.

"I understand that," Himmler said testily. "I have to make sure I can get it moving without . . . undue difficulties, though."

"As you say, sir!" Heydrich was all obedience, all subordination. Why not? Himmler played the cards close to his chest, but Heydrich was pretty sure he'd won.

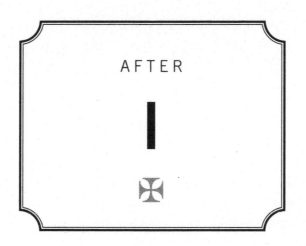

AFTER

I

Lichtenau was a little town—not much more than a village—a few miles south and west of Nuremberg. Charlie Pytlak walked down what was left of the main street, a BAR cradled in his arms. He had the safety off and a round chambered. He knew the Nazis had surrendered the day before, but some damnfool diehards might not have got the word—or might not care. The only thing worse than getting it during the war was getting it afterwards.

He admired the shattered shops and houses and what had probably been a church. The bright spring sun cast his shadow ahead of him. "Wow," he said with profound unoriginality, "we liberated the living shit out of this place, didn't we?"

"Bet your ass, Sarge," said Dom Lombardo. He'd liberated a German submachine gun—a machine pistol, the krauts called it. He kicked a broken brick out of the way. "Got any butts on you?"

"Sure thing." Pytlak gave him a Chesterfield, then stuck another one in his own mouth. He flicked a flame from his Zippo to light both cigarettes; his unshaven cheeks hollowed as he sucked in smoke. He blew it out in a long stream. "Dunno why they make me feel good, but they do."

"Yeah, me, too," Lombardo agreed. "Couldn't hardly fight a war without cigarettes and coffee."

"I sure wouldn't want to try," Pytlak said. "I—"

He broke off. Half a dozen German soldiers came around a corner. A couple of them wore helmets instead of Jerry field caps—a sign they'd likely fought to the end. One of the bastards in ragged, tattered field-gray still carried a rifle. Maybe he just hadn't thought to drop it. Or maybe . . .

"Hold it right there, assholes!" Pytlak barked. His automatic rifle and Dom's Schmeisser swung to cover the enemy soldiers.

The Germans froze. Most of them raised their hands. The guy with the Mauser slowly and carefully set it down in the rubble-strewn street. He straightened and reached for the sky, too. May 1945 was way too late to die.

One of the krauts jerked his chin toward the Chesterfields Charlie and Dom were smoking. He wasn't dumb enough to lower a hand to point. *"Zigarette, bitte?"* he asked plaintively. His buddies nodded, their eyes lighting up. The past couple of years, they must have been smoking hay and horseshit, except for what they could take from POWs.

"I can't give 'em any, Sarge," Lombardo said. "I had to bum this one offa you."

"Fuck. I don't wanna waste my smokes on these shitheads. A week ago, they'd've tried to waste me." Pytlak looked the Germans over. They were pretty pathetic. A couple of them couldn't have been more than seventeen; a couple of the others were nearer fifty than forty. The last two . . . The last two had been through the mill and then some. One of them wore an Iron Cross First Class on his left breast pocket. But they were whipped, too. You could see it in their eyes.

Charlie flicked the BAR's safety on. He leaned the weapon against a wall and dug in his pocket for more cigarettes. As he started toward the Germans, Dom said, "I'll cover you."

"You goddamn well better, Ace."

But there was no trouble. The German soldiers seemed pathetically grateful as Pytlak passed around the Zippo. And well they might have. The way things were in the ruins of the *Reich* these days, he could have got blown for half a dozen Chesterfields. He really was wasting them on these guys.

He scooped up the rifle the one guy had carried. Its safety was off, too. He took care of that. Then he tapped the other kraut's Iron Cross. "Where?" he asked. The guy just looked at him. "Uh, *wo?*" Like most GIs, he'd picked up a few words of German.

"Ah." The Jerry got it. "Kharkov." He pointed east. "Russland."

"Right," Charlie said tightly. If you listened to the Germans, all of them had done all their fighting on the Eastern Front. Trouble with that was, Uncle Joe's boys fought back a hell of a lot harder than the Nazis figured they would. As the war wound down, all the Germans wanted to do was get away from the Red Army so they could hand themselves over to Americans or Englishmen.

Well, these guys had made it. Charlie carried the rifle back to Dom and handed it to him. "Here. You can handle this and your grease gun. I've gotta lug the BAR around."

"Thanks a bunch," Dom said, slinging the Mauser. But Charlie knew he was right. The Schmeisser didn't weigh even half as much as a Browning Automatic Rifle. And he was a sergeant, and Dom nothing but a PFC. What point to rank if you couldn't use it?

They marched the Germans out of Lichtenau. There was a camp of sorts a couple of miles outside of town: a big barbed-wire cage in a field, now rapidly filling up with Jerries. If the surrendered soldiers had to sleep out in the open and eat U.S. Army rations for a while—well, too goddamn bad.

A truck's carcass lay by the side of the road. It wasn't a big, snorting GMC model from the States, but some shitty little German machine. It must have been machine-gunned from the air and then burned like a son of a bitch. Later, a tank or a bulldozer shoved it to one side so it wouldn't block traffic.

A German in civvies was fiddling around in the wreckage. "Wonder what he's up to," Charlie said.

"Scrap metal—waddaya wanna bet?" Dom returned. "Fucking scavengers are gonna be everywhere for months. Years, probably."

"Yeah, I guess." Charlie laughed. "We turned this whole stinking country into scrap metal and garbage. Just what the assholes deserved, too."

"I ain't arguing," Dom said.

The POW camp looked to be getting more organized by the minute. Charlie had to sign a paper saying he'd brought in six krauts. The corporal who manned a typewriter actually gave him a receipt for them. "The fuck'm I supposed to do with this?" Pytlak asked. "I feel like I just got into the slave-trading business."

"Hang on to it," the typist said. "We need to ask you anything about these guys, now we can."

"Hot damn," Charlie said, and then, "Jesus! I gotta figure out how many points I have. Sooner I get out of the Army, happier I'll be."

You earned discharge points for time in the service, for time overseas, for medals, for campaign stars on theater ribbons, and for kids under eighteen back home. Eighty-five would bring you home. Till now, Pytlak hadn't worried about them much. But the war was over. That still took getting used to; damned if it didn't. *And damned if I wanna hang around on occupation duty, either,* he thought.

"Don't get hot and bothered, man," the typist advised him. "They're gonna ship all our asses to the Pacific so we can punch Hirohito's ticket for him, too."

Charlie's reply was detailed and profane. Dom also chimed in with some relevant opinions. The corporal just grinned. He'd got under their skins, so he won the round. The really evil thing was, on top of that he was liable to be right.

Finally, in disgust, Pytlak said, "I'm gone. Next to this crap, Lichtenau looks goddamn good. You with me, Dom?"

"Oh, hell, yes," Lombardo said.

They were both shaking their heads as they trudged back toward the town. "Fight the fuckin' Japs," Charlie muttered. "That's just what I fuckin' need. Time they ship my butt home, I'll have a long white beard."

Dom was more than ready to help him bitch. Dom was always ready to help a guy bitch. He'd been pretty handy with that Schmeisser when they really needed it, too. Before long, it'd be nothing but a souvenir—that or more scrap metal, one. Charlie had heard they weren't letting GIs ship weapons home. One more chickenshit regulation, almost as bad as getting a receipt for POWs.

He and Dom came up to the corpse of the German truck. The scrounger who'd been messing around there was gone. "Who's that asshole gonna sell his scrap to?" Charlie said. "Us—you wait and see. We're dumb enough to pay good money to put these mothers back on their feet now that we stomped 'em."

"Yeah, that's like us, all right," Dom agreed. "We—"

The truck blew up. Next thing Charlie knew, he was sprawled on the ground a surprisingly long way from the road. Dom—no, a piece of Dom—lay not far away. Charlie tried to reach out. His arm didn't want to work. When he looked down at what was left of himself, he understood why. It didn't hurt. Then, all at once, it did.

His shriek bubbled through the blood filling his mouth. Mercifully, blackness enfolded him.

LIEUTENANT LOU WEISSBERG LOOKED AT THE CRATER BY THE SIDE OF the road. "Son of a bitch," he said. "Looks like a five hundred-pound bomb went off here."

That won him the first respectful glance he'd got from the ordnance sergeant already on the scene. "Damn near, sir," Toby Benton agreed, his slow Texas or Oklahoma drawl halfway to being a different language from Lou's clotted New Jersey. "Reckon some Jerries snuck one of their two hundred and fifty-kilo jobs into the truck an' then touched the mother off. Blew two of our guys to hell and gone." He pointed over to the corpses.

They'd left the GIs where they lay, so Weissberg could look them over and use his brilliance to pull a Sherlock Holmes and tell everybody what was what. To ordinary soldiers, the Counter-Intelligence Corps did stuff like that. Lou belonged to the CIC. He wished like hell he could do stuff like that. Unfortunately, unlike ordinary soldiers, he knew better.

He went over anyway and trained a camera on the bodies. "I hate taking pictures of these poor guys, you know?" he said, snapping away anyhow. "But I gotta have something to bring back to Nuremberg so the big shots there can see what happened."

"You better be careful, sir," Sergeant Benton said.

"How come? Is the ground mined?" Lou stood as still as if he intended to take root right where he was. And if Benton nodded or said yes, that would be about the safest thing he could do.

But the noncom shook his head. "Nah—didn't mean that. You

keep talkin' the way you are, though, people're liable to reckon you're a human being or somethin'."

"Oh." Lieutenant Weissberg wondered how to take that. To ordinary grunts, CIC officers probably *weren't* human beings, if by human beings you meant those who lived the same way they did. Lou had fired his carbine exactly once during the war, when his outfit almost got overrun during the Battle of the Bulge. He'd slept warm and eaten well, unlike most mudfaces. Therefore . . . this was likely a genuine compliment. He treated it as one, answering, "Thank you, Sergeant."

"You're welcome, sir," Benton said seriously. "I figured you'd be one o' them behind-the-lines assholes . . . uh, no offense. But you don't want to be doing this shit, neither."

"You better believe it," Lou said. "Somebody has to, though. German army surrendered. Unfuckingconditionally surrendered. If they think they can get away with crap like this . . ."

"What do we do about it?" Benton asked. "Take hostages and shoot 'em if the mothers who did this don't turn themselves in? That's what the Jerries woulda done, and you can take it to the bank."

"I know." Lou's voice was troubled. "All kinds of things the Jerries would've done that I don't want anything to do with."

Toby Benton eyed the CIC man in a way he'd seen before: as someone who knew the straight skinny and might be tempted into talking about it. "That stuff they say about those camps—Dachau an' Belsen an' them all—they really that bad?"

"No," Lou said tightly. Just when Benton started to breathe a sigh of relief, he went on, "They're worse. They're a thousand times worse, maybe a million. Far as I'm concerned, we should hang all the *mamzrim* who ran 'em. And you know what else? I think we're going to."

"If that shit is true—Jesus!—we ought to." Sergeant Benton paused. "The what? Mom-something?"

"Oh." Weissberg realized what he'd said. "It's Yiddish. Means *bastards*. And they are."

"I ain't arguin'." Benton eyed him again, this time not as a source but in another way he'd seen before. "Yiddish, huh? You're, uh, a Jewish fella?"

"Guilty," Lou said. How many Jews had the sergeant seen before? If he came off an Oklahoma farm, maybe not many. And was he a Regular Army guy or a draftee? Lou thought he might be career military, and not many Jews were.

"You *really* don't like the krauts then, right?"

"You might say so, Sergeant. Yeah, you just might. If they were all in hell screaming for water, I'd pull up with a gasoline truck."

"Heh." Benton let out only a syllable's worth of laughter, but his eyes sparked. "I like that—damned if I don't."

"Glad you do." Lou came back over to the crater. "Me, I don't like *this*. If the Germans think they can fuck around with us while we're occupying their country . . ." His voice trailed away. What exactly could—would—the United States do about it?

"Awful lot of guys just want to head on home an' pick up their lives where they left off," Sergeant Benton remarked. "Hell, I sure do." He *was* a draftee, then.

"I know. So do I," Lou said. He'd been teaching high school English in Jersey City when the Japs bombed Pearl Harbor. Nothing would make him happier than going back to diagramming sentences. But he was not the master of his fate or the captain of his soul. The master of his fate was back in Nuremberg, waiting to hear what he had to say about this. He sighed. What *could* he say that wasn't obvious?

Benton's eyes slid to what was left of the two GIs' bodies. Those would either get buried in a military cemetery here or go back to the States in sealed coffins, probably with sandbags to keep them company and make them weigh what they should. Lou hoped the Graves Registration people would plant them here. The less these guys' relatives knew about what had happened to them, the better.

He walked over to the jeep that had brought him out from Nuremberg. Benton had his own jeep. A bored-looking private sat in Lou's machine, checking out a magazine full of girls in pinup poses. Reluctantly, the driver set down the literature. "Take you back now, sir?" he asked. Violation of the surrender terms? A honking big crater and two mangled bodies? He probably didn't care much about anything, but he cared more about the leg art than this business.

And maybe he had the right attitude, too.

"Yeah, let's go," Lou said.

The driver started the engine. Jeeps were almost as reliable as Zippos. They fired up first time every time. Not much traffic on the road. What there was was nearly all U.S. military: olive-drab vehicles marked with a white star, usually inside a white circle.

Lou didn't get his ass in an uproar about trucks and jeeps and half-tracks that ran. He didn't worry about the Germans he saw, either, even though a lot of them still wore *Feldgrau* and some hadn't handed in their weapons yet. But he flinched whenever he rolled by crumpled metal wreckage—and there was plenty of it. If those Nazi *schmucks* had booby-trapped one dead truck, who could say they hadn't done it to more than one?

Nuremberg looked as if God had jumped on it with both feet and then spent a while kicking it, like a kid throwing a tantrum. The town where the Nazis threw their big wingdings, the town where Leni What's-her-name filmed *Triumph of the Will,* was the biggest rubble field in the world.

Or maybe not. Lou hadn't seen Berlin yet. The Russians played for keeps. And well they might. Hitler's team had come that close—*that* close—to doing unto them instead, and they had to know it. It never occurred to most Americans that they might have lost the war. The Atlantic and Pacific didn't shield the USSR from nasty neighbors. Fighting their way west across their own smashed and shattered country, Red Army men could see what a narrow escape they'd had.

Lou suddenly snickered, which made the driver look at him as if he'd started picking his nose. He didn't care. Suppose that truck had been sabotaged by organized diehards who weren't ready to quit. Maybe they thought Americans were too soft to give them what they deserved. Maybe they were even right.

But he would have bet dollars to doughnuts that the surviving Nazis had too much sense to piss off the Russians. He laughed again, louder this time. If the krauts didn't have that kind of sense, the Reds would be happy—fucking delighted—to pound it into them.

MARSHAL IVAN STEPANOVICH KONIEV WAS ABOUT AS UNHAPPY AS A jubilant man could be. His First Ukrainian Front had done everything an army group could do to smash the last German defenses in the east. It had broken into Berlin, and paid its share in blood to take Hitler's capital away from him and throw the Third *Reich* into the coffin it deserved.

So far, so good. But Stalin's orders gave the most important targets in Berlin to Marshal Zhukov's First Byelorussian Front. "*Yob tvoyu mat'*, Georgi Konstantinovich," Koniev muttered.

No matter what he said about Zhukov's mother, Koniev hadn't really expected anything else. Hoped, yes; expected, no. Zhukov was Stalin's fair-haired boy, and that was that. Stalin trusted Zhukov not to try to overthrow him: the kind of trust a dictator didn't give lightly—or, sometimes, at all. Having given it, Stalin could afford to be extravagant in giving Zhukov anything else he fancied.

That Zhukov was a damned good general had nothing to do with anything, not so far as Koniev was concerned. Without false modesty, the commander of the First Ukrainian Front knew he was a damned good general himself. So did Zhukov. And so did Stalin.

All the same, Stalin had only one favorite. Koniev knew he wasn't it. Zhukov was. So Zhukov's men got the Chancellery and the *Führer*'s bunker. It seemed unfair. It certainly did to Koniev, whose men broke into Berlin ahead of the other marshal's.

"*Nichevo,*" Koniev said. And it *couldn't* be helped, not unless he felt like quarreling with Stalin. He might be—he was—irked, but he wasn't suicidal.

Scrawny Germans, many still in threadbare uniforms, trudged gloomily through Berlin's wreckage-strewn streets. They got out of the way in a hurry when Red Army men came by. If they didn't, they'd pay for it. The stench of death hung in the air. Corpses still lay in the gutters, and sometimes in the middle of the street. Quite a few of them had got there after the surrender. No surviving Germans wanted to give the conquerors an excuse to add more.

Off in the distance, a woman shrieked. A Russian a few meters from Marshal Koniev chuckled. "One more cunt getting what she deserves," he said. His buddies laughed out loud.

Koniev didn't. The Red Army had avenged Nazi atrocities inside the USSR ever since it crossed the *Reich*'s borders. Berlin was no exception. Who'd wanted to say the Russian and Asiatic soldiers couldn't have their fun after the war's last battle? They owed the Germans plenty. But discipline was supposed to be returning. That scream—and others like it Koniev had heard in the ten days since the surrender—argued it still wasn't all the way back.

Which went a long way towards explaining why almost all the Germans Koniev could see were men. German women feared Red Army soldiers would drag them off and gang-rape them if they showed themselves. They might have been right, too. They'd be safe enough in a few weeks. Not yet.

A driver came up to Koniev and saluted. "Comrade Marshal, your car is ready," the man said.

"Good," Koniev said. "Very good. I won't be sorry to get out of this place for a while. It stinks."

"Sure does." The driver didn't seem to care. "If you'll come with me, sir . . ."

The car was a captured *Kubelwagen*—the German equivalent of a U.S. jeep—with red stars painted all over it to keep trigger-happy Russians from shooting it up. The driver carried a PPSh41 submachine gun to fight off not only stupid friends but stubborn enemies. Little dying spatters of resistance went on. Massive reprisals killed plenty of Germans, and would eventually snuff out the resistance, too—Koniev was confident of that.

Even a couple of kilometers outside of Berlin, the air improved. And then, abruptly, it got worse again: the *Kubelwagen* rattled past the bloated carcasses of a dozen cows in a cratered meadow. Koniev scowled at the stink, and also at the waste. "Our men should have butchered those animals," he said.

"Sorry, Comrade Marshal." The driver sounded afraid Koniev would think it was his fault. He added, "I never saw the beasts till this minute."

"All right, Corporal." While the fighting was still going on, Koniev might have looked to blame . . . somebody, anyhow. With the war over, he could afford to be more easygoing.

Artillery had chewed up the woods outside of Berlin, too. Some trees still stood straight. Others leaned at every angle under the sun. They'd been down long enough that their leaves were going from green to brown. Some of them would have fallen on the road from Berlin to Zossen—the former *Wehrmacht* headquarters, now taken over by the Red Army. Koniev wondered whether Red Army engineers or German POWs had cleared it. He would have bet his countrymen put the Germans to work.

Three or four men in field-gray scrambled off to the side of the road when they heard the *Kubelwagen* coming. "Those fuckers better move," the driver said. "They stand there knocking pears out of the trees with their dicks, I'll damn well run 'em over."

"Right." Marshal Koniev had to fight to swallow laughter. Russian profanity—*mat*—was almost a language in itself. The driver might have said *If they stand there goofing off . . .* Or he might not have. Even generals sometimes felt like using *mat*.

The road bent sharply. The driver slowed down. Something stirred among the dead trees near the asphalt.

Alarm stirred in Koniev. "Step on it!" he said urgently. If he turned out to have a case of the vapors, the driver could tell everybody he didn't have any balls. Koniev wouldn't mind, not one bit.

As the driver's foot came down on the gas, somebody—a man in a gray greatcoat—stood up. He aimed a sheet-metal tube at the *Kubelwagen*. "*Panzerfaust!*" the driver yelped. He grabbed his submachine gun at the same time as Koniev reached for the pistol on his belt.

Too late. Trailing fire, the bazooka-style rocket roared toward the car. Marshal Koniev ducked. That did him exactly no good. The *Panzerfaust* was made to smash tanks. A soft-skinned vehicle like the *Kubelwagen* was nothing but fire and scrap metal—and torn, charred flesh—an instant after the rocket struck home.

FACES BLANK AS IF THEY WERE SO MANY MACHINES, SOVIET SOLDIERS led out ten more Germans and tied them to the execution posts. Some were men, some women. All were in the prime of life. Orders from Moscow were that no old people or children be used to avenge Marshal Koniev. For him, the defeated enemy had to give their best.

The Germans had to give, and give, and give. Blood puddled at the bases of those posts. Flies buzzed in the mild spring air. The iron stink of gore made Captain Vladimir Bokov's nose wrinkle. He turned to the officer commanding the firing squads. "Smells like an outdoor butcher shop."

"Er—yes." That officer didn't seem to know how to respond. He was a Red Army major, so he nominally outranked Bokov. But the arm-of-service color on his shoulder boards was an infantryman's maroon, and infantry majors were a kopek a kilo.

Bokov's shoulder boards carried four small stars each, not one large one. His colors, though, were bright blue and crimson. He wore a special badge on his left upper arm: a vertical sword inside a wreath. No wonder a mere infantry major treated him with exaggerated caution—he belonged to the NKVD.

"Well, carry on," he said.

"Very well, Comrade Captain," said the infantry officer—his name was Ihor Eshchenko. That and his accent proclaimed him a Ukrainian.

He gestured to the troops tying the hostages to the posts. *Make it snappy,* the wave said. The men blindfolded the Germans. Eshchenko glanced at Bokov, but the NKVD man didn't object. Moscow hadn't said the executioners couldn't grant that small mercy.

A fresh squad of Red Army soldiers came out to shoot the hostages. The local commanders didn't make their men kill and kill and kill in cold blood; they rotated the duty whenever they could. One man in each squad had a blank in his weapon, too. If the soldiers wanted to think they weren't shooting anybody, they could.

"Ready!" Eshchenko called. The soldiers brought up their rifles. "Aim!" he said. A couple of the Germans waiting to die blubbered and moaned. They might not understand Russian, but they knew how firing squads worked. *"Fire!"* Major Eshchenko shouted.

Mosin-Nagant carbines barked. The Germans slumped against their bonds. Back in pagan days, a chieftain who died took a retinue with him to the next world. Good Marxist-Leninists didn't believe in the next world. All the same, the principle here wasn't so different.

Some officers in charge of executions armed their men with submachine guns and let them blast away at full automatic. Major Eshchenko seemed to have too much of a feel for the military proprieties to put up with anything so sloppy. Vladimir Bokov had watched and taken part in plenty of executions, and this one was as neat as any.

One drawback to using rifles, though: two or three hostages weren't killed outright. Eshchenko drew his pistol and gave each the coup de grâce with a bullet at the nape of the neck.

Stone-faced Germans carried away the corpses. Once Germans were dead, the Red Army stopped caring about them. "Nicely done, Major," Bokov said as Eshchenko came back. "Cigarette?"

"*Spasibo,*" Eshchenko replied, accepting one. He leaned forward to let Bokov give him a light. After taking a drag, he added, "This American tobacco is so mild, it's hardly there at all."

"I know." Bokov nodded. "Better than going without, though."

"Oh, you'd better believe it." The infantry officer inhaled again. He blew out a perfect smoke ring—Bokov was jealous—and said, "Better than the horrible crap we smoked at the start of the war, too."

Bokov sent him a hooded look. Though the NKVD man's eyes were blue, they were narrow like an Asiatic's: good for not showing what he was thinking. All he said was "*Da.*" Tobacco was wretched after the German invasion because the Nazis overran so much fine cropland. A vindictive man—or even a man with a quota to fill— might construe Eshchenko's remark as criticism of Comrade Stalin. A word from Bokov, and the major would find out more than he ever wanted to know about Soviet camps.

But Bokov had other things on his mind today. As if picking that from his thoughts, Major Eshchenko said, "Naturally, we also seized prisoners for interrogation. We've already, ah, questioned several of them. The rest we saved for you."

Questioned, of course, was a euphemism for *worked over.* Well, a marshal was dead. You couldn't expect the Red Army to stay gentle after that. And the GRU, the military intelligence unit, thought it knew as many tricks as the NKVD. The two services were often rivals. Not here, though. "Any real leads?" Captain Bokov asked.

Eshchenko shrugged. "None I've heard about. But I might not."

Bokov nodded. If the infantry officer didn't need to know something, nobody would tell him. That was basic doctrine. The NKVD man asked, "So where are these prisoners?"

"Over there, in that cow barn." Eshchenko pointed to a big wooden building surrounded by shiny new barbed wire and a couple of squads' worth of Soviet guards. The major snorted. "Damned thing is fancier than we'd use for people, fuck your mother if it's not."

He was taking a chance, talking like that. What he wanted to say was, *I'm a regular guy, and I figure you are, too.* But if Bokov decided he meant the insult personally, he was dead meat. Again, Bokov had bigger worries than a major with a loose tongue. All he said was, "I'll see what I can get out of them."

His blue and crimson arm-of-service colors got him past the junior lieutenant in charge of the guards. The lieutenant did give him a couple of men with submachine guns, saying, "My orders are not to let anybody go in amongst the Nazis by himself."

The kid spoke of them as if they were lions or bears. His orders made sense, too. If the Germans took a hostage . . . Well, it wouldn't do them any good, but they might be too stupid to realize that. And Bokov was sure the Soviets would deal with the hostage-takers without caring what happened to the man they held.

One of the soldiers opened the barred door. The stink that wafted out said the barn didn't have much in the way of plumbing. Most likely, it didn't have anything. "Give the swine the works," the trooper said.

"I aim to, Corporal," Bokov said. Then he switched to German and shouted, "Prisoners, attention!" He'd learned the language before the war started. Only luck, he supposed, that that hadn't made someone suspect him.

How the Germans scrambled to form neat lines! They all wore uniform, and ranged in age from maybe fourteen to sixty-five. Bokov found himself nodding. Whoever'd taken out Marshal Koniev had used a military weapon, and used it like someone who knew how. So the occupying troops would have hauled in as many men in field-gray as they could catch.

Bokov could see which Germans had already been interrogated. They were the ones who stood there with fresh bruises and scrapes, the ones who had trouble standing up at all. He pointed to a fellow who still wore a senior sergeant's single pip on each shoulder strap. "You. *Feldwebel.* Come with me."

Gulping, the man came. He hadn't been thumped yet. Plainly, he thought he was about to be. And he was right. But the Red Army men would have shot him on the spot had he even peeped.

"Tie him to a tree," Bokov told the troopers. "Do a good job of it." They did. From somewhere, one of them produced wire instead of rope. The *Feldwebel* wouldn't be going anywhere, no matter what. Bokov took out a pen knife. He started cleaning his nails with it. The

German watched the point with fearful fascination. Casually, Bokov asked him, "What do you know about Marshal Koniev's murder?"

"Only that he's dead, sir," the noncom said quickly. Too quickly? Well, Bokov had all the time in the world to find out.

He slapped the German across the face, forehand and backhand. "That's just a taste of what you'll get if I decide you're lying. Now— let's try it again. What do you know about this murder?"

"Nothing. On my mother's honor, sir, I—" Another pair of slaps interrupted the *Feldwebel*. Blood and snot ran from his nose. Bokov eyed him with distaste. He didn't particularly enjoy this, but it was part of the work. If he got something useful from this poor bastard, his bosses would remember. Unfortunately, they'd also remember if he didn't.

With some help from the troopers, he did what he needed to do. The *Feldwebel* didn't enjoy it, but he wasn't supposed to. Bokov soon became sure he wasn't the fellow who'd fired the *Panzerfaust*. That didn't mean he was a born innocent. At a certain point in the proceedings, he shrieked, "Jesus Christ! Why are you doing this to me? Why don't you torture the Werewolves? They're the ones who really know something!"

"Werewolves?" Vladimir Bokov paused to light another mild American cigarette. He blew smoke in the prisoner's eyes. "Tell me more. . . ."

Reinhard Heydrich hardly noticed the distant *put-put* from the generator any more. He hardly noticed the faint smell of the exhaust, either. He hoped he—or somebody—would notice if that smell got stronger. The ventilation system down here was supposed to be as good as anybody knew how to make it, but carbon monoxide could still get you if your luck turned sour.

His mouth twisted. This past month, Germany's luck had turned sour. The *Führer,* dead by his own hand! Himmler dead, too, also by his own hand! The whole country prostrate, surrendered, occupied from east and west. Almost all the important officials of State and Party in the Western Allies' hand; or, worse, in the Russians'.

I'm on my own, Heydrich thought. *It's up to me. If they think we've quit, then we've really lost. If we think we've quit, then we've really lost.*

Thinking of the Western Allies' hands, and of the Russians', made him glance down at his own. The light from the bare bulb was harsh. Even so, he was amazed how pale he'd got, this past year underground. He'd always been a man who rejoiced in the outdoors. He'd always been a man who tanned as if someone had rubbed his skin with walnut dye, too.

When he proposed this scheme to Himmler, when he proposed himself to head it, he hadn't grasped everything it entailed. If you were going to fight a secret war, a guerrilla war, against enemy occupiers, you had to disappear yourself. And so . . . he had.

"I'll come out in the sun again when Germany comes out in the sun again," he murmured.

"What was that, *Herr Reichsprotektor?*" Hans Klein asked. His onetime driver was with him still. After the assassination attempt in Prague, Heydrich knew he could count on the veteran noncom. Klein had loudly and profanely turned down promotion to officer's rank. The mere idea affronted him.

"Nothing." Heydrich said it again, to make himself believe it: "Nothing." But it wasn't. He shouldn't have let Klein see what was going on inside his head, even for a heartbeat.

The *Oberscharführer* had too much sense to push it. Instead, he asked, "Anything interesting in the news bulletins?"

Of course they monitored as many broadcasts as they could. Their own signals were few and far between, to keep from leaving tracks for the hunters. Since the *Reich* collapsed, they had to do the best they could with enemy propaganda and the military traffic they could pick up and decipher. Heydrich fiddled with some papers. "They've found paintings and some other art that Göring salted away."

That made Klein chuckle. "The Fat One wasn't in it for the money, but he sure was in it for what he could grab."

"*Ja.*" Heydrich admitted what he couldn't very well deny. "But when I said he salted stuff away, I meant it. They took this art out of an abandoned salt mine."

"Oh. *Scheisse.*" Hans Klein might not have much book learning, but he was nobody's fool. "Does that mean they'll start poking around other mines?"

"I hope not," Heydrich answered. "We have ways to keep them from finding the entrance." He sounded confident. He had to, to keep Klein's spirits up. But he knew things could go wrong. Anyone who'd survived in Germany knew that. And, of course, one traitor was worth any number of unlucky chances. He had endless escape routes, and didn't want to use any of them.

"What else is in the news?" Klein inquired. Maybe he didn't want to think about everything that could go tits-up, either.

"The Americans say they've almost finished conquering Okinawa." Heydrich had needed to pull out an atlas to find out just where Okinawa lay. He had one to pull out; when Germans set out to do something, they damned well did it properly.

His former driver only sniffed. "They've been saying that for a while now. The little yellow men are making them pay."

"They are," Heydrich agreed. "And these suicide planes . . . If you can use an airplane to sink a warship, that's a good bargain."

"Not one I'd want to make myself," Klein said.

"It all depends," Heydrich said in musing tones. "It truly does. A man who expects to die is hard to defend against. The Russians taught us that, and the Japanese lesson is a different verse of the same song. We have men dedicated enough to serve that way, don't you think?"

"You mean it." Klein considered the question as a senior sergeant might. "Well, sir, I expect we could, as long as they saw they were taking a bunch of those other bastards with 'em."

"Our enemies need to understand we are in earnest," Heydrich said. "One thing to win a war. Quite another to win the peace afterwards. They think they can turn Germany into whatever they please. The Anglo-Americans go on about democracy—as if we want another Weimar Republic! And the Russians . . ."

"*Ja.* The Russians," Klein echoed mournfully. One thing Stalin's men were doing in the lands they'd occupied: they were proving that all the frantic warnings Nazis propagandists had pumped out were understatements. And who would have believed *that* beforehand?

"Well." Heydrich pulled his mind back to the business at hand. "We have some more planning to do. And then—to work!"

BERNIE COBB HAD PLAYED BASEBALL IN HIGH SCHOOL. ALL THE same, nobody would ever confuse him with Ty. For one thing, he was no Georgia Peach; he'd grown up outside of Albuquerque, New Mexico. For another, even in that light air he was no threat with the bat, though he could field some.

He wasn't as fast as he had been then. He'd frozen his feet in the

Battle of the Bulge, and they still weren't back to a hundred percent. Instead of short or center, he played third in the pickup game outside of Erlangen.

The town, northwest of Nuremberg, had come through the war pretty well. The way it looked to Bernie, it wasn't big enough to plaster. Maybe it had a few more people than Albuquerque—which ran about 35,000—but that didn't make it any threat to New York City, or even Munich.

They played on a more or less mowed meadow just outside of town. The pitcher on the other side claimed he'd spent three years in the low minors. He could throw hard, but he needed a road map and a compass to find the plate. Maybe that was why he never got to the high minors. Or maybe he was talking through his hat.

A fastball at Bernie's ribs made him spin out of the box. "Ball four! Take your base!" the ump bawled. He was a first sergeant with a face like a clenched fist. He wasn't much of an umpire, but nobody had the nerve to tell him so.

Tossing the bat aside, Bernie trotted down to first. "Way to go, man!" one of his teammates yelled. Bernie was just glad he hadn't got drilled. A couple of GIs clapped. They weren't buddies of his; maybe they had money on his team.

Along with the American soldiers were a few Germans: mostly kids out for candy or gum or C-rats or women out for whatever they could get. Fraternizing with them was against regulations, which didn't stop it. Bernie hadn't come down venereal, but not from lack of effort. He knew half a dozen guys who had. They hardly cared—not the way they would have while the war was on. They only wanted to go home. If they couldn't do that, they wanted to fuck. Well, so did Bernie. Why not? Even if you caught something, pills or shots could cure you quick nowadays.

No more than three or four German men watched the game. One was an old fart in a suit, a town councillor out to see what the conquerors did in their spare time. Another was talking to a GI Bernie knew, a guy who spoke no German. Maybe the kraut had spent time in the States before the war.

"Strike!" the ump yelled. Bernie thought the pitch was high by six inches, but what could you do?

The pitcher threw over to first. Bernie dove back to the bag. *You stupid asshole,* he thought as he picked himself up. *With my bad feet, am I gonna run on you?*

"Ball!"

To Bernie, that pitch looked better than the one before. If he said so, the umpire would probably rip out his spleen.

He took a very modest lead. The pitcher stared over at him anyway. Bernie ignored the big dumb rube. There was one other German guy in the crowd. He was the same age as most of the GIs, which meant he'd likely been a soldier himself, but he wore baggy, nondescript civvies. They weren't what made Bernie notice him as he pressed his way in among the soldiers back of third base. The guy had the worst thousand-yard stare Bernie'd ever seen, and he'd seen some lulus.

"Ball!" the ump said. And it was a ball—it sent the batter staggering away from the plate like the last one to Bernie a couple of minutes before.

Blam! Bernie flattened out before he knew he'd done it. It might be July, but he still had his combat reflexes. An explosion made him hit the dirt faster than a high hard one at his ear.

"What the fuck?" That was the first baseman, sprawled a few feet away from him. "Christ, we playin' on a goddamn minefield?"

Bernie cautiously raised his head. He didn't have a sidearm, let alone his M1. The war was *over,* dammit.

It was sure over for some of the guys who'd been watching behind third. Over permanently. Bodies and pieces of bodies lay everywhere. Half of somebody's left leg bled ten feet in front of the low mound. Other gruesome souvenirs spattered the left side of the infield.

Screams rose from wounded American soldiers. So did cries for a medic. Bernie ran over to do what he could for the injured men. It wasn't much. He didn't carry wound dressings or a morphine syrette, the way he would have while the war was still cooking. By the helpless looks and muffled profanity that came from the other unhurt GIs, neither did anybody else.

Bernie crouched by a guy who was clutching at a bloody leg. "You want a tourniquet on that?" Bernie asked him. He could improvise one with a shoelace and a stick. When the hell would an ambulance show up?

"I don't think so. I ain't bleedin' *that* bad," the other answered. In a wondering voice, he added, "He blew himself up."

"Huh?" Bernie said brilliantly. "Who?"

"That fuckin' kraut. He blew himself to kingdom come. Blew half of us with him, too, the goddamn son of a bitch."

"He didn't step on a mine? *Somebody* didn't step on a mine?"

A siren warbled, approaching from the direction of downtown Erlangen. The warble meant it was a German vehicle. Bernie wasn't inclined to be fussy, not right now. The guy with the gash in his leg went on, "Nah, not a chance. Look at what's left of the asshole."

Not much was, and even less between the knees and the neck. Bernie gulped and looked away in a hurry. He'd hoped he would never see shit like that again. No such luck.

Just as the ambulance pulled up, the wounded GI yanked what looked like a tenpenny nail out of his leg. "Jesus!" he said, staring at three inches of pointed iron. "The mother didn't just have explosives. He had his own fuckin' shrapnel!"

"That's nuts," Bernie said. "Who ever heard of a kamikaze Nazi?"

"Maybe you better put somethin' around my leg," the other guy said. "It's bleeding more now that I pulled that sucker out."

"Okay." Bernie sacrificed a leather shoelace to the tourniquet.

Three krauts hopped out of the ambulance. They stared at the carnage in disbelief. *"Der Herr Jesus!"* one of them blurted. Another one crossed himself. Then they got to work. Their unflustered competence made Bernie guess they'd been *Wehrmacht* medics up till a few weeks earlier.

One Jerry spoke some English. Unhurt and slightly wounded men followed his orders as if he were an American officer. He plainly knew what he was doing.

But when he started to pick up the remains of the fellow who'd blown himself up, the sergeant who'd been doing umpire duty pushed him away. "Leave what's left of that bastard right where he's at," the noncom said.

"Warum?" the German asked, startled out of his English. He got it back a moment later: "Why?"

"On account of our guys are gonna have to try and figure out how come the shithead went kablooie," the sergeant said. "It's a murder, right? You don't fuck around with the scene of a crime." More to himself than to the guy from the ambulance, he added, "The stuff you pick up from mystery stories."

How much of what he said did the German get? Enough so he didn't go near what was left of the human bomb, anyhow. Bernie Cobb understood all of it. It made much more sense than he wished it did.

LOU WEISSBERG WANTED TO GO BACK TO THE STATES. HE DIDN'T want to examine any more mangled flesh. He didn't want to smell the sick-sweet stench of death any more, either. (Not that you could avoid it in Germany, not in towns where the Army Air Force or the RAF had come to call . . . and in a lot of places the Army'd gone through, too.)

That stench was mild here, two days after the bombing with most of the dead meat taken away. Mild or not, it was there, and it made his stomach want to turn over. Toby Benton's mouth twisted, too. "Hell of a thing—uh, sir," the sergeant said.

"You better believe it." Lou's nod was jerky. "Twenty-three dead, they're saying now. And almost twice that many wounded bad enough to need treatment."

"Shit." Benton's drawl almost turned it into a two-syllable word. "Good thing the Jerries didn't get so many of our guys for every one of theirs while the fighting was still going on. We had more people than they did—more stuff too—but not that much more."

"Mm." Lou hadn't thought of it in those terms, which didn't mean the ordnance sergeant was wrong. "If you were out to turn somebody into a walking bomb, how would you go about it?"

"Same way these fuckers did, I reckon," Benton replied. "The Nazis bite the big one, but nobody ever said they couldn't handle shit like this. Explosives—around the guy's middle, I guess, so they wouldn't show so much. Scrap metal, nails, whatever the hell for shrapnel. A battery. A button to push. And *kapow!*"

"Yeah. *Kapow!*" Lou's echo sounded hollow, even to himself.

"What do we do about shit like this, Lieutenant?" Benton asked. "If this asshole wasn't just your garden-variety nut, seems to me like we got ourselves some trouble. The way we fight is, we want to live, and we want to make sure the other sons of bitches don't. Always figured the krauts played by the same rules. But if all of a sudden-like they don't give a shit no more, sure as hell makes 'em harder to defend against."

"I know." Lou clenched his fist and pounded it against the side of his thigh. He didn't notice he was doing it till it started to hurt. Then he quit. "God damn it to hell, Toby, the war in Europe is over. They surrendered. We can do whatever we want to their people, and they've got to know it."

"Yes, sir," Sergeant Benton agreed. "That's how come I hope he was a nut. If they've got waddayacallems—partisans . . . Russians and Yugoslavs gave old Adolf a fuck of a lot of grief with guys like that. I guess even the froggies caused him some trouble." After hitting the beach on D-Day, his opinion of France and things French could have been higher.

"Well, it's not my call, thank God," Lou said. "I haven't got the stomach for lining rows of people up against a wall and shooting 'em. Even Germans—except camp guards and mothers like that." His voice went ferocious. He'd done Latin in college before the war, and remembered coming across the Roman Emperor who wished all mankind had one neck, so he could get rid of it at a single stroke. Back then, he'd thought that was one of the most savage things he'd ever heard. He felt the same way about SS men himself these days.

"Shit, sir, it wouldn't be so bad if it was only them. But all these chickenshit civilians and *Wehrmacht* guys who swear on a stack of Bibles they didn't know squat about any concentration camps . . . No, sirree, not them. My ass!" Benton made as if to retch, and for once the death reek had nothing to do with it.

"Uh-huh." Lou nodded. "And the real pisser is, they expect us to *believe* that crap. How dumb do they think we are?" He knew the answer to that: your average German—your average German with a guilty conscience—thought your average American was pretty goddamn dumb. By the way some U.S. officers were willing to use Nazis to help get the towns they were in charge of back on their feet, maybe your average German hit the nail right on the head, too.

"You gonna talk with the town councillor who was here?" Benton asked. "What the hell's his handle, anyway?"

"Herpolsheimer," Lou said with a certain gloomy relish. "Anton Herpolsheimer. Jeez, what a monicker. Yeah, I'll talk to him. Don't know what he would've seen that our GIs didn't, but maybe some-thing."

Herr Herpolsheimer's house stood next to the post office on the Hugenottenplatz. Once upon a time, the Germans had taken in perse-cuted French Protestants instead of clobbering them. Worth remem-bering they could do such things . . . Lou supposed.

"Hey, Joe, got any gum?" a kid maybe eight or nine years old called in pretty fair English as Lou and Sergeant Benton neared the house. Benton ignored him. Lou shook his head. He wasn't feeling sympathetic to Germans, even little ones, right then. The kid dropped back into German for an endearment: "Stinking Yankee kikes!"

"Lick my ass, you little shitface," Lou Weissberg growled in the same language. "Get the fuck out of here before I give you a noodle"— German slang for a bullet in the back of the neck. He might have done it, too; his hand dropped toward the .45 on his belt before he even thought.

The kid turned white—no, green. How many uncomprehended in-sults had he got away with? He damn well didn't get away with this one. He disappeared faster than a V-2 blasting off.

"Wow!" Benton said admiringly. "What did you call him?"

"About a quarter of what he deserved." Lou pushed on, his thin face closed tight. The ordnance sergeant had the sense not to push him.

Lou took some satisfaction in banging on Anton Herpolsheimer's front door. If the town councillor thought the American *Gestapo* was here to grill him . . . it wouldn't break Lou's heart.

When the door didn't open fast enough to suit him, he banged some more, even louder. "We gonna kick it down?" Sergeant Benton didn't sound bothered.

"If we need to." By then Lou looked forward to it.

But the door swung wide then. A tiny, ancient woman in a black dress—housekeeper?—squinted up at the two Americans. "You wish . . . ?" she asked in a rusty voice, as politely as if they were holding teacups with extended pinkies.

"We must see *Herr* Herpolsheimer at once," Lou said. If she tried to stall, she'd be sorry, and so would the councillor with the funny name.

But she didn't. She nodded and said, "*Jawohl, mein Herr.* Please wait. I will bring him." Then she hurried away.

" '*Jawohl,*' huh?" Sergeant Benton didn't know much German, but he followed that. "The way she talks, Lieutenant, you're one heap big honcho."

"I should be—not 'cause I'm me, but 'cause I'm an American," Lou said. "We tell these German frogs to hop, they'd better be on the way up before they ask, 'How high?' "

"Now you're talkin'!" Benton said enthusiastically. Lou nudged him—here came Councillor Herpolsheimer.

Nobody'd told Lou that the bomber had wounded Herpolsheimer. But the old German walked with a limp. His left arm was in a sling. An almost clean bandage was wrapped around his head. "Good day, *Herr* Herpolsheimer," Lou said, more politely than he'd expected to. "I'm here to ask some questions about the, ah, unfortunate events of the other day."

"Unfortunate events? I should say so!" Herpolsheimer had a gray mustache and bushy gray eyebrows. (Lou could see only one of them, but the other was bound to look the same.) The old German added, "That maniac!"

"Do you know who he was? Had you seen him before?" Lou asked.

"No. Never." Herpolsheimer winced a little as he shook his head. Maybe he had a concussion to go with his more obvious injuries. He said, "I fought in the last war. That's where I got this." He used his good hand to brush his leg, so he'd had the limp before he went out to watch the Yanks play baseball. The gesture was oddly dignified, almost courtly. "I fought in the last war," he repeated. "No one back then would have done such a thing—not a German, not a Frenchman, not an Englishman. Nobody. Not even an American." He seemed to remind himself what his interrogator was.

"*Danke schön,*" Lou said dryly. "How about a Russian?"

"Well, I fought in Flanders, so I didn't face them," the town councillor replied. "But I never heard of them doing anything like that."

"Do you think the fellow who blew himself up was a German?" Lou inquired.

"Until he did . . . that, I didn't pay much attention to him," *Herr*

Herpolsheimer said slowly. "I might have paid more had I thought he was a foreigner. But he didn't seem to stand out. Oh, he looked like someone who'd been through a lot, but a lot of people look like that nowadays." He stuck out his wattled chin, as if to say, *And it's all your fault, too.*

Lou didn't think it was all the Allies' fault. If Hitler hadn't swallowed Austria, raped Czechoslovakia, invaded Poland, invaded Denmark and Norway, invaded the Low Countries and France, bombed the crap out of England, sunk everything he could in the North Atlantic, invaded the Balkans and North Africa, and then invaded Russia . . . *Details, details,* Lou thought.

But arguing politics with a Jerry was a waste of time. "It seemed like this guy, whoever he was, placed himself to hurt as many Americans as he could before he, uh, exploded himself." That wasn't supposed to be a reflexive verb, but nobody'd had to talk much about human bombs before.

Herr Herpolsheimer understood him, which was the point of the exercise. The old man nodded. "Yes, I thought so. He did it with definite military effect."

"*Wunderbar,*" Lou muttered. If he'd been speaking English, he would have said *Terrific* the same way.

Herpolsheimer eyed him. "Your German is quite good, *Herr Oberleutnant,* but I do not think I have heard an accent quite like yours before."

"I wouldn't be surprised. Half the time, it isn't German, or isn't exactly German—it's Yiddish." Lou waited. *Come on, you old bastard. Let's hear the speech about how you didn't know what those wicked Nazis were doing to the Jews here. No, you had no idea at all.*

The town councillor clicked his tongue between his teeth. "My niece had a Jewish husband," he said after a moment.

"Had?" Lou didn't like the sound of that.

"Max hanged himself in 1939, after *Kristallnacht,*" Herpolsheimer said. "He could not get a visa to any foreign country, and he could not live here. In his note, he said he did not wish to be a burden on Luisa. She did not believe he was one—but, the way things went, she might have come to do so. . . ."

What were you supposed to say after something like that? Lou couldn't think of anything, so he got out of there as fast as he could.

Then he had to tell Sergeant Benton what Herpolsheimer had said, which made him feel great all over again. "Son of a bitch," the ordnance sergeant said when he got done. "*Son* of a bitch. Ain't that a bastard?"

"*Mazeltov,* Toby," Lou said. "That may be the understatement of the year."

"Hot damn," Benton said. "So what the hell are we going to do about this asshole who turned himself into a bomb?"

"What you said, pretty much—hope he's one lone nut and there's no more like him," Lou answered. "Past that, I have no idea—I mean, none. And I may be breaking security to tell you the higher-ups don't, either, but I don't think I'm surprising you much."

"Nope," Sergeant Benton said. "I only wish to God you were."

THE EXPLOSION HAD TAKEN OUT MOST OF A CITY BLOCK. THE DAMage wasn't so obvious in fallen Berlin. The lost capital of the *Reich* had already taken more bombs and shells and rockets and small-arms fire than any town this side of Stalingrad. After all that, what difference did one more explosion make?

Captain Vladimir Bokov knew too well the difference this one explosion made. The bloodstains on still-standing walls and on the battered pavement were noticeably fresher than most in Berlin. And he could also make out bits and pieces of the GMC truck some clever German had packed with explosives before driving it up to some parading Russian soldiers and blowing them up—and himself with them.

"You see, Comrade Captain," Colonel Fyodor Furmanov said. He'd led those parading Red Army troops. Only dumb luck no flying piece of truck got him in the kidneys—or in the back of the neck. He had burns and scrapes and bruises, nothing worse . . . and he seemed embarrassed to remain alive while so many of his soldiers didn't.

"Oh, yes. I see," the NKVD man said. Colonel Furmanov flinched. He knew his next stop might be a labor camp somewhere north of the Arctic Circle. "What kind of precautions did you take to keep that truck from getting close to your men?"

Furmanov flinched again. Bokov eyed the decorations on his chest. They said the Red Army officer had had himself a busy war. He spread his hands now. "Comrade Captain, I took none. The responsibility is mine. I thought the war was over. I thought no one would strike at us. I was wrong—and my poor men paid the price for my mistake."

"You didn't expect that the Fascist would be willing to blow himself up if that meant he could strike at the Soviet Union?" Bokov asked.

"No," Colonel Furmanov said stonily. "If you believe what the Yankees are saying, the Japanese fight like that. But the Germans don't—didn't, I should say. Not before the surrender, they didn't. You must know that as well as I do, Comrade Captain."

His words said the right things. His tone said he doubted whether an NKVD man knew anything about what had gone on at the front— but didn't say so blatantly enough to let Bokov call him on it. Abstractly, the captain admired the performance. The only way he could respond to the challenge was by pretending not to notice it. And so he simply nodded and said, "Yes. I do know."

"Well, then." Colonel Furmanov sighed. He'd been right to come out and accept responsibility. It would have landed on him anyhow. Being ready for it made him . . . look a little better.

Bokov lit another of his American cigarettes. When he handed Furmanov the pack, the older officer stared in surprise before taking it. Furmanov leaned close to get a light from Bokov's cigarette. After giving it to him, the NKVD man spoke slowly and deliberately: "It seems, Comrade Colonel—it seems, I say—that some Nazis have decided to continue resistance in spite of the regime's formal surrender. This bomb in the truck . . . is not an isolated incident."

He didn't want to admit that. Coming out and saying it made the USSR—and, maybe even more to the point, the NKVD—look bad. Easier by far to let this officer vanish into the gulag. Maybe he'd come out in ten years, or more likely twenty-five. Or maybe they would use him up before he finished his sentence, the way they did with so many.

If this were an isolated incident, Furmanov would be gone. As things were, though . . . "There are reports from the American occupation zone of Germans using explosives to kill U.S. soldiers—and killing themselves in the process."

"*Bozhemoi!*" the infantry colonel exclaimed. "In the American zone, too? There really is a resistance, then!"

"It would seem so, yes," Bokov said. "We are also trying to see whether these bombings are connected to Marshal Koniev's assassination."

Colonel Furmanov said "My God!" again. Then he cursed the Nazis with a fluency Peter the Great might have envied. And then, after he ran down, he asked, "What can we do about it?" He held up a hand. "Can we do anything about it that leaves more than maybe three motherfucking Germans alive?"

"That is the question." Bokov impersonated Hamlet. After a moment, he added, "Why do you care? I promise you, nobody in Moscow will." The Nazis had come much too close to wiping the Soviet Union off the map. Anything to help ensure that that never happened again seemed good to the men who shaped Soviet policy. It seemed good to Vladimir Bokov, too, not that his opinion on such things mattered a fart's worth.

"Comrade Captain, if we send Germans up the smokestack the way the SS got rid of Jews, I'll wave bye-bye to them while they burn. You'd best believe I will," Furmanov said. "You can see by my record that I'm not soft on these fuckers. But if we do something that makes them desperate enough to go after my men without caring whether they live or die themselves . . . That I care about, because it endangers Soviet troops for no good reason."

"The Germans aren't doing what they're doing because of how we're treating them." Now Bokov spoke with authority. "Like I said, they're pulling the same damned stunts in the American zone, and you know the Americans go easy on them—Americans and Englishmen are halfway toward being Fascists themselves."

"Yes, that's true," Colonel Furmanov agreed. "So why are they doing it, then?"

"I told you why. Some of them don't think the war is over yet," Bokov said. "Our job here will have two pieces, I think. One will be to hunt down the bandits and criminals who are to blame for these outrages."

"Da." Furmanov nodded. "You don't commandeer a truck and load it full of shit like that by yourself. You're right, Comrade Captain—some kind of conspiracy must lie behind it."

Russians saw conspiracies as naturally as Americans saw profits. Like Americans chasing the dollar, they often saw conspiracies that weren't there. Not this time, Bokov was convinced. Furmanov had it straight—somebody who put a lot of explosives in a truck and set it off had to have an organization behind him.

Then Furmanov asked, "What's the other piece of your puzzle?"

"What you'd expect," Bokov replied. "Somewhere out there are Germans who know about this conspiracy without being part of it. We have to find out who they are and make them tell us what they know. And we have to make all the Germans left alive more afraid to help the bandits than anything else in the world. If even one of them betrays us, they all have to suffer on account of it."

Colonel Furmanov nervously clicked his tongue between his teeth. "This is what I was talking about before, Comrade Captain. With policies like this, we risk driving Germans who would stay loyal— well, quiet, anyhow—into the bandits' arms."

"They'll be sorry if they make that mistake." For all the feeling in Bokov's voice, he might have been talking about the swine at a pig farm. "But they won't be sorry long."

"When the Hitlerites invaded the Soviet Union, they didn't try to win the goodwill of the workers and peasants. Because they didn't, the partisan movement against them sprang to life."

Colonel Furmanov walked a fine line here, and, again, walked it well. He didn't point out that the Nazis had enjoyed plenty of good-will when they stormed into places like the Baltic republics and the Ukraine. That was true, but pointing it out could have won him a stretch in the camps. He also didn't point out that Stalin's policy here would be the same as Hitler's there. That would have been even more likely to let him learn what things were like in a cold, cold climate. And he didn't point out that the Russian partisans got massive amounts of help from unoccupied Soviet territory. Who would help these diehard Nazis?

Nobody. Captain Bokov hoped not, anyway.

Instead of arguing with Furmanov or even pointing out any of those things, Bokov said, "We'll do all we can to track down the Fascists. The place to start, I think, is with the truck. How did the Germans get their hands on it?"

He hadn't expected an answer from the infantry officer, but he got one: "So much stuff is going back to the motherland, Comrade Captain, that nobody pays much attention to any one piece. Maybe that truck was ours to begin with, or maybe it was one the Germans captured from us or from the USA. If somebody told one of our sentries he was taking it somewhere on somebody's orders, the sentry might not have bothered to check. He'd figure, *Who'd lie about something like that?* Or do you think I'm wrong?"

Bokov wished he did. A German with nerve could probably disappear a truck just the way Furmanov described. "Shit," Bokov said wearily. "One more thing we have to tighten up. I suppose I should thank you."

"I serve the Soviet Union!" Furmanov said, which was never the wrong answer.

"We all do," Bokov agreed. But, while it wasn't the wrong answer, it might not be the right one, either.

When Tom Schmidt thought of Nuremberg, he thought of *Triumph of the Will*. He was a reporter. He knew he wasn't supposed to do stuff like that. But how could you help it if you'd seen the movie? Precision marching. Torchlight parades. Searchlights stabbing up into the air, building the columns for a cathedral of light. (Nobody then had mentioned that the searchlights were also part of the city's aircraft-defense system.)

And Hitler haranguing the faithful. Tom's German grandparents had settled in Milwaukee—well, one of his grandmothers was from Austria, but it amounted to the same thing. His own *Deutsch* wasn't great, but it was good enough. Hitler didn't say anything wonderful in the film, but the way he said it. . . .

Even on the screen, it made Tom sit up and take notice. And the shots of the people listening to it live—! The men in their brown or black uniforms and the boys in *Hitler Jugend* shorts stared in awe. They might have been listening to the Pope, or to the Second Coming of Jesus.

The women, though, were the ones who really got to him. Wide eyes; open mouths; slack, ecstatic features . . . They looked as if they were on the edge of coming themselves. If old Adolf could do that without laying a finger on them—well, it was plenty to make Tom jealous.

So that was what he thought of when he thought of Nuremberg. Postwar reality was a little different. *Yeah, just a little,* he thought with a wry chuckle. It was a field of wreckage as far as the eye could see. A U.S. Army information officer told him the town had suffered ninety-one percent destruction. That included the vast majority of the public buildings, though a couple of churches might prove salvageable. About half the prewar housing was ruins now.

That helpful information officer said there were something like 12,000,000 cubic meters of rubble to clear away. The first big raids came in late 1943, the last in early 1945. Tom wondered how many years hauling away the bricks and timber and plaster and concrete would take. By the way Nuremberg looked now, it might take forever.

If it did, he wouldn't be heartbroken. Along with the rubble, today's Nuremberg had something else *Triumph of the Will* didn't show: fear. American soldiers here, as throughout the U.S. occupation zone, didn't travel in groups smaller than four. They always went armed. Representing the *Milwaukee Sentinel,* Tom was officially a noncombatant. That hadn't kept him from acquiring a helmet and a grease gun. The M3A1 was almost as ugly as a British Sten gun, but it could chew up a lot of bandits at close range. Since it could, Tom didn't sweat the aesthetics.

He did wish he had eyes in the back of his head. When he mentioned that to a GI, the dogface laughed at him. Then the fellow said, "Sorry, Mac. If I don't laugh, I bang my head against a wall. Laughing hurts less—I guess. We're all as jumpy as cats in a room full of rocking chairs."

"Nice to know it isn't just me," Tom said. "But it shouldn't be like this. They surrendered. If they mess with us now, we can treat them however we want. It's all in the laws of war, right?"

"Like I know from the laws of war." The soldier wore a PFC's single stripe. No, he wouldn't be chewing the fat with Patton or Eisenhower any time soon. "All I know is, we've shot hostages, and it don't do no good. Fuckin' krauts still shoot at us and plant mines and blow themselves up like they're Japs. Me, I quit goin' to movies on account of they go after us double when there's crowds of us like that."

"Uh-huh." Tom wrote that down. "Doing without movies is a real hardship. What do you do instead?"

"Waddaya think I do, man?" the GI returned. "I do *without,* like you said."

Tom wrote that down, too; it was a good line. "How do we get a handle on these German tactics?"

"Hanging that Heydrich item up by the balls'd make a decent start, I guess," the PFC answered. "He's the one supposed to be back of this shit, right? What's the reward for his worthless carcass up to?"

"Half a million bucks—tax-free if an American bags him," Tom said. "Not exactly worthless, not if you're the one who hits the jackpot."

"You know what I mean. I—" The soldier paused as a couple of Germans mooched past. One of them was in civvies; the other wore a beat-up *Wehrmacht* uniform with all the trim removed. The guy in the uniform glanced over at the Americans as if wondering what his chances for a handout were. The other man, who was older, kept his head down. With all the stones and broken bricks and other bits of crap on the ground, that wasn't the worst idea in the world.

And if he doesn't make eye contact and get us nervous, his odds for seeing tomorrow bump up, Tom thought.

"Okay. Now they're out of range," the GI said. He relaxed—fractionally.

"They wouldn't go after just two of us . . . would they?" Schmidt wished he'd managed to swallow the last two words, but he knew what they said about wishes and horses.

To his relief, the PFC didn't seem to think he was yellow. "Well, you wouldn't think so," the man answered seriously. "When they blow themselves up, they try to take out more than two of us at a time. But you don't wanna drop your guard, you know? If you look like you ain't payin' attention, who knows what one of those cocksuckers'll try?"

"Yeah. Who knows?" Tom's voice sounded gloomy, even to himself.

"I'll tell you somethin', man," the soldier said. "I ain't got near enough points for them to hand me a Ruptured Duck and ship my sorry ass home—I didn't get over here till pretty late in the game. But if they want to throw me on a boat and send me to fight the Japs, I'd sooner do that than this. That's an honest war, anyways. You know who the bad guys are. They get in your way, you fuckin' grease 'em. This . . . Truman said it was over when the Nazis signed the surrender papers, but does it look like it's over to you?"

"Well . . . it did for a little while," Tom said.

"I know. I figured this occupation shit'd be duty you could handle standing on your head." The American broke off to give another German the once-over. She was young and kind of cute, but that wasn't why he eyed her the way he did. As she walked off, he sighed and spat in the rubble. "Standing on your goddamn head. Yeah, sure. And then you wake up."

"Have you heard of any women blowing themselves up?" Tom asked.

"There was one, a coupla weeks ago. Down near . . . where the fuck was it? It was in *Stars and Stripes*—you can look it up. Down near Augsburg, that's where the cunt did it."

Tom asked one more question: "So if you had your druthers, what would you do with the Germans now?"

"Beats me, man," the GI said. "Way it looks to me is, we either gotta kill 'em all or else walk away from 'em. Neither one of those is what you'd call a real good answer."

"I know," Tom said.

"You got any better ones?" the soldier asked. "You can go all over the place. You ain't stuck yakking with guys like me—you can talk to officers and shit. Hell, you can even talk to the krauts if you want to, huh?" He made that sound as strange as talking to Martians. To him, maybe it was.

"I could, yeah. If I did, I don't know how many folks back in Milwaukee'd want to read about it, though." Tom held up a hand. "And before you ask me, I haven't run into any officers with ideas much different from yours."

"Jeez." The PFC spat again, mournfully. "We are fubar'd, then. But good."

Soviet troops shouted orders—in Russian. The Germans they were herding onto trains mostly didn't understand. The Germans weren't happy to be in the train station to begin with. The Soviets had hauled them out of their houses and flats and shacks and tents and wherever else they were staying. Some Germans carried a duffel's worth of worldly goods. More had only the clothes on their backs.

"Where are we going?" "Where are they taking us?" "What's going on?" "What are they doing?" Germans called out the questions again and again. Hardly any of the soldiers understood. Nobody answered.

Watching the chaos unfold, Vladimir Bokov smiled. The NKVD officer had no trouble following the Germans' worried questions. In broad outline, he knew the answers to them. But he kept his mouth shut. He was there to observe, not to ease the Germans' minds. His smile got broader. What he could say wouldn't make these people feel any better.

A train pulled in. Soviet soldiers already aboard opened the cars' doors. An indignant German voice rose above the general din: "*Was ist hier los?* Some of these cars are for transporting freight or—or livestock, not human beings!"

He was right, not that it did him any good. The troops started herding—and then cramming—people onto the train. Men shouted. Women screamed. Children wailed. That did them no good, either.

The NKVD colonel standing next to Bokov chuckled nastily. "Let the pricks find out what it's like, eh? Not like they didn't do it to plenty of other people."

"That's right, Comrade," Bokov agreed. No need to worry that Colonel Moisei Shteinberg would prove disloyal to the Soviet state, not when it came to dealing with the Hitlerites. Lots of Jews in the old Russian Empire became revolutionaries because the Tsars mistreated their people. Well, what the Tsars did to Jews was like a kiss on the cheek compared to what the Nazis gave them.

That angry German man protested again, crying, "This is inhumane!" Then a grinning soldier who doubtless understood not a word he said shoved him into a cattle car. The Red Army men forced more and more Germans in after him.

"Why are you doing this to us?" a woman asked the soldier who was pushing her into another car. "Where are we going?"

Bokov would have bet rubles against rocks that the soldier didn't follow her questions. The fellow had swarthy skin, high cheekbones, and dark, slanted Asian eyes. He bared his teeth in a feral grin. "Suck my cock, bitch!" he said. Luckily for the woman, she didn't understand him, either. She squawked when he put both hands on her backside to get her in there. He only laughed.

In slow, schoolboy Russian, a German man said, "For what you do? I not harm you."

He was over sixty, so he might have been telling the truth, at least in the literal sense of the words. Maybe he hadn't carried a Mauser or served a 105mm howitzer. But even if he hadn't, he'd almost certainly made weapons or munitions or uniforms or something else the Nazis had used against the USSR. Not many people here had clean hands.

The soldier he addressed didn't answer him in words, not at first. Instead, the Red Army man hit him in the side of the head with the stock of his submachine gun. The German crumpled with a moan. The Red Army man kicked him in the ribs. Then he shouted, "Fuck yourself in the mouth! Get up, you stupid, ugly prick!"

Slowly, the old German did. He had a hand clutched to his temple. Blood rilled out between his fingers and ran down his cheek. "Why have you done that?" he choked out. "Not understand."

"I ought to kill you, is what I ought to do. I ought to gutshoot you," the Soviet soldier said. "You didn't harm me, you lying sack of shit? Who the fuck shot me?" He pointed to one arm, then to the other leg. "Who burned down the *kolkhoz* where I grew up? Who raped my sister and shot her afterwards? Was it the Americans? Or was it you *Heil, Hitler!* bastards?"

How much of that did the stupid old German get? Here, for once, Bokov was tempted to translate. The losers needed to hear stuff like this. They'd see what they bought when they invaded the USSR four years ago. And they'd see plenty of other things, too—for as long as they lasted.

More and more people kept going into the cars. It was almost like a comic turn in a film. When it ran in reverse after the train got to wherever it was going, how many people would come out alive? Fewer than had gone in—he was sure of that. The idea didn't break his heart.

He turned to Colonel Shteinberg. "How well do you think this will work, sir?"

"Well, we shook up the Baltic republics as if we were stirring soup," the Jew answered. "Anybody who might have been anti-Soviet, away he went. Or she went—we shipped out plenty of Baltic bitches, too." He chuckled reminiscently; maybe he'd been involved in that. But then the grin faded. "We could ship as many loyal Russians back in as we needed—the Baltics are legally part of the USSR now. We can't do that so well here."

"No," Bokov agreed. Germany, however prostrate it was, remained a separate country. "Too bad."

"Isn't it?" Shteinberg said. "So we have to depend on scaring the devil out of the Fritzes we don't send to camps."

"That will work against most people. Will it work against the diehards?" Bokov asked.

"I doubt it." Colonel Shteinberg sounded so indifferent, Bokov looked at him in surprise. The other NKVD man condescended to explain: "Sooner or later, we'll scare one of the ordinary ones enough to make him sing. He'll think, *If I sell out, they won't take my daughter* or *They won't shoot me* or whatever bothers him the most. And once we get our hooks into the diehards' network, it'll start coming to pieces. They always do."

"Ah." Bokov thought about it. "Yes, sir, you're probably right."

"You'd better believe I am," Shteinberg said. "We'll make every miserable German in our occupation zone sure hell's not half a kilometer away from his front door. Some of them will decide they'd rather kiss our behinds than keep on getting it in the neck 'cause they're making like tough guys."

He talked like a tough guy himself—actually, like a *zek*, a man who'd been through the camps. Maybe he'd been a guard at one of them. Or maybe he had a term in his past. Plenty of people who went into the gulags in '37 or '38 came out again after the Hitlerites invaded. Some of them became Heroes of the Soviet Union, too, which didn't mean they wouldn't go right back into a camp if they sneezed at the wrong time. Even men like Tupolev, the great aircraft designer, had the camps hanging over their heads like the sword of Damocles.

The Red Army men made sure the cars were shut good and tight.

Each one boasted impressive locks and bars that hadn't been on them while they were part of the German railway system—unless the Germans used them to haul people to *their* concentration camps. Similarly, metal gratings and barbed wire across passenger-car windows made sure nobody would leave that way.

Smoke poured from the locomotive's stack. The train pulled out of the station, heading east. Vladimir Bokov wondered if any of the Germans on board had the slightest idea how far east they were likely to go. Well, if the sons of bitches didn't, they'd find out pretty damn quick.

Colonel Shteinberg watched the train go with no expression at all on his face. "A good job, eh?" Bokov said.

Shteinberg looked at him as coldly as he'd eyed the train. "They could put every German ever born on trains like this, and it still wouldn't be enough to pay them back for what they did," he said. His voice was also cool and quiet, but Bokov realized there were people who liked Fritzes even less than he did.

LOU WEISSBERG WAS EATING BREAKFAST AT THE BARRACKS IN NUREM-berg when somebody came in waving the *Stars and Stripes*. "Look at this!" the guy shouted. "Look what we done to the goddamn Japs!"

"Hold the stupid thing still, willya?" somebody else said, more irritably than Lou would have—maybe this fellow hadn't had his coffee yet. "Give us a chance to see what it says."

"Oh. Sorry." The guy with the paper did hold it still—and upside down. After assorted hoots from the soldiers shoveling food into their faces, he turned it right side up.

Upside down or right side up, the headline screamed about an atom bomb. "What the hell is that?" a major asked.

"They dropped one on this, uh, Hiroshima place, and the town is gone. Right off the map," said the man with the *Stars and Stripes*.

"Well, they firebombed the living shit out of Tokyo not long ago, too, and they pretty much burned it off the map. So what's such a big deal about this?" The major seemed determined not to be impressed—or maybe he didn't fully grasp what was going on.

Either way, the guy with the paper spelled it out for him: "Yes, sir, but that was hundreds of planes and gazillions of incendiaries—Christ only knows how many. This Hiroshima place, this was one plane and one bomb. One."

"What? One bomb? A whole city? My ass! That's impossible!" the major said. If not for the enormous headline, Lou would have felt the same way."

"Here's what the President said." The man with the *Stars and Stripes* opened it and read from a story: " 'Sixteen hours ago an American airplane dropped one bomb on Hiroshima, an important Japanese army base. That bomb had more power than 20,000 tons of TNT. It had more than two thousand times the power of the British "Grand Slam" which is the largest bomb ever yet used in the history of warfare.' "

The guy beside Lou stubbed out his cigarette and crossed himself. Lou knew just how he felt.

" 'The Japanese began the war from the air at Pearl Harbor. They have been repaid many fold,' " read the fellow with the paper. " 'And the end is not yet. With this bomb we have now added a new and revolutionary increase in destruction to supplement the growing power of our armed forces. In their present form these bombs are now in production and even more powerful forms are in development.

" 'It is an atomic bomb. It is a harnessing of the basic power of the universe. The force from which the sun draws its power has been loosed against those who brought war to the Far East.' "

"Son of a bitch," the skeptical major whispered. That summed up what Lou was feeling, too.

" 'Before 1939, it was the accepted belief of scientists that it was theoretically possible to release atomic energy. But no one knew any practical method of doing it.' " The guy who had the *Stars and Stripes* didn't read especially well. Or maybe he was as flummoxed as everybody else. He went on, " 'By 1942, however, we knew that the Germans were working feverishly to find a way to add atomic energy to the other engines of war with which they hoped to enslave the world. But they failed. We may be grateful to Providence that the Germans got the V-1's and V-2's late and in limited quantities and that they did not get the atomic bomb at all.' "

"Oh, son of a bitch." From Lou, it came out as more prayer than curse. Imagining the Nazis with a bomb that could take out a city at one shot scared him worse than anything he'd seen in the war, which was saying a lot.

" 'The battle of the laboratories held fateful risks for us as well as the battles of the air, land, and sea, and we have now won the battle of the laboratories as we have won the other battles.' " The soldier folded the *Stars and Stripes* shut again.

"Wow," said somebody at another table. "I wouldn't believe a story like that if it was in *Superman,* and here it is in *Stars and Stripes.*"

All through the mess hall, heads solemnly bobbed up and down. Lou understood what the other American meant, but he didn't nod. He had to fight not to wince, in fact. British and French officers were amazed—and politely dismayed—at how many of their allies from across the Atlantic read comic books. Right this second, Lou understood how they felt.

The major who hadn't wanted to believe in atom bombs said, "We ought to bring some of those mothers over here. If the Jerries want to keep blowing themselves up, we can drop one on Munich and one on Frankfurt and one on this fucking place, too. That'd teach 'em not to screw around with us, by God!"

He got even more nods than the guy who'd talked about *Superman.* "Uh, sir," Lou said, "how do we make sure our own people are out of places like this before we blast 'em? Sounds like one of these things takes out about a mile's worth a ground, maybe more, when it goes off."

"Hell, we'd do it. That kind of stuff is just details." The major was in artillery, which meant he'd never needed to worry about "that kind of stuff." Everything always looked easy to somebody who didn't have to do it.

"How many short rounds did your batteries fire?" somebody asked, not quite quietly enough.

"Who said that, goddammit?" The major turned the color of molten bronze. He jumped to his feet. "Who said that? Whoever it is can step outside, if he isn't too yellow."

"Oh, sit down, Major. Button your lip while you're at it," a gray-haired chicken colonel said. "I got a Purple Heart and a week in the hospital from a short round. That kind of thing happens more often than anybody wishes it did."

Instead of sitting, the major stormed out of the mess hall. Somebody snickered as he got to the door. That only made his back stiffer and his ears redder.

Lou drained his coffee before he stood up. He couldn't imagine the Japs staying in the war much longer, not after a right to the chin like this. Maybe the Nazis had bailed out at just the right time. If the USA had had an atom bomb while the fighting was still going on, it sure would have dropped one on Munich or Berlin.

Now . . . This wasn't a war any more, not officially. What it was was a running sore. Would we blow a city off the map because guerrillas bombed a barracks? Lou shook his head. It'd be like burning down a house with a flamethrower to kill a wasp.

But if you didn't kill the wasp, it would keep buzzing around. And it would keep stinging. So how were you supposed to get rid of it? There was a good question. So far, nobody'd found anything resembling a good answer.

When Hans Klein first heard reports about the American atom bomb, he said two things. The first was *"Quatsch"*—rubbish. The second was *"Unmöglich"*—impossible.

That also pretty much summed up Reinhard Heydrich's reaction. He'd had much better connections than Klein's. He knew German physicists had tried to make a uranium bomb. He also knew they hadn't come close to succeeding. If German scientists couldn't do it, odds were nobody else could, either.

Odds were only odds, though. Sometimes snake eyes would come up four times in a row with honest dice. Not often, but sometimes. So maybe the Americans really had come up with something new. Maybe.

Three days after they claimed to have destroyed Hiroshima, they claimed to have destroyed Nagasaki. And, less than a week after that, the Japanese Empire surrendered unconditionally. Well, not quite: the Japanese wanted to retain the Emperor. But close enough. Heydrich was astonished, to say nothing of appalled. He'd counted on the little yellow men to bloody the Americans who landed on their beaches to

take their islands away from them. That would help make the occupiers sick of holding Germany down.

Would have made. Now the German resistance would have to go
it alone. Reluctantly, Klein said, "I guess the American pigdogs really
do have these fancy bombs."

"I'd say so," Heydrich agreed.

"Can we get *our* hands on one, sir?" the *Oberscharführer* asked.
"That'd teach the enemy a thing or three."

"I don't think we can sneak one from America to here," Heydrich
said. Klein gave back a glum nod. Heydrich continued, "If we can
find out where our own scientists were working and how far they
got . . ."

"Don't you know?" Klein seemed astonished that Heydrich
wouldn't.

But Heydrich had to shake his head. "No. I never found out much
about the project—it was highly secret. And, of course, it came to
nothing, so I thought it wasn't important. It seems I was wrong."

Hans Klein had been through a lot with Heydrich. It took a lot,
then, to surprise him. But his eyebrows leaped toward his hairline
now. "Meaning no disrespect, sir, but I don't think I ever heard you
say that before."

"No, eh?" Heydrich smiled a thin smile: the only kind apt to fit on
his long, lean face. "Well, maybe it's because I don't make mistakes
very often. And maybe it's because, when I do make one, I don't talk
about it afterwards—and neither does anybody else."

"Er—yes, sir," Klein said hastily. Anyone in the *Reich* who talked
about Heydrich's mistakes—with the sole exception of Heinrich
Himmler—would have counted himself lucky if he only ended up in a
camp.

"Now . . ." Heydrich pulled his attention back to the business at
hand. "What can we do about this? Dammit, I really don't know
much about uranium or radioactivity. Can we get our hands on someone who does?"

"Beats me, sir," Klein said. "If you don't know much about this
business, well, me, I know less than nothing. But I do wonder about
something."

"What's that?" Heydrich snapped. Facing the blue glare of his attention was like standing up against a pair of lit Bunsen burners.

Gulping, Klein said, "If we piss the Americans off enough, will they use one of these hellish things on us? One bomb, one city gone." He shuddered.

"*Donnerwetter*," Heydrich said softly. "The whole country is hostage to them." His fingers drummed on the desktop. "This place is safe against any ordinary bombs, even the big British ones. But what would happen if one of those things blew up right on top of us?"

"Beats me," Klein said. "How would we go about finding out?" He glanced up uneasily at the ceiling—and at the many, many meters of rock above the ceiling. He'd never worried about ordinary bombs, either. But how could you help worrying about these atom bombs, especially when you didn't know exactly what they could do?

Dryly, Heydrich answered, "Well, I don't want to make the experiment. Maybe we'd live even if they did it—we're a devil of a long way underground. But if they dropped one of those things on us, that would mean they knew where we were. And the only way they could do that would be to squeeze it out of somebody who already knows."

"What will we do when they start capturing our people?" Klein asked. "They will, you know, if they haven't by now. Things go wrong."

Heydrich's fingers drummed some more. He didn't worry about the laborers who'd expanded this redoubt—they'd all gone straight to camps after they did their work. But captured fighters were indeed another story. He sighed. "Things go wrong. *Ja.* If they didn't, Stalin would be lurking somewhere in the Pripet Marshes, trying to keep his partisans fighting against us. We would've worked Churchill to death in a coal mine." He barked laughter. "The British did some of that for us, when they threw the bastard out of office last month. And we'd be getting ready to fight the Amis on their side of the Atlantic. But . . . things went wrong."

"Yes, sir." After a moment, Klein ventured, "Uh, sir—you didn't answer my question."

"Oh. Prisoners." Heydrich had to remind himself what his aide was talking about. "I don't know what we can do, Klein, except make sure our people all have cyanide pills."

"Some won't have the chance to use them. Some won't have the nerve," Klein said.

Not many men had the nerve to tell Reinhard Heydrich the unvarnished truth. Heydrich kept Klein around not least because Klein was one of those men. They were useful to have. Hitler would have done better had he seen that.

Heydrich recognized the truth when he heard it now: one more thing Hitler'd had trouble with. "I don't know what we'll do," Heydrich said slowly. "We'll play it by ear, I suppose. I don't know whether the enemy will treat our men as prisoners of war or as *francstireurs,* or—"

"The Russians won't treat us like POWs," Klein broke in. "They'll jump on us like they're squashing grapes to make wine."

"*Ja.*" Heydrich scowled. Keeping the resistance going in the Soviet zone was harder than it was in the parts of Germany the Western democracies held. The Russians played by the rules only when it suited them. Otherwise, the NKVD was at least as ruthless as the *Gestapo* had been.

"And so?" Klein was persistent. This must have been on his mind for a while now.

"We've done what we can," Heydrich said. "We work in cells. The cell leaders don't know where their orders come from—only that they'd better follow them. Losing men won't make the system unravel. Even if our government surrendered, it's still a war. What else can I tell you?"

"Nothing, I suppose," the *Oberscharführer* answered. He didn't sound happy.

"Nothing at all," Heydrich said firmly. "It is still a war, dammit. We hurt the enemy as best we can. Sometimes he hurts us. That's a part of war, too, as much as we wish it weren't. Eh?" He wouldn't have wasted time cajoling many other people—maybe no one else still alive—but he and Hans went back a long way.

"*Ja.* I suppose so," Klein said. "But . . ."

"But what?" Heydrich snapped. Even with his old driver, he ran out of patience quickly. He was too used to automatic obedience to be comfortable with anything less.

"But we can't afford to get hurt much any more," Klein said. "If we do, the resistance movement will fall to pieces."

Heydrich sucked in a deep breath, ready to scorch the obstreperous noncom with hot words. He exhaled with Klein still unscorched. How could you come down on somebody who was obviously right?

Only long habits of discipline, obedience, and patriotism would make a man go out and blow himself up to hurt the occupiers. If the troops in the field had no one of suitable authority to obey . . . Germany would be ruined forever.

"They haven't found us. They won't find us. Even if they discover this place, we've got others to go to." Heydrich realized he was bucking up his own spirits as well as Klein's. And why not? His morale mattered, too. "We are going to win this fight, Hans. However long it takes, we'll do it. And the *Vaterland* will be free again."

"*Ja, Herr Reichsprotektor.*" Klein didn't sound a hundred percent convinced, but he didn't call Heydrich a liar with his tone, either. That was something, anyhow. In this uncertain twilight struggle, Heydrich took whatever he could get.

GEORGE PATTON HAD THE BAD HABIT OF SITTING UP VERY STRAIGHT in his jeep. Sometimes he'd even stand up behind the pintle-mounted .50-caliber machine gun the jeep carried. Not for the first time—not for the twentieth, either—his driver said, "General, I wish to Christ you wouldn't do that so much, especially when the road runs through woods like this."

Not for the first time—not for the twentieth, either—the commander of the U.S. Third Army laughed as if he'd just heard the juiciest joke ever. "Take an even strain, Smitty," he said. "The Huns are whipped."

"My ass . . . sir." Smitty hunched low behind the jeep's wheel. He had a wife and two kids in Dearborn, and he wanted to get home to see them again—he had just about enough points to do it, too. "They string that piano wire between trees just above windshield level, and no way in hell you can see it till it catches you in the neck. I hear they've taken two guys' heads clean off."

"Sounds like bullshit to me," Patton said. "Stories always get bigger in the telling. Do you know either of these unlucky souls? Can you put names to them?"

"Well . . . no," Smitty admitted.

"There you are!" Patton said triumphantly. "The Huns *are* whipped, I tell you. Maybe a few of them don't know it yet, but we'll keep licking them till they do. I promise you that."

"Yes, sir." Sometimes you couldn't win. Smitty'd done all the fighting he cared to do before the Germans surrendered. He didn't want to keep on doing it three and a half months later. But if he said so, Patton would go up like a Bouncing Betty. Smitty did say, "I sure wish you'd leave that chromed helmet back in the barracks, though. It's like you're wearing a SHOOT ME sign, y'know?"

"Nonsense!" Patton said. "The Germans fear me, and I don't fear them—not one bit, d'you hear me? Let them see trouble's heading their way."

He stood up again. He swung the big, heavy machine gun back and forth. Sure as hell, he had plenty of firepower at his disposal. But God didn't issue anybody eyes in the back of his head.

Not to Patton, and not to Smitty, either, however much the driver longed for them. The jeep's rearview mirror made a piss-poor substitute. Smitty didn't see the man in ragged *Feldgrau* get up on one knee in the roadside bushes and launch his *Panzerschreck*.

He did see the burst of flame from the antitank rocket. The *Panzerschreck* was a German copy of the U.S. bazooka round. The Germans didn't just copy it, either; they improved it. A *Panzerschreck* had more range and penetrated thicker armor than its American prototype.

This one didn't need the extra range. Smitty had time to go "Aw, shit!" He was starting to yank the wheel hard left when the rocket hit the jeep's right rear and flipped it over. Patton's startled squawk cut off abruptly when a ton and a half of metal and burning gasoline came down on top of him.

Smitty was luckier—he got thrown clear of the jeep. He put his teeth through his lower lip and broke several of them when he met the road facefirst, but he could crawl dazedly away from the inferno that engulfed the general.

He'd had a grease gun beside him on the seat. He couldn't find it now. If the kraut with the *Panzerschreck* came after him, he was history. But the German seemed content with blasting the jeep—he bailed out. And why not? He'd just scragged a four-star general.

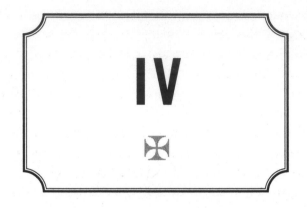

IV

Erlangen was shut down tight—"tighter'n a fifty-buck whore's snatch," one GI put it—for General Patton's funeral procession. Sandbagged machine-gun nests outside of town made sure nobody unauthorized got in. Mustangs and Thunderbolts buzzed overhead, ready to strafe infiltrators or shoot down any enemy airplanes that tried to interrupt the proceedings.

Lou Weissberg wondered how much good all that would do. If the fanatics—a name for the diehard Nazis the papers were using more and more often—already had people in town, they wouldn't need to sneak in more now. He wondered why nobody with a grade higher than his seemed to have thought of that. No one to whom he mentioned it seemed to want to listen.

He also wondered why the occupation authorities were making such a show out of Patton's rites. As far as he was concerned, Old Blood and Guts was a blowhard, a good fighter with few other virtues. During the war, his men worshipped and despised him in about equal numbers. Since . . . If he could have stirred up a war with the Red Army, he would cheerfully have rearmed the Jerries and sent them into battle alongside the U.S. Army. He cared not a pfennig for Eisenhower's denazification orders.

Rumor said Eisenhower was about to remove him from command of Third Army when the krauts removed him permanently. Lou didn't know whether the rumor was true. He wouldn't have been surprised, though. Eisenhower and Patton had been banging heads since the invasion of Sicily, two years ago now.

But here came Ike, driven down Erlangen's *Hauptstrasse*—main drag—in a jeep, a look of pious mourning on his face. Another jeep followed, this one with Patton's coffin on a standard Army quarter-ton trailer hooked up behind. An American flag covered the coffin.

The *Hauptstrasse* led to the *Altstädter Kirche*—the Old City Church—north of the market square. American soldiers lining the parade route fell in behind the jeep to crowd into the square. Germans who tried to do the same were discouraged, more firmly than politely. Again, Lou hoped it would matter.

A couple of GIs with scope-sighted rifles peered out from the church's steeple. *Snipers,* Lou thought. *Terrific.* But maybe having them there was better than not having them. Maybe.

Newsreel cameras recorded the goings-on. One of them peered up at the riflemen. And how would they look to folks back home, here months after peace was supposed to have come? What were they thinking on the far side of the Atlantic? How much did they like this festering aftermath of war?

Eisenhower climbed down from his jeep. Two unsmiling dogfaces with Tommy guns escorted him to a lectern in front of the church's steps. The sun glinted from the microphones on the lectern . . . and from the pentagon of stars on each of Ike's shoulder straps. "General of the army" was a clumsy title, but it let him deal with field marshals on equal terms.

He tapped a mike. Noise boomed out of speakers mounted to either side of the lectern. Had some bright young American tech sergeant checked to make sure the fanatics didn't try to wire explosives to the microphone circuitry? Evidently, because nothing went kaboom.

"Today it is our sad duty to pay our final respects to one of the great soldiers of the twentieth century. General George Smith Patton was admired by his colleagues, revered by his troops, and feared by his foes," Ike said. If there were a medal for hypocrisy, he would have won it then. But you were supposed to speak only well of the dead. Lou groped for the Latin phrase, but couldn't come up with it.

"The fear our foes felt for General Patton is shown by the cowardly way they murdered him: from behind, with a weapon intended to take out tanks. They judged, and rightly, that George Patton was worth more to the U.S. Army than a Stuart or a Sherman or a Pershing," Eisenhower said.

"Damn straight," muttered the man standing next to Lou. He wore a tanker's coveralls, so his opinion of tanks carried weight. Tears glinted in his eyes, which told all that needed telling of his opinion of Patton.

Eisenhower's voice hardened, his Midwestern accent stern as weathered granite: "But these Nazi cowards also judged they could scare us out of Germany by murdering General Patton. They judged they could run us out of Germany, and they judged they could take over again once we cut and ran—take over and start getting ready for the Third World War. That's what they thought. That's how they thought."

He looked out at the assembled GIs. "Well, folks, I am here—I am right here, in Erlangen, in the American occupation zone—to tell them they are wrong."

Lou whooped. He clapped. He was one of many, very many. The soldiers here had seen too much of what Hitler's thugs had done ever to want to see any more of that.

"We are doing all we can to put an end to their wicked violence," Eisenhower went on. Then he used the word of the moment: "Because they're fanatics, our enemies are taking longer than they should to realize they can't hope to defeat the might of the United States of America."

He got another round of applause, louder than the first. The tankman next to Lou joined in, but he also murmured, "Son of a bitch, but I wish I was back in Omaha."

Lou wished he were back in New Jersey, too. Unfortunately, wishing wouldn't put him there. Cleaning up the leftover Nazis just might. It looked like his best chance, anyhow.

"I have one more message for you men, and for the SS goons who skulk in the woods and in the darkness," Eisenhower said. "It's very simple. We are going to stay here as long as it takes to make sure Germany can never again trouble the peace of the world."

He probably expected more cheers then. He got . . . a few. Lou was one of the men who clapped. The guy in the tanker's coveralls edged away, as if afraid he had something contagious. That saddened him without much surprising him. He wondered how many of the others who applauded there were also Jewish. Quite a few, unless he missed his guess.

Yes, Eisenhower had looked for more in the way of approval there. He'd acted professionally grim before. Now his eyes narrowed and the corners of his mouth turned down. He wasn't just grim any more; he was pissed off.

"We would waste everything we've done up till now if we walked away too soon," he said, and Lou thought he was speaking off the cuff rather than from prepared remarks, as he had earlier. He pointed south. "Down in Nuremberg, we're going to try the thugs who are the only reason we had to come here at all. And after that I'd be very much surprised if we don't hang 'em higher than Haman."

This time, Lou clapped till his palms hurt. Most of the soldiers in the market square joined him. They wanted to see the war criminals get what was coming to them, all right.

Eisenhower looked a little happier after that—not much, but a little. "And if we catch *Reichsprotektor* Heydrich by then, we'll try him and hang him, too," he said. "Or maybe we won't bother trying Mr. Heydrich, not when the maniacs he leads have done so much dirty work after the surrender."

More hot, fierce applause. Heydrich was Public Enemy Number One these days, sure as hell. Lou and the Counter-Intelligence Corps were responsible for that. Posters displaying Heydrich's rather lizardy features were plastered to everything that didn't walk. They promised the famous $500,000, tax-free to GIs, for information leading to his capture . . . or to his body. To a dogface making fifty bucks a month—and, with luck, to a kraut, too—that had to look pretty damn good.

It also looked pretty damn good to Lou: 250 years' worth of a first lieutenant's salary. He glanced around. Lots and lots of GIs. No Reinhard Heydrich, dammit. Heydrich was too cool a calculator to risk himself for the glory of it. He'd be hiding away somewhere, cooking up more trouble.

"And there's one more reason we don't want to step away before it's time." Eisenhower looked east. "The fanatics have hurt the Soviet Union, too. Remember, they killed Marshal Koniev before they got General Patton. But whatever Heydrich's men do over in the Russian zone, they won't drive drive out the Red Army. You can bet your bottom dollar on that."

Lou looked around again. That comment didn't raise much applause, but it made a good many soldiers nod thoughtfully. Almost the only thing that kept the USA and USSR on speaking terms was that they both hated and feared the Nazis worse than they hated and feared each other. Without the fanatics, they might have squabbled even more. *There's irony for you,* Lou thought.

Having got in his licks, Eisenhower stepped away from the lectern. After that, Patton's memorial service was in religious hands. It wasn't Lou's religion, but that wasn't why he stopped listening. Ike had surprised him a couple of times. The preacher sounded canned. You knew what he'd say three sentences before he got around to saying it. Nothing was wrong with his remarks, exactly, but they got bloody dull.

Somebody not far from Lou enlivened the proceedings by passing out. He'd stood in the sun too long, and was fine as soon as they flipped water on him. But the near-panic when he pitched forward on his face told how jumpy all the GIs were. No German snipers, no nothing—only jitters. Enough jitters, though, and you didn't need anything else.

As the memorial broke up, a corporal talking to his buddy delivered his own verdict on Patton: "Sure he was a ballbuster, but he was *our* ballbuster." The buddy nodded. So did Lou. That made more sense than most of the highfalutin blather he'd listened to before.

LIKE ANY SOVIET CITIZEN, VLADIMIR BOKOV HAD LEARNED MORE about what war could do than he ever wanted to know. Leningrad: besieged by the Germans and Finns for three years, with hundreds of thousands dead of bombs and shells and hunger and cold and disease. Stalingrad: blasted from the air, then systematically pounded flat by two armies till one could fight no more. Kharkov and Rostov-on-the-Don: both taken by the Nazis, retaken by the Red Army, taken back by the Nazis, and finally seized for good by the USSR, with each side slaughtering the other's collaborators and toadies as soon as it grabbed power.

And those were only a few of the high points—or the low points, if you thought that way.

But despite everything Captain Bokov had learned, despite everything he'd seen, despite his utter lack of sympathy for the folk who'd come too close to enslaving the Soviet Union forever, Dresden gave him the willies. British and American bombers had visited hell on the city in the winter before the war . . . was alleged to have ended.

"*Bozhemoi,*" Bokov muttered, surveying square kilometers of barrenness, of charred shells of buildings, of places where asphalt had puddled and then run like rivers. The twin stenches of burning and death still thickened the air. He suspected they would linger for years.

"Cunts had it coming," said his driver, a stolid peasant named Gorinovich.

"Oh, no doubt," Bokov agreed. Not only did he really feel that way, but you never could tell to whom Gorinovich reported. An NKVD man saw wheels within wheels whether they were there or not. In the USSR, and in Bokov's line of work, they commonly were. He did add, "If the Americans could do *this* without their fancy new bombs, screw me if I know why they needed them."

Gorinovich grunted in response to that. Then he said, "You were going to Division HQ, sir?"

"*Da.*" Bokov nodded.

"All right. I'll get you there."

And he did. The paving was chewed up and sometimes nonexistent, but neither mud nor gravel nor anything else fazed the two-and-a-half-ton American truck. U.S. tanks had thin armor, weak guns, and highly inflammable gasoline engines. The planes the Americans gave the Soviet Union were mostly ones they didn't want themselves. But nobody ever said a bad word about their trucks. The Red Army would have had a devil of a time winning the war without them.

With a word of thanks, Bokov hopped out of this one in front of the battered house flying the divisional commander's flag. Sentries with submachine guns stood in front of the door. Like most of their kind, they scrambled out of the way with comic haste when they spotted his arm-of-service colors.

In a way, that wasn't so good. A Nazi who got hold of an NKVD cap and shoulder boards might bluff his way in to see—or to assassinate—almost anybody. *Worry about it later,* Bokov told himself. *One thing at a time.* He turned the knob and walked into the house.

Major General Boris Antipov was drinking tea and laughing with a pretty redhead half his age. When Bokov came in, she turned red, exclaimed in German, and disappeared with a rustle of silk. She'd landed on her feet in postwar Germany—or more likely on her back.

"Who the—?" Antipov growled. Then he too noticed Bokov's shoulder boards and cap. Some of the hostility left his voice as he went on, "Oh. You're the fellow they sent from Berlin."

"That's me," Bokov said. "Does your, ah, friend speak Russian?"

"Not a word of it. But she fucks like it's going out of style, so who cares? Why do you—?" Antipov broke off again and clapped a meaty hand to his forehead. "Son of a bitch! Are you thinking Trudi's a spy? That's the craziest thing I ever heard."

"I'm not thinking that," Bokov said carefully—even the NKVD had to pick its spots before it risked pissing off a general. "But you should recognize the possibility even so. And I wanted to make sure we could talk without her eavesdropping."

"Well, we can," Antipov said. "You'll want to know about the prisoner, eh?"

Bokov leaned forward like a hunting dog taking a scent. "Yes. I'll want to know about the prisoner." His voice was soft and eager.

"Can't tell you a whole hell of a lot," Antipov said. "What I mainly know is, his bomb didn't go off. Maybe it was a dud, or maybe he chickened out at the last second. But my boys noticed him acting weird, so they jumped on him. When they found his vest, they tied him up good and tight and let me know. I called you people. That kind of stuff is your baby."

"Thanks," Bokov said. Some Red Army men would have tried putting the screws to an important prisoner themselves. In fact, maybe Antipov had. Casually, Bokov asked, "Get anything out of him?"

"His name, his rank, his pay number—that's about it. Like I said, we didn't work him over much. Figured that was your business," Antipov answered. "Oh. And he says he's a prisoner of war."

"Prisoner of war, my dick," Bokov said. "Not after the Hitlerites surrendered, he's not. He's nothing but a fucking bandit. And even before . . ."

General Antipov nodded. The USSR treated German prisoners only slightly better than the Nazis treated captured Soviet troops. Hundreds of thousands of German POWs went into the gulags. Maybe some would come out one day. On the other hand, maybe none would. Bokov wouldn't lose any sleep over that.

"I'll take him back to Berlin, where we can interrogate him properly," the NKVD man said. They would get answers out of the German. Bokov was sure of that. The NKVD had ways of finding out what it needed to know. They weren't pretty, but they worked.

"Come on, then." Antipov got to his feet. For a moment, Bokov thought the general himself would take him to the prisoner, but he didn't. As soon as they got outside, Antipov bawled for some men. A squad appeared on the double. The soldiers were well turned-out and looked very alert. "Take him to the German," Antipov told them. "Do whatever he says."

"Yes, Comrade General!" the men chorused. Their sergeant saluted Bokov. "Come with us, sir."

They'd disarmed the would-be bomber and stowed him in a shed a couple of hundred meters away. Four soldiers with submachine guns stood guard around it. That German wasn't going anywhere. At Bokov's nod, one of the guards unbarred the door. *"Heraus!"* he shouted. It might have been the only word of German he knew—or needed.

Slowly, the Fritz emerged. He had bruises and scrapes on his face and a cut lip. By the way he cradled his right wrist in his left hand, it was sprained, maybe broken. Well, the soldiers wouldn't have been gentle when they grabbed him.

"Ought to string him up by the nuts," one soldier said.

"Roast him over a slow fire," another agreed.

The way the captive watched them made Bokov wonder. "Do you speak Russian?" he asked in German.

"Sir, my name is Fenstermacher, Gustav Eduard Fenstermacher. My rank is *Obergefreiter.*" Gustav Eduard Fenstermacher rattled off a serial number. "I am a prisoner of war. Under the Geneva Convention, I don't have to say anything else."

He was about twenty-five—a few years younger than Bokov—
with blue eyes and brown hair. The *Wehrmacht* had several ranks
between senior private and corporal; he held one of them. He wore
ragged *Feldgrau* as if it were new and pressed and kitted out with his
rank badges and medals.

Bokov laughed in his face. "Fuck you, fuck your mother, and fuck
the Geneva Convention, too." It would have sounded better in Russian, but German would do. "You're dead meat. You're dogshit,
nothing else but. Have you got that?"

Fenstermacher stood mute. Bokov murmured to a Red Army man
beside him. Grinning, the trooper stepped up and whacked the German on his bad wrist. Fenstermacher wailed. He went white. He
started to sag to his knees, but managed to catch himself.

"Have you got that, dogshit?" Bokov asked again. *Obergefreiter*
Fenstermacher hesitated. "Don't screw around with me," Bokov advised him. "If you were a hero, you would've died yesterday. Last
chance, arselick—have you got that?"

The German licked his lips. "*Ja,*" he whispered, just before Bokov
told the soldier to give him another lick.

"Better," Bokov said. And it was. Once a girl who'd been holding
out let you get a hand between her legs, everything else was easy. In-
terrogations worked the same way. "So . . . do you speak Russian?"

Another hesitation—a shorter one this time. "Not much. Mostly
bad words," Fenstermacher said.

Plenty of Russians Bokov knew spoke bits of German the same
way. Which didn't mean this snake was telling the truth. The right lie
now could give him his chance later. He'd think so, anyhow. Bokov
didn't intend to let anything like that happen.

The U.S.-built truck waited not far from the house General Antipov had commandeered. The driver stood outside, leaning against a
fender and smoking a cigarette. By the look of him, Gorinovich didn't
care whether he stayed there another half hour or another week.

"Tie the German up," Bokov told Antipov's men. "Don't hurt him
more than you have to unless he gives you trouble. You, you, and
you"—he pointed to three soldiers, one after another—"you'll come
back to Berlin with us and make sure nothing happens to him. Get
moving."

They did. Had he said they were going to London, they would

have done the same. After they hogtied Gustav Eduard Fenstermacher, they half-frogmarched, half-lugged him over to the truck. When
they were about to throw him in the back, he finally asked the question that must have burned in his mind since Bokov got him out of the
shed, or more likely since he let himself be taken alive: "What . . . will
you do to me?"

Images formed in the NKVD officer's mind. A cell too small to
stand up or lie down in. Not nearly enough food. Not nearly enough
sleep, which could be even worse. Bright lights. Pain. Fear. Always fear.

Fenstermacher had to be imagining most of those same things. For
Vladimir Bokov, they weren't imaginary. They were the tools of his
trade, like a mechanic's wrench and pliers or a sculptor's mallet and
chisel. But that was all right . . . to Bokov. Imagination and anticipation were tools of his trade, too. What a prisoner imagined his captors
doing to him could break him faster than what they did.

Bokov trotted out a couple of small tools: a pitying sigh and a
shake of the head. "You won't like any of it," he said. "And by the
time it's over, you'll tell us everything. You'll be glad to, and you'll
wish you could tell us more."

"I won't." Even Fenstermacher had to hear how hollow his defiance sounded.

"Oh, you will," Bokov promised him. "One way or another, you
will. . . . You *could* come clean before it all starts. Believe me, it won't
change anything in the end, except you'll be a lot happier." He eyed
the German. "Think about it on the way to Berlin. I'll ask you again
then. If you say no—you'll find out just what we do to you, that's all."

"I—" Fenstermacher began.

"Chuck him in the truck," Bokov told the Red Army men, cutting
him off. Let him stew in his own juices all the way back to the ravaged
capital of the ravaged *Reich*. After that . . . The NKVD would get its
answers. Captain Bokov didn't much care how.

DIANA MCGRAW WAS JUST STARTING TO DUST THE SPARE BEDROOM
when the doorbell rang. "Damn!" she said, and then looked around
guiltily to make sure Ed hadn't heard. But the rattle and squeak of the
old lawnmower out back told her he was still working on the yard.
That was a relief. He didn't like her to swear, not even a little bit.

She hurried downstairs: a slim woman in her late forties, going from blond to gray but not all the way there yet. She muttered wordlessly as she opened the door. Her daughter and son-in-law were half an hour early. That was annoying, even if they would have little Stan with them.

"Oh!" she blurted. It wasn't Betsy and Buster and the baby out there. It was a kid in a dark green jacket with brass buttons.

"Mrs., uh, McGraw?" The kid had to look down at the pale yellow envelope in his right hand to get the name. He was just about old enough to start shaving. When Diana nodded, he thrust the envelope at her. "Wire for you, ma'am."

"Uh, thanks," she said in surprise. She hadn't got a telegram in months. "Hold on a second. Let me grab my handbag."

But when she came back with the purse, the Western Union delivery boy was bicycling down the street, pedaling hard. Her mouth fell open as she stared after him. He hadn't waited for his tip! How far behind on his work was he? Far enough to be scared of getting fired if he didn't go like a bat out of you-know-where? That was the only thing that made even a little sense to her.

Then she opened the envelope, and everything stopped making sense. The wire was from the War Department. In smudgy, carbon paper–like printing, it said, *The Secretary of War deeply regrets to inform you that your son, Patrick Jonathan McGraw, private, U.S. Army*—Pat's serial number followed—*was killed outside of Munich, Germany, on 19 September 1945.*

There was more, all of it over the typed signature of a lieutenant colonel. But all Diana saw was *Son. Patrick Jonathan McGraw. Killed.* That looked big as the world, and blotted out everything else.

She staggered toward the back of the house as if Joe Louis had landed an uppercut right on the button. After a moment, she reversed course long enough to shut the front door.

It was impossible. The war in Europe was over. It had been for months. Oh, there were stories in the paper about fanatics and diehards. They'd even killed General Patton. But Pat's letters assured her everything was quiet in his sector. Like a fool—like a mother—she'd believed him.

Son. Patrick Jonathan McGraw. Killed.

"Ed?" she said when she got to the back door. One syllable was all she had in her.

The lawnmower stopped. Ed McGraw's bald head gleamed under the end-of-summer Indiana sun. "Dang!" he said—he wouldn't swear in front of her, either. "They here already?" Then he got a good look at her face. The half-rueful, half-annoyed grin on his own faded. "What is it, hon? What's the matter?"

So she had to find more syllables after all. She managed two: "Pat. He—" But she couldn't say that. She *couldn't*. She held out the telegram instead. It had the words. *Son. Patrick Jonathan McGraw. Killed.*

Ed McGraw stumped over to her. He'd lost the last two toes on his left foot in France in 1918. In spite of that, he'd tried to reenlist the day after Pearl Harbor. They wouldn't take him. They probably wouldn't have if he weren't maimed—he was well overage. So he went on working at the Delco-Remy plant in Anderson, the way he had since he came home with eight toes, making good money and socking away a nice chunk of it.

Anderson, halfway between Indianapolis and Muncie, was almost as big as the latter. But people all over the country had heard of Muncie. Plenty of people in Indiana had no idea Anderson existed. Neither Diana nor Ed cared about that. They liked Anderson fine. They'd raised two good kids there, and expected a fine crop of grand-children. It had already started coming in. Now . . .

Diana had just started to cry when Ed took the wire from her, say-ing gently, "Your mother?"

Her mother was seventy-seven, frail and starting to be forgetful. If, God forbid, something were to happen to her, it would be sad, but it would be part of the natural order of things. But when a parent had to put a child in the ground . . .

Ed held the yellow sheet out at arm's length. He wasn't wearing his reading glasses, not to mow the lawn. Diana wondered if he'd be able to see what it said. If he couldn't, she'd have to read it to him or tell him, and she thought she would rather die herself.

"Oh, Jesus Christ," he said hoarsely. He could read it, all right. When he raised his face to her, it bore the same blind, helpless look she had to be wearing herself. "Pat . . ." He was stumbling over things, too. "Germany . . . Those crazy fucking assholes . . ."

Even now, she stared at him. He didn't say things like that. Oh, maybe at the factory, but never around the house. Never. Except he just did. And why not? What else were the Germans who'd murdered Pat?

"It's wrong." If Diana didn't say what was wrong, maybe she wouldn't have to think about that. So much. Quite so much. Maybe. "It's *wrong*. The war is *over.* They've got no business doing *that.*" Close call there.

"Pat . . ." Ed said again. He was a minute or two behind her. Right now, a minute or two bulked big as a mountain. "What are we going to do without Pat?"

He'd come closer to actually talking about death than Diana had. "We have to make it stop," she said. "The war's *over.* How many people are still getting wires like—" She broke off, her mouth falling open. No wonder the Western Union boy pedaled away so fast! She'd heard they didn't take tips when they brought news like that. It seemed to be true.

"Hello!"

Diana almost jumped out of her skin. There stood Betsy, holding Stan. And there beside them was her husband, Buster Neft. He had a limp worse than Ed's: he'd come back from the South Pacific a year and a half before with a Bronze Star and a Purple Heart. He'd been an outstanding high-school tackle before the war. He'd talked about playing college ball, but a shellburst made damn sure he wouldn't. Now he worked at Delco-Remy, too. Close to half of Anderson did.

Betsy went on, "We knocked at the front door, but nobody came. Bus heard you guys talking back here, so we came around and. . . ." She ran down when she noticed her folks weren't responding the way she'd expected them to.

Her husband saw the telegram still in Ed's hand. "What happened?" he asked sharply. When Ed didn't answer, Buster came up and took the wire. He didn't need to hold it away from himself to read it. "Oh, no!" he said, and threw his free hand in the air in anguish. "God damn those motherfucking sons of bitches to hell!"

Part of Diana thought those were the words she'd been looking for herself but couldn't find. Part thought they didn't go nearly far enough.

"What is it?" Betsy snatched the telegram away from Buster.

"Pat!" she wailed, and let out a shriek that set the baby howling. Buster took him. Betsy ran to her mother and father. They clung together.

That shriek brought neighbors out to see who was murdering whom, and why. They converged on the McGraws' house. Several of them had lost somebody in their family, or at least had somebody hurt. They knew what the McGraws were going through because they'd done it. And the ones who hadn't—the lucky ones—all knew people who had. How could you not?

Somebody—Diana forgot who—pressed a cold tumbler into her hands and said, "Drink this up." She did, thinking it was 7-Up. It turned out to be gin and tonic, and almost went down the wrong pipe. But she felt a little better with it inside her. It built a thin wall between her and everything else. She could still see through the wall, and hear through it, too. She could even reach over it and feel what was there. But the bit of distance the gin gave was welcome.

"Such a crying shame," a neighbor said. She was crying; it made her mascara run. "Pat was a good boy."

Everybody nodded. "If you didn't like Pat, you didn't like people," another neighbor said. "I don't know a soul who didn't." Everyone nodded again.

"Such a . . . waste." With women all around him, Buster swallowed some of what he might have said. "I mean, when I got hit, we were fighting the Japs. I knew why I was on that beach—to make the slant-eyed so-and-so's say uncle. But to get killed on occupation duty? That's a joke, or it would be if it was funny. What the heck are we wasting our time—wasting our people—over there for now that the . . . darn war's done?"

"That's what I said when I showed Ed the wire," Diana exclaimed. "That's just exactly what I said. Isn't it, Ed?" She blinked—she was talking very loud and very fast. The gin must have hit her harder than she thought.

"You sure did, honey." Ed had a glass in his hand. Where did that come from? Diana had no idea. Not surprising, not when she didn't know who'd given her that welcome gin.

"I wonder how many people all over the country are going through the same thing for no reason," Betsy said. Her mascara was all over her face, too. Most of the women's was.

"Too many," Diana said. "One would be too many. One is too many." *Son. Patrick Jonathan McGraw. Killed.* Yes, she could feel what was there.

"It's a lot more than one," Buster said. "All these loonies with bombs strapped on . . . But I don't know how many. I wonder if anybody outside the War Department does. Papers sure don't talk about it. You just pay attention to them and the radio, everything's fine over there."

"And that's not right, either," Ed said. His face was redder than the sun should have made it. Whoever'd handed him that drink had fixed him a doozie. Well, why not? Wagging his index finger in the air, he went on, "I can see why we didn't talk so much about casualties while the war was still cooking. Hitler and Tojo'd find out stuff they didn't need to know? But now? What makes a difference now?"

"Brass hats don't want folks back here to find out how bad they snafu'd things over there," Buster said wisely.

Ed nodded, vigorously enough to make the flesh of his double chin shake. So did most of the men gathered there: the ones who'd served in either war, Diana realized. She only blinked again, in confusion. "Snafu'd?" She wasn't sure she'd even heard it right.

"It's short for 'situation normal—all, uh, fouled up,' " her son-in-law explained. Even at a time like that, Ed managed a grin and a grunted chuckle. Diana wondered why. Then she saw it could also be short for something else. She blamed the drink for slowing her wits. She wasn't about to blame herself—no, indeed.

"We ought to know the truth about what's going in," she said. "Isn't that what we fought the darn war for?" The news about Pat had horrified Ed into swearing in front of her. She couldn't imagine a calamity that would make her swear in front of the neighbors.

"You're right," Betsy said. She took Stan back from Buster.

The baby was eight months old. He had two teeth. He could say "dada" but not "mama" yet, which irked Betsy. He smiled whenever anybody smiled at him or whenever he just felt like smiling. Why not? He had no idea what was going on, the lucky little guy.

Betsy's face crumpled. "He'll never get to know his Uncle Pat now," she said—almost the same thought as Diana's. Betsy started crying again. Stan stared at her. He could cry whenever he felt like it, too—could and did. He wasn't used to seeing Mommy do the same thing.

A neighbor touched Diana on the arm. "If there's anything we can do over the next few days, sweetheart, you sing out, you hear? Anything at all, and don't be shy," she said. "If we don't help each other, who's gonna?"

"Thanks, Louise. God bless you." That made Diana think of something else. She still could think straight if she worked at it. "Ed! We've got to call Father Gallagher."

"We sure do." He shook his head, which made his jowls wobble some more. "So much to take care off. And for what? For a waste, a big dumb waste."

"That's what it is, all right. Nothing else but. And nobody should have to die on account of a big, stupid waste," Diana said. "Not Pat, and not nobody—uh, anybody—else, either. It's wrong, don't you see? It's *wrong*." More nods said her neighbors thought so, too.

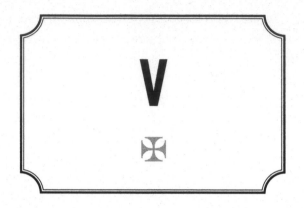

V

If Lou Weissberg hadn't known what he was looking for, he never would have found it. Even knowing, he almost walked right past the forest bunker. Sergeant Benton saved him, pointing and saying, "Reckon that's it, sir."

"Is it?" Lou turned back—and got a raindrop in the eye. Mud squelched under his boots. It was a miserable day to go poking through the woods. But he finally saw the join between the regular forest floor and artfully camouflaged dug-up ground. "Yeah, I guess you're right." He gestured to the squad of GIs who'd come with them. "Okay, guys—we're here. Spread out and form your perimeter."

"Right." The corporal in charge of them sounded no happier to be futzing around in the middle of the Bavarian woods than Lou was. Nobody'd asked his opinion, though, and nobody was likely to. "Take your positions," he told his men. "And for Chrissake watch out for trip wires unless you want your balls blown off."

Thus encouraged, the soldiers moved out around the bunker. Half of them carried M-1s, the others grease guns. If they had to, they could put a lot of lead in the air. Nobody touched off a Bouncing

Betty, for which Lou thanked the God in Whom he'd had more and more trouble believing since he found out about Dachau and Belsen and the murder camps farther east.

He would rather have come out here by himself, or just with Toby Benton. Several horrors had proved that Americans traveling alone or in pairs weren't safe, though. And so he had a squad along to remind the krauts that they'd been defeated and surrendered and given up.

Of course, he wasn't exactly safe even with the hired muscle along. As the corporal had reminded his men, Heydrich's goons liked booby traps. The fanatics were too goddamn good at concealing them, too.

Sergeant Benton was an artist in his own right. He also had some specialized tools: a battery-powered detector to find metallic mines and a long, thin wooden probe to find the ones that weren't. And he had wire-cutters to take care of the trip wires he—like the corporal— assumed would be there. And they were.

"Okey-doke, Lieutenant," he said after a good deal of careful work. "Looks like we can dig now."

Lou nodded to the corporal. That worthy said, "Rojek!"

One of the GIs jerked as if stung by a wasp. "What'd I do to deserve this?"

"You was born lucky," the corporal answered. "C'mon. Get your ass over here."

Muttering bitterly, Rojek did. He used his entrenching tool with a marked lack of enthusiasm. "I oughta write my Congressman," he said.

The corporal gave him the horse laugh. "Yeah, like they give a shit about us. Now tell me another one."

Before long, Rojek banged the tool against a roof of logs and planks. "Can't go through that," he said with some satisfaction. "I ain't no beaver."

"You want beaver, go back to Nuremberg and fraternize with some," the corporal said.

"We've got saws along," Lou said. The look Private Rojek gave him proved glares weren't lethal.

But the corporal spread the wealth. Another GI got to play woodsman. He cut through enough logs to open a space a skinny man could use to get in. Lou filled the bill. Before dropping down, he shone a flashlight into the bunker. He didn't want to land on a detonator—or on a bunch of knife blades or bayonets pointing up. The fanatics came up with lots of ways to make the occupation more . . . interesting.

This time, he didn't see anything like that. "I knew I should've been a dentist," he remarked as he lowered himself into the hole. "Then I wouldn't've had to mess around with crap like this. But no. I wanted to study English lit, so when I volunteered they put me in CIC. My mother gets to say 'I told you so.' "

He let himself drop, and landed with a thump on the floor of hard-packed dirt. A damp, musty smell filled his nostrils. Nobody'd been in this bunker for a while. A prisoner had told the Americans about it, though, so they had to find it and take it out of circulation.

Which would do how much to win the fight against the fanatics? How many of these bunkers were scattered all over Germany—and Austria, and the German-settled parts of Czechoslovakia, and maybe other places, too? Heydrich was a son of a bitch, no two ways about it, but by all the signs he was a goddamn thorough son of a bitch.

Lou turned slowly, playing the flashlight around the bunker. A small stove sat in one corner, with a pipe leading up through the roof to the forest floor above. Neither he nor Benton had spotted where the stovepipe emerged. However much you hated them, nobody could say the Jerries weren't good at what they did.

The walls were planked. Neat metal brackets on them held Mausers and Schmeissers and close to a dozen of the halfway-between weapons the Germans had started fielding in the last year of the war. Assault rifles, they called them; some people said Hitler himself hung the handle on them. True or not, it wasn't a bad monicker. They used a longer, heavier cartridge than a submachine gun's pistol round, and fired at full automatic out to three or four hundred yards. GIs who'd run into them said they were very bad news.

Sergeant Benton's head and shoulders appeared above, blocking most of the cold, gray light that drizzled in through the hole. "Is it the goods, Lieutenant?" he asked.

"Looks that way," Lou said.

"Shucks." Benton sounded disappointed. "Reckon Ludwig gets to keep his family jewels after all. Too goddamn bad."

"Heh," Lou said tightly. He didn't think CIC would have made the prisoner sing soprano if he'd tried to string his U.S. interrogators along, but he wasn't sure. With the war allegedly over, nobody seemed sure what the rules were for Germans captured in arms against the occupiers. Some U.S. officers called them *francs-tireurs* and shot them without trial. Some grilled them mercilessly, declaring that the Geneva Convention didn't apply. And some treated them as POWs. There were no orders from on high; the brass was as confused as everyone else.

Just to make matters even more delightful, the fanatics kidnapped GIs and murdered them and left their bodies in prominent places with placards saying things like VENGEANCE FOR OUR FALLEN COMRADES. Sometimes they would just cut a man's throat. Sometimes they'd get more creative. Lou remembered the poor bastard with his cock stuck in his. . . . He shook his head—shuddered, really. He didn't want to remember that.

He used the flashlight again. A makeshift desk—a filing cabinet, a couple of crates, and boards across them—stood in the corner opposite the stove. Lou walked over to it. He started to open the top file-cabinet drawer. Then he thought better of it.

"Hey, Toby!" he called.

Benton came back. "What have you got, Lieutenant?"

"Stick your head in a little further and see." Lou lit up the desk. "Just the kind of thing the Jerries'd booby-trap, looks like."

"Want me to pull its teeth?"

"If you think you can. Maybe we'll get lucky. The Germans love paperwork. If they give us a roster of half the bastards who've been driving us buggy—"

"We'll take it. Yeah." Sergeant Benton nodded. "Okay. I'll have me a look." His shoulders were wider than Lou's; he had to wiggle to fit through the hole. He dropped into the bunker.

"Don't do anything you're not sure about," Lou told him. "A booby trap here could be wired to enough TNT to blow up this whole fucking forest."

"Uh-huh. Don't I know it?" Benton advanced on the desk with unhurried calm. "I ain't gonna get cute—believe you me I ain't. I aim to climb on a ship and go home one of these days whether the krauts like it or not."

"Sounds good to me," Lou agreed.

As if he hadn't spoken, Benton went on, "So if I think they're getting sneaky, I'll just back off. I'm good at this business, but I know there's guys where I'm not even in their class. So . . ."

He went to work on the top drawer. Lou stood there and waited. He did his best to act relaxed, but sweat trickled from his armpits down his sides. Sweat was supposed to cool you off. These beads felt boiling hot. He told himself that was his imagination. It had to be, but so what?

Benton started to open the drawer, then paused. With a grunt, he went around to the side of the file cabinet and shone his flashlight into the narrow space between its back and the wall. "Uh-*huh*," he said on a thoughtful note.

"What's up?"

"Looks like a wire goin' back there—two wires, matter of fact, one for top and one for bottom. If I'd've pulled . . . Well, who knows? But I don't aim to find out."

"Can you cut 'em?"

"Oh, sure." Benton seemed surprised he needed to ask. "Be a second or two—gotta fit the wire-cutters to the extensions so they'll reach. Can you lean over and shine a light down while I work? Otherwise I kinda need three hands. Lean *over* the desk, I mean. Don't touch nothin' if you can help it, you know?"

"I'll try." Lou did, wishing he were six inches taller so he had more to lean with. "How's that?"

"Over to the left a tad . . . There you go." Lou couldn't see what Benton was doing. He heard a couple of clunks, then one soft twang, then another. The sergeant sighed. "Okay—now I've pulled all its teeth. Let's see what we've got."

Are you sure? Not asking was as tough as standing there radiating unconcern had been. If Lou didn't trust Benton to do this job right, he should have brought someone else along. Doubting him out loud would piss him off, and might hurt his confidence. That could make him goof later, which neither of them would enjoy.

Lou opened the top drawer. Nothing blew up. He wasn't astonished to find the drawer full of potato-masher grenades. "No sweat, Lieutenant," Benton said. "I cut the wire that woulda tripped those fuckers right away."

"That's nice," Lou said. "You do the bottom drawer, too?"

"Better believe it."

Thus encouraged, Lou also opened that one. He found more grenades. Whistling between his teeth, he turned the flashlight on the papers in the crates. To his disappointment, they weren't anything he could use to track more fanatics. Some were comic book–style four-panel illustrations of how to fire the *Panzerfaust* and the *Panzer-schreck*. Others were propaganda posters showing bestial-looking American soldiers assaulting Aryan children while a mother watched in horror. The German caption read *Roosevelt sends kidnappers, gangsters, and convicts in his army.*

Toby Benton read as much German as he read Choctaw. The pictures told their own story, though. "Nice to know they love us," he said dryly.

"This is old stuff," Lou said. "They printed it while the war was still going on—before FDR died."

"Well, we'll still get rid of it," Benton said. "We'll clean out all this crap, and that'll be one bunker the bastards'll never use again."

"Sure it will. And that'll leave—how many just like it?" Lou'd had this unhappy thought not long before. "A million? Nah, let's look on the bright side—a million minus one."

Benton gave him a quizzical look—not the first he'd got from the stolid noncom. "Would you sooner leave it here?"

"No, no." Lou shook his head. "But I was hoping it'd give us a lead to more of the diehards, and it doesn't look like it will. Shutting down places like this won't put out the fire."

"Neither will not shutting 'em down," Sergeant Benton answered, and Lou couldn't very well tell him he was wrong.

CONGRESSMAN JERRY DUNCAN SCRAWLED HIS SIGNATURE ON A LET-ter commending a constituent for collecting a ton and a half of scrap aluminum. With the war over, people would find different things to do with their spare time and energy. They'd still need letters of commendation from their Congressmen, though. Jerry Duncan was morally certain of that.

Plump and smooth and well-manicured, he was morally certain of a good many things. Like most Republicans, he was morally certain four terms were too many for any one President, and especially for a Democrat. Well, God had taken care of that. Now that That Man wasn't in the White House any more, 1948 looked a lot rosier for the GOP.

So did 1946. With any luck at all, his party would recapture at least one house of Congress for the first time since the Hoover administration. Duncan had just been getting his feet under him in his law practice in those days. Another world back then, one without Hitler, without the atom bomb, without FDR's alphabet-soup agencies, without American boys stationed all over the world and trying to figure out what the hell was going on . . .

Well, people right here in Washington were trying to figure out what the hell was going on, too. Jerry Duncan knew damn well he was. So much had happened so fast since the Japs bombed Pearl Harbor. And even after V-E Day and V-J Day, things didn't seem to have slowed down.

His secretary stuck her head into his inner office. "What's up, Gladys?" Jerry asked, glad to escape his own thoughts.

"That woman from Anderson is here to see you, Congressman."

"She is?" Duncan glanced at his wristwatch in surprise. "How'd it get to be three o'clock already?" He'd been doing this, that, and the other thing. By what he'd accomplished, it shouldn't even have been lunchtime. Plenty of people lived their whole lives three steps behind where they should have been. He supposed he ought to be glad he didn't get the feeling more often. But it still rattled him. He tried to pull himself together. "Well, tell her to come in."

"Sure." Gladys withdrew without closing the door all the way. He heard her say, "You can go in now."

"Thank you." The door opened again. Duncan got to his feet. The woman who came in was about as old as he was. She must've been hot stuff when she was younger. She wouldn't have been bad now if she weren't wearing black . . . and if the look on her face didn't say hot stuff was the furthest thing from her mind. "Congressman Duncan?" she said. Automatically, Jerry nodded. She held out her hand. "I'm Diana McGraw."

As automatically, Duncan shook it. Her grip was firm but cool. "Pleased to meet you, Mrs. McGraw," he said. "And I was very sorry to hear about your tragic loss. Please accept my sympathies. Too many boys are dead."

Her nod was bitter and determined at the same time. "Yes. Too many boys are dead," she agreed. "And for what, Congressman? *For what?* Why did Pat have to die, after the war was supposed to be over?"

Gladys came in with a tray. "Coffee?"

"Please." Jerry was glad for the interruption. "Won't you sit down, Mrs. McGraw?" he asked while Gladys poured two cups.

"Thank you." She sat stiffly, as if her machinery needed oiling. Gladys put cream and sugar into Jerry's cup, then looked a question at her. "Black is fine," Mrs. McGraw said.

"Here you are, then." The secretary set cup and saucer near the edge of Jerry's desk, then went out again.

Without preamble, Diana McGraw said, "Do you know how many American soldiers besides my Pat have been killed since the Nazis said they surrendered?"

Congressman Duncan started to answer, but caught himself. "No, I don't know, not exactly. The War Department hasn't publicized the numbers, whatever they are."

"It sure hasn't," Mrs. McGraw agreed with a sniper's smile. "How many do you think, if you don't mind my asking?"

"Over a hundred—I'm sure of that," Jerry said. "Some of the atrocities do get into the papers. I wouldn't be surprised if it were twice that number, maybe even three times."

She smiled that frightening smile again. It made Jerry Duncan want to dive for cover. "The true figure is at least a thousand dead. *At least.*" She seemed to repeat herself for emphasis. "That doesn't count wounded. All since the so-called surrender."

Cautiously, Jerry asked, "How do you know?" *Do you really know?* was what he meant. Still picking his words with care, he went on, "As I say, the War Department doesn't go out of its way to talk about figures."

"Would you, if you had to talk about figures like that?" Diana McGraw returned. "As for how I know, well, I have connections." She held up a hasty hand. "Not political connections, not the kind you usually think about. But when Pat and Betsy were in school, I was in the PTA. I was Central Indiana vice-chairwoman for several years, as a matter of fact. I went to a couple of the national conventions. I know mothers all over the country. Ever since Pat . . . died, I've been on the phone. I've been sending wires. My friends have been asking questions where they live. That's what they've found out, and I believe them."

Jerry whistled softly. "I believe you," he said, and meant it: she radiated conviction. "Over a thousand? Good Lord!"

"You have to understand," she said. "If some German killed Pat in the Battle of the Bulge, I wouldn't be here talking with you now. I'd be as sorry as I am, but not quite the same way. War is war, and things like that can happen. But we're at peace now, or we're supposed to be. Why did Pat have to die almost five months after the war was supposed to be over? Why have a thousand American kids died after it was supposed to be over?"

"That's . . . a better question than I thought it would be when you made this appointment," Jerry said slowly. Like a lot of Midwestern Republicans, he'd wanted nothing to do with the war in Europe when it broke out. He hadn't called himself an isolationist, but he hadn't been far from thinking that way, either.

Then Japan bombed Pearl Harbor. Of course he voted for the declaration of war. He wanted to—he was as furious as anybody else. And if he hadn't, his district would have tarred him and feathered him and ridden him out of Congress on a rail.

Hitler declared war on the USA. That saved him from wondering how he would have voted when Roosevelt asked for war against Germany. Maybe not knowing was just as well.

"What do you want me to do, Mrs. McGraw?" he asked.

"Get some answers," she said at once. "Why are we still over there now that the war's over? What are we doing over there that could possibly be worth a thousand lives? Why is the War Department trying to hush up everything that's going on over there?"

Those were all good questions. Jerry Duncan said so. They were especially good questions for a Republican to ask, since they could hold a Democratic administration's feet to the fire. "And what will you be doing yourself?" Jerry inquired.

"Me?" Diana McGraw sounded surprised he needed to ask. "I'm going to the papers and the radio stations. You can't keep things secret forever, Congressman. You just can't."

"You're right," Duncan said. "You're absolutely right. Some of the mistakes we made in the first part of the war . . . Well, thank God we didn't lose on account of them. Sometimes I wonder why we didn't. Believe me, I do. And the public still doesn't know about a lot of them."

"A few weeks ago, I would have been shocked if you told me something like that. Shocked. Now I believe you," she said. "Why do those people want to sweep everything under the rug?"

"To keep folks from pointing a finger at their mistakes." Again, Jerry replied without hesitation. With a politician's facility, he chose not to remember that he'd voted against the draft bill that passed by a single vote the summer before Pearl Harbor, and that he'd also voted against more money for the War and Navy Departments before the USA actually got into the fighting. Pointing a finger at the administration's mistakes was easy. Pointing a finger at his own . . .

"High time somebody did," Mrs. McGraw said. "Germany's smashed. It's knocked flat. It's not going to magically come back to life if we bring our boys home."

"I hope not." Jerry did remember that people had said the same thing after World War I. But nobody'd blown up American doughboys in the aftermath of that fight. Who could say now what would have happened had the Germans tried it then?

"Let's get on with it," she said crisply. "How many GIs will the fanatics have killed by this time next week or next month or next year? And why will those GIs have died? For what?"

"For making sure the Nazis don't come back and start up again." Jerry knew exactly what his Democratic colleagues would say. He said it himself, to see how Diana McGraw responded.

She snorted. She looked at him as if she'd found half of him in her apple. She was nothing but a housewife, but she made him flinch. "Oh, nonsense," she said, and somehow she got more scorn into that than a cigar-puffing committee chairman would have from *Oh, bullshit.* "How do you hold down a whole country?" she went on. "And how do you fight people who'll blow themselves up to get rid of you? If they're already willing to die, what can you do to make them quit?"

Jerry Duncan opened his mouth. Then he closed it again. Nobody in America had been able to find a good answer to that. One of the things the public didn't know was how much damage Japanese kamikazes had done. How much more would they have inflicted if the USA'd had to invade the Home Islands? Jerry silently thanked God for the A-bomb. It had saved one hell of a lot of American casualties.

Probably kept a good many Japs from joining their ancestors, too, not that he gave a rat's ass about them.

"It's a good question," he said, hoping his pause wasn't too noticeable. "I'll be honest with you—I don't know. Maybe some Army officers do—"

"Fat chance," Mrs. McGraw broke in.

"I was going to say, but if they do, they sure haven't given any sign of it."

"No. They haven't." Her bitterness was hidden while she planned action. It came back now. "And Pat's dead, and my grandson will grow up never knowing his uncle, and my husband stumbles around like a man in a daze—no, like a man who's stopped caring. And he has. And how can you blame him, if Pat died for nothing?"

"If—" Jerry began.

She interrupted him again: "If we get our troops out of there because of what happened to Pat, it may turn out to be worthwhile after all. It may. If we don't . . ." She shook her head, then brushed at the bit of transparent black veiling that came down over her eyes from her hat.

She left a few minutes later, back straight, stride determined. She had a Cause, and she'd stick with it come hell or high water. Jerry Duncan stared after her, even though she'd closed the door when she went out. Damned if she hadn't given him one, too.

BRESLAU WASN'T IN GERMANY ANY MORE. FOR THAT MATTER, BRESLAU wasn't Breslau any more. Stalin had shoved the USSR's border several hundred kilometers west, and shoved newly resuscitated Poland west about as far at Germany's expense to make up for it.

The Poles were calling the place Wroclaw, which they pronounced something like *Breslau*. Captain Vladimir Bokov didn't give a damn what they called it. He also didn't give a damn that he was in Soviet-occupied Poland rather than Soviet-occupied Germany. As long as the Red Army was around, nobody except the Fascist bandits he was trying to root out would give him any trouble. Local officials sure as hell wouldn't.

Breslau, Wroclaw, whatever you wanted to call it, had its share of bandits and then some. Its garrison, surrounded on all sides, had held out till just before the general surrender. The Poles were trying to solve their German problem by resettling their countrymen from Lwow and other cities to the east who didn't want to live under Soviet rule, and by uprooting the local Germans and marching them west toward the new border—at gunpoint, if necessary. That would probably work . . . in the long run. For the time being, it gave the remaining Germans every reason to support the fanatics.

Thus, the local Polish governor had just come to a sudden and untimely end. A sniper had put a Mauser round through his head from close to a kilometer away. Shooting Poles had its points; Bokov had done it himself, more than once. Even shooting Communist Party members was sometimes necessary, as anyone who'd worked through the purges of the late 1930s could attest.

But shooting someone who was in the Soviet government's good graces went over the line. And so Vladimir Bokov had come east to do something about it. The highway to Wroclaw was wide and fine. It had been part of the German *Autobahn* system. Now the Poles got to use it.

There was an American film where one police official told another, "Round up the usual suspects." The local authorities in Wroclaw, Polish and Russian, seemed to have followed that rule. To them, the usual suspects seemed to include anyone who thought the city should still be called Breslau . . . should, in other words, stay German.

They'd rounded up hundreds of *Wehrmacht* veterans. They'd added all the butchers, bakers, and candlestick makers who'd ever said anything bad about Poles or Russians. In a town like Wroclaw, that gave them plenty to choose from.

A captain in a *csapka* met Bokov outside the wire-fenced camp where the locals were stowing their prisoners. Bokov thought the square-crowned Polish headgear looked asinine, but that wasn't his worry. After a couple of false starts, he and Captain Leszczynski conversed in German. He could almost understand Leszczynski's Polish, but Leszczynski didn't want to try to follow his Russian. The Pole wore three Red Army decorations on his chest, but he was plainly a nationalist as well as a Communist.

One day, no doubt, Leszczynski would get purged. Bokov was sure of it. Maybe the proud Pole knew it, too. But they were on the same side now.

"These damned Werewolves are driving us nuts," Leszczynski said. Bokov was highly fluent in German; he'd studied it for years. Leszczynski spoke it like a native. Before the war, he'd likely used it as much as Polish. The Poles might hate and fear their western neighbors, but they leaned toward them as if drawn by a magnet. In Russian, a traveling fort with a cannon in the turret was a *tank,* as it was in English. The Poles borrowed *pancer* from the Germans.

"We'll deal with them. One way or another, we will," Bokov said confidently.

"Jawohl. Aber natürlich." Irony filled Captain Leszczynski's voice. Poles didn't like Russians much better than they liked Germans. They looked down their noses at Russians, though, and hardly bothered to hide it. So did Germans, of course. It was almost less annoying from them than from fellow Slavs.

"We will," Bokov insisted. "If we have to kill them all, we'll do that."

"Hmm. Well, maybe." Captain Leszczynski seemed to be reminding himself they were allies here. "Which prisoners will you want to interrogate?"

"The ones you think likeliest to know something about Comrade Pietruszka's murder," Bokov answered. Before the Pole could say anything, he added, "The ones who hate us worst."

"Oh, they all hate us," Leszczynski said. "The only question is, which ones did something about it?"

Adrian Marwede said he'd been a *Wehrmacht* noncom. He still wore a ratty field-gray service blouse. Bokov eyed a slightly darker ring on the left sleeve near the cuff: the sort of ring a cloth cuff-title might leave after it was removed. Only a few *Wehrmacht* divisions used cuff-titles. However . . . "You were really in the *Waffen-SS, nicht wahr?"* All their outfits had them.

Marwede turned pale. "Well—yes," he muttered.

But then Captain Leszczynski took Bokov aside. "When Breslau surrendered, all the defenders were promised life, personal property, and eventual return to Germany—the SS included."

"What?" Bokov couldn't believe it. "Who made such an idiotic promise?"

With a certain somber relish, the Pole replied, "Lieutenant General Gluzdovsky, commander, Soviet Sixth Army, First Ukrainian Front."

Bokov gave him a dirty look. The truth could be far more irritating than any lie. "All right, I won't knock him around for being an SS swine," the NKVD man said. "I'll knock him around because he may know something about what happened to Pietruszka. Does that make you happy?"

"Pietruszka was a solid man," Leszczynski said, which could have meant anything.

Whatever it meant, Bokov could worry about it later. He turned back to Adrian Marwede. "So, SS man . . ." he said, and watched Marwede flinch. In a Russian's mouth, that was all too likely a death sentence in and of itself. Bokov let him stew for a few seconds, then asked, "What do you know about Reinhard Heydrich, SS man?"

"He's supposed to be a tough bastard." Marwede sounded less impressed than he might have. He explained why as he went on, "How tough can you be when you hardly ever get near the front?"

Captain Bokov didn't care whether Heydrich was personally brave. Things he'd heard made him think Heydrich was, but it didn't matter one way or the other. The man was a goddamn nuisance—worse than a goddamn nuisance—and needed suppressing. "What do you know about what Heydrich's up to, SS man?"

"What? You think the *Reichsprotektor* talks to the likes of me?" Marwede raised an eyebrow.

Without changing expression, Bokov slapped him across the face, forehand and backhand. That was good technique; not only did it hurt, it humiliated. The German staggered. "Don't screw around with me," Bokov said evenly. "Tell me what I want to know, and don't give me any shit. You answer another question with a question and what happens next'll make that look like a love tap. Get me?"

Marwede spat—spat red, in fact. He nodded gingerly. "Yes, I get you."

He got that his life lay in an NKVD officer's cupped palm. Well, what else did he need to get? If Bokov decided to squeeze . . . "What do you know about what Heydrich's up to?"

"Not much." Hastily, Marwede went on, "Nobody up at the front ever found out much of what he was up to. All we knew was, there were times we couldn't get the guns or the ammo we needed. When that happened, people would swear at Heydrich. He was squirreling the stuff away, or guys said he was."

"I've heard that before," Captain Leszczynski remarked.

"So have I," Bokov said. He knew why, too: it was true. He also knew why Heydrich was squirreling that stuff away—to do just what he and his merry thugs were doing now. The Russian eyed Marwede. "What else do you know? What else have you heard?"

"Well . . . nothing I can prove," Marwede said. Bokov gestured impatiently. The German continued, "Sometimes guys'd go back with light wounds, things that wouldn't keep them out of action more than two, three weeks, tops. Only they wouldn't come to the front again when they should've healed up. That'd drive our officers crazy."

"What happened to them?" Bokov asked. "And don't tell me you don't know, either. You Fritzes have paperwork coming out your assholes. I've never seen people for paperwork like Germans. If you wanted to find out where these troops were, you could."

Marwede held up his right hand with index and middle fingers raised together: the gesture Germans used when they were swearing an oath. "Honest to God, I don't know. Our officers *couldn't* track those guys. It was like they fell off the face of the earth. They just disappeared. Nobody knew where. Nobody could find out where. People said Heydrich had 'em. I don't know if he did, but people said so."

"I've heard that before, too," Leszczynski said.

"Me, too," Bokov agreed. He glowered at the SS man. "When did this start happening?"

"I don't know exactly." Marwede set himself for another blow. When it didn't come, he continued, "First couple of people I can remember disappearing like that were right after Kursk, I think."

"Fuck your mother!" Bokov exclaimed in Russian. Marwede scowled; he must have learned what that meant. The NKVD man didn't care. If the Germans had started collecting holdouts as early as the summer of 1943 . . . they'd have a devil of a lot of them, and the bastards could raise all kinds of hell. Which, when you got right down to it, was nothing he didn't know already.

"That I hadn't heard," Captain Leszczynski said with calm either commendable or excessive, depending on how you looked at things.

"Neither had I. As far as I know, nobody's heard that before,"

Bokov said. He wanted to slap the SS man around for no better reason than giving him bad news. The look he gave Marwede should have knocked him over by itself. "Listen, cuntface, if you're lying to me just to make me trip over my own dick, I'll hunt you down and cut your balls off and stuff 'em down your throat."

He wasn't lying. Adrian Marwede had the sense to realize as much. "Not me," he said, using that oath-taking gesture again. "I've done plenty of stupid things, but I'm not dumb enough to screw around with the NKVD."

So he recognized the collar tabs and cap, did he? That was interesting. "You were dumb enough to join the SS," Bokov growled. "You're dumb enough for anything." 1943? *Summer* 1943? *Bozhemoi!*

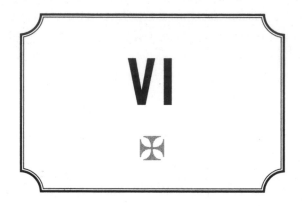

VI

The Indiana state Capitol was one impressive building. Diana Mc-Graw had never seen it before, not in person, even though Anderson was only about twenty miles outside of Indianapolis. A housewife in a suburban town didn't need to hobnob with state legislators. But, since she'd already seen her Congressman, the idea of coming here intimidated her less than it would have before.

Now that she'd seen the U.S. Capitol, this one also seemed a little less splendid than it would have. It was built in the same neo-Roman style, but the dome was smaller and narrower, the proportions altogether less grand. Well, so what? Indiana wasn't Washington, and most of the time that was a good thing.

Dressed in black, she got out of the family Pontiac. Ed sat stolidly behind the wheel, lighting a Chesterfield. This wasn't his show—it was hers. He mourned their son by himself, within himself. Diana was the one with the fiery conviction that what had happened to Pat shouldn't happen to any other mother's son. She was the one who was damn well going to do something about it, too.

She glanced at her watch. It was still a quarter to ten. Of course she'd made sure she got here early. Things wouldn't start for another forty-five minutes. And when they did . . . She wasn't sure what would happen then. You couldn't be sure till you went and did something.

A man across the street whistled and waved. It wasn't a wolf whistle—he was trying to get her attention. When she looked up, he called, "Mrs. McGraw?"

"That's me." She nodded automatically.

He loped across the street toward her, dodging cars like a half-back. He wore a snap-brim fedora and a sharp suit that didn't hang well on his pudgy frame. Behind him came a bareheaded guy in his shirtsleeves who carried a big camera. "I'm E. A. Stuart, from the *Times*," the man in the lead said. "S-T-U-A-R-T. No W. We talked on the phone. This sounds interesting. Jack here'll take photos."

"Hi," Jack said around the stub of a smelly cigar.

"Pleased to meet you both," Diana said. "What does the 'E.A.' stand for?"

Jack grunted laughter. E. A. Stuart sighed. "You really want to know? Ebenezer Amminadab," he answered resignedly. "My ma read the Bible too darn much, you want to know what I think. But that's how come I use E.A."

"Amminadab," Diana echoed in wonder, hoping she was pronouncing it right. "Well, now that you mention it, yes. About your mother, I mean."

"He was the only kid in kindergarten who went by his initials," Jack said.

"Oh, shut up," E. A. Stuart told him, and Diana was sure the reporter had heard the joke way too many times before. Stuart turned back to her. "How many people you expect here?"

"Hundreds," she said, more confidently than she felt. Where were they? She'd made phone calls. She'd sent wires. She'd got answers. No, more: she'd got promises. Satan surely fried people who said they'd do something and then didn't come through. That wouldn't do her any good, though. If this fizzles . . . I'll try something else, that's all, she told herself. Quitting never entered her mind.

Another woman wearing mourning got out of a car. The old De Soto drove off. The woman, who shouldered a sign as if it were an M-1, came over to Diana.

So did another reporter. He introduced himself as Chuck Christman, from the *Indianapolis News*. The photographer he had in tow might have been Jack's younger brother. The way the newspapermen razzed one another showed they'd been covering the same stories for a long time.

The other woman was Louise Rodgers, from Bloomington. She was about Diana's age—no big surprise there—and she'd lost a boy to a roadside bomb two weeks after the German surrender. "The papers and the news on the radio just whitewash everything," she told E. A. Stuart and Chuck Christman.

"We're here now," Christman pointed out.

"Months late and how many lives short?" Louise Rodgers said. "Till I heard from Diana, I didn't think I could do anything about David—that's my son; no, *was* my son—except sit around the house and cry all day. But if we can keep other mothers from crying, that's better."

"You said it," Diana agreed. The reporters scribbled.

More women drifted in. Some of them had lost sons after the Nazis allegedly gave up, too. Others hadn't, but still hated the idea of so many soldiers dying after the war was supposed to be over and victory won. Some men joined them, too—not many, but some. Two were veterans who'd been wounded in France or Germany. Another, older, was like Ed; he'd caught a packet in 1918.

"They called the last one the war to end war. This time, the stupid war can't even end itself," he said. The reporters liked that. They both wrote it down.

Diana went back and opened the Pontiac's rear door. She took her own picket sign off the backseat. BRING OUR BOYS HOME FROM GERMANY NOW! it said. "Come on," she told the other demonstrators.

Heart thuttering, she led them to the sidewalk in front of the capitol. She'd never done anything like this before. Till Pat got killed, she'd never imagined doing anything like this. Nothing like a kick in the teeth to boot you out of your old routine.

HOW MANY DEAD? one sign asked. TOO MANY DEAD! another answered. WHY ARE THEY STILL THERE? another demanded. ISN'T THE WAR OVER YET? a sign inquired rhetorically. STOP THE WAR DEPARTMENT'S LIES! another said. 1000+ DEAD SINCE SURRENDER! another sign declared. Anybody who carried one without either a question mark or an exclamation point seemed out of place.

Another contingent of picketers came up the street. ILLINOIS MOTHERS SUPPORT BRINGING TROOPS HOME! announced the sign their leader carried. GERMAN OCCUPATION WASTES AMERICAN LIVES! another one said. A decorated veteran carried that sign.

"Good to see you!" Diana called to the Illinoisans. She could hear how relieved she sounded. Well, she'd earned the right, by God. They'd said they would come down. It was an easy train trip from Chicago. But promises were worth their weight in gold. She remembered what she'd thought a little earlier about the Devil and people who didn't come through.

Now, where were the people from Ohio? They'd promised, too. Which meant . . . She'd have to see what it meant, or whether it meant anything.

A man driving a battered Model A Ford stopped right in the middle of Capitol Street. The bakery truck behind him almost rearended him, but he either didn't notice or didn't care. He leaned out the window and shouted, "Communists! You're all nothin' but a bunch of lousy Reds!"

"We're Americans, that's what we are!" Diana shouted back. The demonstrators near her cheered. *We have to carry flags next time,* she thought, and wished she could write that down so she wouldn't lose it.

"Communists!" the man in the Model A yelled again. He shook his fist at the people on the sidewalk.

The bakery-truck driver leaned on his horn. So did somebody stuck in back of him. The man in the Model A shook his fist once more, maybe at them, maybe at the picketers, maybe at the world. He put the decrepit old car in gear. It wheezed on down the road.

"Well, people are noticing us," said the woman at the head of the Illinois group. Her name was Edna Somebody—right this minute, Diana couldn't remember what.

She nodded. "That's the idea. Now where are those folks from Columbus and Cincinnati? They said they'd be here."

"Isn't that them?" Edna Somebody pointed up the street. Lopatynski, that was her name. *No wonder I couldn't come up with it for a second,* Diana told herself.

Sure enough, here they came, like the cavalry riding up over a hill in the last reel of a Western serial. OHIO SAYS TOO MANY HAVE DIED

FOR NOTHING! their leader's sign said. THE WAR DEPT. STILL WANTS WAR! declared another. And a haggard woman's sign poignantly asked, WHAT DID MY ONLY SON DIE FOR?

Another car stopped on Capitol, this one with a screech of brakes. "Traitors!" yelled the man inside. His face was beet red; he all but frothed at the mouth. "They oughta string up the lot of you!"

Diana worked hard to stay calm. She'd feared—no, she'd known—people would shout things like that. She'd done her homework, too. "The Constitution says we can peaceably assemble and petition for a redress of grievances. My son got blown up months after the surrender. Isn't that a grievance?"

The red-faced man's arm shot up and out in a salute the Germans had made odious all over the world. "*Heil* Hitler!" he said. "You fools want the Nazis back again." He drove off before horns blared behind him.

Edna Lopatynski's laugh was shaky, but it was a laugh. "Well, Diana, are we Communists or are we Nazis?"

"No," Diana answered firmly. "We're Americans. If the government is doing something stupid, we've got the right to say so. We've got the right to make it stop. And that's what we're doing." She looked around. Chuck Christman and E. A. Stuart were both close enough to hear what she'd said.

Yes, she'd expected to get called a traitor and a Communist. That anybody could think she was trying to help the Nazis after Heydrich's lunatics murdered Pat . . . Her free hand folded into a fist. She wanted to clock that guy. The nerve!

Several cops stood around watching the picketers go back and forth. One of them ambled over to Diana and fell into step beside her. "You running this whole shebang?" he inquired.

"I organized it, anyhow," she said. "I don't know that anybody's in charge."

"Yeah, well, if it goes wrong you're the one we'll jug," the policeman said. "Keep doing like you're doing. Stay spaced out. Let people through. Stuff like that. Long as you play by the rules, we won't give you no trouble. I think you're full of hops myself, but that's got nothin' to do with what's legal."

"My son got killed for no reason," Diana said tightly. "President

Truman never has said why we still need to be in Germany. I don't think he knows, either."

"He's the President of the United States." The cop sounded shocked.

"He was a Kansas City machine politician till FDR dumped Henry Wallace," Diana retorted. "He's only President 'cause Roosevelt died. He's not infallible or anything."

"Huh." Shaking his head, the policeman went away.

Several men who looked like state legislators—they were mostly portly, they had gray hair, and they wore expensive suits—came out onto the Capitol steps to watch the demonstration. Some of them shook their heads, too. *They must figure we're a bunch of crackpots,* Diana thought. *Well, we'll show 'em!*

One of the legislators got into an argument with his colleagues. Another man ostentatiously turned his back on him. Diana wondered if the first guy was on her side. She could hope so, anyhow.

A car horn blared. The driver stuck his left hand out of the window, middle finger raised. He didn't bother slowing down.

Lobbyists and lawyers with briefcases passed through the picket line on the way to doing business in the Capitol. "You should be ashamed," one of them said, but he took it no further than that. More ordinary people went through, too—men in work clothes, women in dresses they'd got from the Sears catalogue or made themselves.

A couple of them said unkind things, too. But one fellow who looked like a mechanic said, "Give 'em hell, folks!" and flashed a thumbs-up. Diana wanted to kiss him. Not everybody hated them! She'd hoped that was true, but she hadn't been sure.

A fat, middle-aged man stood on the sidewalk watching the demonstrators. Every time Diana turned around and got another look at him, he got hotter and hotter. Edna Lopatynski also saw it. "That fellow's going to make trouble," she said quietly.

"I'm afraid you're right," Diana answered. "But what can we do about it?"

They went back and forth twice more before the fat man blew a fuse. "Commies!" he yelled. "Nazis!" He didn't know which brush to tar them with, so he used both. Then he charged into them, fists flailing.

A woman squalled when he hit her. Another woman stuck out a foot and tripped him as he rampaged past her. A man sat on him and kept him from doing anything worse than he'd already done.

The Capitol police came over in a hurry this time, and came over in force. The fat man yelled obscenities. "I dink he boke by dose," said the woman he'd hit. Her nose was sure bleeding: red spotted the front of her white blouse. Jack and the photographer from the *News* both took pictures of her.

"You can't haul off and belt a lady like that, buddy," one of the policemen said. "You're under arrest."

"Lady?" The fat man found several other things to call her, none of them endearments. Then he said, "You oughta haul her off to jail for doing crap like this. You oughta haul every goddamn one o' these yahoos off to jail, and you oughta lose the key once you do."

"They may be jerks, but they aren't breaking any laws," the flat-foot answered. "Assault and battery, now . . ." He clicked his tongue between his teeth. "You should be ashamed of yourself. She ain't even half your size."

"A rattlesnake isn't big, either, but it's still poison." The fat man had strong opinions.

So did Diana. She wanted to tell the cops to haul him off and lose the key. No matter what she wanted, she made herself go on marching without saying anything. The police didn't like her. They wouldn't appreciate her sticking her oar in. If she just let them do their job . . .

They did it. They got the fat man up onto his feet, cuffed his hands behind him, and led him away. He swore a blue streak all the way, which did him exactly no good.

"Bring our boys home from Germany!" Diana chanted. The other picketers joined her. Together, they made more noise than the fat man. Diana thought it was obvious they made more sense, too.

"HERE YOU ARE, CONGRESSMAN." GLADYS PLOPPED THE DAY'S PAPERS onto Jerry Duncan's desk.

"Thanks," he said. "Could you bring me another cup of coffee, too? Can't seem to get myself perking this morning."

She grabbed the cup and saucer. "I'll be right back."

"Thanks," he said again, absently this time. He was already starting to study the papers. You had to keep up with what was going on if you wanted any chance to keep your head above water. The *New York Times* came first. It was much more pro-administration than Jerry was, but had far and away the best coverage of foreign affairs.

Gladys brought back the fresh cup, steam rising from it. Jerry Duncan sipped without consciously noticing where the coffee'd come from. After the *Times,* he went through the *Wall Street Journal* for economic news, and the *Washington Evening Star,* the *Post,* and the *Times-Herald* to find out what was going on in his second home.

Those done, he reached for the *Indianapolis News* and the *Indianapolis Times,* then for the *Anderson Democrat.* You also had to stay current with what was going on in your district. If you decided Washington was your first home, not your second, the folks back in Indiana would likely throw you out on your ear next chance they got.

Right in the middle of the *News'* front page was a photo of cops dragging off a wild-eyed fellow who could have dropped a few pounds, or more than a few. A woman with a picket sign and what looked like bloodstains on her face and on her blouse watched him go. *Man arrested after attacking demonstrator,* the caption said.

The story under the photo was almost studiously neutral. It identified the leader of the demonstration as "Diana McGraw, 48, of Anderson." She was "moved to oppose government policy on Germany after her son, Patrick, was killed there in September, long after the formal German surrender."

"Hmm," Jerry said, and went to see what the *Times* had to say: it was the more liberal paper in town. Because it backed the Democrats, it looked down its nose at anyone presuming to protest against their polices. But even its tone was more-in-sorrow-than-in-anger. Its editorial said, "While we understand Mrs. McGraw's grief and outrage, and those of other similarly afflicted, the United States must persist in its mission of returning Germany to civilization and democracy to Germany."

As for the *Anderson Democrat,* it didn't seem to know which way to jump. Its name told where its politics lay. On the other hand, Diana McGraw was a home town girl, doing something that got noticed beyond the home town's borders—not easy, not if your home town was

Anderson. "What would you do if it were your son?" she'd asked the *Democrat*'s reporter after the demonstration ended.

As far as Jerry was concerned, that was the sixty-four-dollar question. Even the *Democrat* and the *Indianapolis Times* seemed to understand as much. How could you condemn people who'd lost their boys in combat for wanting to know why? And wasn't that all the more true when they'd lost boys in combat when there wasn't supposed to be combat any more?

You might disagree with them—both papers plainly did. But you'd have a devil of a time calling them disloyal. A dead son gave someone carrying a picket sign a decided moral advantage.

Jerry realized he wouldn't be the only Congressman reading these reports. Come to think of it, he might not have been the only Congressman Diana McGraw saw when she came to Washington. If he wanted to stay in front on this issue, he couldn't sit on his hands. He had to stand up, or someone else would get ahead of him. His colleagues could and would draw the same conclusions he was drawing.

His own party desperately needed a club with which to clobber the Democrats. The other side had dominated Congress since the start of the 1930s. They'd just won the biggest war in the history of the world. That might set them up to keep winning elections forever if the GOP couldn't find a shillelagh.

If over a thousand GIs dead since V-E Day weren't a shillelagh . . . then the Republicans would never come up with one. Jerry started scribbling notes.

The House was debating a bill that would finish rationing by the end of the year. There wasn't much debate, because nobody worth mentioning opposed the bill. The whole country hated rationing. The sooner it disappeared forever, the happier everyone would be.

When Jerry raised his hand that afternoon, then, he had no trouble getting the floor. Speaker Rayburn pointed his way and said, "The chair recognizes the gentleman from Indiana." The wily Texan no doubt hoped Jerry would speak out against the bill. If a Republican wanted to commit political suicide, Sam Rayburn would gladly hand him a rope.

"Thank you, Mr. Speaker." Jerry liked the House's ritual courtesies. "Mr. Speaker, I rise to discuss a related kind of rationing—the rationing of our troops' lives in Germany."

Bang! Down came Rayburn's gavel. "You are out of order, Mr. Duncan!"

"Our occupation policy is out of order, Mr. Speaker," Jerry said.

Bang! "You are out of order, Mr. Duncan!" Rayburn sounded like God right after the children of Israel did something really stupid. If you could imagine God moon-faced and pouchy and bald, he looked like Him, too.

"Mr. Speaker!" "Point of order, Mr. Speaker!" The cries of protest came from a dozen Republican throats, maybe more. Jerry had wondered whether anyone else would back his play. There'd been a one-paragraph AP squib about the demonstration on page fourteen of the *New York Times,* nothing more. The same squib showed up in the *Evening Star.* The *Times-Herald* and the *Post* didn't bother running it. Maybe the other Republicans had noticed anyhow.

Maybe Sam Rayburn had, too. He shook his head, glowering down from his high seat on the marble dais. "This has nothing to do with the measure under consideration, and the gentleman from Indiana knows it."

"May I address that point, Mr. Speaker?" Jerry called.

"Briefly," Rayburn growled.

"Thank you. It seems to me, Mr. Speaker, that the bill we were debating mainly has to do with how best to wind down from the war. That's what I want to talk about, too, because the fighting in Germany's gone on and on, even though the Nazis said they surrendered last spring. Don't we need to wind that down?"

Rayburn scowled at Jerry from on high. Then the Texas Democrat said, "That damnfool woman who led her silly march comes out of your district, doesn't she?"

"Minus the unflattering adjectives, yes, Mr. Speaker, she does," Jerry answered. Sure as hell, Sam Rayburn didn't miss much.

"All right, then. Say your say, and after you're done we'll ease back to the business at hand. It won't matter one way or the other." The Speaker of the House sounded indulgent. He knew the kinds of things Representatives had to do for their constituents.

He might not miss much, but he missed something that day when he didn't quash Jerry Duncan before Jerry was well begun.

"Thank you, Mr. Speaker," Jerry said once more. "I want to know why the United States Army, the mightiest army in the history of the world, hasn't been able to stamp out these German fanatics. I want to know why we haven't been able to hunt down this Reinhard Heydrich, who seems to be the brains of the outfit. I want to know why upwards of a thousand servicemen have been killed in Germany since the so-called surrender. And I especially want to know why the War Department is doing its level best to hide all these deaths and to pretend they never happened."

Members of his own party applauded him. Democrats jeered. A couple of them shook their fists. "President Truman knows what he's doing!" one man shouted.

"You're soft on the Germans!" another Democrat added.

"I am not!" Jerry said indignantly. "When we try those thugs we capture, I hope we shoot them or hang them or get rid of them for good some other way. And I expect we will. That has nothing to do with why we're wasting so many lives in Germany. It has nothing to do with why we can't stop the insurgency, either. What are we doing in occupied Germany, and why aren't we doing it better?"

"Sellout!" that Democrat yelled.

"Isolationist!" someone else put in. The minute the Japs hit Pearl Harbor, isolationism became a dirty word.

Bang! Bang! Bang! Speaker Rayburn plied his gavel with might and main. "The House will come to order!" *Bang! Bang!* "Mr. Duncan, how do you propose to find out what you want to know?" *You don't really care,* Rayburn's words implied. *You're just making political hay.*

Jerry pretended not to hear that. If you didn't notice, you didn't have to react. He simply responded to what Rayburn actually said: "Questioning some War Department officials would make a good first step, Mr. Speaker."

"You think so, do you?" Rayburn rasped a chuckle. With a large majority in both House and Senate, Democrats controlled who got questioned. The Speaker made it plain he didn't aim to let anybody ask the War Department anything inconvenient or embarrassing.

Shrugging, Duncan said, "You can pull a rug over a pile of dust, but the dust doesn't go away. It just leaves an ugly lump under the rug."

Bang! "That will be quite enough of that," Sam Rayburn said. "Now, returning to the bill we were actually considering . . ."

Sam Rayburn didn't want to look at the lump under the carpet. Neither did Robert Patterson, the Secretary of War, even though his department had done most of the sweeping that put it there. And Harry Truman *really* didn't want to look at it, and didn't want anybody else looking at it, either.

Well, too bad for all of them, Jerry thought. *It's there, and they put it there, and I'm damn well going to tell the country about it.*

REINHARD HEYDRICH WAS A THOROUGH MAN. WHEN HE REALIZED HE would have to fight a long twilight struggle after the *Wehrmacht* and *Waffen*-SS went under, he prepared for it as best he could. He studied English and Russian. He'd never be fluent in either one. But, with a dictionary and patience, he could manage.

English should have been easier. It was German's close cousin, and used the same alphabet as Heydrich's birthspeech. But he found himself understanding the Soviets much more readily than the British—to say nothing of the Americans.

Soviet authorities reacted to the holdouts much as he'd expected. Deportations, executions, brutality . . . That all made sense to him. It was the way he would have attacked the problem were he running the NKVD. It was the way the *Reich* had attacked the partisan problem in Russia and Yugoslavia. The Germans hadn't done so well as they would have liked, and Heydrich hoped the Soviets wouldn't, either. But it was a good, rational approach.

The Americans, on the other hand . . .

On his desk sat a three-day-old copy of the *International Herald-Tribune.* The patriot who'd put the paper in a secure drop had circled a story on an inside page in red ink. Heydrich had already read the piece three times. He knew what all the words meant. He even understood the sentences—individually, anyhow. But the story as a whole struck him as insane.

"I thought this must be a joke," he told Johannes Klein. "A joke or a trick, one."

"What does it say?" Klein asked. The veteran *Oberscharführer* did fine in German, and cared not a pfennig's worth for any other language.

"It says there are rallies in America protesting the soldiers we've killed since the surrender. It says the people protesting demand that the Americans take their soldiers out of Germany so we can't kill any more of them," Heydrich answered.

"Fine," Klein said. "When do the machine guns come out and teach these idiots some sense?"

"That's what I wondered," Heydrich answered. "That's what we did to those White Rose traitors, by God." He shook his head, still angry at the college kids who'd had the gall to object to the *Führer*'s war policy—and to do it in public, too! Well, they'd paid for it: paid with their necks, a lot of them, and just what they deserved.

"Of course it is," Hans Klein said. "What else can you do when a fool gets out of line?"

"The Yankees aren't doing anything to them. Zero. Not even taking them in for questioning. Madness!" Heydrich said. He added the clincher: "One of their Congressmen is even making speeches taking the demonstrators' side. Can you imagine that, Hans?"

His longtime comrade shook his head. So did Heydrich. He tried to picture a *Reichstag* deputy standing up in 1943 and telling the *Führer* the war was lost and he ought to make the best peace he could. What would have happened to a deputy who did something like that? As near as Heydrich could tell, he wouldn't just die. He would cease to exist, would cease ever to have existed. He would be aggressively forgotten, the way Ernst Röhm was after the Night of Long Knives.

As usual, Klein thought along with him. "So what are they doing to him?"

Heydrich brought a fist down on the newspaper. "Nothing!" he burst out. "This foolish rag goes on about freedom of speech and open discussion of ideas. Have you ever heard such twaddle in all your born days?"

"Not me," Klein said.

"Not me, either," Heydrich said. "I read this, and I thought the Yankees were trying to trick us. But a couple of our people have lived in America. They say it really works this way. Any crackpot can get up and go on about whatever the devil he wants."

"How did they lick us?" Klein asked. No German asked that about the Russians. Stalin put out a fire by throwing bodies on it till it smothered. He commanded enough bodies to smother any fire, too, which had come as a dreadful surprise to the *Führer* and the General Staff. But the Americans were . . . well, *different* seemed a polite word for it.

After some thought, Heydrich said, "That may be the wrong question."

"Well, what's the right one, then?"

"If they really are this naïve"—Heydrich still had trouble believing it, but didn't see what else he could think if the *Herald-Tribune* story wasn't made up—"how do we take advantage of it?"

"Ah. *Ach, so.*" Once Klein saw the right question, he focused like the sun's rays brought to a point by a burning glass. Like any long-serving noncom, he had a lot of practice taking advantage of officers with more power but less subtlety. His predicament with them was much like the *Reich*'s with its occupiers. Heydrich waited to see what he could come up with. After a few seconds, Klein said, "We have to keep fighting the Amis—"

"*Aber natürlich!*" Heydrich broke in.

"We have to keep fighting, *ja.*" The *Oberscharführer* seemed to remind himself of where he'd been before he got to where he was going: "But we should also let them down easy, give them something these people who want to go home can latch on to and use for an excuse so they don't look like a pack of gutless quitters."

Like the pack of gutless quitters they really are, Heydrich thought. But Hans Klein wasn't wrong. The enemy's morale mattered. Germany had done well with propaganda against the Low Countries and France, then completely botched it against the Russians. Treating them like a bunch of niggers in the jungle wasn't the smartest thing the *Reich* could have done. A little late to worry about that now, though. Heydrich leaned forward intently. "What have you got in mind?"

"Well, sir, way it looks to me is, we ought to say something like we're only fighting to get our own country back again. We ought to let 'em know how much that means to us, and to ask 'em how happy they'd be if some son of a bitch was sitting on their head. And we ought to say we'll be mild as milk if they just pack up and go away."

Klein winked at Heydrich. The *Reichsprotektor* laughed out loud. He couldn't remember the last time he'd done that. Of course Germany would rearm the moment it had the chance. And of course German physicists would get to work on atom bombs as soon as they could. That sparked another thought.

"As long as they've got this fancy bomb and we don't, they have the whip hand, too," Heydrich said. "We should tell them we understand that."

"And we should promise we'd never go after the bomb. We should promise on a big, tall stack of Bibles." Hans Klein winked again.

And damned if Heydrich didn't laugh again. After the last war, the Treaty of Versailles said Germany couldn't have all kinds of weapons. Her top aeronautical engineers designed civilian planes. Other engineers tested panzers in Russia—the Soviet Union was another pariah state. Artillery designs for Sweden, U-boats for Holland . . . When Hitler decided it was time to rearm, he didn't have a bit of trouble. If Germany needed atom bombs to get ready for the next round, she'd have them.

"Can we do something like that, sir?" Klein asked.

"You'd better believe it." Heydrich got up from his desk and walked over to a file cabinet under the *Führer*'s framed photo. It held a complete run of *Signal,* the *Reich's* wartime propaganda magazine. *Signal* was a slick product, printed in many languages; people said enemy publications like *Life* and *Look* had stolen from its layout and approach. That wasn't why Heydrich started poring over back issues, though. They'd run an article he could adapt. He remembered it had come late in the war, after things on the Eastern Front went bad. That helped him narrow things down. He grunted when he found the copy he needed. "Here we go."

"What have you got?" Hans Klein inquired.

"See for yourself." Heydrich held out the magazine to him. The article was called "What We Are Fighting for." It showed a wounded *Wehrmacht* man on one page, his left arm bandaged and bloody, his mouth open in a shout of anger and pain. On the facing page was a closeup of a blond, blue-eyed little girl, perhaps five years old. The two photos summed up exactly what the *Reich* was fighting for, but text went with them. That text was what Heydrich wanted.

Klein's eyes lit up. "Wow! Amazing, sir. I saw this, too. I remember, now that you're showing it to me again. But I never would have thought of it, let alone come up with it just like that." He snapped his fingers.

"Words are weapons, too," Heydrich said. "You need to know

where you can get your hands on them. Why don't you go grab yourself some chow? I want to fiddle with this for a while."

As soon as Klein left, Heydrich sat down again and started writing. He worked in German; he knew he'd make a hash of things if he tried to compose in English. But it would get translated. Other people would suggest changes and add things, too. That was all right. He was fighting again.

VII

In Nuremberg, the city jail was near the center of town. The Palace of Justice—a fancy name for the local courthouse—lay off to the northwest. It had taken some bomb damage. That didn't surprise Lou Weissberg. In Nuremberg, it was much easier to list the buildings that hadn't taken bomb damage than to set down the ones that had.

Bomb damage or not, the Allies were going to try the Nazi big shots they'd captured at the Palace of Justice. The American judge and his opposite numbers from the UK, France, and the Soviet Union would give Göring and Hess and Ribbentrop and Streicher and Jodl and Keitel and the rest the fair trials they hadn't given to countless millions. And then, without the tiniest bit of doubt, most of those goons would hang or face a firing squad or die in whatever other way that extraordinary court decreed.

In the meantime, the Nazis cooled their heels in the Nuremberg jail as if they were ordinary burglars or wife beaters. Well, not quite. They had a wing of the jail all to themselves. They had a lot more guards in that wing than anybody in his right mind would have wasted on burglars or wife beaters.

And the jail was surrounded by barbed wire and sandbagged machine-gun nests and concrete antitank barriers. The pointed obstacles looked to Lou like German designs. They'd probably been yanked from the Siegfried Line and carted back here. In a way, Lou appreciated the irony. The obstacles intended to slow up American and British tanks were now going into action against the krauts who'd made them.

In another way, that irony was scary. Almost six months after the alleged surrender, the occupation authorities needed to stay buttoned up tight to make sure the Germans didn't liberate their leaders.

If they somehow did, that would give the United States a godawful black eye. All the same, Lou wondered how much Reinhard Heydrich wanted to have to do with men who might have the rank to order him around. Somebody like Göring wouldn't be able to resist trying. And Heydrich, damn his little shriveled turd of a soul, was managing just fine by himself. Anybody who tried to jog his elbow might come down with a sudden and acute case of loss of life.

Lou eyed the jail again. "Fuck," he said softly. Despite all the barbed wire and the antitank barriers and the machine-gun nests and the swarms of jittery dogfaces manning the position, somebody'd managed to stick one of the fanatics' new propaganda sheets on the wall.

Shaking his head, Lou walked over and tore the sheet down. It was what Europeans used for typing paper, a little taller and a little skinnier than good old 8½ x 11. Lou had seen English and German versions of the propaganda sheet. A printer was giving the fanatics a hand. If the occupation authorities caught him at it, he'd be sorry. Lou snorted under his breath. That didn't seem to worry the bastard one whole hell of a lot.

This was the English version. It was obviously translated from the German, translated by somebody better with German than with English. WHAT ARE WE FIGHTING FOR? it said: smudgy type on cheap paper.

What Germans desire to acquire by victory is the fulfillment of the idea that an individual shall be respected for his own self. This is what makes life worth living for us.

"Assholes," Lou muttered. The Nazis had sure respected Jews and Gypsies and Russians for their own selves, hadn't they?

We fight for the sake of our own culture, the propaganda sheet went on. *If you had invaders ruthlessly occupying your own land, you too would rise up against them. How can a brave folk do anything else?*

"Assholes," Lou said again, louder this time. Tito's guerrillas, Russian partisans, the French *maquis*—what did the SS and the *Wehrmacht* do to real freedom fighters when they caught them? Everybody knew the answer to that one. Lou had seen a photo a German soldier took of a hanged Russian girl maybe eighteen years old. Around her neck the SS had put a warning placard in German and Russian: I SHOT AT GERMAN SOLDIERS.

Once we have once more our own state back in our hands, we solemnly vow that we seek no new foreign conflict. Europe has seen enough of war, the sheet declared, as if Hitler hadn't had thing one to do with that war and the way the Nazis fought it. *All we seek is a fair peace and our own national self-determination, which is the proper right of any free people.*

What kind of self-determination did the *Reich* give Poles and Scandinavians and Dutchmen and Belgians and Frenchmen and Yugoslavs and Greeks and Russians and . . . ? But Germans had a knack for feeling a shoe only when it pinched *them.*

Lou started to crumple the sheet and toss it aside. Then he caught himself, even though CIC already had plenty of copies. A major with a double chin was giving orders to some GIs. Lou walked over to him and said, "Major, I just found this stuck to the wall here. How come somebody was able to put it up?"

The major snatched the paper out of his hand, gave it one quick, scornful glance, and barked, "Who the hell are you, Lieutenant, and who the hell do you think you are?"

"I'm Lou Weissberg, Counter-Intelligence Corps," Lou said calmly. "And who are you . . . sir?"

By the way he said it, he made the title one of reproach, not respect. The major took a deep breath and opened his mouth to scorch him. Then the man had very visible second thoughts. Even a lieutenant in the CIC might have connections that could make you sorry if you crossed him. As a matter of fact, Lou did. Raising when you really held a full house gave you confidence that showed.

"My name's Hawkins—Tony Hawkins," the major said in a different tone of voice. He took a longer look at the propaganda sheet. "You found this goddamn thing here—at the jail?"

"Just now, like I said. Right over there." Lou pointed. "You've got this whole shebang around the building, and I wondered how some Jerry snuck this thing in here and put it up without anybody noticing."

"Goddamn good question," Major Hawkins said. "Fuck me if I know for sure, but my best guess is—"

His best guess got interrupted. The explosion wasn't anywhere close by, but it was big. The ground shook under Lou's feet. One of the soldiers said, "That an earthquake?"

"You California jerks think everything's a goddamn earthquake," another GI answered. "That's a motherfucking bomb going off, is what that is. One huge honker of a bomb, too."

That echoed Lou's thoughts much too well. He looked around in all directions. At least even money the jail's gray bulk would hide whatever had just happened . . . But no. There it was, off to the northwest: a swelling cloud of black smoke and dust.

Major Hawkins had already proved he had a foul mouth. He outdid himself now. Then he rounded on Lou. "What do you wanna bet that's the fucking courthouse? You CIC cocksuckers are such hot shit, how come you didn't keep the fanatics from blasting it to the moon?"

"Oy!" Lou clapped a hand to his forehead. That hadn't occurred to him. But as soon as he heard it, he would have bet anything he owned that Hawkins was right. The older officer's words had that oracular feeling of truth to them. A bomb there couldn't be anything else. Well, it could, but he was only too sure it wasn't. A moment later, he said, "Oy!" again, and, "Aren't the judges working in there now?"

If they could have bottled what Major Hawkins said then, they could have heated water in every house in Nuremberg for a year. "In spades," the portly major added, in case Lou didn't think he meant it.

Lou had other things on his mind. "C'mon!" he said. "Maybe we can do some good hauling people out of the ruins."

"You go on, Lieutenant," Hawkins said, shaking his head. "Me, I aim to sit tight and do what I'm supposed to be doing. For all we know, those mothers are trying to lure us away from here so they can rush this place and spring the big prisoners while we're all making like a Chinese fire drill."

"Right," Lou said tonelessly. And the major was, no two ways about it. That didn't make Lou like him any better. Sketching a salute, Lou took off.

He trotted on parallel to the Pegnitz, the river that ran through town. The river made a better guide than the streets. With so much of Nuremberg ruined, what was street and what was rubble weren't always easy to tell apart. As he hurried toward the Palace of Justice, he sadly clucked several times. The fanatics could sound reasonable. That sheet they'd put out would make some people back in the States go, *See? They only want to run their own affairs and be left alone.* But, no matter how they sounded, they went and did something like this. . . .

Lou loped past a pile of wreckage about a story and a half tall. That gave him his first good look at the Palace of Justice—or rather, what had been the Palace of Justice. He skidded to a stop, gravel and shattered bits of brick scooting out from under his boots. "Holy crap," he yelped.

Somebody must have screwed up. That was the first thing that occurred to him. The American occupiers had gone out of their way to protect the jail. They hadn't taken so many precautions at the Palace of Justice. The authorities must have thought no one would attack it till the Nazis honchos went on trial.

Oops.

What the American authorities had thought might have been reasonable. That turned out not to matter when reasonable was also wrong. Somebody—who?—would have to answer questions now that the pooch was screwed. *We did everything we reasonably could . . .* In his mind, Lou could already hear the calm, sober voice explaining things. Whoever the voice belonged to, it would be calm and sober. He was sure of that. Would calm sobriety be enough to save the dumb fuckup's career? It might. You never could tell.

But that would be tomorrow's worry. Today's was more urgent. Shattered wreckage of a truck—probably one of the ubiquitous GMC deuce-and-a-halfs—blazed in front of what was left of the Palace of Justice. Three wings had projected out from the main body of the building. One of those wings—the central one, the one in front of which the truck had stopped—was just gone, clean off the map. The other two were shattered, tumbledown, smoking, ready to fall down any second now.

Christ! How much TNT did that fucking truck carry? Lou wondered. The sleepless, analytical part of his mind instantly supplied the answer, and a sneer to go with it. *Two and a half tons, dummy.* The Palace of Justice sure as hell looked as if a 5,000-pound bomb had gone off right in front of it.

Some of the rubble shook. Lou thought more of it was falling down, but that wasn't what was going on. A dazed, bleeding American soldier pushed a door off of himself and tried to stand up. He keeled over instead.

Lou hurried over to him and pulled away more bricks and stones and chunks of woodwork. The wounded man's left ankle bent in a way an ankle had no business bending. Lou fumbled at his belt. Sure as hell, he still carried a wound dressing and a morphine syrette. The guy needed about a dozen bandages, but Lou covered up a nasty cut on the side of his head, anyhow. The morphine was probably also sending a boy to do a man's job, but it was what he had. He stabbed the wounded soldier and bore down on the plunger.

To his amazement, the GI opened his eyes a few seconds later. "What happened?" he asked, his voice eerily calm. Maybe the morphine was doing more than Lou'd thought it could.

"Truck bomb." Lou added the obvious: "Great big old truck bomb."

"Boy, no shit," the man said. "You musta stuck me, huh?" When Lou nodded, the guy went on, "You think you can splint my ankle while the dope's working? Best chance I'll get."

"I'll try. I'm not an aid man or anything."

The wounded soldier waved that aside. Lou got to work. He had no trouble finding boards, and he cut up the other GI's trouser leg to get strips of cloth to tie the splint into place. Morphine or no morphine, the guy wailed when he straightened that shattered ankle as best he could.

Some aid men were there. More ambulances rolled up, bells clanging, as Lou wrestled with the splint. Some soldiers set up a .50-caliber machine-gun position, too. Lou wondered if they'd gone Asiatic till one of them said, "Assholes ain't gonna run another truck in here and blow up all the guys who came in to help." That hadn't occurred to Lou, but some of the Americans seemed properly paranoid. He supposed that was good.

Stretcher bearers carried a groaning wounded man past him and the fellow he was helping. All badly hurt men sounded pretty much the same, no matter where they came from. But Lou happened to look up at just the right moment. He saw a not-so-familiar uniform on the stretcher.

"Holy cow!" he blurted, in lieu of something stronger. "Is that General Nikitchenko?" He was proud of knowing the name of the Soviet judge for the upcoming trial.

To his surprise, the man on the stretcher knew some English. "I is Lieutenant Colonel Volchkov," he said. "Alternate to Iona Timofeyevich. The general, he is—" He broke off, gathering strength or looking for a word. After a moment, he found one: *"Kaput."* It wasn't exactly English, but it wasn't exactly *not* English, either. Lou had no trouble understanding it, anyhow.

"We're gonna get you patched up, Colonel. Don't you worry about anything right this minute—you'll be fine," one of the medics said, and then, to his own comrade, "Get moving, Gabe. Soon as he goes into an ambulance, we'll come back for this poor sorry son of a bitch." His hands were full; he pointed with his chin at the soldier Lou was splinting.

"Who you callin' a sorry son of a bitch?" the GI demanded, and Lou's admiration for morphine leaped forward again. The medics didn't bother arguing. They lugged Volchkov away, then returned for the man with the broken ankle.

More wounded people staggered from the wreckage. Some were women. Secretaries? Clerks? Translators? Cleaning ladies? Lou had no idea. All he knew was, bombs weren't chivalrous. That also applied to the American bombs that had leveled most of Nuremberg, but he didn't worry about those.

Corpsmen and other GIs also carried women out on stretchers, in blankets, or sometimes just in their arms. Wounded women were slightly shriller than wounded men; otherwise, there wasn't much difference between them. Most of the casualties here, not surprisingly, seemed to be men.

Lou thought for a moment that someone in a dark robe had to be a woman. Then he saw the person was wearing a man's black dress shoes—one, anyhow, because the other foot had only a sock on it. *A judge,* he realized dully. American? French? British? That hardly mattered.

The medics didn't bother with some of the bodies—and pieces of bodies—they found in the smoking wreckage. They piled them off to one side: a makeshift morgue, one growing rapidly. And they cursed the fanatics with a weary hatred that made the close-cropped hair at the nape of Lou's neck try to stand on end. Turn the guys who wore Red Crosses loose on the Nazis and they might clean them out in twenty minutes flat.

Or, worse luck, they might not.

That enormous explosion hadn't just brought American soldiers out to see what had happened and do what they could to help. Shabby, scrawny Germans stared at the wreckage of the Palace of Justice and at the rows of corpses off to one side. They didn't seem especially horrified—but then, they'd seen plenty worse.

"Doesn't look like they'll have their trial any time soon," a middle-aged man remarked to his wife.

She shrugged. "So what? It wouldn't have been anything but propaganda anyhow," she said. He nodded. He took out a little can of tobacco—scrounged from butts, no doubt—and started rolling himself a cigarette.

Lou wanted to kick him in the nuts and punch his stringy *Frau* in the nose. But the goddamn kraut was right. God only knew when the authorities would be able to try Göring and Ribbentrop and the rest of those jackals. And who'd want to sit on the bench now and judge them? Hell, who'd dare?

"Goddamn Heydrich to hell and gone," Lou muttered. But damn him or not, his fanatics had won this round.

THE McGRAWS HAD A FANCY RADIO SET. IT DID EVERYTHING BUT show you pictures of what was happening at the other end. And now, with this newfangled television thing, that was coming, too. Back before the war, when people first started talking about it, Diana figured it was all Buck Rogers stuff and would never come true.

Well, these days it didn't do to laugh too hard at Buck Rogers. Look at rockets. Look at the atom bomb. And television was plainly on the way, even if it wasn't here yet.

Once upon a time, the telegraph and typewriter and telephone were Buck Rogers stuff, too—except Buck wasn't around yet to give them a name. Diana's mouth tightened. She wished the telegraph had never happened. Then she wouldn't have heard about Pat. . . . She shook her head. That wasn't the point. The point was, he never should have got killed in the first place.

She'd timed it perfectly. The tubes needed a little while to warm up. Almost the first thing she heard once they did was "This is William L. Shirer, reporting to you from Nuremberg."

He'd been reporting from Europe since before the war started. He'd covered it from Berlin during the Nazis' first fantastic run of triumphs. She and Ed had both read *Berlin Diary*. Now he was back on the other side of the Atlantic, broadcasting from the undead corpse of the Third *Reich*. And the photos she'd seen of him—he was a skinny little bald guy who wore a beret and smoked a pipe—didn't detract (too much) from his authoritative voice and plain common sense.

"As you will have heard by now, Reinhard Heydrich's brutal diehards bombed the Palace of Justice in this city. The leading captured war criminals from the Nazis regime were to have gone on trial there for war crimes in a few days. Now those trials have been indefinitely postponed. Many people here doubt whether they will ever take place."

"Ain't that a . . . heck of a thing?" Ed said.

Diana shushed him. She wanted to hear William L. Shirer. "The death toll is known to be close to two hundred," the correspondent went on. "Among the dead are the French, Russian, and American judges and the British alternate. The Russian and British alternates are among the badly wounded, as is Judge Robert Jackson, the American prosecutor."

"Two hundred dead," Diana echoed, her voice rising in disbelief. "And for what? To give those thugs the kind of trial they don't begin to deserve."

Now Ed raised a hand to quiet her. William L. Shirer continued, "American authorities believe the fanatic who drove the truck loaded with explosives up to the Palace of Justice died in the blast he touched off. Before General Patton's recent death, he said the idea wasn't to die for your country but to make the so-and-so's on the other side die for theirs. Like the Japanese, the German fanatics seem to have taken this idea too much to heart. After these messages, I'll be back with an American officer who will talk about the problems posed by enemies who don't care whether they survive."

A recorded chorus started singing the praises of a particular laundry soap. Diana knew from painful experience that it wasn't worth the money if you used it with hard water. If you listened to the chorus, it was the greatest stuff in the world. But then, you deserved whatever happened to you if you took radio advertisements seriously.

William L. Shirer returned. "With me is Lieutenant Louis Weissberg of the U.S. Army Counter-Intelligence Corps," he said. "Thanks for coming on, Lieutenant."

"Thanks for having me, Mr. Shirer." By the way Weissberg talked, he was from New York City or somewhere not far away.

"Tell us a little about why it's harder to defend against enemies who plan to die after completing their missions."

"For all the reasons you'd expect." Lieutenant Weissberg didn't say *You dummy,* but you could hear it in his voice. Shirer wasn't a dummy—nowhere close—but he remembered that some of the people in his audience were. After a beat, Weissberg went on, "They don't have to worry about escape routes. And they can take chances ordinary soldiers never would, because they don't expect to get away anyhow. If you have the nerve to press the detonator, it's all over in a hurry."

"Isn't it just?" Shirer agreed ruefully. "We're standing here in front of what would have been the courtyard for the trial of the century— the trial that would have warned the world no one can get away with wars of aggression any more—and there's not much left, I'm afraid. Do you have any idea how the fanatic in the truck was able to pull up right in front of the building?"

"Well, Mr. Shirer, if a jeep isn't the most common military vehicle in Germany these days, a deuce-and-a-half is. We've got more of 'em here than a dog has fleas. Put a guy in an American uniform in the driver's seat—and you can bet that kraut was wearing one—and nobody paid any attention to him till too late," Weissberg said.

William L. Shirer asked the same question Diana McGraw would have: "Isn't that a severe security breach?"

"Sure," Weissberg answered, which took Diana by surprise. "We slipped up, and we paid for it. We have to hope we don't do it again, that's all."

"Who was responsible for protecting the Palace of Justice?" Shirer asked. "And what's happened to him since the bombing?"

"Sir, I don't have the answer to either of those questions," Weissberg replied. "You gotta remember, I'm just a lieutenant. I see little pieces of the picture, not the whole thing. You'd do better asking General Eisenhower or somebody like that."

"For the record, I have asked General Eisenhower's headquarters," Shirer said. "Spokesmen there declined to comment. They claimed that anything they said might damage an officer's career. What do you think of that?"

Weissberg ducked again: "If they aren't going to say anything about it, you can't really expect me to, can you?"

"Never hurts to try," Shirer answered easily. "Thank you for your time, Lieutenant Weissberg."

"Sure," Weissberg said. William L. Shirer went off the air. The commercial this time was for a brand of cigarettes that, in Ed's memorable phrase, tasted like it came out of a camel's rear end.

Diana was steaming. "You see how things go?" she demanded of her husband. "Do you see? They know who was supposed to take care of that building. They know he was asleep at the switch. But will they say so? Don't hold your breath! Will anything happen to him because he was asleep at the switch? Don't stay up late waiting for that, either."

"Army always takes care of its own," Ed said.

"Two hundred dead," Diana said one more time. "They aren't just sweeping dirt under a rug. They're shoveling it onto graves. That's wrong." *That's wrong, dammit!* was what she wanted to say, but the habits of her whole adult life with Ed suppressed the swear word.

"You're doing everything you know how to do," Ed said. "You're in the papers. You're on the radio, for cryin' out loud. Me, I couldn't get in the newspaper if I robbed a bank. That suits me fine, too."

"It suited me fine—till Pat got murdered," Diana answered. "But this craziness won't stop till we make it stop. If I have to get my name in the paper to do that, I will."

"Babe, I'm not arguin' with you," her husband said. *You'd better not, not about this,* Diana thought. That wasn't fair, though, and she knew it. Ed had backed her play as much as was in him to do. It wasn't his fault that she was the more outgoing one in the family.

And speaking of outgoing, or going generally . . . "I'll need to make another trip to Washington," she said.

He grunted. "Can we afford it?" he asked. A reasonable question: he'd always brought in the money, while Diana figured out how to spend it. The arrangement worked well for them, but it meant she had a better notion of what was in the checkbook and the savings account than he did.

She nodded briskly. "Not to worry. We could swing it by ourselves, but we won't have to. We've got donations coming in like you wouldn't believe. I've started . . . oh, I guess you'd call it a business account. Mothers Against the Madness in Germany, I'm calling it."

Ed grunted again. "What'll it do to our taxes? And can the government use it to come after us if we don't keep everything straight? They got Al Capone on a tax rap when they couldn't nail him for anything else, remember. If they sent him to Alcatraz, they can sure take a whack at us."

"They wouldn't do that," Diana answered with the sublime confidence of one sure of the righteousness of her cause. On a more practical note, she added, "And I've talked to a bookkeeper. He says he knows how to keep everything straight."

"Okay. I hope he knows what he's talking about," Ed said. "From what I hear at the plant, tax law is pretty much whatever the government wants it to be."

"I asked around. Abe is supposed to be the best in town, bar none," Diana said.

"You got Abe Jacoby?"

"I sure did," she said, not without pride.

"How about that?" Ed sounded relieved. "If a smart sheeny like him can't keep us outa trouble, nobody can. Those people know money like they invented it. Maybe they did—wouldn't surprise me one bit."

"I was thinking the same thing," Diana said. "He doesn't work cheap—"

Ed guffawed. "There's a hot headline!"

"Yeah, I know." Diana laughed, too, a little sheepishly. "But, like

I said, the money's there. And he's charging less than he might have, too."

"How come? You bat the baby blues at him?" Ed winked to show he was kidding.

"I did no such thing!" Actually, Diana thought Abe was kind of good-looking, which made her sound stuffier than she would have otherwise. "He's got a nephew in Munich, and he wants to help make sure Sheldon stays safe."

"Gotcha. That sure makes sense. Blood's thicker than water. I guess sometimes it's thicker than money, too."

"Let's hope so," Diana said. "I won't be the only one going to Washington, either. If we can get into the papers all over the country for picketing in front of the Indiana state Capitol, think what'll happen after we picket in front of the White House."

"They'll arrest you, that's what," Ed predicted.

"No, they won't, not if we stay peaceful—and we will," Diana said. "That chowderhead jumped our people in Indianapolis. We didn't start any brawls. We won't in Washington, either. But Truman has to know we won't put up with stalling around in Germany."

"Well, you've got that right." Ed paused a moment, thinking. "Make sure you tell the papers and the radio before you go. That way, they can be there ready to get the story and the photos—the papers can get the photos, I mean."

"I understood you." Diana walked over to him, bent down, and gave him a kiss. "And I've already talked to the Indianapolis papers, and to the ones in Washington, and to the *Chicago Tribune* and the *New York Times*. If you want a story to go all over the country, those last two are the papers to aim for. I haven't got hold of NBC and CBS yet, but I will."

"Attagirl! I might've know you were a jump ahead of me." Ed chuckled. "Truman doesn't know what he's up against, poor sap. When you start something, you don't stop till you get it done."

Maybe he was kidding again, maybe not. Diana didn't care. "This needs doing, darn it," she said, and Ed didn't try to tell her she was wrong—not that she would have listened if he had.

WHEN THE JEEP CARRYING TOM SCHMIDT CAME TO THE FIRST CHECK-
point on the outskirts of Munich, the dogface behind the wheel let out
a sigh of relief and lit up a Lucky. "Made it through Injun country one
more time," he said.

"Is that what you guys call it?" The reporter took out a little notebook bound with a spiral wire and wrote it down.

"You betcha, Charlie." The GI, who answered impartially to Mel
or to Horseface, nodded emphatically. "Liable to be some asshole behind a tree, behind a rock, hiding inside any old ruined house or
barn—and there sure are enough of 'em." The cigarette jerked as he
spoke.

He wasn't wrong. Munich and its suburbs had taken sixty-six air
raids during the war. The estimate was that it held something like
9,000,000 cubic yards of rubble. And the rubble still held bodies—
nobody knew how many. But even in this chilly weather the stink of
dead meat hung in the air.

The guards at the checkpoint weren't delighted to see them. One
made Mel pop the hood. Another got down on his stomach and slid a
long-handled mirror under the jeep. Tom's papers got examined with
a jeweler's loupe. "Do you do this to everybody?" Tom asked the MP
going over them.

"Sure do," the noncom answered. "Goddamn krauts can get our
uniforms. Stealing a jeep's easy as pie. And they're damn good forgers."

"You must spend a lot of time doing it, then," Tom said.

"Yes, sir," the MP said. "Better than letting some bastard through
with a bomb, though. They caught a guy a couple of days ago at another checkpoint."

"What did they do to him?"

"When he saw they were gonna search the car, he hit the switch
and blew himself up. He got four of us—one of 'em was a buddy of
mine."

"Sorry." It wasn't enough, but it was all Tom could say.

"Yeah. Me, too," the MP replied. "You look legit, though." He
turned to his comrades. "The jeep clean?" When they told him it was,
he nodded. "You can pass on."

Getting to the *Vier Jahreszeiten*—the Four Seasons, the hotel
where Ike was staying—wasn't easy. Munich had been plastered to a

faretheewell, all right. The roads were all potholes or worse. The jeep also had to clear two more checkpoints before they got to the hotel. And the fortifications around it would have done credit to Stalingrad.

"After what happened up in Nuremberg, Mac, we don't take no chances," said the GI who patted Tom down. He was so intimate, Tom halfway expected to be asked to turn his head and cough. But, after the blast at the Palace of Justice, how could you complain? Finding nothing more lethal than notebook, fountain pen, wallet, and a box of cherry cough drops, the soldier let him through.

A generator chugged outside the *Vier Jahreszeiten*. The biggest part of the city didn't have power yet. The hotel had taken bomb damage. Tom would have been surprised if it hadn't. Most of downtown Munich was nothing but bomb damage. But you could tell this had been a hotel once upon a time, which put it ahead of a lot of places.

He had to cool his heels for forty-five minutes before Eisenhower would see him. That was also par for the course. He'd managed to get an appointment with the American proconsul. At last, a spruce young major led him in to the great man. "You've got half an hour," the youngster said.

Terrific, Tom thought. He started with a big one: "How do you see things in Germany now?"

"We're making progress," Eisenhower said. "Rubbish getting cleared. Power and sewage works coming back. Industry starting up again. People getting fed. We are making progress." He repeated it, as if to reassure himself.

"How much trouble are the fanatics causing?" Tom asked.

"More than we wish they were. Less than they wish they were," Ike answered. "They can't go on forever. Sooner or later, they'll run out of men willing to die for a dead cause." How could he know that? Was he whistling in the dark?

Instead of asking directly, Tom said, "How much support do they have among the people?"

"Well, some Germans aren't sorry they fought the war. They're only sorry they lost," Eisenhower said. "They wouldn't mind getting in the saddle again—I'm sure of that. But I'm just as sure it won't happen."

"What do you think about the movement in America to bring home the occupation troops?" Tom asked.

The room wasn't warm to begin with. The temperature suddenly seemed to drop twenty degrees. "I'm a soldier. I'm not supposed to have political opinions. But I think that would be a poor policy," Eisenhower snapped.

"In spite of all the casualties we can't seem to stop?"

"Yes." Ike bit off the word. He cut the interview short, too. Tom Schmidt was disappointed but, on reflection, again not surprised.

VIII

Bernie Cobb swore as he tramped through the woods and fields outside of Erlangen. Fog puffed from his mouth and nose at each new obscenity. When he looked back over his shoulder, he could see his footprints in the snow.

"Fuck this shit," he said. "I was doin' this same crap a year ago, when the krauts hit us in the Bulge. That's how—"

"You got frostbite in your feet," Walt Lefevre finished for him. "We heard it before, Bernie."

"Yeah, well, this is still a crock," Cobb said. "War's been over since May, for cryin' out loud. So how come I'm still lugging a fucking grease gun around and making like there's bandits in the woods?"

"On account of there *are* bandits inna woods." Sergeant Carlo Corvo talked out of the side of his mouth. He'd never said he had Mafia connections, but he'd never said he didn't, either. Connections or no, he was a bad guy to screw around with. "We gotta make sure the cocksuckers stay hid and don't come out an' make trouble, see?"

"Good luck," Bernie said. Sergeant Corvo gave him a dirty look. But he couldn't say Bernie was wrong, not when the fanatics had kicked up so much trouble already. Warming to his theme, Bernie went on, "I wish I had my Ruptured Duck, goddammit. I didn't sign up to chase diehards through the boonies after the war was done."

"You signed up to do whatever the fuck Uncle Sam tells you to do," Sergeant Corvo said. "If he wants you to dig latrines from now till 1949, you'll fuckin'-A do that. And you'll like it, too, 'cause he'd find somethin' worse for ya if ya didn't. Right now he wants you to go asshole-hunting. You oughta be good at it."

Experience taught you how much you could argue with a noncom. Corvo took less kindly to backtalk than most. *He isn't Uncle Sam, even if he thinks he is,* Bernie thought bitterly. But Corvo's three stripes made him a more than unreasonable facsimile.

"Look for tracks," Corvo went on. "That's what we gotta do. With the snow on the ground and the leaves off the trees and the bushes, those Nazi shitheels can't hide out here no more. We've already found a buncha bunkers on account of that."

At least one of those bunkers had blown sky-high while American soldiers were searching it, too. Maybe more than one. If Bernie were in charge of things, he would keep stuff like that as hush-hush as he could. But he'd known one of the guys who went up in this particular blast. Pete would never try and draw to an inside straight again.

"Something moved over there." Walt pointed towards a stand of trees a couple of hundred yards away.

"A bird? A deer, maybe?" Bernie didn't want it to be anything worse.

Lefevre shook his head. "I don't think so. It ducked back behind a trunk, like."

"Fuck," Sergeant Corvo said. For once, Bernie agreed with him completely. "Spread out, youse guys," Corvo went on. "If that asshole's got one o' them automatic rifles, it's like goin' up against a BAR, 'cept the German piece only weighs half as much."

Two grease guns and an M-1. Not impossible odds, but not good, either, not against a weapon that fired full automatic out to . . . farther than this. *How come the krauts made the good tanks and the good guns?* Bernie wondered. *We're fuckin' lucky we won. . . . Or did we?*

He had a finger on the trigger as he slowly approached the trees. He felt all alone. Hell, he was all alone. One burst wouldn't get everybody that way. But one burst could sure chop him down. When the surrender came, he'd thought he'd got free of this kind of dread. He licked dry lips. No such luck.

Something stirred behind one of those skeleton-branched trees. *"Halt!"* Bernie yelled. *"Hände hoch!"* His accent was horrible, but at least he remembered to use German, not English.

He hit the dirt while he was yelling. A good thing, too, because three or four bullets cracked past the place where he'd stood a second earlier.

He started shooting—not aimed fire, but plenty to make the diehard keep his head down. Walt and Carlo were banging away, too. If the fanatic was a kid, maybe he wouldn't know which way to answer. If, on the other hand, he was a *Waffen*-SS vet who'd swing for war crimes if they caught him, he damn well would.

He fired at Sergeant Corvo, who had the M-1. That could hit from farthest away, so it was the right move. Wanting to run, Bernie scuttled forward instead. He could smell his own rank fear. The Jerry headed back to another tree. Bernie squeezed off a burst of his own. At least one round caught the kraut in the back. He pitched forward onto his face in the snow.

"Good shot!" Corvo called. He was up and cradling his rifle, so the fanatic hadn't done anything too drastic to him. "Let's see what we got. Careful, now—liable to be trip wires for mines around here. You don't want your balls bounced, watch where you put your clodhoppers."

With so much free and almost-free pussy over here, Bernie took good care of his balls. He raised and lowered his booted feet with utmost caution. The Germans used a trip wire so thin you could barely see it even when you were looking for it.

The fanatic was still twitching when Bernie came up to him, but he wouldn't last. He'd caught the whole burst: one in the lower left part of his back, one as near dead center as made no difference, and one just below the right shoulderblade. He turned his head to look at the American. *"Mutti,"* he choked.

"Your mama ain't gonna help you now, kid," Bernie said roughly. The other two GIs came up behind him. He bit down on the inside of his lower lip, hoping he wouldn't heave. The diehard was a kid: with those smooth cheeks, he couldn't have been more than fifteen. Well, he wouldn't see sixteen now.

"Fuckin' good shooting, Cobb," Sergeant Corvo said. "They're all the same size when they pick up a gun." Just to be on the safe side, he grabbed the fanatic's piece. Sure as hell, it was one of those nasty new automatic rifles. It looked ugly as sin, all plastic and rough metal, but it was very bad news. That big, banana-shaped clip held what looked like a week's worth of ammo.

"*Mutti,*" the German said again, on a weaker note now. No, he wouldn't last long. Well, good riddance. But even so . . .

Bernie spat in the snow. "I don't like shooting kids, goddammit," he said. "And those Nazi cocksuckers are using more of them all the time."

"Sure they are," Walt said. "Kids don't mind shooting you, not even a little bit. It's cowboys and Indians for them—a game, like."

"Sure—that's what bothers me," Bernie said. "They don't even know the score. Doesn't seem fair to point 'em at us. This little asshole probably didn't even figure he could get hurt—"

"Till you put three in his ten-ring," Corvo broke in. "Get it through your head, man—fair went out the window as soon as these guys didn't come out with their hands up after the surrender. They catch you, you ain't goin' into no POW camp. They catch you, they'll cut your cock off and shove it down your throat. You think this half-grown fucker wasn't playin' for keeps?"

"Unh-unh." Bernie didn't hesitate there. He'd come too close to getting ventilated.

"Okay. Maybe you ain't as dumb as you look. Maybe." Corvo turned the kid over. That seemed to finish killing him—close enough, anyway. Bernie didn't notice exactly when he quit breathing for good. The sergeant went on, "We'll go through his pockets. Maybe he's stupid—maybe he carried something the CIC guys can do something with."

But he didn't. About the most interesting things on the kid's corpse were three or four little one-pfennig coins: cheap zinc, dark with corrosion, but still displaying the Nazi eagle and swastika. They weren't legal tender any more. The occupation authorities had come down like a ton of bricks on symbols of the old regime. Well, maybe even a fanatic needed to remind himself what he was fighting for.

Mournfully, Walt said, "Now we'll have to search this whole goddamn wood, see if there's a bunker hidden here somewhere. Boy, I'm really looking forward to that."

"Gotta be done," Sergeant Corvo said.

Lefevre didn't argue with him. Neither did Bernie Cobb. The noncom wouldn't be down on his belly probing. He wouldn't be doing pick-and-shovel work, either. Bernie knew he and Walt damn well would. No wonder Corvo didn't mind the prospect so much. Who ever minded the hard work somebody else was doing?

CAPTAIN HOWARD FRANK SLAPPED A FILM CANISTER DOWN ON LOU Weissberg's desk. Lou eyed it as if wondering if it had an explosive charge inside. Truth to tell, that wouldn't have much surprised him. *"Nu?"* he asked.

"Nu, nu," Frank agreed, one Jew to another. "And a new headache, too."

Lou could have done with a Bromo-Seltzer. He tried to make light of it: "I thought you were going to appoint me morale officer and have me show the troops the latest Western."

"Ha. Funny," his superior said—about as much as the joke deserved. "I had to rout out a morale officer, 'cause I needed a projector to run this *verkakte* thing. It's even got sound. Somewhere, Heydrich's assholes have themselves a regular photo lab."

"What . . . exactly is it?" Lou wondered if he wanted to know. A photo lab? What the hell were the fanatics doing now?

"It's trouble, that's what. Come see it. I'll watch it again, too. Maybe one of us'll spot something I missed the first time. I can hope so, anyway."

"Okay." Lou got up. Captain Frank grabbed the canister and carried it off.

The morale officer actually had rigged a screen and a projector in one room of the rambling Nuremberg hotel the CIC had taken for its own. "Why'd you have me take it out of the machine if you want me to run it again?" he asked Captain Frank.

" 'Cause I'm dumb, Bruce," the captain answered. "Do it anyway, okay?"

"Sure." Bruce was a ninety-day wonder with one gold bar on each shoulder. He wasn't about to argue. He threaded the film through the projector. He did that very well. For all Lou knew, he was a morale of-

ficer because he'd been a projectionist before Uncle Sam grabbed him.
As he turned on the machine, he said, "Hit the lights, will you?"

Lou stood closest to the switch, so he flicked it. Squiggles and
scribbles filled the screen as leader ran through. Then, without warning, a scared-looking young man stared out at him. The man wore
U.S. uniform and looked as if he'd been worked over. His eyes kept
sliding to the left, toward something off-camera. *A rifle, aimed at his
head?* Lou wondered. Something like that, unless he missed his guess.

"My name is Matthew Cunningham, private, U.S. Army." He
paused to lick his lips and glance left again. Then he rattled off his serial number and went on, "I am a prisoner of the German Freedom
Front. They say they will, uh, execute me if U.S. authorities don't
meet their, uh, just demands. For now, I'm being well treated." The
mouse under one eye, the split lip, and the fear all over his face gave
the lie to that.

"U.S. forces are to leave Germany at once. Germany is to be free
to determine its own destiny like any other nation. The struggle for
national liberation will go on until victory is won, no matter what.
You cannot hope to outlast the aroused German folk. So-called prisoners of war must also be released to return to their loved ones.
Germany demands peace and justice." Cunningham gulped, then
whispered one more word: "Please."

He disappeared. More squiggles flashed across the screen. Then it
showed pure white, which faded as Bruce turned off the projector.
Lou turned on the room lights. "Jesus," he said.

"You betcha," Captain Frank agreed: a slightly chubby, funda-
mentally decent man in a hell of an unpleasant place. "How'd you
like to get one of those every week, or maybe every day?"

"Jesus!" This time, Bruce beat Lou to the punch.

"Is he really a GI?" Lou asked. "Not just a kraut who speaks good
English?"

"A Matthew Cunningham was reported as AWOL in Frankfurt
last week," Frank answered. "We're bringing in some of his buddies
to make sure this is really him, but for now it's a pretty good bet."

"Yeah." Lou nodded. The kid on the screen sounded just like a
Yank. "Shit. What do we do next?"

"That isn't for the likes of you or me to decide," Captain Frank said. "But you can bet your last dime we won't pack up and go home. You can bet we won't turn all the Jerry POWs loose, either. How many divisions' worth of new recruits would we give Heydrich if we did?"

"What about the chuckleheads back home?" Bruce said. "What'll they do when they see this thing? How loud will they squawk?"

"We ain't gonna show it to 'em," Frank said. "We ain't gonna say boo about it. You want to spend the next twenty years in the Aleutians, son? You'll be lucky to get off that easy if you open your big yap where a reporter can hear. Got it?"

"Oh, yes, sir," Bruce said solemnly. "But how do you know this is the only print those Nazi bastards made?"

"Fuck," Captain Frank whispered. "I didn't even think of that."

Lou hadn't thought of it, either. He realized he should have. Maybe Bruce really had worked in a movie theater. That would have got him used to thinking about more than one copy of a film at a time. To Lou, a movie was a movie. But how many people, in how many theaters all over the country, could watch the same movie at the same time? Lots. Lots and lots.

The captain visibly tried to pull himself together. "Lou, when you were watching this . . . this piece of crap, did you see anything that gave you a clue about maybe where it was made?"

"Let me think, sir," Lou said. It wasn't easy. All he'd looked at was the GI's face. Behind it were . . . planks. That didn't help much.

"By the lighting, it was shot with floods, not with the sun," Bruce said. "You could tell by the shadows."

"He's right." Lou wished he would have come up with that. It was obvious . . . once somebody else pointed it out.

"Yeah." Captain Frank nodded. "Good one, Bruce. You think it was in one of their goddamn bunkers, then?"

Now he's asking the shavetail, Lou thought resentfully. Well, Bruce knew more about this stuff than he did himself.

"Probably," the morale officer said. "And they've got—how many of 'em?"

"Too many, that's for sure," Frank said gloomily. "Could've been in the woods, could've been inside Frankfurt somewhere, could've been . . . any place at all, near enough. *Gevalt!*"

"Brass're gonna spit rivets when they see this," Lou said.

"Now tell me one I *don't* know," his superior replied. "Half of me thinks we just ought to ditch this film, pretend we never got it."

"Except that'd be curtains for Cunningham," Lou said.

"Yeah." Captain Frank sighed heavily. "But it's curtains for him anyway, if those Nazi shitheads follow through. You think we'll get out of Germany to keep them from shooting a hostage? Don't make me laugh."

Lou didn't think so, not for a minute. But something else occurred to him. "If Bruce here is right—and I bet he is—this isn't the only copy around. If another surfaces after we make this one disappear, we'll spend the rest of our days in Leavenworth, making big ones into little ones."

Frank sighed again. "Well, you ain't wrong. I wish like hell you were. All right, already. I'll kick it up the line. Somebody with more rank than me can figure out where we go from here." He paused to light a cigarette and smoked half of it in short, savage puffs. "And you're right about something else, too, goddammit."

"What's that, sir?"

"Any which way, poor Cunningham's fucked."

FRATERNIZING REMAINED AGAINST REGULATIONS FOR GIs. THAT didn't mean as much as the brass wished it did. The Americans occupying Germany were as horny as any other young men. They had a prostrate nation at their feet. And plenty of *Fräuleins* were cute and persuadable. Quite a few didn't need much persuading. They figured lying down with one of the conquerors was the best way to land on their feet. More often than not, they turned out to be right.

The same held true for American reporters, only more so. The occupying authorities couldn't give them orders against fraternizing. Some had wives back home but didn't care. Tom Schmidt was single and thirty-two. Sometimes he felt like a kid in a candy store. Sometimes he was a lot happier than that.

His latest flame, Ilse, was small and dark and slim—skinny, if you wanted to get right down to it. There weren't many fat Germans these days, and a lot of the ones who were fat had been Party *Bonzen* and weren't to be trusted. Ilse was close to his age. She didn't wear a ring, but a pale circlet on the third finger of her left hand said she had. Had

Fritz or Karl gone to the Eastern Front and not come home? Or did he lie in or under some field in Normandy? Ilse hadn't volunteered answers, and Tom hadn't gone looking for them. As long as she said yes often enough, he didn't require anything else.

She lived in a cellar. Most surviving Nurembergers did, because so much above ground was only wreckage. She had a couple of lanterns and a little coal stove that kept the place warm enough. Thanks to Tom, she had plenty of fuel for them, and plenty to cook on the little stove.

He sometimes wondered whether one person could eat that much and stay that skinny. But if she had kids, he never saw them. He never saw their clothes or toys when he came to call. Again, he didn't push it. No, answers weren't what he wanted from her.

There weren't many places to take a girl for a date. No movie houses, except the ones for American soldiers. No fancy restaurants. The only public eateries open were soup kitchen–style places that served potatoes and cabbage and U.S. Army rations to keep people from starving. You could walk in the parks, if you didn't mind bomb craters and shattered trees and a reek of death whenever the wind swung the wrong way.

Or you could get down to basics and go to bed. Tom didn't mind. If that wasn't a guy's idea of heaven, he didn't know what would be. Ilse never complained. If she had, he would have looked for someone else. It wasn't as if he didn't have other choices. Oh, no.

One evening, he brought her a carton of K-rations—less romantic than long-stemmed roses, maybe, but the way to a girl's heart in occupied Germany. She received them with hugs and kisses and promises of even better things later on. Then she surprised him, saying, "And I have for you also *etwas* . . . something." She'd learned some English in school before the war, then forgotten most of it till she turned out to need it again. Tom had about that much German. They managed.

"What is it, babe?" he asked now.

"I know not." She gave him a small parcel wrapped in old newspapers.

He frowned. "Where'd you get it?"

"A man give it to me." He knew what the look on his face must have said, because even by the light of two kerosene lanterns he could see her flush. Hastily, she went on, "Not that kind of man. Not a man I ever see before. He give. He say, 'Give to the *Amerikaner.*' He go."

"Hah." Tom wondered if he ought to open it. It was small for a bomb, but you never could tell. "What did he look like?"

"A man." Ilse shrugged. "Not big. Not small. Like a man who go through the *Krieg* . . . the war." That meant almost every male here from fourteen to sixty.

"Okay." Tom wasn't sure it was, but what else could he say? He pulled out a pocket knife to cut the string holding the parcel together, then tore the newspaper. He didn't know what he'd expected, but a reel of movie film wasn't it. "Huh!" He couldn't do anything with it till he found somebody with a projector—probably somebody from the Army. "Would you recognize this guy if you saw him again?"

"What is 'recognize'?" Ilse asked.

"Know. Uh, *kennen.*"

She thought. "*Vielleicht.* Um, it might be. Or it might not."

He could watch the gears turning in her head. She was no dope. Who would give her something to give to an American reporter? Well, anybody might, but the best bet was one of Reinhard Heydrich's merry men. And if you admitted to recognizing one of those bastards, you were much too likely to die before your time. No wonder she stayed cagey.

And a lot of her mind was on other things: "Shall I make for us supper?"

"Sure, babe. Go ahead," Tom answered.

Ilse could do things with K-rats to turn Army cooks green with envy—Army cooks who didn't just want to get the hell out of Germany and go home, that is, assuming there were any such animals. And Tom was able to show his appreciation in a way much more enjoyable than helping with the dishes (he'd done that once, but only once—having a man volunteer help with housework bewildered her).

Afterwards, sprawled over him warm and naked under the covers, Ilse said, "You will with this *Kino*—this film—careful be?"

"You betcha, sweetheart," Tom assured her.

"*Das ist gut.*" She nodded seriously. "I do not want you to lose."

Was that because he made a good meal ticket, or did she actually fancy him between the sheets? One more question Tom was liable to be better off not asking. Tom ran a hand along her slim curves and let it rest on her backside: almost like a boy's but not quite. No, not quite. *Let's hear it for the difference,* he thought. Aloud, he said, "Don't you worry about a thing. I'll be fine."

One of the lanterns had gone out. The other was guttering low. Even in the dim red light remaining, he could read her expression: she thought she'd just heard something really and truly dumb. "Always I worry," she said.

Tom needed a couple of days to track down a corporal whose duties included running movies to keep the GIs happy—well, happier. "Yeah, I can show you that," the two-striper said, eyeing the reel. "What is it? Stag film?" The idea perked him up. "I can sure as hell show you that, buddy."

And watch it yourself, too, Tom thought, amused. "I don't know what it is. I got it in town." He didn't say anything about Ilse. "Run it and we'll both find out."

"Sound and everything—how about that?" the projectionist said as he set things up. "Gonna look a little washed out—this room ain't as dark as it oughta be. Well, let's see what we got." He clicked a switch.

The projector whirred into action. Tom didn't think a German would have handed Ilse a dirty movie to pass on to him, but he didn't know what else to expect. It wasn't a sweaty kraut grappling with a buxom blond *Fräulein.* It was . . .

"My name is Matthew Cunningham, private, U.S. Army. My serial number is—"

Tom gaped while the captured American soldier poured out the German Freedom Front's demands. Only after the short film ended did he realize he should have been taking notes. He was sitting on the biggest story of the—what? Day? Week? Month? Not the year, not in 1945. But the biggest one since the Nuremberg Palace of Justice went up in smoke, anyhow.

"Run it again," he said urgently.

"I dunno if I oughta," the corporal answered. "You should take this straight to the brass."

"I will." Tom had no idea whether he'd keep the promise. "But I've got to know what's in it first."

"We oughta kill all of them kraut motherfuckers," the GI said as he rewound the film. "Either that or get the hell outa here and let 'em kill each other off. I sure as shit wouldn't mind seeing Rochester again, I'll tell ya that."

"You and Jack Benny both," Tom said. The corporal laughed way more than the joke deserved. After horror, that often happened. And if Matthew Cunningham's terrified face wasn't the face of horror . . . then the shambling skeletons at Dachau and Belsen and the murder factories the Russians found in Poland were. The Nazis had so god-damn much to answer for. How could anybody turn his back on that? But how could anybody keep soaking up casualties after the surrender that wasn't, either?

"My name is Matthew Cunningham, private, U.S. Army. . . ."

"I AM NIKOLAI SERGEYEVICH GOLOVKO, SUPERIOR PRIVATE, RED Army. . . ."

Vladimir Bokov watched the film to the end. It didn't take long. Then he turned to Colonel Shteinberg, who'd summoned him to see it. "All right, Comrade Colonel. There it is. What are we going to do about it?"

Moisei Shteinberg steepled his fingertips. The senior NKVD officer had a pale, thin face, a blade of a nose, and a dark, heavy beard shadow. He looked like the Jew he was, in other words. "What would you recommend?" He could sound like a bruiser, yes. But, like a lot of Jews Bokov had known, he could also use Russian like a highly educated man.

"Well, it's tough luck for Golovko, of course." Captain Bokov dismissed the hostage right away. The Soviet Union wasn't going to bend because some stupid senior private let himself get nabbed. The Nazis who'd taken him had to know that, too. They wouldn't have bent, either—they also played for keeps. "The motherfuckers must be trying to put us in fear, or else to embarrass us."

"Yes, I think so, too." Even though Shteinberg often sounded tough, Bokov rarely heard him actually cuss. Listening to him, you were tempted to forget there was such a thing as *mat*. "How do you propose to make them change their minds?"

"How many from their organization are we holding?" Bokov asked.

"Here in Berlin, or all over our occupation zone?"

"I think Berlin will do, Comrade Colonel."

"Eight or ten we're sure of—I know we've cracked a couple of the bandits' cells. Another few dozen who may or may not be involved. You know how it is." Colonel Shteinberg shrugged. "Once you start arresting people, you may as well keep going. You don't want to miss anybody by mistake."

"*Da.*" Bokov nodded—he felt the same way. "Well, if it were up to me, I'd kill off three or four of the real ones and leave their heads or their balls or whatever for the Nazi pricks to find, along with a message saying they can expect twice as much the next time they want to screw around with us. Best way I can think of to pay back Nikolai Sergeyevich."

Shteinberg paused to fill and light a pipe. Stalin smoked one, so a lot of Soviet officials naturally imitated him. Shteinberg brought it off better than most, maybe because Hebraic features weren't so different from those common in the Caucasus. After a couple of meditative puffs, the Jew said, "Fuck your mother, but that's a good notion. Go take care of it."

Bokov's jaw dropped. Just when he thought Shteinberg didn't use *mat,* the Jew dropped the basic Russian obscenity on him. And he used it the way a real Russian would, too: to say something like *This really needs doing, so handle it.*

"I will, Comrade Colonel," Bokov said. "Give me a written authorization to take the bastards out of prison and, ah, deal with them. And where do you think I should leave the, ah, remains? We want to make sure the message gets to the right people."

Still puffing, Shteinberg scrawled the requisite order. "Anybody asks you questions, tell him to talk to me," he said, handing Captain Bokov the scrap of paper. Bokov nodded again. He didn't think anybody would quarrel with an NKVD officer, but the world could be a strange old place. His superior went on, "As for the other, put the bits . . . Hmm. There's a place on Stalin Allee they use sometimes. That should get the message across."

The USSR was busily turning its chunk of Germany into a proper Socialist state. Where it could, it used German Communists who'd survived the Nazi epoch. But it changed the landscape, too. Lots of streets in Soviet Berlin—and other places in eastern Germany—had new, Marxist-sounding names. Bokov hoped Hitler was spinning in his grave because Stalin had a street named for himself here in the Fascists' capital. And, on Armistice Day, the Russians had unveiled a huge monument in the Tiergarten, commemorating the Red Army men who'd died taking Berlin away from the Hitlerites. Adolf's ghost could look at that as much as it pleased.

Bokov brought his mind back to the business at hand. "Give me the address, sir. I'll take care of everything." He wouldn't have even wiggled without orders. Now that he had them, he couldn't get in trouble for carrying them out.

He turned out not to need to show the jailer Shteinberg's authorization. "Do whatever you please with those people," the man told him. "If you need to take them all, go ahead. I don't want them around. The anti-Soviet bandits on the outside are liable to try and liberate them."

"They won't liberate these four fuckers, but you've got to hang on to the rest," Bokov said. "We may sweat more out of them."

"Yes, Comrade Captain." The jailer was the one doing the sweating.

Bokov shot the prisoners, one after the other. He was no butcher, though. At his orders, a sergeant took care of the necessary mutilation. "These cunts have it coming, eh?" the underofficer said.

"Of course," Bokov answered. The sergeant didn't seem to care much one way or the other. He was just making conversation while he worked.

Carrying the relevant remains in a canvas duffel—a damned heavy duffel now—Bokov went out onto the chilly streets of Berlin. A large number of the men out and about were Red Army soldiers. With padded jackets and felt boots, they were equipped for worse weather than this. Most of them also carried either a rifle or a submachine gun. If anyone gave overt trouble, they were ready. But what could you do against a fanatic with a bomb under his clothes or in a pushcart— or, worst of all, against a fanatic driving a truck full of explosives?

Most German men mooched around in shabby, threadbare *Wehrmacht* greatcoats. German winter gear had been a joke the first year of the war, though Bokov doubted the Hitlerites thought it was funny. They'd got better at it later on, but their stuff was never as good as what the Red Army used.

Quite a few German women wore *Wehrmacht* greatcoats, too.

The ones in civilian clothes looked as mousy as they could. They scuttled here and there like cockroaches, trying not to get far from a doorway or alley into which they could escape. Nothing like the orgy of rape that accompanied Berlin's fall went on any more, but the local women stayed scared. *Good,* Bokov thought.

Four men in sharp Western suits and topcoats strolled up Stalin Allee, chattering in what had to be English. They stood out like peacocks in a flock of crows. One of them pulled out a notebook and wrote something in it.

Who does he think he is? the scandalized Bokov wondered. *Can he spy so openly?* But the American or Englishman or whatever he was certainly could. Russians could go freely into the U.S., British, and French zones in Berlin, and it worked the other way, too. That was just wrong. One of these days, somebody would have to do something about it.

Catching Bokov's eye, one of the foreigners tipped his snap-brim fedora. The NKVD man wouldn't have minded wearing a hat like that. It had style. He touched the brim of his own officer's cap and walked on.

Idly, he wondered how well the Americans and British were dealing with bandit troubles in western Germany. He knew they had some; their papers, and those they permitted their Germans, gabbled about them in ways no Soviet censor would have tolerated for an instant. It surprised him. At the end of the war, the Nazis seemed eager to give up to the Western allies but went on fighting like maniacs against the USSR. Heydrich and his followers took on everyone. They really *were* fanatics, then. Bokov hoped they'd pay for it.

Finding the building he wanted wasn't easy. Half the houses and shops and offices along Stalin Allee had been flattened or burned. A lot of the others had taken damage of one kind or another. Street numbers were few and far between.

He could have asked a Berliner. He snorted, fog bursting from his nose and mouth. He was damned if he would. Then he snorted again, on a higher note. A Berliner wasn't just somebody from Berlin. It was also the local word for a jelly doughnut. He could have done with one of those right now.

He finally found what had to be the place. By the way people went in and out, it looked to be a cheap eatery, or maybe a tavern. That made some sense. The fanatics could use the flow of customers to hide whatever they were up to.

Bokov went in. It was a tavern, one of the shoddiest excuses for one he'd ever seen. Three men scurried out a hole in the side wall as soon as they glimpsed his uniform. The bruiser behind the bar kept his hands out of sight. What did he have under there? A Schmeisser? Bokov wouldn't have been surprised.

In his best German, he said, "There's a cordon around this place. They've already nabbed the rats who ran. If I don't come out in ten minutes, nobody here will like what happens next." He was bluffing, but the Germans didn't know that. He hoped.

"So what'll it be, then?" the barman asked.

"Beer," Bokov answered. If they had anything, they had that.

He laid a ten-mark occupation note on the bar. The man took it and started to make change. Bokov waved for him not to bother. With a grunt, the fellow gave him a seidel. "Drink fast," he suggested.

"Don't worry—I will." Bokov did. The beer was surprisingly good. He set the duffel down beside him and turned a little to one side to keep an eye on the men sitting at the battered table. They watched him, too.

"You got your nerve, Ivan, poking your nose in here," the barman said.

With a shrug, Bokov set down the mug. "All part of a day's work." He started out.

"You forgot something," a man called after him.

"Keep it. You'll know who needs to hear about it, anyhow." Bokov didn't sigh with relief till he'd got a hundred meters away.

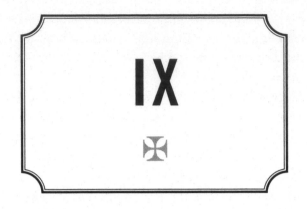

IX

Diana McGraw was packed. She was ready. Tomorrow morning, Ed would put her on the train for Washington. Tonight, they were going to see *The Bells of St. Mary's* along with Betsy and Buster. Diana knew Ed would stare at Ingrid Bergman every instant she was on the screen, and never mind that she was playing a nun. Diana didn't mind . . . much. If you were male and didn't stare at Ingrid Bergman, you were probably dead. And . . . something interesting might happen after her daughter and son-in-law went home to their baby. Inspiration—or something—was where you found it.

"Shall we go, babe?" Ed said.

"Sure." Diana put on her coat. It was down in the twenties: nothing out of the ordinary, not in Anderson in December. The weatherman said it wouldn't snow for another couple of days, but what did the weatherman know?

They went out. Ed started up the Pontiac. When you worked for Delco, they looked at you funny if you drove anything but a General Motors car. They didn't usually say anything, but they remembered.

"Glad I've got a heater," Ed remarked, pulling the lever that got it going.

"It'll start putting out hot air right about when we get there," Diana said. Ed grunted, but didn't try to tell her she was wrong. The Bijou was only a few blocks away. In summer, they would have walked over. They still could have, but the car was nicer, especially with gas rationing gone at last.

Downtown Anderson was bright lights and tinsel and stores open late to snag more Christmas shoppers. With the war over, with money in their pockets and purses, most people were in a festive mood. Diana would have been, but. . . . "I wish Pat were here, too," she said as Ed slid into a parking space.

"Oh, boy, me, too." He shook his head and stuck the key in his pocket. He didn't bother locking the car—nobody was likely to steal it. He didn't put a nickel in the parking meter, either. It was after six o'clock.

He paid for their tickets at the box office. Then he and Diana walked into the lobby. Betsy and Buster were already there, buying Cokes and popcorn. Ed got some, too. "We're free!" Betsy exclaimed, adding, "For a few hours, anyway."

"Free, nothing," Buster said. "I'm gonna have to pay Karen Galpin a buck and a half when we get home."

"Worth it," Betsy declared. Diana remembered how glad she'd been to get out of the house once in a while when Betsy and Pat were little. Babysitters were worth the money, and then some.

The Bijou had seen better days. Too many feet had trodden the carpet. Too many bottoms had worn through the velvet on the seats. Even the curtain looked shabby and faded. During the war, people'd had more important things to worry about. Now, most of them didn't.

But the war's not over, not for everybody, Diana thought. *It should be, but it's not.*

She sat down. The seat creaked under her—yes, the Bijou needed work. Well, the management would likely be able to afford it. The place was filling up fast. Everybody wanted either to stare at Ingrid Bergman or to listen to Bing Crosby.

People sighed with anticipation when the house lights went down.

Then they laughed or whistled or let out catcalls, because the curtain got stuck while it was still half closed. A guy in overalls lugged out a tall ladder as the lights came up again. A teenage kid scaled the ladder, nimble as a squirrel. He fiddled with something out of sight, then flashed a thumbs-up. The curtain moved freely. The audience gave him a hand as he descended. He waved, his face red. The lights dimmed once more.

Naturally, the newsreel came first. There were scenes of tiny, exquisite Japanese women in kimonos bowing to GI's who seemed half again as tall. *They know they're licked. Why don't the Germans?* Diana thought resentfully. But, beside her, Buster muttered, "Miserable little monkeys." Japanese fire had made sure he wouldn't play football again.

By what the smooth-voiced announcer said, everything was peachy in Japan, at least if you were an American—and who cared what happened to the Japs? Then, echoing what had just been in Diana's mind, the man went on, "But on the other side of the world, things are harder. One of our correspondents in the American zone in Germany obtained this disturbing footage for us. Anonymous U.S. Army sources assure us it's genuine."

There on the big screen, a battered, frightened young man said, "My name is Michael Cunningham, private, U.S. Army. . . ."

Diana crossed herself. She murmured a prayer for the soldier's family. There were even worse things than what had happened to Pat. She'd read the stories in the paper, of course. Seeing the poor kidnapped soldier was a thousand times worse.

"Naturally, the United States could not yield to the fanatics' demands," the announcer said. "I am sad to have to tell you that Private Cunningham's body was discovered not far from Regensburg, which is northeast of Munich." Diana watched a couple of GIs tenderly lift a canvas-wrapped bundle into the back of a jeep. The announcer went on, "The Army is pursuing the heartless fanatics who murdered Private Cunningham, and expects to make arrests soon."

Diana wondered why the Army expected to do that. To look good in the newsreels? She was getting more and more suspicious of everything the government claimed. The Army sure hadn't had much luck getting rid of the fanatics up till now.

The newsreel went on with floods and spectacular car crashes and highlights from football games. Diana couldn't care about any of them. The Flash Gordon serial that followed also left her cold. Spaceships! What a bunch of nonsense that was! (But then, she would have said the same thing about atom bombs a few months earlier.)

Even *The Bells of St. Mary's* had trouble cheering her up. That told her how far down she was more clearly than anything else could have. But Ed and Betsy and Buster enjoyed it. She could enjoy their enjoyment, even with none of her own.

Afterwards, as they went out into the cold, Betsy sighed and said, "Back to the pressure cooker."

"It gets better. It gets easier," Diana said. She wondered if she would ever feel the same way about the burden she carried.

After she and Ed got back to the house, they talked for a few minutes about nothing Diana remembered the next day and then went to bed. She wasn't amazed when he reached for her under the covers. She didn't quite feel like it, but she let him pull her close. If he didn't fully please her, he never knew it. He went into the bathroom for a minute, then came back and started to snore right away.

She lay on her back, staring at the ceiling. She had to get up early tomorrow to catch the train for Washington, but sleep stayed away. The ticking clock sat on his nightstand. She looked over at it, but couldn't read the dimly glowing hands. Her sigh sounded just like her daughter's. After what seemed a very long time, her eyes slid shut at last.

CAPTAIN HOWARD FRANK WAS NOT A HAPPY MAN. HE STARED AT LOU as if over the sights of a machine gun. "You know this *mamzer* Schmidt?"

"I've run into him a few times." Lou told the truth. If he didn't, his superior could find out easily enough. And when he did . . . Lou didn't care to think about that. He wanted out of the Army, yeah, but not with a court-martial giving him a boot in the seat of the pants.

Frank drummed his fingers on the card table that did duty for his desk. "What d'you think of him?"

Lou shrugged. "He's a reporter. He'll never make anybody forget Shirer or Howard K. Smith."

"He's doing his goddamnedest." The CIC captain drummed harder. "What d'you know about how he got his hands on that film?"

Ice walked up Lou's back. Did the brass think he had something to do with that? "Only what he's said, which isn't much."

"Which isn't *bupkis*," Frank snapped. "A German gave it to him! That only cuts it down to eighty million people. Maybe to forty million, if it's a fucking kraut from the American zone. Hot damn!"

"We ought to get more than that out of him," Lou said.

"No kidding! But he's a civilian. He goes on about not revealing his sources. All we can do is ship his sorry ass back to the States." Captain Frank made as if to tear his thinning hair. "Yeah, throw *me* in the briar patch, too, why don't you? And you know what else?"

"No, but you're gonna tell me, aren't you?" Lou said.

"You better believe it. The isolationist chowderheads who want us to bring all the boys home day before yesterday, they'll make a hero out of him." Frank lit a cigarette. He looked mad enough to breathe fire and smoke without one. "They'll say he was telling the truth, and the Army's trying to hide how horrible things are over here. They'll wrap him in the First Amendment and beat us over the head with it."

The Army *was* trying to hide how bad things were in Germany. It would have been crazy not to, as far as Lou was concerned. You did what needed doing. And if holding down the resurgent Nazis didn't need doing, he'd never seen anything that did. But these—*chowderheads* struck him as much too nice a word—wanted to joggle Truman's elbow.

"What can we do about it, sir?" Lou asked.

"Find out where his footage came from—that'd make a halfway decent start," Captain Frank answered. He blew out more smoke. "And relax, for cryin' out loud. I'm pretty sure you're clean, 'cause we checked you out. . . . That surprise you?"

"Not for this, sir," Lou said slowly. "I would've hoped you could've trusted me, but. . . . With this, you want to know. It's the Army."

"Hey, they've been on my ass, too," Frank said reproachfully. He rolled his eyes. "*Gottenyu,* have they ever. They really want to know how this Schmidt item got his hands on that movie."

"What's your best guess?" Lou asked.

"Same one Bruce the morale officer made when I first showed it to you," Frank answered. "Heydrich's goons figured we'd try and sit on it, so they made more copies and spread 'em around. Schmidt got his hands on one some kind of way."

"Makes sense to me." Lou's chuckle held no real mirth. "If we were the *Gestapo,* we'd ram splinters under his fingernails and set 'em on fire. He'd sing—he'd sing like a goddamn canary. Or even if we were the NKVD, over in the Russian zone." His gaze sharpened. "How bad is it, over in the Russian zone? D'you know?"

Captain Frank hesitated. "Officially, you didn't get this from me."

"Get what, sir?" Lou was the picture of innocence.

"Okay." His superior's laugh sounded as dry as his had a moment before. "From what I hear, if the fanatics don't want us occupying them, they *really* don't want the Russians occupying them. So they're kicking up their heels in the Russian zone and in what Poland's holding and in the Czech mountains, too. But the Russians aren't Mr. Nice Guy like we are. They aren't taking the gloves off, on account of they never put the gloves on to begin with. So things are kinda rugged over there right now."

Lou nodded thoughtfully. "Yeah, I bet. They ever ask how things are going over here?"

"Not through channels, or not that I've heard of, and I think I would have," Frank answered.

"Too bad. It'd be nice if we were still making like allies on something, you know?" Lou said.

"It would, wouldn't it?" Frank agreed. As soon as the Germans went down for the count, the USA and the USSR started glaring at each other over the fallen body—and in the Far East, too. Berlin wasn't going to be the capital that ruled the world. Washington and Moscow both had ambitions along those lines. Neither liked the idea that the other had ambitions. Lou didn't know what he could do about that. Well, actually, he did know what *he* could do—*bupkis,* as Captain Frank had said. But he didn't know what anyone else could do, either.

"I wonder if we ought to talk to their people," Lou said. "We might do better against Heydrich's boys if we were all fighting the same war, not two separate ones—know what I mean?"

"Yeah, I do," Frank said. "But you are not to talk to the Russians without orders from somebody above you. That's a direct order, Lou.

You try sliding around it and I promise the brass will crucify you. When they aren't looking for Nazis under the bed, they're looking for Reds. You hear me?"

"Yes, sir," Lou said resignedly—he knew Frank was right.

"Besides," the captain went on, "we aren't fighting two separate wars against the fanatics. We're fighting four. Well, we do work with the English some, but the French are almost as prickly as the Russians—and almost as rough on the Jerries, too."

"I've heard that. Breaks my heart," Lou said, which won him another wry laugh from Captain Frank. They weren't the only American Jews who wouldn't have been sorry to see their own government come down harder on the Germans it ruled, not by a long shot. Lou added, "French're getting some of their own back for four years under the Nazis' thumbs."

"Sure they are," Frank said. "But it still rubs me the wrong way when de Gaulle goes on about turning France into a great power again when it wouldn't be diddly-squat if we weren't propping it up."

"Me, too," Lou said. "He thinks he's Napoleon—except he's a big guy. I saw him once, when I was on leave in Paris. He's gotta be six-three, maybe six-four."

"Didn't know that," Captain Frank replied. "What I do know is, if we didn't prop him up, Stalin would in a red-hot minute. De Gaulle knows it, too. It lets him bite the hand that feeds him, like."

"As long as he takes a good, big chomp out of the fanatics, I don't much care what else he does, not right now," Lou said.

"We're on the same page there—that's for damn sure," Howard Frank said.

WHEN DIANA MCGRAW WENT TO WASHINGTON TO TALK TO HER CONgressman, she could hardly get over being there. The Capitol, the Washington Monument, the White House . . . Even though Pat's loss was still fresh as a gash, she'd been a tourist, or partly a tourist, anyway. How could you help it the first time you came to the capital?

You couldn't. But when you came back again, the scenery faded into the background. You had work to do. Right now, she didn't feel like a PTA official. She felt like a third-grade teacher trying to get her class lined up and on the way to where it was supposed to go.

Like most of the people who were marching on the White House with her, she was staying in one of the hotels near Union Station. They weren't after anything ritzy. Most of them couldn't afford anything ritzy. Diana was paying for her trip out of donations from the cause, but even so. . . . They were a middle-class bunch.

Diana stood on the corner of Fourth and F, right by Judiciary Square. The U.S. District Court, the U.S. Court of Appeal, Juvenile Court, the Municipal Court, even the Police Court—and she cared about none of them. All she wanted to do was head west toward the White House and get on with things.

She looked down at the slim watch on her left wrist. "Where is everybody?" she exclaimed, her breath smoking. It wasn't anywhere near as cold here as it was back in Anderson, but it wasn't summer, either.

"Take it easy, Diana," Edna Lopatynski said. Nothing rattled Edna. If Gabriel were to sound the Last Trump, she'd ask him to wait till she finished dusting. And she'd get him to do it, too. She went on, "It's only half past eight—not even. We don't start moving till nine . . . if we're lucky. I bet none of these things ever gets going on time."

"This one sure won't," Diana said fretfully. "I know we're here early, but I expected more people would've shown up by now."

"Nah." The woman from Ohio shook her head. "The ones who show up real early are the organizers and the—well, I don't like to call 'em fanatics, not with what's going on in Germany, but you know what I mean."

And Diana did. Edna's calm good sense helped her make her own butterflies quit fluttering so much. Most of the regional leaders were here, and they were taking charge of the people from their areas. Or they were trying to, anyhow. Edna was right. Some of the ones who showed up early looked as if they'd rather be carrying rifles than picket signs. Diana hoped like anything that nobody'd stashed a pistol in pocket or purse. That wouldn't be so good, which was putting it mildly.

Someone driving by shook a fist at the gathering crowd. Attorneys going into one court building or another stared at the ordinary-looking people with the signs on their shoulders. And a sizable contingent of Washington, D.C.'s, finest gathered to keep things peaceable—or maybe to arrest anybody who got the least bit out of line.

At nine on the dot, one of the policemen sauntered over to Diana. Before she could wonder how he knew she was in charge of things, he tipped his hat and said, "Time to get 'em moving, ma'am."

"Not everybody's here yet," she protested.

The cop looked over the crowd. "You've got enough," he said. "You're all up and down F Street, and you're starting to mess up traffic. The ones who can't get out of bed quick enough know where they're supposed to go, right?"

"Yes, but—"

"No buts. Get 'em moving, like I said, or I can write you up for blocking the streets here." *I can write you up* had to mean *I will write you up*.

Diana considered. Several reporters were watching what went on. She recognized E. A. Stuart from Indianapolis (Ebenezer Amminadab! what a handle!). What would they say—what would they write?—if the police broke up the demonstration without letting it get started? But her people really were starting to spill into the street. Not all the car horns that blared at them were political. Some were just plain annoyed.

She looked a question at Edna Lopatynski. Edna nodded back. Diana nodded, too. She raised her voice: "Come on, folks! The President needs to find out what we think! So does the whole country! Let's go show them!"

She started west, toward the White House, holding her sign high. HOW MANY DEAD IN "PEACETIME"? it asked. Behind her, Edna called, "Regional leaders, bring your people along!"

"We might as well be in the Army ourselves," somebody grumbled.

If you were going to run something this size, you had to have organization. Otherwise, you only thought you were running it. But if all the people did whatever they wanted, what you really had was a mob.

Not quite a mile from the gathering place to Presidents Square. The gray, enormous Greek Revival Treasury Building, on the east side of the square, blocked the view of the White House. Better planning, Diana thought, would have kept something like that from happening.

But better planning would have done all kinds of things—like winning the war sooner, and like making sure it was really over when it was supposed to be.

Diana looked back over her shoulder again. She wanted to see how many men she had here, especially men who'd fought in this war. She nodded to herself. Enough, she judged. Without them, people would think this was only a women's movement. She was old enough to remember how much that had slowed the suffragettes.

E. A. Stuart trotted across the street toward her. A cop shook his nightstick. "I oughta run you in!" he boomed. "Jaywalkin's against the law."

"I'm a reporter," Stuart answered, as if that freed him from obeying laws he didn't happen to like. From what Diana had seen of reporters the past few months, it was liable to do just that. Stuart poised notebook and pencil. "How do you think things are going here, Mrs. McGraw?"

"Fine." Diana was damned if she'd admit to any worries, no matter what. She asked a question of her own: "How can you walk and write at the same time?"

"Practice. Lots of practice." When Stuart grinned, he looked like a kid. Then he got serious again: "What do you aim to accomplish today?"

"I want the President to know not everybody supports his policy in Germany. I want him to see the faces of the people whose sons and brothers and husbands he's killed. I want the whole country to see them, too," Diana answered. "I want everybody to know we're not a bunch of nuts. We're just ordinary people. If this happened to other ordinary people, they'd be out here, too."

A car zoomed by. The driver gave the marchers the finger out the window. It was nothing Diana hadn't seen before. "What do you have to say to people like that?" E. A. Stuart asked.

Before Diana could say anything, Edna Lopatynski beat her to the punch: "They can go get stuffed." Diana stared—that wasn't like Edna at all. But the Polish woman went on, "I mean it. If people want to talk with me, I'm glad to talk with them. But if all you're gonna do is something disgusting like that, to heck with you, buddy."

They walked past Ford's Theater. *Lincoln got shot there,* Diana thought. She would have torn down the place after something like

that, but they hadn't. Then something else crossed her mind. Even as
things were, Lincoln got a lot more time than a lot of the kids he sent
into battle. And he got a lot more time than Pat had or ever would,
too.

The National Theater stood another few blocks farther on. Diana
didn't know one thing about it. In a way, that came as a relief. Nothing horrible had happened there, except maybe some of the produc-
tions.

She turned right on Fifteenth Street, in front of the Treasury
Department building. As soon as she got past it, there was the White
House on the left. Leaves had fallen from the trees on the White House
grounds, so she could see it really well. They'd had at least one hard
frost here, because the grass was going all yellow-brown, the way it
did back in Anderson.

Left this time, onto Pennsylvania Avenue. The White House was at
1600—probably the one address besides their own that all Americans
knew. Somebody behind Diana said, "It looks like a postcard." She
smiled. She'd had the same notion at almost the same time.

Several men waited for the marchers right in front of the gate that
led into the White House grounds. Some of them were reporters. A
newsreel camera crew filmed the demonstration. People all over the
country might see this. The mere idea made Diana automatically pat
at her hair with her free hand.

And one of the men in suits . . . Diana waved frantically. "Congressman Duncan!" she called. "Thanks so much for coming!" He
hadn't promised he would. He must have wondered whether showing
up would gain him votes or cost them. And he must have decided it
wouldn't cost him too many, anyhow.

"Diana." Edna tapped her on the shoulder. When Diana didn't answer fast enough to suit her, she tapped again, harder. "Diana!"

"What?" Diana said impatiently. "That's the Congressman from
my district there, and—"

"And the guy next to him—the guy in the gray hat—is Senator
Taft," Edna broke in. "That counts for more, you ask me."

"Senator Taft?" Diana whispered. And it was, sure enough. She
recognized him now that Edna pointed him out. She thought she
would have done it sooner if the hat hadn't covered up his bald

head—and kept it warm, too, she supposed. But she didn't see Taft's picture every day. Edna was from Ohio, so chances were she did.

Some of the other men gathered with Jerry Duncan and Robert Taft were probably Senators and Representatives, too. Their home states and districts knew what they looked like, but Diana didn't. Maybe a book somewhere had pictures of all of them. Diana had never seen or heard of one like that, but it would sure be a handy thing to have if you were a political kind of person. *And I am—now,* she thought. *I really am.*

"More of them here than I expected," Edna said. "Have we got enough signs for them all?"

"We will," Diana declared. If they didn't, if they had to rob a few ordinary Peters to let the political Pauls picket, she would do that without a qualm. The country needed to see not all politicians blindly followed Harry Truman's lead.

"Hello, Mrs. McGraw." Jerry Duncan came up to her with a big smile—a politician's smile—spread across his face. "May we join you?"

"I hope you will," Diana said. "Who are your, uh, colleagues?"

Duncan introduced Senator Taft first, as she'd hoped—he was the heavy hitter in the group. "Very pleased to meet you," Taft said, his voice raspy. "You're making people think, and that's never bad."

Diana wanted to make people feel. That would make them get out there and do things. But she didn't want to argue with the Senator from Ohio, so she nodded. Edna handed Taft a picket sign that said ISN'T AMERICA ENOUGH? He gruffly thanked her and nodded at the sentiment. Diana nodded to herself. Being from his home state, Edna would know the kind of thing he wanted to say.

Jerry Duncan presented more politicos: from California, from Idaho, from Illinois, from Alabama, from Mississippi. "We're not all Republicans here, you see," he said.

"Sure." Diana nodded. The Congressmen—or were they Senators?—from the Deep South might call themselves Democrats, but they'd be more conservative than most Republicans. Diana didn't care whether they worshipped at the shrine of the donkey or the elephant. As long as they wanted GIs to stop dying in Germany, they were on her side.

Duncan's sign said DIDN'T THE NAZIS SURRENDER? Reporters shouted questions at the politicians as they tramped back and forth in front of the White House along with the ordinary demonstrators. "This is pretty good," Edna said. "Now the flatfoots'll leave us alone. They won't get tough where big shots can see 'em do it."

"Yup." Diana nodded. In Indianapolis or in Washington, the cops paid attention to power. They had to. What were they but power's hunting dogs? Diana went on, "This is pretty good, Edna. But you know what? Next time we come here, we'll fill that whole park with people." She pointed across Pennsylvania Avenue to Lafayette Square.

"Wow! You don't think small, do you?" Admiration filled Edna's voice.

"If I thought small, I'd still be sitting at home crying 'cause Pat's dead. We'd all be sitting at home, crying alone 'cause our boys are dead," Diana answered. "But sitting at home and crying doesn't help. If we don't do anything but that, nobody else will, either. We've got to get people moving. And we will."

"Damn right." Edna could swear like a trooper when she felt like it. To her, it was just talk, not filthy talk.

A car going by on Pennsylvania Avenue honked its horn. "Traitors!" the driver yelled.

"Jackass!" Senator Taft said crisply. "This is just as much a part of government as all the wind and air up on Capitol Hill." The man in the car couldn't hear any of that, of course. But the reporters could. Several of them took down what he said. Most seemed to share E. A. Stuart's knack for writing on the move.

Back and forth. Back and forth. They had several hundred people there—nowhere near enough to fill Lafayette Square, but enough to be noticed. *Enough,* Diana thought, *to look like more when they film us.* The majority of the picketers came from the East and the Midwest. The majority of people in the country lived in those parts, and they were closest to Washington. But a man was here from Nevada, and a woman from Washington state, and a couple from New Mexico, and several people from California. When something like this happened to you, it hit you hard. You wanted to do something about it. No—you *had* to.

After a while, the newsreel crew took their camera off its tripod.

They loaded the gear into a van and drove away. Reporters drifted off. Diana hoped they were going to write up their stories, not to hoist a few in the nearest bar.

Some of the Representatives and Senators left after a bit, too. They must have felt they'd made their point—and they'd got filmed doing it, which was even better. Jerry Duncan and Robert Taft stayed. Diana had expected Duncan to; she thought of him as *her* Congressman, and didn't worry about whether he thought the same way. But she was delighted about Taft. People said he was thinking of running for President in three years. If he did, if things changed then . . . Diana shook her head. Things needed to change right away. That was why she was doing all this.

A couple of men came around the corner of Pennsylvania Avenue and Seventeenth Street, on the far side of the White House grounds. They wore ordinary off-the-rack suits, and hats that might have come from Sears, but they looked like combat soldiers just the same. Diana had seen men who looked like that too often to doubt her snap judgment. And, a moment later, she understood why they did. Behind them strode Harry Truman.

Diana's knees knocked. That was the President of the United States, the most powerful man in the world, even if he did look like a small-town druggist in his Sunday best, right down to his bright bow tie. She'd never dreamt he would come out of the White House. Too bad the newsreel crew was gone.

He pushed past his bodyguards—they didn't look happy about it—and walked straight up to her. In person, he seemed a little smaller, a little older, than he did when he got his picture in the paper or showed up in a newsreel on the big screen.

"You're Mrs. McGraw, aren't you? The woman who started this whole silly thing." His voice was familiar, too, and yet not quite so: it had a different timbre coming from his own mouth rather than booming out of a speaker.

"Uh, yes, sir." Diana knew her own voice shook. She forced it to firmness as she went on, "Only I don't think it's silly."

She kept walking as she answered; the demonstration would have bogged down if she hadn't. Harry Truman kept pace with her. With her! Only later would she think about how surreal that was.

"Well, yes, I can see how you'd feel that way," Truman said. "I commanded an artillery battery in the last war. We must've had four-leaf clovers in our pockets—we only took a couple of minor wounds. Most other units weren't so lucky. Always unfortunate when you lose people, but that's war."

"Yes. That's war." Diana nodded. "But the war in Europe's been over since May. That's what everybody says, anyhow. What are we still doing over there if the war's been over since May?"

"Making sure it doesn't start up again for real." Truman had an agreeable Missouri twang. It made him sound like a small-town druggist, too. "Parts of Germany got occupied after World War I, too, remember. The Nazis are more dangerous than Kaiser Bill ever was, so this time around the Allies have to sit on the whole blamed country."

He wasn't the first one Diana had heard who argued that way. She'd had to study up since starting her crusade. She couldn't afford to sound like a jerk when she came up against somebody who thought she was talking through her hat. "But the Germans weren't killing our soldiers in 1919. How many men have we lost since they said they surrendered? Must be close to two thousand by now. And what about England? And France? And Russia?"

Truman's face hardened. "Yes, what about Russia? Stalin isn't acting like good old Uncle Joe any more. Now that Hitler's gone and Germany's *kaput,* he wants Russia to fill her shoes and then some. Suppose we do what you want. Suppose we come home with our tails between our legs. What happens next? That's what you haven't thought about, Mrs. McGraw. Either Heydrich's goons come out of hiding and start getting ready for the next war or Stalin marches in where we marched out . . . and starts getting ready for the next war."

"Oh, piffle!" One more thing Diana had never imagined was that she might one day say *piffle!* to the President, but that day seemed to be at hand. "If they get out of line, we drop one of our atom bombs on them, or more than one if they need that the way the Japs did. Then we go in and pick up the pieces—except there won't be any pieces left to pick up, will there?"

"It's not so simple as you make it sound. Do you know, nobody told me about the atom bomb till after I was in the White House? I was Vice President, and nobody told me. That's how secret it was." Truman sounded plaintive—and who could blame him? "One thing is plain—it's not something you can use casually. It's like swatting a fly by dropping a Sherman tank on it."

"And so we have this running sore instead," Diana said. "How long will the Germans go on murdering GIs, sir? Will we still have soldiers over there in 1949? In 1955? Do you think the American people will let something this senseless go on that long?"

"Holding down the Nazis and holding out the Reds isn't senseless," Truman insisted. "If we'd done things the right way after World War I, we never would've had to fight World War II."

"Getting thousands of soldiers killed after everybody said the war was over is senseless." Diana could dig in her heels, too. "Grandchildren who'll never be born . . ." She told herself not to puddle up. That wasn't easy, but she managed.

"I have to do what I think is right," Truman said. "I have to think of the long term, not just today and tomorrow."

"If you foul up today and tomorrow, what's the long term worth?" Diana retorted. "And if you foul up today and tomorrow, the American people will throw you out before you can do anything about it later on."

"Chance I have to take," Truman said.

"You'll be sorry, sir," Diana told him. "I am already, and you will be."

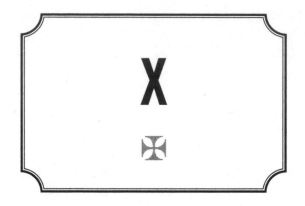

X

New Year's Eve. New Year's Day. The big holiday in the Soviet year. Behind Christmas in the Gregorian calendar, but conveniently ahead of the old Julian reckoning the Orthodox used. This year, celebrating the slide from 1945, the year of victory, to 1946, the year of . . . what? The year when the Soviet Union didn't need to worry about victory any more. Not much, anyhow.

And, here in Berlin, the year where the Russians could celebrate in style. Here where Fascism had grown, here where it had done its bloody-handed best to annul the Revolution and destroy the Soviet people . . . How many officers would swill up the loot of a conquered country? How many frightened German barmen would pour the drinks? How many frightened German barmaids would serve them? How many of those frightened German barmaids would serve the conquerors in other ways later on, whether they much wanted to or not?

Three days earlier, Vladimir Bokov had been looking forward to getting his own drunken blowjob from some blond German bitch.

Life wasn't fair. He'd thought so for a long time. Now he was sure of it. Instead of going off and drinking till he puked and getting his cock sucked, he lay tossing on the meager mattress of a steel-framed cot, knocked flat by the nastiest case of influenza he'd ever had.

Colonel Shteinberg lay one cot to his left. Shteinberg looked like hell. No doubt Bokov looked like hell, too, but he couldn't see himself. He and his superior were both running a fever close to forty Celsius. Bokov's head ached. So did every other part of him. Sometimes he shivered and wished he had more blankets. Five minutes later, sweat would river off of him.

He was, in short, a mess. So was Moisei Shteinberg. The only difference between them was that Bokov remembered liking Christmas when he was a small, small boy before the Revolution. Shteinberg never would have given a damn about it.

A male nurse—a Red Army private who'd done something wrong and was lucky not to have drawn some worse punishment—brought them aspirins and glasses of heavily sugared hot tea. The tea stayed down. Some of the other things Bokov had tried didn't want to. He had vivid memories of that, and wished he didn't.

The sullen nurse moved no faster than he had to. No doubt he wished he were out carousing, too. And he had plenty to keep him busy. Bokov and Shteinberg weren't the only ones down with the grippe—not even close. As the aspirins lent Bokov's wits brief clarity, he thought, *You'll probably catch it yourself, you sorry fucker.*

"This is shit," Colonel Shteinberg said—maybe the little white tablets were also helping him think straighter. "We'll be flat on our backs for days more, and then feeling steamrollered for another week after that. Pure shit, nothing else but."

"Don't worry about it, Comrade Colonel," Bokov said.

Shteinberg gave him a bleary stare. "Don't worry? Are you out of your mind? Why not?" He plucked at the cold compress on his forehead—except, if it was anything like Bokov's, it wasn't cold any more.

"Because all the officers out drinking tonight will be just as bad off as we are," Bokov answered. "They'll have more fun getting there"— no German girl was going to suck him off tonight, not when he couldn't get it up with a crane—"but they'll be fucked over, too."

"Maybe," Shteinberg said grudgingly. "But do you suppose the stinking Heydrichite fanatics will drink themselves blind tonight? Not likely! They're no fools, damn them—they know how we do things. And you just wait and see if they don't try something while we're plastered out of our minds."

That struck Captain Bokov as much too likely. He shrugged anyway. It hurt—but what didn't right now? This was even worse than a hangover, and he hadn't even had the pleasure of getting plastered himself. Definitely unfair.

"Comrade Colonel, the two of us can't do a thing about it," he said.

"Too right we can't," Shteinberg agreed. "I feel like dogshit."

"*Da.*" Bokov looked around for that private. He wanted more tea, and he wanted his compress soaked in cold water again—or, better yet, in the snow outside.

He didn't see the fellow. Where the devil had he gone? Was he off smoking a cigarette? Or had he cached a flask somewhere? Was he swigging right this second? Bokov's spirit lusted after vodka. His body told his spirit it had to be kidding. Sometimes you had to listen to your body, even if you didn't want to.

The orderly came back. He didn't look so sullen now. Sure as hell, he'd found some way to make himself feel better. And if the men he was supposed to be taking care of got short shrift, that was their hard luck. They were already sick, weren't they?

Bokov drifted into a restless, uneasy sleep—the only kind he'd had since this miserable thing landed on him like a *Katyusha* rocket. His dreams were confused and dark. That was all he remembered of them.

Then a doctor with a thin, clever Jewish face much like Colonel Shteinberg's was shaking him awake. Another doctor, this one an authentic Slav, was waking the NKVD colonel. "Get up," the Jew told Bokov. "We need you."

"What is it?" Bokov tried to sit up. His head swam. "I beg your pardon, Comrade Physician. I am not well." He gulped, hoping the juices in his stomach would stay down. He wasn't kidding, not even a little bit. In the next bed, Shteinberg was also feebly protesting.

"You don't have time to be sick," the Jewish doctor said bluntly.

"The fucking Nazis have poisoned half the officer corps in Berlin, maybe more. You've got to track them down and pay them back. Give me your arm."

"*Bozhemoi!* How?" Bokov exclaimed. Automatically, he stuck out his left arm. The doctor undid the cuff on his uniform tunic, then rolled up his sleeve and tapped at the inside of his elbow to bring up the veins there. As soon as he found one, he stuck a hypodermic needle into it and pushed in the plunger. Bokov shook, not only from the influenza but also because he flat-out hated needles. The doctor knew his stuff; he didn't let the hypodermic slip out of the vein till he'd finished the injection. "What did you shoot me with?" Bokov asked. "I didn't think there was any medicine for the grippe."

"There isn't," the doctor said. "You'll still be sick. But with enough benzedrine in you, you'll be able to work anyhow. We'll feed you pills from now on, but we want to get you up and moving right away."

He knew how to get what he wanted. The dose he shot into Bokov was brutally effective. The NKVD man's heart pounded as if he'd drunk fifty cups of strong coffee all at once. His snot dried up. So did his mouth. So did his eyeballs. His brain felt on fire. He knew he still had the influenza. He also knew he'd have to pay for this artificial vitality, and that he'd be even sorrier later than he was before the injection. But all that would wait. Right this second, he was raring to go.

"Poisoned? How?" he demanded. Far from being fuzzy with sickness, his wits raced at triple time. He beat the doctor to the answer: "Fuck my mother if they didn't put something in the booze for the New Year's bash!"

"Right the first time—wood alcohol," the Jew said. "Lots and lots of wood alcohol. They must have been setting this up for weeks, the fucking cunts. It's the best thing in the world to use if you're poisoning liquor. You won't notice it while you're drinking. Most people even like the taste. But afterwards . . . Afterwards, it'll kill you if you drink enough. And it'll leave you blind even if you don't."

Bokov nodded. He knew what wood alcohol could do. Plenty of illicit liquor got cooked up in the Soviet Union. Some of it was as good as any you could buy in the government stores. Some was better: a labor of love. But some was pure poison. He'd heard people say you could get rid of the bad stuff if you filtered booze through a loaf of black bread. Bokov didn't know whether that was true—he'd never tried it. He did know they wouldn't have filtered their drinks at the New Year's feast. They'd have poured them down as fast as they could.

Over in the next bed, Colonel Shteinberg had also risen like a drug-fueled Lazarus. "You will have held the bartenders and the serving women?" he demanded of the doctor who'd injected him back to life.

The only answer he got was a broad-shouldered shrug. "They told me to run my cock over here and start your motor," the man answered. "I don't know what all else they're doing. If it weren't for the commotion in the hall, they wouldn't even've told me how come I had to do that."

Like so many Red Army officers, he'd carried out his orders precisely and to the letter, and hadn't taken one step beyond them. Stalin had terrified initiative out of the whole country. If being wrong landed you in the gulag, you couldn't take the chance. That kind of caution had cost casualties, maybe even battles. What would it cost here?

Would anybody at the banquet hall have kept his head enough to think to make the necessary arrests? Bokov had to hope so. (Would the barmen and barmaids have been the ones who poisoned the liquor? No way to know till you started hurting them.)

"Come on," Shteinberg said, and then, "Where the devil are my *valenki*?" Bokov had already found his own felt boots under his cot. He was pulling them on. His superior grunted when he came up with his.

"Here." The Jewish doctor gave Bokov a vial of pills. "Take two of these whenever you start slowing down. They'll keep you going for three or four days. Eat a lot. Drink a lot. If you were an airplane, you'd be running on your reserve tank."

"Right." Bokov could feel that. He wrapped his greatcoat around himself. "Ready, Comrade Colonel?"

"You'd best believe it." Shteinberg barked hard, mirthless laughter. "See? We get to go to the party after all."

"Just what I wanted," Bokov said in a hollow voice. Benzedrine or no benzedrine, the colonel's chuckle also sounded less lively than it might have.

A jeep waited outside the barracks. Bokov and Shteinberg piled in.

the jeep took off toward the south and west. "Potsdam?" Shteinberg asked. "Again?"

"Yes, sir. That palace with the German name," the driver answered.

"The Schloss Cecilienhof." Bokov didn't make it a question. The Red Army noncom behind the wheel nodded. Bokov muttered. That was where Stalin had met with the American President and British Prime Minister. More recently—not even two months ago now—the Red Army had celebrated the anniversary of the Russian Revolution there. And now this.

"We got careless. We got predictable." Moisei Shteinberg took the words out of his mouth. "We came back to the same place three times in a row, and the fucking Nazis went and made us pay."

"Somebody should answer for that, sir," the noncom said. "Even in the trenches, you don't stick your head up in the same place three times. A sniper'll put one through your ear if you're dumb enough to try it."

Voice dry as the inside of his own mouth, Bokov said, "Whoever planned our party would have gone to it himself. Chances are decent he's a casualty, too."

He was shivering by the time the jeep got to the Cecilienhof. It wasn't just the cold—it was the influenza trying to jump on him again. He choked down two of the pills the doctor had given him. Colonel Shteinberg did the same thing.

They had to pass through several belts of security. That would have been funny if it weren't so grim. No fanatics could get in and shoot up the place—but nobody'd bothered to vet the booze. Shteinberg said it: they'd got careless. And they'd played right into the bandits' hands.

An English country house for the Kaiser's daughter-in-law: that was how the Schloss Cecilienhof got started, just before World War I. *Country house, nothing,* Bokov thought, the benzedrine making his heart drum again. *It's a goddamn country palace, is what it is.*

And, at the moment, it was a country palace in one of the nastier districts of hell. Spotlights spread harsh light on the snow-covered grounds around the main buildings—and on the uniformed bodies stacked there like cordwood. One of the bodies wasn't uniformed, but wore black tie and boiled shirt. A barman had poured it down on the sly . . . and got what the officers he was serving got. "*He* didn't know the shit was poisoned," Bokov said, pointing to the corpse in the fancy suit.

"You wouldn't expect many to," Shteinberg answered. "Some American said three can keep a secret if two of them are dead. He knew what he was talking about."

"Sensible, for an American," Bokov said. He jumped down from the jeep. The noises from inside the Cecilienhof sounded like something from a low-rent district in hell, too. He didn't want to go in there, and he knew he had to. Then he stopped almost in spite of himself. "Comrade Colonel, tell me—please tell me—that isn't Marshal Zhukov."

"It is." Shteinberg's voice was hard and flat. "The revenge Stalin will take . . . Unless . . ." He quickly shook his head and went inside.

Unless what? Bokov wondered. Unless Stalin decided to get rid of the popular Zhukov and blame it on the Heydrichites? Was that what the other NKVD man meant? Even if it was, Bokov didn't believe it. If Stalin wanted Zhukov shot, shot Zhukov would be, and never mind that he was the leading soldier in the Red Army. But that Bokov could wonder—and that Shteinberg could, too—spoke volumes about how the system they lived under worked.

Bokov had no time to read those volumes, and no interest in them. He was, after all, part of the system himself. He followed his superior into the Cecilienhof.

It was as bad as he'd expected, maybe worse. The palace stank of sweat and smoke and vomit and shit. Men reeled here and there, some clutching their bellies, others rubbing frantically at their eyes. "Who turned out the lights?" a major shouted furiously. The lights were blazing. His eyes had gone dark. *Wood alcohol, sure as the devil,* Bokov thought.

"The NKVD men!" a sergeant shouted. "They'll take over!"

"Thank God!" another noncom exclaimed. *Now the monkey's off our backs,* he meant. Nobody could blame the poor underofficers for screwing up if they weren't in charge.

"No officers here still on the job?" Shteinberg asked, in the tones of a man hoping against hope.

But the two noncoms shook their heads. Bokov wasn't surprised, either. Why else would a man come to a New Year's festival, except to drink himself blind? And how many Red Army officers had done just that here tonight?

"Have you got the Germans under guard?" Bokov asked.

The two underofficers gave each other apprehensive looks. "Comrade Captain, we have . . . some of them," answered the one who'd spoken first. "Some went home before people started getting sick." He paused unhappily. "Some may have slipped out when the Devil's grandfather got loose, too. Things were pretty confused there for a while."

Whenever a Russian hauled the Devil's kin into a conversation, he knew he was in the middle of a mess. Bokov knew it, too. As far as he could see, things were still plenty confused. Part of him wanted to lie down and forget about everything but the influenza. But neither duty nor benzedrine would let him.

A word from him or Shteinberg could destroy these noncoms. What point, though? They hadn't done anything wrong. Most of the ones who had screwed up were poisoned, which served them right. *If I weren't sick, I'd be poisoned, too,* Bokov thought.

"Comrade Captain, what do we do if the Nazi bandits rise up now?" the other conscript asked. "Who'd give orders to help us fight back?"

"People like you," Bokov answered. "And if they try it, we'll whip them right out of their boots. I hope they do—fuck your mother if I don't. If they come out and fight fair, we'll smash them like the cockroaches they are. The one way they can hurt us is by sneaking around like this."

"Unfortunately, they're too damned good at sneaking." Colonel Shteinberg's voice was dry as usual. Only the way his hands shook and the unnatural glitter in his eyes told of the war between disease and drugs inside him. He went on, "Take us to the Germans. Let's see what we can get out of them."

Guards with submachine guns stood outside the door to the room where the servers were corralled. Nobody was going anywhere now. Of course, it was much too likely that anyone with guilty knowledge had already got away. As Bokov and Shteinberg went in, one of the guards muttered to another: "Never thought I'd be glad to see the damned Chekists get here."

"Shut up," the other fellow hissed. "They'll hear you."

If Bokov didn't have bigger things to worry about . . . But he did. If Moisei Shteinberg heard the whispers from the Red Army men, he also gave no sign.

Inside the splendid chamber—a plaque said it had been the smoking room—huddled a gaggle of scared-looking Fritzes. Bokov nodded glumly to himself: sure as hell, the women were chosen for looks and figures. The Red Army men in charge were careful about that. About some other things, things that turned out to matter more, they weren't.

Colonel Shteinberg pointed to one of the women, a statuesque brunette. "You, bitch—come outside with us," he snarled. He wasn't really speaking German at all, but Yiddish. She'd be able to follow it, though. And it ought to frighten her even more. Most Germans hadn't had anything direct to do with killing Jews. But they'd had a notion of what was going on even so. They didn't like the idea of Jews holding power over them now. They feared revenge—and well they might.

Her lower lip trembled, but she came. As soon as she got out into the hall and the door closed behind her, Bokov slapped her in the face. She stared at him, her mouth an O of injured astonishment. She had eyes green as jade.

She didn't squawk, which wasn't what he wanted. "Scream your head off," he told her. "Give those other pigdogs back there something to worry about."

When she obeyed, he felt as if he were standing in front of an air-raid siren. "Enough, already!" Shteinberg said, and she shut it off as abruptly as she'd let loose. The Jewish NKVD man went on, "So you're one of the ones who thought you could wipe out the Red Army, eh?"

"I work in a shoe factory," the dark-haired woman said. "One of your men pulled me out and said he would shoot my little son if I didn't come here and give your officers drinks and—" She stopped, then made herself finish: "—and anything else they wanted."

Bokov didn't know if she was telling the truth. Her story sounded as if she could be, though. "Tell us what happened here," he said.

"They gave me these clothes to wear," she said. The black and white maid's outfit didn't cover that much of her. After a sigh, she continued, "I brought drinks. I brought food. I got groped a couple of times, but nothing worse."

The Red Army officers would still have been more or less sober. And the sour resignation in the woman's voice said she might have been on the receiving end of worse when the Russians took Berlin. Nobody knew how many rapes there'd been then. A lot, though; no doubt of that.

"Go on," Bokov told her. "When did people start getting sick?"

"A little before midnight," she answered. "At first we thought it was because they were drinking like . . . well, because they were drinking so much." She had sense enough not to tell a Russian that Russians drank like swine. But Bokov already knew that—knew it from experience. He could have been lying out there stiffening in the snow himself. When he remembered how much he'd looked forward to this feast, and how pissed off he'd been when he came down sick . . . When he remembered all that, he quickly thought about something else.

"Do you know any of the people—the Germans, I mean—who got out of here before the poison showed itself?" he asked.

"*Nein, mein Herr.*" Curls bobbed back and forth as the woman shook her head. "I never saw any of them before. Your man must have liked my looks and thought I would make a good whore here." She looked defiance at him, daring him to deny that was what the Red Army man had in mind. When Bokov just waited, she shrugged and went on, "I think most of the women got picked that way. The men behind the bar might be a different story. They didn't get chosen for their looks, anyhow."

She made good sense, even if she was trying to get the NKVD men to leave her alone. Colonel Shteinberg went back into the smoking room, presumably to grab one of the barmen.

Bokov carried on alone with her. "Show me your papers," he snapped. He wrote down her name: Elfriede Taubenschlag, a hell of a mouthful. Then he said, "So you have a boy, eh? Where's your husband?"

"He died in an air raid last year," she answered bleakly. "He was home, getting over a wound, and he was out drinking beer with some other soldiers in the same boat, and the tavern got hit. I think most of what we buried was him. I hope so."

If she was looking for sympathy, she was looking in the wrong place. Bokov slapped her again, almost hard enough to knock her over. "Hitler shouldn't have started the war if he didn't want it to come home," he snapped.

"If you treat us like this, no wonder we give you poison," she said.

This time, he did knock her down. She might not have wanted to yelp, but she did anyway. Bokov had to fight the urge to murder her right there. If he hadn't thought it came from the benzedrine roaring through him, he wouldn't have bothered fighting. "We'll kill all of you if we need to, cunt. Nobody'd miss you a bit. It's what you tried to do to us."

Elfriede Taubenschlag kept quiet. She could see he would kill her if she argued. He could read her face, now bruised, too. Like so many Germans, she wasn't sorry Hitler had started the war. She only regretted losing.

Bokov shoved her back toward the smoking room. "Any luck?" Colonel Shteinberg asked him, pausing with a barman whose flat nose and scarred forehead said he'd done some prizefighting.

"Not much," Bokov answered, eyeing the German to see if he followed Russian. Seeing no signs of that, he went on, "Since the bitches were chosen for their looks, the barmen look like a better bet."

"So we'll see what Uwe here knows," Shteinberg said. Then he fell back into rasping, guttural Yiddish: "And if he doesn't sing like a damned canary, we'll see how he likes Siberia."

"I don't know nothin' about nothin'," Uwe said—like most Germans, he had no trouble with the Jews' dialect.

"No, huh? If we strip off your monkey suit, will we find an SS tattoo under your armpit?" Shteinberg asked. The Red Army often liquidated SS men it captured. As the war wound down toward disaster for them, some of the Nazi supermen had their blood-group marking surgically removed so it wouldn't betray them. But a fresh scar right there could also be a death sentence.

"Got no tattoos," Uwe said stolidly. He pulled up one trouser leg to show he did have an artificial foot. "Goddamn French 75 nailed me outside of Dunkirk in 1940. I tended bar ever since I got out of the hospital. Even the *Volkssturm* wouldn't take me with a leg and a half."

Bokov had thought the only prerequisite for the Germans' last-ditch militia was a detectable pulse, but maybe he was wrong. The answer didn't faze Shteinberg, who asked, "How about Heydrich's crowd? You don't have to run fast to pour wood alcohol into the vodka."

"I don't know nothin' about that, and I ain't no fuckin' Werewolf," Uwe said. "Fuckin' war's over. We lost. All I want to do is get on with my life."

"If you know who poisoned it, you'll live better," the Jew told him. "We help people who help us."

Uwe grunted. "Happens I know a couple of dykes who're pretty much Reds. They make it through the war without the SS grabbing 'em. Red Army shoots its way into Berlin at last. Dykes come out waving and yelling, 'Kamerad!' Know what happens next? They get gangbanged. Believing Goebbels' bullshit cost me my foot. What do I win for believing yours?"

A trip to the gulag, Bokov thought. You ran your mouth like that, you were asking for it. "Let's see your papers," Bokov said. "We may want to ask you more questions later, and we'll need to know where to find you."

By his documents, the German was Uwe Kupferstein. Bokov carefully noted his name and address. He didn't know whether they'd need to question Kupferstein some more or just stuff him onto an eastbound train so he could see how he liked life as a *zek*. Well, that was a worry for another time.

"How are you doing?" Shteinberg asked as the barman stumped back away. The fellow had had practice with that foot; he hardly limped at all.

"I've been better, Comrade Colonel, but I'll keep going as long as the pills let me," Bokov answered. "How are you?"

"About the same." The Jew sighed and clicked his tongue between his teeth. "We won't find the answers here tonight—this morning, I should say." The eastern horizon was starting to lighten.

"I don't suppose we will, either." Bokov sighed, too. "But we've got to try."

"Oh, yes. And we have to be seen trying, too." Maybe the influenza and the benzedrine were what made Shteinberg sail close to the edge: sail over it, really. Shaking his head at what had come out of his mouth, he added, "Let's go interrogate two more." Feeling in his pocket to make sure he still had the vial the doctor had given him, Bokov followed him back to the smoking room.

WHEN LOU WEISSBERG PASSED FROM THE AMERICAN ZONE TO THE British, the way the Tommies inspected his papers and examined his jeep told him things were just as rugged here as they were where he'd come from. "Having fun with the diehards, are you?" he said.

To his way of thinking, the corporal checking his documents had his chevrons on upside down. The man was pale, almost pasty, and had an ugly scar on his left cheek. He wore a new-style British helmet, halfway between the old tin hat and the American pot. "Too bloody right we are," he answered, his accent even further from Lou's than Toby Benton's drawl was. "When we catch them, they die hard, all right."

Officially, the Americans didn't do things like that. Germans caught in arms after the surrender weren't legally POWs—they were classed as enemy combatants instead. Still, orders were to give them at least a drumhead hearing before shooting them. Lou happened to know those orders didn't always get observed. The French thought their mere existence absurd: Frenchmen were practical people. Evidently Englishmen were, too.

"You seem to pass muster, Leftenant." Yes, the corporal spoke English, but not the kind a Yank from New Jersey would use. He gestured with his Sten gun. "Pass on—and for Christ's sake keep your bleedin' eyes open."

"Always good advice," Lou agreed. He tapped his driver on the shoulder. "On to Cologne."

"Yes, sir." The driver had make jokes about smells and perfume till Lou was sick of them. For a wonder, the guy seemed to realize as much, and cut it out. Maybe the age of miracles wasn't dead after all.

The British zone lay northwest of the bigger stretch of territory the USA administered. Signs in German lined the road. THE FANATICS HURT YOU! they said, and THE WAR IS OVER, and DON'T LET THE MAD-MEN GET AWAY WITH IT. Lou didn't know how much the propaganda helped, but it sure couldn't hurt. He wished U.S. military authorities were trying more of the same thing.

There'd been more fighting here than in most of the American zone. Wrecked trucks and tanks—U.S., British, and German—still lay by the side of the road and in the fields. They made Lou nervous: too many of them offered perfect hiding places for a diehard with a *Panzerschreck* or a Schmeisser or even a Molotov cocktail. Hastily dug graves were scattered over the countryside, some still marked by no more than a bayoneted rifle thrust into fresh-dug earth, sometimes with a helmet on it, sometimes without.

Only makeshift bridges led across the Rhine to Cologne. Bombing had destroyed some of the real ones, and the Nazis the rest. In the Rhineland, relatively close to England, Cologne had got the hell bombed out of it all through the war, and then the Germans fought in the ruins. Lou hadn't thought a city could be in worse shape than Nuremberg, but this one was.

He presented his papers at an enormous tent near the ruins of the train station. "Care for a glass of beer?" asked the British Intelligence major who cleared him.

"I'd love one. Thanks," Lou answered. "Although after what the Jerries did to Ivan last week . . ."

"They've played with poisoned liquor here, too. Haven't they in your zone?"

"Yeah, but with hard stuff, not beer. And they've done it by nickels and dimes, not all at once like they did with the Russians."

"By nickels and dimes," the major murmured. Lou realized people from the other side of the Atlantic sometimes needed to pause and decipher American lingo, too.

The beer was excellent, far better than anything you could get back in the States. The Germans might be murderous, *"Heil!"*-screaming brutes, but by God they could brew.

Lou was halfway down his stein when the man he was waiting for strode into the tent. The British major—his name was Hudgeons—introduced them in fluent German: "*Herr* Adenauer, this is *Oberleutnant* Weissberg, of U.S. Counter-Intelligence. *Oberleutnant,* this is Konrad Adenauer, former lord mayor of Cologne, former denizen of one of the late regime's concentration camps, and current founder of the Christian Democratic Union."

"Pleased to meet you, sir," Lou said. Most Germans these days claimed to have been anti-Nazi. Adenauer really had been. He was around seventy, with thin, foxy features and a perpetually worried air. Well, he'd earned the right to that.

"A lieutenant," Adenauer said sadly. "Well, I suppose I am pleased to meet you, too. Not your fault your superiors don't take this more seriously." No matter what he claimed, he was affronted. Europeans set more stock on status and rank than Americans did; Lou'd seen that before. Adenauer thought he deserved a colonel or something. Chances were he was right, too.

"Tell me about your new party, *Herr* Adenauer," Lou urged.

"Before 1933, I belonged to the Catholic Center. Thanks to the Nazis, though, this party is now *kaput*. No point trying to make a dead body into Lazarus," Adenauer said, and Lou nodded. He only wished the Nazis made as quiet a corpse as the Catholic Center Party did. Hudgeons' batman or whatever the noncom was called fetched Adenauer a mug of beer. After a healthy swig, the German went on, "So we try something new, eh? Germany needs a responsible conservative party. We will not work with those, ah, to the right of us. We know better."

"Hope so," Lou said. Back in 1933, plenty of conservatives thought they could work with the Nazis. Hitler's henchmen chewed them up and swallowed them.

"We do—from experience," Adenauer said. "If Germany is to become a democracy—a proper democracy—she must sooner or later have her own parties. And they must be independent, and be seen to be independent. Otherwise, our folk will think they are tools of the occupiers, and will not want much to do with them. They will instead work with Heydrich's maniacs . . . and with those on the left. We also aim to form a bulwark against Communism."

Maybe the American occupation authorities had sent Lou to Cologne instead of somebody more senior so they wouldn't seem too interested in the Christian Democratic Union. That was possible, but Lou didn't believe it. His superiors didn't have the subtlety for a move like that. They were paying for the lack, too.

"Heydrich's goons take Konrad seriously," Major Hudgeons put in. "A bloke with a bomb under his clothes tried to take him out, but the bloody thing didn't go off. We nabbed him, and we've learned some interesting things about how the fanatics operate in our zone."

"I lit a candle in the church of St. Pantaleon to thank the Lord for sparing me," Adenauer said. "I take it as a sign that I am meant to succeed. And if I fail, what is left for Germany but the old dreadful choice between brownshirts and Reds?"

"Sooner or later—sooner, with luck—Germany will need to stand on her own two feet again," Hudgeons said. "So we see it, anyhow. The only other choice is sitting on this country forever, and that would be . . . difficult."

Lou thought it was just what Germany deserved. Whether the rest of the USA felt the same way was liable to be a different story. People with picket signs marching in front of the White House? Congressmen and Senators with them? If they'd done that while the war was still going, it would have been treason, or something close to it. It still felt that way to Lou, even though the fighting was officially over. But more and more Americans seemed to think otherwise. And fewer and fewer dogfaces on occupation duty wanted to do anything more than pack up and go home in one piece.

"We can stand up, stand alongside of the United States and Britain and France as a free and prosperous democracy," Adenauer said. "We *can*. But we will not, not until people are able to go about their business without worrying whether a fanatic will blow himself up in the market square or explode a truck in front of the church on Sunday morning. However much you may hate it, fear is a weapon."

He had a point. Lou wished he knew how to keep Heydrich's men from making everybody else afraid. No one seemed to know how to do that, not yet. Could something like the Christian Democratic Union make a difference? Lou didn't know—but if it could, he was all for it.

XI

Sometimes you stepped on a dog turd and came out smelling like a rose. Sometimes the bread landed butter side up. Sometimes, even in the newspaper game, you had to go easy on the clichés and just write.

When the Army booted Tom Schmidt out of Germany, he'd been afraid he would have to quit reporting and find a real job. If he didn't have to go that far, he'd figured he would end up on a weekly in Michigan's Upper Peninsula that never got word of his fall from journalistic grace.

He'd been doing what he thought was right when he passed on the fanatics' film of luckless Private Cunningham. He'd had the nasty feeling that would make him a villain to almost everyone outside the news business. To his surprise, he turned out to be wrong. A startling—and growing, which was even more startling—number of people back in the USA were loudly calling for President Truman to bring all the GIs home from Germany. They weren't always people he was comfortable with, but he was in no position to be choosy.

He was, for instance, a staunch New Dealer. The *Chicago Tribune* had gone after FDR from the minute he got nominated to run against Hoover. The *Tribune* showed no signs of letting up on Democrats just because a new fanny sat in the Oval Office swivel chair, either. But when it offered him a slot in Washington at twice the money he'd been making before he had to come home, how could he say no?

He couldn't. He didn't even try. He had no trouble snagging an apartment in Washington. Now that the war was over, or mostly over, or whatever it was, more people flowed out of the capital than came in. His landlord was almost pathetically eager to have him.

He didn't have much trouble finding a replacement for Ilse, either. An awful lot of people left in Babylon by the Potomac were secretaries and clerk-typists. Making connections wasn't hard. Myrtle was more expensive than Ilse; she wouldn't put out for K-rations. What the hell? You couldn't have everything.

When Tom applied for a White House press credential, he wondered if the flunkies there would tell him to fold it till it was all corners and then stuff it. But, after one of them made a phone call to a higher-up, everything went snicker-snack.

"Thanks," he said, wondering how his vorpal blade managed to slice through red tape.

"It ain't your pretty face, buddy," the press secretary's subordinate replied. "If we turned you down, how much crap would you crank out about how we were stifling free expression? So we won't stifle it. You want to ask the President questions, go ahead. Five gets you ten he spits in your eye."

Roosevelt had been a gentleman right down to his paralyzed toes. From what Tom heard, Harry Truman was anything but. If he thought you were a son of a bitch, he'd call you one. Well, it made for good copy. "I'll take my chances," Tom said.

"You sure will." The other man sounded as if he looked forward to it.

If Truman cussed him out . . . Tom had been cussed out by experts. You couldn't quote a President cussing—there were unwritten rules about such things, as there were about reporting on, say, a Senator's lady friends—but you could probably get the idea across one way or another.

Tom's chance came on a blustery day in the middle of January. He presented his pass at the front gate of the White House, wondering if the guards would turn him away at the last minute. But they didn't. One of them said, "Lucky stiff—you get to go inside. Goddamn cold out here."

They wouldn't have had anything to complain about in the White House press room. Tom figured he'd come out as a ham: thoroughly cooked, and just as thoroughly smoked. His own Old Gold added only a little to the tobacco haze. Truman's press secretary came in and said, "Ladies and gentlemen, the President of the United States." Charlie Ross was a longtime Missouri newspaper man. He was an even longer-time friend of Truman's; they'd gone to high school together. Rawboned, with a lock of gray hair that flopped down onto his forehead, he stood several inches taller than the President.

But Truman ran the show. He bustled in and started sassing several correspondents he knew well. They returned fire. Truman wasn't Stalin—giving him a hard time wouldn't cost you your head. He looked out over the crowd of reporters. When his eyes met Tom's, he said, "Haven't seen you here before. You new?"

"Yes, sir. Tom Schmidt, from the *Chicago Tribune*."

"Oh. You're him." Truman looked as if somebody'd just farted. "Charlie wanted to give you the bum's rush, but I said no. You don't have to go sneaking around any more, Mr. Schmidt. If you've got something to say, say it to my face. Believe me, I can take the heat."

"Thanks, Mr. President," Tom said. "I wouldn't've had to sneak if your people in Germany weren't hiding how badly things are going there."

"They're still fighting in Germany, Mr. Schmidt, in case you hadn't noticed," Truman said tartly. "We don't want to spread information that can help the fanatics." He might be tart, but he was also smart: he didn't use the word *war*. The war, after all, was over.

Sure it is, Tom thought. "Well, yes, sir," he replied. "But since the Nazis were the ones who kidnapped that poor GI and then filmed him, don't you think they already knew what was going on?"

Truman glowered at him over the tops of his metal-rimmed glasses. Tom felt as if he were getting grilled by his principal after some high-school scrape. No doubt the President wanted him to feel just that way. "During the War Between the States, Abe Lincoln asked why he had to order a young deserter shot but let the clever so-and-so who conned him into deserting go free," Truman said. "All these years later, it's still a damn good question. Or don't you think morale matters?" He skated around war again.

"Of course I do, Mr. President," Tom said. "But I think truth matters, too. Or what are we fighting for? Hitler was the one who went in for the big lie."

Truman's nostrils flared as he snorted angrily. "I suppose you think we should have pointed a big arrow with neon lights at the Normandy beaches and run up a billboard that said 'We're going to invade here.' Some things need to be kept secret, that's all. Go ahead—tell me I'm wrong."

"Not me." Tom shook his head. "But you can hide anything you want behind that kind of smoke screen. Like I said, we weren't keeping this from the Nazis. We were keeping it from our own people. I don't think that's right."

"Heydrich's so-and-so's didn't snatch Private Cunningham because they figured we'd yield to those demands they made him mouth," Truman snapped. "They released that movie because they wanted to confuse decent Americans and to scare them. *Schrechlichkeit*, they call it. Frightfulness. We tried to suppress it to keep that from happening—at my order, in case you're wondering. But you played straight into their murderous hands. Thank you one hell of a lot, Mr. Schmidt. I hope you're proud."

Tom had thought the President would say his commanders in Germany had made the decision and he backed them because they were the experts and they were on the spot. Something like that, anyhow. But Harry Truman didn't seem to work that way. He'd done what he'd done, and he was ready to argue about it. Right or wrong, he had the courage of his convictions.

"And now I've wasted enough time on you," he continued. "Too much time, to tell you the truth. Let's get back to business. Who else has got a question for me?" Hands shot into the air. Truman pointed at a heavyset bald man. "Drew?"

"How long can we keep troops in Germany if the American people decide they don't want to any more?" Drew Pearson asked.

If the look the President sent him didn't scream *Et tu, Brute?*, Tom had never seen one that did. "Since I don't believe the American people are going to decide any such thing, that isn't worth answering," Truman said.

"Diana McGraw will tell you you're wrong, sir," Pearson responded.

"I respect Diana McGraw. I sympathize with her, too, and with all the good people who've lost loved ones because of Heydrich's fanatics. Hitler called Heydrich the man with the iron heart, and for once Adolf wasn't lying." Truman deigned to shoot Tom another glare. Then he went on, "I talked with her when she came to picket the White House last month. I'm convinced she's sincere. I'm also convinced she's wrong. If we run away from Germany without finishing the job we set out to do there, we'll be worse off in the long run than if we stay. And not in the very long run, either."

"More and more people seem to agree with what she's saying," Drew Pearson observed.

"Well, so what? That doesn't make them right." Yes, Truman could be as stubborn as a Missouri mule. "And just because there are more of them than there were, that doesn't mean there are very many of them. Most Americans can see farther than the end of their nose—and a good thing, too." He nodded to another correspondent. "What's on your mind, Walter?"

Walter Lippmann asked him a question about farm legislation. Truman answered it with every sign of relief. Most of the time, foreign-policy issues weren't what swayed elections. In the aftermath of the biggest war in the history of the world—no, not in the aftermath, dammit, because it wasn't over yet, no matter who'd signed which surrender documents—the usual rules might not apply. But they would if Truman had anything to do with it.

Tom Schmidt remembered the line from *The Wizard of Oz*. "Pay no attention to the man behind the curtain," the Wizard had said desperately. That was only a movie, but the President was trying to pull the same stunt for real. Could he make Germany disappear from voters' minds? To Tom, that would be a bigger trick than any the Wizard managed.

He wasn't the only one with such thoughts on his mind. When Truman pointed to another reporter, the man said, "Seems like the Republicans want to use Germany as a club to hit you over the head with in the upcoming elections. What will you do if you have to deal with a Republican Congress next year?"

"Ha! That'll be the day!" Truman was a dumpy little guy, but he had an actor's control of his expressions and attitudes. His whole body radiated contempt.

"Work with me, Mr. President," the newspaperman urged. "Suppose they do win the election. Then they'll be holding the purse strings. What can you do if they decide not to appropriate any money for the occupation?"

FDR would have set his granite chin and looked indomitable. Harry Truman didn't have that kind of chin. He didn't look indomitable, either—he looked pissed off. "They wouldn't dare," he snapped. Before the reporter could even try to follow up, Truman shook his head. "I know what you're gonna say, Bernard. Suppose they do, right? Okay, I'm supposing. And this is what I suppose. No matter what kind of stupid stunts the Republicans try and pull with the budget, this country still only has one commander-in-chief, and you're looking at him. The United States of American isn't a box turtle, no matter what some people think. It can't pull its head and its legs inside its shell and pretend the rest of the world isn't out there. That got us in trouble before the war. It'd be a lot worse now."

Yet another reporter said, "If you were to try to do something after Congress said you couldn't . . . That's how Andrew Johnson got impeached."

"Congress has no business telling me how to run the country's foreign policy," Truman retorted. "And this is all moonshine, anyhow. I'm just indulging Bernie there. Everything in Germany will be fine. The Republicans won't win in November. And even if they do, they aren't asinine enough to play games with the public purse."

"You hope," the reporter said.

"No, I hope they do try it. They'd give me all the platform I need to bang on 'em like a drum in 1948," Truman replied. "But they're just not that stupid. . . . Well, a few of them are, but not many."

"What if they run Eisenhower against you?" Walter Lippmann asked.

"Nobody knows whether Ike's a Republican or a Democrat. I'm not sure he knows himself," the President answered. He got a laugh; even Tom chuckled. Truman went on, "But I am sure of one thing:

Eisenhower likes the idea of pulling out of Germany even less than I do. And they said it couldn't be done! For the isolationists to line up behind him would be as foolish as for the antiwar Democrats to line up behind General McClellan against Lincoln in 1864."

"But the Democrats did do that," Lippmann pointed out. Tom thought he remembered the same thing, but hadn't taken American history in a hell of a long time.

"Damn straight they did—and they got their heads handed to them that November," Truman said. "If the Republicans want to try what didn't work for my party in 1948, good luck to 'em."

He didn't lack for confidence. Tom had known that before. Seeing it face to face was more than a little daunting, though. He had to remind himself that being confident and having good reasons for confidence were two different critters. Would Harry Truman remind himself of the same thing? Off this morning's performance, Tom didn't think so.

"GOD DAMN THE RUSSIANS TO HELL AND GONE!" REINHARD HEY-drich ground out.

Hans Klein made sympathetic noises. "No one ever hit them a lick like the one we gave them New Year's Eve," he said. "Not even Stalin purged their officers the way we did."

"*Wunderbar,*" Heydrich said sourly. "Just killing them didn't matter. Killing them and accomplishing something does."

"The new men in those slots won't be as sharp as the ones we got rid of," Klein said. "That's bound to help us later on."

"*Wunderbar.*" Heydrich sounded even more morose this time. He didn't know what the hell to do about the Russians. In the western occupation zones, the resistance was going as well as he'd hoped, maybe better. Lots of Americans and Englishmen and even some Frenchmen were yelling that holding Germany down was more expensive than it was worth.

They hadn't taken a blow even close to the one poisoned liquor gave the Red Army. But the Russians didn't miss a beat. They hanged Germans and shot them and deported them and hunted Heydrich's underground more ferociously than ever. Nothing seemed to faze them. The *Reichsprotektor* couldn't understand it.

Well, Hitler hadn't understood it, either. He'd said one good kick would bring the whole rotten structure of the Soviet Union crashing down. And he'd proceeded to deliver the good kick with 3,000,000 men, 3,000 panzers, and 2,000 planes. And the USSR staggered and lurched and reeled . . . and then, like one of those toys weighted at the bottom, bobbed upright again in spite of everything. And it started kicking back, and didn't stop kicking till the *Reich* lay prostrate under its boot.

The same thing was happening now. Knock out that many top French or British or American officers—hell, knock out that many top German officers—and the army you'd just sucker-punched would do its best imitation of a chicken right after it met the hatchet.

(Which reminded Heydrich: what would happen to the resistance if he went down? Jochen Peiper, his number two, was a pup—he'd just turned thirty. He was a damned capable pup, though. He ought to be able to carry on. Heydrich had to hope so.)

As for the Red Army, the Germans had seen too often, to their dismay and discomfiture, that it had an almost unlimited supply of human spare parts. Take out a bunch of people and Stalin would simply bolt on replacements and carry on as before. Maybe the military engine ran rough for a while. But it kept running. Since it hadn't had much luck rooting out Heydrich's fighters, it avenged itself on the German people as a whole.

When Heydrich growled about that, Johannes Klein said, "It's bad for even more reasons than you're talking about, sir."

"Oh? What am I missing?" Heydrich was always ready to acquire fresh fuel for his righteous indignation.

"They aren't just killing Germans for the fun of killing Germans. Maybe they're raping for the fun of it, but not killing," the veteran noncom answered. Heydrich snorted. *Oberscharführer* Klein went on, "They're being horrible to try and detach the *Volk* from us. If people start thinking helping us—or even keeping quiet about us—means they'll get strung up, they'll blab. You bet they will. They'll blab like you wouldn't believe."

Heydrich thought that over, but not for long. *"Scheisse,"* he said crisply. "Well, when you're right, you're right, dammit. Now what do we do about it?"

"Beats me, sir," Klein said, which made the *Reichsprotektor* want to clout him in the ear. Oblivious to that, or at least affecting to be, Klein continued, "As long as we look strong, we've still got a decent chance. The Russian partisans weren't that much trouble till they saw we wouldn't take Moscow, and our Frenchies stayed in bed with us till the Anglo-Americans landed. Hell, some of 'em stayed longer than that."

A mocking smile stretched Heydrich's thin lips. Some of the French collaborators had indeed clung to the *Reich* till the bitter end. What called itself Radio Paris went on broadcasting from Sigmaringen in southwestern Germany long after the real Paris fell. And some of Berlin's last defenders were troops from the SS *Charlemagne* division (so-called; it never really got above regimental strength): Frenchmen with a few German officers and noncoms.

But things were different here. Now Heydrich's followers needed the goodwill—or at least the silence—of the people among whom they moved. They tried not to compromise the wider populace . . . but how could you fight back at all without endangering them, especially when you faced a ruthless foe like the Russians?

You couldn't. And, as Hans Klein reminded him, that carried risks of its own. Thinking out loud, Heydrich said, "I don't want to have to pull out of cities in the Russian zone and in the parts of the *Reich* the Poles and Czechs are stealing from us. Harder to strike at the enemy if we stick to fields and forests."

"Yes, sir." Klein nodded. "Chances are it wouldn't do us any good anyway. Just 'cause we move out of Breslau, say, nothing to keep the Russians from reaching in and hanging a hundred people there, or a thousand, on account of we blew up a panzer somewhere else."

"*Himmeldonnerwetter*," Heydrich muttered. The *Oberscharführer* was right again, however much Heydrich wished he weren't. All the Germans in the land lost to the Soviet Union were hostages. The NKVD wouldn't need long to figure that out, if it hadn't already. And it would be as vicious as Stalin decided it needed to be . . . and if Stalin's viciousness had a limit, the world hadn't seen it yet.

Although Hitler was almost eight months dead, even thinking that someone else might be harder than he was made Heydrich want to look over his shoulder and make sure no *Gestapo* or *Sicherheitsdienst* man was standing there and writing him up for disloyalty.

Heydrich knew that was ridiculous. If anyone qualified as *Führer* these days, he did. But, like the men he led, old habits died hard. And knowing in your head was different from knowing in your belly. As far as Heydrich's belly was concerned, Hitler still ruled the *Reich* from Berlin.

I will rebuild it, mein Führer. *I promise I will,* the *Reichsprotektor* thought. *I'll make it as much the way you would have as I can.*

"*Herr Reichsprotektor,* I've got another question for you, if you don't mind too much," Klein said.

You would, flashed through Heydrich's mind. But he forced himself to patience; as he'd seen, the noncom sometimes thought of things he'd missed himself. And so his voice held no snap—or he hoped it didn't, anyhow—when he asked, "What is it?"

"Suppose the Amis do decide to pack up and go home. Then suppose they don't like what we're doing once we come out of the caves and mines and bunkers and start running things. Will they drop one of those goddamn atom bombs on us?"

"I don't know if they will, but they can. I'm sure of that—how could we stop them?" Heydrich said. "That's why we've got to get one for ourselves as soon as we can. Till we do, you're right—we live on their sufferance. So do the Russians, but Russia's a lot bigger than Germany."

"We found that out the hard way," Klein remarked.

"Didn't we just! I was thinking the same thing a little while ago. And that reminds me of something else. . . . Where the devil did I see it?" Heydrich pawed through papers. He didn't like being an administrator; he craved action. But unless he knew what was going on, he wouldn't know what to act on. His desk wasn't especially neat, but after a few seconds he found what he was looking for. "They grabbed as many of our nuclear physicists as they could catch and took them over to England right after the surrender."

"Did they? I hadn't heard that, but it doesn't surprise me." Klein nodded to himself. "Nope, doesn't surprise me one goddamn bit. The British'd want to grill 'em, and they wouldn't want the Russians to grab any of them."

"Right on both counts," Heydrich agreed. "Same kind of race with them as there was with the engineers who built our rockets. You can bet the Ivans got their hands on some of both groups, too, damn them. But that's not the point."

"Well, what *is* the point, then, sir?" Klein asked reasonably.

"The point is that ten of these fellows with the high foreheads came back to Germany on the . . ." Heydrich paused to check the sheet of paper he'd uncovered. "On the third of January, that's when it was. Just a couple of weeks ago. They landed at Lübeck, in the British zone. Now they're staying at a tricked-out clothing store in Alswede, not far away."

"Lübeck? Alswede?" Dismay filled Klein's voice. "That's up by the Baltic—and no more than a long spit from the edge of the Russian zone. The Tommies'd better hope the NKVD doesn't try a snatch-and-grab."

"They do have *some* security," Heydrich admitted reluctantly. "And they make sure the physicists can't just go wandering off on their own. They have an evening curfew. The brains can't leave the British zone, and their families are hostages to make sure they behave. The Tommies don't say that's how things are, but it's what they amount to."

"Better than nothing, I suppose. Still not good," Klein said.

Now Heydrich nodded; he felt the same way. But he turned the talk in a different direction: "I've made inquiries up there. The British are going to really start letting people go any day now. Harteck and Diebner plan to go the Hamburg. Heisenberg and Hahn aim to start up their old institute in Göttingen. Von Weizsäcker and Bagge and some of the others are thinking about joining up with them there. They all know more than they did during the war. If nothing else, they've learned a lot from the enemy. And that means . . ." He let his voice trail away and waited.

People talked about watching a light come on on somebody's face. Heydrich watched it happen with Johannes Klein. "Sweet suffering Jesus!" the *Oberscharführer* exclaimed. "We can grab 'em ourselves, put 'em to work making bombs for us!"

"We can sure grab them. I aim to try," Heydrich agreed. "That way, we deny them to the British—and to the Russians. I don't know how much they can actually do for us. We won't have a lot of the equipment they'd need, and we may not be able to take it—steal it— without giving away too much. Still, all we can do is try."

"Yes, sir!" Klein's eyes glowed. "When we've got a bomb like that for ourselves, nobody will be able to kick us around any more, not ever again."

"That's right, Hans. As a matter of fact, we'll be able to do some kicking ourselves." Reinhard Heydrich's predatory smile said he looked forward to it. But then the smile faded like an old photograph left too long in the sun. He started shuffling through the papers on his desk again.

"What's up, sir?" Klein inquired.

"Some other business that needs taking care of," Heydrich said: an answer that wasn't. "All this stuff happens at the same time, and you can't let any of it get away from you or you're screwed. It's a miracle the *Führer* handled so much so well for so long."

"And then after a while he didn't," Klein said. Heydrich gave him a look. The noncom stuck out his chin. "Oh, c'mon, sir. you know it's true. He screwed up the Russian war like nobody's business. And when we still weren't doing real bad, you know, nobody'd make terms with us, 'cause the Anglo-Americans and Stalin only figured the *Führer* would use the time to rebuild and then jump 'em again. And he would have, too. Tell me I'm wrong."

Heydrich couldn't. Every word was gospel. All the same . . . Klein must not have had that internalized *Führer* looking over his shoulder. "Will you say the same thing about me?" Heydrich asked dryly.

"Sure hope not, sir," the *Oberscharführer* answered. "But wouldn't you rather have somebody tell you to your face you're going wrong instead of being too scared to open his mouth till after everything's down the shitter?"

If you told Hitler he was wrong to his face, you'd pay for it. If you were lucky like some of his generals, you'd retire whether you wanted to or not. If you weren't . . . well, that was one of the things concentration camps were for.

"A point, Hans," Heydrich admitted. "Still, even if you do tell me I'm going wrong, I reserve the right to think you're full of crap."

"Oh, sure," Klein said. "Officers always do. Every once in a while, they're even right." He sketched a salute and ambled out into the rocky corridor. Heydrich stared after him. Noncoms who'd been around for a long time always thought they deserved the last word.

Every so often, you had to remind them why you were in command.
Every so often—but maybe not today.

LOU WEISSBERG HELD UP A COPY OF THE *INTERNATIONAL HERALD-
TRIBUNE*. It had a front-page story about a demonstration in California against the continued American occupation of Germany. The
story called the demonstration "the largest and loudest yet."

Captain Howard Frank grimaced when he saw the paper. "I already read it," he said. "Hot damn."

"Yup." Lou nodded. "Story didn't make the *Stars and Stripes*.
Funny how that works, huh?"

"Funny, yeah. Funny like a truss." Captain Frank made a small
production out of lighting a cigarette. He held out the pack to Lou.
"Want one?"

"Thanks." Lou flicked a Zippo to get his started. After a couple of
puffs, he said, "Y'know, we can lick our enemies. We knocked these
Nazi assholes flat. If Stalin fucks with us, we'll wallop him into the
middle of next week. He's gotta know it, too. But how the devil are
we supposed to beat the people who say they're on our side?"

"Good question. If you've got a good answer, go tell Eisenhower.
Hell, write it up and tell Truman," Frank said.

"Thanks a bunch—sir."

Howard Frank held up his hand. "Hey, I'm not kidding—not
even a little bit. We can't stay here if the folks back home decide we
ought to pack up and leave. If your Congressman tries to buck 'em,
they'll throw him out on his ass this November. If Truman tries, they'll
throw him out in '48. And where will we be then?"

"Up shit creek, that's where. And they'll be '*Sieg heil!*'ing from
what used to be the American zone twenty minutes after the last C-47
takes off," Lou said.

Frank stubbed out the cigarette and lit another one. "Maybe not,"
he said. "Maybe we can hang around long enough to teach the Germans how to stand on their own two feet. You said that Adenauer guy
over in Cologne impressed you. Gotta be more where he came from."

"I'm sure there are." But that wasn't agreement, because Lou went
on, "But if we leave the way that McGraw broad and her pals want
us to, those guys won't have the chance to stand up for themselves.

The Nazis'll bump 'em off, first chance they get. And then we start worrying about World War III, all in one lifetime."

"Maybe not," Frank said. Lou made a rude noise. In a more rules-conscious army, it might have landed him in the stockade. Captain Frank just laughed. "You said Stalin's scared of us. Well, yeah, but he's fucking terrified of the Germans. If we do pull out, he's liable to head for the Rhine to make sure we don't get round two of the Third *Reich*."

"We can't let him do that. France shits its pants if he does—same with Italy," Lou said gloomily. "So we go to war against him on account of the fucking krauts? God, that'd be a kick in the nuts, wouldn't it? And it sounds a hell of a lot like World War III, too."

"It does, doesn't it?" Captain Frank eyed the glowing coal of his cigarette. "You'd think that when everybody says a war is over, it'd really be over."

"Yeah. You would." Lou put out his cigarette, too. The ashtray was soldier-made from the base of a 105mm shell. "I figured I'd be home by now. I figured my wife'd be expecting another baby by now."

"Okay. I understand what you mean. Morrie'd probably be getting a little brother or sister if they'd given me a Ruptured Duck when I thought they would," Frank said. "But things after the surrender didn't work out the way anybody hoped. You know that. And what we're doing here is worth doing. You know that, too. Hell, everybody knows that."

"Not Diana McGraw and her crowd. And it seems like her crowd gets bigger every day." Lou tapped the *Herald-Trib* with his index finger. "That guy who smuggled out the Cunningham film is with these people, too. Tom Shit, whatever the hell his name was."

"Schmidt," Captain Frank corrected primly. Then he shot Lou a dirty look. "Funny guy. You and Danny Kaye and Groucho Marx. You ought to have your own radio show. You'd sell tons of toothpaste and shaving soap."

"All *Yehudim*. If Hitler had his way, he would've *made* us into shaving soap." Lou hesitated, then went on, "Some of the Jewish guys over here, they don't hardly seem to give a damn. Sure doesn't stop 'em from laying German broads."

"Nope. Me, I'd sooner jack off. If I fucked one of those bitches, I'd break every mirror I own," Frank said. Lou nodded; he felt the same way. But, a moment later, his superior went on, "Other people see it different, that's all. I heard one guy say he was getting his revenge nine inches at a time."

Lou snorted. "A fucking braggart. Or maybe a braggart fucking— who knows?" Captain Frank sent him another severe look. He ignored it; he was used to them. "More fun than going up against the *Wehrmacht* or the *Waffen*-SS, I will say that."

"Or than going up against the fanatics," Frank said. "Know what I heard?"

" 'Fraid I don't. But you're gonna tell me, aren't you?" Lou said.

"Sure am. The MPs here grabbed a couple of German broads with VD who say people told 'em not to get cured. They wanted these gals to make as many of our guys come down venereal as they could."

"Makes a twisted kind of sense," Lou said. "Or it did, anyway, before sulfa and penicillin. A guy with a drippy faucet's just as much a casualty as a guy who got shot in the leg. He was, anyway, till you could cure him with a needle in the ass or a handful of pills."

Captain Frank suddenly looked alert. He pulled a fountain pen from his left breast pocket and scribbled a note. "Something to remember: Heydrich and the other bastards down in the salt mines or wherever the hell they are don't know everything we can do. They've got old German intelligence reports—"

"And new newspapers," Lou broke in.

"Mm-hmm. And those." Howard Frank nodded. "And which bunch has more crap mixed in with the good stuff is anybody's guess."

"Well, you've got that right, sir. If Hitler's intelligence on us were any good, he never would've taken us on. Christ, if his intelligence on Russia were any good, he would've let Stalin alone, too," Lou said.

"Back toward the end of '41, the Germans had already wiped out as many divisions as they thought the Red Army had," Frank said. "At the start, they didn't know the Russians had the T-34, either. You kinda lose points with your bosses when you miss stuff like the best tank in the war, y'know?"

"Oh, maybe a few," Lou said, which wrung a dry chuckle out of the captain. Then Lou asked, "What are we missing that we ought to see?"

For a moment, Captain Frank looked almost comically astonished. He was in the intelligence racket, too. Did he really imagine he saw everything there was to see? Didn't imagining something like that take colossal—almost Germanic—arrogance? Captain Frank started to say something, then closed his mouth. What he did say was probably quite different from what had almost come out: "You're a disruptive son of a bitch, you know that?"

"Thank you, sir," Lou said, which earned him another pointed glance. "But I'm serious. God knows the Nazis have their blind spots, but so do we. If we try to shrink 'em, maybe we can."

"Japs sure blindsided us when they hit Pearl Harbor. We never dreamt they'd be dumb enough to jump on us like that, so they caught us flat-footed," Frank said. "They were tougher all kinds of ways than we expected. We didn't know any more about the Zero than the Germans knew about the T-34. And kamikazes . . ." His voice faded.

"Before the Japs finally quit, we played down how much trouble an enemy who didn't care if he lived could be," Lou said. "I guess we were smart—the Japs would've done more of that shit if they knew how bad it hurt us. But it seems to me we believed our own propaganda. We didn't think the krauts could give us much trouble if they pulled stunts like that. Shows what we knew, huh?"

"Other thing we didn't think was that they would pull shit like that," Lou said. "Before the surrender, they didn't hardly. The Master Race must've learned something from the Japs. Who woulda believed it?"

"Not me." Captain Frank held up a sheet of paper. "Word is that that Adenauer guy you brought from Cologne is gonna speak at Erlangen. You really think he's the straight goods?"

"He's no Nazi, if that's what you mean," Lou replied. "If you mean, is he the Answer with a capital A, hell, I don't know. But I sure hope like hell somebody can make the Germans run their own government and not automatically go after all their neighbors. If nobody can—"

"Then we've got to do it ourselves," Frank finished for him. Unhappily, Lou nodded. That was what he'd been thinking, all right. His superior went on, "And God only knows how long we'll stay here."

"We need to," Lou said.

"No shit. But what we need to do and what we're gonna do,

they're two different beasts, and the jerks back home sure aren't helping. Time may come when we have to go home, prop up whatever
half-assed German government we've patched together in the meanwhile, and hope like hell Heydrich and the Nazis don't knock it over
as soon as we're gone."

"It won't happen right away." Lou took what comfort he could
from that. "Not till after the fall elections, anyhow."

Captain Frank lit another cigarette. He blew out smoke and shook
his head. "You're such a goddamn *American,* Lou."

Whatever Lou had expected from the other CIC man, that wasn't
it. "I sure hope so, sir." He hesitated, then asked, "What exactly
d'you mean? I'm damn glad I'm an American, but you don't make it
sound like a compliment."

Frank sighed. "I don't mean it for an insult, either. But the Europeans play a deeper game than we do, 'cause they know how to wait
and we don't. Heydrich figures if he can put the Nazis back on top ten
years from now, or maybe twenty, he's won. And he's right, too, God
damn him to hell. But us? We get bored, or we find something new to
worry about, or we get sick of spending lives a few here, a few there,
when it's got no obvious point. And so you're right—we won't do
anything much till after the elections. But that's only this fall, remember. If the Republicans take Congress—and if they take Congress because they're yelling, 'What are we doing in Germany now that the
war's over?'—what can Truman do about it? Not much, not if he
wants to get elected in '48."

Lou thought about that. He shivered, though a coal stove kept
Captain Frank's office toasty. Then he covered his face. "We're
screwed. We are so screwed."

"That's how it looks to me, too," Captain Frank said. "I hoped
like anything you'd tell me I was wrong."

XII

Diana McGraw paid attention to the newspapers in ways she never had before Pat got killed. Back in those prehistoric days, she'd looked at the funnies and the recipes and the advice and gossip columns. Foreign news? As long as the Americans and their allies kept moving forward—and, from 1942 on, they pretty steadily did—who worried about foreign news?

She did, now. The Indianapolis papers didn't carry as much as she wanted, as much as she needed. And so the postman brought her the *New York Times*. She got it a few days late, but that was better than not getting it at all. The same went for the *Washington Post*. If you wanted to find out what was going on in Congress, you had to read a paper that covered it seriously.

She was reading the *Times* when she looked up and said, "Ha!"

Ed was rereading *The Egg and I*. He'd stop and chuckle every so often. Diana had read it, too. The only way you wouldn't stop and chuckle was if you'd had your sense of humor taken out with your tonsils when you were a kid. But that *Ha!* was on an entirely different note. "What's up, sweetie?" Ed asked.

She pointed to the story that had drawn her notice. "This German politician named Adenauer"—she figured she was messing up the pronunciation, but she hadn't taken any German in high school—"is coming into the American zone to talk to the Germans there."

"He's not a Nazi, is he?" Ed answered his own question before Diana could: "Nah, he wouldn't be. They wouldn't let him get away with it if he was. So how come you think he's a big deal?"

"I think we're pushing Truman and Eisenhower and all the other blockheads running things over there—pushing 'em our way, I mean," Diana said. "If they set up some kind of German government, that gives 'em an excuse to say, 'Well, we've done what we need to do, so we can bring our boys home now.' "

"Sounds good to me," Ed said.

She nodded. "To me, too. So let's hear it for Mr. Konrad Adenauer." She tried the name a different way this time. Ed only shrugged. He'd come back from Over There with a few scraps of German, but he'd forgotten it in the generation since.

The phone rang. She picked it up. "Diana McGraw," she said crisply. The phone rang all the time these days. She had to answer it as if she were running a business. What else was she doing, when you got right down to it? She was just glad she wasn't on a party line; the ringing that wasn't for them would have driven all the other people crazy.

"Hello, Mrs. McGraw. This is E. A. Stuart," the reporter said.

She'd already recognized his voice. She'd never imagined she would get to know reporters so well, but it didn't impress her. She would gladly have traded everything—travel, getting acquainted with prominent people, even meeting the President—to have her only son back again. But God didn't make deals like that. Too bad. It was almost enough to tempt you into atheism.

Since she couldn't have what she wanted, she did what she could with what she had. "What can I do for you, Mr. Stuart?" She used other reporters' first names. With Ebenezer Amminadab Stuart, formality seemed a better choice.

"I was wondering if you had any comment on the speech Senator Taft made this afternoon," Stuart said.

She would see that speech when today's *Post* or *New York Times* got to Anderson . . . three or four days from now. "Can you tell me

what he said?" she asked. "If it got reported on the radio, I missed it."
Radio news made even the local papers look thorough. When you
had to shoehorn everything into five minutes' worth of air time . . .
Well, you couldn't. That was about the size of it.

"Basically, he said Truman doesn't know what he's doing in Germany. He said Truman had won the war, but he was losing the peace.
He said we heard all through the war how wicked the German people
were. If that's true, he said, they aren't worth any more American
lives. And if it's not true, why were the President and the whole government lying to the American people from Pearl Harbor to V-E
Day?"

"Wow!" Diana said.

"That's not a, mm, useful remark," E. A. Stuart reminded her.

"Sorry. You're right, of course," Diana said. "Let me see. . . . You
can say I agree with everything the Senator said, and he put it better
than I could have."

"Okey doke." She could hear Stuart's pencil skritching across
paper. "Yeah, you may not like Taft—an awful lot of people don't—
but you have a devil of a time ignoring him."

"No kidding," Diana said. "Has Truman answered him yet?"

"Yup. He doesn't waste any time—when somebody pokes him
with a stick, he pokes right back." E. A. Stuart sounded admiring and
approving. Diana understood why: Truman made good copy. To a lot
of reporters, nothing mattered more. They didn't much care what
public figures said or did, as long as it sold newspapers. *Mercenaries,*
Diana thought scornfully. She had to deal with people like that, and
to be interesting in her own right for them. She didn't have to like
them.

When Stuart showed no inclination to go on, Diana prodded him:
"Well? What did Truman say?"

"He said Taft is like a guy yelling from the bleachers. He's never
been a manager in the dugout, let alone a player on the field. He said
Taft doesn't know what he's talking about, but what can you expect
from a guy up in the cheap seats?"

"The only reason he's not in the bleachers himself is that FDR
died," Diana snapped. She had the uneasy feeling that Roosevelt
wouldn't have wanted to pull troops out of Germany, but she didn't
mention it to E. A. Stuart. The less you said that could make the peo-

ple on your side unhappy with you, the better off you were. She'd learned all kinds of unsavory but needful lessons about how to run a political campaign.

Stuart chuckled. "He'd probably call that baptism by total immersion. He'd have a point, too."

"Phooey," Diana said. "And you can quote me."

"Well, maybe I will," the reporter answered. "Won't take up any more of your time now. 'Bye." The line went dead. *I've got other things to do,* he meant: one more polite lie. Diana had learned a raft of them the past few months.

"What did Stuart want?" Ed asked.

"My comments on something Senator Taft said, and on the President's answer to it." Diana had said things like that often enough by now that she almost took them for granted—almost, but not quite. "Taft makes good sense. Truman's full of malarkey."

"Well, what else is new?" her husband said.

GERMANS AMBLED INTO THE MARKET SQUARE IN ERLANGEN TO HEAR what Konrad Adenauer had to say. Bernie Cobb didn't give a damn about the politician from the British zone. He wouldn't be able to follow the speech anyhow. He'd picked up a little more German since the so-called surrender: enough to order drinks and food, and enough to get his face slapped if he tried to pick up the waitress afterwards. Politics? Who cared about politics?

He and the other GIs at the edge of the square weren't there to listen to the speech. They were there to frisk the krauts mooching in, to make sure nobody was carrying a Luger or wearing an explosive vest. All Bernie knew about the Adenauer guy was that he was anti-Nazi. Well, no kidding! Otherwise, the occupying authorities never would've let him open his yap.

But if the American authorities liked him, you could bet your last pfennig that Heydrich and the fanatics wouldn't. Which was why U.S. soldiers were searching the German men who came to listen to Adenauer.

"What I want to do is pat down the broads," Bernie said. "Not all of 'em—you can keep the grannies and stuff. The cute ones. Hey, it'd be strictly line of duty, right?"

"Line of bullshit is what it'd be, Cobb," said Carlo Corvo. The sergeant pointed toward the WACs and nurses who were searching German women. "See? It's taken care of."

One of the gals they were checking was a tall, auburn-haired beauty—just the kind Bernie'd had in mind. "Yeah, but they don't put their hearts into their work the way I would."

"Your heart? Is that what you call it these days?" Sergeant Corvo asked. But he was leering at the good-looking German gal, too.

None of the Jerries they frisked had anything lethal on him. Nobody else yelled out an alarm, either. And none of Heydrich's goons blew himself up, and a few dogfaces with him, in frustration because he couldn't get close enough to Konrad Adenauer.

The German politico came out to what Bernie thought of as extremely tepid applause. Hitler would have had the Germans screaming themselves sick. Maybe they'd learned better than to get too excited about politicians. More likely, Adenauer was about as exciting as soggy corn flakes without sugar. He was an old fart with a sly face that would have served him well in a poker game.

An American officer introduced Adenauer to the crowd in what sure sounded like fluent German to Bernie. Quite a few officers and some enlisted men could go pretty well *auf Deutsch*. Some had studied in school. Others, like this Lieutenant Colonel Rosenthal, came by it in different ways.

Bernie wondered what Adenauer thought of having a Jew present him to his own countrymen. Or did Keith Rosenthal's being an American count for more? Wasn't Adenauer trying to show that Germans could handle their own affairs? Well, sure they could—as long as the occupying authorities said it was okay.

Despite the lukewarm hand Adenauer got, he waved as he stepped up to the microphone. Maybe the krauts had had all their political enthusiasm knocked out of them by now. If they had, that probably wouldn't be such a bad thing. When Bernie said so, Sergeant Corvo nodded. "You better believe it wouldn't," he opined. "Or maybe this Adenauer guy is as much of a boring old shithead as he looks like."

Corvo always said exactly what he meant. Whether Adenauer was getting his message across was liable to be another story. If he fired up the krauts in the crowd, they hid it well. Again, chances were that was good news.

"You know a little of the lingo, right, Sarge?" Bernie said. "What's he going on about?"

"He says Germany has to . . . do something with England and France."

"Germany sure did something to 'em," Bernie said.

"Shut up," Corvo snapped. "When you talk, I can't make out what he's going on about. . . . He says Germany needs to reconcile, that's what it is. He says Germany has a lot to atone for. . . . Yeah, he's a Catholic, all right. Catholics like to talk about atoning for shit."

"If you say so," answered Bernie, a Methodist who hadn't seen the inside of a church any time lately. New Mexico was full of Catholics, of course: well, as full of them as a mostly empty state could be. But he paid even less attention to their religion than to his own.

How long would Adenauer go on? Some of Hitler's rants had lasted for hours, hadn't they? Did the Jerries expect all their politicians to match that? If they did . . . If they did, they were even screwier than Bernie Cobb gave them credit for, which was saying a mouthful.

Fighting through France and Germany, Bernie'd hated land mines worse than anything else. They lay in wait for you, and if you stepped on one or tripped over a wire, that was all she wrote. Right behind them—*right* behind them—came mortar rounds. Ordinary artillery announced itself. Somebody yelled, "Incoming!" and a bunch of dogfaces hit the dirt or dove for holes. But half the time you didn't know the bad guys had opened up with a mortar till the first bomb tore your buddy's leg off . . . or maybe yours.

Bernie heard a faint hiss, a faint whistle, in the air. He had a second or two to pretend he didn't. It could have been a flaw in the microphone and speakers. It could have been the wind, which was nasty and cold. It could have been . . .

Bam! An 81mm round burst right in the middle of the crowd of krauts listening to Konrad Adenauer. Next thing Bernie knew, he was as flat on the cobblestones as if a deuce-and-a-half had run over him. He wasn't hurt. In a way, discovering his combat reflexes still worked was gratifying.

Carlo Corvo had flattened out beside him. Quite a few of the German men were also down on their bellies. Yeah, they'd been through the mill, too. Shrieks said some people were down because the mortar bomb had knocked them down.

And then another round came in, and another, and another. A trained two-man crew could fire ten or twelve a minute. Morons could use an 81mm once it was aimed. You dropped a bomb down the tube and you made sure it didn't blow your head off when it came out again. It wasn't near as tough as designing an atomic bomb.

"Where the fuck you think they are?" Corvo yelled as fragments whined not nearly far enough overhead.

"The mortar guys, you mean?" Bernie said. Corvo nodded without raising his head. Bernie's shrug actually hunched him down lower. "Could be anywhere. With a full charge, one of those cocksuckers'll shoot a mile and a half."

He tried to imagine securing everything within a circle three miles across centered on the market square. His imagination promptly rebelled. Somewhere—in a fenced-in yard or a back alley or up on a roof—a couple of mortarmen were having a high old time. And they could just leave the tube and bipod behind when they finished. How many mortars—German and American and British and Russian—littered the local landscape? Thousands, maybe even millions.

"C'mon, get up! Get moving!" Corvo shouted. "We gotta make sure Adenauer's okay. Fanatics are bound to be after him."

Bernie hadn't even thought about that. He hadn't thought about getting up under fire, either. He'd done it more often than he cared to remember during the war, but the war was over . . . wasn't it? But seeing the sergeant stand up brought Bernie to his feet, too.

Several other U.S. soldiers were also up. Most of them headed for the platform from which Adenauer spoke. Another mortar bomb scythed one of them down. Bernie looked away. You didn't want to remember what explosives and jagged metal fragments could do to flesh.

The mortar rounds stopped falling then. Either somebody'd caught the guys serving the nasty little piece or they'd figured they'd done their duty and bugged out. Bernie knew what he hoped. He also knew what he thought. They weren't the same.

There lay the auburn-haired gal he'd wished he were searching. Nobody'd want to feel her up now. A bad chest wound, a worse head wound. . . She was still moving and moaning, but Bernie didn't think she'd last long. Too bad, too bad.

He jumped up onto the platform, pointing his M-1 this way and that. It was dumb—he knew as much even while he did it. The bastards who'd done this weren't close enough for the rifle to do him a nickel's worth of good. Everybody here in the square with him probably hated the mortarmen as much as he did. But you wanted to hit back somehow, even when you couldn't.

"Oh . . . motherfuck." Sergeant Corvo used his rifle, too, pointing with the muzzle.

One of the mortar bombs had blasted Konrad Adenauer off the platform. He lay on his back, staring up at the sky. His thinning gray hair was mussed. A single drop of blood splashed the end of his long, pointed nose. Other than that, his face was untouched. He looked mildly surprised.

Below his face . . . Bernie looked away. The mortar rounds had done worse to Adenauer than they had to the pretty woman with the dark red hair. "Motherfuck," Carlo Corvo said again.

"You got that right," Bernie agreed. "He ain't gonna be making more speeches any time soon. I mean, not unless it's to St. Peter or the Devil, one."

A groan from a little farther away drew their attention to Lieutenant Colonel Rosenthal. He leaned against a wall, clutching one arm with his other hand. Blood leaked out between his fingers.

"Can I bandage that for you, sir?" Bernie called.

"I don't think you'd better." Rosenthal sounded eerily calm, as wounded men often did. "I'm holding it closed better than a bandage could. If you want to yell for a medic, that'd be good." He paused as if remembering something. And he was, for he asked, "How's Adenauer?"

Bernie wished he could lie, but didn't see how it would help. "Sir, he bought a plot." He raised his voice: "Corpsman! We need a corpsman over here!"

"Shit!" Rosenthal sounded furious. Then he said "Shit" again, this time in the way Bernie'd heard much too often before: the wound was starting to get its claws into him. Baring his teeth, the American officer went on, "Adenauer was the best hope we had for a Germany that isn't either Nazi or Red."

" 'Was' is right, sir. He's a gone goose." Bernie pointed toward the politician's crumpled body. People always looked smaller when they were dead. He didn't know why that was true, but it was.

"Shit," Keith Rosenthal said yet again. "Score a big one for Heydrich and his assholes, then. Who's gonna have the nerve to try and stand up to 'em after this?"

From in back of Bernie, Carlo Corvo said, "Here comes a medic."

"That was quick." For a moment, Bernie was admiring. Then he wondered how come the aid man had got here so fast. Had the American authorities feared trouble and put the medics on alert, maybe even posted them close by? What did that say about Konrad Adenauer, who'd trusted U.S. security arrangements? It said he'd been a jerk—that was what.

And what did it say about how things were going in Germany generally? Nothing good. Bernie Cobb was goddamn sure of that.

VLADIMIR BOKOV HAD BEEN THROUGH THE INFLUENZA BEFORE. YOU spent a week flat on your back. Then you spent another week feeling as if you'd been beaten with knouts. After that, you were pretty much all right.

Running on benzedrine while you were at your sickest meant that afterwards you felt as if you'd been beaten with knouts and chains. And you felt that way for three weeks, not one.

All of which got him scant sympathy from his superiors—not even from Moisei Shteinberg, who was as miserable as he was. "Did influenza keep anyone from holding the Nazis out of Moscow and Leningrad?" Shteinberg demanded. "Did it keep anyone from throwing them out of Stalingrad?" He paused for a coughing fit.

Influenza probably kept some Red Army men flat on their backs during those fights. Bokov knew better than to say so. Instead, he said, "The Western imperialists have lost one of their reactionary politicians. I suppose we need to protect the leaders of the Social Unity Party of Germany."

"I suppose so. Ulbricht is . . . useful, no doubt about it." Shteinberg spoke with the same not so faint distaste Bokov had used.

They had their reasons. Walter Ulbricht *was* useful. He headed the Social Unity Party of Germany, the front through which the USSR intended to rule its chunk of the dead *Reich*. Like Lenin, he was bald and wore a chin beard. There the resemblance ended. Lenin, by all accounts, had been loyal to no one and nothing but himself—and the revolution.

Ulbricht, by contrast, was Stalin's lap dog. He'd spent the war in exile in the USSR, returning to Germany in the Red Army's wake. He would do exactly what the Soviet Union told him to do, no more and no less. If Heydrich's hooligans blew him off the face of the earth, Moscow might have to turn to someone less reliable—to say nothing of the propaganda victory his death would hand the bandits.

With a sigh, Shteinberg went on, "I'm not really enthusiastic about keeping *any* Germans alive these days, if you want to know the truth."

"Well, Comrade Colonel, plenty who were alive on New Year's Eve are dead now, and plenty more will be," Bokov said.

"They had it coming," Shteinberg said coldly. Mass executions in Berlin and all through the rest of the Soviet zone warned the Germans that having anything to do with the Fascist bandits was a bad idea. Far bigger mass deportations drove home the same lesson. How the camps in the Arctic and Siberia would absorb so many . . . wasn't Bokov's worry. You could always plop prisoners down in the middle of nowhere and have them build their own new camp. If some of them froze before the barracks went up, if others starved—it was just one of those things.

Bokov had been through the Germans' murder camps. They sickened him—the Soviet Union had nothing like them. They also struck him as wasteful. They didn't squeeze enough labor out of condemned people before letting them give up the ghost. *Zeks* were to use, not just to kill. So it seemed to him, anyhow.

Shteinberg lit a cigarette. That made him cough, too, which didn't keep him from smoking. "We never did catch the swine who poisoned the booze," he wheezed, sucking in more smoke.

"Has to be the Germans who laid in the supply," Bokov said. "If the barmen and serving girls knew anything, we would've pulled it out of them." He and Shteinberg and their comrades had pulled all kinds of things from the people who'd been at the Schloss Cecilienhof that night. All kinds of things, but not what they wanted—what they needed.

"There should be a list of those people," Shteinberg said. "There should be—but there isn't."

"Maybe nobody bothered to keep one," Bokov said. Had Germans given the orders—"Round up that liquor!"—they would have kept a list. Since the command probably came from a Soviet quartermaster, who could say? Russian efficiency was no byword. Bokov added, "If someone did keep one, somebody else made it disappear."

"If we can find out who did that—" Shteinberg broke off, shaking his head. "Anybody who's smart enough to make a list disappear is smart enough to make himself disappear, too."

"*Da,*" Bokov agreed glumly. "I used to wonder how the Red revolutionaries could operate right under the noses of the Tsar's secret police. Why didn't they all get arrested and shipped to Siberia? *Bozhe-moi!* Why didn't they all get arrested and killed?"

"Some of the Tsar's men were secretly on our side. Some were soft. Some were stupid." Shteinberg stopped again. "And some were very good at what they did. We had to kill a good many of them. But others . . . others we reeducated. Some of them still serve the Soviet Union better than they ever served the Tsars."

A young, able lieutenant or captain from 1917 would be a colonel or a general or even a marshal now . . . if he'd lived through all the purges in the generation between. Some would have made it. Some could—what did people say about Anastas Mikoyan?—some could dance between the raindrops and come home dry, that was it.

Something else Shteinberg had said made Bokov mutter to himself. "How many of our people are secretly on Heydrich's side?"

"Not many Russians. You'd have to be a Vlasovite—worse than a Vlasovite—to side with the Nazis now," Shteinberg said. Bokov nodded. The Germans had captured General Andrei Vlasov in 1942, and he'd gone over to them, even if they never quite trusted him. Anyone who'd served in his Russian Liberation Army was either dead or in a camp wishing he were dead.

"But the Germans who say they're on our side . . ." Bokov said. He felt the same way about those Germans as the Hitlerites had felt about Vlasov and his fellow Russians: they might be useful, but would you really want to have to rely on one of them at your back?

"Yes. We shall have to go through them. That seems all too clear. Heydrich's men want us to think they're ordinary mushrooms when they're really amanitas." Shteinberg would have gone on, but he had another coughing spasm. "This damned grippe. I don't think it'll ever let go."

Bokov displayed a vial of benzedrine tablets. "They still help—but I have to take more to get the same buzz."

"I have some, too," Shteinberg said. "I try not to take them unless I have to. Sometimes, though, there's no help for it. So, Volodya—how do we get the amanitas out of our mushroom stew?"

REINHARD HEYDRICH'S CHIN AND CHEEKS ITCHED. HE'D LET HIS beard grow for a couple of weeks before emerging from the mine where he'd sheltered for so long. He wore beat-up civilian clothes, with an equally ragged *Wehrmacht* greatcoat over them: the kind of outfit any German male of military age might have.

Hans Klein sat behind the dented, rusty *Kubelwagen*'s wheel. Heydrich hadn't wanted to risk using an American jeep—it might have roused suspicion. "Are you sure you should be doing this at all, sir?" Klein asked.

Since Heydrich wasn't, he scowled. But he answered, "The operation is too important to leave to anyone else."

"If you say so." Klein didn't believe him. Klein thought he was using that as an excuse to come out and do his own fighting. Klein was much too likely to be right, too. But Klein was only an *Ober-scharführer*. Heydrich was the *Reichsprotektor*. If he decided he had to come out, none of the other freedom fighters had the rank to tell him he couldn't. And if anything went wrong, Jochen Peiper, fidgeting inside another buried command post, would take over and do . . . as well as he could, that was all.

So far, everything was fine. They'd already made it from the American zone up into the one the British held. Their papers had held up at every inspection. Things would have been harder where the Russians ruled. The Russians did Heydrich's men the dubious courtesy of taking them and their uprising seriously. Neither Amis nor Tommies seemed eager to do that. They *wanted* the fighting to be over, and so they did their best to pretend it was.

A jeep with four British soldiers in it came down the road toward Heydrich and Klein. The jeep carried a machine gun. The Tommy behind it aimed it at the battered *Kubelwagen*. Heydrich had seen that was only an ordinary precaution. The fellow wouldn't open up for the fun of it. He just feared that the *Kubelwagen* might be full of explosives, and the men inside willing to blow themselves up to kill him and his mates, too.

Not today, friend Tommy, Heydrich thought as the vehicles passed each other. *We've got something bigger cooking.*

After a while, Klein pulled off onto the shoulder. He started messing around in the *Kubelwagen*'s engine compartment, as if he'd had a breakdown. Heydrich watched the road. When it was clear in both directions, he said, "Now."

They jumped back in. Klein drove into the woods till trees screened the *Kubelwagen* from the road. "You'll know where the bunker is?" he asked.

"I'd better," Heydrich answered confidently. Inside, though, he wondered. How far out of practice was he, and how much would finding out cost?

To his relief, a scrap of hand-drawn map in his greatcoat pocket (written with Russian names, to make it look like a relic from fighting much farther east if he were searched) and a compass brought him to a hole under a fallen tree. The hole led to a tunnel. The tunnel took him to the bunker.

Three men waited there. Despite exchanged passwords, they all pointed Schmeissers or assault rifles at the entrance till Heydrich and Klein showed themselves. "All right—it *is* you," one of them said, lowering his weapon.

"*Ja,*" Heydrich said. "Let's get what rest we can. We move at 0200."

The underground hideout had bunks enough for all of them. Alarm clocks clattered to wake them at the appointed hour. They armed themselves and went up and out into the quiet German night. No blackouts any more, which seemed unnatural to Heydrich. He could see the little town ahead, even though it was mostly dark in the middle of the night.

Soft-voiced challenges and countersigns showed more Germans gathering around Alswede. This assault would be in better than platoon strength. The fighting wolves hadn't shown their strength like this before.

Into the town they strode. Some wore the *Stahlhelm*. Others used American or Russian helmets instead. Their weapons were a similar blend. And the Tommies didn't even seem to realize they were there.

The British had converted the fancy clothier's emporium where they housed the German physicists into a residence hall. It stood near the center of Alswede. Heydrich hoped to bag all the brains, because they had to be back at their new residence by sundown every day.

As his ragged little force converged on the emporium, he imagined himself a field marshal on the Eastern Front, moving armies and corps like chessmen on the board. But those methods had failed the *Reich.* Maybe this platoon's worth of men would do more for Germany than an army group had in the Ukraine. *It had better,* Heydrich thought.

Yawning Tommies stood sentry outside the physicists' quarters. The British weren't altogether idiots. But the sentries didn't expect trouble.

"Hands up!" an English-speaking German called to them. "If you surrender, you will not be harmed."

A burst from a Sten gun answered him. Unlike the tin Tommy gun that had almost murdered Heydrich in Prague, this one worked fine. But so did the Germans' assault rifles and Schmeissers and grenades. The sentries went down one after another. Lights came on all over Alswede as people woke to the firefight and tried to figure out what the hell was going on.

Heydrich's raiders charged into the haberdashery. *"Schnell!"* he called to them. "We have to be gone before the Tommies come in force." He didn't know how long they had. Fifteen minutes, he judged, would be uncommon luck.

Long before fifteen minutes were up, the raiders came out again, herding along men middle-aged and elderly in their nightclothes. "We've grabbed nine of them!" a captain yelled to Heydrich. "Let's get out of here."

"Where's the last one?" As long as they were in Alswede, Heydrich wanted to make a clean sweep.

But the captain answered, "He's *kaput*—caught a bullet in the head, poor bastard." He jabbed a thumb toward the ground.

"All right." As long as the loose end was cleared up, Heydrich wouldn't fuss. He'd known going in that they took that chance if the British resisted. They were lucky—more than one of the slide-rule boys might have stopped something. Heydrich raised his voice: "Withdraw! Plan One!"

Some of the raiders left Alswede heading north. They made a hellacious racket, whooping and shouting and firing their weapons into lighted windows. Everyone in town could tell exactly where they were—and could tell the British exactly where they'd gone.

Along with the captured physicists—who were now starting to shiver in the late-night chill—Heydrich and the rest of his men quietly retreated to the south. Far fewer locals would pay them any attention. Far fewer would be able to tell the Tommies where they'd headed. And, with luck, the British would be slow to figure out they were the important group. How important could they be if they didn't fire off everything they were carrying?

One of the scientists—a middle-aged fellow with rumpled, greasy hair and thick glasses—asked, "Why did you shoot poor Heisenberg?"

"Shut up, Professor Diebner, or we'll shoot you, too." Heydrich was pleased with himself for recognizing who'd spoken. "Heisenberg was an accident." *An unfortunate accident, too,* he thought. Heisenberg was—had been—a high-horsepower physicist. Coldly, Heydrich went on, "We will shoot you on purpose, though, if you slow us down or give us away."

"Give you away? I don't even know who you are," Diebner said.

"A man who believes in a free, strong Germany," Heydrich answered. "A man who doesn't believe the war is over yet, or lost."

Behind the spectacle lenses, Diebner's eyes were enormous. Maybe the lenses magnified them; Heydrich wasn't sure. He didn't care much one way or the other. "But—" Diebner began, and then clamped his mouth shut. That made sense; he was in no position to argue.

He and the others had probably spilled their guts while the enemy held them in England. Heydrich didn't even reckon it treason. Obviously, the Anglo-Americans were ahead of Germany in nuclear physics. He would have grabbed American scientists if he could. But his countrymen were the best he could get his hands on. Maybe they'd be able to come up with . . . something, anyhow.

Out of Alswede. Into the woods. The raiders divided into smaller groups, splitting the physicists among them. Gunfire broke off to the north. Heydrich smiled wolfishly. His distraction was working just the way he'd hoped it would.

"Be damned, sir," Hans Klein said. "I think we pulled it off."

"I said we would," Heydrich answered. Klein kept his mouth shut. Officers and leaders said all kinds of things. Sometimes they delivered. Sometimes . . . Sometimes your *Vaterland* ended up occupied by unfriendly foreigners. But Heydrich had delivered. And maybe Germany wouldn't stay occupied too much longer.

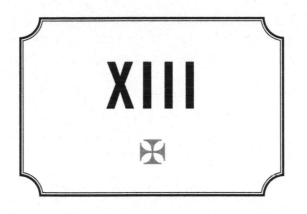

XIII

Cold rain pissed down out of a gray, curdled sky. Bernie Cobb manned a checkpoint outside of Erlangen and steamed. The rain blew into his face and dripped down the back of his neck, which did nothing to improve his mood. He looked this way and that—he tried to look every which way at once. Visibility wasn't much more than a hundred feet, so looking didn't do him a hell of a lot of good. The only consolation was, a Nazi sniper couldn't see any farther than he could.

"What did they stick us out here for?" Mack Leff asked for about the tenth time.

Leff wasn't a bad guy, but he'd got here after V-E Day, so Bernie didn't trust him as far as he would have trusted somebody who'd been through the mill. "Beats me," Bernie said. "Something's screwed up somewhere, though—that's for goddamn sure. Otherwise they wouldn't have put so many of us out on patrol at once."

"Yeah," Mack agreed mournfully. His left hand moved inside the pocket of his field jacket. Bernie knew what that meant: he was feeling a pack of cigarettes in there and wondering if he could keep one lit in this downpour. He must have decided he couldn't, because he didn't try to light up.

Bernie had already made the same glum calculation and come up with the same answer. He wasn't twitchy from missing a smoke yet, but he sure wanted one. "The orders we got are all bullshit, too," he went on—he could always piss and moan, even if he couldn't light up. "Check everybody's papers. Hold anybody suspicious for interrogation. Suspicious how?"

"You come out in this weather at all, you ought to have your head examined," Mack Leff opined.

"Got that right." Bernie wondered if he could peel the paper off a cigarette and chew the tobacco inside. He'd always thought a chaw was disgusting (to say nothing of hillbilly), but out in the open in weather like this. . . . "Rained this hard when we got over the Rhine last year. Then, at least, we could lay up in a house or a barn or somethin' and stay out of it sometimes."

"Uh-huh." Leff nodded. "Musta been good when you knew who the enemy was, when you didn't have to worry about everybody from the grocer to the old lady with a cat. You didn't have to watch your back so hard then."

"Fuck," Bernie muttered. Mack actually thought he'd had it easy when the real war was on. How was that for a kick in the nuts? The really weird thing was, the new guy might have a point. You kinda had to look at things sideways to see it, but when you did. . . .

He became aware of a new noise punching through the endless hiss of rain off paving and fields. "Heads up, Mack," he said. "Car's comin'."

The jeep they'd ridden out here made a decent obstacle after they'd pulled it across the road. If you wanted to go around it, you'd probably get stuck in the mud and you'd probably get shot, too. Bernie had the safety off on his M-1. If Mack Leff didn't, he was too dumb to deserve to live.

Only worry was whether whoever was in the oncoming car could spot the jeep in time to stop. They did, which impressed Bernie—that *Kubelwagen* had seen plenty of better years. Hitler's equivalent of a jeep could do most of the stuff a real one could, only not so well.

Two men sat in the *Kubelwagen*. If they weren't vets, Bernie'd never seen any. "Cover me," he told Leff as he came out from behind the jeep. He raised his voice and used some of his terrible German: "*Papieren, bitte!*" Then, hopefully, he added, "You guys speak English?"

Both krauts shook their heads. Bernie sighed; he might've known they wouldn't. It was that kind of day. They passed him the papers. The guy behind the wheel was Ludwig Mommsen, the documents said. The other fellow, whose long, thin nose kind of leaned to one side and who needed a shave like nobody's business, was Erich Wisser.

"You—in *Krieg*?" Bernie asked them. They looked at each other. "Where?" he said. "Uh, *wo?*"

"*Ostfront,*" Wisser answered. "Danzig." Mommsen nodded again, to show he'd served over there, too.

Bernie grunted. You couldn't get a Jerry to admit he'd ever taken a shot at an American. If you listened to those guys talk, nobody'd fought between Normandy and central Germany—not a soul. Bernie wished he didn't know better.

These guys seemed legit, though. He handed back their documents. "*Wo gehen Sie?*" he asked.

"Nürnberg," Mommsen answered, pronouncing it the way a kraut would instead of *Nuremberg* like an American.

They were on the right road. "Okay," Bernie said, and then, louder, "Move the jeep, Mack!"

Leff did. The Germans put the *Kubelwagen* back in gear and drove off to the south. "That wasn't so bad," Leff said.

"Sure wasn't," Bernie agreed. "They should all be so easy."

LOU WEISSBERG READ THE REPORT HOWARD FRANK GAVE HIM. THEN he handed it back to his superior officer. He didn't have rank enough to get his own copy. For that matter, neither did Captain Frank. He'd have to give the report to his own superior, who would stow it in a stout safe where no unauthorized eyes could see it.

"Jesus Christ!" Lou exclaimed. He and Captain Frank exchanged self-conscious half-smiles. That was a hell of a thing for a Jew to say, but plenty born in the States did it all the time. "Did the limeys screw the pooch or what?"

"They sure did," Frank said. "They screwed it like you wouldn't

believe. And so now the fanatics have nine first-rate atomic physicists . . . somewhere."

"Can they make a bomb?" Lou asked. "The guy who wrote your
little paper doesn't think so, but does he know his ass from third
base?"

"How am I supposed to tell? Do I look like Einstein?" Frank returned. "One thing I will say is that making a bomb seems to take a
lot of fancy equipment. Heydrich's baboons have all kinds of shit,
damn them, but I don't see 'em having that kind of gear. So I'd bet
against it."

"Mm." Lou nodded. That made sense—a certain amount of it,
anyhow. "If they *can't* make a bomb, how come the diehards nabbed
'em?"

"Maybe to make us yell and scream and jump up and down like
we've got ants in our pants," Captain Frank answered. "Or maybe
just for the hell of it—they don't *think* the slide-rule boys can pull a
rabbit out of the hat, but they don't want to take the chance they
might be wrong. If you were in Heydrich's shoes, what would you
do?"

"Hang myself and save everybody else a lot of trouble," Lou said
promptly. He won a snort from his superior. After a moment, he went
on, "Been a week since they made the snatch, right?"

"Yup," Frank said.

"And nobody's caught any physicists since. Not many diehards,
either."

"Nope." The captain turned downright laconic.

"Well, shit," Lou said. "Chances are that means they got away
clean."

"Yup," Frank said one more time. "If we'd caught 'em, people like
you and me never would have got to see this report. Now it's gonna
be up to us to try and track the bastards down."

"My aching back!" Lou said. That didn't satisfy him, so he added,
"Gevalt!" Howard Frank's head bobbed up and down. Lou took the
name of the Lord in vain. "The fanatics'll stash 'em underground
somewhere way the hell down south. How many places have they got
in the mountains there?"

"Too many—and we haven't found a tenth of 'em yet," Frank
said. "They were ready for the collapse, damn them. They started get-

ting ready two years before the surrender. That's what the interrogation reports say, anyhow. Way things look, you've got to believe it, too."

"Uh-huh." Lou sounded as uncomfortable as his superior. Interrogators didn't always bother playing by Geneva Convention rules when they caught diehards alive. The *Reich* had surrendered, after all. And they needed information, and didn't much care how they got it—especially since the krauts weren't playing by the rules, either. If a hotshot lawyer or a reporter who sided with the let's-run-away-from-Germany people back home found out what went on questioning fanatics, the fur would fly. Oh, boy, would it ever! And the *Chicago Tribune* and the other anti-administration papers would print every goddamn word.

"Well, now you've got all the good news," Captain Frank said. "Where we go from here, God only knows."

"If He does, I wish He'd tell us." Lou scowled. God didn't work that way. If anybody'd had any doubts, what went on during the war would have quashed them. "And I wish He'd tell us why He decided to throw all the *Yehudim* from France to Russia into the fire." Nobody knew how many were dead for no other reason than that they were Jews, not even to the closest million.

"Nobody has a good answer for that," Frank said heavily. "God doesn't have a good answer for that." The words should have sounded like blasphemy. To anyone who'd seen the inside of a German concentration camp, they seemed only common sense. Reputable German firms had taken contracts for crematoria and bone crushers and all the other tools that went along with industrialized murder. Lou had followed more paper trails than he cared to remember. And they all led back to businessmen who said things like, *We didn't know what they'd be used for. And how could we say no to the government?* The scary thing was, they meant it. Sometimes saying no to the government was the most important thing you could ever do, but try and explain that to a German.

"And Heydrich wants to start it all up again, only worse this time," Lou said.

"Worse. Yeah," Captain Frank said gloomily. "Who woulda thought that was possible after the Nazis surrendered? Nothing could be worse'n what they already did, right? Then along comes the atom bomb, and we find out maybe that's not right after all. Swell old world we got, huh?"

Before Lou could answer, the phone on his desk rang. It was an Army field telephone, patched into a network that also included what was left of the German national telephone system. He picked it up: "Weissberg here."

"You da guy in charge o' going after the fanatics?" By the way the GI on the other end of the line talked, he was from New Jersey, too, or maybe Long Island.

"I'm one of 'em," Lou said. "How come?"

"On account of I got a kraut right here who's ready t'swear on a stack o' Bibles he seen that Heydrich drive through town a little while ago."

"Jesus Christ!" Lou exploded, this time altogether unself-consciously. "Put him on."

The German knew some English, but proved more comfortable in his own language. "He had a beard, but I recognized him," he said. "His picture was all over the papers when the English tried to kill him in the war. There is a reward for me if you catch him, *ja*?"

"*Jawohl*," Lou agreed. The reward for Heydrich, dead or alive, was up to a million bucks. Lou had no idea who this German was or what he'd done between 1939 and 1945. Whatever it was, it was nothing next to Heydrich's list.

"What's cooking?" Frank asked. One hand over the mouthpiece, Lou told him. The captain almost jumped out of his skin. "We can catch him! We really can! Find out how long ago this guy saw him and which way he was headed. We can spread the net ahead of him so tight a hedgehog couldn't sneak through."

Lou got back on the phone. He asked the Jerry Captain Frank's questions, then relayed the replies he got: "Less than an hour ago, and heading southeast."

"Son of a bitch!" Howard Frank said reverently. "We've got him!"

REINHARD HEYDRICH HAD SERVED IN THE NAVY BEFORE THE WAR— till he left it abruptly after not marrying the senior officer's daughter he'd seduced. He'd flown combat missions over Poland and the Soviet Union. The only experience he had as a foot soldier was getting away from the Ivans after his 109 crash-landed between their lines and the Germans'.

Squelching through a swamp and ducking down into the mud and the water plants wasn't his idea of fun. But Hans Klein had the perfect spur for him: "Do you *want* the fucking Amis to catch you, sir?"

"Now that you mention it, no," Heydrich admitted.

"Well, then, don't stand straight up and down like a heron looking for frogs. Get down here with me," Klein said. He hadn't had much ground combat experience himself—certainly none since he became Heydrich's driver. But he sure talked like somebody who knew what he was talking about.

"If you'd been able to fix the *Kubelwagen* when it broke down for real—" Heydrich began peevishly.

But that didn't wash, either. The *Oberscharführer* let out a derisive snort. "*Ja, doch,* then what? I'll tell you what . . . sir. I'd've driven us straight into a Yankee ambush, that's what, and they'd've filled both of us full of holes."

Again, he was altogether too likely to be right. That made Heydrich love him no better when freezing water filled his shoe . . . again. Maybe infantrymen really were the heroes of the war, even if pilots and panzer commanders got more ink from Goebbels. Infantrymen put up with more shit—no possible doubt about that.

The *Kubelwagen* had flatulently expired about ten kilometers outside of Nuremberg. The horrible noises it made told Klein he didn't have the tools to fix it. They started off for a farmhouse they could see a couple of kilometers off the road. Maybe the farmer would have the tools. If he didn't . . . If he didn't, they would think of something else, that was all.

They'd just trudged into a grove of apple trees not far from the farmhouse when Klein looked back over his shoulder and said, "Mm, *Herr Reichsprotektor,* I think maybe we don't want to go back no matter what."

"Are you out of your—?" Heydrich had begun. Then he'd looked over his shoulder, too. American jeeps and an armored car and U.S. soldiers in their pot helmets and ugly greenish khaki uniforms swarmed around the dead *Kubelwagen.* When Heydrich turned to say as much to Klein, Klein wasn't there. He was down on the ground, and reaching out to tug urgently at Heydrich's trouser leg. Heydrich needed a second to get it, which proved him no infantryman. Then he hit the dirt, too.

They crawled away from the car that had chosen such an opportune moment to crap out. No bullets chased them, so the Amis hadn't spotted them before they went down.

"Have they got dogs?" Klein whispered as they slithered away.

"I don't think so. I didn't see any," Heydrich replied, also in a low voice. Low voice or not, he had trouble hiding his scorn. The Russians would have had dogs. The Russians, damn them, were serious about this twilight battle. The Americans didn't seem to be. They thought his men annoyances, nuisances. They wanted everything peaceful and easy and smooth. Well, you didn't always get what you wanted, even if you were an Ami.

After a while, Klein found another question: "Do you know of any bunkers around here?"

A map formed inside Heydrich's mind. He had an excellent, even outstanding, memory and a knack for visualization. After a moment, he nodded. "*Ja*. There's one maybe three kilometers east of here."

"Can you find it? Shall we go there?"

"I can find it," Heydrich said confidently: what he promised, he could deliver. The other half of Klein's question wasn't so easy to answer. After some thought, the *Reichsprotektor* said, "I'd rather not go to ground if I can help it. If they track us to the bunker, we're trapped like a badger inside its sett."

"Well, yes," Klein returned, also after a pause to think. "But they can run us down in the open, too, you know."

If Heydrich made it back to his underground headquarters, he didn't plan on coming out again any time soon. In the meanwhile . . . "As long as we're above the ground and moving, we've got a chance to get away. I think the risk that they can follow us to the bunker and dig us out is just too big."

Had Klein argued, he might have convinced his superior to change his mind. As things were, the *Oberscharführer* only sighed. "Well, you're right about one thing, boss—we can get screwed either way."

They weren't screwed yet. The Americans made a ham-fisted job of going after a pair of fugitives. Without false modesty, Heydrich knew the SS would have caught up with him and Klein in short order.

For that matter, so would the NKVD. Professionals knew what they were doing. The Americans . . .

How the devil did they win? They were brave—Heydrich couldn't deny that. And there were lots of them. And what came out of their factories . . . Few Germans had imagined just how much the USA could make when it set its mind to it. Bombers, fighters, tanks, jeeps, trucks . . . Yes, each man from the *Wehrmacht* or *Waffen*-SS was better than his enemy counterpart. But he wasn't enough better, not when the other side had so many more troops and so much matériel.

And, however clumsy the other side was, it hadn't given up here. American soldiers stumbled across the landscape. How far south and east the search extended, Heydrich didn't want to think. Sooner or later, the Amis were much too likely to blunder across him and Klein by sheer luck. If they did . . .

If they do, I'm a dead man, Heydrich thought. So was Klein, but Hans could do his own worrying. If the noncom did, it stretched no further than himself. Heydrich also worried about the fate of the whole National Socialist uprising. It would go on without him; he knew that. Whether it would go on so well and sting the enemies from the east and west the way it had was a different question. Yes, Jochen Peiper was capable—he wouldn't have been second in command if he weren't. Still, Heydrich didn't think anybody could match Heydrich.

"What are you idiots doing screwing around in this swamp?" The question came in such a broad Bavarian dialect that Heydrich barely understood it.

He almost plugged the man who asked it any which way. He'd had no idea anybody but Hans was anywhere within half a kilometer. But this wizened little grinning bastard appeared from behind a tussock as if he were a sprite in one of Wagner's lesser operas. Now, was he a good sprite or the other kind? He was a sprite who was wary of firearms, that was for sure—he stood very still and kept his hands where Heydrich could see them.

"Hey, buddy, you don't want to do that," he said, his grin slipping only a little. "You shoot me, all the American pigdogs'll come running this way."

"Are you loyal to the *Grossdeutsches Reich*?" Heydrich demanded. He knew about the ever-rising price on his head. If this scrawny son of a bitch decided to play Judas, he'd get a lot more than thirty pieces of silver. *But he won't live to enjoy them if he does,* the *Reichsprotektor* promised himself.

"Got out of the Ukraine in one piece. Got out of Romania in one piece. Hell, got out of Hungary almost in one piece—they grazed me while I was hightailing it over the border. Got stuck in Vienna after that, and got away there, too," the Bavarian said. "We still owe folks a thing or three."

Maybe he was telling the truth. Maybe he was spinning a line to lull Heydrich and Klein. The underofficer came straight to the point: "Can you get us out of here without tipping off the Amis?"

"Not a sure-fire deal, but I think so," the Bavarian answered. "Want to come along and see?"

Heydrich and Klein looked at each other. They both shrugged at the same time. Heydrich didn't see how he could leave somebody who might be a betrayer at his back. He also didn't see how he could quietly dispose of the fellow. Yes, the man might take them straight to the Amis. Sometimes you just had to roll the dice.

"Let's go," Heydrich said after a barely perceptible pause.

"Get moving, then," the Bavarian replied. Off they went.

"Are you sure this is a good idea?" Klein whispered.

"No," Heydrich returned. "Are you sure it isn't?" The *Oberscharführer* answered with another shrug.

After a few minutes, Heydrich became convinced the Bavarian wasn't going straight to the Americans. He wasn't going straight at all. His turns seemed at random, but they all took him and the half-trusting men at his heels deeper into the swamp. Bushes and scraggly trees—the edges of the Lorenzerwald—hid them ever more effectively.

"Right season, you can get all kinds of mushrooms around here." Their guide smacked his lips.

"I believe it." Hans Klein sounded more as if he was thinking of death and decay than of a thick slice of boiled pork smothered with mushrooms. Since Heydrich's train of thought ran on the same track, he couldn't very well tell Klein to shut up. The Bavarian chuckled. Not only was he at home in this miserable countryside, he was enjoying himself.

"How will you get us past the enemy?" Heydrich asked. One of his wet shoes was rubbing at the back of his heel. Pretty soon, like it or not, he'd start limping. He wondered if he'd do better barefoot. If he had to, he'd try that. But running something into his sole wouldn't slow him up—it would stop him cold. He resolved to hang on to his shoes as long as he could.

"Oh, there are ways," the other man said airily.

They came to a shack beside a little stream. The shack might have been built from junk salvaged after the surrender, or it might have been leaning there in growing decrepitude since the days of Frederick the Great . . . or Frederick Barbarossa. "Nice place," Hans Klein said dryly.

The Bavarian chuckled. "Glad you like it. Follow me around back."

Around the back, a stubby wooden pier stuck out into the stream. Like the shack, it might have been there a few months or a few hundred years. The boat tied to the pier wasn't new, but also wasn't obviously a remembrance of things past.

"Get in," the Bavarian told Heydrich and Klein. "Then lie flat. It's roomier down there than it looks."

And so it was. This fellow probably didn't smuggle fugitive National Socialist fighters every day. If he didn't smuggle something every day, or often enough, Heydrich would have been astonished. Just to make sure of things, the Bavarian draped a ratty tarpaulin over them. The tarp smelled of mildew and tobacco. Heydrich nodded to himself. *Thought so—cigarette smuggler.* These days, cigarettes were as good as money in Germany. In a lot of places, they were money, near enough.

"Off we go." The man's voice came from the other side of the tarp like the sun from the far side of a cloud.

"What happens if the Americans make you stop?" Klein asked.

"We'll worry about that when it happens, all right?" The Bavarian didn't lack for nerve.

The boat began bobbing in a new way. It was floating down the stream now. Pretty soon, the Bavarian sat down and started rowing to help it along. The oarlocks creaked. Time stretched, all rubberlike. Heydrich didn't know whether to be terrified or bored. Beside him, Klein started snoring softly. Heydrich found himself jealous of the underofficer. Sometimes not thinking ahead made life simpler.

After a while, Heydrich jerked awake and realized he'd been dozing, too. Hans Klein laughed softly. "You snore, *Herr Reichspro-tektor.*"

"Well, so do you," Heydrich said. "How far do you suppose we've come?"

"I dunno. A ways."

"Shut up, you two," the Bavarian hissed. "Amis on the banks."

Sure as hell, a voice called out in accented but fluent German: "Hey, Fritzi, you old asslick, you running Luckies again?"

"Not me," the Bavarian answered solemnly. "Chesterfields."

He got a laugh from the American. But then the enemy soldier went on, "You seen a couple of guys on the lam? High command wants 'em bad—there's money in it if you spot 'em."

"Your high command must want them bad if it's willing to pay," the Bavarian observed, and won another laugh. "But me, I've seen no-body." He kept rowing.

If the American called for—Fritzi?—to stop . . . But he didn't. The boat slid on down the stream. Heydrich wished he could see what was going on. He could see the bottom of the boat, the tarp, a little of himself, and even less of Hans. It wasn't enough. He kept his head down anyhow.

After a while, the Bavarian said, "We gave that lot the slip. Shouldn't be any more for a while. And even if there are, I can make it so they never see us."

"Good by me," Klein said.

"And me," Heydrich agreed. One of the basic rules was, you didn't argue with somebody who was saving your ass. Heydrich had broken a lot of rules in his time, but that one made too much sense to ignore.

LOU WEISSBERG COULD COUNT THE TIMES HE'D BEEN ON A HORSE ON the fingers of one hand. He thought of a jeep as the next best thing, or maybe even the equivalent. A jeep could go damn near anywhere and almost never broke down. The *Stars and Stripes* cartoon of the sad cavalry sergeant putting a hand over his eyes as he aimed his .45 at the hood of a jeep that had quit only reinforced the comparison in his mind.

Mud flew up from under this jeep's tires as it roared toward the edge of a two-bit stream. The PFC driving it gave it more gas. "Don't worry, Lieutenant," the guy said cheerfully. "I'll get you there—and I'll get you back, too."

"I wasn't worried," Lou answered, and he was telling the truth— about that, at any rate. He was worried about Heydrich getting away. If the report was true, they should have grabbed the son of a bitch by now. They'd found the *Kubelwagen,* or *a Kubelwagen,* not too far from here. That much checked out. But no Heydrich. That Jerry hoping for a big chunk of change had to be sweating bullets right now, for all kinds of reasons. If the kraut was bullshitting, the Americans would come down on him hard. If he wasn't, who'd want to sell him life insurance?

The jeep half skidded to a stop. Lou hopped out. Carrying a grease gun, he trotted over to the GIs by the side of the stream. The mud tugged at his boots, but he'd been through plenty worse, plenty thicker. "Seen anything?" he called to the dogfaces.

He'd been thinking of *Stars and Stripes.* One of the soldiers had a bent nose and a dented helmet, just like Joe of Willie and. "Not a goddamn thing," he said, adding, "Uh, sir," a beat later when he noticed the silver bar painted onto Lou's steel pot. "Only Fritzi running smokes like usual."

"Who's Fritzi?" Lou asked.

The GIs looked at one another. Lou could tell what was going through their minds. *This guy is supposed to help run things, and he doesn't know stuff like that?* Patiently, the one who looked like Joe explained, "He's this kraut who lives in the swamp around here. He gets cigarettes—hell, I dunno where, but he does. And he makes his living turning 'em over, y'know what I mean? He's a good German, Fritzi is."

"How do you know that?" Lou had met any number of Germans who'd done things that would make Jack the Ripper puke, but who were kind family men and never kicked the dog. You just couldn't tell.

"Oh, you oughta hear him cuss Hitler and the generals," the soldier answered. "Far as he's concerned, they screwed things up like you wouldn't believe."

"Terrific," Lou said tightly. "You searched the boat, right?"

They eyed one another again. At last, the guy who looked like Joe said, "Nah, we didn't bother. Fritzi's okay, like I said. And we woulda had to notice the cigarettes, and that woulda just complicated everybody's life." His buddies nodded.

"Suppose he was carrying Heydrich?" Lou snapped.

"Then we fucked up," the GI said, shrugging. "But what're the odds?"

"Okay. Okay. But when the prize is this big, we gotta tie up all the loose ends," Lou said. "If all he's got're cigarettes, I don't give a shit. But all the krauts hate Hitler—now. Ask 'em five years ago and you woulda got a different answer. So which way did this goddamn boat go?"

"Thataway," the soldier said, as if he'd watched too many Westerns. He jerked a thumb toward the southeast.

"Then we'll go after him," Lou declared. He had a radio in the jeep, and turned back towards it. "I'll call in reinforcements."

"Call in a bunch—sir," the dogface told him. "You go much farther and things start getting tricky-like." Again, his pals' heads went up and down.

Lou shrugged, too, in a different way. "Fine. So things get tricky. I will call in a bunch." And he did.

Then he had to wait for the reinforcements to get there. When they did, his heart sank. They were new draftees—you could always tell. They didn't want to be there, and barely bothered to hide it. They squelched into the swamp like guys ordered to take out the Siegfried Line with slingshots.

"Just remember the price on Heydrich's head, guys," Lou called to them. "A million bucks, tax-free. You're set for life if you nail him." Anything to get the reluctant soldiers moving. If he thought they would have believed him, he would have promised them a week of blowjobs from Rita Hayworth.

They did move a little faster, but only a little. One of them said, "Yeah, like this fuckin' kraut's really in there. Now tell me another one." Like any other soldier with an ounce of sense, the American GI was a professional cynic. These fellows didn't know much about soldiering yet, but they'd sure figured that out.

Sometimes there was no help for a situation. Sometimes there was. Lou knew one that front-line officers had often used before the surrender. "Well, follow me, goddammit!" he snapped, and plunged past the draftees into the swamp himself. They muttered and shook their heads, but they did follow.

That accomplished less than he wished it would have. He rapidly discovered why the troopers who knew Fritzi had set up their checkpoint where they did. Past that, the stream split up into half a dozen narrow channels that crossed and recrossed, braided and rebraided, like a woman's pigtail woven by a nut. Some of what lay between the channels was mud, some was bushes, some was rank second-growth trees. All of it was next to impossible to get through.

"Have a heart, Lieutenant," one of the draftees panted after a while. "If that what's-his-name asshole came this way, he'll never make it out again." Several of the other new fish nodded.

"My ass," Lou said sweetly. "You wouldn't be dogging it if the Jerries were plastering this place with 105s—I guarandamntee you that."

Behind him, the GIs muttered. Nobody directly answered him, though. He knew what that meant. It meant just what he'd thought: these guys were fresh off the boat from the States. They'd never been under fire, and they had no idea what the hell he was talking about.

Something fair-sized and brown splashed into the water and swam away. Lou came *that* close to opening up on it before he realized it was an animal . . . one that walked on four legs. Most of the GIs came out with variations on "What the fuck was that?" But one of them said, "Hey, Clifton, that a muskrat or a nutria?"

"Muskrat, I betcha. Nutria's even bigger." Clifton sounded froggier than most of the Frenchmen Lou'd met. Five got you ten he was born within spitting distance of the Louisiana bayou. After a moment, he went on, "Damfino what either one of 'em's doin' here. They's American critters."

"Waddaya wanna bet the krauts brung 'em over to raise for fur and they got loose, way nutrias did when we shipped 'em up from South America?" his buddy answered. "My uncle raise nutrias for a while. Then he go bust and sponge offa Pa."

Lou didn't give a muskrat's ass about escaped rodents or the soldier's sponging uncle. "Spread out," he told his none too merry men. "God damn it to hell, we are gonna comb this swamp and see what's in here."

He hadn't gone another fifty yards before he realized it was hopeless. A regiment could have gone through here and missed an elephant standing quietly in the shade of the trees. No elephants, or none he saw—the Jerries wouldn't have brought them in for fur. But with the best will in the world the platoon he led couldn't have searched the whole swamp in under a year.

And these clowns didn't have the best will in the world, or anything close to it. They pissed and moaned. They dragged their feet. Reward or not, they couldn't have cared less about catching Reinhard Heydrich, because they didn't think he was within miles. As for Fritzi and his rowboat full of illicit tobacco . . . The only thing that mattered to them was that they were getting muddy and their poor little tootsies were soaked.

More than once, Lou had heard krauts—especially krauts who didn't know he spoke German—wonder out loud how the hell the USA won the war. He'd never been tempted to wonder the same thing himself . . . till now.

A gray heron almost as tall as a man made him nervous—all the more so because its plumage was only a little lighter than *Feldgrau*. But no *Landser* ever born came equipped with that cold yellow stare or that bayonet beak. The heron's head darted down. A carp wriggled briefly, then disappeared.

The sun sank toward the western horizon. Clifton said, "No offense, Lieutenant, but we ain't gonna find him."

"Yeah," Lou said, and then several things quite a bit warmer than that. Maybe the GIs posted on the far side of the swamp would scoop Heydrich up when he came out. Lou had to hope so. He wasn't going to be the hero himself. The *Reichsprotektor* shouldn't have got away—but it looked like he had.

XIV

A teletype chattered. Tom Schmidt pulled the flimsy paper off the machine. The dateline was Munich. The headline said, HEYDRICH MOCKS PURSUERS AFTER ESCAPE. The story was . . . just what you'd expect after a headline like that. The boss of the German national resistance was back in hiding again, and thumbing his nose at the blundering Americans who'd let him slip through their fingers.

"Well, Jesus Christ!" Schmidt said in disgust. "We really can't do anything right over there, can we?"

"What now?" asked another reporter in the *Tribune*'s Washington bureau. He was interested enough not to light his cigarette till he got an answer.

Schmidt gave it to him, finishing, "What d'you think of that, Wally?"

Wally did light up before replying, "I think it stinks, that's what. What am I supposed to think? First the krauts grabbed a bunch of guys with slide rules, then when their own big cheese put his neck on the chopping block we couldn't bring the goddamn hatchet down. Somebody's head ought to roll if Heydrich's didn't."

"Sounds right to me," Tom said. "You know what else?"

"I'm all ears," Wally said. He wasn't so far wrong, either; he really did have a pair of jug handles sticking out from the sides of his head.

"I'll tell you what." Tom always had liked the sound of his own voice. "This part of the war is harder on us than whipping the *Wehrmacht* was, that's what."

"How d'you figure?" Wally asked.

" 'Cause when we were fighting the *Wehrmacht* we knew who was who and what was what," Tom said. "Now we're in the same mess the Nazis got into when they had to fight all the Russian partisans. You can't tell if the guy selling cucumbers likes you or wants to blow you to kingdom come. And does that pretty girl walking down the street have a bomb in her handbag? How are you supposed to win a fight like that if the other side doesn't want to let up?"

"Kill 'em all?" Wally suggested.

"We aren't gonna do that," Tom said, and the other reporter didn't disagree with him. After a moment, he added, "Hell, even if we wanted to, I don't think we could. Hitler's goons pretty much tried it, and even they couldn't pull it off. Besides, d'you really wanna imitate the goddamn SS?"

"They didn't have the atom bomb, so they had to do it retail," Wally said. "We could do it wholesale."

"Maybe we could, but we won't," Tom said. "Ain't gonna happen—no way, nohow. I almost wish it would. It's the only thing that could get us out of the deep shit we walked into."

"Either that or just packing up and going home," Wally said. "You oughta write the rest of it up. It'd make a good column, y'know, especially if you use the Heydrich story for a hook."

"Damned if it wouldn't." Tom carried his filthy mug over to the coffee pot that sat on a hot plate in the corner of the room. The pot had been there since sunup, and it was late afternoon now. The black, steaming stuff that came out when he poured would have stripped paint from a destroyer's gun turret. Adulterated with plenty of cream and sugar, it also tickled brain cells.

Tom ran a sheet of paper into his Underwood and started banging away. When things went well, he could pound out a column in forty-five minutes. This was one of those times. He passed it to Wally when he finished.

"Strong stuff," the other reporter said, nodding. "Truman'll call you every kind of name under the sun."

"Okay by me," Tom said. "Only thing I want to know now is, what'll the guys back in Chicago do to me?"

"If you don't like getting edited, you shoulda written books instead of going to work for the papers," Wally said.

"Nah," Tom replied. "I'll never get rich at this racket, but I won't starve, either. You try writing books for a living, you better already have somebody rich in the family. Yeah, I don't like what the editors do sometimes, but I can live with it. A regular paycheck helps a lot."

"You think I'm gonna argue with you?" Wally shook his head. "Not me, Charlie. I got two kids, and a third on the way."

Schmidt's column ran in the *Tribune* the next day. At the President's next press conference, Truman said, "I didn't imagine anybody could make me think a guttersnipe like Westbrook Pegler was a gentleman, but this Schmidt character shows me I was wrong." Tom felt as if he'd been giving the accolade.

Then Walter Lippmann, who was staunchly on the side of keeping American troops in Germany till the cows came home, attacked him in print. Up till then, Lippmann had never deigned to acknowledge that he existed, much less that he was worth attacking. Tom fired back in another column, one that drew him even more notice than the first had. He was as happy as Larry.

Every once in a while, though, he got reminded of what his happiness was built on. As if to celebrate Heydrich's escape, the diehards blew up an American ammunition dump on the outskirts of Regensburg. The blast killed forty-five GIs, and wounded a number the War Department coyly declined to state. It broke windows ten miles away.

A survivor was quoted as saying, "I thought one of those atomic whatsits went off."

How do we let things like this happen? Tom wrote. *And if we can't keep things like this from happening, why do we go on wasting our young men's lives in a fight we can't hope to win? Wouldn't it be better to come home, let the Germans sort things out among themselves, and use our bombers and our atomic whatsits to make sure they can never threaten us again? Sure looks that way to me.* He paused. That wasn't quite a strong enough kicker. He added one more line—*Sure looks that way to more and more Americans, too.*

No brigadier general summoned to testify before Congress ever looked happy. In Jerry Duncan's experience, that was as much a law of nature as any of the ones Sir Isaac Newton discovered. This particular brass hat—his name, poor bastard, was Rudyard Holmyard—looked as if he'd just taken a big bite out of a fertilizer sandwich.

Which didn't stop the Indiana Congressman from trying to rip him a new one. "How do we let things like this happen?" Duncan thundered. If a newspaper columnist had put it the same way a few days earlier, well, it was still a damn good question.

"Um, sir, when both sides have weapons and determination, you just aren't likely to pitch a perfect game," Holmyard said. "We found that out the hard way in the Philippines at the turn of the century, and again in the Caribbean and Central America during the '20s and '30s. Sometimes you get hurt, that's all. You do your best to prevent it, but you know ahead of time your best won't always be good enough."

"One of those things, eh?" Jerry laced the words with sarcasm. General Holmyard nodded somberly. Jerry went on, "When we were fighting in the Philippines at the turn of the century, though, we didn't have to worry about the guerrillas getting the atom bomb, did we?"

"No, sir," the general replied. "Of course, we didn't have it ourselves, either."

Would we have dropped one on the Philippines if we'd had it then? Duncan wondered. His guess was that we probably would have. How could Teddy Roosevelt have carried a bigger stick? And the Philippines were a long way away, and the people there were small and brown and had slanty eyes. They weren't quite Japs, but. . . . Yeah, Teddy would have used the bomb if he'd had it.

With an effort, the Congressman pulled his thoughts back to the middle of the twentieth century. "Why haven't we been able to recapture any of the physicists the fanatics kidnapped?" he asked.

General Holmyard looked even gloomier; Jerry hadn't thought he could. "A couple of points there, sir," he said. "First, we don't know for a fact that the missing scientists ever entered our occupation zone. They may be under British or French administration, or even Russian."

"So they may. The only thing we're sure of is that they're under Reinhard Heydrich's administration. Isn't that a fact?"

A muscle in Holmyard's jaw twitched. But his nod seemed calm enough. "Yes, sir," he said stolidly. "Another thing I need to point out is that, unfortunately, a nuclear physicist looks like anybody else when he's not wearing a white lab coat. Coming up with these guys is like looking for multiple needles in a heck of a big haystack."

"Terrific," Jerry said, at which point the Democrat running the committee rapped loudly for order. "Sorry, Mr. Chairman," Duncan told him. He wasn't, but the forms had to be observed. "I only have a few more questions. The first one is, how likely are the fanatics to be able to manufacture their own atom bombs now that they know it's possible?"

"Very unlikely, Congressman. I have that straight from General Groves," Holmyard replied. Jerry winced; having run the Manhattan Project to a successful conclusion, Leslie Groves owned a named to conjure with. General Holmyard continued, "Atom bombs may be possible, but they aren't easy or cheap. You need a sizable supply of uranium ore, and you need an even bigger industrial base. The Nazi fanatics have neither."

"You're sure they can't get their hands on uranium?" Duncan said.

"When we entered Germany, we had a special team ordered to take charge of whatever the Germans were using to try and build their own bomb," Rudyard Holmyard said. "That team did a first-rate job The War Department is confident Heydrich's goons can't come up with anything along those lines."

"The War Department was also confident the Germans would stop fighting after they signed their surrender," Jerry pointed out. The chairman banged the gavel again. Jerry didn't care. He'd wanted to get in the last word, and now he had. "No further questions," he said, and stepped away from the microphone.

None of the other Congressmen raked General Holmyard over the coals the way Jerry had. Of course, the majority of the committee members were Democrats, but the rest of the Republicans also stayed cautious. The Democrats wished the issue of Germany would dry up and blow away. Too many men on the same side of the aisle as Jerry Duncan didn't have the nerve to reach out and grab it with both hands.

Of course the majority were Democrats. . . . Jerry muttered to himself as he went back to his office. Ever since the Depression crashed down, the Democrats had ruled Congress. These days, most people took their comfortable majorities for granted. Jerry didn't. He thought Germany was a prime way to pry them out of the chairman- ships and perquisites they'd enjoyed for so long. He only wished more Republicans agreed with him.

As usual, a fat pile of correspondence awaited him when he sat down at his desk. Actually, two piles: one from within his own dis- trict, the other from outside it. Before he made a name for himself about Germany, nobody outside the area that stretched northeast from Anderson and Muncie had cared a nickel for him. That had suited him fine, too.

Now, though, people from all over the country sent him letters and telegrams. Some said he should run for President. Others called him a fathead, or told him he would burn in hell, or said he had to be a Nazi or a Communist or sometimes both at once. And still others— sadly, fewer than he would have liked—were thoughtful discussions of what was going on in Germany and what the United States ought to do about it.

This latest stack of mail from all over would have to wait a while. His district came first. Any Congressman who didn't get that didn't stay in Congress long. More people from Indiana seemed to understand what he had in mind. Not only did he know his district, but he'd represented it long enough to let it get to know him, too.

Oh, there were a couple of burn-in-hell letters here, and one un- signed one decorated with swastikas. But you couldn't make every- body happy no matter what you did. The local mail wasn't anything that made Jerry doubt he'd win in November.

And winning in November was what he had to do. Once he'd taken care of that, he would look around and see everything else he needed to deal with. But if he lost the upcoming election—well, there wasn't much point to anything after that, was there?

REINHARD HEYDRICH DIDN'T BOTHER WITH FULL DRESS UNIFORM very often. What was the point, God only knew how many meters un- derground? The other resisters down here knew who he was and what he was and that he had the authority to command them. What more did he want—egg in his beer?

Sometimes, though, he needed to impress—no, to intimidate—people. And so today he wore the high-peaked cap, the tunic with the SS runes on the black collar patch and the eagle holding a swastika on the right breast, the Knight's Cross to the Iron Cross at his throat, and the rest of his decorations on his left breast. It was all devilishly uncomfortable, but he looked the part of the *Reichsprotektor,* which was the point of the exercise.

Hans Klein, also in full SS regalia, came in and said loudly, "*Herr Reichsprotektor,* the scientist Wirtz to see you, as you ordered!"

"Send him in, *Oberscharführer,*" Heydrich replied.

"*Zu befehl, Herr Reichsprotektor!*" Klein clicked his heels. They never would have bothered with that nonsense if Karl Wirtz weren't out in the corridor listening. But they had to make Wirtz and the other captured physicists believe the *Reich* was still a going concern. And, to a certain degree, they had to believe it themselves.

Klein strode out. He returned a moment later with Professor Wirtz. The scientist looked to be in his late thirties. He was tall and thin, with a hairline that had retreated like the *Wehrmacht* on the Eastern Front, leaving him with a forehead that seemed even higher than it would have anyhow.

Heydrich's right arm snapped up and out. "*Heil* Hitler!" he barked.

Wirtz gaped. "Er—Hitler's dead," he muttered.

"You will address the *Reichsprotektor* by his title," Hans Klein rumbled ominously, sounding every centimeter the senior underofficer.

"The *Führer* may be dead," Heydrich said. "The *Reich* he founded lives on—and will live on despite any temporary misfortunes. And you, *Herr Doktor* Professor Wirtz, will help ensure its survival."

"M—Me?" If the prospect delighted Wirtz, he hid it very well. "All I ever wanted to do was come home from England and get back to my research."

"You are home—home in the *Grossdeutsches Reich,*" Heydrich said. "And we brought you and your comrades here so you could conduct your research undisturbed by the English and the Americans."

"You want us to make a bomb for you . . . *Herr Reichsprotektor.*" Wirtz wasn't altogether blind—no, indeed.

"That's exactly what we want, yes," Heydrich agreed. "With it, we are strong. We can face any foe on even terms. The Americans, the Russians—anyone. Without it, we are nothing. So you will give it to us."

Wirtz licked his lips. "It makes me very sorry to say this, *Herr Reichsprotektor,* but what you ask is impossible."

He was sorry to say it, Heydrich judged, because he feared what the *Reichsprotektor* would do to him. And well he might. But, though Wirtz didn't know it, Heydrich had already heard the same thing from several other physicists. All he said now was, "Why do you think so?"

"You do not have the uranium ore we were using before, do you? The ore from which we would have to extract the rare pure material we need for the bomb?" Wirtz said. When Heydrich didn't answer, the physicist went on, "And you do not have the factories we would need to perform the extraction. The Americans spent billions of dollars to build those factories. Billions, *Herr Reichsprotektor*! When I think how we had to go begging for pfennigs to try to keep our research going . . ." He shook his head. "We were fighting a foe who was bigger than we are."

Again, Heydrich had heard the same thing before. He liked it no better now than he had then. "Can you get the uranium you need?"

"I have no idea where we would do that . . . sir," Professor Wirtz said. "We were working at Hechingen and Haigerloch, in the southwest, when the war ended. French troops, and Moroccans with them"—he shuddered—"captured the towns and captured us. Then American soldiers took charge of us and took charge of the uranium we were using."

Hechingen and Haigerloch were still in the French zone. The French fought Heydrich's resisters almost as viciously as the Red Army did—no doubt for many of the same reasons. Still, something might be managed . . . if it had a decent chance of proving worthwhile. "The uranium is all gone? Everything is all gone?"

"Yes," Wirtz said, as the other reclaimed scientists had before him. But then, as none had before, he added, "Except perhaps—"

Heydrich leaned forward abruptly enough to make the swivel chair creak under his backside. "Except perhaps what, *Herr Doktor* Professor?" he asked softly.

"When the Amis captured us, we were making a new uranium pile." The actual word Wirtz used was *machine*, a term Heydrich had already heard from the other scientists he'd questioned. The physicist continued, "We also had about ten grams of radium. One of the technicians hid the metal under a crate that had held uranium cubes. The Americans took the uranium, of course, but I am sure they did not take the radium. As far as I know, it is still in Hechingen."

Excitement tingled through Heydrich. Radium was potent stuff. Everybody knew that. Everybody had known that even before anyone imagined atomic bombs. And ten grams! That sounded like a lot. "Can you make a bomb with it?" Heydrich asked eagerly.

"*Nein, Herr Reichsprotektor.* If you expect me to do that, you'd better shoot me now. It is impossible." Wirtz's voice was sad but firm. He understood the way Heydrich thought, all right.

Heydrich didn't want to believe him, but decided he had no choice. If Wirtz was lying, one of the other physicists—Diebner, most likely—would give him away. And then Heydrich *would* shoot him. He had to understand that. "Well, if you can't make a bomb, what can you do with ten grams of radium?" Heydrich demanded. "You must be able to do something useful, or you wouldn't have brought it up in the first place."

"Let me think." Wirtz did just that for close to a minute. Then he said, "Well, you know radium is poisonous even in very small doses."

"How small? A tenth of a gram? A hundredth?" Heydrich asked. A poison that strong could make assassinations easier.

Karl Wirtz actually smiled. "Much less than that, *Herr Reichsprotektor.* Anything more than a tenth of a microgram is considered toxic." He helpfully translated the scientific measurement: "Anything more than a ten-millionth of a gram."

"*Der Herr Gott im Himmel!*" Heydrich whispered. He did sums in his head, and then, when he didn't believe the answer, did them again on paper. "Ten grams of radium could poison a hundred million people?" That stuff could kill off everybody still alive in Germany, with almost enough left over to do in France, too.

"Theoretically. If everything were perfectly efficient," Wirtz said. "You couldn't come anywhere close to that for real."

"But we could still do a lot of damage with it." Heydrich waited impatiently for the physicist's response.

Wirtz slowly nodded. "Yes, you could. I have no doubt of that. I am not sure of the best way to go about it, though."

"Well, that's why you and your friends are here." Heydrich's grin was as wide and inviting as he knew how to make it.

SPRING WAS IN THE AIR. VLADIMIR BOKOV WAS ALMOST BACK TO HIS old self again. Everything should have been easy. After all, hadn't the Fascist beasts suffered the most devastating military defeat in the history of the world? If they hadn't, what was the tremendous victory parade through Red Square all about? Where had all those Nazi standards and flags that proud Soviet soldiers dragged in the dust come from?

The only trouble was, the Germans didn't want to admit they were beaten. The Russian zone in what was left of the shattered *Reich,* what had been eastern Germany and was now western Poland, what had been East Prussia and was now split between Poland and the USSR, western Czechoslovakia, the Soviet zone in Austria . . . Rebellion bubbled everywhere.

Bokov would have suspected the Western Allies of fomenting the trouble—the Soviet Union's greatest fear had always been that the USA and Britain would end up in bed with Hitler, not Stalin—if he hadn't known they had troubles of their own. They might even have had worse troubles than the USSR did, because they put them down less firmly.

Poland and Czechoslovakia were kicking out their Germans. The Soviets were doing the same thing in their chunk of East Prussia. What had been Königsberg—a town the Nazis fought for like grim death—was now called Kaliningrad, after one of Stalin's longtime henchmen. Reliable Russians poured in to replace the Germans, who were anything but.

Once Poland and Czechoslovakia were German-free, the uprisings there would fizzle out. That delighted Bokov less than it might have. You couldn't expel *all* the Germans from the Soviet zones in Germany and Austria . . . could you? Not even Stalin, who never thought small, seemed ready for that.

And so the NKVD had to make do with lesser measures hereabouts. Mass executions avenged slain Soviet personnel. Mass deportations got rid of socially unreliable elements—and, often enough, of people grabbed at random to fill a quota. The survivors needed to understand they'd better not help or shelter Fascist bandits.

All that might have scared some of the remaining Germans into staying away from the bandits. Others, though, it only cemented to what should have been the dead Nazi cause.

Which was why Bokov bucketed along in a convoy of half a dozen jeeps, on his way south to Chemnitz. One jeep took the lead. Four more followed close together. The last one did rear-guard duty. The hope was that the formation would defeat bandits lurking by the side of the *Autobahn* with *Panzerschreck* or *Panzerfaust*—or, for that matter, with nothing fancier than a machine gun.

Bokov certainly hoped the stratagem worked. His neck, after all, was among those on the line here. This ploy was new. The bandits would take a little while to get used to it. After that . . . He knew his countrymen better than he wished he did. They would go on repeating it exactly—and the Germans would get used to it, and would find some way to beat it. Then the Red Army would take too long to figure out what to do differently.

Chemnitz wasn't quite so devastated as Dresden had been. But Anglo-American bombers had visited the Saxon city, too. The old town hall and a red tower that had once been part of the city wall stood out from the sea of rubble.

In the old town hall worked the burgomeister, a cadaverous fellow named Max Müller. "Good to meet you, Comrade Captain!" he said, shaking Bokov's hand. He belonged to the Social Unity Party of Germany, of course the Russians wouldn't have given him even the semblance of power if he hadn't. And he might well have spent the Hitler years in Russian exile with Ulbricht if he so readily recognized Bokov's rank badges.

"You've had a string of assassinations here," Bokov said. Red Army soldiers had established a barbed-wire perimeter around the town hall. They wanted to keep Müller alive if they could. He was the fourth burgomeister Chemnitz had known since the surrender.

"We have," he agreed now. Sweat glinted on his pale forehead, though the day was far from warm. He had to be wondering what the

Heydrichites were plotting now—and who could blame him? "Neither our own resources nor those of the fraternal Soviet forces in the area have quelled them."

He certainly sounded like a good Marxist-Leninist. All the same, Bokov's voice was dry as he asked, "And what makes you think one more officer will be able to set things right like *this*?" He snapped his fingers.

"Oh, but, Comrade Captain, you're not just one officer! You're the NKVD!" Müller exclaimed.

"Well, not all of it," Bokov said, more dryly still. He was glad this Fritz respected and feared the Soviet security apparatus. But he meant what he'd said before: there was only one of him.

"You have the rest behind you," Müller declared in ringing tones.

The other NKVD men were probably goddamn glad they were nowhere near Chemnitz. The place stank of death. So did a lot of Germany, but this was worse.

A labor gang of Germans—old men in overalls, younger men in *Wehrmacht* rags, and women in everything under the sun—dumped rubble into wheelbarrows and carted it away. How many wheelbarrows full of broken bricks and shattered masonry did Chemnitz hold? How many did all the Soviet zone hold? How many did all of Germany hold? How many years would it take to clear them, and how big a mountain would they make added together?

A tall one, Bokov hoped. Then he wondered how big a mountain the rubble in the USSR would make. Leningrad and Stalingrad weren't much besides rubble these days. Plenty of cities, some of them big ones, had changed hands four times, not just twice. As the Nazis fell back, they'd destroyed everything they could to keep the Red Army from using it against them.

How long would the Soviet Union take to get over the mauling the Fascist hyenas had given it? Vladimir Bokov scowled, not liking the answer that formed in his mind. Germany had caught hell, no doubt about it. But, even though the Red Army finally drove the invaders off with their tails between their legs, it was plain the USSR had caught whatever was worse than hell.

How many dead? Twenty million? Thirty? Somewhere between one and the other, probably, but Bokov would have bet nobody could have said where. He knew—everybody knew, even if it wasn't something you talked about—the Germans had inflicted far more casualties on the Red Army than the other way around.

But that wasn't all. That was barely the beginning. The Germans had slaughtered Jews, commissars, intellectuals generally. Would the USSR's intelligentsia ever be the same? And so many civilians had starved or died of disease or simply disappeared under German occupation.

It wasn't all one-sided. The labor gang dug up an arm bone with some stinking flesh still clinging to it. As nonchalantly as if such things happened every day (and no doubt they did, or more often than that), a scrawny old geezer with a white mustache shoveled the ruined fragment of humanity into a wheelbarrow with the rest of the wreckage.

One of the women in the gang sent Bokov a look full of vitriol. He stared back stonily, and she was the first to drop her eyes. He and the Red Army hadn't had anything to do with this death. It lay in the Anglo-Americans' ledger. Captain Bokov only wished the bombing had done more, and done it sooner. Then fewer Soviet citizens might have died.

The woman muttered something the NKVD man didn't catch. By the way several of the other Germans nodded, she was bound to be lucky he couldn't hear her.

He thought about seizing her anyway, and the laborers who'd nodded. He could; rounding up a few Red Army men to take them away would be a matter of moments. The only question was whether it would be worthwhile. It would teach these Germans they couldn't flout Soviet authority.

But it would also make their friends and families—who wouldn't understand the progressive Soviet line toward provocations—more likely to throw in with the Heydrichites or at least to keep silent about their banditry. That calculation made Bokov stalk off instead of yelling for Russian soldiers.

It also made him stop in dismay a few paces later. If he was calculating about the Heydrichites as if they were serious enemies . . . "Fuck my mother!" he exclaimed. If he was thinking of them that way, then they really were. Diehards, fanatics, bandits . . . Names like those minimized them. They were enemy combatants, and this was still a war.

Lou Weissberg didn't speak French. Captain Jean Desroches didn't speak English. They were both fluent in German. Lou felt the irony. He couldn't tell what, if anything, Desroches felt; the French intelligence officer had a formidable poker face.

"Hechingen. Something's up with Hechingen," Lou said *auf Deutsch*.

"And what would that be?" Desroches inquired.

"I don't exactly know," Lou answered. "But a couple of the fanatics we've caught lately have talked about it. I don't mean men we caught together, either—one we nabbed up near Frankfurt and the other by Munich. So something's going on."

"Unless they want you to think something is while they really strike somewhere else," Desroches said. "I mean—Hechingen?" He rolled his eyes. "The most no-account excuse for a town God ever made."

"I don't know much about the place," Lou admitted. "But I'll tell you something you may not know—Hechingen is where the German nuclear physicists got captured."

"You mean, before Heydrich's *salauds* captured them back?" Desroches used one word of French, but Lou had little trouble figuring out what it meant. His opposite number went on, "Besides, what difference does that make now?"

"I don't know what difference it makes." Lou was getting tired of saying he didn't know, even if he didn't. "But it's liable to make some, and you guys ought to be on your toes on account of it."

"You tend to your zone, Lieutenant," Desroches said icily. "We will handle ours."

"We can send some men if you're short," Lou offered.

He knew he'd made a mistake even before the words finished coming out of his mouth. Poker face or no, Captain Desroches gave the impression of a blue-haired matron who'd just been asked to do something obscene. "That will not be necessary," he said. After a moment, as if feeling that wasn't enough, he added, "You offer an insult to a sovereign and independent power, *Monsieur*."

"I didn't mean to," Lou said, instead of something like *Will you for God's sake come off it?*

France threw its weight around as if it would've had any weight to throw around if the United States and Britain—de Gaulle's scorned

"Anglo-Saxons"—hadn't saved its bacon. But you couldn't tell that to any Frenchman, not unless you really wanted to piss him off. Lou didn't have the nerve to ask Desroches how he came to know German so well. Life in France had been . . . complicated from 1940 to 1944.

The Frenchman lit a cigarette: one of his own, a Gauloise. To Lou, the damn thing smelled like smoldering horseshit. He fired up a Chesterfield in self-defense. Through the clouds of smoke, Desroches said, "I will take you at your word." Everything about the way he glared at Lou shouted *You lying son of a bitch!*

Since Lou was lying, or at least stretching the truth, he couldn't call Desroches on it. He said, "If you don't want our soldiers—"

"We don't," Desroches broke in.

"You don't have to use them," Lou went on, as if the other man hadn't spoken. "But do keep an eye on Hechingen. If anything happens there, I sure hope you'll let us know. My superiors—all the way up to General Eisenhower—sure hope you will."

"Is that a threat?" Desroches demanded. "What will happen if we don't?"

"I'm only a lieutenant. I don't make policy. But the people above me said it could be important enough to affect how much aid France gets." Lou eyed Captain Desroches, who was wearing U.S.-issue combat boots and a U.S. Army olive-drab uniform with French rank badges. Most of the French Army was similarly equipped, from boots to helmets to M-1 rifles to Sherman tanks (though they were also using some captured German Panthers). French soldiers ate U.S. C- and K-rations and slept in U.S. pup tents.

Desroches followed Lou's gaze down himself. He went red. "You Americans have the arrogance of power," he said.

"Aw, bullshit," Lou said in English. As he'd figured, Captain Desroches got that just fine. In German, Lou went on, "Hitler had the arrogance of power. If we had it, you guys would be going '*Heil* Truman!' right now."

Desroches turned redder. He stubbed out his foul cigarette and lit another one. "Perhaps you are right. I phrased it badly. I should have said that you Americans have the arrogance of wealth."

That did hit closer to the mark. Lou was damned if he'd admit it. "We have some worries about Hechingen—that's what we have. France and the USA are allies, *ja?* We pass the worries on to you, the way allies are supposed to. If anything happens there, we hope you're ready and we hope you'll let us know—the way allies are supposed to."

Captain Desroches sent up more smoke signals. "I will take this report back to my superiors, and we will do . . . whatever we do. Thank you for this . . . very interesting session, Lieutenant. Good day." He got up and stamped out of Lou's crowded little Nuremberg office.

"Boy, that was fun," Lou said to nobody in particular. Dealing with the French was more enjoyable than a root canal, but not much.

He went to Captain Frank's office down the hall. Frank was talking to a German gendarme—who also wore mostly U.S.-issue uniform, though dyed black—and waved for him to wait. Lou cooled his heels in the hallway for fifteen minutes or so. Then the Jerry came out looking unhappy. Lou went in.

"*Nu?*" Frank asked. Lou summarized his exchange with Desroches. His superior muttered to himself. "You sure we were on the same side?"

"That's what folks say," Lou answered.

"Are they going to pay any attention to Hechingen?" Captain Frank asked.

"My guess is, it's about fifty-fifty, sir," Lou said. "They sure are touchy bastards, aren't they?"

"Oh, maybe a little," Frank said. They both laughed, but neither smiled.

"Other thing is, sir, we don't know for sure the fanatics'll hit Hechingen, and we don't know for sure the froggies'll tell us if they do," Lou said.

"Uh-huh. Ain't we got fun?" Frank tacked on another mirthless laugh. "Gotta be something to do with the damn bomb scientists, doesn't it?"

"Looks that way to me," Lou agreed. "That's where we grabbed those guys in the first place. But it *could* be something else, I guess. If they've got a big old stash of mortar rounds or *Panzerfausts* or something outside of town, they might be all hot and bothered about those instead."

"Yeah. They might." Howard Frank didn't sound as if he believed it. Well, Lou didn't, either.

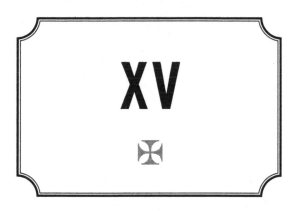

XV

Jerry Duncan got back to Anderson whenever he could. He got to see his wife, Betsy, more that way. They'd been married for going on thirty years, and still got on well.

And he'd long since decided that any Congressman who turned Washington into his full-time home town deserved to lose his next election—and probably would. He also knew he was liable to lose his next election anyhow. The Democrats were putting up a decorated and twice-wounded veteran named Douglas Catledge.

Even though it was still spring, Catledge's posters and signs were everywhere. VOTE CATLEDGE! they shouted. SUPPORT OUR PRESIDENT! SUPPORT OUR TROOPS!

When Jerry spoke at the local American Legion hall, he met that one head-on. "Anybody who says I don't support our troops is a liar," he declared. "It's just that simple, folks. I don't support keeping our troops in the wrong place at the wrong time for all the wrong reasons. I'm afraid Harry Truman does. We did what we needed to do in Germany. To do what Truman wants, we'll need soldiers there for the next fifty years. If that's what you've got in mind, you'd better vote

for the Democrats. But I'll tell you what I think. I think it's no accident they use a donkey to stand for their party."

He got a few chuckles and more than a few smiles. Plenty of the
guys who hung around the hall had known him for years. After he
made his speech, everybody went to the bar and hoisted a few. A
younger guy wearing a Ruptured Duck on the lapel of his tweed
jacket stuck a forefinger in Jerry's chest and declared, "The Germans
deserve every goddamn thing that happened to them. I was there. I
saw . . . Hell, Mr. Duncan, you don't want to know most of what
I saw." He gulped down his highball.

"I don't say they don't. I've never said they don't," Jerry answered.
"What I do say is, our boys don't deserve what's happening to them
in Germany right now. We won the war. We knocked the Nazis flat.
Isn't that enough?"

"They aren't knocked flat enough," the newly returned soldier
said. He hurried back to the bar and reloaded. Then he planted himself in front of Jerry Duncan again.

"They won't cause any more trouble now," Duncan said confidently. "They can't. We've got the atomic bomb, and they don't. If
they get out of line—*wham!* We blow 'em off the map."

"What about the Russians?" asked the guy with the Ruptured
Duck.

"Well, what about the Russians?" Jerry said confidently. "If you
believe General Groves, it'll be years and years before they figure out
how to make an atom bomb—if they ever do. And they won't let Germany get too big for its britches, either."

"Mm—maybe." The younger man didn't sound convinced. He
jabbed a forefinger at Jerry again. "And you waste too much time
with that crazy McGraw gal."

Before Jerry could answer that, a middle-aged guy in a chambray
shirt and dungarees spun the youngster toward him. "Diana McGraw
isn't crazy. My daughter graduated high school with her boy Pat. I've
known her and Ed since dirt. He fought the krauts the last go-round,
same as me, and he's been at Delco-Remy ever since. And Diana . . .
How do you expect her to feel when her only son gets bumped off
after the goddamn war's supposed to be over and done with?"

" 'Supposed to be' is right. Thanks, Art," Jerry said.

"Any time, Jerry," Art answered. "Me, I dunno if I'd go whole hog, the way Diana went and did. But, hey—I've got girls. They didn't have to head out and get their asses shot off. Uh, pardon my French."

"Maybe," the new vet said again. Then he went off to finish the fresh highball somewhere else.

Art laughed. "We whipsawed him, you and me."

"I guess we did," Jerry agreed. That wasn't exactly what he'd had in mind. Showing the other guy he was wrong—or showing him he'd get popped in the snoot if he kept mouthing off—wasn't how you won his vote. You made him like you. If he liked you, he wouldn't care whether you kept a cashbox marked BRIBES on your desk back in Washington. He'd vote for you because he thought you were a good fellow, and he wouldn't need any better reason.

Hell, there was no better reason.

Another man, one more of Jerry's vintage, came over to him and said, "Y'know, I hate like the dickens to cut and run in Germany."

"If you make a mistake, don't you try and get out from under it?" Jerry said. "If what we're doing in Germany isn't a mistake, what would you call it, Ron?"

Ron grinned—the Congressman remembered his name. Jerry remembered a gazillion names, but his constituents didn't think about that. They just noticed that he remembered *theirs*. Jerry nodded to himself. *Make them like you,* he repeated silently. Nothing made somebody like you more than recalling his name. It made him seem important in your eyes . . . regardless of whether he really was.

"Well, we did mess up some," Ron allowed now.

"Oh, maybe a little," Jerry allowed. In another tone of voice, it would have been polite agreement. The way he said it, it sounded more like the understatement of the year.

Several of the guys standing around laughed. Two or three, though, scowled instead. One of them made a point of turning his back on Jerry. In Nazi Germany or Red Russia, that kind of rudeness would have bought him a ticket to a concentration camp, or maybe to a firing squad. In Anderson, Indiana, it only meant he wouldn't vote Republican when the election rolled around.

As far as Jerry was concerned, that was bad enough. He wasn't ready to hang out his shingle and go back to practicing law, even if he would make more money here in Anderson than he did in Washington. Politics was as addictive as morphine. To Jerry, it had a sharper kick, too.

A PRIVATE STUCK HIS HEAD INTO LOU WEISSBERG'S OFFICE. "SIR, there's a Frenchy outside who wants to talk to you," the kid said.

"Yeah?" Lou set down his pen. "Does he speaka da English?"

"No, sir. But he had a piece of paper with your name written on it. He's a skinny guy; looks kinda mean, y'know? Got a scar right here." The private ran a finger along the side of his jaw.

"Ah. Okay. I know who he is." Lou was depressingly aware he might make a good target for Heydrich's fanatics. But if that wasn't Captain Desroches, the Nazis had come up with somebody who could play him in the movies.

"You want I should bring him in?" the GI asked.

Lou pushed back his swivel chair. "Nah. I'll go out there and talk to him. Any excuse to get outside is a good one."

Spring was in the air. So was the stench of death, which winter chill had muted, but Lou ignored that. Pigeons and house sparrows hopping on the rubble-strewn street crowded hopefully around his boots, looking for handouts. Starlings in shiny breeding plumage trilled from any high spot they could find. He might have seen and heard the like back in New Jersey. He wished like anything he were back in Jersey.

But he wasn't, so. . . . So he watched storks build a big, untidy nest of sticks on top of a chimney. He wouldn't have seen that in New Jersey, and neither would Roger Tory Peterson.

Captain Desroches, by his expression, didn't give two whoops in hell about spring, pigeons, sparrows, starlings, or storks. The Gauloise he was puffing on insulated him from the death reek, though it might have smelled worse.

Lou wondered why the Frenchmen had ridden all the way to Nuremberg. As soon as Desroches saw him, Lou stopped wondering. The French officer's face lit up in an I-told-you-so sneer. It couldn't possibly be anything else.

And it wasn't. "A good day to you, *Herr Oberleutnant,*" Des-

roches said in his Gallic German. "I have for you news from Hechingen."

"*Guten Tag, Herr Hauptmann,*" Lou answered resignedly. "Tell
me the news, whatever it is."

"There was indeed a fearsome raid by these vicious and savage
German renegades." Desroches was as good at the mock-epic as anybody this side of Alexander Pope.

"I'm glad you survived." Mock-epic was beyond Lou. Sarcastic he
could manage, even in German.

"Oh, yes. A great relief. The terrible monsters struck . . . the rubbish heap outside the building where some of the Nazi scientists got
seized last year." Captain Desroches stubbed out his butt and started
another smoke screen.

A sparrow darted in to grab the dog-end, then spat it out after one
taste. Lou's sympathies were with the bird. Before long, though, some
German would gladly scavenge the butt. Collect three or four of them
and you could roll one nasty cigarette of your own and either smoke
it or use it to buy something you needed more.

But that was by the way. "Did the fanatics get anything?" Lou demanded.

"Rubbish, I assume." Desroches inhaled till his already hollow
cheeks looked downright skull-like. "What else is there in a rubbish
heap?"

"Well, I don't exactly know." That was truer than Lou wished it
were. Nobody above him wanted to tell him much about what went
into making an atomic bomb. He couldn't blame his superiors for
that, but ignorance made his job harder. "Maybe you'd better tell
your story to Captain Frank."

Desroches exhaled an exasperated cloud of smoke. "This is a
waste of my time, Lieutenant."

"If you wasted enough time to drive to Nuremberg and gloat, you
can damn well waste a little more. Come on."

They glared at each other in perfect mutual loathing. But Captain
Desroches came. "Hello, Lou," Captain Frank said when Weissberg
led the French intelligence officer into his cubbyhole. "Who's your
friend?"

"Sir, this is Captain Desroches. He doesn't speak English, but he's fine with German," Lou answered in the latter tongue. He nodded to Desroches. "Please tell Captain Frank the story you just told me."

"If you insist." Desroches had the air of a man humoring an obvious lunatic. He gave Frank the tale almost word-for-word the way Lou had heard it. "But for the warning from your bright young lieutenant here," he finished, plainly meaning anything but, "we never would have noticed the garbage-hounds at all. As things were, we fired a few shots, they fired a few shots, and then they ran away. It was, I assure you, nothing to get excited about."

Captain Frank didn't look assured. "You say this was outside the place where the German scientists got caught?"

"Yes, I do say that. But so what?" Any comic who wanted to play a Frenchman on the stage would have studied Desroches' shrug. "A scientist's rubbish is no different from anyone else's, *nicht wahr?*"

"I don't know about that—but I think I'd better find out."

As far as Lou could tell, Captain Frank didn't know much more about atom bombs than he did himself. The French captain watched alertly as Frank spoke. Lou suspected Desroches followed more English than he let on.

After talking with somebody, Captain Frank hung up and called someone else. He told Desroches' story over again. There was a long, long pause at the other end of the line. Then whoever was there shouted, *"Son of a motherfucking bitch!"* Lou heard it loud and clear. So did Captain Desroches, who raised an eyebrow. It must have damn near blown out Frank's eardrum.

The other officer went on at lower volume for some little while. Captain Frank listened. He scribbled a couple of notes. When he finally rang off, he nodded to Captain Desroches. "Well, thank you for bringing the news. Now we know what we're up against, anyhow."

"Which is?" Desroches inquired acidly.

Howard Frank looked right through him. Lou admired that look, and wanted to practice it in front of a mirror. It would cow every rude waiter and sales clerk ever born. "Sorry, but I can't tell you," Frank said. "You haven't got the clearance or the need to know."

"This is an outrage!" Desroches was almost as loud as the fellow who'd talked with Frank on the phone. Lou looked for him to breathe flame, or for steam to pour out of his ears. "You have no right—"

"I have my orders, Captain," Frank replied. "I'm sure you understand." *I'm sure you understand you can fuck off,* he meant.

Desroches called him several things in German. Captain Frank only smiled blandly. Desroches switched to French. Lou hadn't thought French was much of a language to cuss in. He discovered he'd never heard an expert before. Captain Desroches sounded electrifying, or possibly electrified.

Captain Frank never lost his smile. When the Frenchman slowed down a little, Frank said, *"Et vous. Et votre mère aussi."* Even Lou could figure out what that meant. Desroches stormed out. He slammed the door behind him. It didn't fly off its hinges, but not from lack of effort.

"Wow," Lou said, listening to Desroches roar down the corridor like a tornado with shoulder boards. Then he asked, "So what was that all about?"

"I talked with this guy named Samuel Goudsmit. He's a colonel, I think—some kind of science officer," Frank said.

"Goudsmit," Lou said musingly. "Kraut?"

"Dutchman," Captain Frank replied. "And now I know what the fanatics were after—what it looks like they got."

"Nu?" Lou said.

"Ten grams of radium, Goudsmit says. The physicists snatched it there when we grabbed them, and one of them must've blabbed to Heydrich."

"Fuck," Lou muttered. Then he asked, "How can Goudsmit know that?"

"When the German big brains were in England, they were wired for sound, only they didn't know it. A couple of them talked about this radium."

"Fuck," Lou said again. "If we knew about it, how come we didn't go in there ourselves and take it away?"

"Good question—damn good," Frank said. "Best answer I can give you is, we didn't want to tip off the frogs that they were sitting on something important."

Lou clapped a hand to his forehead. *"Gevalt!* And so the Nazis get it instead. Ain't that a kick in the nuts? What can Heydrich do with the shit?"

"Like I know. I told you once already, I ain't no Einstein," Captain Frank said. "But you've gotta figure they think they can do *something,* anyhow. Otherwise, they wouldn't have gone after it, right?"

"Right," Lou said glumly. "Can they make a bomb with it?"

"Beats me." Frank held up a hand. "No, I take that back. I bet they can't. We used B-29s to clobber Hiroshima and Nagasaki, so those bombs musta been big old mothers. Ten grams isn't much. It's like—what? Half an ounce? Not even. So I figure no way in hell they make it go boom. You think I'm wrong?"

"Well, the way you say it, it makes sense, but I'm no slide-rule jockey, either," Lou said. "If they can't make a bomb out of it, what can they do?"

Captain Frank's shrug wasn't so elaborate as Captain Desroches', but it got the message across. "Goudsmit says he'll let our guys with the thick glasses know about it. We'll see where we go from there, that's all."

"From there, or from wherever the fanatics take us." After a moment, Lou added, "Too bad we didn't trust our own allies with the news about the radium."

"Uh-huh." Howard Frank nodded. "But if all these Frenchmen are like Desroches, you can see how come we didn't, too."

DIANA MCGRAW WONDERED WHEN A SECRETARY OF STATE HAD LAST made a speech in Indianapolis. She wondered whether a Secretary of State had ever made a speech in Indianapolis before. A Secretary of Agriculture or a Secretary of Commerce, possibly—probably, even.

But State? Indianapolis wasn't where you went when you talked about foreign policy. Only now it was. And Diana knew why, too, or thought she did. Would James Byrnes have come here if she didn't live in nearby Anderson? Would he have talked about Germany here if she hadn't started the movement to get Americans out of the defeated country? She was sure he wouldn't have. You dropped a bucket of water where something was already burning, didn't you?

Secretary Byrnes spoke inside the Indiana National Guard Armory, a formidable pile of yellow-brown brick—the color of diarrhea, actually—up on North Pennsylvania. Nobody'd advertised his speech in the papers. No one on the radio had mentioned that he would be there.

So what? Diana thought. She had connections now. She'd known for most of a week that Byrnes would be here. And so she and her cohorts marched outside the armory. These past months, she'd grown intimately familiar with the way a picket sign's stick pressed against your collarbone as you paraded. Her sign today said HOW MANY MORE WILL DIE FOR NOTHING?: bloody red letters on a white background.

Bored-looking cops stood by the entrance to make sure her people didn't try to go inside and disrupt the meeting of the Indiana Internationalists or whoever they were. *Byrnes' stooges. Truman's stooges,* Diana thought scornfully. The cops were bored because they'd seen she and her people played by the rules.

She would have loved to storm the podium in there. She would have loved to scream at Secretary Byrnes. Come to that, she would have loved to chuck a grenade at him. But going over the line like that lost supporters. *Not drawing to an inside straight,* Ed called it. Diana played bridge, not poker, but she understood what her husband meant.

The Indiana Internationalists—or whoever they were—had rigged up loudspeakers so the pickets could hear the Secretary of State even if they weren't allowed inside. Maybe they thought wise words of wisdom spoken wisely would show the poor heathens out on the sidewalk the error of their ways and lead them back to the true faith.

If they did, they were even dumber than Diana gave them credit for. She wouldn't have believed such a thing was possible, but hey, you never could tell.

"We will not forsake Europe." Heard through big, cheap speakers, James Byrnes' voice grated unpleasantly. "I want no misunderstanding. We will not shirk our duty. We are staying there."

People inside the armory applauded. People outside booed. For a while, Diana couldn't make out what the Secretary of State was saying. She shrugged, which made the stick shift against her dress. What difference did it make whether she heard or not? Anybody who spoke for the government would be telling lies anyhow.

When the noise subsided, Byrnes was continuing in the same vein: "In 1917 the United States was forced into the first World War. After that war we refused to join the League of Nations. We thought we could stay out of Europe's wars and we lost interest in the affairs of Europe."

"What a buncha baloney!" Ed McGraw yelled from right behind Diana. Marching back and forth hurt his poor torn-up foot, but he'd come along tonight.

She was the one who drew the attention, though. "What do you think of the Secretary of State's speech so far?" E. A. Stuart asked her, poising pencil above notebook to await her reply.

"It's nothing we haven't heard before. It's nothing we haven't heard way too often before," Diana answered. "The Truman administration is going to do whatever it wants to do, and it won't pay any attention to what the little man wants, to what the people want."

The reporter's shorthand spread pothooks and squiggles across the page. "How do you propose to change his policies?"

"By showing him he has no popular support. By winning lots of seats for people who oppose his occupation policies in November," Diana said.

James Byrnes' voice kept on blaring from the tinny loudspeakers: "We will not again make that mistake. We have helped to organize the United Nations. We believe it will stop aggressor nations from starting wars. The American people want to help the German people to win their way back to an honorable place among the free and peace-loving nations of the world."

More applause inside. More boos outside. Diana turned to E. A. Stuart. "Whenever the President or one of his flunkies talks about what the American people want, they're really talking about what Harry Truman wants." Stuart wrote down the quote without slowing up.

Diana stopped then, because she wanted to tell the reporter something else. "Keep moving, there!" one of the cops called, setting a hand on his billy club.

She kept moving. She didn't want to give the police any excuse to get rough. As she marched, she bitterly added, "How peace-loving do the German people seem to *you*, Mr. Stuart?"

"They have their ups and downs, all right," Stuart agreed.

So did the Secretary of State. After his series of polite phrases, he got down to the meat of his speech. So it seemed to Diana, anyhow, though she wasn't so sure Byrnes would have agreed. "The United States is not about to abandon Europe," he declared. "Security forces will probably have to remain in Germany for a long period. Some of you will know that we have offered a proposal for a treaty with the major powers to enforce peace for twenty-five or even forty years."

"There!" Diana pounced. She felt as if the enemy—for so she thought of James Byrnes—had delivered himself into her hands. "Did you hear that, Mr. Stuart? *Did* you? He's talking about American soldiers in Germany *in 1986*! Forty years from now! That's what Truman really wants!"

"He did say that. I heard it." Wonder filled E. A. Stuart's voice. He scribbled some more as he walked beside Diana. "We've got another guy listening inside, but I can't afford to let that get by. Forty years from now. Oh, boy."

Not everybody seemed to have caught it. Maybe most people out here weren't listening so closely. Or maybe they just didn't want to believe what they'd heard. How could you imagine trying to hold Germany down in 1986? Didn't you have to be a little bit nuts, or more than a little bit, to think you could get away with something like that for so long?

Of course you did. Diana McGraw had no doubts on that score. Why, Jesus Himself hadn't lived for forty years. If God wouldn't have been able to hold things together that long, who did Harry S Truman think he was?

Somebody in a Studebaker driving up Pennsylvania honked and yelled, "Goddamn Commies!" A moment later, somebody driving down Pennsylvania really leaned on his horn and shouted, "You stinking Nazis!"

Diana laughed. "Doesn't that bother you?" E. A. Stuart asked her.

"Not any more. It used to, but now I don't care," she answered truthfully. "If some people think we're Reds and some people think we're Nazis, chances are we're really right where I want us to be—in the middle. We're the genuine Americans. The ones who screech at us, they're the lunatic fringe."

"Huh." That was one of the more thoughtful grunts Diana had ever heard.

Inside, Secretary Byrnes finally finished his speech. The blind fools who'd sat there listening to all that hot air—so they seemed to Diana, anyhow—gave him a big hand. To get one like that after such a speech, he had to be the best hypnotist since . . . What was the name of that character in the potboiler novel? They'd made a silent movie about him, too. Diana grinned as she dredged it up. The Phantom of the Opera, that's who he was.

James Byrnes didn't want to play the Phantom of the Armory. As Truman had in Washington, he came out to talk to the people protesting his policies. City policemen and khaki-uniformed state troopers with drill-sergeant hats surrounded him, but loosely. Experience had taught them that Diana and her group wouldn't try anything drastic.

Experience had its virtues. If you relied on it too much, though . . .

"You murderer!" a woman screamed, and hurled herself at the Secretary of State. "How much American blood's on your hands?" She had blood—or, more likely, red paint—all over hers. She left James Byrnes with one messy scarlet handprint on his jacket and another on his white shirt and necktie.

Before she could do anything else to him—if she had anything else in mind—the startled police officers woke up and wrestled her to the ground. "You're under arrest!" an Indianapolis policeman yelled.

"Assault on a federal official!" a state trooper added. "That's a felony!"

Another trooper rounded on Diana. "Clear your people out of here right now, lady," he snapped. "They stick around, we'll run 'em in for conspiring with this gal here. That goes for you, too."

"We'll go," Diana said. "I don't know who that woman is—I want you to know that. I never saw her before."

"Yeah, I'd say the same thing if I was in your shoes," the state trooper retorted. "That doesn't make it true. And even if it is—well, so what? You go around talking nonsense all the time, of course you'll draw the loonies. A magnet picks up nails, right?"

"We aren't talking nonsense," Diana said indignantly. "Were you there?"

"Better believe it. I was lucky. I just got a little crease in my, uh, backside. My brother Matt lost a leg. We run home now, we'll only have to do it all over again before too long."

"I don't think so," Diana said. "And the war isn't over, no matter what kind of papers the Germans signed a year ago. We're *already* doing it all over again. Can't you see that's wrong?"

"No." Hostility roughened the trooper's voice. He glanced down at his wristwatch. "You and your chowderheads have one minute to get lost. After that, we start arresting people. One minute from . . . *now*. Fifty-nine . . . Fifty-eight . . ."

"Chowderheads!" Diana exploded. But, thanks to that woman who'd gone too far, whoever she was, the trooper had the law on his side. And Diana was bitterly certain the cops would seize the excuse to keep a closer eye on her people whenever they tried to march. She wanted to cry. She wanted to swear. All she could do was retreat.

BERNIE COBB DROVE ONE OF THE MIDDLE JEEPS IN A CONVOY BOUND from Erlangen up to Frankfurt. The Americans had taken longer than the Russians to adopt that approach, but it seemed to work . . . as well as anything did. A jeep traveling alone in Germany was in deadly danger, as General Patton could have testified if he were in a position to testify about anything. A jeep in the middle of a convoy was just in danger.

German POWs cleared brush and shrubs back from the sides of the road. GIs with grease guns guarded them. "We shoulda started doin' that a long time ago," drawled Bernie's passenger, an ordnance sergeant named Toby Benton. "If they can't hide, they can't shoot their goddamn rockets at us."

"Hot damn," Bernie said. "So they lay back a few hundred yards and cut us into dogmeat with their goddamn Spandaus instead. Is that better?"

"Some," Sergeant Benton said. He looked very ready to use the jeep's machine gun, a big, beautiful .50-caliber piece. It outranged and outshot any German MG42. But the son of a bitch behind a Spandau could wait in ambush till he found a target he liked, squeeze off a burst, and then disappear. Clearing roadside bushes back a hundred yards would make things tougher for assholes with a *Panzerschreck* or *Panzerfaust*. It wouldn't come within miles of curing all the Americans' problems here.

Which reminded Bernie . . . "How come they want you up in Frankfurt, anyway?"

Benton only shrugged. "Some kind of rumor that the fanatics planted a bomb in our settlement there. I'm supposed to check it out.

If anybody can find that kind of shit, I'm the guy." He spoke like a master plumber: he was the fellow other plumbers called when they couldn't find a leak or fix one themselves.

"You really that good?" Bernie was impressed in spite of himself.

"I've been doin' it since before the surrender, and I'm still in one piece. So are a bunch of other guys," Benton answered. "The krauts, they're pretty sneaky, but I've learned to be sneaky the same way."

"Sounds good to me." Bernie swerved around a freshly repaired pothole. Maybe the fix was legit, or maybe it concealed a land mine. Sure as hell, the diehards were pretty sneaky. He noticed every jeep in front of him had also dodged the pothole. Either the ones behind him also swerved or else it really was okay, because nothing went boom. Things not going boom was one of the sweetest sounds Bernie had ever heard.

He hadn't been up to Frankfurt before. Erlangen hadn't suffered badly during the war. Nuremberg had. Frankfurt was bigger than Nuremberg—say, about the size of Pittsburgh or St. Louis. It looked as if God had stomped on the town and then ground in his heel. And so He had, except He'd used B-17s and B-24s and Lancasters instead of a mile-long boot.

"Boy, oh boy," Bernie said. "You look at a place like this, you wonder how anybody lived through the bombing."

"People always do," Toby Benton said. "I guess maybe that's how come we made the atom bomb. Drop one of those suckers and that's all she wrote."

"I'd drop one on Heydrich in a red-hot minute if it'd stop all the crap we've gone through," Bernie said. The ordnance sergeant nodded. Bernie couldn't think of a single dogface in Germany who wouldn't make that deal.

He honked his horn to warn the Jerries in a labor gang to get out of his way. They stepped aside, though none of them moved any faster than he had to. Regulations said German men weren't supposed to wear *Wehrmacht* uniform any more, but these guys either hadn't got the news or, more likely, didn't have anything else. They were skinny and pale—hell, most of them looked green—and badly shaven.

"Some master race, huh?" Benton said.

"You betcha," Bernie agreed. Looking down your nose at the Germans was easy—unless one of the bastards carried an antitank rocket or had dynamite and nails under his raggedy tunic or drove a truck full of explosive till he found a bunch of GIs all together and pressed down on the firing button wired to his steering wheel.

Hausfraus queued patiently for cabbages or potatoes or whatever the guy in the shop was doling out. Most of them looked shabbier than their menfolk. They'd got even less in the way of clothes than German soldiers had. The stuff they were wearing was falling to pieces and years out of style and had been dumpy to begin with. A couple of them had on cut-down *Feldgrau*—probably the only cloth they owned. Their complexions were also fishbelly pale. A few of them had put on rouge and mascara. It made things worse, not better— Bernie thought of so many made-up corpses.

A block or two farther on, a buxom young *Fräulein* walked hand in hand with a GI. Nothing wrong with *her* complexion, by God—she was radiantly pink. She had meat on her bones, too: luxuriantly curved meat. Her dress didn't cover all that much of her, and clung to what it did cover. The American soldier on whom she bestowed her favors looked as if he'd invented her—but not even Thomas Edison was that smart.

"Some hardass MP spots them, he'll get in trouble for fraternizing," Sergeant Benton said.

"Worth it," Bernie declared. The ordnance specialist didn't try to tell him he was wrong.

Right in the middle of Frankfurt, behind a barbed-wire fence nine feet high, was another world. The Army had built what amounted to an American suburb for something close to a thousand families of U.S. occupation officials and high-ranking officers.

Close to half a million Germans lived in postwar misery all around them, but they had it as good as they would have back in the States— better, because they couldn't have afforded servants there. Except for those servants, the enclave was off-limits to Germans. Electricity ran twenty-four hours a day there, not two hours a day as it did in the rest of Frankfurt. The enclave boasted movie theaters, beauty shops, a gas station, a supermarket, a community center, and anything else the homesick Yankee soul might desire.

"Holy Moses," Bernie said as he drove up to the gate in front of the guardhouse. "No wonder they keep this place behind barbed wire. If you were a kraut, you wouldn't need to be one of Heydrich's goons to want to blow it to kingdom come."

"Yeah, that's crossed my mind a time or three, too," Toby Benton agreed. "But if you're just a little guy like us, what can you do about it? Try and make sure the fanatics don't sneak in any bombs—that's all I can see. And that's what I'm here for."

Guards inspected the jeep with microscopic care before they let it into the enclave. The kids playing there didn't wear rags. They didn't look as if a strong breeze would blow them away. Fords and De Sotos rolled along the clean, rubble-free streets. Bernie wondered for a second where the hell he really was.

Yeah, if the Jerries saw this . . . But Bernie Cobb shook his head. *If they don't like what they've got now, they shouldn't have lined up behind Hitler back then,* he thought.

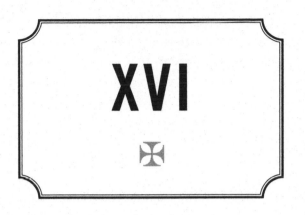

XVI

Vladimir Bokov watched Germans go back and forth between the Russian and American zones in Berlin. The spectacle struck him as too anarchic for comfort. He turned to Moisei Shteinberg. "Comrade Colonel, we need to tighten this up," he said. "People we should keep can get into one of the Western Allies' Berlin zones easy as you please, and from there they can leave the Soviet zone of Germany altogether. And the Western Allies have such bad security, bandits can hide in their zones for as long as they want. Then they cross over and attack us."

Shteinberg nodded. Captain Bokov hadn't expected anything else. No NKVD man could go far wrong talking about the need to tighten up. And Shteinberg worried about things Bokov hadn't even thought of: "It wouldn't surprise me if the Anglo-Americans let Heydrich's hyenas move about freely in their zones here. There always was talk about the USA and Britain lining up with the Hitlerites against the Soviet Union."

"*Da.* There was," Bokov agreed. No NKVD man could go far wrong by assuming all the enemies of the USSR were plotting together, either. "If we have to, we ought to build a wall between our zone and theirs, to make sure only the proper people pass from one to the other."

"I'd like that," Shteinberg said. "I'd like blockading the Western Allies' Berlin zones to force them out of here even better. They didn't spend their blood taking this city. We did. It should be ours by right of conquest. But . . ."

"But what?" Bokov said. "That's a wonderful idea, sir! We ought to do it! We ought to start right away!"

"Unfortunately, the international situation does not permit it. Believe me, Comrade Captain, I've had discussions with our superiors about this." Shteinberg sighed mournfully. "They fear deviating from the Four-Power agreement on Berlin would touch off a war. The military's judgment—and the Politburo's—is that we can't afford one now."

"Well . . ." Bokov had trouble arguing with that. Anyone who'd seen what the fight against the Nazis had done to the Soviet Union would. Yes, Eastern Europe obeyed Marshal Stalin's every wish and busily remade itself on the Soviet model. Yes, the hammer-and-sickle flag flew in Berlin. But oh, the price of planting it here . . . !

"And there is another concern," Shteinberg continued inexorably. "If we fight the United States, we risk the atom bomb. Till we also have this weapon, we have to be more cautious than we would if it did not exist."

"Well . . ." That also made more sense than Captain Bokov wished it did. "How long till we build our own?"

"I don't know, Volodya," Shteinberg said with a shrug. "Till the Americans used one, I never dreamt anything like that was possible. I'm sure our people are doing everything they can."

"Oh, so am I!" Bokov exclaimed. If all the free physicists in the USSR and all the ones who'd gone into the gulag for one reason or another (or for no reason at all—nobody knew better than an NKVD man that you didn't always need a reason to end up in a camp) weren't working twenty-one-hour days in pursuit of uranium, he would have been astonished.

"And we will have taken some German physicists back to the motherland, I'm sure, the same as we've taken some rocket engineers," Shteinberg said.

Bokov nodded. "No doubt. Everybody knows the German rocket engineers are good, though—the Americans have grabbed the ones we didn't. But the Fascists couldn't make an atom bomb—"

"A good thing, too, or they would have used it on us," his superior broke in.

That seemed too likely even to rate a nod. Bokov went on with his own train of thought: "How good are their physicists? How much can they help us?"

"If they can't, they'll be sorry." Cold anticipation filled Shteinberg's voice. A German brought to the USSR who earned his keep might get good treatment. A German who didn't . . . was gulag fodder. If he died in a camp, well, the gulags never ran short of bodies.

But Bokov found something else to worry about. "What about the physicists the Heydrichites snatched up, the ones England turned loose in Germany?" he said. "How much harm can they do? They're probably better men than the ones we took." He was resigned to the fact that the more capable German scientists and engineers had wanted to get captured by the Anglo-Americans, not the Red Army.

"They can't make Heydrich a bomb." Shteinberg sounded completely confident about that. "And if they can't make him a bomb, they're a nuisance, a propaganda coup, an embarrassment to what passes for England's security system."

"We understand propaganda. So do the Fascist jackals—Hitler made a point of it in *Mein Kampf*. But the Anglo-Americans?" Bokov shook his head. "Only when it bites them." He went on, "Do you think the bandits can actually make them take their troops out of the zones they occupy? The last thing we need is a Germany where the Nazis are running free again."

"You think so, do you?" Shteinberg's irony had as many barbs as a porcupine's quill. He was an NKVD man. He was a Soviet citizen. Though no doubt officially an unbeliever, he was a Jew. Even Jews who didn't believe remained Jews; like most Russians, Bokov was convinced of that. The colonel continued, "I have no idea what the Anglo-Americans will do next. I often think they have no idea what they'll do next."

"But if they should walk away from the occupation?" Bokov persisted. "What do *we* do then?"

Moisei Shteinberg's gaze put Bokov in mind of Murmansk winter.

The junior officer was glad it wasn't aimed straight at him. "In that case," Shteinberg said quietly, "we do whatever we have to do."

"No, no, no," a Democratic Congressman said, exasperation filling his voice. "No one is talking about pulling American troops out of Germany, and—"

"If the distinguished gentleman from New York doesn't think anybody is talking about bringing our boys home from Germany, I suggest that he'd better pull his head out of the sand," a Republican broke in.

Bang! Sam Rayburn rapped loudly for order. "That will be enough of that," the Speaker of the House declared. "As a matter of fact, that's too much of that."

"Sorry, Mr. Speaker." The Republican sounded anything but. Still, he observed the forms.

It's getting rough, Jerry Duncan thought. After Pearl Harbor, foreign policy had been thoroughly bipartisan. Before Pearl Harbor, with the exception of a few war-related measures like Lend-Lease, foreign policy had barely been on the House's radar screen (and nobody'd ever heard of radar). But now the two sides were going at each other like a bucket of crawdads.

"Thank you, Mr. Speaker," the Democrat from New York said pointedly. "If I may take up my remarks from the point where I was interrupted . . . No one is talking about pulling our troops out of Germany. And even if we were to remove them for any reason, the Russians would not proceed to occupy the western zones. I can guarantee that, because—"

He got interrupted again, by a different Republican this time: "How can you guarantee it? Who told you? God? God's the only one who knows what the Reds are liable to do next."

Bang! Speaker Rayburn wielded the gavel again. "If you let the gentleman finish, maybe he'll tell you how he can guarantee it."

"*Thank* you, Mr. Speaker," the Democrat repeated. "As a matter of fact, I was about to do that. The Russians won't invade western Germany because we will drive them out with atom bombs, if necessary."

"Or maybe we'll just let them keep it," another Democrat put in.

"We know we can deal with Uncle Joe—we've been doing it since 1941. But does anybody want to let the Nazis get up off the mat after all we did to knock 'em flat? That's what taking our troops out of Germany means, whether you like it or not."

Jerry muttered under his breath. That was the administration's trump card. Truman and his backers tried to make anybody who favored removing troops from Germany seem pro-Nazi. As far as Jerry was concerned, it wasn't even slightly fair. "Mr. Speaker!" he called, jumping to his feet.

"Mr. Duncan has the floor," Sam Rayburn intoned.

"Thank you, Mr. Speaker. The problem is, thousands of our men are getting killed and maimed for no good reason. Thousands, Mr. Speaker, more than a year after this war was alleged to be over. And for what? For what? Are we one inch closer to putting down the German fanatics than we were the day after what was called V-E Day? If we are, where's the evidence?"

"Are you asking me, Mr. Duncan?" Rayburn inquired. "I am not a military man, nor do I pretend to be."

"I understand that, Mr. Speaker," Jerry said. "But the military men have no answers, either. They say so-and-so many fanatics have been killed. So-and-so many bunkers have been uncovered, and so-and-so many weapons have been captured or destroyed. And I say, so-and-so what? They don't say the fanatics will quit any time soon. They don't say the fanatics will quit at all—which seems wise, because they show no signs of quitting. But if these men show no signs of quitting, if we can't put them down, *what are we doing there?* Besides wasting American lives and American taxpayers' money, I mean?"

"I will speak to that," the Democrat from New York said.

"By all means," Rayburn told him. "Please go ahead."

"Thank you, Mr. Speaker," the New Yorker said.

He had even more reason to be polite than Jerry did. Jerry was on the other side; he wouldn't get anything out of Sam Rayburn no matter what. But a Democrat who offended the Speaker of the House could find himself almost as unhappy about his office space and his committee assignments as your run-of-the-mill Republican. Like a lot of politicians, Rayburn had a long memory for slights.

The Democrat from New York turned to Jerry Duncan. "What

we're currently doing in our occupation zone—and what our allies are doing in theirs—is very simple. We are preventing Heydrich and the Nazis from taking over Germany again. President Truman thinks that's a job worth doing. I agree with him."

It was certainly the strongest argument the Democrats had. Nobody in the United States—hell, nobody in his right mind—had a good word to say about the Nazis. "Is this the best way to do that, though? Is this even close to the best way?" Jerry asked. "We were supposed to have knocked the Nazis over the head last May. How long will we have to stay in Germany? The Secretary of State talked about forty years. Do you want your grandsons shot at by German partisans in 1986? Do you think the American people will put up with spending forty years and God knows how many billions of dollars trying to drain a running sore?"

"If we leave, Heydrich wins. Do you want that?" the New Yorker said.

"If we stay, we throw away thousand—tens of thousands—of lives and those billions of dollars. Do you want *that*?" Jerry countered.

"We can't let the fanatics drive us out," the Democrat said.

"We can't let them bleed us white, either," Jerry Duncan said. "They pick their spots. They plant mines under a road or bombs in wreckage beside it. Our boys can't pick up an ashtray without being afraid it'll blow up in their hand. They can't take a drink without being afraid it's poisoned—look what the fanatics did to the Russians on New Year's Eve. And when one of those maniacs with a truckload of explosives blows himself up, he costs Heydrich one man. He doesn't cost him a truck, 'cause that's one of ours, stolen. He takes out anywhere from a dozen to a hundred GIs. And we can't stop it. By all the signs, we can't even slow it down. Are you looking forward to forty more years of that?"

By the look on the Democratic Congressman's face, he was looking forward to getting the hell out of there and having a long, stiff drink—or maybe three or four long, stiff drinks. "We are paying a price," he said. Sam Rayburn jerked like a man who'd just found out he had a flea in his shorts. Democrats weren't even supposed to admit that much. Doing his best to make amends, the New Yorker hurriedly went on, "But we'd pay a much higher price if we cut and run. We might pay the price of World War III."

"So you're saying it's worthwhile to go right on bleeding till 1986?" Jerry asked.

"I don't believe we'll have to do that, or anything like that," the Democrat from New York said. "I think we can defeat the fanatics in a reasonable amount of time. I think we will, too."

Jerry pounced: "Then you'd favor a timetable for getting all our troops out of Germany?"

"I didn't say that!" the New Yorker squawked.

"Sure sounded like you did," Jerry said. By Sam Rayburn's glower, he felt the same way.

"President Truman has said a timeline is unacceptable. I agree with him. A timeline just tells the enemy how long he has to wait before he wins," the Democrat from New York said.

"In that case, you *don't* really believe we can lick Heydrich's goons in some reasonable time," Jerry said. "You believe we'll still be stuck there when that time is up. And you know what? I think we will, too. So what's the point of waiting around and taking more casualties? Let's bring the boys home now!"

Several people listening to the debate up in the gallery started to applaud. Sam Rayburn used his gavel. "Order! Order!" he called. They went on clapping. He banged the gavel some more. "We must have order," he declared. "I will have the gallery cleared if this continues."

Slowly, the people who'd applauded quieted down. Jerry figured he'd made his point, at least to them. The unhappy look on the New York Democrat's face said he did, too.

"Wow!" Lou Weissberg eyed the swarms of GIs with grease guns and M-1s, the halftracks, and the Pershing heavy tanks surrounding the Nuremberg jail. Mustang fighters roared low overhead. "We could've captured half of Germany with a force this big."

"Yeah, well . . ." Howard Frank let his voice trail off. He needed a few seconds to find a way to say what he was thinking. When he did, it turned out to be bleakly, blackly cynical: "Look how much all our security helped old Adenauer."

Lou grunted. In a way, that was applicable. In another way, it wasn't. "Heydrich's goons wanted Adenauer dead. You gotta figure they'll try a rescue here if they try anything at all."

"Who knows? Who the hell knows anything any more?" Captain Frank said wearily. "We've given 'em a big concentration of our own troops to shoot at, and an asshole with a mortar is awful hard to catch." Another P-51 thundered past at just above rooftop height. "Even with planes overhead, he's still hard to catch," Frank continued with a mournful sigh. "And besides, maybe Heydrich wants the other Nazi big shots dead. Then nobody can claim he doesn't deserve to be *Führer.*"

"If he lets us try 'em, we'll take care of that for him," Lou said. "But he doesn't want to do that, either." He pointed northwest, toward the shattered Palace of Justice. "If the fanatics had let the trial go on, we would've hanged those bastards by now. Better than they deserve, too."

"You don't need to tell me, Lou. I already know." Frank might have been on the point of saying something more, but the doors to the jail opened. Out came MPs with grease guns, followed by the Nazi prisoners in civilian clothes. Göring and Hess were easy to recognize, even though they'd both dropped a lot of weight. The rest . . . Without their uniforms, without the power those uniforms conferred, they looked like a bunch of small-town shopkeepers and tradesmen, with maybe a lawyer and a doctor and a preacher thrown in.

There were almost two dozen of them all told. The MPs hustled them into four halftracks. Guards also scrambled up into the armored personnel carriers. The tanks and other armored vehicles rolled away to take the lead in the convoy. One by one, the halftracks with the important captives followed. The rear guard was at least as strong as the force that had gone before.

More American troops and vehicles waited along the route the armored convoy would take. Still more were posted along routes it might have taken but wouldn't. "I wonder how much this little move is costing the taxpayers," Lou remarked.

"You'll find out," Captain Frank said. "As soon as the jerks who want to make Heydrich happy and go home hear what the number is, they'll shout it from the housetops. Grab a copy of the *Chicago Tribune* or any Hearst paper and you'll see it."

"That's what I'm afraid of," Lou said. "Don't people understand the war's still cooking even if the krauts did sign a surrender?"

"Hey, if you get a scoop, who gives a shit what happens to the

poor goddamn dogfaces on the other side of the ocean?" Yeah, Frank
was in a cynical mood, all right.

Lou also had a strong opinion about what people like that could
do to themselves. It violated several commandments and other Biblical prohibitions, to say nothing of the laws of anatomy, physiology,
and probably physics. He expressed it anyhow. His superior laughed.
"Sideways," Lou added.

"Well, it's not like I don't feel the same way," Howard Frank said.
"But I'm just a poor goddamn dogface on the other side of the ocean,
too, far as they're concerned."

"Uh-huh." Letters from Lou's family—and, even more, letters
he'd tried and failed to write to them—had painfully proved to him
that he wasn't a civilian any more. He wondered if he ever could be
again. He had his doubts.

"But I think they're just what you called 'em," Frank said, "I'm
not gonna worry about 'em—not unless they make so much noise,
they don't let us do what we've gotta do over here."

"Sounds good to me, too, sir," Lou said. The last Pershing—
finally, an American tank that could match up with a Panther, only
it got to the battlefield a couple of months before Panthers went out
of business—rumbled away. Exhaust fumes choked the air.

"I just hope everything goes good on the other end, too," Captain
Frank said.

"Boy, me, too," Lou said. "Next stop . . ." He dropped to a whisper. He wasn't supposed to say where, even if the only guy who could
possibly hear already knew anyway. Bringing out the place had a
thrill of the forbidden: "Frankfurt."

THE TRUCK WAS A DEUCE-AND-A-HALF PAINTED OLIVE DRAB. WELL,
what the hell else would it be in Germany these days? The English
used them. So did the French. So did the Russians. And the Jerries had
used all the big American brutes they could capture. These babies
beat the crap out of the Opels and the other hunks of tin the krauts
had manufactured for themselves.

"Papers?" said the guard at the entrance to the American compound in Frankfurt.

Without a word, the driver passed them to him. The guard looked them over. They were in order. They looked in order, anyhow. It wasn't the same thing, but the guard didn't think of that.

"I've got to inspect your cargo," he said. The driver only nodded. The guard eyed him. "Watsamatter? Cat got your tongue, buddy?" The driver mimed tipping back a stein, or maybe a bottle. He held his head in both hands and rolled his eyes. The guard laughed. "Okay, okay. I've tied one on a few times, or maybe a few times too many. But I still gotta look at your stuff."

With a hesitant nod, the driver waved him on. The man was as pallid as if he'd got plastered the night before—that was for sure. The guard went around to the back of the truck. He scrambled up onto the rear bumper so he could look over the gate at what the canvas-covered truck body held.

Then he jumped down in a hurry. His own face felt as if it were on fire. He knew it had to be beet-red. Carton after cardboard carton, all with KOTEX printed on them in big, embarrassing scarlet letters. Soldiers' wives, officers' grown and mostly grown daughters . . . Sure, they'd need stuff like that, but a nineteen-year-old draftee didn't want to get reminded of it.

"Well, go on, goddammit." He tried to make his voice rough and deep, but it broke in the middle of the curse. Mortified anew, he waved the deuce-and-a-half forward.

It should have headed straight for the PX, which was for all practical purposes a supermarket. Instead, it made for the community center, right in the middle of the American compound in Frankfurt.

"Hey," the GI said to his companion, who hadn't bothered coming out of the guard shack. "What does he think he's doing?"

"What is he doing?" The other guard emerged to look. He was a year older, which only meant his whiskers rasped more when he rubbed his chin. "Sure doesn't know where he's going, does he?"

"No, and he oughta, unless . . ." A sudden, horrid suspicion filled the kid who'd waved the truck through. He raised his grease gun, and his voice. "Hey, you! Halt, or else I'll—!"

Too late. If there are two more mournful words in the English language, what could they possibly be? The truck was out of voice range, and almost out of grease-gun range. It hadn't been full of Kotex after all. It blew sky-high.

I'm in deep shit, the guard thought as he went ass over teakettle.

That was pretty goddamn mournful, too, but it needed more than two words. Then he slammed into what was left of a wall across the street from the compound. A rib broke. It stabbed him from the inside out. "Motherfuck!" he gasped, and got stabbed again. That wasn't mournful; it was half automatic, half furious.

At that, he was one of the lucky ones. When the German fanatic pressed the button on the steering wheel or wherever the hell it was, he'd got 300 yards—maybe even a quarter mile—into the compound: almost to the community center. He blasted himself to kingdom come, of course. He blew up twenty-nine U.S. soldiers, and seventy-three women, and nineteen children under the age of ten. The papers were very particular about that, for some reason. *Children under the age of ten,* they all said. The exploding truck wounded more than twice as many as it killed.

So the papers proclaimed right after the fanatic killed himself to strike at the USA. The luckless guard lay on a cot in a crowded room in a crowded Army hospital. His chest was bandaged so tight, he could hardly breathe. He had nothing to do—nothing he could do—but read the papers and listen to the radio that sat on a wall shelf in one corner of the room.

A broken rib. That wasn't so much. After a while, you'd get better. Except the guard didn't. He lost his appetite—easy enough to do with Army chow, but still. . . . When he scratched his head, his hair started coming out. He didn't feel good at all, not even a little bit.

A frowning nurse gave him a blood test. Not too much later, a frowning doctor came in and asked him, "How long have you been anemic, son?"

"Huh? What? Me?" The guard didn't even know what the word meant. "How come I'm going bald?"

The doctor didn't answer, which pissed him off. It would have made him even madder if he'd felt better. He threw up that night, and the vomit had blood in it.

A tech sergeant walked into the ward much too early the next morning. He carried a metal box with . . . things attached to it. The guard, still nauseous, wasn't inclined to curiosity just then. One of the . . . things was a set of earphones. The tech sergeant steered the other one over the guard. Something clicked in the earphones; even the sick guard could hear it. The sergeant looked down at a gauge on top of the metal box. "Jesus Christ!" he muttered, and got out of there in a hurry.

They carried the guard out of the ward later that day. The medics who moved him wore gas masks and thick gloves. "What the hell's going on?" he asked. "I ain't Typhoid Mary. I ain't got smallpox or nothin'. I know I ain't—I been vaccinated. All I got's a coupla cracked ribs, right?"

"Well, no." Coming through the gas mask, the medic's voice sounded otherworldly.

"What is it, then? How come I feel so crappy?" the guard asked.

"After we A-bombed the Japs, the docs called it radiation sickness," the medic replied.

"Son of a bitch!" The guard would have got more excited, but he did feel crappy. "That thing the fuckin' kraut touched off—that was an atom bomb? How come I ain't dead?"

The medic hesitated. *Maybe you will be*—something like that had to be going through his mind. The guard would have been more upset had he been less wrung out, too. At last, the medic said, "Well, it wasn't a real atom bomb. What blew up was just TNT, that kinda shit. If it was a real atom bomb, Frankfurt wouldn't be there any more—one gone goose. But the fuckin' krauts put some kinda radio-active crap in with the explosive, and the blast spread it all over the place. You musta been pretty close to where it went off."

"Yeah, I sure was. That's how I got the ribs," the guard agreed. "What happens now? Am I gonna die?" He wished he cared more.

"See how much of that crap you took in. See if you get better or not." The medics who were lugging the guard stopped at a door with ISOLATION painted above it in big letters that looked new. A nurse held the door open for them. She was a blonde with a nice shape—Betty Grable legs—but a gas mask kept the guard from telling whether she was cute or not. He also wished he cared more about that. If he didn't give a damn about what a girl looked like, he had to be much too close to buying a plot.

Several other guys already lay in the isolation ward. A couple of them seemed pretty chipper. Others looked even worse than the guard felt. The medics got him up onto a bed. He lay there like a lump, wondering what happened next or if anything happened next. He had a hard time caring one way or the other.

ROBERT PATTERSON DIDN'T LOOK HAPPY ABOUT COMING BEFORE Congress. Jerry Duncan didn't give a good goddamn about how the Secretary of War looked. "Let me get this straight, Mr. Secretary," Jerry said. "We had this enormous enclave in Frankfurt for American officers and their dependents, constructed at taxpayer expense for several million dollars. Is that right?"

"Yes, Congressman." Patterson looked even less happy. Jerry hadn't been sure he could.

"Okay," Jerry said. It wasn't—not even close—but sometimes you had to soften 'em up before you bored in for the kill. "We had this enclave. Now we can't use it any more, because this damned German fanatic blew himself up right in the middle and left it radioactive. We were going to try the German war criminals there, but now we can't do that, either. Is all that right?"

"Yes, Congressman. Unfortunately, it is." There had to be some bottom to the Secretary of War's gloom, but he hadn't found it yet.

"How did the German drive his truck into the middle of our enclave?" Jerry inquired, acid in his voice. "Was the guard asleep at the switch?"

"It appears the guard was deceived, sir, if that's what you mean," Patterson answered stolidly.

"What would have happened if the guard wasn't asleep at the switch?" Jerry liked his own phrase better. It made the guard and the Secretary of War look bad. "Wouldn't the whole enclave have been saved?"

"Well, sir, I think the most likely thing is that the fanatic behind the wheel would have touched off the vehicle at the first sign of trouble," Patterson replied. "There was a lot of explosive in that truck. It still would have blown up a large area, and it would have spread the, uh, radioactive material far and wide any which way."

Damn, Jerry thought. That seemed likely to him, too, even if he wished it didn't. He tried a different jab: "How did Heydrich's fanatics get their hands on radioactive material in the first place? How did they know what to do with it?"

Patterson licked his lips. "They kidnapped physicists out of the British zone. The radioactive material came from the French zone."

"So none of this is the War Department's fault? Is that what you're saying?" Jerry asked. "The bomb blew up in the American zone, didn't it? It contaminated the American zone, didn't it?"

"Yes, sir," the Secretary of War said.

"And this, uh, radioactive material the fanatics got from the French zone—how did they know it was there?" Jerry pressed.

"I presume one of the German physicists told them," the Secretary of War said.

"Now, we knew the stuff was there? But we didn't try to get it because we didn't want to alert the French to its presence? Isn't that right?" Jerry said.

Patterson sipped from the glass of ice water in front of him before answering, "Yes, Congressman, I believe it is."

In his shoes, Jerry would have been sweating, too, and would have wanted to cool down. "We held our cards too close to our chest, wouldn't you say?" Jerry asked.

"It did turn out that way, yes, sir. Hindsight is always twenty-twenty," Patterson said.

"How many people got blown up by the bomb, Mr. Secretary? How many will die of radiation sickness or cancer because of it? Couldn't we have used some twenty-twenty foresight?" Jerry demanded.

Bang! The committee chairman used his gavel. "There will be no badgering of witnesses," he declared. "You need not respond to that, Mr. Patterson."

"Sorry, Mr. Chairman," Jerry said. But, when he thought about the stories the papers would run, he wasn't sorry one bit.

SOME SOVIET PRINTER IN BERLIN HAD RUN OFF COUNTLESS COPIES OF the latest ukase from Moscow. The fellow must have, if one appeared on the desk of an officer as junior as Vladimir Bokov. With the order in hand, he went down the hall to see what his superior thought of it.

Colonel Shteinberg was reading the pronunciamento when Bokov came in. "Hello, Volodya," he said. "You've seen this?" He held up the sheet of cheap pulp paper.

"*Da,* Comrade Colonel." Bokov displayed his own copy. "What do you make of it?"

"It will be a little inconvenient, maybe, but of course we'll do it, because the order comes straight from Marshal Stalin," Shteinberg said.

"Of course," Bokov agreed, straight-faced. Anyone who didn't follow an order from Stalin would regret it the rest of his life, which might not be long but would be unpleasant. "We will have to help organize postage and reparations to make sure everything is examined by Geiger counter before it proceeds to the motherland." He paused, then asked, "Comrade Colonel, how many of these Geiger counters are there in the Soviet zone, and what are they for?"

"They measure radioactivity. I found that out with a phone call to a doctor who did a course in physics before the war," Shteinberg replied. "At the moment, I believe we have seven in the Soviet zone. But more are coming from the USSR."

"Good. That's good," Bokov said with what he thought of as commendable optimism. Every motherland-bound letter, parcel, truck, soldier, dismounted factory? Seven of these Geiger counters? Yes, they needed more—thousands more!

All the same, he thought he understood why Stalin gave the order. Radioactivity could kill, and kill invisibly. The bandits' bomb in Frankfurt must have put the Little Father's wind up. If the Heydrichites still had any of their radioactive material—whatever it was—left, they could strike a blow at the very heart of the Soviet Union. Of course Stalin would do everything he could to block it.

Another question formed in Bokov's mind. "What do we do if we find something that's, uh, radioactive?" He had only the vaguest notion of what the word meant.

"Ah. They must not have issued you the supplement." Moisei Shteinberg brandished another sheet of paper. "In that case, we are to find out who delivered it, and where, and where he got it. This may give us some leads on who gave it to him."

"Yes. It may." Bokov didn't believe that, but he had to sound like someone who did. Well, it wasn't as if he hadn't had practice.

"And so we have our orders, and so we will carry them out," Shteinberg declared. "At my suggestion, the Red Army's postmasters have directed that all mail to the motherland be routed through Berlin. Six of the seven Geiger counters are here, in this city. All rail traffic between the Soviet zone and the USSR will be centralized here, allowing us to inspect soldiers and functionaries."

"Very good, Comrade Colonel. What about Germans assigned to camps?" Bokov asked.

"Oh, I don't think we need to worry about them," Shteinberg said with a certain savage satisfaction. "They won't be going any place where they can endanger people who matter."

Bokov nodded. "Makes sense to me. We won't have to take any of these counters away from important work, then."

"We'll be stretched thin enough as is," Shteinberg agreed.

"Can we borrow Geiger counters from the Anglo-Americans?" Bokov wondered. "They're imperialist powers, I know, but they're still our allies against the Fascist jackals."

Shteinberg pondered, then clicked his tongue between his teeth. "Not a good idea, Comrade Captain. We will not show England or the United States that we are weak in any way." When he put it like that, Bokov couldn't possibly argue. Even trying would have been dangerous, so he didn't.

XVII

Ravens were nasty birds. Lou Weissberg hadn't seen many—truth to tell, he couldn't remember seeing any—back in New Jersey. He hadn't even seen that many crows. But he'd found out more than he ever wanted to know about ravens in the months before the German surrender. They pecked out corpses' eyes and worried at wounds to make them bigger and get at the exposed flesh. Sometimes they didn't wait till what they were pecking at was a corpse.

Here they were again, on the road between Nuremberg and Munich. The day before, a squad's worth of fanatics had tangled with about an equal number of GIs. More often than not, the krauts' assault rifles and Schmeissers would have given them a firepower edge over American troops. Not this time—three of the dogfaces were BAR men. The Brownings chewed up the fanatics and left them . . . ravens' meat.

Vultures prowled the grass along with the ravens. European vultures were hawkier than their American equivalents. They looked as if they wouldn't mind going out and killing something when the carrion ran short. Well, they didn't need to do any extra work today. The GIs with the BARs had taken care of that for them.

The Americans had lost one dead and three wounded. The Germans were mostly dead. They'd given themselves a nasty surprise, sure as hell. But the GIs had captured a couple who were only wounded—he didn't get to interrogate fanatics all that often.

Plenty of U.S. soldiers surrounded the tent that housed the wounded Aryan supermen. Most of the time, the Jerries would have gone to a hospital in Munich or Nuremberg. Not today, Josephine. So soon after the radioactive attack on Frankfurt, the brass wasn't sure Heydrich's goons wouldn't try another one. A tent in the middle of nowhere didn't make a promising target for that kind of thing.

Jumpy troopers made Lou show his ID three different times and frisked him twice before he got inside the tent. In the Far East, he'd heard, Army discipline was going right down the crapper. The Japs actually believed they were licked. American troops might not want to be in Europe, but they didn't get slack and dick around here. Nothing concentrated the mind like the possibility you might get your head blown off.

A medic—no, a doc: he wore captain's bars—looked up when Lou ducked into the tent. "You Weissberg? Heard you were coming."

"Call me Lou." Lou had captain's bars of his own, brand new ones. That was more for time served than for anything he'd actually accomplished, and he knew it too well. He went on, "I wish your watchdogs woulda got the word. They wouldn't've felt me up like I was Jane Russell. How're the krauts?"

"One of 'em's got a sucking chest. He's in bad shape—dunno if he'll make it," the Army doctor answered. "Other guy's got a smashed-up leg. Maybe I'll have to amputate, maybe not. Penicillin and sulfa give him a chance to keep it, anyhow. Ten years ago, it would've been gone for sure. You can talk to him—he's with it. The one with the chest wound keeps going in and out, know what I mean?"

"Oh, yeah. I've seen fellows like that before," Lou said.

"Our guys waxed these assholes—cleaned their clocks," the doctor said. "Sure hope it gets into the papers."

"Me, too, but I can't do a thing about that," Lou said. "So, I can talk to this one, huh?" He pointed to the German with a leg wrapped in bloody bandages.

"Yeah. He's got plenty of morphine in him, too—he needs it. So if he's flying, maybe he'll sing for you. You can hope, anyway."

"I sure can." Lou leaned over the German, who wore a neater, less raggedy *Feldgrau* tunic than he'd seen for a while. And the man still had on a set of shoulder straps, with a senior sergeant's rank badges, which had been against regulations since the dreadfully misnamed V-E Day. Well, the Jerry had bigger things than that to worry about. Lou switched to Deutsch: "Hey, you! *Herr Feldwebel!* Can you hear me?"

The kraut's eyes opened. They were aluminum-gray, a genuinely scary color. But they also looked back at Lou from a million miles away. *Plenty of morphine and then some,* Lou thought. "I'm not a goddamn *Feldwebel,*" the German said. "I'm a *Scharführer,* and don't you forget it." Contempt and weariness warred in his voice.

He had to be doped out of his skull, or he'd never admit to owning *Waffen-SS* rank. Lou decided to roll with it. "Sorry, *Herr Scharführer,*" he said. "Tell me who sent you out on this dumbheaded mission that got you shot."

"God damn Egon to hell and gone. He can lick my asshole, the son of a whore." Lou thought the *Scharführer* would bust right open, but he didn't. No matter how full of drugs he was, he knew what he was supposed to say when somebody started interrogating him. "My name is Bauer, Rudolf Bauer. I am a *Scharführer, Waffen-SS.*" He gave Lou his serial number. "By the Geneva Convention, I am not required to tell you more."

"Pigdog!" Lou yelled, loud enough to make the doctor jump. "Do you think the Red Army gives a rat's ass about the Geneva Convention?"

Bauer's aircraft-skin eyes widened. Lou watched him try to fight the morphine. "But—" he sputtered. "But—I am in the American zone. You are wearing an American uniform."

Shit, Lou thought. But *shit* wasn't what came out of his mouth. Once upon a time, somebody who'd come back from a visit to smashed Berlin had taught him how to cuss a little in Russian. He'd never imagined that would come in handy, but maybe it did now. "*Gavno!*" he yelled, and, for good measure, "*Yob tvoyu mat'!*"

Hearing him, a real Russian likely would have laughed his ass off. A drugged and wounded SS man was in no position to realize what a lousy accent he had. Rudolf Bauer gulped. The way his Adam's apple swelled and contracted, he might have been in a Bugs Bunny cartoon.

He started to give his name, rank, and pay number again—he had nerve.

"Shut up!" Lou yelled. "Tell me who sent you out! What's Egon's whole name?"

Had he been a real Russian interrogator, he probably would have kicked that wounded leg about then. Morphine or no morphine, Bauer would've gone right through the roof of the tent. Lou didn't have the stomach for it, even if the doctor wouldn't have reported him. But Bauer didn't have to know that.

The *Scharführer* gulped again. Then he whimpered; the leg had to hurt in spite of everything. "Talk, you stinking turd!" Lou screamed. In a horrible way, it was fun. He could see why SS and NKVD men enjoyed what they did for a living . . . and he wondered if he'd be able to look at himself in the mirror when he shaved tomorrow morning.

In a very small voice, Bauer whispered, "He is *Hauptsturmführer* Steinbrecher."

Aha! "Where do I find this cocksucker?" Lou demanded.

He's dead. A BAR blew his brains out. If Bauer said that and stuck to it, how could anybody prove he was lying—short of kicking his leg, anyhow? But once a prisoner started talking, he often sang like a nightingale. "He lives in the town of Pförring, outside Ingolstadt," Bauer said. "He is a mechanic there."

"How about that?" the doctor muttered—he spoke German, then.

"Yeah—how about that?" Lou agreed. "A break. Maybe. Sure could use one." The fanatics were good. You couldn't break into their cells very often. But if this Egon Steinbrecher was happily repairing stuff in Pförring, and if Lou and some GIs dropped in (you never could tell if somebody kept a Schmeisser handy) . . . "See you later, Doc."

Lou tore out of the tent. He corralled some of the guys guarding the scene of the firefight. They piled into three jeeps and roared off toward Pförring, about twenty minutes away.

Most of the small town was intact. One block on the outskirts and then two more a little farther on had had the bejesus knocked out of them. Lou'd seen that kind of thing before. Those were the places where the krauts tried to make a stand when the American army came through.

At Lou's order, the jeep stopped by an old woman carrying a few sticks of firewood. "Where do I find Egon Steinbrecher, the mechanic?" Lou asked her.

"Three blocks that way and one block up." She pointed. "A brick house with a shed to one side." If she was lying, she was damn good on the spur of the moment.

The dogface driving the jeep didn't know German. Lou gave him the directions. The other two jeeps zoomed after his.

There was the house. There was the shed. There was the guy who had to be Steinbrecher, working on something broken with a pair of pliers. Lou pointed a grease gun at his midsection. "Hold it right there!" Lou yelled. "Drop the pliers! Hands high!"

Clank! The pliers fell on the cement floor. *"Was ist los?"* Steinbrecher said as he raised his hands. "I have done nothing wrong."

"We'll see about that," Lou said in German, and then, in English, to one of his men, "Frisk him, Sandy. And check under his arm for the tattoo."

"Sure thing, Captain." The GI patted Steinbrecher down. He found nothing more lethal than a clasp knife. But, when he undid the German's shirt and looked under his left armpit, he grunted and nodded. "Yeah, he's got it." Wearing your blood group on your skin made transfusions quick and easy and safe even if you were badly hurt and couldn't tell the doctor what group you were. Egon Steinbrecher hadn't bothered getting his tattoo removed as the war wound down.

"Bring him along, then," Lou told Sandy. "We'll question him back in Nuremberg."

"But I have done nothing wrong!" Steinbrecher bleated again.

"Yeah, tell me another one," Lou answered. He didn't remember the last time he'd felt so good. Something had actually worked out for a change.

A MAJOR IN DRESS UNIFORM READ FROM A STATEMENT IN A PENTA-gon press room: "Nine of Heydrich's fanatics were killed and two captured. One of them later died of his wounds. An SS captain was also captured afterwards. American losses in the skirmish were one dead, three wounded. We believe the captured officer will give us valuable information about the fanatics' organization and resources." He looked out at the reporters. "Questions, gentlemen?"

Tom Schmidt's hand shot up. When the major nodded to him, he said, "Why should a story like this impress us? Germany surrendered more than a year ago. Shouldn't it be quiet over there by now?"

One of the things Tom had learned in Germany was how to read campaign and decoration ribbons. Among others, the major wore one for a Purple Heart with two tiny oak-leaf clusters attached. He also wore an expression that said he wanted to scrape Tom off the bottom of his shoe. "When you grow up, Mr. Schmidt, you learn there's a difference between what ought to be and what is," he said in the flat voice of formal hostility. "And you learn you have to deal with what is, not what ought to be."

Some of the reporters in the briefing room snickered. They weren't all administration backers, either. Tom's ears felt incandescent. "Well, let me ask that another way, then, Major," he said, doing his best not to show his own fury. "How could we have dealt with what was a year ago so we wouldn't have this mess on our hands today?"

"Sir, I am trying to show you progress in the fight against the fanatics, and you don't want to look at it," the briefing officer complained.

Tom sniffed. "We won a skirmish. Hot diggety dog. A year ago, did you expect we'd still be having skirmishes today?"

"My opinion on these issues doesn't matter," the major said.

"Okay, fine. Did anybody in the War Department or the State Department or the White House expect we'd still be fighting a shooting war in Germany halfway through 1946?"

"That doesn't matter now," the major insisted. "The point now is that we have to win it, and we're going to win it, and we are winning it. This fight we just had—"

"How many years before we can go back into Frankfurt? How many people from there are refugees?" Tom broke in. "Does that say we're winning?"

The briefing officer turned brick red. "Maybe it would be better if someone else asked questions for a while, Mr. Schmidt."

"Better for who?" another reporter inquired.

"For whom?" yet another man corrected. Assemble a bunch of people who made their living with words and somebody was bound to turn copy editor on you.

"For people who want full and accurate information, that's for whom." The major answered what had probably been a rhetorical question. "The papers only seem interested in bad news. When anything good happens, you don't want to talk about it."

Maybe he didn't know how big a can of worms he was opening. Or maybe he had orders from people above him to try to put the fear of God into the Washington press corps. If he did, it didn't work. Even the people who'd laughed when he mocked Tom Schmidt started screaming at him now. Tom was sure of that: as far as he could tell, *everybody* in the briefing room started screaming.

"I've had enough!" someone shouted—a variation on one of the Republicans' campaign slogans.

"To err is Truman!" another reporter added, this time parroting the Republican line. Then he said, "And you're right up there with him, Major."

"I don't know how we got such an unpatriotic press," the briefing officer said. "You people are worth regiments to Heydrich and his maniacs. Here I'm trying to show you we're making progress, and you don't want to listen."

Tom didn't laugh out loud, but he felt like it. The major had delivered himself—and, with him, maybe the Truman administration— into the reporters' hands. Accuse them of supporting the other side and they'd tear you into bloody chunks . . . all in the name of freedom of the press, of course.

They screamed at the major. They demanded to know what he was talking about. "Are you saying we're card-carrying Nazis?" one of them yelled. " 'Cause I'll make you sorry if you are!" He was short and fat and wore thick glasses: a born 4-F if there ever was one. The major might have been wounded three times, but as long as he wasn't in a wheelchair he wouldn't have any trouble with a twerp like that. Which didn't stop the reporter, and might even have spurred him on.

The briefing officer didn't try to back down or cover his tracks the way he should have. He scowled back at the gentleman of the fourth Estate and answered, "I don't know what you guys are. I wonder what the FBI would turn up if it tried to find out."

That was blowing on a fire. They told him all the reasons the FBI had no right to do anything like that. They told him how they'd sue J. Edgar Hoover if he tried, and for how much. They didn't ask him any more questions. They swarmed out of the briefing room, swarmed out of the Pentagon, to write their stories and file them with their papers.

They weren't the kind of stories the Truman administration would have wanted.

ARMY SUPPRESSES TRUTH! was the headline under which Tom's piece ran. As those things went, that was one of the milder ones. Tom Schmidt smiled when he saw some of the others. If the Army fucked with him, he'd fuck with it right back.

LOU WEISSBERG LIT A CIGARETTE. IN GERMANY, THAT MADE HIM A rich man—he could afford to smoke his money. Major Frank—the other man's promotion had come through about the same time as his own—was smoking too. Well, of course they were rich here. They were Americans, after all.

"I was talking to a guy who hit the beach at D-Day," Lou remarked.

"Yeah?" Howard Frank tried to blow a smoke ring. It was a ragged botch.

"Uh-huh." Lou nodded. "He told me his LCI was a few hundred yards from the beach when it got hit by a round from an 88."

"He's lucky he's still here to tell you the story, in that case," Frank said. The German 88—antiaircraft gun, antitank gun, and main armament in the Tiger tank and the *Jagdpanther* tank destroyer—was one hellacious piece of artillery.

"No shit," Lou agreed. "Only reason he is, is the Jerry gunners loaded an AP round instead of high explosive. So the damn thing went through the side of the landing craft, went through two of his buddies, and went straight out through the bottom."

"Okay. I'm hooked. Give me the next reel of the serial," Frank said.

"Well, the LCI started to sink like you'd expect," Lou said. "Not real quick, but it took on more and more water and rode lower and lower . . . till finally it scraped up onto the beach and the guys who hadn't got ventilated got out and headed for the war."

"Mmp." Major Frank essayed another smoke ring, with no better luck than before. He looked disgruntled, maybe at the miserable puff of smoke, maybe at Lou. "And you're telling me this story because . . . ?" By the way he said it, he didn't believe Lou had any reason.

But Lou did. "On account of it kinda reminded me of what we've been doing here since the surrender. We've been sinking an inch at a time, like. You know what I mean, sir?"

"I only wish I didn't." Frank stubbed out the cigarette in his shell-casing ashtray and promptly lit another. As he took a deep drag on the new coffin nail, he asked, "So where's the beach?"

"The beach? . . . Oh. I was hoping you could tell me," Lou said. "If we can't make it that far before we go under, all we leave is a trail of bubbles, and then we're gone for good." He got a fresh smoke going, too. The inside of his mouth felt like sandpaper. Still, the little nicotine buzz was worth it. He'd tried quitting a time or two, but that hurt, so he hadn't.

"One more time," Major Frank said, and tilted his head back. This smoke ring was . . . not good, but better, anyhow. As if it helped jog his brain, he continued, "Maybe if we kill Heydrich . . ."

"Maybe," Lou allowed. "If one of our bombs had blasted Hitler in 1943, that would've kicked over the anthill for sure."

To his surprise, Howard Frank looked less than enthusiastic. "They might've fought the war better if old Adolf did go to hell halfway through, you know. He told 'em to do a lot of dumbass things, and nobody had the nerve to go, 'Wait a minute. You're out of your goddamn mind.' "

Lou grunted. No doubt his superior had something there. Something for the *Reich* in 1943, for sure. Now? Wasn't now a different story? "You think Heydrich's *meshiggeh,* too?" Lou asked.

"*Meshuggeh,*" Frank said. "It's a miracle the krauts can understand you, the kind of Yiddish you talk. It's all in the front of your mouth."

"Yeah, yeah, bite me," Lou said—they'd gone around that barn before, a time or twelve. "I did proper German in college, too. You know that. But do you think Heydrich's squirrelly?"

"Bite me, *sir,*" Major Frank said without rancor. He paused to chew on the real question. Reluctantly, he shook his head. "Nah, I guess not. Coldhearted son of a bitch, but that's not the same thing. For somebody with a crappy hand, he's played it damn well. Or do you think I'm wrong?"

"Wish I did," Lou answered. "Boy, do I ever. But I'm not sure how bad his hand really is, y'know? Yeah, his guys can't fight us straight up any more, like they did before the surrender. But so what? They sure can drive us nuts, same as the Russian partisans did with them. And those assholes were ready for this. They started gearing up a couple of years before the *Wehrmacht* threw in the towel—stashing guns, getting men out of regular units and salting 'em away. . . . Not a lot of men, not when you're talking about a real army. For partisans, though, they got plenty."

"Ain't it the truth?" Frank said mournfully. "And how do you stop somebody who doesn't care if he kills himself as long as he gives you a good one in the balls?"

"Two atom bombs made the Japs believe they honest to God lost," Lou said. "Our guys over in the Pacific don't have any trouble now—lucky bastards."

"You don't like it where you're at, you can always put in for a transfer," Major Frank said. "I'll endorse it like nobody's business."

Lou sent him a reproachful look through the smoke that hazed the office. "You know I don't want to do this. I want to clobber these Nazi mothers. I've got millions of reasons why, too, same as you do. I just wish to hell I knew how we were gonna do it, and that Congress would let us do it."

As if to punctuate his words, the thump of not-too-distant explosions rattled the windows that gave Major Frank a look at the devastation outside. Lou tensed, ready to hit the dirt. Before he did, a veteran's judgment told him he didn't have to. Howard Frank didn't dive under his desk.

"Only a mortar," Lou said. Frank nodded. Mortars were the small change of this war. Unless one came down close to you, you didn't have to worry about them. (*Much good that did old Adenauer,* Lou reminded himself.) But trucks full of explosives and Heydrichite fanatics wearing vests stuffed with TNT and nails were what you really needed to worry about.

The Germans had surrendered more than a year before. This kind of picayune crap—maybe a couple of GIs wounded, maybe just something smashed—looked as if it could go on forever. *Are we ready to hold these shitheads down forever?* Lou wondered. He was. He was much less sure about the rest of his country.

———————

LIGHTS FROM LIGHT BULBS. SLIGHTLY STALE AIR. THE HUM OF FANS in the background. Reinhard Heydrich hardly heard them any more, not unless he made a conscious effort and listened. Nowadays, this was where he belonged: deep underground. The raid into the British zone that netted the German physicists only rubbed his nose in the truth. However much he wished he were, he wasn't a field operative any more.

This is what happens to a field marshal . . . or to a Führer, he thought. The Allies spread stories about how Hitler had gone mad down in his bunker. Heydrich didn't think that was happening to him . . . but he'd changed, no doubt about it.

He was damn glad his wife and children made it to Spain while things were falling apart in the *Reich*. A lot of people had used that escape route, and Franco wouldn't give them up. Of course, the whole war would have gone differently if Franco had let the *Wehrmacht* take Gibraltar away from England. . . . Hitler came back from that meeting saying he would rather have three teeth pulled than dicker with the *Caudillo* again.

At least Heydrich didn't have to worry that the Yankees would try to use Lina and the kids against him. Better still, he didn't have to worry that the Russians would. Whatever they tried wouldn't have swayed him—he was sure of that—but it might have clouded his judgment. He couldn't afford that, not when he had to fight this unbalanced, unequal kind of war.

Oberscharführer Klein came in with the latest stack of newspapers from all over Germany—and from beyond. He laid a copy of *Le Figaro* on Heydrich's desk and pointed to a photo on the front page. "Isn't this disgusting?" he growled. "They're so damned proud of themselves because they tied themselves to the Amis' apron strings."

The photo showed a French panzer rumbling down the Champs Élysées. It looked rather like a Panther; Heydrich knew the French army was using some of those it had taken more or less intact. His French was rusty, but he could make sense of the story under the photo. It bragged about how the French-built panzer showed that France was a great power again.

Heydrich wanted to spit on the newspaper. "How great was France in 1940?" he growled.

"That's what I was thinking, *Herr Reichsprotektor.*" Hans Klein leered. "I was on leave in Paris in '42, and the girls were pretty great—I'll tell you that. Leave a few Reichsmarks on the dresser and they'd do whatever you wanted. They'd smile while they did it, too." He chuckled reminiscently. "Those were the days, all right."

"And now the same girls suck off the Americans—some great power," Heydrich said. Klein laughed out loud. Heydrich's eyes, already narrow, narrowed further. "We ought to teach them a lesson, Hans. We really should. Maybe another one for the English, too. As if England could have beaten us if she hadn't let herself get overrun by American niggers and Jews."

"Damn right, sir." Klein sounded hearty, but only for a moment. Then he asked, "Um . . . What have you got in mind?"

"I don't know yet," Heydrich admitted. "But something. There has to be something. No security to speak of in France or England— not like here. Getting people and the stuff they need across the border should be easy as you please."

"*Ja.*" Klein nodded. "You've got that right—for France, anyway. England may be harder, though. Miserable Channel."

Heydrich nodded, too, unhappily. England's natural moat wasn't even a good piss wide, but it had been plenty to frustrate the *Reich* in 1940. "Moving our personnel—that should be manageable," the *Reichsprotektor* said, thinking out loud. "What they need . . . there's the hard part."

"Shame we don't have any U-boats left," Hans Klein remarked.

That made Heydrich think some more. A few of the submarines that had surrendered had put in at German ports. Regretfully, he shook his head. "We haven't got the people to man one. And even if we did, the Allies would shit bricks if one of those boats went missing. Can't have that, not when we're trying to keep a secret."

Klein grunted. "Yeah, you're right, sir. Too damn bad, but you are."

"A fishing boat, maybe?" Heydrich wondered. "That might work." He had no idea how many fishing boats were setting out from German ports these days. Up till this moment, he'd never had any reason to worry about it. And the North Sea and the Baltic were about as far from his redoubt as you could get and still stay in the *Reich*. "Have to see what we can find out."

"Whatever it is, the Tommies won't like it," Klein predicted.

Heydrich didn't smile very often, but he did now. "That's the idea, Hans."

SUMMER PRESSED DOWN ON ANDERSON, INDIANA, LIKE A HOT, WET glove. Diana and Ed McGraw went to movies on weekends and whenever Ed didn't come home from the plant too tired during the week. What was playing? They didn't much care. The theaters had air-conditioning. That counted for more than what went on the screen. The movie houses were packed whenever they went, too. They weren't the only ones who wanted to beat the heat for a couple of hours.

"I wonder what it'd cost to air-condition the house," Diana said when they left a theater one night. It was after ten, but still sweltering outside.

"I can tell you what," Ed answered. "More than we can afford, that's what. I make pretty good money, but not that kind." He opened the Pontiac's passenger door. Diana slid in. She knew he was right. Ed went around to get in on the street side. As he started the car, he went on, "You'll be taking your trips, anyway. The trains are air-conditioned, and so are the hotels, right?"

"A lot of the time, anyhow," Diana agreed.

"Well, that's something, anyways." Ed put the car in gear. "Where do you go next? Detroit?"

"No, Minneapolis," she said.

He thumped his forehead with the heel of his hand. "That's right. I forgot. Detroit's later. But they were both up north, and I mixed 'em up. It's a wonder you can keep everything straight. Maybe it'll be cooler up there. You can hope."

"Sure," Diana said, and then, after cautious silence, "Does it bother you that I'm gone so much?"

"Nah." To her relief, Ed didn't hesitate even a little bit. "It needs doin'. I couldn't hack anything like that. I ain't got the waddayacallit— the personality. But you're goin' great guns. Pat'd be proud of you. Honest to God, babe, he would."

"Thanks." Tears stung Diana's eyes. She did sometimes wonder what their son would have thought of her campaign against the government. That was foolishness. She never would have started it if one of Heydrich's fanatics hadn't killed him and opened her eyes.

Minneapolis turned out to be hot, too. The paper there said the heat wave ran all the way up to Winnipeg, on the other side of the border. The Canadians were lucky. They didn't have to try to help hold Germany down.

The ground around Minneapolis was as flat as if it had been ironed, and puddled with ponds and lakes of all sizes. Most of the people were tall and fair. They spoke with a slight singsong Scandinavian accent, and said *"Ja"* when they meant yes. Most of the time, they didn't seem to notice the way they talked. Every once in a while, they would grin wickedly and put it on twice as thick to drive an out-of-towner loopy.

Signs printed in red on white—STOP THE BLEEDING IN GERMANY! RALLY AT LORING PARK!—were tacked to telephone poles and pasted to walls everywhere on the short car ride from the Great Northern depot to Diana's hotel. "Looks like you folks have done a terrific job getting ready," Diana told the couple who'd met her at the station.

"Well, we try," said Susan Holmquist, who ran the Minnesota fight against the war.

"Ja, we do," agreed her husband, Sven. They both seemed surprised at her praise. Other places, people acted as if they wanted a medal for pitching in. Not here, not with the Holmquists.

Quietly, Susan added, "Danny would have wanted it this way. If you do something, do it right." Sven nodded. They'd lost their son at almost the same time as Diana lost Pat. A German wearing explosives under his clothes blew himself up in a crowd of GIs, and Danny Holmquist was one of the unlucky ones.

Loring Park had—inevitably—a two-lobed lake at its heart. Susan said the ice skating was terrific during the winter. Diana had tried ice skating exactly once, and sprained an ankle. Besides, just then she was amazed the little lake wasn't steaming. The air shimmered under the swaggering sun.

A bunting-draped platform with a mike stood near a statue of Ole Bull. A plaque at the base of the statue explained that Ole Bull was a nineteenth-century Norwegian violinist. A good thing, too, because Diana wouldn't have known otherwise. What he was doing immortalized in bronze in a Minneapolis park . . . Well, it was a Scandinavian part of the country.

Picketers paraded and chanted. Their placards carried all the slogans Diana had seen so often before. Some of them, she'd come up with herself. By now, she had trouble remembering which ones those were. They all blurred together.

People who disagreed with the picketers shouted and hooted. Bored-looking cops kept them from doing anything more. In places like New York City or Pittsburgh, the cops wouldn't have looked bored. A lot more of them would have been here, too. Even so, they might not have been able to keep the two sides apart. Folks in these parts seemed to have better manners.

Susan Holmquist made a speech. The crowd in front of the podium—not too big, not too small—listened politely. They applauded politely at the right places. Reporters took notes. Photographers photographed. It was all very civilized. If everybody behaved like this, World War II probably never would have happened. But . . .

Susan introduced Diana, who got a bigger hand. Stepping up to the microphone, Diana thought of how scared of public speaking she'd been when she started out. She wasn't any more. She'd done it often enough to let it lose its terrors.

She hammered away at the points she'd made so many times before. Why was the USA still in Germany? Why had so many young men died after victory was declared? Why couldn't the Americans— or anyone else—squash the German fanatics? How long would it go on? How much more money and how many more lives would it cost?

She cut her speech shorter than usual. They were going to do something different here. They were going to read out, one after another, the names of all the servicemen and -women killed in Germany since what was laughably called V-E Day.

Sven Holmquist came up with a typewritten sheet of paper. "Irving Sheldon Aaronson," he intoned. "Hovan Abelian. Creighton Abrams. Manuel José Acevedo . . ."

Diana found herself nodding as she listened to name following name. It was oddly impressive, oddly dignified. And it brought home, one name at a time, just what the United States had already thrown away.

Maybe she wasn't the only one who felt that way. A man in a suit bustled out of the crowd and headed toward the speakers' platform. He had a pointed chin and a high forehead—he was going to lose his hair, but he hadn't lost too much yet. Diana noticed his person less than she noticed that the police were letting him through. "Who is that guy?" she whispered to Susan. "What's he doing?" *Is he safe?* was what she really meant.

"That's Mayor Humphrey. Hubert Humphrey," Susan answered. The name meant nothing to Diana. The Minneapolis woman went on, "He's pro-administration all the way."

Humphrey hopped up onto the platform. "May I say a few words?" he asked. His voice was a light tenor, a bit on the shrill side.

"This isn't your show, Mr. Mayor," Sven Holmquist said. "This is ours."

But Hubert Humphrey grabbed the mike anyway. "Folks, I just want you to think about one thing," he said loudly. Diana got the idea that there would be no such thing as *a few words* from him. He went on, "If we run away from Germany, the Nazis win. All the soldiers who've died will have died for nothing. For nothing—do you hear me? We will have wasted years and tens of thousands of lives and tens of billions of dollars. Is that what you want? Cutting and running won't—"

Diana took the microphone away from him. He looked astonished—he wasn't used to people doing anything like that. "Mr. Humphrey, Mr. Holmquist was right. This is *our* show," Diana said. "If you want your own, you can have it, I'm sure."

"I only meant—" Humphrey began.

"I don't care what you meant, sir." Diana cut him off. It wasn't easy—he was used to talking through or over other people. But, with the mike in hand, she did it, adding, "When I was a girl, Wilson talked about the War to End War. What did he know? Was he right? What do politicians ever know? Let the people decide, if you please."

The crowd really applauded then. Hubert Humphrey looked amazed all over again. He eyed Diana as if he were seeing her for the first time. "There's more to you than meets the eye," he said.

"I don't know about that. I don't care, either," Diana answered. "All I know is, this is our show, and we're going to run it. Get down off this platform before I ask the police to run you in for interfering with a public meeting."

He blinked. "You would, wouldn't you?"

"Mr. Humphrey, it would be a pleasure. Now get down," Diana said. And Humphrey did, because he had to know she wasn't bluffing.

She gave the microphone back to Sven Holmquist. "If you'd go on from where you were interrupted, please . . ."

"Yes, ma'am," he said, something not far from awe in his voice. "Donald Andrew Barclay. Peter LeRoy Barker . . ."

A ROOM. A COUPLE OF ARMED GUARDS. A BRIGHT LIGHT. A PRIS-oner. An interrogator. How many times had that scene played out during the war, and in how many countries—to say nothing of how many movies? Now Lou Weissberg was in the driver's seat. The light shone into *Hauptsturmführer* Egon Steinbrecher's face. They'd been through several sessions by now. Lou was fast running out of patience with the captured German.

"Look," he said in reasonable tones, "you're a dead man. The Geneva Convention doesn't apply. Your side surrendered. If you fight on after that, it's your tough luck."

The SS captain licked his lips. He'd been slapped around a little, but nothing more. Lou and the Americans generally didn't like tor-ture. Unless you had to tear something out of somebody right this sec-ond, what was the point? And Steinbrecher didn't know anything like that. Lou got the feeling he wasn't up to being a suicide warrior, the way too many of Heydrich's fanatics were. But he tried to hold a bold front: "So why have you not killed me, then?"

"Why do you think?" Lou said. "So we can squeeze you. If you sing pretty enough, we may even let you keep breathing. Who all was in your cell?"

"You already know that," Steinbrecher said. "They had bad luck when they attacked your men."

"Those were the only ones?" Lou asked. The German nodded. Lou laughed in his face. "Tell me another one."

"It is the truth." Steinbrecher sounded affronted that anyone could doubt his word. He yawned. He hadn't had much sleep since he got nabbed. That wasn't quite torture, not to Lou's way of thinking. And it could soften a guy up, or at least make him punchy and stupid.

"How do you get your orders?" Lou asked.

"There is—there was—a drop in a hollow tree fifty meters behind my shop," Steinbrecher said. "Sometimes a piece of paper would show up there. It would tell me what to do. I would do it. I do not know who put the paper in, so you need not ask me that."

"I'll ask you whatever I damn well please," Lou snapped. The trouble was, he believed Steinbrecher here. That was how undergrounds all over the world ran their operations. If you didn't know who gave you your orders, you couldn't tell the other side if they caught you. Lou grimaced; this wasn't going the way he wanted. He took another stab at it: "You can't do any better, it's time for the blindfold and cigarette."

This time, the SS man gulped. And he named half a dozen names, all of them men living in Pförring. "They all hate you," he declared.

"We'll check it out," Lou said. He left the interrogation room and made a telephone call. An hour and a half later, he got an answer. The men were . . . just men. Nothing showed they had any connection with the fanatics.

An hour after that, *Hauptsturmführer* Egon Steinbrecher stood tied to a pole in front of a wall. He declined the blindfold, but accepted a cigarette—ironically, a Lucky—from Lou, who commanded the firing squad. "I die for Germany," he said as he finished the smoke.

"You die, all right," Lou agreed. He stepped aside and nodded to the half-dozen GIs. "Ready . . . Aim . . . Fire!" Their M-1s barked. Steinbrecher slumped against the pole. He died fast; Lou didn't have to finish him off with his carbine. That was a relief, anyhow. He'd had this duty before, and he hated it.

He also hated not getting more—hell, not getting anything—out of Steinbrecher. Maybe he hadn't known the one right question to ask, the one that would have made the German sing. Maybe there hadn't been any one right question. All he had now was one more dead Nazi, which wasn't bad, but wasn't good enough.

In the first days of the occupation, they'd taken newsreels of executions like this and shown them in German theaters. That quickly stopped; the films raised sympathy for Heydrich's goons, not the fear U.S. authorities wanted. No camera crew here. Just the squad, and a couple of the GIs looked as if they wanted to be sick.

Lou cut Steinbrecher's body down. "Bury this crap," he said. Sometimes nothing went the way you wished it would.

XVIII

Jürgen had been in Paris twice before. He'd paraded through the City of Light in June 1940. Everything seemed possible then. Hell, everything seemed likely. The *Wehrmacht* had done what the Kaiser's army never could. France lay naked at Germany's feet.

With a smile, Jürgen remembered how tired he'd been as he marched under the *Arc de Triomphe*. Tired? Hell, he'd been out on his feet. So had most of the *Landsers* who tramped along with him. They'd had a month of hard fighting to get to where they were, and they'd felt every minute of it.

But great days, great days. England would give up next, and that would end the war. The *Reich* would take its rightful place in the sun. Everybody would be happy, and he could take off the *Feldgrau* and go back to being a longshoreman again.

Only things worked out a little differently. *Yeah, just a little,* Jürgen thought wryly. When he came back to Paris, it was December 1943. The Red Army had just chased his division out of Kiev. He'd been on the Eastern Front for a couple of years. He'd stopped one bullet and one shell fragment by then. His left elbow didn't bend much, but if you were right-handed you could live with that.

Paris . . . wasn't the same. Winter, sure. But also shortages of everything. Electricity only a few hours a day. Not much heat. The streets empty of cars. Skinny, shabby people on foot or making do with bicycles. The restaurants couldn't cook what they couldn't get. Even the whores just went through the motions.

Well, Jürgen wasn't the same as he'd been in 1940, either. He'd only imagined he was tired back in the old days. He hadn't had exhaustion seep into his bones, into his very soul. In 1943, he'd hibernated like a dormouse all the way across Europe in his railway car. He'd hardly looked out to notice what Lancasters and B-17s and B-24s were doing to the *Vaterland*.

He'd seen bad things fighting through France. He'd thought he'd seen everything. What the hell did he know? He was just a kid. What he'd seen in Russia, what he'd done in Russia . . . Even now, he shied away from remembering that. And it wasn't as if the Ivans didn't play the game the same filthy way. What they did to some of the guys they captured . . . Jürgen shied away from remembering that, too. You always saved one cartridge for yourself. You didn't want them getting hold of you. Oh, no!

So he wasn't afraid of doing himself in. He might have needed to do it long before this if *Reichsprotektor* Heydrich's men hadn't plucked him from the depot and turned him into a holdout. He still wanted to live, but all that soldiering had taught him you didn't always get what you wanted.

So here he was in Paris again, in the cab of a U.S. two-and-a-half-ton truck. He wore olive-drab American fatigues that fit pretty well but not quite well enough. He had papers that showed he was somebody called Paul Higgins. It was the kind of name even a German who knew no English could pronounce well enough. He'd traveled across France with it. He didn't have far to go now.

Once more, Paris wasn't the same. It was nighttime. All the lights were on. That struck him as perverse. But Paris didn't worry about air raids now. And it seemed to have been captured by Americans. Olive drab was everywhere. So were trucks just like the one he drove. They made traffic on the narrow, winding streets horrendous.

After a while, he realized not all the olive-drab uniforms had

Americans in them. A French *flic* directing traffic in a kepi looked like an Ami from the neck down. Maybe not all the deuce-and-a-halfs had American drivers. Jürgen chuckled. He knew one that damn well didn't.

He checked the map on the seat beside him. That was funny, too. He could see where he was going, by God! He just had to find the right way to get there. Also on the seat lay a *Sturmgewehr* and a couple of extra magazines. He'd taken them out of hiding when he got into town. He might need to do some shooting on the last leg of the trip. Extra steel sheets armored his doors. Heydrich's mechanics hadn't had to do that. The Ami who'd driven the truck before it was stolen had taken care of it. He hadn't wanted to stop a German bullet. Jürgen didn't want to stop an American round, or even a French one. Not now. Not when he'd come this far.

He came up alongside the Champ du Mars: a rectangle of greenery and geometrically precise garden in the heart of Paris. The Eiffel Tower loomed ahead. Beyond it lay the Pont d'Jena. Napoleon had beaten the Prussians at Jena; Jürgen knew that. The French named their bridges for battles they'd won. There wouldn't be a Pont d'Ardennes in Paris any time soon.

Well, he wasn't going as far as the Pont d'Jena anyhow. He cut hard left and made for the base of the Tower. A *flic's* whistle shrilled—he wasn't supposed to do that. He started to reach for the assault rifle. Spraying a few bullets around would buy him the time he needed.

But nobody opened up on him. Nobody tried to block him. The Paris cop blew his whistle again, furiously. He thought Jürgen was a drunk Ami on a joyride. Jürgen laughed. Sorry, *flic*.

Orders were to see if he could drop the Tower straight down onto the Pont d'Jena, to double the damage from its fall. One look told Jürgen that wouldn't happen. The supports were positioned so it had to go down diagonally to the bridge. Nobody back in Germany had remembered that.

Well, if it went into the Seine, that would screw things up pretty goddamn well. Jürgen thought it was tall enough to reach. As he drove under the more northerly of the riverside supports, somebody—probably that policeman—fired a pistol at the truck. Too little, too late: like everything the French did.

Jürgen's finger found the detonator button on the side of the steering column. He wished he could watch what was about to happen. It ought to make one hell of a show. Oh, well. You couldn't have everything. *"Sieg heil!"* Jürgen said, and stabbed the button hard.

Lou Weissberg stared at the front page of the *International Herald-Tribune.* Some photographer was going to win himself a Pulitzer Prize for this pic, the way that guy in the Pacific had for his shot of the flag-raising on Iwo Jima the year before.

There was the Eiffel Tower, still mostly lit up, leaning at a forty-five-degree angle to the rest of the skyline. But it didn't keep leaning, the way the Tower of Pisa did. It crashed all the way down, the last hundred feet or so going right into the Seine.

"What a mess," Lou muttered. "What a fucking mess!"

He read the story, though the headline—TOWER FALLS!—and the photo got the message across by themselves. Sometimes the details carried a morbid fascination of their own. He learned that, counting radio antenna, the Tower was (had been) more than a thousand feet high: taller than anything manmade except the much newer Empire State Building. It weighed about 10,000 tons, or as much as the water a heavy cruiser displaced. And now . . . it was 10,000 tons of scrap iron.

Shaking his head, Lou turned to the *Continued on page 3.* The inside page had another shot of the toppled Tower, this one taken in the cold gray light of dawn. As it lay on the ground—and in the river—it reminded him of nothing so much as one more soldier shot dead in the war.

The story said eighty-one people had died when the Eiffel Tower fell. Some had been on it, others under it or caught in the blast of the exploding truck that sheared through one of its enormous feet. And a weatherman who'd been up at the very top reading a barometer got pitched into the Seine and was fished out with nothing worse than a broken wrist.

"Fuck!" Lou said when he read that. "Sometimes you'd rather be lucky than good." If he were that weatherman, he thought he'd go out looking for wallets.

Next to the inside photo and the continuation of the story from the front page was another one. Seeing its headline—GERMAN FREE-

DOM FRONT CLAIMS BLAST—Lou ground his teeth. Heydrich's goons had released a statement by planted communiqués, telephone calls, and their clandestine radio station. The stinking bastards didn't miss a trick, God damn their black-hearted souls to hell.

If you believed them (and Lou, unfortunately, had no reason not to), the fellow who'd brought the tower down was an *Unteroffizier*—a lousy corporal—named Jürgen Voss. *He gave up his life gloriously for the future liberation of the Fatherland and its folk,* the statement said. *Let all who dare to oppose us beware!*

Of course, a lousy corporal from the last war, a fellow by the name of Hitler, had done a lot more damage than this Jürgen Voss ever dreamt of. But it sure wasn't bad for a first try.

General de Gaulle's statement only made page four. Lou thought putting Heydrich ahead of him was chickenshit, but what could you do about newspapermen? "The Tower shall rise again," de Gaulle declared. "Nazi Germany never will." Slowly, Lou nodded. That had style. If only he could be as confident himself as de Gaulle sounded.

Harry Truman's response went right next to the French leader's. "Today, we are all Frenchmen," the President said. That was pretty good, too. Truman went on, "This latest vile Nazi atrocity shows the desperation of the madmen who refuse to accept the verdict of history."

Lou frowned. That also sounded good. Chances were it'd play well back in the States. It was a vile atrocity, no two ways about it. But were Heydrich and his chums madmen? Were they desperate? If they were, they hid it much too well.

Fighting the USA—and the UK, and the USSR—toe-to-toe hadn't worked out so well for the Third Reich. Fighting a partisan war was a whole different story, dammit. If you were trying to drive the other guy nuts and hurt him way worse than he could hurt you . . . Well, if you were trying to do something like that, how could you play your hand better than Heydrich had?

It was nine in the morning. Lou headed for the officers' club anyway. He needed something to turn off part of his brain. Right now, bourbon would do.

Like so much of the American presence in Nuremberg these days, the Quonset hut that housed the officers' club cowered behind rings of barbed wire and sandbagged machine-gun emplacements. The GIs who manned those emplacements seemed extra jumpy this morning. Lou would have, too. If Heydrich's goons could knock over the Eiffel Tower, for Christ's sake, what was one stinking officers' club?

Not worth noticing. Lou hoped.

Even so early, the place was more crowded than it usually was at night. Tobacco smoke hazed the air. Almost every man in there, from lowly second lieutenant to bird colonel, held a copy of the *Herald-Trib* or of *Stars and Stripes,* which also had that picture of the Tower in mid-fall. And almost every man in there was drinking hard.

"What'll it be, sir?" asked the PFC tending bar when Lou squeezed up to him. Once upon a time, a Jerry had worked back there. After what happened to the Russians in Berlin, that didn't look like a good idea any more.

"Bourbon on the rocks," Lou said. "Make it a double. I've got some catching up to do."

"Yes, sir. Comin' up." The kid poured in two generous jiggers of Kentucky lightning and some ice cubes. "Hell of a mornin', ain't it?"

"Man, you said a mouthful." Lou looked around. Major Frank was sitting with a tough, skinny major named Ezra Robertson. Robertson, who was from Vermont or New Hampshire—Lou couldn't remember which—was supposed to help the prosecutors in the war-crimes trials. If the twice-derailed trials ever got off the ground, no doubt he would.

Frank waved. Lou snagged a chair and joined the two majors. He raised his glass. "Mud in your eye." Frank and Robertson both had glasses in front of them. They drank with him. The bourbon ran down his throat like sour-mash fire. "Whew!" He shook his head. "Tastes funny this time of day."

"Yeah, it doesn't go with powdered eggs, that's for damn sure." Major Robertson waved his hands. "Sure isn't stopping anybody, though."

"It's like it was us. This is even worse than that radium bomb in Frankfurt. Who would've thought anything could be?" Howard Frank said gloomily. He put his head in his hands. Had he drunk himself sad already? Not a world record, maybe, but pretty fast. His voice was muffled as he went on, "We are screwed. We are so fucking screwed."

"Not yet, goddammit," Robertson said. "The fanatics can annoy us. They can embarrass us. But they can't beat us. They can't make us pack up and go—not a chance in church, gentlemen. They flat-out aren't strong enough. The only people who can beat us is us." He frowned. "Uh, are us? Hell, you know what I mean."

"Yeah," Lou said. "That's why we're screwed. Elections coming up. What happens when all the people who're squealing 'Get out of Germany now!' go into Congress?"

"So fucking screwed," Frank intoned again, as if it were a dirge. And so it was much too likely to be.

"Red Army doesn't have to worry about this election shit," Robertson said. "Uncle Joe tells 'em hop, and up they go."

"Fanatics are giving them a hard time, too," Lou said. "They're finding out how much fun the other end of a partisan war is."

"They don't like it for beans, that's for sure," Robertson agreed. "Their war-crimes people—all officers, you know—cuss as much as they can in English or German. Then they go back to Russian and really cut loose."

"We ought to do more with their Intelligence people. By God, we really should," Lou said. "We've got the same enemy, just like we did before V-E Day."

A considerable silence followed. Lou considered it—unhappily—while Major Frank and Major Robertson looked at each other. How far into his mouth had he stuck his foot? At last, voice gentle, Frank said, "That won't go very far if you try to push it up the line. I told you so before."

The bourbon at an unaccustomed hour might have hit Lou harder than he figured, for he said, "Why, dammit? About time somebody did."

Ezra Robertson looked down into his now-empty glass. "You know what 'PAF' stands for, Captain?" he asked quietly.

Lou nodded. You picked up all kinds of weird stuff in the CIC. Most of it you put right back down again, because you couldn't use it. But bits and pieces stuck whether you could use them or not. "Premature Anti-Fascist," Lou said. "Guys who went to Spain to fight for the Republic and like that."

"Yeah. And like that," Robertson agreed. "Guys who could've given us a lot of special help during the regular fighting, too. Only most of 'em never got the chance, on account of we didn't trust 'em as far as we could throw 'em. You go yelling we should team up with the NKVD, you'll end up in that same basket, y'know."

"I'm no Red," Lou said. Some of the Americans who'd come over to administer prostrate Germany had had those leanings. A few of them were now working directly for Uncle Joe, because they'd headed for the Soviet zone one jump ahead of the internal investigators.

"We know you aren't," Major Frank said. "But if you start talking about working with the Russians, you'll bump up against people who've never heard of you before."

"And they'll nail you to the cross," Ezra Robertson added.

"*Oy,*" Lou said dryly. Howard Frank snorted. Major Robertson didn't get it. Lou hadn't expected him to—*goys* would be *goys*. Lou only wished he thought the New Englander was wrong. With a sigh, he went on, "Might almost be worth throwing away my Army career for. I think it needs doing."

"Wouldn't just be your Army career," Robertson said. "You'd fubar your whole life. Every place you looked for a job, people would go, 'He's the one who . . .' You don't believe me, find one of those guys who fought in the Lincoln Brigade and see how much fun he's had wearing 'PAF' ever since."

He might have been talking about the weather. He couldn't have been much more matter-of-fact if he were. And he seemed more likely to know what he was talking about than most weathermen of Lou's acquaintance. (Lou remembered the Frenchman who'd gone into the Seine. Talk about luck!)

"Shit," Lou said. He got back up and headed for the bar again. One double wasn't enough to get him where he wanted to go. As the PFC built him a refill, he decided two might not get him there, either.

OBERSCHARFÜHRER KLEIN CAME INTO REINHARD HEYDRICH'S OFFICE with a stack of newspapers that had found their way . . . here . . . from the French zone and from France itself. They all went on and on about the downfall of the Eiffel Tower, and about what France was doing to pay the Germans back.

After quickly flipping through them, Heydrich asked, "Have you seen these, Hans?"

"I've looked at a few of 'em, anyhow," the veteran noncom answered. "Sounds like the Frenchies are pissing themselves—and pissing on us."

"It does, doesn't it?" Heydrich said, not without satisfaction. "And it sounds like there's a regular partisan war going on in the French zone. Plenty of people will pick up a rifle when they think what happens to them if they don't will be worse."

"*Ja,* I saw that, too," Klein said. "More than one of the stories blame it all on us. 'Heydrichite fanatics,' they say." He sounded proud of the label.

"*Scheisse,*" said Heydrich himself. "Our people aren't doing anything in the French zone right now. Nothing, you hear me? I ordered our cells there to stay quiet, because I knew the French would go out of their minds for a while if Voss managed to bring the Tower down."

"They're bad enough anyway—much worse than the Englanders or the Americans. Sometimes they're worse than the damned Russians, too," Klein said.

"Well, the damned Russians really did beat the *Wehrmacht* in the end. That makes them feel better," Heydrich said. "The French never did—the Anglo-Americans had to rescue them. So they're still afraid their cocks are too small, and they act tough to try and make up for it."

Hans Klein guffawed. "That's telling 'em, sir!"

"The only thing they'll do in the occupation zone is get us more recruits," Heydrich said. "Anybody who's willing to grab a gun and fight them on his own is liable to be someone we can use."

"If our people are lying low, how do we find 'em? How do they find us?" Klein asked.

Heydrich only shrugged. "We'll manage. We'll do it later if we don't do it right away. We're in this for the long haul, Hans. If we're still down here in 1955 or 1960, then we are, that's all."

Klein looked down at his hand. "If we are, I'll be pale as a ghost."

"Remember to take your Vitamin D tablet," Heydrich said. "But I don't think we'll still be down here then. We have the will for the struggle, however long it takes. Do our enemies? I don't think so."

————

SOUND TRUCKS BLARED JERRY DUNCAN'S MESSAGE TO THE PEOPLE IN his district: "Reelect Duncan! Bring our boys home from Germany! Keep us prosperous!"

Jerry knew *Reelect* was the magic word. Once you got in, you had to do something pretty stupid to make the voters want to throw you out. Or things had to go into the toilet, the way they had in the Depression. Herbert Hoover dragged his whole party down the drain with him.

But they had a chance to come back here in '46. *At last!* Jerry thought. Germany was Harry Truman's mess, nobody else's. More and more Democrats winced every time they stood up to support the President. Douglas Catledge's posters said DON'T THROW VICTORY AWAY! How much of a victory was it, though, when the Eiffel Tower lay in ruins?

"President Truman doesn't want to listen to the American people!" Duncan shouted at a speech in a park in Anderson. His wife stood on the platform with him, along with the mayor of Anderson and a couple of councilmen. The weather was gray and cool: summer giving way to fall. The forecast had said it might rain, but that seemed to be holding off. Jerry was glad—he had a good crowd on this Saturday afternoon. "Truman doesn't want to listen!" he repeated, louder this time. "He doesn't want to bring our soldiers home from Germany! Well, if he doesn't want to, we just have to make him, that's all!"

People clapped their hands. They cheered. Oh, a few hecklers lurked in the crowd. They jeered and hooted. Some of them tried to start a *"Sieg heil!"* chant. That was Truman's best argument—tarring people who'd had enough with the Nazi brush. But Jerry's backers didn't let the *"Sieg heil!"* chorus get started. They hustled the chanters away. A few scuffles broke out, but cops kept things from getting out of hand.

"When you don't have a plan of your own, you smear the man who does," Jerry ad-libbed, and got another hand. He went on, "We don't have any business in Germany any more. We're just getting sucked deeper and deeper into this swamp." He held up a newspaper. "Yesterday, six more GIs got killed in what people call the American zone. Another thirteen got wounded. Lucky thirteen, right?"

The laugh that rippled up was bitter, scornful—not at him, but at the President. "No more Truman! We need a new man!" somebody yelled. That won a hand, too—a bigger one than Jerry had got.

"We do need a new man," Jerry agreed. "But we have to wait two more years for that. In the meantime, we have to bring the man we've got to his senses. No more blank checks for our stupidity across the Atlantic. No more money to keep our soldiers in Germany unless we start bringing them home right away!"

That did it. The crowd erupted. More hecklers tried to break up the tumultuous applause. They got shouted down. "Take a look at what's happening in the French zone," Jerry said. "The French tried to get revenge for the Eiffel Tower, and what did they end up with? Their very own shooting war, even worse than the one we're stuck with in our zone. And do you know what'll happen next? I'll tell you what. They'll come begging us to pull their chestnuts out of the fire. We had to do it in 1918. We had to do it two years ago, too. They sure can't take care of themselves. They've proved that over and over again."

More cheers. You couldn't go wrong taking shots at France. Jerry had thought about trotting out the French war debt from World War I, but held off. Clobbering Truman was more likely to get his followers all hot and bothered.

And he had plenty to clobber Truman about. Foreign policy was one thing. If you had a son or a brother or a husband stuck in Germany, it mattered to you. But if you didn't, what happened overseas didn't seem to count so much.

On the other hand, everybody had to eat. "How many of you've tried to buy hamburger any time lately?" Jerry asked. A forest of hands went up. "How many of you managed to do it?" he asked. Quite a few of the hands went down. "How many of you paid less than a dollar a pound?" he inquired. Not a single hand stayed up. Jerry waved to show he got it. "Didn't think so. I know my wife paid a dollar and seven cents—didn't you, sweetheart?" Betsy Duncan nodded. Jerry finished, "And I'll tell you something else I know, too. I know that's a shame and a disgrace and a crime!"

Had he got hands like that every time he went up onto the stump, he could have been elected President himself. President? Hell, he could have been elected Pope—and he wasn't even Catholic.

———

VLADIMIR BOKOV FELT HIMSELF CAST BACK IN TIME TO THE BAD DAYS, the dark days of 1941 and 1942. The Hitlerites had had the bit between their teeth then. They did whatever they chose to do, and the Soviet Union had to react to it.

Well, the Soviet Union *did* react, and react well. Otherwise, Captain Bokov wouldn't have been prowling through the ruined streets of Berlin. Instead, some *Sicherheitsdienst* officer would have stalked through wrecked Moscow, trying to keep stubborn Soviet partisans from damaging the city any more.

"Bozhemoi!" Bokov muttered, shaking his head. This work had to be getting to him if pictures like that formed in his head.

It was. He knew it was. And he knew why. Despite the biggest military victory in the history of the world, the USSR was reacting to the Nazis again. The Heydrichites blasted radium all over the heart of Frankfurt. Soviet technicians had to check everything and everyone bound for the motherland from Germany to make sure no radium went along. Inconvenient? So what! Expensive? So what! Time-consuming? Again, so what! So said Moscow, against whose orders there was no appeal.

Now the Fascist bandits had managed to knock over the Eiffel Tower. Which meant . . . To Moscow, it meant all prominent cultural monuments in Eastern Europe needed special guards to keep the same thing from happening to them. Inconvenient? Expensive? Time-consuming? So what! Stalin had decided that the USSR wouldn't be humiliated the way France had been.

Bokov had heard that Stalin couldn't stand de Gaulle. Visiting Moscow, de Gaulle had called the battle of Stalingrad "a symbol of our common victories over the enemy." Stalin hadn't asked, *What French victories?*—though Bokov thought he himself might have, were he in the Marshal's position. But Stalin never took de Gaulle seriously again after that, either.

More guards protected the monument commemorating the Red Army's liberation of Berlin than any others. That was the one that had to gall the Heydrichites the most. The troops around it understood. "Oh, yes, Comrade Captain," said a Red Army major commanding a battalion. "We know they may try and hit us. Well, they can try, but they won't get through unless they've gone and stashed some tanks nearby."

"There's a cheery thought!" Bokov exclaimed. "Do you think they could have?"

"No. That, no." The major shook his head. "And even if they did, they wouldn't get far. Everybody in our T-34s and Stalin tanks would start shooting off everything he had the second he laid eyes on one of those slab-sided Nazi contraptions."

"*Da,*" Bokov said. The bandits had stowed away small arms and antitank rockets and mortars in truly horrendous quantities. But those were all small and easy to hide. Panzers weren't. Which didn't mean you couldn't play games with them. Bokov remembered one stunt the *Wehrmacht* and the Red Army had each used against the other before the surrender. "Are you sure the Fascist hyenas can't steal any of our tanks and use them to fuck us over?"

The major blinked, whether at the idea or the language Bokov wasn't sure. "Comrade Captain, I am not responsible for tank security," the man said slowly. "I command infantry. The tanks are under the jurisdiction of the division's armored regiment."

Not many Red Army officers were willing to move even a centimeter beyond their stated duties. They would follow orders (no matter how harebrained or suicidal) or die trying (knowing there was no excuse for disobedience). When it came to showing initiative . . . They didn't. Say what you would about the Germans, they could think for themselves in the field. This major wore decorations on his chest. He still dared not do anything outside his assigned sphere.

And do I? Bokov wondered. He looked west. If the Soviets worked with the Anglo-Americans (and even the French) against the Heydrichites instead of apart from the Western Allies . . . If he proposed it, his superiors would tell him no; Colonel Shteinberg was dead right about that. If he tried to do it without proposing it . . . He sighed. If he was lucky, they'd shoot him for espionage. If he wasn't, they'd spend a long time hurting him and then shoot him for espionage.

So much for my *initiative and moral courage.* Chastened, Bokov dragged himself back to the business at hand. "I will consult with the officers in armor, then," he said. He saw the relief in the major's gray eyes as he took his leave. The Red Army had more guns, but the NKVD still made people shiver.

Talking with the commanders from the armored regiment turned out to be a good idea. They hadn't thought the bandits might try to hijack a tank or two. "We will strengthen the guard force around the tank park immediately, Comrade Captain," a lieutenant colonel— Surkov, his name was—said. "Thank you for bringing this to our notice. If something had gone wrong—" He made a small choking noise. That was about what would have happened to him, all right—again, if he was lucky.

Even now, the lieutenant colonel might get reprimanded for inadequate readiness. But he wouldn't get his shoulder boards torn off. He wouldn't get shipped to a gulag. And Vladimir Bokov went back to his office and drafted a memo about alertness in the armored forces.

It went out to units all over the Soviet zone—and, for all he knew, elsewhere in Eastern Europe, too. It might do some good. Whether it would do as much as cooperating with the Anglo-Americans . . . he didn't have the initiative to find out.

"OH, THIS HERE WAS CUTE," SERGEANT TOBY BENTON SAID.

"Watcha got?" Lou Weissberg asked. They were only a couple of hundred yards outside the barbed-wire perimeter around American headquarters in Nuremberg.

"You see how this painting's got a wire coming off it—looks like it might be part of the wire that hung it to the wall," the explosives expert said.

"Right." Lou nodded. He saw it when the Oklahoman pointed it out. He'd learned a lot from Benton. But he wouldn't make an ordnance man if he lived another fifty years. And he wouldn't live anywhere near that long if he tried the trade.

"Painting's old. Looks like it might be worth a little somethin'. But the dogface who found it reckoned it might be booby-trapped, so he didn't pull it off the wall. He called the explosives guys—me— instead. Good thing, too, on account of that wire leads to a Bouncing Betty in the wall."

"Oh, my!" Lou said in shrill falsetto. He crossed his hands in front of his crotch like a pretty girl surprised skinnydipping. Some Nazi engineer must have won himself a bonus for the Betty. When the mine went off, a small charge kicked the main charge up in the air. The main charge blew up at waist height and sprayed shrapnel all around. Too many American soldiers were singing soprano for real.

Benton nodded. "Uh-huh. But that ain't the worst, Captain."

"*Gevalt!*" Lou said. Toby Benton had worked with him often enough to have a notion of what that meant. After a moment, Lou went on, "So what's worse than a Bouncing Betty?"

"I tore up the wall to get at the son of a bitch," Benton answered, "but I didn't want to lift it out right away, y'know? Maybe I watched too many movies or somethin'. I kinda got to thinking, *This here is mighty slick—maybe even a little too slick.* So instead of taking out the Bouncing Betty like I usually woulda done, I dug down *underneath* the bastard instead."

"Yeah?" Lou said.

"Yeah." Sergeant Benton nodded. "And I found me *another* wire, goin' down below the building. An' *that* son of a bitch was attached to a ton and a half of TNT, with a delay fuse so it woulda gone off after there was a good old crowd here takin' care of the poor sorry shitheel who blew his nuts off with the Bouncing Betty . . . or to pat the explosives guy on the back when he really wasn't smart enough."

"Wow!" Lou said. That didn't seem remotely adequate. He tried again: "I'll write you up for a medal."

"Write me up so I can go on home, sir," Toby said. "I'd like those orders a fuck of a lot better, an' you can sing that in church."

"Yeah, well, I believe you," Lou said. "Shit, I'll even try. God knows you just earned yourself a ticket to the States. But it won't do any good. I can tell you right now what the brass'll say. 'This guy is good. We can't afford to discharge him, 'cause too many people'll get hurt if we do.' "

"Well, if that don't beat all," Benton said disgustedly. "If I do me a crappy job, I get my sorry ass blown up. If I do me a great job, they make me stick around—so's I can get my sorry ass blown up." He spat on the filthy floor. "Ought to be a name for somethin' like that, where you get fucked over comin' an' goin'."

"Yeah, it's a heller, all right. One of these days, I bet there will." Lou got a strange kick out of thinking like an English teacher instead of a counterintelligence officer. "A guy who's been through the mill will write a story or a book about it. He'll hang some kind of handle on it, and from then on everybody'll call it that."

Toby Benton let out a thoughtful grunt. "Well, maybe so. Till then, 'fucked over comin' an' goin' ' works good enough."

"Sure does," Lou agreed. He shook his head. The classroom inside it vanished. He was back in bombed-out, stinking, fanatic-infested Nuremberg again, doing Uncle Sam's job, not his old one. *Aw, shit,* he thought wearily. "How long would it've taken for Heydrich's fuckers to set this up?"

"Well, you don't sneak in a ton and a half of explosives an' bury 'em overnight, not if you don't want the sentries yonder and the patrols and all to spot you while you're doin' it," Benton answered.

"Yeah." Lou's voice was sour. "I figured you'd say something like that. So we've got fanatics hiding out inside of Nuremberg, huh? And there's bound to be ordinary krauts who know just who the assholes are, too. Only stands to reason. But have they said anything to us? Don't you wish?"

"Ain't there a reward for that kinda information?" Toby asked.

"Certainly." It came out more like *Soitainly,* as if Lou were Curly from the Three Stooges. "You know how long a German who turns stoolie usually lives afterwards?"

Sergeant Benton chewed on that. He grunted again. Then he said, "Likely makes my line of work look downright safe by comparison."

The average guy in his line of work had a life expectancy measured in months—sometimes in weeks. He was far above average, which (along with fool luck, especially at the start) was why he was still breathing.

And, unfortunately, he was dead right here. "We have to make the Jerries like us better than they like the fanatics, or we have to make 'em more afraid of us. So far, we haven't managed either one. You find an answer there, Sergeant, and I'll get you home if I have to carry you on my back," Lou said.

"Won't hold my breath. You smart guys can't fix it, don't expect me to," Benton said.

Lou sighed. "I will write you up for the medal. Whether you want it or not, it's something I can do." It seemed a GI could only get what he didn't want. *Fucked over comin' an' goin'* rang in Lou's mind again.

XIX

Bernie Cobb was not a happy man. Occupation duty in Erlangen hadn't been so bad. Oh, you looked sideways at about every third Jerry you passed on the street, but he'd kind of got used to that. And Erlangen wasn't a big city. Yeah, the fanatics had bumped off that Adenauer guy there, but that was just one of those things. (Half-remembered bits of Cole Porter spun through his head—something about gossamer wings. He wished he had some right this minute.)

What he was doing now wasn't occupation duty. It was war—no other name for it. He was part of a skirmish line combing through a valley somewhere in the Alps, looking for—well, anything that didn't belong there. Some of the things that didn't belong here were krauts with rifles and Schmeissers and machine guns. Not all of them were Heydrich's diehards. The rest were just brigands. They'd lived by robbery all through the war, and hadn't felt like quitting after the surrender. But they could kill you every bit as dead as any fanatic.

Yeah, those gossamer wings would come in handy, all right. Bernie imagined flying above the rocky landscape, spying out trouble that'd be hard to spot from the ground. Then he imagined some asshole in a ragged *Wehrmacht* greatcoat doing antiaircraft work with an MG42. His imagination came back to earth with a thump, the same way he would if the bastard shot him down.

His breath smoked. His short Eisenhower jacket didn't keep him warm enough. Fall was here, sure enough. Erlangen was cooler than Albuquerque—all of Europe that he'd seen was cooler than Albuquerque—but in summer that was okay. Now, tramping through these miserable mountain valleys . . . He shook his head and exhaled more fog.

Haystacks dotted the valleys. All the grass was going yellow because of the night freezes, so the stacks were less picturesque than they would have been a few weeks earlier. That didn't mean they were any less dangerous. Haystacks were great to sleep in and to hole up in. Bernie'd found that out for himself plenty of times before the surrender.

He and his buddies warily approached the closest stack. They fanned out so they could make sure nobody was hiding on the far side. Inside was harder to be sure about. *"Raus!"* Bernie yelled. *"Hände hoch!"*

Nobody came out with his hands up. "Want me to give it a burst?" another dogface asked, hefting his grease gun.

"Bet your ass, Roscoe," Bernie said. The rest of the GIs stood clear. Roscoe sprayed three short bursts through the haystack. Nobody staggered out bleeding and wailing, either.

"Okay. This one's clean," another soldier said.

"Is now, by God," Bernie agreed. If some German hiding in there had just quietly died with his brains blown out, Bernie wouldn't shed a tear. Son of a bitch had the chance to give up. That was more than he would've given the guys hunting him.

The Americans tramped on. Bernie lit a cigarette. A few hundred yards off, a GI in another group of troops waved, silently asking what the gunfire meant. Bernie's answering wave said everything was jake. The distant soldier gave back one more flourish to show he got it. Then he returned to his own hunt.

Bernie's bunch came to a farmhouse and outbuildings. The farmer was about fifty, so maybe he'd put in his time and maybe he hadn't. His skinny wife eyed the Americans as if she'd just taken a big swig of vinegar. They had a daughter who might've been cute if she hadn't looked even more sour than her ma.

And, on the mantel, they had a framed photo of a young man in the uniform of a *Wehrmacht* junior noncom. Bernie pointed at it and raised an eyebrow. *"Ostfront,"* the farmer said. *"Tot?"* A sad shrug. *"Gefangen?"* Another one.

"Dead or captured fighting the Russians," said Roscoe, who had the usual GI bits and pieces of German.

"Yeah, I got it, too," Bernie said. He pointed at the farmer. *"Soldat? Du? Westfront? Ostfront?"*

"Nein. Bauer durchaus Krieg," the man replied in elementary *Deutsch.* German for morons, not that Bernie cared. He got the answer he needed—the guy claimed he'd farmed all through the war.

And maybe the kraut was even telling the truth. He was wearing patched overalls, like an Okie fleeing the Dust Bowl in the '30s. His shirt and shoes weren't *Wehrmacht* issue, either. A lot of Germans hung on to their army clothes because those were all they had. This stuff wasn't any better than what the Jerries got from the *Wehrmacht,* but it was different.

"Let's search the joint," Bernie said.

Maybe Mother and Daughter Vinegar Phiz knew some English, because they looked even nastier than they had before. It did them exactly no good. They might have got themselves shot if they did anything more than glare, but they didn't.

The GIs turned the place upside down and inside out. They opened drawers and scattered clothes all over the floor. Some of them got a giggle out of throwing women's underwear around. They poked and prodded the mattress and bedclothes, and lifted them up to check underneath. They found a stash of dirty pictures, with plump, naked *Fräuleins* doing amazing things to men with old-fashioned haircuts. Those were good for a giggle, too. Several guys helped themselves to the best ones. Bernie wondered how the farmer would explain them to his pickle-faced wife. That wasn't his worry, thank God.

What they didn't find were any weapons. The most lethal things in the place were the kitchen knives. They went out to the barn and the other outbuildings. Guys who'd grown up on farms back in the States led the search there. Again, they came up with nothing. Maybe these people really didn't hang around with bandits.

"Danke schön," Bernie said as the soldiers started to leave. He tossed the farmer a pack of Luckies. It wouldn't square things, but it might help.

By the farmer's expression, and by some of the things he muttered under his breath, it didn't. If any of Heydrich's fanatics wanted to hide here from now on, the guy would probably serve them roast goose and red cabbage. Well, too goddamn bad.

As the GIs trudged away, the farmer's wife started screeching at him. "Oh, boy, is he gonna catch it," Roscoe said, not without sympathy. He had one of the farmer's finest photos carefully tucked into a breast pocket.

They hadn't gone more than a few hundred yards when they came to the place where a mineshaft plunged into the hillside. It wasn't much to look at: a roughly rectangular hole, a little bigger all the way around than a man was tall. Bernie went in as far as the light reached, which wasn't very. Spider webs shrouded support timbers that looked as if they'd stood there since Napoleon's day, or maybe Martin Luther's.

But you never could tell. This was the kind of stuff they'd been sent out to find. One of the guys had a radio set on his back instead of his ordinary pack. He was already on the horn to divisional HQ when Bernie came out of the shaft. Bernie told him what little he'd seen, and the radioman passed it on.

He listened for a little while, then gave the word: "They'll send a search team and a demolition team. We're supposed to wait till they get here, and then support the search team."

"Suits," Bernie said. He flopped down in front of the big, black hole in the ground and lit a cigarette. Some of the dogfaces dug out K-ration cans and chowed down. Others promptly started snoring. Bernie had lost the knack for sleeping on bare ground, and wasn't sorry he had. But if they kept giving him shit like this to do, he might have to get it back.

The demolition squad and the searchers showed up a couple of hours later. Bernie wasn't anxious to go back into the mine, but he did it. The search team brought flashlights that could have doubled as billy clubs.

"You oughta sell these suckers to MPs," Bernie said, turning his this way and that. All he saw was carved-out gray rock and more of those ancient support timbers. His boots thumped on the stone floor of the shaft.

"Not a half-bad notion. Damn snowdrops'd be dumb enough to

fork over," said a corporal on the search team. Bernie snickered. The MPs' white helmets and gloves gave them the scornful nickname.

"Hold up," somebody called from ahead. "Big old cave-in here. This is the end of the road." Bernie glanced at the corporal. The two-striper was already turning around. Bernie wasn't sorry to follow him out—not even a little bit.

"Everybody out?" a man from the demolition squad yelled into the shaft. No one answered. Bernie looked around. All his people were standing outside the mine. The sergeant in charge of the search team seemed to have all his guys, too. The demolitions people placed their charges. They backed away from the opening. Again, Bernie wasn't sorry to follow. The man who'd yelled used the detonator.

Boom! It wasn't so loud as Bernie'd expected. Dust spurted out of the shaft. When it cleared, the hole was gone: full of fallen rock. "That'll do it," he said.

"Yeah," agreed the soldier who'd touched off the blast. "Nobody going in or out of there. Now all we gotta do is seal off about a million more of these motherfuckers and we've got it licked."

"Er—right." Bernie wished he hadn't put it that way. It made him think he'd be tramping through these miserable mountains forever. He looked around. Hell, he was liable to be.

Boom! The explosion was a long way off, which didn't mean Reinhard Heydrich didn't hear it. He swore. The Amis had just plugged one of the ways into and out of his underground redoubt. They didn't know they'd done that, of course; all the shafts that led down here were artfully camouflaged to look as if they deadended. Even so . . .

Things had picked up. The Amis wanted him dead. They'd wanted him dead before, of course, but now they *really* wanted him dead. They wanted him dead enough to put some real work into killing him: into killing him in particular because he was what and who he was, not because he was some Nazi diehard.

I should thank them for the compliment, he thought wryly. He'd got under their skin. He'd hurt the enemy enough to make the enemy want to hurt him back. No, to make the enemy *need* to hurt him back. This wasn't just war. It was politics, too. American elections were coming up soon. If the Amis could show off photos of Reinhard Heydrich's mutilated corpse, their hard-liners would win votes.

"Ladies and gentlemen, we got him!" It would go out over the radio, in the newspapers, in their magazines. And the oppression of Germany would go on.

Clausewitz said war was an extension of politics by other means. Hitler had often—too often—forgotten that. Now that the *Führer* was dead, Heydrich could look at him and his policies more objectively. And Heydrich didn't have the mighty *Wehrmacht* at his back. The mighty *Wehrmacht* was rotting meat and scrap metal. Heydrich couldn't bludgeon foes out of the way. He had to keep stinging them, wasplike, till they decided Germany was more trouble than it was worth and left on their own.

He wanted to stay alive, too. He wanted to enjoy the free Germany he'd created. And he especially didn't want to die if dying gave the occupying powers an advantage and hurt the rebuilding *Reich*.

Hans Klein walked in. "They aren't coming after us."

"Good." Heydrich nodded. "I didn't think they would. We spent a lot of time and a lot of Reichsmarks making the holes in the ground that lead in here look like holes in the ground that don't go anywhere."

"When you're playing bridge, one peek is worth a thousand finesses," Klein said. "When you're playing our game, one traitor's worth a thousand tonnes of camouflage."

Heydrich grunted. Nothing like a cynical noncom to put his finger on your weakness. "We haven't had to worry about that so far," the *Reichsprotektor* said.

"We've been lucky so far," Klein retorted.

Again, Heydrich couldn't very well tell him he was talking through his hat. Klein damn well wasn't. At least Heydrich had the sense to see as much. Plenty of people who'd yelled *"Heil* Hitler!*"* as loud as anybody were serving the Anglo-Americans now. Or they were licking the lickspittle Frenchmen's boots, or else kowtowing to Stalin the way they'd once bowed down to their proper *Führer*.

When such folk made conspicuous nuisances of themselves, Heydrich's men disposed of them. A sniper from 800 meters, a bomb planted in an automobile or posted in a package, poison at a favorite eatery . . . There were all kinds of ways. Collaborators knew they had to be careful. Some of them decided the risk wasn't worth it and quit collaborating. Every one like that counted as a victory.

But the enemy also had his weapons. One of them was cold, hard cash. Heydrich remembered the huge price on his head. A million U.S. dollars now, wasn't it?

Would that be enough to tempt some sniveling little Judas who'd got sick of staying cooped up in a hole in the ground for years? Heydrich nodded to himself. A million dollars was plenty for a traitor to buy himself an estate and a Rolls and the kind of pussy that went with an estate and a Rolls. Then all he'd need to worry about was his former friends' revenge.

He might figure the resistance movement would die with Heydrich. He might be right, too, though the *Reichsprotektor* didn't think so. If the resistance had gone on after Hitler died, it would go on after Heydrich, too. Jochen Peiper was more than capable in his own right—and freedom for Germany was more important than any one man.

Which didn't mean treason couldn't hurt. "People do have to keep their eyes open," Heydrich said.

"That's right," Klein agreed. "You can't push it too hard, though, not when we've all been down here so long. Folks stop listening to you. Anything you have to say over and over starts sounding like *Quatsch* . . . uh, sir."

"And you not even a Berliner," Heydrich said with a mock-sorrowful shake of the head. But the slang word for *bilge* was understood all over Germany these days. After some thought, Heydrich nodded much more seriously. "That is one of the troubles with a fight like this. Well, if you think the warnings get to where they do more harm than good, let me know."

"Will do, *Herr Reichsprotektor*," Klein promised. Heydrich had no doubt he would, too. Klein was solid. You couldn't win a war without leaders, but you also couldn't win it without reliable followers. Heydrich would have paid a reward of his own to bring in more just like Hans Klein.

Meanwhile . . . "We've lost one doorway. We've still got plenty. If they think we can't hurt them now—they'll find out."

NOVEMBER 5. ELECTION DAY. SUNNY BUT CHILLY IN ANDERSON. Early in the morning, Jerry Duncan and his wife made the ceremonial stroll from their house to the polling place a couple of blocks away. Sure enough, two or three reporters and their accompanying photographers stood waiting on the sidewalk.

"Wave to the nice people, Bets," Jerry said in a low voice, and followed his own advice.

Betsy Duncan did, too. Also quietly, she answered, "I know what to do. It's not like this is the first time."

"Nope," Jerry agreed. The one who'd be sweating rivets was Douglas Catledge. Duncan didn't think the Democrat had ever run for anything before he came back from the war.

"Who you gonna vote for, Congressman?" one of the reporters called.

"Who do you think, E.A.?" Jerry said. E. A. Stuart grinned. One of the other reporters laughed out loud. It was funny, and then again it wasn't. About every other election, you heard of some little race—school board, maybe, or town councilman—decided by one vote. Sometimes it was decided when—oops!—one candidate chivalrously voted for his opponent. Like any serious politician, Jerry believed in winning more than he believed in chivalry.

The polling place was in the auditorium of an elementary school. Jerry shook hands with people in there till an election official—a skinny old lady and undoubtedly a Democrat—said, "No electioneering within a hundred feet of the polls."

"I wasn't electioneering—just meeting friends," Jerry lied easily.

He got his ballot, went into a booth, and pulled the curtain shut behind him. After he'd marked his ballot, he folded it up and gave it to the clerk in charge of the ballot box. That worthy stuffed it into the slot. "Mr. Duncan has voted," he intoned ceremoniously. Betsy came out of her booth a moment later. The clerk took her ballot, too. "Mrs. Duncan has voted."

Flashbulbs from the photographers' cameras filled the dingy auditorium with bursts of harsh white light. The walk back to the house was attended only by E. A. Stuart. Jerry'd hoped he would get to be an ordinary human being on the way home, but no such luck.

"What will you do if the Republicans win a majority today?" Stuart asked.

"Celebrate," Betsy answered before Jerry could open his mouth.

Chuckling, Jerry said, "She's right. You can write it down. I think the first thing we'll do after that is try and bring our boys home from Germany."

"President Truman won't like it," E.A. Stuart predicted. Jerry tried to remember his full handle, but couldn't. It was something ridiculous and Biblical—he knew that. No wonder he went by his initials.

"Truman's had a year and a half to fix the mess," Jerry said. "He hasn't done it—not even close. Things are worse now than they were right after the surrender. If he won't get cracking on his own, we'll just have to make him move."

"And if the Democrats hold on?" Stuart asked. Jerry and Betsy Duncan made identical faces. The reporter laughed. "I can't quote expressions, folks," he said.

"Awww," Jerry said, and E. A. Stuart laughed again.

He tried another question: "Would you oppose the occupation so strongly if Diana McGraw hadn't mobilized opinion against it?"

Betsy's step faltered, ever so slightly. She was jealous of Diana. Jerry hadn't given her any reason to be, but she was. (What she didn't know about a few young, pretty clerk-typists back in Washington wouldn't hurt her.) He picked his words with care: "Of course Mrs. McGraw comes from my district." He stressed *Mrs.* for his wife's benefit. "That makes me pay some extra attention to her views. But the President's disastrous policy would have sparked opposition with her or without her. I have to think I would have been part of it."

"Okay," Stuart said, scribbling. "Now—"

Jerry held up a hand. "Can we hold the rest for tonight or tomorrow? Then I'll know what's what. Right now I'd just be building castles in the air, okay?"

"Well, sure." E. A. Stuart smiled crookedly. "But that's half the fun."

"Maybe for you." Jerry turned into his own walk. A man's home was his castle, and reporters and other barbarians could damn well wait outside.

The polls closed at seven. Jerry and Betsy were at his campaign headquarters—a storefront three doors down from the Bijou—at five past. Radios turned to CBS, RCA, and Mutual stations blared returns. Some people had trouble straining information out of election-night chaos. Not Jerry. He could pick the East Coast nuggets from all the random chatter.

And all the nuggets seemed pure gold. Democrat after Democrat was losing or "trailing significantly," as the pundits liked to say. Republican after Republican claimed victory. Excitement made Jerry's fingertips tingle. It had been so long, so very long.

"And now we have the first returns from Indiana," one of the radio announcers said. Everybody at campaign headquarters yelled for everybody else to shut up. While people were yelling, the announcer read off the returns. In spite of Jerry's ear, he couldn't make them out.

"Downstate," someone said. "We're leading three to two."

"Is that all?" Someone else sounded disappointed. Downstate Indiana, down by the Ohio River, was as solidly Republican as anywhere in the country. Still, three to two wasn't half bad, not by any standards. And most of the votes might have come from some local Democratic stronghold. Till you knew provenance, you had to be careful about what the raw numbers meant.

"In the suburbs of Indianapolis," the announcer went on, "incumbent Jerry Duncan leads his Democratic challenger. The totals are 1,872 to 1,391 in what are still preliminary results."

Cheers erupted. So did a few four-letter words aimed at the man on the radio. People from Anderson and Muncie didn't like to hear their towns called suburbs of Indianapolis. When you got right down to it, they were, but folks didn't like to hear it or think about it.

"What were the numbers like two years ago? I don't remember exactly," Betsy said.

"Not as good as they are now. I was only up by maybe a hundred votes at this stage of things." Like most politicos, Jerry had total recall for all the returns in every election he'd ever contested. But he was also cautious: "Can't tell too much yet. Besides, who knows where these votes come from?"

"Okay," Betsy said. "But I sure like it a lot better than I would if you were behind by that much."

He laughed. "Well, when you put it like that, so do I."

The air got thick with cigarette smoke and the odd pipe and cigar. Then it got thicker. Jerry was puffing away like everybody else, but he didn't like it when his eyes started to sting and water. That took a good thing too far.

More good news kept blaring out of the radio. "This does look like a repudiation of Harry Truman's domestic and foreign policy," a broadcaster said. "Unless things out West dramatically change the situation, the Republican Party stands to gain control of both houses of Congress for the first time since the Hoover administration."

More cheers. Jerry shouted along with everybody else. But he couldn't help wishing the guy on the radio hadn't mentioned Hoover. If ever there was a jinx . . .

But not even the ghost of Hoover and the Depression could jinx the GOP tonight. Around half past ten, when Jerry's lead had swelled to over 5,000 votes, one of the telephones at campaign headquarters jangled. The staffer who answered it waved to try to cut the hubbub in the room. Not having much luck, he bellowed, "It's Douglas Catledge, Congressman!"

Jerry jumped to his feet and hurried over to the phone. The campaign workers yelled and clapped and stamped their feet. But when Jerry waved for quiet, he got it. He grabbed the handset, saying, "Thanks, Irv." He talked into the telephone: "This is Jerry Duncan."

"Hello, Congressman. Doug Catledge here." The young Democrat sounded tired and sad but determined: about the way Jerry would have sounded in his shoes. *One of these days, I will sound that way. Going to Washington is always a round-trip ticket. But not today, thank God,* Jerry thought. After an audible deep breath, his opponent went on, "I called to congratulate you . . . on your reelection."

"Thank you very much, Doug. That's mighty gracious of you," Jerry said. "You ran a strong campaign. I was worried right up till the polls closed." He hadn't been; he'd thought things looked pretty good. But if the other fellow was gracious you had to follow suit.

"Kind of you to say so," Catledge replied. "If you don't mind my two cents' worth now, I do hope you'll soft-pedal the pullout foolishness you spouted the past few weeks."

Jerry frowned. Douglas Catledge had lost not least because he backed Truman's policies, and he was telling Jerry what to do? *Go peddle your papers, sonny.* Jerry came *that* close to saying it out loud.

But no. Just because the other guy couldn't mind his manners didn't mean Jerry had to imitate him. What he did say was, "The fight over there costs more men and more cash than we can afford. Our dollar is falling against the Swiss franc and the Canadian dollar and even the Mexican peso. It would be falling against the pound, but England's stuck in this flypaper, too."

"If we run away from Germany, either the Russians grab all of it or the Nazis come back in and start getting ready for World War III," Catledge said. "I don't think either one helps the United States."

"I don't think either one is anything we've got to worry about, not as long as we have the atom bomb," Jerry answered. "Good night, Mr. Catledge." He wasn't about to argue, not tonight.

"Good night," Douglas Catledge said sadly. "I still think you're making a bad mistake."

"I know you do. But the voters don't." Jerry said "Good night" once more and hung up. He'd got the last word. So had the voters: the only word that mattered in an election. Jerry stood up and held up his hands. Everybody in the crowded room looked his way. "My opponent has just generously conceded," he told the campaign workers. "I want to thank him, and I want to thank all of you for making my victory possible. I'm the one who's going back to Washington, but I couldn't possibly do it alone. Thanks again to every one of you from the bottom of my heart."

He got another round of applause. He went over and kissed Betsy. Then somebody stuck a lighted cigar in his mouth. He didn't usually smoke them, but he took a few puffs with it held at a jaunty angle while the photographers snapped away. It was like a victory lap at the Indianapolis 500. As soon as the photographers were done, he stuck the cheroot in an ashtray and forgot about it.

Diana McGraw walked into the campaign headquarters about fifteen minutes later. The campaign workers gave her a hand, too. Jerry joined in. His wife, he noticed, didn't. No, Betsy never came out and said anything about Diana, but she didn't need words to make her feelings plain.

"Congratulations," Diana said. "When the radio said Catledge had conceded, I figured I could come over without causing too much distraction."

"We're going to have another term," Jerry said. Betsy's smile might have been painted on.

"Another term," Diana agreed. "How long do you think it will take to get the bonehead in the White House to bring our men home?"

"Good question. If Truman's shown one thing, it's that he's at least as stubborn as FDR ever was," Jerry answered.

"But Congress holds the purse strings," Diana said. "If you don't give him the money to keep troops in Germany—"

"Have to see what things look like, what the lineup is after they count all the votes," Jerry said. He'd been trying to make that calculation himself. Knowing the numbers of Republicans and Democrats in the upcoming Eightieth Congress would help only so much. Some Democrats would steer clear of Truman for fear of losing the next time around, while some Republicans would stick with him because they were scared of Stalin—or just because the people in their districts thought occupying Germany was still a good idea.

Diana, of course, had her sights set on one thing and one thing only. "The sooner the boys come home, the sooner no more mothers will start hating the Western Union delivery boy," she said.

How were you supposed to answer that? Jerry couldn't, all the more so because he thought she was right. But she seemed sure the election would make things happen as if by magic. As a multiterm Congressman, Jerry Duncan knew better. There'd be plenty of horse trading and log rolling before anything got done. Washington was like that. It always had been. If it ever changed, he would be astonished.

"If Truman won't see reason, you ought to impeach him and throw him out on his ear," Diana said.

Jerry held up a hand like a traffic cop at a busy intersection. "Don't even try to get anybody to talk impeachment. You'd only be wasting your time, and no one would listen to you," he said. "Truman's not doing anything unconstitutional. He's just wrong. There's a big difference."

"If they impeached everybody in Washington who was wrong, the place'd be empty inside of two weeks," Betsy said.

"If you're wrong enough—" Diana began.

Maybe she had something, too. If Roosevelt had been on the point of losing the war, wouldn't people have run him out of town on a rail? Jerry suspected they would . . . which, in those days, would have left Henry Wallace President of the United States, a genuinely scary thought. Truman had no Vice President at the moment. That would make the Speaker of the House President if he got impeached. And the new Speaker would be a Republican. . . .

ED MCGRAW READ THE PAPER WHILE HE ATE BACON AND EGGS OVER easy and toast with butter and jam and smoked a cigarette. "Well," he said, "looks like you've got the kind of Congress you're gonna need."

"What are the final numbers?" Diana asked around a mouthful of toast—she was eating breakfast, too.

Her husband read from the front-page story: " 'If present trends continue, the House in the Eightieth Congress will consist of at least 257 Republicans, 169 Democrats, and one American Labor Party member. The final eight races are too close for a winner to be declared. In the Senate, there will be at least fifty-three Republicans and forty-two Democrats. Again, the final Senate race is still up in the air.' "

"That's amazing," Diana said. "The Democrats had big majorities in both houses of Congress the last time around."

Ed rustled the newspaper to show he wasn't done yet. " 'This historic reversal is surpassed in recent times only by the Democratic sweep that went with Franklin D. Roosevelt's election,' " he read. " 'Pundits believe many of the voters who turned to the GOP yesterday did so in protest against President Truman's costly and bloody occupation of Germany. Diana McGraw's opposition movement galvanized voter unhappiness.' " He grinned at her around the cigarette, which was about to singe his lips. "How about that, babe? You and zinc and sheet metal." In the nick of time, the butt went into the ashtray.

"How about that?" Diana echoed. She didn't quite get the joke, but Ed had been making factory jokes she didn't quite get ever since they were newlyweds. She went on, "Jerry said something like that last night, but he's on the same side as we are, so it's hard to take him all that seriously."

"Jerry . . ." Ed McGraw shoveled in a forkful. He took a bite of toast. Then he lit another cigarette. "Ever figure you'd call a Congressman by his first name?"

"You've got to be kidding." Diana started to say that the Congressman's wife didn't like it very much. She swallowed the words before they came out. Why have Ed wondering whether Betsy Duncan had a good reason not to like it? That would set Ed wondering, too, which wouldn't be good when nothing was going on between her and Jerry. And, she realized a beat later, it would be even worse if something *were* going on.

"You're hot stuff, kiddo." Ed took the cigarette butt out of his mouth long enough to drink some coffee. After that, it went right back in. "But I've known you were hot stuff since high school."

"Oh, you—!" she said fondly. She never had confessed some of the things that went on in the back seat of his beat-up old Chevy before they got married. What the priest in the booth didn't know wouldn't hurt him . . . and God, of course, had already seen it.

"So how does it feel?" he asked. He'd never looked for any of the limelight himself. He wasn't that kind of man. All he cared about were his house and his job and their family. "You know all these big shots. You met the President and everything. You get your name in the papers."

"I wish nobody'd ever heard of me," Diana said. "That would mean we had Pat back. To hell with all this other stuff."

No, she didn't usually swear in front of her husband. She hardly noticed doing it this time. Ed didn't notice at all. His big bald head bobbed up and down. "You got that right. Oh, boy, do you ever. I'd trade anything for another minute with him, even. But you don't get those chances over again."

"You sure don't." Diana drained her own coffee mug. She looked at the clock above the stove. It always ran fast, but she made the correction without conscious thought. "You'd better get going."

"I know. I know." Ed stood up. He grabbed his sheet-metal dinner pail. "Tongue sandwich in here?"

"Sure."

"Good—one of my favorites." Ed leaned down and brushed his lips across hers, leaving affection and the smell of tobacco smoke behind. Then he was out the door and heading for work, right on time.

Ever since they got married, he'd been as reliable as the machines he tended.

Diana smiled as the Pontiac backed down the driveway and chugged out into the street. Ed was reliable here, too—not just on the job. She didn't want him to think she was running around, even if he didn't always leave her glowing in bed any more. He'd never given her any reason to think he was, not even during the war, when all those Rosie the Riveter types flooded into the plant. Some of them—plenty of them, in Diana's jaundiced opinion—were looking for more than work. If they'd found it, they hadn't found it with Ed.

Reaching across the kitchen table, Diana snagged the newspaper. Ed always got it first, because he had to hustle out the door—and, not to put too fine a point on it, because he was the man. But she could look it over now. It had maps and charts showing Senators and Representatives by party in the old Congress and the new.

No doubt Jerry was right (*yes, I do know my Congressman by his first name,* Diana thought): some Republicans would back the occupation, while some Democrats would vote against it. But the more Republicans in Congress, the better the chances it would end soon. You didn't need a crystal ball to see that.

"We *will* bring them home," Diana said, there in the empty kitchen. It would have been empty even if Pat did come home: he would've gone off to work with Ed. But it would have been a different empty. It wouldn't have been such an aching emptiness. Pat would have been gone, but he wouldn't have been *gone*. Diana nodded to herself. Pretty soon, nobody else would have to worry about the aching kind of emptiness. She hoped.

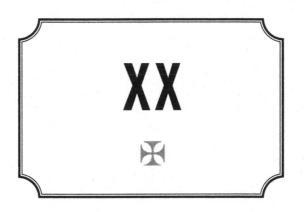

XX

More than a year and a half after the war in Europe was supposed to have ended, London remained a sorry, miserable place. Food was still rationed. So was coal. People wore greatcoats even indoors. Demobilized soldiers seemed to huddle in theirs as they ambled along looking for work—but jobs were as hard to come by as everything else in Britain these days.

Police Constable Cedric Mitchell counted himself lucky. He'd had his position reserved for him when he came back from the war—if he came back. Plenty of his mates hadn't. He'd made it across the Channel from Dunkirk in a tugboat that got strafed by two Stukas. Then he'd gone to North Africa, and then on to the slow, bloody slog up the Italian boot. Now he had a Military Medal, a great puckered scar on the outside of his right thigh, and nightmares that woke him up shrieking and sweating once or twice a week.

He also had a new dream that wasn't so nasty: to retire to Algiers or Naples or somewhere else with decent weather one day. Down in those countries, winter didn't mean long, long nights and fogs and endless coughs and shivers. He wouldn't have believed it if he hadn't seen it with his own eyes, but he damn well had.

"Italy's wasted on the bloody Eyties," he muttered, his breath adding to the mist that swirled in front of Parliament. "Fucking wasted."

He walked his beat, back and forth, back and forth. The most lethal weapon he carried was a billy club. Thinking of that made him snort, which also added to the mist. No Jerry'd sneak up behind him and cut his throat here. No stinking dago who still loved Mussolini'd chuck a German potato-masher grenade into his foxhole. He didn't need a Sten gun or a fighting knife or an entrenching tool—which could be a lot more lethal than a knife if you knew what to do with it, and he did.

A fellow in American pinks and greens—khaki trousers and olive-drab jacket—looked left before he stepped out into St. Margaret's Street. "Watch yourself, Yank!" PC Mitchell shouted. The American froze. A truck rumbled past from the direction in which he hadn't looked.

"Jesus!" he said. "Why don't you guys drive the right way?"

"We think we do," Mitchell answered. "And since you're over here, you'd jolly well better think so, too."

"That's the third time the past two weeks I almost got myself creamed," the Yank said.

Do you suppose you ought to suspect a trend? But Mitchell didn't say it. Even though the Americans were two years late getting into the war—a year better than the last time around, at that—they'd done all right once they got going. He'd fought alongside them in Italy, so he knew they'd paid their dues. And Britain would have gone under without the supplies they sent. So . . .

"Well, have a care crossing," was what did come out of Mitchell's mouth. His sergeant would have been proud of him. He beckoned the American on. "Seems safe enough now."

"It *seemed* safe enough before," the Yank said darkly. But he made it from the houses of Parliament to Westminster Abbey without getting run down. Not that many cars were on the road. Petrol was still rationed, too, and hard to come by.

PC Mitchell wondered how long the country would need to get

back to normal. Then he wondered if it ever would. India wanted to leave the Empire, and nothing short of another war seemed likely to keep it in. Without India, what was left wasn't worth tuppence ha'penny. And there wouldn't be a war on the far side of the world when Germany, only a long spit away, had turned into a running sore.

Blam! No sooner had Mitchell heard the explosion than he was flat on his belly. It hadn't knocked him over—he'd hit the dirt. That was a hell of a big bomb going off somewhere not far enough away— not close enough to hurt him, but nowhere near far enough away.

Across the street, the Yank in pinks and greens had also flattened out like a hedgehog smashed by a lorry. *He's seen action, too, then,* Mitchell thought as he started to scramble to his feet.

Lorries. No sooner had they crossed his mind than a big one—one of the kind the USA had built by the millions during the war—came tearing down the middle of the street toward him. It was as if the driver knew he ought to stay on the left but had trouble remembering. "Jesus!" Mitchell said, furiously blowing his whistle. Just what the poor sorry world needed: a drunken Yank driving a deuce-and-a-half like he'd just been let out of the asylum.

Then PC Cedric Mitchell got one glimpse of the driver's face as the fellow swerved across the street toward Westminster Abbey. The bloke was a nutter, all right, but not *that* kind of nutter. Not barking mad but exalted mad. He had the face of someone about to do something marvelous, and the devil with the consequences. He had a face that made PC Mitchell hit the dirt again.

Right after Nazi fanatics bombed the Eiffel Tower, soldiers had appeared in front of Parliament and Westminster Abbey and Buckingham Palace and St. Paul's and a few other places. Then, when nothing happened, they vanished again. Mitchell had most of a second to wish men with rifles and Sten guns were anywhere close by—or even that bobbies like him carried firearms.

Then the fanatic in the truck—and he couldn't have been anything else—touched it off. The other explosion had been too close for comfort, frightening but not dangerous. This one . . . When this one went off, it was like getting stuck in the middle of the end of the world.

Much too much like that, in fact.

Blast picked PC Mitchell up and slammed him into something

hard. "Oof!" he said, and then, "Ow!" He could barely hear himself, even though that second noise came closer to a shriek than a yelp. Blast had also smashed at his ears.

Had the Nazi struck at Parliament, Mitchell would have been nothing more than a smear on the sidewalk. But he'd steered his truck into Westminster Abbey before detonating it . . . and God help that poor bloody American in his smart uniform.

Broken glass clattered and clinked down around the bobby. A big, sharp shard shattered between his legs. He shuddered. A foot higher up and that one would have cut it right off him or left him with no need to shave for the rest of his days.

He snuffled as he staggered to his feet. A swipe at his nose with his sleeve showed he was bleeding there like a mad bastard. No great surprise: he realized he was lucky he was still breathing. Blast could tear up your lungs, kill you from the inside out, and not leave a mark on you. He'd seen that more than once, fighting north through Italy.

No broken ribs grated and stabbed when he moved. That was nothing but fool luck. And his bobby's helmet had kept him from smashing his head. It wasn't anywhere near so tough as an army-style tin hat, but evidently it was tough enough.

Across the street . . . Every English or British sovereign since William the Conqueror was crowned in Westminster Abbey. The bulk of the structure dated from the reign of Henry III, in the late thirteenth century. Not all of it was ancient; the Tomb of the Unknown Soldier from the last war was in the west nave.

No. Had been in the west nave. The Abbey'd come through the Blitz and the later unmanned German Doodlebugs and the even more terrifying V-2s without much damage. But Cedric Mitchell couldn't imagine a building in the world that would have come through unscathed if a deuce-and-a-half stuffed to the gills with high explosives blew up alongside it. And Westminster Abbey hadn't.

Through rags of mist and through much more roiling dust—literally, the dust of centuries—he saw the Abbey was nothing more than rubble and wreckage. But for the size of the pile, it might have been an Italian country-town church hit by shellfire. Flames started licking through the brick and stone and timber. Wood burned—Mitchell shook his head, trying to clear it. *Of course wood burns, you bloody twit. So does anything with paint on it.*

To his slack-jawed amazement, people came staggering and limping and crawling out of the rubble. A priest in bloodied vestments lurched up to him and said—well, something. Police Constable Mitchell cupped a scraped hand behind his right ear. "What's that, mate?" he bawled. His mouth was all bloody, too. Was he also bleeding from the ears? He wouldn't have been a bit surprised.

"More caught in there," the priest shouted, loud enough this time for Mitchell to make out the words. "Will you help?"

"I'll do my damnedest," Mitchell answered. The words didn't seem blasphemous to him till later. The injured priest took them in stride.

Another wall went over with a crash that made Mitchell flinch. Anything loud enough for him to hear was liable to be frightening. He followed the priest across St. Margaret's to the ruin. They both had to skirt the crater the exploding lorry had blown in the pavement. Water was rapidly filling it.

"Bloody Nazi must have wrecked the pipes," Mitchell said. The priest, a pace in front of him, didn't turn around. The other man's ears must have suffered in the blast, too.

A woman's legs lay under some bricks. Together, the bobby and the priest pulled some of them off her. Then Mitchell twisted away, wishing they hadn't. What was left of her upper body wasn't pretty.

"How do we get revenge for this?" he bawled into the priest's ear.

"I don't know," the man answered. "It may be un-Christian of me to say so, but we need to do that, don't we? Here and St. Paul's—"

"That's where the other one was?" PC Mitchell broke in. The priest nodded. Mitchell swore, not that that would do any good, either. Would anything? He didn't think so.

NOW LOU WEISSBERG HAD SEEN BOTH *STARS AND STRIPES* AND THE *International Herald-Trib.* No English shutterbug seemed to have matched the photographer who'd snapped the Eiffel Tower in mid-topple. No picture of St. Paul's splendid dome collapsing, nor of Westminster Abbey falling down. Only rubble and wreckage and bodies.

And rage. Some of it came from Clement Attlee's Labour government. "The Germans show why their ancestors were named Vandals," Attlee thundered—as well as a mild little bald man with a scrawny mustache could thunder. "Destruction and murder for the sake of destruction and murder will settle nothing, and will only rouse the hatred of the entire civilized world."

That was good, as far as it went. A lot of Englishmen didn't think it went nearly far enough. Winston Churchill, wandering in the wilderness after the electorate turned him out of office the year before, aimed his thunder *at* the Labour government. "How could these barbarous swine smuggle the tools of their filthy trade into our fair country?" he demanded. "How could they do so altogether undetected? 'Someone had blundered,' Tennyson said. The poet never claimed to know who. I hope we shall do rather better than that in getting to the bottom of our shameful failure here."

Major Frank walked into Lou's office while he was drowning his sorrows in coffee. Somehow this latest outrage didn't make him want to run out and get crocked the way the fall of the Eiffel Tower had. Maybe you could get used to anything, even enormities. Wasn't that a cheery thought?

Howard Frank pointed to the picture of the ruins of St. Paul's on the front page of the *Herald-Trib*. "Well, the fuckers got the frogs and they got the limeys," he said. "Next thing you know, they'll make it to Washington and blow up the Capitol."

Lou eyed him. "If they wait till the new Congress gets sworn in next January before they try it, they'll do the country a big favor."

"Now, now." Frank clucked at him like a mother reproaching a little boy. "We have to respect the will of the people."

"My ass," Lou said, and then, a long beat later, "sir."

"Dammit, we really do," Major Frank said. "If we don't, what's the difference between us and the fucking Nazis?"

"What did Trotsky tell one of the guys who followed him? 'Everybody has the right to be stupid, Comrade, but you abuse the privilege.' Something like that, anyhow," Lou said. "Well, the American people are abusing the privilege right now, goddammit, and we'll all end up paying 'cause they are."

"Treason," Frank said sadly.

"Damn straight," Lou agreed. "Call the MPs and haul me off to Leavenworth. I'll be a hell of a lot safer in Kansas than I am here."

"If they don't get to take me away, they don't get to take you, either," Frank said. "And I ain't going anywhere."

"Ha! That's what you think," Lou told him. "Fucking isolationists in Congress won't give Truman two bits to keep us here. We'll all be heading home pretty damn quick. Got a cigarette on you?"

"You give me all this crap I don't need and then you bum butts offa me?" Major Frank shook his head in mock disbelief. "I oughta tell you to *geh kak afen yam*." Despite the earthy Yiddish phrase, he tossed a pack down onto the newspapers on Lou's desk.

When Lou picked it up and started to extract a cigarette, he paused because his eye caught a phrase he'd missed before. "Here's Heydrich, the smarmy son of a bitch: 'Thus we remind the oppressors that the will to freedom still burns strong in Germany.' And we're gonna turn our backs on this shit and just go home?" He did light up then, and sucked in smoke as hard as he could.

Frank reclaimed the pack. He lit a cigarette of his own. "Way you talk, I'm one of the jerks who want to run away. I'm on your side, Lou."

"Yeah, I know, sir. Honest, I do. But—" Lou's wave was expansive enough to cover two continents' worth of discontent and the Atlantic between them. "Do these people *want* to fight another war in fifteen or twenty years? Do they think the Nazis *won't* take over again if we quit? Or the Russians if the Nazis don't?"

"What we need is Heydrich's head nailed to the wall," Howard Frank said. "If we get rid of him and things start settling down, maybe we can make the occupation work after all."

"That'd be something," Lou agreed. "Not much luck yet down in the mountains, though. A few weapons caches, but those are all over the fucking country. No Alpine Redoubt—or if there is, it's as close to invisible as makes no difference."

"Those may not be the same thing," Frank said thoughtfully.

"Huh," Lou said, also thoughtfully, and then, "You've got a point. Redoubt or not, though, you know what Germany is these days?"

"Sure, a fucking mess," Frank answered.

"I mean besides that," Lou said. "It's like one of those small-town china shops with a sign in the window that goes YOU DROP IT, YOU BREAK IT, YOU PAY FOR IT. And we dropped it, and we broke it, and—"

"We're paying for it. Boy, are we ever," Major Frank said. "But what the folks back home can't see is, we'll end up paying even more later on if we bail out now. Hell, could you see that if your kid came home in a box a year and a half after Hitler blew his brains out and the Nazis surrendered?"

"I don't know, sir—honest to God, I don't." Lou stubbed out his cigarette, which had got very small. All the butts in the ashtray would get mixed in with the general trash and then thrown out. And once the stuff got beyond the barbed-wire perimeter, the krauts would pick through it like packrats and get hold of every gram of tobacco and every scrap of crust of burnt toast. Times were tough here. That it was the Jerries' own goddamn fault made it no less true.

"Well, there you are, then." Frank had kept on with the conversation while Lou's wits wandered.

"Yeah, here I am," Lou agreed. "And you know what else? No matter how fucked up this lousy place is, I need to be here. So do you. So do we—all of us. But how much longer will all the big brains back in Washington let us do what we gotta do?"

"You get that one right, Lou, you win the sixty-four dollars," Howard Frank said.

BERLIN WAS A RAVAGED CITY: NO TWO WAYS ABOUT IT. AND YET, Vladimir Bokov had come to realize, it could have been worse. The *Wehrmacht* had done the bulk of its fighting off to the east, trying to hold the Red Army away from the German capital. Blocks in Berlin— especially blocks around the seat of the Nazi government—had got smashed up, certainly. But not every block, every house, had been fought over till one side or the other could fight no more. In that, Berlin differed from Stalingrad or Kharkov or Warsaw or Budapest or Königsberg or . . . a hundred or a thousand other places, large and small, on the Eastern Front.

The Germans would be able to rebuild Berlin faster because of that. The women and kids and stooped old men chucking broken bricks into bins one by one had only millions to dispose of, not tens of millions the way they would have if every building had been wrecked. Captain Bokov grimaced. The Soviet line proclaimed that the German people weren't the USSR's enemies: only the former Hit-lerite regime and the Heydrichite bandits who wanted to resurrect it.

Bokov wasn't stupid enough to criticize the Soviet line. An NKVD officer who did something like that—assuming anyone could be so idiotic—would soon discover just how far north of the Arctic Circle his country built camps. But, even if he wouldn't say so out loud, Bokov was a lot more suspicious of the German people than Soviet propaganda suggested he ought to be.

That kid with the peach fuzz and the drippy nose and the mittens full of holes who was chucking rubble into a bucket . . . was he old enough to have toted a rifle or a Schmeisser the last year of the de-clared war? Sure he was. The *Volkssturm* had sucked in plenty of younger guys. And the scrawny bastard working next to him, the one with the gray stubble and the limp . . . What had he done before he got hurt? He warily watched Bokov, letting his eyes drift down or away whenever the NKVD man looked in his direction.

He probably wasn't wearing an explosive vest right now—he was too skinny. But if he put one on, with a raggedy greatcoat to camou-flage it, and went looking for a crowd of Russians . . . No, the only Germans Bokov was sure he could trust close to him were naked women. Even then, he'd heard stories that some of them deliberately spread disease to put occupiers out of action.

He didn't *know* that was true, but it wouldn't have surprised him. He'd seen that the Germans deserved their reputation for thorough-ness. No one who'd been through one of their murder factories could possibly doubt it. Why *wouldn't* they use infected prostitutes as a weapon?

Then a bullet cracked past his head. He forgot about subtle weapons like syphilitic whores. Not a goddamn thing subtle about rifle fire. He heard the report as he threw himself flat in the wreckage-strewn street. Had to be a sniper shooting from long range, if the round beat its sound by so much.

Another bullet pierced the air where he'd stood a moment before. It spanged off a paving stone behind him. A woman screeched and clutched at her arm. The ricochet must have got her.

Three or four Red Army soldiers, most of them carrying PPSh submachine guns, trotted purposefully in the direction from which the gunfire had come. The Germans in the work gang—except the wounded woman—started making themselves scarce. They knew the Soviet Union took hostages when somebody fired at its troops. They knew the Russians shot hostages, too.

Bokov didn't have time to worry about that right now. He wriggled behind the burnt-out, rusting carcass of a German halftrack that had sat there since the last battle. One of these days, somebody would haul it off for scrap metal, but that hadn't happened yet.

He waited for another shot. Unlike a soft-skinned vehicle, the halftrack really would protect him against small-arms fire. But the sniper didn't shoot at Bokov or at the Red Army men now going after him. Since he'd failed, he seemed to want to get away and shoot at somebody else another time.

Cautiously, Captain Bokov peered out from behind the halftrack's dented front bumper. If the sniper had outguessed him, if the son of a bitch had drawn a bead on the front end of the halftrack and was waiting for him to show himself . . . Well, in that case Bokov's story wouldn't have a happy ending.

But no. Bokov's sigh reminded him he'd been holding his breath. The soldiers were heading for a block of flats that had to be almost a kilometer away. Yes, a marksman could hit from that range. Bokov didn't like turning into a target—which wouldn't matter a kopek's worth to the damned Heydrichite with the scope-sighted rifle.

No more gunfire from the distant apartment block. Bokov stood up straight and brushed dust and mud off his uniform. He started toward the flats himself. His eyes flicked back and forth. If the sniper missed him again, he wanted to know where to dive next.

More soldiers came around a corner. They also headed for the apartments. They went in. Germans started coming out. Any of them over the age of twelve might have been the gunman. Bokov didn't think any of them was. If the shooter wasn't long gone, he would have been surprised.

A senior sergeant who'd been with the first bunch walked up to him. Saluting, the man said, "Well, Comrade Captain, we have enough of these bastards for the firing squads."

"Good enough," Bokov answered. "Did your men find any weapons or anti-Soviet propaganda in the flats?"

"No weapons, sir." The underofficer suddenly looked apprehensive. "We weren't really searching for propaganda. We could go back. . . ."

"No, never mind," Bokov said. The sergeant's sigh of relief wasn't much different from the one he'd let out himself behind the German halftrack. "If you had found something like that, it might have told us who'd want to harbor one of the bandits. Since you didn't . . ." He shrugged. "Question the lot of them. If you don't learn anything interesting, give them to the firing squads. If you do, bring the ones who know something over to NKVD headquarters and execute the rest. Have you got that?"

"*Da*, Comrade Captain!" With another sharp salute, the senior sergeant repeated Bokov's orders back to him. He wore several decorations. Bokov wouldn't have been surprised if he'd led a company during the war. More than a few underofficers had, casualties among lieutenants and captains being what they were. His look and manner proclaimed him a competent man.

"All right, then. Carry on," the NKVD officer said.

"*Da*," the sergeant repeated. Then he added something he didn't have to: "Glad the son of a bitch missed you, sir. This kind of crap just goes on and on. There doesn't seem to be any end for it, does there? And too damned often we've got to carry off the poor bastard who stopped one. That's no good, you know? We *won* this fucking war . . . didn't we?"

Bokov could have sent him to the gulag for those last two imperfectly confident words. He could have, but he didn't. The senior sergeant made it plain he cared whether an NKVD man lived or died. From a Red Army trooper, that was close to miraculous. By the way they talked, most Soviet soldiers had more sympathy for Heydrichites than they did for Chekists.

When Bokov got back to his office, Moisei Shteinberg greeted him with, "Well, Volodya, I hear you had an adventure this morning."

"Afraid so, Comrade Colonel," Bokov agreed. "Sniper missed me—missed me twice, in fact. He got away afterwards, dammit. The Fascist bandits will probably reprimand him for bad shooting."

"I shouldn't wonder." Shteinberg was so serious, he destroyed Bokov's small pleasure at his own joke. After a moment, the colonel went on, "We've been lucky over here for a while now. The Heydrichites haven't used any radium against us, and they haven't pulled off any outrages against us, either, the way they did in Paris and London."

"How long can that last?" Bokov wondered aloud.

Colonel Shteinberg's eyes were dark, heavy-lidded, and narrow (not slanted like a Tartar's—or like those of so many Russians, Bokov included—but definitely narrow). They were also very, very knowing. A Jew's eyes, in other words. Bokov had never thought of them that way before, but when he did the notion fit like a rifle round in its chamber. Yes, a Jew's eyes.

After studying Bokov a long moment, the Jew—the senior NKVD officer—gently inquired, "Have you no confidence in the ability of the Soviet system to defend itself against the Fascist bandits?"

What a minefield lay under one innocent-sounding question. "I have perfect confidence that our system will triumph in the end." Captain Bokov answered with the greatest of care—and also took care not to show how careful he was. "But no one can know ahead of time the road by which it will triumph, or how strongly the reactionaries will be able to resist."

"*Khorosho,* Volodya. *Ochen khorosho.*" The smile that flickered across Shteinberg's face said he appreciate the response no less than he might have savored a particularly lovely passage in a new Shostakovich symphony. "Still, even if it's a good answer, it doesn't tell us how to keep such disasters from happening to us."

Shrugging, Bokov said, "We work hard. We hope we stay lucky." He paused, wondering whether to press his own luck. With Colonel Shteinberg pleased with him, he decided to: "And maybe we really ought to work more with the Anglo-Americans."

No matter how pleased Shteinberg was, he shook his head without the least hesitation. *"Nyet,"* he said firmly. "Don't even waste your time thinking about it. It won't happen, and you've got no idea how much trouble you'll end up in if you suggest it to anybody but me. I keep trying to tell you that, but you don't want to listen."

"All right, Comrade Colonel." By the way Bokov said it, it wasn't, but his superior wouldn't come down on him for that. "Still seems a shame, though . . ."

"Sending a good officer to Kolyma would be a shame, too," Shteinberg observed. Since Kolyma, in far eastern Siberia, was one of those places that lay well above the Arctic Circle, Bokov decided not to press the argument any further. Too bad, but you did have to live if they'd let you.

"STAND CLEAR!" THE DEMOLITIONS GUY YELLED.

Bernie Cobb figured he was already well beyond anything the charge in the throat of the old mine could throw. He backed up a few more paces just the same. Some chances he got paid—not enough, but paid—to take. This wasn't one of them.

Several other GIs also retreated a few steps. The first sergeant with the detonator looked around one more time. "Fire in the hole!" he yelled, and rammed the plunger home.

Boom! Bernie had heard a lot of explosions like this one. He watched dust and a few rocks fly out of the mouth of the shaft. None of the rocks came anywhere near his buddies and him. They all knew how far to back up by now.

As the dust settled, he saw that the shaft was closed, presumably for good. He nodded to himself. The fellow with the explosives knew what he was doing, which was reassuring. If you handled that shit, you needed to know what was going on. Anyone who didn't would end up slightly dead, or more than slightly. And a butterfingers was liable to take some ordinary dogfaces with him, too.

The thought had hardly crossed Bernie's mind before something out of the ordinary happened. Most of the time—all the time up till now—there'd been the explosion, and the roar as the mouth of the shaft fell in, and that was it.

Except that wasn't it, not today. Things down underground kept falling over. It was like listening to a house of cards collapse, if you could imagine cards made of rock and each about the size of a bus.

"Holy Moses!" said one of the GIs standing alongside of Bernie.

"Son of a bitch!" another one added, meaning about the same thing.

"Jesus H. Christ!" said the first sergeant with the detonator. "I figured this was a little blind shaft like all the others I closed off. Sure don't seem like it. God only knows what all's under there. We sure as shit can't get at it from here any more—you can sing that in church."

For a bad moment, Bernie'd feared the top kick would order the men to get out their entrenching tools and start digging through the rubble clogging the top of the shaft. But, for a wonder, the man had better sense. Maybe he realized he'd get the shaft if he tried giving an order like that.

"Whatever was in there, you're right—we won't get at it now," Bernie said, to drive home the point.

"Nope," the demolitions man agreed. "Sounded like a whole bunch of dominoes falling over down below."

"Yeah. It did!" Bernie grinned. The other guy'd come up with a better figure of speech than he had himself. Somewhere back in the States, an English teacher would have been happy if only she knew.

"Maybe we could use POWs to dig it out," the first sergeant said thoughtfully.

"Yeah. Maybe." Bernie didn't want to come right out and say he didn't think that was such a hot idea. He let his tone of voice do it for him.

And the demolitions man's rueful chuckle said Bernie had got the message to Garcia. "Or maybe not," the explosives expert said. "Some of those guys hate the Nazis worse'n we do. Can't blame 'em, either—the Nazis got their asses shot off."

"Sure, Sarge. But most of the POWs who hate the Nazis hate 'em because they lost the war, not because they started in the first place," Bernie said.

"I know. But I wasn't done yet," the demolitions man answered. "Some of 'em hate the Nazis, like I said before. But there's others—if they saw a chance to duck into a tunnel and run straight to Heydrich's assholes, they'd do it like *that*." He snapped his fingers. "Boy, would they ever. So maybe putting POWs to work here ain't the smartest notion since Tom Edison came up with the fucking light bulb."

Bernie grinned at him. "You find a couple of those fucking light bulbs, pass one on to me. All I've seen is the regular kind."

"Shit, you don't need a special light bulb to fuck these kraut broads," the first sergeant answered. "A pack of Luckies'll do it, or a few cans of K-rats. You can't get your ashes hauled here, you ain't half tryin', man."

Since Bernie'd discovered the same thing, he would have left it right there. But one of the guys in his squad—a new draftee, poor devil—said, "What about the orders against waddayacallit—against, uh, fraternization?" He pronounced the word with the excessive care of somebody who wasn't sure what it meant.

"Well, what about 'em?" the first sergeant returned. "Look, buddy, nobody's gonna make you fuck one of these German gals. But if you want to, they're pushovers. Hell, after the Jerries knocked France out of the war, the French broads lay down and spread for 'em like nobody's business. Now *we're* the winners. And if you see how skinny some of these German gals are, you'll know why they put out, too."

"It's against orders," the new guy said. Some people were like that: if somebody told them what to do and what not to, they followed through right on the button. And they were happy acting that way. Bernie'd seen it before: it saved them the trouble of thinking for themselves. He figured a hell of a lot of Germans worked that way. What else did such a good job of explaining how they'd lined up behind Hitler?

"Fine. It's against orders." The demolitions man spoke with exaggerated patience. "I look at it this way. If the broads ain't playing Mata Hari with me—or if they are, long as I don't tell 'em anything they shouldn't know—I'm gonna have me a good time. And the way things are nowadays, even if I come down venereal, so what? A couple of shots in the ass and I'm ready to hop in the sack again. Hell of an age we live in, ain't it?"

"You come down venereal, the brass'll give you a bad time," the draftee observed.

"Sure they will—if they hear about it," the first sergeant agreed indulgently. "Some people, though, some people know a corpsman or a sawbones who'll give 'em some of this penicillin shit and not bother filling out all the paperwork afterwards, know what I mean?"

After some very visible thought, the new guy decided he did know. By his expression, he hadn't been so surprised since his mother regretfully informed him the stork didn't bring babies and leave them under cabbage leaves. And how long ago had that been? Maybe six months before he got his Greetings letter from Selective Service? Bernie wouldn't have been surprised.

But what the kid knew about the facts of life wasn't Bernie's problem. This underground collapse was, or could be. "Maybe we don't use POWs to find out what happened under there," he said. "We ought get there some kind of way, though."

"Bulldozer crew. Nah, a coupla dozers," the first sergeant said. "Beats working. Those mothers can dig faster'n a company's worth of guys with picks and shovels."

That idea Bernie did like. "You have the pull to get 'em?" he asked.

"Oh, hell, yes," the demolitions man answered. "The first sergeant in an engineering battalion, he owes me from before the surrender. I tell him we need a couple of D-7s up here, they'll come pronto. Don't worry your pretty little head about that."

Bernie snorted. "I been called a whole lotta things since I got sucked into the Army, but never pretty. Not till now, anyway."

The demolitions man eyed him. "Yeah, well, I can see why." The other guys in Bernie's squad chuckled. Even the new draftee thought that was funny.

"It's okay. You won't put Lana Turner out of business any time soon, either," Bernie said. The first sergeant grinned at him. They'd probably never see each other again, so they could both sling the sass without getting hot and bothered.

It also wouldn't bother Bernie if the bulldozers uncovered something juicy. He didn't expect it—he'd given up expecting anything much—but it wouldn't bother him one bit.

XXI

One of the first tricks Heydrich's fanatics had tried was still among the nastier ones they used. As a matter of fact, the Germans had trotted this one out even before the surrender, so maybe some bright *Wehrmacht Feldwebel* dreamt it up. Stretch a wire across a road at just above windshield height on a jeep and you'd get anybody who was inside by the neck.

Scuttlebutt said the diehards had decapitated a few GIs with that little stunt. Lou Weissberg didn't believe it, and he was in a better position to know than most American soldiers. He supposed it might be possible, if the wire was stretched good and tight and the jeep was really hauling ass. But the next confirmed report he saw would be the first.

Which didn't mean a wire stretched across a road couldn't put an unlucky or careless dogface in the hospital. In miserable winter weather like this, snow alternating with freezing rain, you'd never see a wire till you were way too close to stop.

That was why the jeep Lou rode in, like most in the American zone, had a wire cutter mounted on the hood. (Most jeeps in the

British, French, and Soviet zones also mounted wire cutters these days.) The contraption, made from a couple of welded steel bars, would part any wire like Moses parting the Red Sea.

These days, casualties from murder wires were few and far between. Lou wondered why the fanatics kept running the risk of stretching them across highways. He supposed it was because they'd got used to doing it when it still accomplished something. It wasn't as if they were the only military force ever to get bogged down in routine.

He remarked on that to his current driver, a swarthy fellow who went by Rocky and had five o'clock shadow at ten in the morning. Rocky swore and spat as the jeep rattled along between Nuremberg and Munich. "Fuck, Lieutenant, nice to think *something* these assholes try don't work so hot," he said.

"Well . . . yeah." Lou hadn't thought of it like that. He wished Rocky hadn't, either. The driver had a grease gun on the seat beside him, where he could grab it in a hurry. Lou carried a .30-caliber M2 carbine, which gave him about as much firepower as a submachine gun. But he also manned the jeep's pintle-mounted .50-caliber Browning. That baby could reach out over a mile, and kill anything it reached. A damn nice weapon to have.

All the same, he and Rocky both kind of hunkered down whenever they passed a wrecked German or American vehicle by the side of the road. They did that at least every few hundred yards— sometimes a lot more often, where fighter-bombers had rocketed or just shot up a column on the move.

You never knew whether some bastard lurked in or behind a burnt-out hulk. If he popped up and let fly with an antitank rocket, your fancy .50-caliber machine gun might not do you one goddamn bit of good. You'd have a *Panzerfaust* up the ass, and he'd duck back down before you could even get a shot off at him.

"Almost 1947," Rocky said after they rolled past a seventy-ton King Tiger tank that some colossal explosion had flipped over onto its side. Lou tried to imagine what it took to do that to one of the fearsomely lethal—and fearsomely immense—panzers. He had trouble coming up with anything plausible.

Answering Rocky seemed easier. "I won't be sorry to see the end of 1946—I'll tell you that," he said.

But then the driver said, "Back when those Nazi cocksuckers signed the surrender, did you figure you'd still be here now?"

"Maybe to get rid of war criminals," Lou said uncomfortably. "I didn't think the fighting'd still be going. Who could have?"

"Yeah. Who?" Rocky gunned the jeep to hustle past a dead Panzer IV. Those babies weren't nearly so dangerous as King Tigers—they made a pretty fair match for, say, a Sherman. The krauts had had a lot more of them than King Tigers, but nowhere near enough. A rocket had blown the turret clean off of this one. When the IV proved really and truly dead, Rocky went on, "Me, I won't be sorry if Congress ships us all home. Only way we'll ever get there, looks like to me."

"You want to fight another war in fifteen, twenty years?" Lou demanded.

"Shit, Captain, I'll worry about that then—or I'll let my nephew worry about it. He's like six or seven now," Rocky answered. "What I know for sure is, I don't want to fight *this* motherfucking war any more. I've paid my dues and then some. Fifteen, twenty years till we go again? I think that sounds pretty goddamn good."

Lou stared at him, as he might have stared at a blue giraffe in a zoo. Were people really shortsighted enough to think like that? Of course they were. Why else was the incoming Eightieth Congress full of folks who wanted to pretend that the United States could walk away from Europe without anything bad happening afterwards? But they weren't pretending. They really believed it. That was even scarier.

They drove through some trees. Lou didn't know whether to swing the heavy machine gun to the left or the right. He feared it wouldn't do much good either way, because he couldn't see very far in either direction. Well, with luck any lurking German fanatics also couldn't see very far.

Only trouble with that was, he couldn't know ahead of time where the fanatics lurked. They already had a pretty good notion where the road was. They could have their rocket launchers or machine guns all sighted in. . . .

Spang! The wire cutter mounted on the jeep's hood did its job. "Greatest thing since—" Rocky started.

He never got *sliced bread* out. The world blew up before he could. That was how it seemed to Lou, anyhow. One second, he was grinning along with Rocky. This $1.29 wire-cutting wonder damn well *was* the greatest thing since sliced bread. American ingenuity and know-how beat the evil fanatics again. It was an ending straight out of a Hollywood serial.

Except it wasn't. The next second, Lou flew through the air with the greatest of ease. He fetched up against a tree trunk on the far side of the road with an *"Oy!"* followed a moment later by a louder, more heartfelt "Shit!" That stab when he inhaled had to mean at least one fractured rib. If he hadn't been a good boy and worn his helmet the way orders said he was supposed to, he likely would have had a fractured skull to go with it. He wasn't a hundred percent positive he didn't anyway. He was sure as hell seeing double as he struggled to sit up.

And, at that, he'd been lucky. Getting blown clear of the jeep was the best thing that could have happened to him. Well, actually, not getting into the jeep at all would have been luckier, but it was way too late to worry about that now. Way too late to worry about the blasted jeep, too. It had slewed sideways and caught fire. Whatever blasted it to hell and gone must have killed Rocky. He wouldn't have been pretty even without the flames. He seemed to be in several chunks. . . .

Muzzily, Lou tried to figure out what the devil had happened. They'd taken care of that damn wire, and then. . . . "Shit," Lou said again, on a different note this time. Cutting the wire must have touched off whatever explosive charge the fanatics had hooked up to it.

Explosive charge and fragments: it wouldn't have done that to Rocky—and to the jeep—without plenty of fragments. A buried 155mm shell, maybe? The blast seemed about right for something like that. If Lou had been Catholic, he would have made the sign of the cross. He realized how lucky he was not to be ground round himself. Lucky, yeah—and Rocky caught some of the fragments that would have torn him up instead.

The only good thing you could say about Rocky was that he never knew what hit him. One second, he was being happy about the wire cutters. The next? *Blam!* No, he couldn't have suffered much, not when he ended up looking like . . . that.

Lou hauled himself to his feet. That made the rib or ribs stab him again. It also informed him that one of his ankles could have been working better.

He scowled at the wire cutters, which he now saw through a curtain of flames and smoke—and through a deeper curtain of apprehension. If you took them off jeeps, the fanatics' wires would start causing casualties again. But if you left them on, how many wires would turn out to be hooked up to big old artillery shells? You'd find out pretty damn quick. Boy, would you ever, the hard way.

Something warm dripped from Lou's nose. Blood, he discovered when he wiped it on his sleeve. No surprise there. Blast could have broken both eardrums as easily as not. It could have torn up his lungs, too, if he'd been inhaling instead of exhaling. If could have done all kinds of things it hadn't—quite—done.

All it did was earn him a Purple Heart. *Just what I fucking need,* he thought, doing his best not to breathe deeply.

After a moment, he realized the improvised bomb had done something else. It had turned Rocky, who wanted to get the hell out of Germany, into a statistic that argued for doing just that. He would be the whatever and sixth GI killed in Germany since what the papers were calling the so-called surrender. And Lou had just made the statistics himself. He would be the whatever and twenty-ninth American soldier wounded since V-E Day.

"Hot damn," he muttered, and then "Shit" one more time.

VLADIMIR BOKOV REMEMBERED LAST YEAR'S NEW YEAR'S EVE MUCH too well. Influenza and benzedrine made a lousy combination. They went even worse with wood-alcohol poisoning. Damn the Heydrichites anyway! They'd taken out far too many first-rate Soviet officers with that stunt. Some of the men who replaced those casualties couldn't tie their own boots without reading the manual first. Others didn't have the brains to read the manual.

"Things could be worse," Colonel Shteinberg said when Bokov complained out loud.

"How's that, sir?" Bokov asked.

"Well, the Heydrichites could be holding their own victory banquet right now," the senior NKVD officer replied.

"You're right," Bokov admitted. "It isn't that bad. But it isn't good, either. For instance, Comrade Colonel—how many times have you been in a jeep that cut a garroting wire stretched across the road?"

"A few. More than a few, in fact. That was a clever gadget our technicians came up with," Shteinberg said. "Why?"

Vladimir Bokov happened to know an American noncom had invented the wire cutters that sat on the hoods of most jeeps in Germany these days. He also knew Shteinberg wouldn't listen if he said anything like that out loud. It was beside the point, anyway. "Be careful if you cut another wire, that's all," was what he did say.

"Oh? How come?" Moisei Shteinberg asked.

"Because Heydrich's bandits have started hooking those wires to 105mm and 155mm shells buried by the side of the road," Bokov answered. "The wire gets stretched, the wire gets broken, and *bam!*"

Colonel Shteinberg understood what that meant, all right. "*Gevalt!*" he exclaimed. Captain Bokov blinked. His superior spouted Yiddish about as often as he spouted *mat*. Shteinberg had to be truly provoked to come out with either. By the way he hastily lit a cigarette, he wanted to pretend he hadn't done it here. He blew out smoke and sighed. "One more way for the Heydrichites to get in our hair."

"I'm afraid so," Bokov said. "Damned if we do and damned if we don't, if you know what I mean. We've already had some casualties on account of this. So have the Americans, I gather."

"Nice to know the Fascist hyenas aren't saving all their cute tricks for us alone," Shteinberg said. "I suppose this report's on my desk, too. It just hasn't surfaced yet."

"Believe me, Comrade Colonel, I understand *that*." Bokov spoke with great sincerity. Even though he swam easily through the sea of Soviet bureaucracy, he said, "What else does more than paperwork to keep us from accomplishing anything really important?"

Shteinberg sent a meditative plume of smoke up toward the ceiling. "Maybe you're right. Maybe I ought to send you to a camp for saying such a thing. Maybe you're right *and* I ought to send you to a camp for saying such a thing."

Captain Bokov laughed. He didn't think Shteinberg was serious. On the other hand, the only way you knew for sure when someone was serious about a crack like that was when the burly Chekists knocked on your door in the wee small hours. Bokov had made it through the frightful nights of 1937 and 1938. He hoped times like those would never come again.

"Besides," Shteinberg continued, as if what he'd just said meant nothing at all (exactly what Bokov hoped it meant), "unless something goes wrong somewhere else, I'm not getting into a jeep tonight, not for anything. I'm not going to drink tonight, either, not unless I have some German taste the booze first."

"Makes sense," Bokov said, remembering last year's madness once more and wishing he could forget it. Perhaps rashly, he asked, "So what will you do, then?"

"Me? I'm playing chess with Marshal Stalin, what else?" Shteinberg said.

Bokov shut up. Whatever his superior would be doing, it had *None of your damned business* written all over it. Bokov didn't know what *he'd* be doing as 1946 turned into 1947, either. Like Shteinberg, and for all the same reasons, he was leery of drinking on New Year's Eve. True, the Heydrichites probably wouldn't try the same stunt two New Year's Eves in a row. But they might decide the Soviets would figure they wouldn't try the same stunt twice running, and try it anyhow to see what happened. Why take chances?

Red Army soldiers—and, no doubt, their French and Anglo-American counterparts—started shooting rifles and pistols in the air about half past eleven. That gave Bokov one more reason for thinking staying quietly indoors was a good idea. If you went outside without a helmet, a falling bullet could punch your ticket for you just fine.

And how many murders were getting committed under cover of that small-arms fire? By Heydrichites? By ordinary robbers? By husbands sick of wives and wives sick of husbands? Most of them wouldn't be the NKVD's worry, for which Bokov thanked . . . *No, not God*, he decided. *I thank my good luck.*

Front-line soldiers had no trouble sleeping through worse gunfire than this. So they insisted, especially after they took aboard a good cargo of vodka. Vladimir Bokov hadn't seen the kind of action that would have inured him to such a racket. He kept waking up whenever a new set of drunks squeezed off yet another annoying volley.

Bokov also kept going back to sleep. No noncom came to shake him out of bed with word of some horrid atrocity from the Fascist bandits. That might not mean a lot of progress, but it meant some. And it meant a halfway decent night's sleep, if not a great one. You took what you could get. If it wasn't too great, you thanked whatever you thanked that it wasn't too bad.

Bokov finally gave up and got out of bed about half past six. It was still dark; the sun wouldn't be up for a while yet. Berlin was only three or four degrees of latitude south of Moscow. It had long summer days and long winter nights. Bokov rubbed his chin. Whiskers rasped under his fingers. His beard wasn't especially heavy, but he'd have to shave this morning.

A jeep started up outside. Bokov went to the window to see what was going on. It might have been raiders taking off after planting a bomb. It might have been, but it wasn't. It was Colonel Shteinberg taking off with an extraordinarily pretty brunette. Sunrise might be more than an hour and a half away, but Bokov had no trouble seeing that. The Soviet barracks blazed with light, to help hold the Heydrichites at bay.

"Well, well," Bokov said softly, and then again: "Well, well." Plenty of Soviet officers were screwing German women: that general he'd visited in Dresden sprang to mind. It wasn't encouraged (though raping German women had been, at least unofficially, as the Red Army stormed into the *Reich*), but the Soviets didn't try to declare it off-limits the way the U.S. Army did. The women were there. They were in no position to say no. Of course men would screw them.

Moisei Shteinberg, though . . . For one thing, he was NKVD, which meant he had more to keep quiet about than most Red Army men. For another, he was a Jew. Was he avenging himself every time he stuck it in there? Or was he just a man who got horny like any other man, even if he'd had his cock clipped?

"Interesting," Bokov murmured. And it might give him a hold on Shteinberg. It also might not, but finding out could be interesting, too.

A NEW FACE UP THERE ON THE ROSTRUM. SAM RAYBURN WAS JUST another Congressman again. Well, not *just* another Congressman— Rayburn remained House Minority Leader. But after you'd been Speaker, House Minority Leader wasn't worth a pitcher of warm piss, as John Nance Garner had famously said (and been famously mis-quoted) about another Washington office.

Jerry Duncan grinned like a fool. Well, pride could do that to a man. Instead of Rayburn's combative, bald, round-faced visage (which made him sound like Churchill, whom he resembled not at all), there was the aristocratic New England countenance of Joseph W. Martin. Joe had represented his Massachusetts district since just after the Indians got chased out of it. He finally had his reward. The GOP finally had its reward. Joe Martin was Speaker of the House.

It was a cold day outside, cold enough to snow. Some of the Democrats staring up toward Joe Martin were bound to be thinking, *A cold day in hell*. Well, maybe Satan was juggling snowballs, because the Republicans had their majority back.

What Jerry was thinking was that traffic would go to hell. Coming from central Indiana, he took snow for granted. Washington didn't. The town didn't get it often enough. People didn't know how to drive in it. The street authority, or whatever they called it here, didn't know how to keep the main highways cleared. It would be a mess till it melted.

Joe Martin raised the gavel and brought it down again. "The Eightieth Congress is now in session," he declared. There. It was official. The Speaker went on, "We have a lot of things to try to set right. The American people expect it of us. No—they demand it of us."

Along with most of the other Republicans, Jerry nodded. He had all he could do not to clap his hands. The Democrats, by contrast, all looked as if they'd been issued lemons and ordered to suck on them. From Pearl Harbor through V-J Day, Congress had shown a biparti-san spirit unusual in its raucous history. That wouldn't go on any more.

It's Truman's fault, not ours, Jerry thought with the smug right-eousness a majority could bring. *If he didn't want to keep on occupying Germany when any idiot can see that's a losing proposition, we could get along with him just fine. But let's see him occupy Germany if we don't give him any money to do it.*

The Speaker of the House said the same thing, only more politely: "It's time to take a long, hard look at our foreign policy. It's also time to get our fiscal house in order. I think we'll see that the two of those go hand in hand."

More solemn nods from the Republicans—and from the Democrats who didn't think they'd make it to the Eighty-first Congress if Truman went on pouring men and money down the German rathole. More scowls from the President's loyalists—and from the Republicans who feared Hitler's ghost or Stalin's reality more than they feared the endless bloody bog through which Truman insisted on wading.

Behind Jerry, somebody called, "And we'll bring our boys home from overseas!" The voice wasn't one Jerry recognized, but that didn't prove anything, not on this Friday, January 3, 1947. Too many new voices, too many new faces. He'd get to know the new kids on the block pretty soon, but he hadn't yet.

All the rage on both sides that had sizzled just below the surface exploded. Congressmen shouted. Congressmen swore. Some Congressmen clapped their hands. Others shook their fists. Things must have felt like this just before the country tore itself to pieces when Lincoln was elected.

"Order! Order! There will be order!" Joe Martin shouted, plying his gavel with might and main. But there was no order. *Bang! Bang!* He tried again: "The Sergeant at Arms will enforce order!"

The Sergeant at Arms looked at him as if he'd lost his marbles. Jerry Duncan wasn't so sure the poor, unhappy functionary was wrong. One man couldn't enforce order on 435 (well, 434, because Joe Martin up on the rostrum wasn't being disorderly) unless they wanted it enforced. And, right this minute, they didn't. All they wanted to do was yell at one another.

"We haven't got the money to pay for even half the things we really need!" another new Republican Congressman bawled. He had a bigger, rougher voice than the fellow who'd first ignited the uproar, and he used it like a top sergeant roaring his men forward through an artillery bombardment: "We're going to spend it to blow up innocent people if we can get enough kids to grow old enough for us to send to Germany to get their heads blown off for the President's amusement!"

Jerry'd only thought things were bad before. A skunk at a picnic, a photographer at a no-tell hotel, couldn't have raised a tenth the ruckus that furious shout did. Not so many Republicans clapped this time. The Democrats, though . . .

"Shame!" some of them cried. "Shame!" And they were the polite ones. What the others yelled would have made a dock worker blush. What it did to the handful of Congresswomen . . . Well, they all seemed to be shouting their heads off, too.

"Order! Order!" Speaker Martin said again, this time in something not far from desperation. He used his gavel so fiercely, Jerry Duncan was surprised the handle didn't break off in his hand. And he got . . . something not far from order, anyhow. Maybe everyone was shocked at how fast things had gone down the drain. Jerry knew he was.

"Censure!" Sam Rayburn shouted, shaking his fist at the new Congressman who'd said what he really thought. "I demand a vote of censure! That gentleman"—he spat the word—"is a disgrace to the House!"

"Now, Mr. Rayburn," Joe Martin said, "if we censure everyone who loses his temper and says something unfortunate—"

"Unfortunate! I don't know whether he should be more embarrassed for spouting claptrap or we for listening to it," Rayburn thundered. "I move that we censure . . . whatever the devil the stupid puppy's name is."

"Second!" That cry rang out from all over the Democratic side of the aisle.

By the look on Joe Martin's face, he was wondering why he'd wanted to be Speaker in the first place. He called for the vote. The motion failed, 196 to 173. Quite a few Congressmen sat on their hands. Jerry voted against the motion, though he didn't think the new Representative had done himself or his side of the argument any good. At least half a dozen Republicans voted in favor of censuring him.

And that was the first day, the day that was supposed to be ceremonial and nothing but ceremonial. The Eightieth Congress got livelier from there.

THEY ISSUED LOU WEISSBERG A CORSET AND A STICK WHEN THEY LET him out of the military hospital. They'd already given him his Purple Heart. He could have done without it, but the brass gave it to him anyway.

When he came back on duty, Major Frank greeted him with, "Well, well. Look what the cat drug in."

"Your mother . . . sir," Lou answered sweetly. "I found out how to fly without an airplane. If it weren't for the honor of the thing, I'd've rather walked." You could do worse than steal your jokes from Abraham Lincoln. You could, and Lou figured he probably would.

"Good to have you back any which way, and more or less in one piece," Howard Frank told him.

"Goddamn good to be back," Lou said. "One piece—with a few cracks and chips and shit like that. They'd put me on the discount table at Woolworth's, you betcha."

"Well, the problem hasn't gone away while you were on the bench, that's for sure," Frank said. "Matter of fact, you found one of the ways it's getting worse. Care to guess how many 155mm shells, and 105s, and 88s, are lying around Germany waiting to get turned into bombs?"

"Too fucking many—that's all I can tell you," Lou replied. "Government didn't issue me a slide rule, or maybe I'd do better."

" 'Too fucking many' is good enough. Bad enough, I mean," Major Frank said. "One of the fanatics' bright boys must've had a brainstorm, 'cause they're starting to play all kinds of cute games with shells lately. Those goddamn trip wires—"

"I found out about those, all right. I found out more than I ever wanted to know," Lou said.

"Yeah, I bet you did. But that's not the only thing they're doing." If Lou was back, Major Frank would bring him up to date come hell or high water. That kind of persistence made Frank annoying, but it also made him a good officer. He went on, "They've got some of them wired so a guy watching half a mile off can blow 'em up when he sees they'll do him the most good—hurt us worst, I should say."

"Figured that out, thanks," Lou said dryly.

"Did you?" Frank gave him a wry grin. "The guy with the detonator's long gone, natch, by the time we trace the wire back to where he was hiding, but the wire does let us do some tracing. So the assholes have one more stunt. Some of these shells, they've got 'em hooked up so they can touch 'em off by radio."

"Fuck!" Lou spoke with great sincerity.

"You said a mouthful," Howard Frank agreed. "Try tracing a radio wave. I know, I know—we can do some of that. We can do more than the Jerries ever thought we could. But a signal that lasts this long?" He snapped his fingers, then mournfully shook his head. "Fanatic's gone, transmitter's gone—it's a major-league snafu, is what it is."

"Sure sounds like one," Lou said. "Does it matter to a kraut if Heydrich pins a Knight's Cross on him instead of Hitler?"

"You don't get a Knight's Cross pinned on. You wear it around your neck," Frank said.

He was right, too. Lou had interrogated several German supermen who'd won the award—it was more or less the equivalent of the Distinguished Service Cross. All the same, Lou made a face now. "They shoulda sent you to law school," he said.

"Nah. I got good at picking nits the times I was lousy," Captain Frank said. Lou winced; he'd had lice more than once himself. If you spent much time in the field, chances were you would. Frank added, "Thank God for DDT, is all I've got to tell you. That shit really works."

"Yeah!" Lou nodded enthusiastically. He'd seen the same thing himself. From what retreads said, nothing they'd tried in the First World War stopped the cooties. But DDT did the trick, sure as hell. It knocked mosquitoes over the head, too. And it didn't poison people. How could you *not* like something that slick?

"Well, anyway, like I said, it's goddamn good to have you back," Frank told him. "I did want to get you up to speed as fast as I could—and I wanted to let you know you aren't the only guy the fanatics did for with their new trick."

"Misery loves company," Lou said. The funny thing was, it was true. If something happened to a bunch of other guys, too, you didn't feel quite so bad when it happened to you. Not that Lou had felt good when that 155 or whatever it was went up, but. . . .

"Well, you've got it," Frank said. "Word is they're working over the Russians the same way, too."

"I bet Ivan loves that to death." Lou knew what the Red Army and the NKVD did when they were unhappy. He would have said they'd learned their lessons from the *Wehrmacht* and the *Gestapo,* but they'd needed no instruction. Hostages, firing squads, mass deportations, concentration camps . . . The Russians knew at least as much about such things as the Germans.

Before he could say anything more, he heard something outside. A shout—and a shout in English, at that. He hadn't heard any gunshots or explosions beforehand, but how much did that prove? Any time people—for the shout had definitely come from more than one throat—in occupied Germany started yelling in English, something had hit the fan somewhere.

"Son of a bitch!" Major Frank's mouth thinned to a pale, furious line. He must have understood the shout, where Lou hadn't. "Those stupid bastards! Boy, are they gonna catch it!"

"Huh?" Lou said brilliantly.

Howard Frank didn't answer. He didn't need to, because the shout rang out again, louder and closer this time. Lou made it out with no trouble at all.

"We want to go home!" The roar was ragged but unmistakable. A moment later, here it came once more, louder still: *"We want to go home!"*

"Oh, good God!" Lou said. If that wasn't mutiny . . .

Major Frank jumped to his feet and hurried to the window in his office. Lou followed more sedately. With corset and cane, he couldn't hurry, but he wished he could now.

And here they came, around the corner toward the command center. There might have been fifty or sixty of them. Most were privates, but Lou saw several corporals and at least one sergeant. *"We want to go home!"* they bawled again.

Quite a few of them carried picket signs, as if they were on strike against, say, an auto-parts factory. And damned if some of the signs didn't say UNFAIR! Others said WHY ARE WE HERE? and demanded HOW COME WE'RE DYING AFTER THE SURRENDER?

"We want to go home!" the unhappy soldiers yelled one more time.

They'd attracted MPs the way a magnet attracted iron filings. But, once attracted, the snowdrops stood around trying to figure out what to do next. They had billy clubs on their belts. Some carried grease guns, others Tommy guns. But the soldiers they confronted weren't rioting. They were demonstrating. Both went against orders, but you

couldn't beat demonstrators or shoot them . . . could you? Lou imagined the headlines if the MPs tried. By the unhappy look on the military policemen's faces, they were imagining the headlines, too.

"We want to go home!" Some of the GIs probably had struck at
auto-parts plants or the like. The line they formed in front of the command center seemed highly practiced. They chanted in rough unison.
The picket signs bobbed up and down. *"We want to go home!"*

"What are they gonna do?" Lou asked hoarsely, meaning not the
demonstrating soldiers but the MPs and the top brass.

Major Frank understood him perfectly. "I don't know," he answered. "They've gotta do something. If they don't, the nuts are running the loony bin."

"Yeah." Lou nodded. That was one way to put it, all right.
Another way was that, if the brass and the MPs didn't do something,
and do it pretty goddamn quick, the U.S. Army in Germany wouldn't
be an army any more. It would be a mob.

The door to the command center opened. An officer came out and
said something to the GIs marching in front of the place. They
stopped chanting long enough to listen to whatever he came out with.
When he stopped, they hesitated, but not for long.

"We want to go home!"

It rocked him back on his heels. Maybe he'd thought he would get
them arguing among themselves, or something. No such luck. They
were more united and more determined than he'd figured. It wasn't
the first time the powers that be had underestimated the rank and file.

When the officer spoke again, the soldiers quieted long enough to
hear him out. Then they gave forth with their much louder counter-
blast.

"We want to go home!"

Okay. You asked for it. The officer didn't say that, but Lou read it
in every line of his body. He gestured to the MPs. They waded in with
their billy clubs; just about all of them, by then, had slung their submachine guns. Some of the demonstrating soldiers tried to resist. They
used the handles on their picket signs to hit back at the military police.

But, while the ordinary soldiers had shown pretty good discipline
for protesters, they couldn't match the well-trained military policemen. The MPs grabbed and handcuffed as many GIs as they could,

clobbering them whenever they thought they needed to. Some of the soldiers who threw away their picket signs ran and escaped. The others were quickly overcome.

"How long in the stockade d'you think they'll earn?" Lou asked as the demonstration came to pieces before his eyes.

"Depends on what they charge 'em with," Major Frank said. "If it's making a mutiny, that's not the stockade. That's Leavenworth—if they're lucky."

"Urk," Lou said. "You can draw the death penalty for making a mutiny, can't you?"

"Don't ask me. I've got nothing to do with the judge advocate's office, and I'm damn glad I don't." Having denied everything, Frank pontificated anyway: "But I think you can, at least during wartime."

"Is this wartime?" Lou asked. "I mean, yeah, the Nazis surrendered and all, but what's the shooting about if it's not?"

"Those guys can figure that out, too." Having pontificated, Frank started denying again. "Only thing I know is, we've got a mess on our hands."

"Yeah, like we didn't before. I wish," Lou said.

"Okay. We've got a bigger mess on our hands now," Major Frank said. "There. You happier?"

"No. I'd be happier if Heydrich was dead. I'd be a hell of a lot happier if I was going home," Lou said. "Only difference between me and those dumb assholes is, I know better than to lay my neck on the block."

"If we kill Heydrich, maybe we do get to go home," Frank said.

"If Congress kills the budget, maybe we get to go home any which way," Lou said. Howard Frank frowned but didn't try to contradict him. Lou wished he would have.

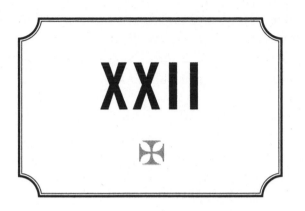

XXII

"Well, boys, here I am again," Harry Truman said. One eyebrow quirked up toward where his hairline had been once upon a time. "You've got to have more fun talking with me than you do with Joe Martin. My God! That man makes oatmeal look like it's made out of chili peppers."

Along with the rest of the press corps, Tom Schmidt chuckled. Truman knew what he was talking about, all right. Joe Martin wasn't the most exciting man God ever made. All the same . . . "How does it feel to be working with a Republican House and Senate?" somebody called.

"I'm going to do something a good Democrat probably shouldn't: I'm going to quote Abraham Lincoln," President Truman replied. "He said he was like the boy who'd got a licking—he was too big to cry, but it hurt too much to laugh."

More chuckles. FDR would never have told a cornpone story like that—Tom was sure of it. But FDR was a year and a half gone: more than that now. Truman was on his own. By all appearances, he was in over his head, too. He was the only one who didn't seem to think so.

"What will you do if Congress passes a bill cutting off funds for U.S. soldiers in Germany?" another reporter asked.

"Veto it," Truman said calmly. "And they know I will."

"What if they override?" the man pressed.

"They haven't got the votes," the President said. "Even with a few Democrats who can't see their nose in front of their face, they haven't got 'em. So let them try." He sounded like a tough little terrier. Roosevelt would have stuck out his chin, but Roosevelt had more of a chin to stick out than round-faced Truman. Roosevelt never had to deal with a Republican Congress, either. Maybe he'd picked the right time to die, or he probably would have.

"What about the soldiers' strikes in Germany, sir?" Tom asked when Truman nodded at him.

"What about 'em?" the President said. "Some of our boys drank some bad schnapps, if you want to know what I think."

"A little more than that going on, isn't there?" Tom said. "Marches, picket signs, petitions? Sounds like more than drunken foolishness to me."

"Oh, it's foolishness, all right." Truman's eyes flashed behind his spectacles. He wasn't FDR—not even close—but in his own way he was also nobody you wanted to mess with. He'd make you sorry if you tried. Eyes still snapping, he went on, "You know what would've happened if American boys tried that kind of nonsense in 1918?"

"Tell us," Tom urged, along with two other reporters.

"I will tell you, by God. They would've got drumhead courts-martial, they would've got blindfolds and cigarettes—miserable French Gitanes, that tasted like horse manure—and *pow!* That would've been that. Good riddance to bad rubbish."

"Can we quote you, Mr. President?" someone asked. Tom swore under his breath; he'd intended to quote Truman any which way.

But the President nodded again. "Go right ahead. The Army's not a factory. You don't have the right to strike against the United States of America. Anybody who thinks he does doesn't think very well. He's going to be sorry pretty darn quick. That's just the way things are, and that's how they'll stay."

"So do you think we ought to shoot these strikers?" Tom asked. "Do you think the Communists got to them, or maybe the Nazis?"

"I don't know who got to them. I don't know if anybody did,"

Truman said. "All that will come out in the courts-martial. I'm sure the military judges will do what the evidence suggests."

"What will you do if some of the soldiers get sentenced to death?" Somebody else beat Tom to the question, which pissed him off. "Will you let the sentence be carried out, or will you commute it?"

"I'm not going to judge anyone in advance," Truman answered. "I don't have all the evidence in front of me now. I'll see what the courts-martial decide and how they decide it. Then I'll do some deciding of my own."

A reasonable response—to Tom, no friend of the administration, too reasonable to be of much use. Well, he could turn the story however he needed it to go. Another reporter asked a question about the civil war in China. Truman said he hoped Chiang Kai-shek's forces would do better. That wasn't useful, either. Who didn't hope Chiang's soldiers would do better? Getting them to do better was the problem.

Then the questions turned to domestic policy, and Tom almost stopped listening. As far as the *Tribune* was concerned, he was there to hold Truman's feet to the fire about Germany. Westbrook Pegler had been tearing the Democrats a new one on domestic issues for years.

At last, Truman said, "That's all for today, boys."

"Bye-bye, donkey," one of the reporters said as they trooped out of the press room. "The elephant's gonna be living here as soon as the voters send Harry T. back to Missouri."

"Dewey? Taft? Stassen? Who do you figure?" Tom asked.

"Whoever makes the most noise about bringing the boys back," the other reporter answered. "Right now, I'd put my two bucks on Taft, but it's early days yet. They aren't even around the first turn."

"Yeah." Tom nodded. Then he grinned. "I think I've got the lead for my next column." He wrote it down so he wouldn't lose it.

IF YOU HAD TO BE ANYWHERE IN JANUARY, LOS ANGELES WAS A PRETTY good place to be. The sun beamed down from a bright blue sky. It was over seventy. Lawns were still green. Flowers bloomed. Every now and then, Diana McGraw saw a butterfly. Birds chirped as if it were spring. Diana even spotted a hummingbird at some of the flowers in front of Union Station.

"My God!" she said to the man who'd organized this protest rally. "Why does anybody live anywhere else?"

"Beats me," Sam Yorty answered. The California Assemblyman was a Democrat. Not only that, he'd served in the Army Air Force during the war. That made him a doubly terrific catch for Mothers Against the Madness in Germany. He went on, "I was born in the Midwest myself, but the only way they'll get me out of California again is feet first."

"What if they send you to Washington?" Diana asked. "Would you go there?"

"If the voters send me to Washington, I'd have to go," Yorty said. "You've got to listen to them." He might not just listen—he might do some talking of his own. And if he did, they might well listen to him. He was pushing forty, with a handsome face, a fine head of curly hair, and a wry, almost impish sense of humor. "Truman isn't listening," he added, "and look what's happening to him."

"Not just to him. To the country," Diana said.

"Sure. I know." Assemblyman Yorty nodded. "More and more people know. More and more people want to do something about it. We were going to hold this rally in the Angelus Temple, but—"

"In the what?" Diana broke in. Then the name rang a bell, and not one she cared for. "Isn't that where Aimee Semple McPherson—?"

Sam Yorty nodded again. "She started it, but she's gone, remember—she died during the war. Anyway, the place only holds 5,300 people. That's not enough. So we've moved things to Gilmore Field."

"Where's that?" Diana asked. Unlike the Angelus Temple, she'd never heard of it.

"In Hollywood. It's a ballpark—the Stars play there. Pacific Coast League," Yorty said. Diana nodded. The Indianapolis Indians of the American Association were the Hoosier heroes. Yorty went on, "Anyway, we can put 13,000 people in there. That ought to do the job."

"I hope so," Diana said. "I never dreamt when I started out that so many people would get behind me."

"I'm only sorry you had to start out," Yorty said. He remembered about Pat, then. Not everybody did, even though Diana talked about her son almost every time she spoke.

Gilmore Field was on Beverly Boulevard. It wasn't that far up and over from her downtown hotel. The rally organizers got Diana earlier than she thought they needed to. When she saw the traffic, she understood. This was a big city, even if it all looked like suburbs.

Picketers marched outside Gilmore Field's grandstand. Cops kept them from going any farther, and from mixing it up with the people filing into the ballpark. *"Heil* Hitler*!"* the picketers yelled at Diana, and *"Heil* Heydrich*!"* and "Communist!" and all the other endearments she'd heard from one coast to the other by now.

The cheers she got when she went out onto the field warmed her. So did the weather, which was still perfect. From what the locals said, you couldn't count on that in January, even in Los Angeles. But God or the weatherman or somebody was smiling on the rally.

Before Diana got to talk, Sam Yorty burned some time introducing celebrities who agreed with her. She'd never imagined she would meet an actor like Ronald Reagan, but there he was, waving up at the people in the stands and blistering Truman in three well-spoken minutes. Several other performers did the same.

"And now," Yorty said at last, "the lady who started this ball rolling! Let's hear it for Mrs.—Diana—McGraw!"

Diana got another hand, louder this time. If those picketers were still out there, this one was loud enough to make them grind their teeth. "Thank you very much," she said into the microphone between second base and the pitcher's mound. "I think I've already been upstaged, but that's okay. We're all on the same side here today, right?"

"That's right!" The cry rolled down on her from all around the single-decked grandstand. She felt as if she'd hit a pennant-winning grand slam in the bottom of the ninth on the last day of the season.

"My son Pat would be proud of you," she said. "He went to Europe to fight to keep us free. He helped win the war—or he thought he did. But after everybody said it was over, he got killed. And for what? For nothing! That's all these poor kids who get murdered every day in Germany are dying for. For nothing! Because Harry Truman's too pigheaded to bring them home, that's why. There's no other reason at all!"

Was this what a ballplayer heard when he did something special and won a big game? If it was, it was worth playing for all by itself. Any money the player raked in after that seemed only a bonus.

"Germany can't hurt the United States any more. We knocked it flat. Even if we hadn't, we've got France and England and the ocean in between," Diana went on. "And we've got the atom bomb, and the Germans all know it. If they even think about making trouble, we can knock them even flatter. Anybody with his eyes open can see that, right? Too bad the President of the United States keeps his shut!"

More cheers. Diana knew they were as much for what she was saying—for what *needed* saying—as for her ideas. She hardly cared. They were as warming as the bright California sun. It was snowing back home. Did it ever snow here?

"Congress is heading our way. Maybe that will push Truman in the right direction. Maybe. But how many more American boys will get blown up on occupation duty that doesn't need doing before the President sees the light? Too many! Even one more would be too many!"

"*That's right!*" If anything, the roar from the packed seats was even louder than it had been before. Diana finished her speech. She waved and flashed a two-finger V for Victory as she stepped away from the mike.

Sam Yorty wrapped things up: "Remember to give, folks, if you haven't given already. Changing people's minds costs money. I wish it didn't, but it does. Please be generous. Show you support our cause."

They did, with everything from nickels to twenty- and even fifty-dollar bills. Quite a few silver dollars ended up in the donation buckets. The government hadn't minted them since 1933, but they still circulated out West. Diana had seen that on other trips across the Rockies. She couldn't remember the last time she'd had a big silver cartwheel in her hand back in Anderson. Probably not since before the war.

"I think we did a heck of a job," Yorty said. When Diana saw what they'd taken in, she wouldn't have dreamt of arguing with him.

"THE MOTHERFUCKERS WERE ORDERED TO SURRENDER ALL THEIR munitions, dammit!" The Red Army lieutenant colonel was almost comically outraged.

Vladimir Bokov looked down his nose at him—not easy, not when the Red Army was several centimeters taller, but he managed. "And you're all of a sudden surprised because the Fascists didn't, Comrade?

They've had mortars and antitank rockets all along. When they figured out something new to do with artillery shells, of course it figured
they'd start pulling those out of their dicks, too."

"Well, why don't you miserable bluecaps stop them, then?" the
lieutenant colonel shouted. "What the hell good are you if you can't
do something like that?"

"What was your name again, Comrade?" Bokov asked softly.

A question like that from an NKVD man should have turned the
Red Army officer to gelatin. It didn't, which made him either very
brave or very stupid. "Kuznetsov. Boris Aleksandrovich Kuznetsov,"
he growled. "If you have to blame me, go ahead. Even a camp's a better bet than going down some of these German roads."

Maybe that proved he didn't know much about camps. On the
other hand, the way things were these days, maybe it didn't. That possibility worried Bokov. He said, "We're not the only ones with the
problem. The Americans have it, too. By the way they squawk, they
have it worse."

"Americans always squawk. It's what they're good for—that and
jeeps and trucks and Spam." Kuznetsov's bulging belly said he'd
probably put away a lot of Spam. Since Bokov liked it, too, he
couldn't mock the Red Army man. Kuznetsov went on, "This is just a
fucking mess. They blow us up, and there's nobody around to avenge
ourselves on. What kind of chickenshit way to fight is that?"

"A damned nasty one," Bokov answered. Lieutenant Colonel
Kuznetsov blinked. Bokov continued, "What do you want us to do?
We shoot people by the thousands. We've shipped so many to Siberia,
pretty soon everybody north of the Arctic Circle will speak German.
We've captured the Devil's grandmother's worth of Nazi artillery."

"This Nazi officer we captured used to intercept our signals. He
said that whenever we started talking about the Devil's relatives, it
was a sure sign things were really fucked up," Kuznetsov said.
"Looks like he was right."

"Huh," was all Bokov said. So even the Germans knew that!

Before he had to come up with anything more, an explosion
rocked the already-battered building in which he worked. All the windows rattled. One of them fell in with a tinkle of shattering glass.
Only luck it hadn't speared him and Kuznetsov with flying shards.
Frigid February air streamed in through the sudden new opening.

"Bozhemoi!" Kuznetsov burst out, and then loosed a stream of *mat* that proved *zeks* in the gulag didn't know everything there was to know about cussing. He finished, "That was too cocksucking close."

"No shit." Bokov jumped to his feet. "I'm going to see what happened—and if I can help."

"Well, you talk like a soldier, even if you've got that blue band around your cap," Kuznetsov said. Instead of wanting to deck him as he should have, Vladimir Bokov felt obscurely pleased. The two men dashed out of Bokov's third-story office together.

They couldn't get down the stairs as fast as they would have wanted, because other NKVD and Red Army men clogged them. Some would be useful when they got to the bomb site. Others would just stand around rubbernecking. Bokov had seen that before.

The crater was in a small square a couple of blocks away. A market of sorts had sprung up there. Berliners traded whatever happened to have come through the war in one piece for food and firewood. Sometimes women who didn't have anything else traded themselves. More than anything else, that was what drew Red Army men to the place. And the Red Army men had drawn the . . .

Truck. It was a truck. Part of the chassis was still recognizable even after blast and fire. The stink of cordite or some high explosive much like it filled the cold air—that and burned rubber and burnt flesh.

Bokov did some swearing of his own. His obscenity wasn't so inspired as Boris Kuznetsov's, but it would have to do. The motionless bodies and pieces of bodies he didn't have to worry about. They were beyond worry now. The Red Army men and locals down and moaning were a different story—if anything, a sadder story, because they were still suffering. What had happened seemed all too obvious. Now Bokov had to do what little he could in its wake.

Lieutenant Colonel Kuznetsov spoke in a voice like iron: "This kind of shit has happened too fucking often. We've got to get a handle on it. We've got to, goddammit. If we don't, those Nazi cunts will run us out of Germany yet."

That kind of defeatist talk could get him sent to a camp, too. But, looking at the crater the bomb had blown in the pavement, at the bodies, at the freshly shattered apartment blocks around the edges of the square—a couple of them on fire—Bokov had trouble feeling anything but defeatist himself.

"They haven't tried one so close to us for a while." Moisei Shteinberg might have appeared out of nowhere. He sounded altogether dispassionate as he surveyed the scene. "I'm surprised they did. They don't seem to have got enough for their bomb."

"You're a cold-blooded prick of a *zhid,* aren't you?" Kuznetsov said.

"I try to think with my head, not with my belly," Shteinberg answered calmly. "Chances are it's lucky for you that I do, too."

Bokov stooped to bandage a Red Army sergeant with gashes in one arm and the other leg. Here it was, going on two years since Berlin fell, and he still routinely carried wound dressings in a pouch on his belt. What did that say? For sure, nothing good.

"*Spasibo,* Comrade Captain." The sergeant managed something between a grimace and a wry grin. "Fuck me if I ever come here looking to get my cock sucked again."

"I don't blame you," Bokov said. "Did you notice the truck before the bomb went off?"

"Nah." The young underofficer shook his head. "I was just looking for a woman who wasn't old enough to be my mother."

Ambulances and fire engines screamed into the square, tires screeching, sirens wailing. The men on one of the fire trucks swore horribly when they discovered the bomb had broken a water main. They got a pathetic pissy dribble from their hose, nothing more. The ambulance drivers and their helpers started loading the injured—Red Army men first—into their vehicles.

With help from Bokov, the wounded sergeant hopped toward the closest one. His mangled leg wouldn't bear his weight. Bokov hoped he would keep it. The sergeant managed one more word of thanks as he flopped into the back of the ambulance.

The bomb hidden in a jeep at the edge of the square blew up then.

Next thing Bokov knew, he was on his hands and knees. His trousers tore. The cement scraped his legs. Dirt and pebbles and bits of broken glass dug into his palms. He felt as if someone had banged his ears with garbage-can lids, or maybe with hatch covers from a Stalin tank.

And the ambulance had shielded him from the worst of the blast. It hadn't flipped over onto him, either, which was a major piece of good fortune. It would have squashed him like a cockroach if it had.

As if from very far away, he heard people screaming. Shaking his head like someone who'd been sucker-punched, he lurched upright. He needed two tries, but he made it.

Colonel Shteinberg had a cut on his forehead and seemed to be missing the bottom of one ear. Blood dripped onto his tunic—ear and scalp wounds were always gory, even when they weren't serious. Whatever had clipped his ear might have taken off the top of his head had it flown a few centimeters to one side.

No sooner did that thought cross Bokov's mind than he got a look at Lieutenant Colonel Kuznetsov, or what was left of him: not much, not from the eyes up. The Red Army man's blood pooled on the pavement. Bokov gulped. It wasn't that he hadn't seen blood, or spilled it, before. But how much a man held always surprised you. Kuznetsov's steamed in the cold.

Shteinberg shouted something at Bokov. Cupping a hand behind his ear, Bokov shouted back: "What?"

The Jew cupped a hand behind his ear, too. That was how he discovered he was missing part of it. He looked absurdly astonished. Limping over to Bokov—one of his knees didn't seem to work right—he bawled in the ear the junior officer had cupped: "Nazi swine planned it this way!"

When Bokov heard that, he knew he was hearing truth. It was just the kind of things the Germans would do. It had their complicated cleverness all over it. Use one blast to create chaos. Wait a bit. Let rescuers and firemen gather. Then take them out with a second bomb.

German tanks were far more complicated than Soviet T-34s. They were easier to drive. They had better fire-control systems. But they broke down more often, too. In tanks, in submachine guns, in strategic plans, the Soviet option was usually the simple one, the one that reliably did what was needed. Complicated gadgets and plans had so many more ways to go wrong. When they went right, though, they could go spectacularly right.

This one had.

Something else occurred to Bokov. "More cars here. Is a third bomb waiting?"

He had to say it three times before Moisei Shteinberg understood. The NKVD colonel clapped a hand to his forehead—and found out he was cut there, too. "We have to make them pay," he said.

Boris Aleksandrovich Kuznetsov would have agreed. But Kuznetsov was dead. So were—how many other Russians? How many Germans? The Heydrichite hyenas didn't care about that. They only cared out hurting the occupiers. They were much too good at it, too.

THE BUDGET WAS USUALLY ABOUT AS EXCITING AS . . . WELL, THE BUD-get. You voted for it or you voted against it. You tried to fish something out of the pork barrel for your district—or your state, if you were a Senator. Jerry Duncan had played the game, and played it well, ever since he came to Congress. Not even he could claim he'd got excited about it.

This session of Congress, things were different. The GOP held the majority. It ran the Ways and Means Committee. The budget started there. And the Republicans were bound and determined that the War Department's appropriation would start without one thin dime for the occupation of Germany.

Oh, how the Democrats screamed! (Actually, some of them didn't—more than a few Southerners, and some others, were sick of the occupation, too. And some northeastern Republicans wanted to leave the troops in place. But the fight came closer to Republicans versus Democrats than anything else.) The Republicans were less than sympathetic. Jerry watched the fur fly. "You people made this mess," the Ways and Means Committee chairman said. "Now you're blaming us for trying to get the country out of it."

"You're getting the country into a worse mess, and you're too blind to see it," the ranking Democrat retorted. "Do you want to fight the Nazis again in twenty years? Do you want to fight the Russians sooner than that?"

"We don't want to fight anybody any more, and we don't have to," the chairman said. "That includes wasting thousands of lives and billions of dollars on an unwar that the administration has proved incapable of ending. And we don't have to fight anybody, either, not in a big way. In the atom bomb, we have Teddy Roosevelt's big stick. If we've got to use it again, we will, that's all."

"What happens when somebody uses it on us?" the ranking Democrat demanded.

Jerry Duncan's hand shot up. "Mr. Duncan," the chairman said.

"Last year, General Groves testified before the Senate that Russia had next to no uranium and was at least twenty years away from making one of these bombs," Jerry said. He'd had people beat him over the head with Leslie Groves. Now he got to quote the general himself. That was a lot more enjoyable.

"And what about the Germans?" the Democrat inquired. "Will they sit quietly like good boys and girls, the way they did from 1939 to 1945?" He got a laugh. The chairman's gavel stifled it. "Will they sit quietly, the way they're still doing now?"

"Who said the surrender in 1945—almost two years ago now!— was the end of the war in Europe? Wasn't that Mr. Truman?" Jerry said. "How right was he? How right has he been about anything?"

"That isn't what you were talking about. You were talking—I should say, not talking—about the chances the Nazis would get the atom bomb if we ran away from Germany," the Democrat said. "They already used one, remember, or close enough, on Frankfurt. Even cleaning up the mess there will take years."

"It wasn't an atom bomb. It used radium, not uranium. The only explosive was TNT." For somebody who'd never heard of uranium before August 6, 1945, for somebody who'd practiced law before going into politics, Jerry'd learned a hell of a lot since. Well, so had plenty of other people, but he'd learned more than most. "You can't call it an atom bomb, not if you want to tell the truth." By the way he said it, he didn't think his Congressional opponent gave a damn.

Said opponent only shrugged. "Okay, fine. Say it wasn't an atom bomb. What if they drop one just like it on midtown Manhattan?"

Best thing that could happen to the place went through Jerry's head. But that was small-town Indiana talking. The press would crucify him if he said it out loud. So he didn't. He did say, "How would they get it over here? There's an ocean in the way. We've got fighter planes. We've got radar to watch for bombers."

"Okay, fine," the Democrat repeated, and shrugged again. "Suppose one of these radium-not-atom bombs goes off inside a freighter in New York harbor?"

Jerry's ears got hot. "You're being ridiculous."

"The Secretary of the Navy sure doesn't think so."

"Then he's jumping at shadows," Jerry said. "If the Germans tried a stunt like that, we'd blast their country off the face of the earth. You know it. I know it. They know it, too. So why are you talking silly talk, unless you're just trying to scare the American people?"

"Mr. Chairman!" The Democrat raised his voice in appeal.

In Congresses gone by, that would have been plenty to get Jerry's ears pinned back. Here in the Eightieth Congress, the chairman came from the GOP, too. "Sounds like a reasonable question to me," he said.

Debate—no, argument—went on. But both sides knew what would happen long before it did. The appropriations bill with no money in it for the U.S. occupation of Germany would come out of the Ways and Means Committee. It would pass the House. If the Democrats in the Senate wanted to filibuster, they could. Then they'd get blamed for holding up the people's business. Sooner or later, a bill pretty much like the one the Republicans wanted would hit the President's desk.

And Harry Truman would veto it. He'd already promised that. And then the fun would really start.

NO NOISE FROM OVERHEAD. NO EXPLOSIONS ECHOING DOWN THE long, lovingly concealed mineshafts. Reinhard Heydrich breathed a little easier. No repair crews rushing to check the latest damage, or to repair the ventilation system after the confounded Americans screwed it up.

Had the Amis known which shafts were blind holes, which ones led to mines that were nothing but mines, and which ones led to paydirt . . . But they didn't, and they were unlikely to find out. The Jews and other camp scum who'd expanded this old mine probably hadn't had any idea why they were digging here. Just to stay on the safe side, afterwards they'd been exterminated anyhow—all of them, as far as Heydrich knew. And their SS guards had gone to the Eastern Front once this little stint was over. Not many of them were likely to survive, either.

Business as usual, then, at the same old stand. Well, almost as usual. The German Freedom Front had to do without a whole mine's worth of munitions and small arms. Two valleys over, the miserable

Americans had collapsed the whole thing when they touched off their damned charges up near the surface. That should never have happened—whoever'd designed that storage system had screwed up in a big way. Which didn't mean Heydrich could do anything about it now.

The struggle went on regardless. Most ways, it went pretty well. The fellow who'd come up with the bright idea of using exploding trucks and cars in sequence to do more damage would win himself a Knight's Cross. That scheme was a beauty—it could hardly work any better. Heydrich had no authentic Knight's Crosses to hand out, but he could improvise. It wasn't as if he hadn't done it before. An Iron Cross Second Class with the proper ribbon—which he did have— would do the job just fine. Everyone would know it stood for a real *Ritterkreuz*. Besides, a medal truly wasn't iron and ribbon—it was a reminder of what the holder had done to earn it.

Heydrich touched the Knight's Cross that hung at his own throat. Even if he weren't wearing it, he would know he had it, and why. That was the only thing that mattered. He went through the latest pile of newspapers and magazines from the outside world that Hans had left on his desk. The French were still vowing to rebuild the Eiffel Tower: de Gaulle had made another speech before their Chamber of Deputies.

Another story in the *International Herald-Tribune* told how the English, apparently without any political speeches, were already re-building Westminster Abbey and St. Paul's. Reinhard Heydrich nod-ded to himself. If he hadn't come upon a fundamental difference between the two races there, he didn't know when he ever would. The English monuments had been bombed later. He had no doubt they would rise again first.

But then, on an inside page, he found a story that interested him even more. The American Congress (a vaguely obscene name for a parliament, he'd always thought) was still wrangling about whether to pay for keeping U.S. soldiers in Germany. Signs were that Congress didn't want to, but the President still did.

Heydrich knew what he would do in Harry Truman's place. The leaders of Congress who didn't want to go along with him would get a visit from . . . what did the Amis call their *Gestapo*? From the FBI, that was it. Then they would see things Truman's way. If they didn't, their funerals would no doubt be well attended.

If Truman had plans along those lines, the *Herald-Tribune* didn't talk about them. It wouldn't, of course. But Heydrich didn't believe Truman would do the obvious, necessary thing. Americans were fools. They were rich fools, fools with enormous factories, but fools all the same. The factories let them smash the *Wehrmacht*. Still, they had no stomach for what came after even a victorious war. . . .

Or did they? A German magazine had a glowing article about the police force the Amis were organizing in their zone. Heydrich already knew about that, naturally. But getting the American slant—for what else was the magazine but an American propaganda rag?—was interesting. Very interesting, in fact.

Before the collapse, the writer had worked for the *Völkischer Beobachter;* Heydrich recognized his name. Well, he'd landed on his feet. He claimed that this new police corps would protect order and guard against extremism, whether from the left or the right. He also claimed the Amis were building it up to be strong enough and reliable enough to do its duty under any conceivable political circumstances.

"Any?" Heydrich murmured. That was a large claim, to say the least. And Heydrich also knew enough to translate it from journalese into plain German. The writer obviously hoped most of his readers didn't. If the Americans decided to hop on their planes and boats and go back across the Atlantic where they belonged, the new police corps would stay behind as their surrogates.

During the war, Germany had set up plenty of police outfits like that. The French *Milice* fought the French resistance harder than any German outfits in France ever did. Latvian and Lithuanian policemen cheerfully delivered Jews to the Germans for disposal. General Nedic's militia in Serbia harried the Titoists.

All of those police forces fell apart when the German military might supporting them waned. Did the Amis think the same thing wouldn't happen to their sheep dogs after they went home? If they did, they really were fools.

And did they think their fancy new police corps wasn't riddled with traitors? Heydrich shook his head. *With true German patriots,* he thought. It depended on how you looked at things, though. Some of Nedic's men had warned Tito's followers what their outfit was up to. Some members of the *Milice* played a double game with the resistance.

Some members of the Americans' German police were in touch with the forces that aimed to restore the *Reich* to greatness, too. Heydrich usually knew what the would-be oppressors had in mind before they tried it. None of their moves had hurt him yet. He had to be careful—the Americans weren't too naïve to plant false information—but so far he'd outsmarted them.

How many men from the *Milice* had de Gaulle's French forces shot or imprisoned? What had the Titoists done to Nedic's militia? How had the Russians treated Germany's Latvian and Lithuanian collaborators? Heydrich slowly smiled. None of that would be a patch on the revenge he aimed to take on the German police who cozied up to the Americans.

"Revenge on the USA, too," he said, as if reminding himself. Von Braun and the other slide-rule soldiers at Peenemünde had made rockets that could hit London from the Continent. They'd planned much bigger beasts: rockets that could hit America from Europe. Only the collapse kept the scientists from building them.

A lot of those scientists were twiddling their slide rules for the United States these days. Others were working for the Russians. But some remained in Germany. And the *Reich* still had plenty of scientists and engineers who could learn rocketry if they needed to.

Which they would. A rocket that could reach New York City with an atom bomb in its nose would teach the Americans they couldn't tell Germany what to do any more. And rockets like that could also reach far into Russia—farther than the *Wehrmacht* ever got. As soon as Germany built them, Stalin would have to think twice before he started any new trouble.

Heydrich could hardly wait.

XXIII

Lou Weissberg's mother had talked about how good it felt *not* to have to wear a corset when they fell out of fashion after World War I. Lou always nodded. What were you supposed to do when your mother went on about something that wouldn't matter to you in a million years?

Except now it did. He'd escaped his own canvas-and-metal contraption not long before. His leg didn't bother him too much, either. He was . . . no, not quite good as new, but getting there, anyway. On this second anniversary of V-E Day, that wasn't so bad.

It was a bright spring morning. Sunshine. Puffy white clouds drifting across the sky. Vibrant greens. Songbirds chirping their heads off. Storks nesting on chimneytops wherever chimneys still stood. And the stink of undiscovered bodies buried in rubble, the stink that never seemed to disappear from Nuremberg but did fade in the chilly wintertime.

Howard Frank snorted when Lou remarked on it. "Yeah, well, those are the krauts we don't have to worry about," Frank said.

"Ha!" Lou said around a mouthful of scrambled eggs and hash browns. "Don't I wish that was funny!"

"I know, I know." Major Frank lit a cigarette. "At ten o'clock we get to listen to General Clay telling us how wonderful everything's going."

"Oh, boy." Lou had no trouble restraining his enthusiasm. General Eisenhower'd gone back to the States at the end of the year before. Staying any longer would have tarnished his reputation as the man who'd won the war in Europe . . . assuming the war in Europe had been won. Germany was Lucius Clay's baby now, and a damned ugly baby to find on your doorstep it was, too.

"Next interesting question is whether the fanatics mortar us while we're listening to Clay tell us how wonderful everything is," Frank said.

"You're chipper today, aren't you?" Lou said. In lieu of answering, his superior smoked his Chesterfield down to a tiny butt, stubbed it out, and lit another one.

German cops on street corners stiffened to attention as the two American officers went to listen to General Clay. The policemen wore their black-dyed American uniforms. Some of them had on American helmets, too. Others wore what had been firemen's helmets, with an aluminum crest to change the outline of what otherwise looked the same as the standard German *Stahlhelm*. And, with shortages everywhere, some of the cops *did* wear the *Wehrmacht*-issue steel helmet.

Pointing to one of those guys—who also carried a U.S.-made submachine gun—Lou said, "That still gives me the willies, y'know?"

Howard Frank didn't need to ask what in particular was eating him. The major only nodded. "Yeah, me, too," he agreed. "But what are you gonna do? They may see action, and it's a damn good helmet. When we switched from the limey-style tin hat to the one we use now, first scheme was to make *Stahlhelms* and just paint 'em a different color."

"Fuck. I'm glad we didn't. That thing screams *Nazi!* at me." Since the Kaiser's engineers had devised the shape in the last war, Lou knew that wasn't completely rational. He didn't care. Hitler's bastards had been trying to kill him, not the Kaiser's—except for some retreads, no doubt. He gave the next German cop he saw a fishy stare. "Other thing is, how many of these bastards are ratting on us to Heydrich?"

"Bound to be some. Hopefully, not too many." Howard Frank sounded somewhere between cynical and resigned.

A couple of other guys in dyed-black U.S. uniform came by. They weren't German police; they had on armbands that said DP. They sure as hell were displaced persons. They talked to each other in some Slavic language—Russian? Polish? Ukrainian? Czech? Serbo-Croatian? Bulgarian?—full of consonants and *y*'s. One of them carried a grease gun like the cop's; the other wore a Luger on his belt.

At least they don't have German helmets, Lou thought. With more and more American soldiers heading home, DPs were doing a hell of a lot of the cooking and cleaning and fetching and carrying. The way things were going, the occupation would probably fall apart without them. On the Eastern Front, the Germans had used Russian POWs—*Hiwis,* they called them, a contraction from their term for "volunteer assistants"—the same way, and for the same reason: to stretch their combat manpower. Now they were getting it done to them instead. *Serves 'em right, too.*

Better not to inquire about what happened to any *Hiwis* who fell into Soviet hands. Lou might want to work more closely with the Russians against the Heydrichites. That didn't mean he thought they were nice people. But they weren't on the Nazis' side, which also counted.

A perimeter of barbed wire, concrete barriers, and machine-gun nests protected the Americans gathering to hear General Clay from German kamikazes driving trucks full of TNT. Mortars . . . Lou shook his head. He'd already worried about mortars once. If they started coming in, he'd hit the dirt, that was all.

Even as Clay stepped up to the microphone, several enlisted men bawled, "We want to go home!"

Clay looked at them. He had bushy dark eyebrows that told what he was thinking without his saying a word. If he wasn't thinking *stockade* right this minute, Lou'd never seen anybody who was.

He had a raspy voice that spoke of a million cigarettes, or maybe a million and one. "I want to go home, too," he said. "We all want to go home. I don't know of a single soldier in Uncle Sam's army who wants to stay in Germany. But we've got what they used to call a job of work to do, and we're going to do it."

When he paused, some of the soldiers yelled, "We want to go

home!" again. They didn't give a damn about a general or anybody else. They were draftees. They sure didn't give a damn about winning the war before they left, the way earlier crops of dogfaces had. After all, the war in Europe had been over for two years—hadn't it? If it hadn't, why were they all standing around on this nice May morning? Why weren't they out trying to pick up German broads with chocolate bars?

But if the war in Europe had been over for two years, why all the tank barriers and machine-gun positions and barbed wire? *Yeah. Why?* Lou wondered, his own thoughts pretty barbed, too.

General Clay charged into that question head-on: "We beat the German army. We walloped the *Waffen*-SS, too. You know it, boys. Some of you helped do it. And some of you saw what the Nazis did while they were on top. You know why we had to lick them. If we hadn't, one of these days before too long they would have done that stuff to our friends and neighbors and families."

"Damn straight," Howard Frank muttered beside Lou. Lou nodded. As far as he was concerned, Lucius Clay was preaching to the choir. He'd never yet heard of a Jewish soldier who went around shouting *We want to go home!* Jews understood in their *kishkas* what this war was all about.

But there weren't enough Jews to go around, goddammit.

"And they still want to," Clay went on. "That's the funny thing about this whole business. Plenty of people back home march around and wave signs and bang drums and yell and scream and shout that we ought to pack up and get the devil out of Germany. But not one of them says the Germans are good guys all of a sudden. Not one of them says the Nazis won't take over again if we do run away."

Lou craned his neck. He didn't see any of the German policemen in their black GI uniforms inside the American perimeter. How hard would they fight the fanatics after the Americans went home? Some of them had spent time in concentration camps under the Third *Reich*. Those guys would give Heydrich's goons a smack in the teeth if they could. The rest? Well, who could say?

And, even if the new kraut cops were willing to mix it up with the Nazis, would they stay that way after a sniper picked off their wife or mother or two-year-old? That was already starting to happen. Or suppose a truck full of explosives blew up a police barracks in the middle of the night. That had already happened more than once, too. What would it do to the cops' morale?

Lost in those gloomy reflections, Lou realized he'd missed some of what General Clay was saying. "—thinks we need to be here," Clay declared. Then he said, "The President is the commander-in-chief of the armed forces of the United States," so Lou figured out what was going on. "As long as the commander-in-chief thinks we need to stay in this country, we will. The sooner our friends and our foes understand that, the better."

It sounded good. It would have sounded even better if one of the fed-up GIs hadn't hollered, "Not if Congress doesn't give him the cash!"

As if on cue, several other men called, "We want to go home!" again.

"Congress will do whatever Congress does. The President will do whatever he feels he has to do. And we will do whatever the President and our superiors tell us to do." Clay stuck out his chin. "And so will I, and so will every one of you, too."

He stepped away from the microphone. Some of the soldiers assembled to listen to him applauded. Lou and Major Frank both made sure they did—but then, they had their reasons. Lou assumed MPs had kept an eye on the hecklers and would give them what-for afterwards. He hoped so, anyway.

Even if they did, though, so what? The mouthy draftees might spend some time in the stockade for disrespect, or whatever other charges had a chance of sticking. While they were there, they'd still have plenty to eat and somewhere soft and dry to sleep. Heydrich's thugs wouldn't be trying to bump them off, either. If all you wanted to do was come home in one piece, the stockade didn't look half bad.

When Lou said as much, Major Frank answered, "Sure, if that's all you want. But it goes on your record, too. It won't look so good when you're trying to land a job once you get home."

"How many of these guys give a damn?" Lou said. "How many of 'em think that far ahead?"

Howard Frank looked as if he'd put down several too many a while ago and his head was banging like Buddy Rich's drums. "*Mazeltov,*" he said sourly.

"For what?" Lou asked.

"For nailing the USA down tight in two goddamn questions, that's for what," Frank answered.

Neither one of them had much else to say on the way back to their offices.

AS FAR AS BERNIE COBB WAS CONCERNED, THE KRAUTS KNEW WAY more about tanks and machine guns and beer than anybody in the United States had ever imagined. The Panzer IVs and Panthers and Tigers (*Lions and tigers and bears! Oh, my!*) were out of business, thank God. You still had to look out for fanatics with MG42s, but not right this minute, also thank God. As for the beer . . .

Bernie had a big old stein of it in front of him. He'd already emptied the mug several times. He expected to empty it several more before the day or the night or whatever the hell was through. A bunch of GIs packed the tavern in the Alpine village with the unpronounceable name. As he'd discovered, there were a lot of Alpine villages with unpronounceable names. This one was more unpronounceable than most, which was—or would have been—saying something.

"Thank you kindly." Toby Benton had taken on a considerable alcoholic cargo, too. The sergeant sounded mushmouthed any old time—that was what coming from Oklahoma did to you. When he was also drunk, you could hardly understand him at all.

"Goin' home." Bernie didn't sound like anybody from the speech and debate team, either. "Man alive . . . You *are* a man alive."

"Sure am." The demolitions expert nodded. "Sure as hell am. Didn't know if I was gonna make it through, 'specially with the way they went an' kept stretchin' our hitches an' stretchin' 'em an'. . . ."

Every guy in the joint growled profane agreement with that, even the fellows who hadn't been over here since before the shooting was supposed to be over. "Way my points added up, I figured I'd make it back in November or December of '45," Bernie said. "I'm still here a year and a half later. God only knows when they'll turn me loose."

"Long as you don't go home in a box, that's the only thing that matters," another GI said. He raised his voice a little: "Anybody here *not* know somebody who got it after fucking V-E Day?"

No one claimed to, not even a couple of kids who'd been here only a few weeks. "It's a bastard, all right," Sergeant Benton said. "Ain't we lucky we won the war?"

"Some luck." Bernie Cobb peered lugubriously into the bottom of his seidel. "I don't even have any beer left."

"You can do something about that, you know," the dogface sitting next to him said.

"Oh, yeah." Bernie needed reminding. He waved to the barmaid. "Hey, sweetheart!"

He wouldn't have called her *sweetheart* anywhere else, and not without a few under her belt, either. She was somewhere in her mid-thirties. She wasn't ugly—she wasn't half bad, in fact, and she had a shape like a Coke bottle. Even drunk, though, he wasn't tempted to put a move on her. She looked tough, was what she looked. He wondered if she'd been through a denazifying trial. If somebody told him she'd been one of the nasty female guards at a German camp, he would have believed it.

Which didn't keep her from filling up his beer mug again. She had serious muscles in her forearms, from hauling around so many steins and pitchers. He gave her a dime. *"Ja,"* she said softly as she made the small silver coin disappear. Would the old man with the gray mustache behind the bar see any of that? Bernie shrugged. It wasn't his worry.

"Gonna get me a job where the most explosive thing I gotta mess with is the carburetor off an old Ford," Benton was saying. "Gonna forget all the shit they learned me. Ain't gonna study war no more, like it says in the Good Book."

"Wow," two or three GIs said together, longing in their voices. The Americans in the tavern amassed an impressive amount of lethal hardware. Nobody went anywhere unarmed these days. You might as well tie a bull's-eye and a SHOOT ME! sign to your back.

"You know what, Sarge?" a soldier said. "Pretty soon we'll all be coming home, regardless of points or whether the Army likes it or any of that crap. Congress'll figure we wasted enough time fucking around over here, and that'll be that."

"Wouldn't bother me none," Benton answered. "Nobody likes the damn Nazis, but nobody wants to get his dick shot off, neither."

"We want to go home!" several men chorused. Then they started laughing fit to bust. Discipline here was still pretty good—not great, but pretty good. From what Bernie heard, some places hardly anybody obeyed orders he didn't happen to like.

Toby Benton called for more beer. "One bad thing about goin' home," he said, "is I'll have to drink the horse piss they put in bottles back in the States." Bernie wasn't the only guy who nodded—not even close. The stuff they brewed over here had been a revelation to him. Beer didn't just get you blasted after you poured down enough of it. It could taste good, too. Who would've thunk it?

The barmaid came over and filled up Benton's stein. He gave her a K-ration can and a pack of Luckies. *"Ja!"* she said, as she had after Bernie handed her the dime, only she sounded a lot happier this time. In a cautious, experimental way, as if he were defusing a mine, Sergeant Benton patted her on the ass.

All the Americans in the tavern tensed. The other half-sloshed GIs must've thought the same thing Bernie did: if you messed with this babe, she'd knock your block off. Which only went to show you never could tell. The barmaid plopped herself down in the demolitions expert's lap, threw her arms around his neck, and gave him the kind of kiss the Hays Office wouldn't let you film. Bernie wondered if she'd screw him right there where he sat, but she didn't—quite.

"Hot damn!" Benton said when he finally came up for air. "I'll miss the easy nookie they got over here, too. Sure as hell can't get an American girl to put out for beef stew and a pack of smokes."

"Our side didn't lose the war," Bernie said.

"Who says theirs did?" Sergeant Benton regretfully untangled himself from the barmaid. She didn't seem anywhere near so tough any more.

"You know what I mean," Bernie persisted. "Other thing is, girls back home don't know what all we've been through."

"And every goddamn bit of it the past coupla years—all the bombs, all the rockets, all the snipers, all the crap—it's been nothin' but a waste of time," Benton said. "You fuckin' wait an' see. We're gonna chuck it in over here. We're gonna go home an' let the Jerries do whatever they want."

"We're gonna pay the price for it down the line if we do," Bernie said.

Benton shrugged—and almost fell off his chair. Yeah, he'd taken on a lot of beer. "It'll be somebody else's headache then," he said. "Long as it ain't chewing on the guys who're in right now, they won't care."

Whether Benton was drunk or not, that seemed like a pretty good bet to Bernie Cobb. And, now that the ice had been broken, so did the barmaid.

HARRY TRUMAN LOOKED HOPPING MAD. SINCE COMING BACK TO Washington, Tom Schmidt had seen the President angry plenty of times. Truman delighted in sticking out such chin as he had and telling the world where to go and how to get there. He could be funny at the same time. He made Tom laugh, and Tom got paid for writing unkind things about him. But today he just looked ticked off.

Overhead lights flashed off his spectacle lenses as he glared out at the assembled reporters. "I called a press conference this afternoon so I could tell the American people why I'm vetoing this joke of a budget bill that has landed on my desk. I warned the Republicans who head up this new Congress—and I warned the Democratic leadership, too—that I would veto any bill that looks like this. They sent me one anyway, and I am sending it back—air-mail, special delivery."

"Nice of him to get his own party mad at him, too," Schmidt whispered to the guy sitting next to him.

The other fellow barely had time to nod before Truman went on, "I'm especially unhappy with the so-called Democratic leaders in the Senate." No, he didn't care if he antagonized them. "They told me this was the best they could do—a bill that cuts off funds for our boys in Germany at the end of the year instead of right away. If this is the best they can do, I'm here to tell them it isn't good enough."

"Why not?" a reporter called.

"I'll take questions when I'm done with my statement," the President said. "But since I was coming to why not anyway, it'll look like I'm answering this one. Congress has got no business tying American foreign policy by the purse strings. Can you imagine what would have happened after Pearl Harbor if Congress told President Roosevelt, 'You've got to win the war by the end of 1943, or we won't give you any more money to fight it'? Can you imagine?" He quivered with indignation. "If Congress did something that stupid, why, Hitler would be holding a press conference here in the White House right now, for heaven's sake!"

Several reporters laughed then. Newsreel cameras ground away. One day soon, people all across the country would see him when they went to the movies. "Is it really the same thing, Mr. President?" Tom called.

"You'd better believe it is," Truman snapped—so much for taking questions after his statement. "We will do what we need to do. It may take longer than we expect right now. It may cost more. We will do it anyway."

Since he'd got one answer, Schmidt tried for another: "But if you think we need to do this, sir, and Congress and most of the American people think we need to do that—?"

"I'm the President," Truman said. "I didn't want the job. I wish Franklin Roosevelt, God love him, were still here to do it. Just by the way, I believe he'd do it the same way I am. But that's neither here nor there. For as long as I am President, I'm going to do things the best way I know how. And that includes keeping American soldiers in Germany to hold down the Nazis and hold back the Russians."

"If you do that, you won't stay President long," said another member of the White House press corps.

"Chance I take," Truman answered calmly. "If I leave, I'll leave knowing I did the right thing. And if whoever the Republicans pick does something else, he'll prove pretty darn quick how right I was."

He didn't lack for confidence. By all accounts, he never had. How much good did that do when he was so out of step with the rest of the country? Herbert Hoover had been confident, too, and look how much good it did him. You could be confident you knew a road, but all the confidence in the world wouldn't help you if you drove off a cliff. You'd go smash at the bottom any which way—and so would all the other people you were driving.

"And let me tell you boys—and you ladies—something else." Truman wagged a finger at the reporters. "You think you know what America thinks. Well, I've got news for you. There are a devil of a lot of Americans who don't march around with placards on their shoulders. They keep their mouths shut and go to work every day and pay their taxes—oh, they don't like paying them (who does?), but they do it. And even though they don't kick up a fuss and get their photographs in the newspapers, they have the sense to know that we are doing the right thing in Germany and that we need to stay the course there. I wouldn't be surprised—no, sir, I wouldn't be one bit surprised—if there were more of them than there are of the noisy kind."

Tom Schmidt's shorthand scribbles barely kept up with the angry President. As Truman finally paused to draw breath, Tom wrote his own comment under the other man's words. *Silent majority? Good luck!* Then he eyed the phrase and nodded to himself. It wouldn't make a bad lead—might even do for a headline.

After that deep breath, Truman returned at last to his prepared remarks. He lambasted the Republican Congress for everything except violating the Mann Act. If you listened to him, everything was Congress' fault. He hadn't made a single mistake himself—not one, not in all his born days.

If you listened to him. How likely were the American people to do that? Looking at the folks they'd sent to Congress, maybe not very.

Truman finally got around to taking the questions he'd planned to take all along. "Does being an accidental President hinder you?" a reporter asked. "Is it harder to do your job knowing nobody elected you to do it?"

"Not even a little bit," Truman said. "People elected Roosevelt President four different times. This last time, he and the Democratic Party chose me as his running mate. There is always the chance that a President of the United States will die in office. In 1944, it was an open secret that President Roosevelt was not a well man. Whoever ran with him might have to succeed him. I wish that hadn't happened— I wish it with all my heart. But it did, and I'm just as much President as if I'd been elected unanimously. So I have to do my best, like I say, and that is what I am doing."

No red meat there, Tom judged. Anybody in the same spot would say the same thing. Too bad.

"Why do you think it's so important to stay in Germany when everybody else is sick of being there?" another reporter asked.

"I told you before, not everybody is," Harry Truman said. Tom underlined *Silent majority.* Truman went on, "Anybody who wants to risk seeing the Nazis come back to power needs to have his head examined too."

Tom's hand flew up. After a pause, Truman nodded his way. "How dangerous can they be in a country that got stepped on?" he asked. "I was over there till—"

"Till you got thrown out, and for good reason, too," Truman broke in.

"I don't think believing in freedom of the press is a good reason to expel a man, sir," Tom said with dignity.

Truman only sniffed. "Believing in getting a better byline is more like it, if you ask me. But to get back to your question. How dangerous can the Nazis be? Why don't you ask the English while they clean up London? Why don't you ask the French after four years of occupation? Why don't you ask the Russians—the survivors, I should say? The only question is whether they lost twenty million or thirty million in the war. Pennsylvania plus California plus maybe Illinois—gone. Gone to graveyards, when people got buried at all. So how dangerous can the Nazis be?"

"What about the atom bomb?" Tom and three other reporters asked the question at the same time. Two of those others worked for papers that normally favored the administration, which was . . . interesting, anyhow.

"Yes, we have it," Truman said. "The first thing the Nazis do will be to try to get it on their own. The radium treatment they gave to innocent civilians in Frankfurt is proof of that. The next thing they'll do is, they'll try to find a way to throw it at us. They could reach London with the V-2, though that isn't strong enough to carry an atom bomb. They had plans on the drawing board for a rocket that could reach our East Coast from Europe. How long do you suppose it will be before they dust off those plans and start building rockets like that?"

A rocket that could reach the East Coast from Europe? It sounded like science fiction, the stuff in the cheap pulp magazines with the lurid covers. Of course, up until August 1945 the atom bomb itself had sounded the same way. So maybe Truman and the German engineers knew what they were talking about. On the other hand, maybe they didn't.

Another reporter beat Tom to the question he wanted to ask: "How do we know this is true? How do we know this isn't just you talking, Mr. President, to try to justify the mess in Germany?"

Truman glared at the man. "I am giving you the information I've got, Wilbur," he said. "Sometimes I cannot give you all the information I've got, because that might help the enemy. But I am not lying to you. I am not making things up. And if you say I am, you can go—" The phrase he used would not be printed in any family newspaper in the United States.

"Love you, too, Mr. President," Wilbur said, which got a laugh from the press corps and even a chuckle from Harry Truman. The reporter went on, "After all the stuff the administration has tried to hide about the way things in Germany are going, can you blame us for having our doubts about the things you say?"

"Blame you? Damn right I can blame you," Truman answered. "You are trying to make me run the country by Gallup poll. I am here to tell you, that does not work. By the nature of things, it can't work. Sometimes you have to stick it out even when things don't look so good at the moment and not everybody likes what you're doing. If nobody pays any attention to what may happen in the long run, you've got yourself a problem."

Truman doesn't care about democracy, Tom wrote. It wasn't a completely fair summary of what the President said, but it wasn't completely unfair, either. If Truman thought he had the right to override the will of the people whenever he felt like it, what were the checks and balances in the Constitution worth? Not even the paper they were printed on.

"What will you do if Congress sends you another appropriations bill like this one?" somebody asked.

"Veto it again," Truman said promptly.

"What will you do if Congress passes the bill over your veto?" the reporter asked.

"What will I do? I'll be very surprised, that's what," Truman said. "If Congress somehow manages to sabotage our foreign policy in that way, it will be a sad day in the history of the United States."

I'm the one who's right. I'm the one with all the answers. That might not be what Truman was saying, but that was what he meant. Tom Schmidt wrote it down. A big part of his job was telling people what he thought the President did mean, regardless of what Truman actually said.

———

Ed McGraw flipped to the editorial page of the *Indianapolis Times*. He'd rarely bothered with it before Pat got killed. He grunted. "Here's a column by your friend Schmidt," he said, and then, "Let me have some more coffee, willya?"

"Sure." Diana poised the pot over Ed's cup and poured. He dumped in sugar and Pet condensed milk. Diana let him take a sip before she asked, "What does Tom say?" She'd never figured she would be on a first-name basis with national reporters, but she was.

Her husband grunted again, to show he noticed how strange that was, too. Then he read out loud: " 'Harry S Truman thinks he knows best. He thinks he can run the country on the basis of what he thinks he knows, regardless of how the American people feel about it. How does that make him any different from Joseph Stalin? For that matter, how does it make him any different from Adolf Hitler?' "

"Wow," Diana said appreciatively. "That's strong stuff." She felt as if she'd poured a slug of brandy into her own morning coffee.

"Wait. There's more. Let me give you the best part." Ed paused for a moment, then resumed: " 'Truman claims a silent majority backs the steps he is taking in Germany and his stubborn refusal to cut his losses—our losses—and come home. The reason this so-called majority is silent appears to be that it is not there. Most things that are not there make very little noise.' How about *that,* babe?"

"Yeah, how about that? I want to applaud," Diana said.

" 'What is Truman accomplishing in Germany? Anything? Anything at all?' " Ed read. " 'The longer this pointless occupation goes on, the less likely that seems. Thousands of men, dead. Billions of dollars, wasted. Down a rathole. What will happen when the United States finally gives up and comes home? The same thing that would have happened if we'd come home right after V-E Day. Everybody knows it. Even Harry Truman probably knows it by now. The trouble is, he's too pigheaded to admit it.' "

"That's about the size of things, all right. Silent majority!" Diana scoffed the idea to scorn. "We'll have to show Truman where the majority is. And we'll have to show him how much noise it can make, too."

"You do that, babe—and I know darn well you will." Her husband let the paper flop down onto the kitchen table. "Me, I gotta go to work." He grabbed his lunch bucket, pecked Diana on the cheek, and headed out the door. In the driveway, the Pontiac started up with a whir and a groan. Ed backed out, put it in first, and drove off to the Delco-Remy plant.

Alone in the house, Diana sighed very quietly. Now that she'd met so many hard-driving men, Ed McGraw seemed . . . well, just a little dull. Or more than just a little. Oh, he made a decent enough living. And he loved her. And he was as reliable as the 1:27 out of Indianapolis. And, while he looked at pretty women, she knew he'd never do more than look.

But . . . The only way Ed would ever show any spark was if he got struck by lightning. Diana hadn't known she missed that till she saw it in other men. *Aren't I entitled to a little spark every once in a while?* she wondered.

Some women, faced with a question like that, took direct action: they went out and found the spark they thought they were looking for. Some took indirect action: they quietly started emptying the cooking sherry or the brandy or the bourbon or whatever along those lines happened to be handy. If they put out the spark in themselves, they wouldn't miss it in anyone else.

And some, like Diana, worked harder than ever at what they were already doing. If they stayed too busy to notice the spark wasn't there, not having it almost didn't matter. Almost.

She grabbed the newspaper and reread the column Ed had read out loud. It just made her madder the second time around. "Silent majority!" she snorted. Then, because no one else was there to hear her, she added, "My ass!" And then she put down the paper, picked up the telephone, and got cracking.

The McGraw household had a new phone line these days, one paid for with funds from Mothers Against the Madness in Germany. That was the one Diana parked herself in front of. She'd never imagined making so many long-distance phone calls. All the local long-distance operators recognized her voice. One had had a son wounded in Austria, so almost all of them were on her side.

Over and over again, across the country, she summarized Tom Schmidt's column for the movement leaders who hadn't seen it yet (several already had, and were just as stirred up about it as Diana was). "Silent majority!" she fleered, again and again. "Do we have time to organize rallies on the Fourth of July? We'll show Truman where the majority is. We'll show him it isn't silent, too. And we'll show him it isn't on his side."

By the time she got hungry enough to think about lunch, she'd made plans to turn the country upside down and inside out. She'd run up the phone bill by God only knew how much, but so what? It wasn't her money. She still kept careful track of every penny of it—all those years in the PTA had ground that into her—but she didn't worry about it any more.

She raided the icebox for leftovers and heated them on top of the stove. As she ate, she read the rest of the paper. Two more poor GIs blown up when a roadside artillery shell went off as their jeep drove by—another soldier wounded, too. She shook her head. Such a senseless waste!

She wished she hadn't had that exact thought. Ed's face appeared in her mind when she did. That wasn't fair, and she knew it. They'd had a lot of good years together. They'd raised two good kids. If Pat had come home right after V-E Day, everything would still be fine. Everything still was fine—unless she decided it wasn't.

Why did Ed have to look so much like a 1933 De Soto with a dented fender and a broken taillight?

"Nothing wrong with Ed. Not a single, solitary thing," she said, there where nobody else could hear.

But that wasn't what bothered her. What bothered her was, there wasn't enough right with Ed.

She got on the phone again. The busier she stayed, the less time she'd have to look at things like that.

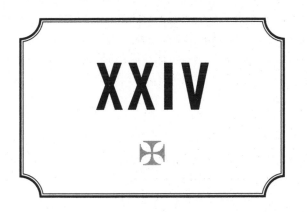

XXIV

Berlin. Broken capital of the Third *Reich*. Quadruply occupied symbol of Allied solidarity, even when there wasn't a hell of a lot of Allied solidarity to go around. A place where Heydrich's fanatics pulled off enough bombings and other atrocities to generate more Allied solidarity than there would have been otherwise.

Lou Weissberg stared at the wreckage—some of it mighty grandiose wreckage, too—for all the world like a tourist. Behind him, Howard Frank also did some tall rubbernecking. Lou lit a cigarette. Smoking helped you not notice the other thing that remained in the air, even two years and more after the fighting was said to be over. A lot of people had died here, and not so many of them lay in graves.

His superior smoked away with him. Major Frank puffed like a steam engine on an uphill grade. "Maybe we'll bring it off this time," he said.

A blackbird chirped, sounding like a robin back home. Like those good old American robins, blackbirds ate worms. What the worms ate . . . was perhaps better left uncontemplated in Berlin.

"Maybe we will." If Lou sounded as if he didn't believe it, that was only because he didn't. "We tried it in '45—and they blew up the Palace of Justice in Nuremberg. We tried it in '46—and Frankfurt is still waddayacallit . . . radioactive. So what the hell will they do here?"

"We got the Nazi big shots here. That's something, anyhow," Frank said. "I wouldn't've given good odds we'd manage that."

"Chances are Heydrich's waiting till they go on trial," Lou said. "Then his merry men will try something really juicy, know what I mean?"

"Merry men, my ass." But Frank's green-persimmon pucker said he knew just what Lou meant, no matter how much he wished he didn't. He glanced east. "Trial's gonna be in the Russian zone, so the security monkey's off our back, anyway."

"Unless they holler for help," Lou said.

"Don't hold your breath," Howard Frank said. "They wouldn't do that unless they were in deeper shit than they are now."

"I guess," Lou said. Scuttlebutt said that back in 1942, when things looked black for the USSR, Stalin asked FDR and Churchill for American and British divisions to fight alongside the Red Army on the Eastern Front. Scuttlebutt even said he'd promised to let them keep their own command structure, which for a Russian leader was like handing over the crown jewels and the key to whatever he used instead of Fort Knox. The Anglo-American troops didn't go. Trucks and avgas and Spam and ammo did, by the bazillions of tons. And Uncle Joe found enough Soviet bodies to make Hitler blow his brains out.

And that was what so many of them turned into, too—bodies. To this day, you could smell them, and the Germans they'd taken with them, in Berlin.

Lou and Major Frank smoked their cigarettes down to teeny-tiny butts before tossing them away and lighting new ones. The tobacco scroungers were on those little, spit-soaked dog-ends like Dracula on a pretty girl's neck. Tobacco fueled what was left of the German economy—and you could even smoke it.

Labor gangs shifted rubble one broken brick at a time. Old people, women who'd probably been chic once upon a time, and shabby demobilized soldiers labored side by side. Everybody was skinny. The ration was supposed to be up to 1,500 calories a day, which wasn't saying much. You'd lose weight doing nothing on 1,500 calories a day. Doing hard physical labor . . .

Considering what the Germans had done in occupied Europe, Lou had trouble working up much sympathy. He suspected the Red Army men in the Russian zone found it even tougher.

Howard Frank was also eyeing the skinny krauts. "Now if we sent everybody who looked at us sideways off to a camp—"

"We'd be just like the Russians. And just like the Nazis," Lou finished for him. "But we're not. Hell, we can't even keep our own guys here."

"Last GI in Germany, close the door on your way out," Frank agreed. "Gotta admire Congress, don't you?"

"God must love idiots, or He wouldn't have made so many of them," Lou said, which might have been an answer or might not.

"Yeah, but how come so many of 'em got elected?" Frank said. "You ready to go back to the States yet?"

"A lot of me is. I've been away from my family way too goddamn long—I mean way," Lou said. "Hate to leave feeling like I didn't do my job, though. If I could punch Heydrich's ticket before I climbed on a plane or a boat or a unicycle or whatever the hell . . ."

"I got a picture of you on a unicycle. I got a picture of you back in the hospital after you fall off the fuckin' unicycle, too," Frank said. Lou Weissberg, not the most graceful of men, maintained a dignified silence.

During the war, there'd been a German propaganda photo of a soldier raising the swastika flag over the ruins of Stalingrad. That didn't quite work out for Hitler's crew. Right before V-E Day, Stalin got his answer: a photo of a Red Army man planting the hammer and sickle on the *Reichs* Chancellery in Berlin. The *Wehrmacht* gave up a few days later, and everything was supposed to be hunky-dory from then on out.

Well, theory was wonderful.

Getting into the Russian zone to see the Chancellery wasn't easy. You had to clear a checkpoint, sign a log, show your ID, and get patted down. You also had to talk to a Red Army lieutenant who spoke American English like a native and probably was one.

"Okay—youse guys are legit," the guy said: a turn of phrase Lou heard all the time from New Jersey high-school kids in his English classes. The Red Army soldier went on, "We gotta keep our eyes open, y'know? Damn Fascist hyenas try and pull all kinds of sneaky stunts."

"Sure," Lou said. He'd heard that hyena line, too—mostly from people who read the *Daily Worker*. It came from Russia there, and it came from Russia here.

If anything, the Russian zone in Berlin looked worse than the American zone. It was the eastern part of the city, and the part where the fighting had been heaviest. The labor gangs here were guarded by Russian soldiers with submachine guns that looked as if they'd been made in somebody's basement. For all Lou knew, they had.

The Chancellery and the other fancy buildings from which the Nazis had run the *Reich* were all smashed wreckage. Lou took out a Brownie and clicked away. "These'll remind me they got some of what was coming to them, anyhow," he said. He wasn't the only Allied soldier photographing the ruins, either. Amateur shutterbugs nodded to one another, all probably thinking the same kinds of thoughts.

"Americans? You have any money? You have any cigarettes?" The guy who asked spoke Yiddish, not German. He rolled up a sleeve on his frayed shirt to show a number tattooed on his upper arm. He'd lived through the death camps, then. His face was all nose and staring eyes. Even now, more than two years after he'd been liberated, he looked as if a strong breeze—hell, a weak breeze—would blow him away.

"Here, buddy." Lou handed him a pack of Luckies and five bucks and half a D-ration chocolate bar he had in a jacket pocket.

Major Frank was similarly generous. "Beat it," he told the displaced person after giving him stuff. "Somebody'll knock you over the head if you hang around."

"Thank you both. If I still believed in God, I would ask His blessings on you," the DP said. He disappeared like a cockroach vanishing down a crack in the floor.

"If I still believed in God . . ." Lou echoed, in Yiddish and then in English. It sounded just as bad either way. But when you'd been through what the DP had, when millions of people who went into the camps came out only as smoke from a crematorium chimney, when God—if there was a God—sat there and watched without doing anything . . . The Chosen People? Chosen for what? For *this*? Lou had done his best not to think about it. If you did think about it, how *could* you go on believing?

Lou started to ask Howard Frank about that. Then, seeing the look on the other Jew's face, he didn't. Frank was wrestling with the same demons. When you did start to think, how could you help it?

One way was to stop thinking about it. They got their chance, and in a hurry. Other beggars had seen them give to the Jewish DP. They might have marked themselves with the brand *Sucker*. Hungry people in threadbare clothes converged on them from all directions, hands outstretched, voices shrill and desperate.

Yes, they all needed food. Yes, they were all broke. But there were too many of them for two U.S. Army officers to help much, even if they stripped themselves naked. Lou wasn't inclined to do that anyway. That almost all the beggars were Germans did nothing to endear them to him any further.

Major Frank said, "No." So did Lou. Then they said, "Hell, no!" Then they said, "Go away!" Finally, it was, "Fuck off!" And Lou wondered if he'd have to draw his sidearm to show he meant business.

Before he did, a couple of Russian soldiers came over to see what the yelling crowd was all about. That got the beggars moving. Did it ever! They didn't want the Russians to pay any special attention to them. Oh, no!

The Russians understood bits of German. Lou explained what had caused the fuss. "Stupid to give to a German," one Russian said.

By the look on his face, he wouldn't have been impressed had Lou told him he'd given to a Jew. Lou didn't try. He just spread his hands and said, *"Ja, sehr dumm."* That gave the Russians nothing to chew on. Having broke up the crowd, they went on their way.

"Ain't this fun?" Major Frank said.

"Oh, boy." Lou nodded. "Some fun."

VLADIMIR BOKOV DIDN'T KNOW A SINGLE NKVD MAN WHO WASN'T nervous. Twice now the United States had failed to try the leading German war criminals. The first failure had cost the court building and most of the jurists who would sit in judgment on the Nazis. And the city of Frankfurt hadn't recovered from the second, nor would it for years.

So it was up to the Soviet Union to do things right this time around. It was up to the Soviet Union to give the thugs who almost overran the world what they deserved. High time for that. Long past time. And if everything went well, the USSR would get the credit for doing what the USA couldn't.

But if things failed to go well, the USSR would get the blame. Marshal Stalin had made one thing unmistakably plain: he did not wish the workers' paradise to be seen as blameworthy in any way. If blame accrued to the Soviet Union, blame would also accrue to the men who should have kept the trial running smoothly. Stalin's blame.

Would accrue to the NKVD.

No wonder Bokov was nervous. No wonder his colleagues twitched if anyone looked at them sidewise, or even if no one did.

They'd found what had been a minor municipal courthouse still standing near the eastern edge of the Soviet zone in Berlin. Most of the buildings around it had already been leveled. They'd finished the job for a kilometer around in all directions. And they'd fortified that two-kilometer circle in ways that would have made the Soviet generals who planned the fieldworks for the Battle of Kursk jealous.

The best estimate—given by people who had reason to know such things—was that it would cost any enemy 250 tanks or a couple of divisions of infantry to batter through those fortifications to the courthouse. And that was before the NKVD and the Red Army started throwing in reinforcements.

Bokov was still nervous. He wasn't the only one, either.

Moisei Shteinberg didn't just twitch. He quivered. As a Jew, he had extra reason to want to see Göring and Ribbentrop and Rosenberg and Streicher and the rest of the brutes dead. And, as a Jew, he had extra reason to fear what would land on him if anything went wrong.

"They cannot get through," he said to Bokov, surveying the fortified belt from the outside.

"No, Comrade Colonel, they can't," Bokov agreed. He was a little easier in his mind than Shteinberg was. He was no Jew. He was no colonel, either. Less blame for any failure would stick to him. He could hope so, anyhow.

He did hope so. With all his heart.

"They can't give it to us up the ass, either." Shteinberg went on worrying as if Bokov hadn't spoken. "We have our own generator. We've sealed off the water lines. We've sealed off the sewer lines. We've got our own water tower by the courthouse. We've got a sealed-off septic tank to handle the drains. The Heydrichites can't possibly get at or get into any of that stuff. They *can't,* dammit."

"You're right, Comrade Colonel," Bokov said. What else was he supposed to say? You couldn't very well go wrong agreeing with your superior officer. And, as far as he could see, Colonel Shteinberg *was* right.

Right, maybe, but not reassured. He looked up into the air. The only planes there were a couple of the ubiquitous C-47s. They were too far away to let Bokov tell if they were American originals or the Soviet copies called Li-2s; the one had its entry door on the left side of the fuselage, the other on the right. It hardly mattered either way. They sure as the devil weren't German.

Even Shteinberg saw as much. "The *Luftwaffe's* dead. I don't miss those wolves at all," he said. "Ever have a *Stuka* bomb your trench?"

"No, sir." Bokov hadn't seen front-line service.

"Only happened to me once, and I'm not sorry," Shteinberg said. "It was early in the war. I had to deal with a major who lost his head." *Lost his head* probably meant something like *retreated without orders.* And *deal with* certainly meant something like *kill.* "I was going to take him away, and this damned thing with a shark mouth painted on its nose screamed down on us, and . . . Well, I didn't have to worry about the major any more. Not enough of him left to bury. It could have been me."

It could always be you. In the Soviet Union, that was as axiomatic as anything out of Euclid. The knock on the door, the tap on the shoulder . . . It didn't have to be nearly so dramatic as a screaming shark-mouthed dive bomber.

No wonder Shteinberg was so jumpy. No wonder everybody with a blue stripe around his cap was.

Another C-47 flew by, this one right overhead. "Don't worry too much, Comrade Colonel," Bokov said. "We'll make it work."

"*Da,*" Shteinberg said, and then, "We'd better."

Red Army sentries discouraged Germans from getting too close to the fortified zone. They shouted one warning—they'd learned to say *"Heraus!"* After that—usually only seconds after that—they opened fire.

They did just that this morning. Bokov heard the sharp, peremptory cry—German was a wonderful language for giving orders. He heard the sharp stutter of a three-round burst from the guard's PPSh submachine gun when somebody didn't listen to the order no matter how wonderfully peremptory it sounded. And he heard a screech that said at least one of those rounds connected.

Sure as hell, somebody was down and thrashing maybe seventy-five meters outside the perimeter. Bokov and Shteinberg loped over to him. He was a half-starved fellow with a beak of a nose and several days' worth of gray stubble on his chin and cheeks. At the moment, he was clutching his left leg and cussing a blue streak.

Seeing two NKVD men bearing down on him only made him turn his indignation on them. "That *verkakte mamzer* went and shot me!" he exclaimed in what came fairly close to German.

"*Nu?* What did you expect him to do? Give you a big kiss?" Moisei Shteinberg replied in the same language. Bokov could follow it well enough to realize what was going on. *A Jew. A DP,* he thought.

The guard came up. He didn't want to see two NKVD men, either. Anxiously, he said, "He didn't move when I yelled. Orders are to open fire if they don't move. I did what everybody above me told me to do."

"It's all right," Bokov told him. "You're not in trouble. Go back to your post." With an enormous sigh of relief and a parade-ground salute, the guard obeyed.

"How bad are you hit?" Colonel Shteinberg asked the wounded man. The fellow pulled up his trouser leg. He had a bloody groove in the outside of his calf. Shteinberg waved dismissively. "That isn't worth getting excited about."

"Easy for you to say. It isn't your leg, either," the Jew—no, the other Jew—retorted. "Hurts like shit." He didn't say *Scheisse;* he said *govno.* Chances were he'd started out in Poland or the Soviet Union, then. Where he'd been since . . .

Bokov spoke German, not Yiddish: "Why didn't you clear out when the guard warned you?"

"*Gevalt!* Some warning!" the DP said—Bokov had figured he'd be able to follow regular *Deutsch*. "The fucking Nazis couldn't kill me off, so now you Russian *mamzrim* try and finish the job for them? A *kholeriyeh* on you!"

"*Mamzrim?*" Bokov asked Shteinberg. It had to be the plural of the earlier insult, but Bokov didn't know what the insult meant to begin with.

"Bastards," Shteinberg supplied economically. He gave his attention back to the DP. "Everybody's got a sob story these days. Some of them are even true. The rest aren't good for wiping your ass."

Muttering under his breath, the skinny man displayed a tattoo on his arm. "Know what that means, you—?" He bit back whatever he'd been about to add: no doubt a good idea.

But Colonel Shteinberg had to nod. Bokov also recognized a death-camp serial number. This fellow had seen hell on earth, all right. If he kept mouthing off, he might get to compare the Nazi and Soviet versions of it, too.

"And before they shipped me to Auschwitz, they had me digging their fucking mines for them in the mountains," the Jew went on. "I go through all that, I live through all that, and your miserable shithead puts a hole in my leg. The way you talk, I should thank him."

"Maybe you should," Shteinberg said. "He could have hit you in the head."

"Wait," Vladimir Bokov said. Both Colonel Shteinberg and the DP looked at him in surprise. Bokov eyed the survivor. "You say you worked in the mines in the mountains. Down in the Alps?"

"That's right," the skinny man said. "What about it?"

"Were you just . . . digging out gypsum or whatever it was?" Bokov asked.

"No—tea with fucking lemon wedges," the DP snapped. "What the devil else would I be doing down there?"

Bokov seldom faced such sarcasm, not from a man he was interrogating. The half-swallowed chuckle that came from Colonel Shteinberg didn't help, either. Doing his best to ignore sarcasm and amusement, Bokov asked, "Did the Nazis care how much you brought up?"

"They cared how much I dug," the wounded Jew answered. "If you didn't do enough to suit 'em, you were a goner right there."

"But did they care how much—fuck, call it gypsum—you brought

up, or just how much you dug?" Bokov persisted, excitement tingling
through him despite his best efforts to hold it down.

"Oh," Shteinberg said softly. "I know what you're driving at."

"I sure don't," the DP said. Shteinberg had spoken Russian, not
Yiddish or German. The DP still followed him.

That didn't surprise Bokov, not after his earlier guesses. "Just answer my question," he snapped, this time with an NKVD officer's authority in his voice.

After frowning in memory—and, no doubt, in pain as well—the
DP said, "As long as we moved rock, they didn't give a shit. Some of
us thought it was funny. Some of us just thought the Nazis were
meshigge."

"Nuts," Shteinberg translated, adding, "That's an ass-end-of-
nowhere dialect of Yiddish he talks."

"Who, me?" The skinny Jew sounded affronted. "I'm no dumb
Litvak who goes *fiss* like a snake when he means *fish.*"

"*Shibboleth,*" Moisei Shteinberg murmured, which seemed to
mean something to the DP even if it didn't to Bokov. Shteinberg took
out a clasp knife and cut some cloth from the DP's already-ragged
trouser leg so he could bandage the bloody gouge. Then Shteinberg
frisked him. He found a small chunk of a D-ration bar and—much
better hidden—a U.S. five-dollar and a ten-dollar bill. "Where'd you
get these?" he asked. "Tell it straight the first time, or you'll be sorry."

"Sorry? I'm already sorry," the skinny man said. Before Shteinberg could say anything else, he went on, "Yeah, I know—I'll be sorrier. You people know how to take care of that. The guys who gave
me the money were a couple of American soldiers. Officers, even, I
think. They gave me the chocolate, too. It's not so great, but it fills
you up. I've been empty a lot."

"Americans, eh?" Bokov sounded less suspicious than he would
have most of the time. His own thoughts were racing in a different direction. Eyeing the DP, he asked, "Were they Jews, too?"

"Yeah. They talked Yiddish to me, not German. Better than him,
too—one of them sounded just like me." The man sneered at Shteinberg. Captain Bokov wouldn't have wanted to piss off an NKVD
colonel, but the DP didn't seem to give a damn. "They treated me a hell
of a lot better all the way around, if you want to know what I think."

"Fat chance," Shteinberg said.

Bokov thought exactly the same thing at the same time. All the same, he asked, "This place where the Nazis had you digging—could you find it again? Could you show us where it is?" He leaned forward, waiting for the answer.

The DP said only, "It ain't in your zone."

"I understand that." Bokov could be patient when he needed to. "But could you?"

"Maybe." The skinny Jew wasn't about to admit anything, not till he knew which way the wind blew.

Shteinberg made a fist and brought it down—on the cement next to the fellow's wounded leg. "Then . . . maybe . . . we won't have to get rough to find out."

"Are you still thinking along with me, sir?" Bokov asked.

The colonel smiled a vulpine smile. "Maybe," he said.

THE FOURTH OF JULY HAD ALWAYS BEEN DIANA McGRAW'S FAVORITE holiday—well, except for Christmas, which was a different kind of thing altogether. The Fourth went with picnics and beer and sometimes going to the park to listen to bands and patriotic songs and speeches and waiting through the long hot sticky day for nightfall at last and cuddling with Ed while fireworks set the sky ablaze above them and the kids went "Oooooo!"

And here was the Fourth come round again. Here she was in a park again, only in Indianapolis, not Anderson. The McGraws had gone to the state capital a couple of times before the war, to see if the fireworks were better. Once they were. They weren't the next time, so the family didn't go back.

Diana looked out at the throng of people in the park with her, at the throng of American flags, at the throng of placards. They stretched from just in front of the speakers' platform to too far away to read, but the ones she couldn't make out were bound to say the same things as the ones she could. If you were here today, you wanted Harry Truman to bring the boys home from Germany.

If you were here today . . . She turned to the Indianapolis police officer who stood on the platform with her and the other people who would talk in a while. "How big a crowd to you think we've got today, Lieutenant Offenbacher?"

Offenbacher's beer belly and double chin said he spent most of his time at a desk. He didn't look happy standing here sweating in the sun. Still, he shaded his eyes with a hand and peered out over the still-swelling mass of people. "From what I can see, and from what I've heard from the men on crowd-control duty, I'd say, mm, maybe fifteen or twenty thousand folks."

Experience had taught Diana that cops cut the size of crowds by at least half—more often two-thirds—when they didn't like the cause. By now, she'd had a good deal of practice gauging them, too. This one looked more like forty or fifty thousand to her. But even Offenbacher's estimate was impressive enough.

"Just think," she said brightly. "We've got rallies like this in every big city from coast to coast—and in a lot of cities that aren't so big, too."

"Yes, ma'am." Lieutenant Offenbacher's voice held no expression whatever.

They had governors and Congressmen and Senators speaking at the rallies, too. It had been less than two years since Diana started her movement. Back then, most politicians wanted nothing to do with it or with her. Jerry Duncan, bless him, was the exception, not the rule. But things had changed. Oh, yes, just a little!

And they also had actors and actresses speaking. It wasn't bad publicity, not any more. They had singers. They had ministers and priests—next to no rabbis. They had baseball players. (Not all of them, of course. What Ted Williams told them to do with their invitation wasn't repeatable in polite company. It wasn't physically possible, either.) They had writers—newspapermen and novelists.

They had some of just about every kind of people who could make other people listen. No, Diana hadn't known what she was getting into when she started out. She also hadn't known how many others she could bring along with her.

And they still had people who hated their guts. The cops Offenbacher led weren't just keeping the anti-occupation crowd orderly. They were also keeping counter-demonstrators from wading into the crowd with their own picket signs—and with baseball bats and tire irons and any other toys they could get their hands on. Some of the chants that rose from their opponents might have made Ted Williams blush.

"Can't your men arrest them for public obscenity?" Diana asked Offenbacher.

"Well, they could," the boss cop allowed. "Maybe if things get worse."

"Worse? How?"

"You never know," Lieutenant Offenbacher said. Diana understood that much too well. The Indianapolis police sympathized with the counter-demonstrators. They wouldn't do anything against them they didn't absolutely have to.

Time to get the show on the road. Diana stepped up to the microphone. "Welcome, ladies and gentlemen," she said, and paused while cheers and applause drowned out the noise from the opposition's peanut gallery. "Thank you for coming out this afternoon. We've got some terrific people lined up to talk to you, and we've got one of the best fireworks shows in town waiting for you after the sun goes down." More cheers, maybe even louder this time. As they ebbed, Diana went on, "But most of all, thank you for being here, no matter why you came. We still need to show Harry Truman and all the people in Washington with their heads in the sand that there are lots and lots of us, and we aren't about to go away!"

A great roar swelled up from the crowd: *"That's right!"*

"It sure is," Diana said. "And now it's my pleasure to introduce our first speaker, City Councilman Gus van Slyke!"

Van Slyke had a belly even bigger than Lieutenant Offenbacher's. He'd made a fortune selling used cars. He hadn't come down one way or the other on the German occupation till a friend's nephew got wounded over there. That convinced him. (That he couldn't stand Truman probably didn't hurt.)

"We won the war. By gosh, we did," he said. His voice was gruff and growly, like a bear's just waking from hibernation. "Now enough is enough. What are we doing over there in Europe? We're getting good young men, our best, killed and maimed. We aren't accomplishing anything doing it. The fanatics are still there, no matter what we've tried. And how much money have we flushed away? Billions and bill—"

When Diana heard the sharp *pop!,* it didn't register as anything but a backfire. But Gus van Slyke fell over. Something warm and wet splashed Diana's arm—she was wearing a sleeveless dress because of the heat. It was blood. She could smell it. She could smell something else, too—van Slyke had fouled himself. His feet drummed on the platform, but not for long. He lay in a spreading pool of his own gore.

Diana jammed a hand in her mouth to keep from shrieking. Out in the crowd, people did start screaming. Some of them tried to run away. They stepped on other people. No, they trampled them—they weren't being polite about it. More screams and yells and wails rang out, which only led to more trampling as chaos spread.

Lieutenant Offenbacher stepped around the red, red pool as he strode to the microphone. "This assembly is canceled," he declared. "This is a crime scene, a murder investigation." That didn't stop the panic in the crowd, either. If anything, it made matters worse.

The fireworks got canceled, too.

OFFICIAL WASHINGTON CELEBRATED THE FOURTH OF JULY ON THE Mall. The President made a speech. No doubt it was full of patriotic fervor. The fireworks display was second to none. With Uncle Sam footing the bill, they could afford to make it lavish.

Tom Schmidt wasn't there. Somebody else was covering President Truman's hot air for the *Chicago Tribune*. Unofficial Washington gathered in Lafayette Park, across Pennsylvania Avenue from the White House, to tell official Washington what it thought of Truman's German policy. Official Washington, of course, was hard of hearing.

"No," Tom muttered as Clark Griffith, who owned the Washington Senators—first in boos, first in shoes, last in the American League— tore into Truman. "Official Washington is hard of listening."

"What's that?" another reporter asked him.

"Nothing. Just woolgathering," Tom lied. He wrote the line down. Sure as hell, it would help the column along.

Griffith finally ran out of words and backed away from the microphone. Next batter up was Congressman Everett Dirksen of Illinois. Dirksen had kind of fishy features, wildly curly hair, and the exaggerated gestures of a Shakespearean ham actor. The combination should have made him ridiculous. Somehow, it didn't. His baritone bell of a voice had a lot to do with that. So did the genuine outrage that poured from him now.

"Out in Indiana, they are killing us—killing us, I tell you!" he thundered, pounding a fist down on the lectern. "Councilman Augustus van Slyke tried to exercise his rights under the First Amendment of our great Constitution. He tried to peaceably petition our government for redress of grievances. And our government has a great many grievances to redress, but I shall speak of that another time. Augustus van Slyke tried to tell the truth to the powers that be, and what became of him? *What became of him?* He was shot dead, my friends, shot down like a dog in the highway, without so much as a bunch of lace at his throat!"

Something stirred in Tom Schmidt as he scribbled notes. That was from a poem. He'd read it in high school. "The Highwayman," that was it, though he was damned if he could remember who wrote it. Well, he could check Bartlett's when he got back to the bureau. Only somebody like Dirksen (though there wasn't really anybody *like* Dirksen—he was one of a kind) would throw a poem into a political speech.

But it worked. The hum that rose from the crowd said it worked. Half the people there, maybe more, must've read "The Highwayman" or heard somebody recite it. Dirksen might be a crazy fox, but a fox he was.

"How dare they? *How dare they?*" He pounded the lectern again. "They are no longer content with lying to us. No, that does not satisfy them any more, for they begin to see that we begin to see through the tissue of their lies. And so, where words will not suffice them, they commence to argue with bullets. But will even bullets stop us, friends?"

"No!" the crowd roared. That cry must have rattled windows in the White House. Harry Truman wasn't there to hear it—he'd be speechifying to his friends right now. If he had any friends. To his supporters, anyhow. Maybe he'd hear it on the Mall, too.

Hammier than any actor, Dirksen cupped a hand behind one ear. "What was that?" he asked mildly.

"No!" That oceanic crowd-roar came again, even louder this time. Tom's ears rang. A little nervously, he wondered how many people here carried guns. Some pulp horror writer—Schmidt couldn't come up with his name, either, and it wouldn't be in Bartlett's—once advanced a rule about raising demons. *Do not call up that which you cannot put down.* Had Everett Dirksen ever heard of that rule? The

White House *was* right across the street. If the crowd tried to storm it, Councilman van Slyke wouldn't be the only one who got shot today. Unh-unh. Not even close.

"They say, in Indianapolis, they have yet to find the murderer—to find the filthy *assassin*." Dirksen hissed the last word with poisonous relish. "He shot a man dead in broad daylight, before witnesses uncounted, and they have yet to find him? My friends, *how hard are they looking?*"

Another roar rose up from the throng gathered together in the hot, sticky July night. This one was wordless, and all the angrier for that. Suddenly, Tom Schmidt wasn't just anxious any more. He was scared green. Politics was what you did instead of shooting people who didn't think like you. But once you started shooting, where did you stop? Anywhere?

If the Second Revolution—or maybe the Second Civil War—starts here, it's a hell of a story, yeah, Tom thought, *but am I gonna live long enough to file it?*

And then he caught a break. Maybe the whole country caught a break—he was never sure afterwards, but he always thought so. Over on the Mall, the super-duper fireworks show began.

The noise was like gunfire, but the polychrome flameflowers and torrents of blazing sparks exploding across the velvet-black sky proclaimed by their beauty their peace. Everett Dirksen looked over his shoulder at them. That was probably sheer reflex to begin with, but he seemed transfixed by the spectacle—he couldn't look away.

At last, he did. He lifted his glasses with one hand and rubbed at his eyes with the other. Then, softly at first but with his great voice swelling as the words poured out of him, he began to sing "The Star-Spangled Banner." It was a bitch of a song to sing, but he did it. He raised his hands, and the crowd joined in.

Tom Schmidt started singing before he quite realized he was doing it. He couldn't carry a tune in a sack, but it didn't matter right then. None of the reporters nearby sounded any better than he did. Chances were most of the people in Lafayette Park wouldn't run Alfred Drake or Ethel Merman out of business any time soon, either. That also turned out not to matter. Added all together, they sounded pretty damn good.

. *"The bombs bursting in air . . ."* Tears ran unashamed down Everett Dirksen's cheek, glistening in the spotlights. Did he mean them, or could he bring them on at command? With Dirksen, you never could tell. But half the hard-bitten newshounds near Tom were sniffling, too, as bombs *did* burst in air. And nobody stormed the White House.

XXV

NKVD Lieutenant General Yuri Pavlovich Vlasov wore a permanent scowl. *I would, too,* Vladimir Bokov thought, warily eyeing Vlasov's pinched, pulled-down mouth and angry, bristly eyebrows. The assistant chief of the NKVD's Berlin establishment was cursed, and would be cursed till the day he died, with an unfortunate family name.

Red Army General Andrei Vlasov was the worst traitor the USSR had had in the Great Patriotic War. After surrendering to the Nazis, he'd commanded what Goebbels called the Russian Liberation Army, a Fascist puppet force of other Soviet traitors. And, after the *Wehrmacht* surrendered, he'd been captured and shot, and better than he deserved, too.

Yuri Vlasov had no family connection to him; the surname wasn't rare. But the stench that went with it lingered. No Soviet citizen could say the word *Vlasovite* without feeling as if shit filled his mouth. Vlasov met the problem the same way Captain Bokov would have were he stuck with it: by acting ten times as tough as he would have otherwise.

So it was no great surprise when Yuri Vlasov's cold, narrow-eyed

glare—he had Tartar eyes like Bokov's, and his were also dark—
swung from the captain to Colonel Shteinberg and back again, as if he
couldn't believe what he was hearing. And it was no great surprise
when he barked, *"Nyet."*

"But, Comrade General, we have this excellent information—new
and excellent information," Moisei Shteinberg said. "We have it, and
we can't do anything with it ourselves. It's like having a pretty girl
when you can't get it up."

Much less earthy than most Russians, Shteinberg hardly ever
cracked jokes like that. Maybe he shouldn't have cracked this one.
Lieutenant General Vlasov's right hand cramped into a white-knuckled
fist; his cheeks and ears blazed red. Had he tried playing games with
some German popsy with big tits and come up short?

Whether he had or he hadn't, he snarled, "Fuck your mother,
Shteinberg. I told you you couldn't go to the American pricks, and
you goddamn well can't. That is an order. Do you understand it?"

"Da, Comrade General," Shteinberg answered tonelessly: the only
thing he could say.

Those fierce Tartar eyes lit on Bokov again. He wished they
wouldn't have. "What about you, Captain?" Vlasov demanded. "Do
you also understand the order?"

"Da, Comrade General," Bokov said, as Shteinberg had before
him.

"Khorosho." But it wasn't good enough to suit Vlasov, for he
rounded on Shteinberg once more. "You're a *zhid* yourself, so you
were born sneaky—just like this so-called informant of yours. Asking
if you understand isn't enough. Will you obey the order?"

Bokov didn't know whether the loophole had occurred to Shteinberg. It had occurred to him: a measure of his own rage and desperation. He waited to see what Shteinberg would say. The Jew said what
he had to say yet again: *"Da,* Comrade General." He sighed afterwards, which did him not a fart's worth of good.

Yuri Vlasov proceeded to nail things down tight: "You will obey,
too, Captain Bokov?"

"Da, Comrade General. I serve the Soviet Union." Bokov did his
best to turn the ritual phrase of acknowledgment into a reproach.

His best wasn't good enough. "All right, then. That's settled,"
Vlasov said, relentless as a bulldozer. "Fuck off, both of you."

They . . . fucked off. Once outside of—well outside of—Yuri Vlasov's office, Bokov began, "I'd like to—"

"Wait in line, Captain. I'm senior to you," Shteinberg said. "So many people like him, and we beat the Hitlerites anyway. Only goes to show Germany was pretty screwed up, too."

"But this Shmuel—" Bokov kept spluttering phrases. "We ought to—"

Colonel Shteinberg took him by the elbow and steered him out of NKVD headquarters before he could splutter a phrase that would cook his goose. "No," Shteinberg said, regretfully but firmly. "He gave us an order. We promised to obey it. If we go back on that . . ." He shivered, though the day was warm enough and then some. "Even if it worked out well, they'd still make examples of us."

That was such obvious truth, Bokov didn't waste his breath arguing it. He did say, "That goddamn fathead will be sorry he gave his stupid order."

"One way or another, things will even out," Shteinberg said. "Unless, of course, they don't."

A CREW OF GERMAN STEVEDORES IN OVERALLS LOADED CRATES INTO the C-47. First Lieutenant Wes Adams eyed his cargo manifest. *Equipment,* it said, which told him exactly nothing. "You know what we're taking to Berlin?" he asked his copilot.

"Buncha boxes and two krauts," answered Second Lieutenant Sandor Nagy—he inevitably went by Sandy.

The krauts were on the manifest, too, at the bottom. "Wonder who they paid off to get a lift," Wes said.

Sandy shrugged. "Beats me. They finagled it, though, one way or another. So we'll haul 'em and kick 'em off the plane and say bye-bye."

The Germans came aboard right on time. They were krauts, all right—probably figured somebody'd execute 'em for showing up five minutes late. The guy was pale and skinny, in a suit that had been new about when the Depression started. The woman would have been pretty if not for a scar on one cheek. The way she scowled at Wes and Sandy made the pilot bet she'd got the scar in a wartime air raid.

Tough shit, lady, Wes thought. He pointed to a couple of folding seats right behind the cockpit. "Sit here. Buckle yourselves in. Stay here till we get to Berlin."

"*Kein Englisch.*" The guy spread his hands regretfully. Wes repeated himself, this time in rudimentary German. "*Ach, ja. Zu befehl,*" the man said, and the gal nodded.

Wes eyed him. *Zu befehl* was what a Jerry soldier said when he got an order, the way an American would go *Yes, sir.* Well, there weren't a hell of a lot of German men who hadn't gone through the mill. And he and his lady friend were settling into the uncomfortable seats peaceably enough. "Let's go through the checklist, Sandy," Wes said with a mental shrug.

"Sure thing, boss," the copilot replied.

Everything came out green. Wes set an affectionate hand on the Gooney Bird's steering yoke. A C-47 would fly through things that tore a fighter to pieces, and take off with all kinds of shit showing up red. He'd done that kind of thing during the war more often than he cared to remember. You didn't have to in peacetime flying, which was nice.

Twin 1,200-horsepower Pratt and Whitney radial engines fired up as reliably as Zippos. Wes and Sandy taxied out to the end of the runway. Taxiing was the only thing that could get tricky in a C-47. In tight spaces, you really needed pilot and copilot both paying close attention. But they had plenty of room here.

When the tower gave clearance, Wes gunned the engines. He pulled back on the yoke as the C-47 got to takeoff speed. Up in the air it went—sedately, because it was a transport, and a heavily laden transport at that—but without the least hesitation. If you wanted to fly something from here to there, this was the plane to do it.

They headed up toward 9,000 feet, where they'd cruise to Berlin. No need to worry about oxygen, not lazing along down here like this. Wes leaned back in his seat. "This is the life," he said over the Pratt and Whitneys' roar.

"Beats working," Sandy agreed. The C-47 bounced a little as it ran into some turbulence. It was enough to notice, not enough to get excited about. Wes had flown straight through thunderstorms. A Gooney Bird was built to take it.

Because of the engine noise, he didn't hear the cockpit door open. Motion caught from the corner of his eye made his head whip around. There stood the German couple. They both held pistols—no, cut-down Schmeissers. "What the fuck?" Wes said.

"Sorry, friend," the man said. He spoke English after all.

That was Wes' last startled thought. Then the submachine guns barked.

LUFTWAFFE OBERLEUTNANT ERNST NEULEN AND THE FORMER FLAK-hilferin he knew only as Mitzi—what you didn't know, you couldn't tell—pulled the Amis' bodies out of their seats. "Good job," he told her as he settled into the pilot's seat himself. It was bloody, but that wouldn't matter for long.

"Vielen Dank," she said primly, as if he'd complimented her on her dancing.

"Go get your umbrella," Neulen told her.

She gave him a smile—a twisted one, because of that scar. Then she went back into the cargo compartment. The forwardmost crate had a trick side that opened easily if you knew what to do. Mitzi did. She shrugged on the parachute she found inside.

That done, she stepped into the cockpit again for a moment. "Good luck," she told him.

"You, too," he answered, his voice far away. He was cautiously fiddling with the throttle. Did it work German-style or like the ones in French and Italian planes, where you had to push instead of pulling and vice versa? Some young German pilots had bought a plot by for-getting the difference after training on foreign aircraft. Oberleutnant Neulen found out what he needed to know and relaxed.

"I'm going to bail out now," Mitzi said.

"Right," Neulen agreed, still getting a feel for the plane. It was a hell of a lot more modern than the trimotored Ju52/3s that had hauled cargo and soldiers for the Reich. He wouldn't have wanted to try to land it, though he'd heard even coming in wheels-up was a piece of cake for a C-47. But he didn't have to worry about that.

Mitzi disappeared again, no doubt heading for the cargo door. Neulen hoped she would make it down in one piece. She'd practiced on the ground, but she'd never jumped out of an airplane before. She'd never really landed, either. Well, all you could do was try and hope for the best.

He also hoped the Americans—or was the C-47 over the Russian zone by now?—wouldn't grab her as soon as she touched ground. How much did she know? Too much: Neulen was sure of that. He hoped for the best again. German patriots on the ground would do their best for her when she landed, anyhow. He was sure of that.

He felt the door open, and heard the howl of the wind inside the cargo bay. Out Mitzi went. He felt that, too. "Luck," Neulen said softly.

He flew on toward Berlin. He was about fifteen minutes outside the city when the radio crackled to life: "You're a little north of the flight path. Change course five degrees right."

"Five degrees right. Roger," Neulen said in English, and made about half the change.

"Still a little north," the American flight controller said. "You okay, Wes? You sound like you got a cold in the head."

"I am okay," Neulen answered, and said no more—less was better.

Pretty soon, the flight controller came back: "You're still off course, and you're up too high, too. Make your corrections, dammit. Is the aircraft all right?"

"All fine," Neulen said. He did come down—why not? How fast could they scramble fighters? Nobody flew top cover over Berlin: someone was liable to go where he shouldn't, and then the Russians and Anglo-Americans might start shooting at one another. Keep them happy as long as he could. Neulen didn't want them phoning their flak batteries either.

He was below 2,000 feet—*600 meters,* he translated mentally— when he overflew the airport. "What are you doing, man? Are you nuts?" the flight controller howled. "They're gonna ground your stupid ass forever!"

"Not that long," Neulen answered. He gunned the C-47, almost straight into the early-morning sun.

"THIS TIME, WE TRY THE BASTARDS. THIS TIME, WE HANG THE BAS-tards," Lou Weissberg said savagely. "I want to watch 'em swing. I want to hear their necks crack. All of 'em—and especially Streicher's, the antisemitic motherfucker."

"That's not a Christian thought," Howard Frank observed.

"Damn straight . . . sir," Lou said. "I'm not a Christian, any more than you are. An eye for an eye and a tooth for a tooth sounds great to me. Let the Nazis turn the other cheek . . . under a hood, in the wind."

"Okay," Frank said. "Ribbentrop and Keitel and Jodl are the ones I want most. The one plotted the war, and the other two fought it. And Göring for the *Luftwaffe,* even if he was pretty useless once the fighting started."

"Worse than useless. Didn't he tell Hitler he could keep the Germans in Stalingrad supplied by air?" Lou said.

"That's what I've heard," Major Frank agreed. "Even so, he was one of Hitler's right-hand men when the Nazis were coming up. If that's not reason enough to put a noose around his neck—"

"Reason enough for all of them. Reason enough and then some. And this time they will get it. Oh, boy, will they ever." Lou eyed the fortified ring the Russians had built around their courthouse. He eyed it from a distance of several hundred yards, because the Russians were liable to start shooting if anybody—anybody at all—got too close. One American officer had already got plugged for not reacting fast enough to *"Heraus!"* Luckily, he'd live. Nobody except maybe the NKVD knew how many Germans were wounded or dead.

Major Frank was looking the other way. "Pretty soon they go through the maze and in."

"Yeah." Lou nodded. Soviet Stalin tanks, U.S. Pershings, and British Centurions would surround the halftracks carrying the accused to justice. The road had been widened—the Russians had blown up the buildings to either side—so the heavy armor could do just that. Demolitions people swept for mines every half hour. Even the sewers were blocked off, as they were around the court. No rescue for the Nazi big shots.

"Won't be long," Frank said, glancing down at his watch. "In they'll go. The judges are already waiting for them."

"Uh-huh. Just like they were back in Nuremberg." Lou ground his teeth together, a split second too late to keep the words from escaping. That goddamn fanatic with his truck full of explosives . . . Lou counted himself lucky not to have been there when the blast went off. Too many of the men who would have tried the Nazis had died in it.

"Kineahora!" Howard Frank exclaimed.

Lou nodded vigorously. He hadn't wanted to put the whammy on what was about to happen—just the opposite.

"Here they come," Frank said.

Hearing the heavy rumble of approaching motors, Lou started to nod one more time. But he didn't, because that heavy rumble was approaching much too fast. And it wasn't coming up the widened road, either. It was . . . in the air? In the air!

The C-47 thundered over them at treetop height, maybe lower. The wind of its passage almost knocked Lou off his feet. "What the fuck?" he choked out—his mouth and eyes and nose were all full of dust and grit that wind had kicked up.

Ahead, a few of the Red Army men guarding the courthouse started shooting at the mad Gooney Bird—but only a few, and too late. Much too late. "It's gonna—" Horror as well as dust clogged Major Frank's voice. He tried again: "It's gonna—"

And then it did. .

It wasn't just a hurtling C-47 crashing into the courthouse. Somehow, the fanatics had loaded the plane with explosives. It could carry more than a deuce-and-a-half could. And when the shit went off . . .

Lou Weissberg and Howard Frank stood more than a mile from the blast. It hammered their ears and rocked them all the same. Lou staggered again, as he had only seconds before when the transport roared by overhead. The fireball that went up dwarfed the courthouse. By then, Lou had seen newsreel footage of what happened when an atom bomb blew up. This wasn't *just* like that. *A baby version. An ordinary blockbuster,* Lou thought dazedly. *Plenty bad enough.*

"*Gottenyu!*" Frank burst out. "The bastards just took out the judges again, and the lawyers, and—"

"*Vey iz mir!*" Lou clapped a hand to his forehead. He heard Major Frank as if from very far away. He wondered if his ears would ever be the same. He'd wondered the same thing plenty of times before the sadly misnamed V-E Day. It had always come back then. Maybe it would now. He also wondered why he hadn't thought of what Frank had. *Because you're punchy, dummy:* the answer supplied itself.

More slowly than he might have, he noticed a rumble and clatter from behind him. He turned. Sure as hell, here came the tanks protecting the Nazi *Bonzen* on their way to trial. On their way to . . . nothing, now. Judges and attorneys had gone up in the fireball, but the foulest criminals in the history of the world were fine. The way things were going, they'd probably die of old age.

Helplessly, Lou started to laugh and cry at the same time. He waited for Major Frank to slap him silly and tell him to snap out of it. That was what happened when you got hysterical, right? But when he looked over at the other officer, he saw Frank doing the same goddamn thing.

VLADIMIR BOKOV DECIDED THE FORTIFICATIONS AROUND THE COURThouse seemed even more impressive from within than when viewed from the outside. Standing in a trench along the route by which the war criminals would at last come to justice, he couldn't actually see very much. Even so, he knew he was in the middle of that maze of trenches and minefields and concrete antitank obstacles and barbed wire and machine-gun nests and . . . everything under the sun. Everything anyone could think of, including artillery and antiaircraft guns and thousands of Red Army and NKVD men.

"They're going to get it. This time, they're going to get it. And we're going to give it to them." He spoke with a certain somber pride. "We are: the workers and peasants of the Soviet Union." And the NKVD, of course, and the Anglo-Americans, and even the afterthought that was France. But he knew the propaganda line, and he needed next to no conscious thought to echo it. Any Soviet citizen had plenty of practice with that.

And Moisei Shteinberg nodded. "We'll do it right. We'll show the Americans how to do it right." That also came straight from the propaganda line. But then he lowered his voice to something not far above a whisper: "I wish we could show the Americans . . ."

"That fucking stupid pigheaded Vlasov." Captain Bokov also whispered. Because of the Soviet traitor, taking the NKVD general's name in vain felt extra filthy. And if the soldiers around them overheard him, they'd think he was cursing the collaborator.

"I—" Shteinberg's head came up, as a wolf's would have at an unexpected noise in the forest. "What's that?"

Whatever it was, it got louder and closer much too fast. "Mothercocksuckingfuck!" a Red Army sergeant shouted, and pointed into the sky.

Not very far into the sky—the C-47 roared by almost close enough to knock off Bokov's cap. That was how it felt, anyhow. Colonel Shteinberg, the damned clever Jew, was quicker on the uptake than Bokov. *"Nooo!"* he howled—a wail of fury and despair—and fired a burst from his submachine gun at the plane.

Here and there, a few other Chekists and Red Army men shot at it. But most, like Vladimir Bokov, watched in frozen surprise. One antiaircraft gun opened up—only one, as far as Bokov could tell. Whatever its shells ended up hitting, they missed the C-47. It slammed into the courthouse at something over 350 kilometers an hour.

The blast knocked Bokov flat even though he was in the trench. He and Colonel Shteinberg fell all over each other, in fact. And they fell on the foul-mouthed sergeant, or he fell on them, and everybody close by was falling over everybody else. And then chunks of masonry and sheet metal and everything else that went into a building and an airplane started falling on them, and some of that was on fire.

Squoosh! If you dropped a rock on a pumpkin from a third-story window, it would make a noise like that. Maybe five meters from Bokov, a brick plummeting from the Devil's sister only knew how far smashed in a soldier's skull. The poor bastard thrashed like a chicken that had just met the hatchet. He was as dead as a chopped chicken, too.

"Those clapped-out cunts! They did it again!" When Moisei Shteinberg swore like that, somebody'd spilled the thundermug into the soup. And the Heydrichites damn well had.

Bokov ever so cautiously looked out of the trench. The courthouse was a sea of flame, with black, greasy smoke already towering high into the sky over it. Hadn't an American bomber slammed into the Empire State Building not so long before? Maybe that was what gave the bandits the idea for this raid.

But the Empire State Building was still standing. The architects who designed it must have seen that it might be a target and strengthened it accordingly. Nobody'd ever imagined a nondescript police courthouse in Berlin might get clobbered by an explosives-packed C-47 going flat out. Who in his right mind would have? And it stood no more.

"Comrade Colonel!" Bokov shouted, suddenly thinking of something else that should stand no more.

He needed to shout several times before he got Shteinberg's notice. Everybody's ears were stunned. At last, the Jew growled, "What is it?" He glowered at Bokov as if he thought all this was his fault.

"Don't get pissed off at me, Comrade Colonel," Bokov said. He had a good notion of whose fault it really was. "I know what we need to do next."

"You do, do you?" Suspicion filled Shteinberg's voice. "And that is . . . ?"

"Sir, we need to go have another talk with Lieutenant General Vlasov."

Moisei Shteinberg thought it over. Slowly, he smiled a smile that should have shown shark's teeth instead of his own yellowish set. As he smiled, he nodded. "You're right," he said. "We do."

YET AGAIN, THE ANGLO-AMERICANS AND THE RUSSIANS (TO SAY NOTHING of the remora French, which was what they deserved to have said of them) would not get to put on their show trial for the leaders of the Third *Reich* and the National Socialist German Workers' Party. A small, cold smile stole across Reinhard Heydrich's face as he went through newspaper and magazine accounts. Some of the photos were truly spectacular.

So were some of the editorials. One American writer feared the German resistance would start what he called "a reign of terror in the air." He imagined fighting men seizing planes full of passengers and flying them into buildings all over Europe and maybe even in the States. He imagined seizing laden planes and crashing them on purpose. He even imagined seizing planes and flying them to, say, Franco's Spain to hold the passengers hostage till the German Freedom Front's demands were met.

He had one hell of an imagination. None of that stuff had occurred to Heydrich. As far as he was concerned, the attack on the Berlin courthouse was a one-off job. But he recognized good ideas when somebody stuck them in front of his nose. He started taking notes.

Only a handful of these hijackings and atrocities would be needed to throw air transport into chaos all over the world, the editorial writer warned. *Would travelers put up with the delays and inconve-*

*niences necessary to ensure no one can smuggle weapons or explo-
sives aboard aircraft? It seems most unlikely.*

It seemed pretty unlikely to Heydrich, too. He wrote himself more
notes. Throw air transport into chaos all over the world? That
sounded good to him. He didn't know whether grabbing a few planes
would have the effect this fellow foretold, but he could hardly wait to
find out.

Hans Klein walked into his office with more papers and magazines. "We've got 'em jumping like fleas on a hot griddle, *Herr Reichsprotektor,*" the noncom said.

"Good. That's the idea. May they jump out of Germany soon."
Heydrich bounced some of the American editorial writer's ideas off of
Klein. "What do you think?" he asked, respecting the veteran's solid
common sense. "Can we do these things? Would they cause as much
trouble as the Ami thinks?"

"They might," Klein said slowly. "We don't have many pilots left
to aim at buildings, but anybody with balls can crash a plane. And if
you were going to fly to Spain instead of crashing, you could likely
point a gun at the regular pilot and make him take you there."

"Well, so you could." Heydrich wrote that down, too. Some men
who weren't willing to throw their lives away for the *Reich* would be
willing to fight for it. They might make good hijackers . . . and quite
a few people from the Third *Reich* had already taken refuge in
friendly—even if officially neutral—Spain.

Oberscharführer Klein's thoughts ran on a different track: "Damn
shame that poor Mitzi gal's chute didn't open when she jumped." His
mouth twisted. "Too much time to think on the way down."

"*Ja,*" Heydrich said, and left it right there. At his quiet orders, the
man who'd packed Mitzi's parachute made sure it wouldn't open.
Why take chances? She was much too likely to get captured and
grilled after she landed.

When you issued orders like that, you had to do it quietly. If it got
out that you'd thrown away someone's life—especially a woman's—
on purpose, your own people would give you trouble. Never mind
that it was the only reasonable thing to do. What you saw as reasonable, they'd see as coldhearted.

And now Heydrich wanted to find a discreet way to dispose of the
man who'd packed Mitzi's chute. As soon as that fellow started push-

ing up daisies, he wouldn't be able to blab to the enemy. He wouldn't be able to blab to his own pals, either.

None of which showed on the *Reichsprotektor*'s face. Once upon a time, the *Führer*'d called him the man with the iron heart. If you were going to hold a position like his, an iron heart was an asset, no two ways about it.

"One more embarrassment for the enemy," he said. "With any luck at all, it will make the Amis squeal even louder than they are already."

"*Ja!*" Klein perked up. He was always eager to look in that direction. "Tomorrow belongs to us."

"Well, of course it does," Reinhard Heydrich said.

LIEUTENANT GENERAL VLASOV HAD LOOKED AND ACTED LIKE A SON OF a bitch the last time Bokov and Shteinberg called on him. He seemed even less friendly now. For twenty kopeks, his expression said, both the other NKVD men could find out how they liked chopping down spruces in the middle of Siberian winter.

However much he hated them, though, he couldn't just tell them to fuck off, the way he had before. He might want to; he plainly did want to. But the Heydrichites had humiliated the Soviet Union before the world when they crashed that plane into what would have been the war criminals' courthouse. Striking back at them any way at all looked like a good idea.

It did to Captain Bokov, anyhow, and to Colonel Shteinberg. Whether it did to Yuri Vlasov . . . *We've got to find out, dammit,* Bokov told himself.

"I know what the two of you are here for," Vlasov rasped. "You're going to try and talk me into sucking the Americans' cocks."

"No, Comrade General, no. Nothing like that," Shteinberg said soothingly. *Yes, Comrade General, yes. Just like that,* Vladimir Bokov thought fiercely. He wanted to watch Vlasov squirm. Maybe they could have kept the crash from happening if only the miserable bastard had put his ass in gear.

"Don't bother buttering me up, *zhid,*" Vlasov said. "Nothing but a waste of time."

"However you please . . . sir." Moisei Shteinberg held his voice under tight control. "My next move, if you keep dicking around with us, is to write to Marshal Beria and let him know how you're obstructing the struggle against the Heydrichite bandits."

"You wouldn't dare!" General Vlasov bellowed.

"Yes, I would. I've already done it," Shteinberg said. "And if anything happens to me, the letter goes to Moscow anyway. I've taken care of that, too . . . sir."

"Fuck your mother hard!"

"Maybe my father did," Shteinberg answered calmly. "But at least I know who he was . . . sir."

Could looks have killed, Yuri Vlasov would have shouted for men to come and drag two corpses out of his office. Bokov wondered whether the general would try something more direct. He also wondered how much good this move would do him and Shteinberg even if they turned out to be right. He shrugged, with luck invisibly. If it helped the fight against Heydrich's bandits, he'd worry about everything else later.

"All right. All right." Vlasov spat the words in Shteinberg's face. "Take this other kike to the Americans, then. Go ahead. Be my guest. They'll probably be a bunch of Jews, too. As far as I'm concerned—" He broke off, breathing hard.

"Yes, sir?" Shteinberg's voice was polite, even curious. Bokov was curious, too. What had Vlasov swallowed? Something like *As far as I'm concerned, Hitler knew what he was doing with you people?* Bokov wouldn't have been surprised. Plenty of his fellow-Russians felt that way. He didn't love Jews himself. But you could damn well count on them to be anti-Fascist.

No matter how much rope Shteinberg fed Vlasov, the NKVD general was too canny to hang himself. "Go on," he barked. "If you're going to do it, go do it—and get the devil out of here."

"If it works, he'll take the credit," Bokov warned once they were safely outside NKVD headquarters.

"Oh, sure," Shteinberg agreed. "But he'd do that anyway." Bokov laughed, not that his superior was joking—or wrong.

———

"AYE," JERRY DUNCAN SAID.

"Mr. Duncan votes aye," Joe Martin intoned, and the Clerk of the House recorded his vote. They weren't going to be able to override President Truman's veto of the bill that cut off funds for the U.S. occupation of Germany. They had a solid majority, including most Republicans and the growing number of Democrats who saw that staying on Truman's side was lucky not to have cost them their jobs in the last election and that it damn well would get them tossed out next time around. A good majority, yes, but not a two-thirds majority. *Too bad,* Jerry thought.

The roll call droned on. Sure enough, when it finally finished, they fell twenty-two votes short of ramming the budget down the President's throat. "Mr. Truman has put himself on record as saying he will not sign a War Department appropriation without money for continuing the occupation of Germany," Speaker Martin said after announcing the results. "I want to put the House of Representatives on record, too. We will not send him an appropriations bill with that item in it."

Members of the majority, Jerry Duncan loud among them, clapped their hands and cheered. Several Congressmen shouted "Hear! Hear!" as if they belonged to the House of Commons in London. People who'd voted against the override booed. Some of them shook their fists. Jerry couldn't remember seeing that kind of bad behavior here. Everybody's temper was frayed. Maybe things had been like this in the runup to the Civil War. The trial of wills over the occupation was tearing the country apart now.

"Order! We will have order!" The Speaker thumped his gavel. "The Sergeant at Arms has the authority to take whatever steps may prove necessary to restore order," Joe Martin continued. The Democrats—and a handful of pro-occupation Republicans—went on booing. He banged the gavel again. Something like order slowly returned.

Out of it, Sam Rayburn bawled, "Mr. Speaker! *Mr. Speaker!*"

Had Jerry been up there in the Speaker's seat, he wouldn't have recognized the Texas Democrat. When Rayburn was Speaker of the House, he'd made a point of ignoring people whose views he didn't fancy. That was one of the perquisites the Speaker enjoyed, and few Speakers had enjoyed it more than Rayburn.

But Joe Martin said, "The distinguished gentleman from Texas has the floor." He clung to courtesy even as it collapsed around him.

"Thank you, Mr. Speaker." Rayburn could also be courtly when he felt like it—and he could be an iron-assed son of a bitch when he didn't. He sounded slightly surprised. Had he expected Martin to pretend not to hear him? It looked that way to Jerry Duncan. Any which way, Rayburn went on, "You do realize, Mr. Speaker, that if you refuse to give the War Department the money it needs to keep holding down the Nazis, you will force us out of Germany in spite of the President's conviction, and the U.S. Army's, that we need to stay there?"

"Yes, Mr. Rayburn, I realize that. And that is the point, after all. In their wisdom, the framers of the Constitution gave Congress the purse strings. Not the President. Not the U.S. Army. Congress. If the President and the Army prove unwise, as they have here, we have the responsibility to exercise wisdom for them," Joe Martin said.

"Hear! Hear!" This time, Jerry shouted it at the top of his lungs. He was far from the only Representative who did. Opponents of cutting off funds for the occupation yelled back. People on both sides took off their jackets and tossed them aside, as if expecting they'd be brawling in the aisles any second.

"Order! There will be order!" the Speaker of the House insisted loudly. The microphone made each blow of his gavel sound like a gunshot. After what had happened to poor Gus van Slyke—whom he'd known for years—Jerry wished that comparison hadn't leaped into his mind, but it was the only one that seemed to fit. Also as if using a gun, Martin aimed a forefinger at Sam Rayburn. "The gentleman from Texas may continue—without, I hope, any undue outbursts this time."

"I hope the same, Mr. Speaker. And I do thank you for recollecting I had the floor," Rayburn said. "You say you and those who agree with you aim to stop the President and the Army from acting unwisely."

"I say just that, sir, and it is the truth," Joe Martin replied. Jerry Duncan nodded vehemently.

"Okay. Fine. You have—the Congress has—this high and fancy responsibility." Rayburn waited.

The Speaker of the House waved in agreement. "I say that also, and it too is the truth."

"All right, then. Here is my question for you: what happens when you exercise that responsibility and it turns out to be the biggest mistake since Eve listened to the serpent in the Garden of Eden?" Sam Rayburn demanded ferociously. "President Truman likes the saying 'The buck stops here.' When something goes wrong, he admits it. When the blame lands on you—and it will, Mr. Speaker, it will—when it lands on you, I say, will you be man enough to shoulder it?"

"If that happens, which I do not expect—" Speaker Martin began.

"Fools never do." Rayburn planted the barb with obvious relish.

Bang! went the gavel. "You are out of order, as you know very well."

"So is the House—the inmates are taking over the asylum."

Bang! Bang! "Enough!" Joe Martin snapped. Rayburn sat down, grinning. Business resumed. Jerry wished the Texan hadn't asked such a prickly question.

XXVI

President Truman had a high, raspy, annoying voice. Diana McGraw had never really thought of it that way till after Pat got killed, but she sure did now. Of course, for the past couple of years Truman had been saying things she didn't like and didn't agree with. That made a difference, whether she thought so or not.

"We will carry the President's radio address live at the top of the hour," the radio announcer said, sounding as proud as if Truman were Moses about to read the brand new Ten Commandments on his station.

Even stolid Ed snorted at the fellow's tone. "Are we supposed to get excited, or what? It's not like Truman can do a Fireside Chat or anything."

"Not likely!" Diana exclaimed. "When FDR said something, you wanted to believe him. Whenever Truman opens his mouth, you know he's going to lie to you. That's all he knows how to do."

The radio filled up most of the time till the top of the hour with commercials. In a way, Diana supposed that was good: it meant there were plenty of things to buy again. During the war, a lot of normal stuff had been unavailable—and a lot of ads went away. Diana had to admit she hadn't missed them. Now the stuff was back, and so were the pitchmen trying to convince people it was wonderful. Everybody knew the war was over . . . except the stubborn Missouri mule—no, jackass—in the White House.

At last, and precisely as if he were selling soap or cigarettes, the announcer said, "And here is the President of the United States!"

A long electric hiss. A burst of static, cut off almost instantly. Then Harry Truman's voice came out of the radio speaker: "Good evening, my fellow citizens. The Nazis still lurking in Germany have proved again how dangerous they are. Laughing at the very idea of justice, they flew a C-47 into the building where their captured leaders would have gotten a fairer trial than any they gave their countless victims. This C-47 was hijacked in the air. As best we can determine, the American pilot and copilot were both callously murdered. The Nazis seem to have been able to smuggle extra explosives onto the airplane. We are still investigating how they did it."

"Because somebody who should've kept his eyes open was asleep at the . . . darn switch," Ed McGraw said. "Anybody can see that."

If anybody can see it, why did you say it? Diana wondered—one more thought she wouldn't have had before a death in Germany turned things upside down and inside out for her. All she said out loud was a quick, "Hush. I want to hear him."

"Much as we wish they weren't, the Nazi fanatics are still dangerous," Truman went on. "Because they are, our soldiers need to stay in Germany until we can be sure the country will stay peaceful and democratic—that's 'democratic' with a small 'd'—after we go home."

"They wouldn't be fighting if we weren't there to give them big, fat, juicy targets!" Diana burst out.

"Some people will say the fanatics wouldn't still be fighting if we weren't in Germany," Truman said, as if he were sitting in the kitchen with the McGraws.

Ed chuckled and lit a cigarette. "They oughta put you in the White House, babe."

"How could I do worse?" Diana said. "It wouldn't be easy."

"The Republican Party in Congress seems to feel that way," Truman said.

"Not just Republicans! Not even close!" Diana said hotly.

"It would be nice if the world were so simple. Or it would be nice if the Republicans weren't so simple." Truman wouldn't—didn't—miss a chance to throw darts at the opposition. "But the fact is, the Nazis have a long history of attacking anybody and everybody they can reach. The world knows that, to its sorrow."

"We've got the atom bomb. They don't," Diana said.

"If we run away from Germany, the first thing the Nazis will do if they get back into power is start working on an atom bomb," the President said. "They will deny it. They will swear on a stack of Bibles that they would never do anything like that. They told the same lies after World War I, and look what happened to the people who believed them then—the Lindberghs and the Liberty Lobby and the rest of the fools.

"And the second thing the Nazis will do if, God forbid, they get back into power is start working on a rocket that can reach the United States from Germany," Truman said. "They had one on the drawing board when V-E Day came and made them shelve their plans. If they build a transatlantic rocket with an atom bomb in its nose, nobody is safe any more. Nobody. Not a single soul. Not anywhere in the world."

"Yeah, yeah, enough with the Buck Rogers bull . . . manure," Ed said. "If pigs had wings, we'd all carry umbrellas." Diana smiled at him. He might not be exciting, but his heart was in the right place. His head, too.

"Do the Republicans in Congress see that?" Harry Truman answered his own question: "They don't. They might as well be ostriches, not elephants, the way they've stuck their heads in the sand. They flat-out refuse to put any money in the budget for keeping our armed forces in Germany. Without money, we will have to start bringing troops home."

"Good!" Diana said. "That's the idea! We should have done it a long time ago. If we had, maybe . . . Pat'd still be alive." Her voice roughened at the last few words; she still couldn't talk about him without wanting to cry.

"I know, hon," Ed said softly, and he sounded husky, too.

There on the radio, Truman kept chattering away: "An old proverb talks about being penny wise and pound foolish. It's so old, it goes back to the days before our independence. Nowadays, we'd understand it better if it talked about penny wise and dollar foolish. The point of it is, you're making a mistake if you only worry about what's right in front of you and not about what happens half a mile or a mile or five miles farther down the road. And that's exactly what the Republicans who are starving our forces in Germany are doing."

"My . . . heinie!" Diana had heard an awful lot of bad language the past couple of years. She'd used more of it herself than she ever did before. But she still tried not to when Ed could hear her.

He chuckled now, knowing—of course!—what she hadn't said. "Way to go, babe. You tell 'em."

"They won't listen to me," Truman said sadly.

"That's 'cause they've got better sense than you do!" Diana also had a lot of practice talking back to politicians on the radio.

This time, the President didn't seem to listen to her. "Trouble is, they're Republicans, and that just naturally means they aren't what you'd call good at listening," he continued. "All the same, they'd better hear this, and hear it loud and clear. If they make us clear out of Germany, if they make us leave long before we really ought to, what happens afterwards is their fault. They'll be responsible for it. I know the situation we have now isn't very pretty. What we'll get if we go their way will be worse. And they will be to blame for it."

A Bronx cheer didn't count as cussing. Diana sent the radio the wettest, juiciest raspberry she could. Ed laughed out loud.

"I wish I didn't have to tell you things like this," Harry Truman said. "But, unlike some people I could name, my job is to tell you what's so, not what sounds good or what might get me a few extra votes. Thanks. Good night."

"That was the President of the United States, Harry S Truman," the announcer said, as if anybody in his right mind didn't already know.

"He's full of . . . malarkey," Diana declared as Ed turned off the radio.

Her husband laughed again. "You better believe it." He bent down and gave her a kiss. Then he nuzzled her neck. "So to heck with him for a little while, anyways."

"Yeah. To heck with him." Diana went upstairs to the bedroom willingly enough. You needed to keep a man happy every so often. She didn't have anything *against* Ed. When it was over and he turned on the nightstand lamp so he could find his cigarettes, he had a big, sloppy grin plastered across his face. Diana made herself smile, too. She'd just started to warm up when, too soon, it was over. Was that happening more and more these days, or was she simply noticing more?

Because she didn't want to make Ed angry or upset, she didn't say anything about it. He finished the cigarette, gave her a tobacco-flavored kiss, then got up to use the bathroom and brush his teeth. Five minutes later, he was snoring.

Diana lay there in the darkness. It should have been better than this, shouldn't it? Once upon a time, it had been better than this, hadn't it? Hadn't it?

She was a long time sleeping.

LOU WEISSBERG WONDERED WHAT THE HELL BRIGADIER GENERAL R.R.R. Baxter's initials stood for. There they were, three R's in a row on the nameplate on Baxter's desk. Readin', 'Ritin', 'Rithmetic Baxter? It seemed as likely as anything else. A company-grade officer couldn't very well come right out and ask a general something like that. Lou would just have to let his imagination run wild.

He glanced over at Howard Frank. Was the same burning question uppermost in Frank's mind, too? The other Jewish officer didn't seem to keep glancing at the nameplate the way Lou did. But did that mean anything?

Baxter had cold blue eyes that bifocals did nothing to warm up. He eyed Lou and Major Frank in turn. If either man impressed him, he hid it goddamn well. *Well, he doesn't impress me, either,* Lou thought. *Except his initials.* A star on each shoulder put R.R.R. Baxter among the Lord's anointed in the Counter-Intelligence Corps. He wouldn't give a rat's ass whether he impressed a lonely subordinate or not.

"How's your German, boys?" he asked in that language. His own *Deutsch* had a strong American accent, but he was plenty fluent.

"*Ganz gut, Herr* General," Howard Frank said. Lou nodded.

"Figured as much, but I wanted to make sure. From what I hear, German will work well enough," Baxter said.

"Well enough for what, sir?" Lou paused, filled by a hope he hardly dared believe. "Has the Red Army finally decided to work with us?"

"Not the Red Army," Baxter replied, and Lou's hope crashed and burned. Then it rose phoenixlike from the flames, for the CIC big wheel went on, "The NKVD. The Russians wanted to try the top Nazis in their zone in Berlin 'cause we screwed it up twice. If they did it right, they figured they could score propaganda points off of us. Well, they ended up with egg on their face, too. They don't like that any better than we would. They're proud people."

"After what they went through against the Germans, pride's about all they've got left," Lou remarked.

"Pride and most of Eastern Europe," R.R.R. Baxter pointed out. "But, yeah, I know what you mean. They paid for everything they got—paid in blood. Now they've got something they can't use themselves. That's all I know about it. Right this minute, that's all anybody who isn't a Russian knows about it. Your job is to find out what it is and what we can do with it."

"Why us, sir?" Frank asked. "Why not somebody with more clout?"

"For one thing, you've both been heard to say we ought to work more with the Russians," Brigadier General Baxter answered. Lou blinked. He had said things like that. How closely were people here monitored, though, if the higher-ups knew he'd said it? Well, that one answered itself, didn't it? Baxter went on, "And the Russians don't want to make a big deal out of this. If it doesn't work out, the blame won't land on them—that's our best guess. So they don't want anything more than a midlevel contact. Not yet, anyhow. You're it, the two of you . . . if you're game, of course."

If you aren't, you're nothing but a couple of gutless, worthless pieces of shit. Baxter didn't say that, but he didn't have to. One other thing he might not have said was *a couple of gutless, worthless Jewish pieces of shit.* Maybe such a rude, unfair thought never once crossed his mind. Maybe. But plenty of American officers still had their doubts about Jews in spite of Hitler.

Which was why Lou said, "Oh, hell, yes, sir!" as fast as he could—but no faster than Howard Frank said, "You'd better believe it, sir!"

R.R.R. Baxter nodded smoothly. He wasn't a general for nothing, Lou realized—he knew how to get people to do what he wanted. He sure did. "Glad to hear it, gentlemen," he said. "We'll work out the details of the meeting with the Russians, and we'll go from there."

"COME ON," VLADIMIR BOKOV SNAPPED AT SHMUEL. "GET MOVING, dammit."

"I'm right here with you," the Jewish DP said. "I'm not going any place but where you tell me to."

"Too fucking right you're not. You wouldn't last long if you did," Bokov said. Maybe there really were snipers with beads drawn on Shmuel's gray head. Or maybe Bokov would have to plug him if he tried to bug out. The NKVD man didn't know for sure. Shmuel couldn't know, either.

Together, they crossed to the south side of the Wittenbergplatz. Whoever'd set up this meeting had an evil sense of humor. Captain Bokov suspected Yuri Vlasov was taking a measure of revenge for having his hand forced. The sign above the tavern proclaimed that it was Fent's Establishment. And so it was . . . now. If you looked closely, though, under Fent's name you could still make out the smeared letters that spelled out who the former proprietor had been.

Up until Berlin fell to the Red Army, this had been Alois Hitler's tavern. From everything Bokov had heard, the *Führer*'s half-brother wasn't a bad fellow. With a different last name, he would have been indistinguishable from a thousand other saloonkeepers. Bokov didn't know what had happened to him in the wake of the *Reich*'s collapse. Alois Hitler hadn't been important enough in the grand scheme of things for anybody to worry about him.

Shmuel didn't seem to know about the tavern. Bokov couldn't resist telling him, just to see the look on his face. It was everything the NKVD man could have hoped for. The DP stopped in his tracks. "I won't go in there!"

"Like hell you won't," Bokov said. "If I've got to, you've got to. A minute ago, you said you weren't going anywhere except where I told you to. And I'm damn well telling you to."

"Hitler's place!" Shmuel cried in horror.

"Hitler's place," Captain Bokov agreed. "But not *that* Hitler, and it hasn't been his place for a couple of years now. So get your sorry old ass in gear."

"Hitler's place!" the DP said again. Shaking his head, he went inside with Bokov.

It smelled like tobacco smoke and beer and sweat: like the inside of a tavern, in other words. The light was dim. Whether the man behind the bar was Fent himself or just a hireling, he looked nothing like any Hitler ever born. That was a relief.

Americans were sitting at two or three tables. Even just sitting there, they irritated Bokov. They had so much, and didn't have the faintest idea how well off they were. An officer at one of the tables nodded to Bokov. The NKVD man walked over and sat down. Again, Shmuel followed. The DP was still muttering to himself.

A barmaid hurried up. She was pretty, although on the skinny side. Bokov thought a lot of German women were skinny, which didn't keep him from laying them when he got the urge. But this gal was skinny even by German standards. He preferred his women with something to hold on to.

He ordered beer. So did Shmuel. The Americans already had seidels in front of them. The barmaid hustled away. A Russian wouldn't have moved so fast, not at a no-account job like that. Germans did apply themselves, no matter what they were up to. It was one of the things that made them dangerous.

Both Americans looked like Jews. That matched Bokov's briefing. The barmaid came back with two more mugs of beer. Bokov raised his and trotted out the phrase he'd been told to use: "To cooperation between allies."

"To nailing down the ironheart!" one of the Americans returned: the proper answer. He went on, "I'm Frank. This is Weissberg."

Maybe those were real names, maybe not. Bokov hadn't been told to hide his identity, so he said, "Bokov." He jerked a thumb at the DP. "And this is Shmuel Birnbaum." He would have identified a new-model mortar the same way—he thought of Shmuel more as a weapon than as a human being.

But a new-model mortar wouldn't have gulped beer as if it would be outlawed tomorrow. A new-model mortar wouldn't have waved to the barmaid for a refill, or pinched her on the butt when she brought it. She glared at him and got out of there in a hurry. And a new-model mortar wouldn't have said, "I can talk for myself."

"We saw you before!" the American called Weissberg exclaimed. "We gave you some chow and some cash."

"You did," Birnbaum agreed. He nodded at Bokov. "This guy and his pal made it all disappear. Well, I got to eat some of the chocolate."

Suspicion sparked in Bokov. This was bending the arm of coincidence if not breaking it. The Americans were both scowling at him, no doubt for abusing a fellow *zhid*. Well, the hell with 'em. As if reporting to his own superiors, he said, "This man was shot by a guard for approaching the perimeter around our courthouse too closely. The guard might have killed him had another officer and myself not intervened. Naturally, we searched the prisoner. Naturally, we confiscated personal property."

"So you're releasing him now, right?" Weissberg said. "Will you give it back?"

"Not our policy," Bokov answered, which was true enough. Colonel Shteinberg had done whatever he'd done with the ten-dollar bill, and Bokov had bought himself a fancy dinner and some fine cigars with the five. And if the Yankees thought Birnbaum deserved to have the money, they could go fuck themselves. If provoked, Bokov was ready to tell them so.

Weissberg looked as if he wanted to press it. The other officer—Frank—said something in English. Weissberg still looked mutinous, but he shut up. Frank spoke directly to the DP: "You know where the Hangman's dug in, do you?"

"Not for sure," Birnbaum said. That took nerve. He had to know he'd be better off going with the Americans than staying in Soviet hands. If these Yanks decided they didn't want him, he'd never get the chance to pinch another barmaid's ass. He went on, "I was digging and digging down in the mountains. Then they sent me to Auschwitz. They hadn't got around to killing me before the Red Army ran 'em out, so I lived."

"You might be grateful," Bokov said.

"For getting rescued? I am. For getting shot? For getting robbed? No offense, Comrade Captain, but I could've done without those," the DP said. The American called Weissberg let out a snide chuckle.

"If you weren't snooping around the perimeter, nobody would have had any reason to shoot you," Captain Bokov said irritably.

"Snooping? What snooping? I was just walking along when that asshole guard yelled something—God knows what—and then he opened up, the dumb *schmuck*," Shmuel Birnbaum said.

"That was his job. We were trying to protect the courthouse, dammit," Bokov said.

"You sure did great, didn't you?" Birnbaum jeered.

Before Bokov could tell him where to head in, the Yankee called Frank said, "Take it easy, both of you. Maybe it all worked out for the best."

"In this best of all possible worlds? I don't think so," Shmuel Birnbaum said.

By the way both Americans winced and pulled faces, the DP had made a joke. Vladimir Bokov almost asked what it was. He didn't get it. Only one thing held him back: the fear of being thought uncultured. *Nye kultyurny* was a muscular insult in Russian. It meant you'd just come off the farm with manure on your boots—or, more likely, on your bare feet. It meant drool ran down your chin. It meant you picked your nose and ate the boogers in public. It meant . . . It meant Bokov kept his mouth shut, was what it meant.

Weissberg said, "We'll want to take him back with us, you know. He'll do a better job going back to the mountains and showing us where he was than he would trying to draw a map or something."

"Yes, I understand that," Bokov said. "I am authorized to turn him over to you. I will want a receipt. And we'll expect better cooperation in U.S.-Soviet affairs, especially if he does you some good."

"You'll want us to do more of what you want, you mean," the Jew called Frank said, which was true enough. "I can't promise, but. . . ."

"*Da, da,*" Bokov said impatiently. Neither one of these guys was of a rank where his promise meant anything. Neither side was dealing at a level like that. Bokov had hoped the Americans would, but they weren't always as naïve as you wished they were.

"A receipt?" Shmuel said. "What am I, a sack of beans?"

"You're a sack of hot air, is what you are." Bokov knew him better than the Americans did, but they'd find out. "We have to hope you're not a sack full of farts. The one thing we know about you is, you hate the Nazis, too. This is our chance to get some of your own back against them."

"Too little, too late," the DP said bleakly. "Everybody who ever meant anything to me is dead—up the fucking smokestack. Most I can hope for is to try and keep that shit from happening again."

"That's . . . better than nothing." Weissberg sounded hesitant about saying even so much. And well he might have, when his country and his loved ones had come through the war with hardly a scratch. Here again, Bokov had more in common with Birnbaum, and more understanding of him, than his fellow Jew did.

Frank had set a piece of paper on the tabletop. He finished writing on it, then passed it and his pen over to Weissberg. The other American officer read it, signed it, and slid it across to Vladimir Bokov.

Bokov had some trouble with it. He was familiar with German cursive. Even using German, the Americans wrote the Roman alphabet in a different way. But the NKVD man puzzled it out. *Received from NKVD Captain Bokov one displaced person, by name Shmuel Birnbaum, believed to possess important information concerning the Nazi resistance.* The two signatures followed.

"Good enough," Bokov said. "I hope this guy does you—does us—does everybody—some good. I put my dick on the chopping block to get him to you people—you'd better believe that."

Both Americans nodded back at him. "Our nuts are on the line, too," Weissberg said. "We kept trying to tell people our side and yours needed to work together better. Against the fanatics, there's only one side."

"It looks that way to me, too." Bokov waved to the barmaid. "Fresh ones all around, sweetheart." When she brought them, she made a point of giving Shmuel Birnbaum a wide berth. The DP's crooked grin said he knew why and didn't give a fuck. Captain Bokov raised his seidel. "Death to the Heydrichites!"

They could all drink to that. "Death to the Heydrichites!" they chorused. Bokov emptied the mug at one long pull. The Germans were motherfuckers, no doubt about it, but they could sure as hell brew beer.

THE CAPTAIN—NAVY CAPTAIN, OR THE EQUIVALENT OF AN ARMY colonel—looked at Tom Schmidt as if he wanted to clean him off the sole of his shoe. "No," the officer said in a voice straight from the South Pole. "I will not authorize your entry into Germany. You may sail to England or France if you like. But if you come under military jurisdiction in Germany, you will be expelled at once, if you don't get tossed in the brig—uh, the stockade—instead."

"That's not fair!" Tom squawked. "Plenty of other reporters get to go see our boys climbing onto ships."

"A technical term applies here, Mr. Schmidt: tough shit." The four-striper had the whip hand. He knew it, and he enjoyed it. "Those members of the press did not violate security arrangements in Germany. They were not sent home from the country. You did, and you were, and you don't get a second chance."

"You were censoring the news!" Tom exclaimed. He sounded more pissed off than he was. He'd figured the military would hold a grudge for what had happened in Germany. But taking a shot at Captain Weyr here for censorship would look good in his column.

And Weyr played straight into his hands, saying, "Sometimes censorship is necessary, Mr. Schmidt. Sometimes it's even essential."

"Yeah, sure," Tom said, as any reporter worth his press credential would have.

"It is, dammit," the Navy officer insisted. "Would you have printed a story that told the Germans we'd hit Normandy, not Calais?" He sent Tom another dogshit-on-my-sole look. "You probably would have."

"Up yours, Captain," Tom said evenly. Captain Weyr's jaw dropped. His subordinates couldn't tell him stuff like that, no matter how much they wanted to. But military discipline didn't bind Tom. And, if the military wanted to make a point of screwing him, neither did ordinary politeness. He went on, "You make it sound like I'm not a patriot or something, and that's a bunch of crap. Of course I know why you had to keep the invasion a secret. The movie of that poor damn GI—Cunningham, that was his name—that's a different story. You didn't want ordinary Americans seeing what was going on in Germany—seeing how the occupation was screwing things up."

"For one thing, I deny that the occupation is screwed up," Weyr said.

"Then you'd better pull your head out of the sand and look around," Tom said. "The lions are getting close."

"Amusing. You should be a writer." Weyr had a Philadelphia Main Line kind of condescension he'd probably been born with. Plenty of officers were snotty or arrogant, but only a blueblood could bring off condescending so well. He continued, "You seem to forget what an important factor in war morale can be."

Bingo! Tom pounced: "You seem to forget the war's over. You want everybody else to forget it, too. The Secretary of State talked about occupying Germany for the next forty years. How can we do that if it's peacetime? How can you imagine the American people will put up with this for the next forty weeks, let alone forty years?" He held up a hand to correct himself. "The Presidential election's a little further than forty weeks off—but only a little."

"I am not the Secretary of State. You have no business taking his words out of context and trying to put them in my mouth," Captain Weyr said. "But do you think you did Private Cunningham's family any favors by making sure that vile film got plastered onto movie screens all over the country?"

Tom did feel bad about that, even if he hadn't felt bad enough to keep from getting the film back to the States. "If I thought the brass was sitting on the film to save his family's feelings, maybe I wouldn't have done what I did," he answered. "But I don't—and neither do you."

"That's twice now you've put words in my mouth," Weyr said.

"Oh, give me a break!" Tom rolled his eyes. "The brass was doing what the brass always does. It was trying to hide the bad news. Sometimes you can get away with that in wartime. See? I admit it! But the war's over and done with. Harry Truman said so. He even acted like it. Rationing's dead as a dodo. He wants it both ways here, though. The war's over and done with . . . except when the brass says it's not. The American people aren't dumb enough to fall for that, Captain."

"I take it back. You should be a politician, Mr. Schmidt, not a writer. You sure seem to like making speeches," Weyr said. "But you can huff and puff as much as you want. You still won't blow the Pentagon down."

"Too big for that, all right. Even flying an airplane into this place wouldn't knock down much of it," Tom said.

As if he hadn't spoken, Captain Weyr went on, "And you can also huff and puff as much as you want, here in my office or in your column, and you won't get to Germany to watch the troops coming home. . . . May I speak off the record? Do you respect that?"

"Yes, I do. And yes, go ahead." Tom wasn't happy about it, but he meant it. If you said something was off the record and then went ahead and used it anyway, in nothing flat nobody would talk to you off the record any more. And you needed to hear that kind of stuff, even if you couldn't use it.

"Okay. This is Ollie Weyr talking, not Captain Weyr. Way it looks to me is, guys like you are a big part of the reason Congress won't pay for the German occupation any more. If you weren't pissing and moaning about every little thing that goes wrong over there—"

"And every big one," Tom broke in.

"Shut up. I'm not done. Maybe Germany'll be fine once we get out. I don't know. You can't know ahead of time. But it's like the President said on the radio not long ago. If things go wrong, if the Nazis get back in, I know where a bunch of the blame lands."

"And you say I make speeches?" Tom laughed in the Navy captain's face. "You ought to look in a mirror some time."

"At least I'm working for my country," Weyr said.

"So am I. Last time I looked, the First Amendment was part of what we were fighting for," Tom retorted. "Too much to expect anybody from the government to understand that."

"Yeah, you hot reporters go on and on about the First Amendment. All I've got to say is, you're using it to help guys who'd stamp it out first chance they got. We had those SOBs squashed a couple of years ago."

"You wish you did," Tom interrupted. "In your dreams, you did."

"If they start running Germany again, it won't be because the military failed," Weyr said. "It'll be because the press and the pressure groups made it impossible for us to do our job."

"Can I quote you on that?" As soon as Tom asked, he wished he hadn't. Now he'd given Weyr a chance to say no.

And Weyr did, or close enough: "That was still Ollie talking, not Captain Weyr. If you want to say it's a military officer's personal opinion, go ahead. It's not the Navy's official opinion. I can't speak for the Army, but I've never heard anything to make me think it's their official opinion, either."

"But a lot of their people believe it, too?" Tom suggested.

Captain Weyr only shrugged. "You said that. I didn't."

Too bad, Tom thought.

BERNIE COBB WALKED THROUGH BAD TÖLZ, LOOKING FOR A PLACE where he could buy a beer. The town sat in the foothills of the Alps south of Munich. The old quarter, where he was, lay on one side of the Isar; the new district, on the other side of the river, was a lot more modern. Mineral-water springs were what brought people here—people who weren't GIs with a few days' leave from prowling through Alpine passes, anyway. And there had been a training school for SS officer candidates here, too. That was out of business now . . . Bernie hoped.

"Cobb!" called another dogface—no, the guy was a three-striper.

"Sergeant Corvo!" Bernie said. "Jesus! I figured they woulda shipped you back to the States a long time ago."

"Not me." Carlo Corvo shook his head. As usual, he talked out of the side of his mouth. Also as usual, a cigarette dangled from one corner. "Draft sucked me in, yeah, but I've gone Regular Army. I got better chances in uniform than I ever would back in Hoboken—bet your ass I do."

"You nuts?" Bernie said. "You got better chances of stopping a bullet or getting your balls blown off."

"Nah." Corvo shook his head. "I don't exactly come from the good part of town—not that Hoboken's got much of a good part. I don't exactly hang around with the nice kind of people, neither. I shoot somebody over here, I don't gotta worry about cops on my tail or spending time in the slammer."

Mob connections? Bernie'd always wondered about that with Corvo. The swarthy sergeant still wasn't exactly saying so. Not exactly, no, but it sure sounded that way.

Meanwhile, Corvo asked, "How come you ain't back in—where was it? Arizona?"

"New Mexico," Bernie answered. "Not enough points. I'm young. I'm single. I was out of action for a while after the Bulge 'cause of my feet, so I missed out on a couple of campaign stars. And besides, the cocksuckers keep bumping up how many a guy needs before they ship him out. A little luck, though, it won't be too much longer."

"You mean the money cutoff?" Sergeant Corvo said.

Bernie nodded. "What else? If they bring everybody home, they can't very well leave me here all by my lonesome. Hope like hell they can't, anyway."

"Stupid fuckin' assholes can't even see the ends o' their pointy noses, let alone past 'em," Corvo said. "We bail out now, we'll just hafta fight the Jerries again later on."

"Later on suits me fine," Bernie said. "Maybe my number won't come up then. I don't owe Uncle Sam one thing more, and he owes me plenty."

Carlo Corvo sighed. "Always useta think you had pretty good sense."

"I do. I'm not gonna catch Heydrich on my own. So why should I care more about the Army than the Army cares about me? I've been away from home more than three years now. Enough is enough. I'm looking out for number one." Bernie paused. "I'm looking for some beer, too. You know any decent joints?"

By the way Corvo hesitated, knowing where to drink in Bad Tölz wasn't the question for him. Whether he wanted to drink with Bernie was. At last, with another sigh, the noncom nodded. "Yeah. C'mon—I'll show you. If you don't wanna be no lifer, can't hardly blame you for thinkin' like you do, I guess."

"Love you too, Ace," Bernie said. He followed Corvo down the narrow, winding street.

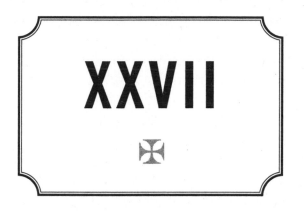

XXVII

To Shmuel Birnbaum, K-rations and U.S. Army field kitchens were the greatest inventions in the history of the world. He ate and ate, and never once worried whether what he was eating had pork in it. "I quite caring about that during the war," he told Lou Weissberg. "If it's food, you eat it."

"What with the little you got after the Nazis came through, who could blame you?" Lou said sympathetically.

"Oh. The Nazis. Sure. But I meant the last war, sonny." One other thing the DP had made the acquaintance of was a safety razor with a limitless supply of blades. His cheeks were as smooth as Lou's these days, but the stubble he'd had when Lou first met him was gray heading toward white, as was his hair. "Since 1914 . . . a war . . . a revolution . . . a civil war . . . a time to watch yourself . . . another war . . . Been a long, long time since I made a fuss about what I got, as long as I got *something*."

"You embarrass me because I had it easy in America," Lou said.

"Your folks were smart—they got out. If I'd been smart, I would've got out, too," Birnbaum said. "But I thought, *It's not so bad. It's even getting a little better, maybe.* Maybe not, too. For sure not, the way things worked out."

"We'll take you to a different valley tomorrow," Lou said. "Maybe this will be the one where they made you dig."

Maybe, nothing. Alevai *this will be the one where they made you dig,* Lou thought. The U.S. Army had been giving Birnbaum a guided tour of all the Alpine valleys in southern Germany. So far, he hadn't found the right one. Lou hoped there was a right one. You never could tell what you'd get when you dealt with the Russians. He'd wanted to for a long time. Now that he had . . .

Would Captain Bokov of the NKVD sit in his Berlin office and laugh his ass off because a no-account DP was getting fat on U.S. Army chow? Had Birnbaum ever been in one of these valleys? No doubt he'd been in Auschwitz; Lou had seen too many of those tattoos to doubt that this one was authentic. But that wasn't reason enough—the Army in its infinite wisdom had decided it wasn't reason enough—to be especially nice to him.

If he didn't come through . . . *Well, what's the worst they can do to me? Discharge me and ship me home to Jersey.* Which, when you got right down to it, would be a hell of a lot more fun than what he was doing here.

But he hated getting played for a sucker. He didn't want the NKVD to do it, and he didn't want a no-account Jew who said he hadn't had a square meal since 1914 to do it, either. He wanted . . . "Heydrich's head on a plate," he muttered.

"I hope I can give him to you," Shmuel Birnbaum said. "They didn't tell us what we were doing. They just told us to dig, and they got rid of anybody who didn't dig fast enough to suit 'em. Then they sent the rest of us to Auschwitz, also for disposal. Just dumb luck they didn't get around to me before the Red Army came."

"Sure," Lou said. Birnbaum's story sounded good. It felt good, which might have counted for even more. Lou had heard a lot of bullshit since he got to the Continent. He didn't think this was more of the same piled higher and deeper. But he'd never know for sure unless the DP delivered.

Birnbaum looked at him. "You don't think I can do it."

"I hope you can do it. I hope like anything you can," Lou said.

"Heydrich . . ." Birnbaum tasted the name. "It wouldn't be enough. There's no such thing as enough, not for that. But it would be something, anyway. And after so much nothing, something's not too bad."

"Yeah." Lou nodded. "You're right." He was sure what Germany would be like if Heydrich and his pals took over: the way it had been when Hitler was running it, only trying to find a place in a new, tougher, more suspicious world. That was . . . about as bad as things could get, as far as he was concerned.

Suppose they squashed the Heydrichites. What would Germany turn into then? Lou had no idea. That politician—Adenauer—had thought it could turn into a civilized democracy like England and France and America. Maybe. But Lou had trouble believing it. If Germany could turn into a democracy like that, wouldn't Adenauer still be alive?

Shmuel Birnbaum stopped shoveling food into his face. "Let's go," he said.

It wasn't so simple, of course. One jeep could rattle along the winding roads that slid through valleys and climbed the passes between them. It might get through. If Heydrich's goons decided it looked harmless, or if they were off making pests of themselves somewhere else, it would. But there was no guarantee—not even close.

And in these parts, it wasn't just Heydrich's goons you needed to worry about. Deserters and brigands and bandits prowled the mountainside, sometimes singly, sometimes in platoon strength. You wanted to show enough firepower to make them decide not to bother you.

Three jeeps with .50-caliber machine guns, two M8 armored cars with 37mm guns. With luck, that kind of convoy would be enough to persuade Werewolves and freelance brigands to leave them alone. The heavy machine guns and the cannon outranged anything the Jerries were likely to pack themselves. All the soldiers had Garands or M2 carbines or grease guns, too.

And so did Shmuel Birnbaum. When Lou first gave him the submachine gun, he asked if Birnbaum knew how to use it. The DP gave back a lizard's stare. "I point. I pull the trigger. If it doesn't shoot, I fiddle with the safety till it does."

"It doesn't even have a safety," Lou said.

"All right, then. So I shoot. What else do I need to know? Anything?" Birnbaum asked. For the kind of fighting he'd need to do—if he needed to do any—he *didn't* need to know anything else. Lou shut up.

They rolled past a monument to American ineptitude, a burnt-out ammo dump. It had gone up in fire and smoke a couple of months earlier, and taken half a dozen GIs with it. Back home, it probably hadn't made more than page four, except in the dead men's home towns. Too many other things were going on in Germany—this was just small change from a guerrilla war.

Birnbaum's gaze flicked to the sooty craters and scattered shell casings that marked the remains of the dump. "How'd they do it?" he asked.

"If I knew, I would tell you," Lou answered. "If we'd known ahead of time, we might have stopped them."

The DP grunted. "They need stopping. Not just for this. For everything."

"You're right. They do," Lou agreed.

"Do I hear straight? Are you Americans really starting to go home from Germany?" Birnbaum asked.

"You hear straight. I wish you didn't, but you do."

"*Meshigge,*" Birnbaum said, and Lou smiled in spite of himself. The DP spoke the same funny Yiddish dialect he did himself, with most of the vowels shifted forward in the mouth. It still meant *crazy,* however you pronounced it.

"And if I don't come through?" the DP asked bleakly. "What happens then? You give me a *kigel*?" Most people would have pronounced that *kugel.* It meant, literally, a noodle. To German guards, slave laborers, and camp inmates, it also meant a bullet in the back of the neck.

"No. We don't do that. We won't give you back to the Russians, either." Lou sighed. "But *vey iz mir,* I want Heydrich dead. If anything will show the folks back home what we're doing here is worthwhile, that's it."

"Me, I just want Heydrich dead, and all the rest of those. . . ." Shmuel Birnbaum broke off, shaking his head. "I can't find a word bad enough. Pogroms? Purges? I didn't know what trouble was till the Nazis came though. That camp . . . What I saw there . . ." He rubbed at the place where the tattooed number he would wear the rest of his life lay under his sleeve. Whatever his eyes were looking at, it wasn't the latest Alpine valley.

Hesitantly, Lou said, "I saw Dachau and Belsen."

"Practice," Birnbaum said scornfully. "The shitheads did those for practice. Once they got it figured out . . . Fuck. What do you know? What *can* you know? Don't expect me to tell you. Like I say, there are no words."

"What's the old fart going on about, sir?" asked the driver, who couldn't have been over nineteen. "Sounds nasty, whatever it is."

Hearing English jolted Lou halfway out of helpless horror. "The murder camps the Nazis built in Poland," he answered. "He lived through one."

"They really did that shit?"

"They really did," Lou said solemnly. "You would've come over here after the surrender, wouldn't you?"

"Uh, yes, sir. All I wanna do is get my ass back to Dayton in one piece, too."

"Right." Lou couldn't talk to the driver, any more than Birnbaum could talk to him. No reason for the kid to have visited any of the camps in Germany. He wouldn't have seen the corpses and the shambling, diseased living skeletons. He wouldn't have smelled what a place like that was like. And he probably wouldn't believe there were worse places. How could you believe that, in a world where God had anything to do with anything?

And if this guy had trouble believing it over here, what about all the safe tens of millions across the Atlantic? What was Reinhard Heydrich to them but a name? What were Dachau and Belsen and Auschwitz and all the others but names? Lou shivered. If the Army did punch Heydrich's ticket, would the folks back home decide the job was really done now and figure it was one more reason to yank the boys out of there and forget the nasty mess ever happened?

But if killing Heydrich made the fanatics give up. . . "Gotta try," Lou muttered.

"What's that?" Birnbaum asked him.

Lou realized he'd used English again. The DP understood *yes* and *no* and *shit* and *fuck*, but not much more. Lou returned to Yiddish: "Maybe the Nazis will quit once we get rid of their leader."

"Maybe they will—but it's about as likely as snow is black," Birnbaum said. Lou snorted; he'd heard that one from his old man more times than he could count.

They passed into another valley. This one wasn't the one where Birnbaum had been made to dig, either. "Hell," Lou said with a sigh. They drove on. Moses had wandered in the wilderness for forty years. The way Germany was unraveling, Lou wasn't sure he had forty days and forty nights. That was . . . what? Noah's flood. But Lou thought this one was flowing the wrong way.

WHEN SOLDIERS CAME HOME FROM EUROPE RIGHT AFTER V-E DAY, they came back to the United States in triumph. Pretty girls greeted them with flowers and kisses. They paraded through the streets. The same for the GIs and Marines coming back from the Pacific.

It wasn't like that now. Harry Truman wasn't bringing men home from Germany because he wanted to. He was doing it because Congress was giving him no choice. He was dragging his heels and grabbing at things as the new anti-occupation majority forced him down this road. And he, and all the branches of government he could still command, were doing their level best to pretend none of this was happening.

No press releases announced when troopships brought soldiers home from Germany. No welcoming committees waited for the returning troops. If the War Department could have disguised them with false noses and false names, it would have.

Diana McGraw didn't think that was right or fair. The way things had gone wrong in Germany wasn't the soldiers' fault. If the American government hadn't put them in an impossible situation . . . But it had, even if it was still too stubborn to believe as much.

And so she waited for a Liberty ship chugging into New York harbor. With her were local leaders of the movement to bring the troops home. And, since it was New York City, with them were more reporters and cameramen than you could shake a stick at.

The press didn't bother her. She kept looking back over her shoulder toward the buildings behind the harbor, though. Any sniper lurking there had a clean shot, all right. The warm wetness of Gus van Slyke's blood splashing her arm . . . She shivered, though the autumn day was mild enough. For several years after Ed came back from Over

There, he'd wake up shrieking from nightmares where he revisited what he'd been through. Now Diana understood why.

"What exactly are you doing here today?" a reporter from the *New York Times* asked her.

She was ever so glad to get away from her own thoughts. "Our troops deserve a proper welcome," she answered. "They haven't done anything wrong." Instead of a picket sign, she carried a big American flag today. Her colleagues had flags, too.

The reporter eyed the tired-looking ship, which tugs were nudging into place against the pier. Soldiers crowded the deck. They were staring at the amazing New York City skyline. Diana understood that, even if she'd looked at the buildings in a different way. You thought you could stay blasé about how New York looked. After all, you'd seen it a million times in the movies, right? But the difference between the movies and the genuine article was about like the difference between a picture of a steak dinner and the real thing on the table in front of you.

After a bit, the reporter's gaze slid from the GIs to their welcoming committee. "Don't you think they would have liked to see people closer to their own age?" he asked.

Diana looked at the people on the pier in a new way. Most of them, like her, had been born in the nineteenth century. And those were definitely twentieth-century men on the ship. "I suppose they would," she admitted, which made the man from the *Times* blink. "But if we weren't here, they wouldn't see anybody at all. That would be wrong, no matter what Truman thinks. So here we are."

She wasn't quite right. At the base of the pier stood a big olive-drab tent, with MPs flanking it. A sign above the open flap said U.S. ARMY DEPROCESSING CENTER, and, in smaller letters just below, ENTRY REQUIRED. Of course there would be paperwork to finish before soldiers could set foot in the United States again. But the soldiers or clerks or clerk/soldiers inside the tent weren't what a returning GI wanted to see and hear.

The tugboats pulled away from a Liberty ship. Sailors pushed through the soldiers so they could lower the gangplank. The far end thudded down onto the pier. The young men in olive-drab cheered and whooped.

"Welcome home!" Diana and the rest of the welcomers shouted, waving their flags. "Welcome back!"

Still in neat Army single file, the soldiers tramped past them toward the deprocessing center. "Who are you folks, anyways?" one of them asked.

"We're the people who got you out of Germany, that's who," Diana answered proudly. Moses might have told the children of Israel *I'm the person who got you out of Egypt* in the same tone of voice.

And the way the returning soldier's face lit up told her she hadn't wasted her time with him. "Much obliged, ma'am!" he exclaimed, and marched on.

Several other young men thanked the welcomers, too. But a skinny kid with curly brown hair and a nose like the business end of a churchkey opener stopped in front of Diana and said, "You're Mrs. McGraw, aren't you?"

Diana smiled. "That's right," she said, not without pride.

"Well, you can *geh kak afen yam,*" the kid told her. She didn't know what it meant, but it didn't sound like a compliment. And it wasn't, because the soldier went on, "You've gone and messed up the whole country, that's what you've done. We need to be in Germany. We need to stay there. If the Nazis grab it again, that'll be the worst thing in the world."

"We aren't stopping the Nazis," Diana said.

"We sure were slowing 'em down," the soldier said. "Once we're all gone—"

She went on as if he hadn't spoken: "All we were doing—are doing—over there is bleeding for no reason." She'd had this argument dozens of times before. She was ready to have it again. Ready? She was eager.

And so was the returning GI. "It's not for nothing," he insisted hotly. "It's—"

The guy behind him, who was half again his size, gave him a shove and cut him off. "C'mon, Izzy. Move it, man. This ain't the place for politics. I wanna go get my Ruptured Duck, darn it." Having ladies around kept even most soldiers talking clean.

Izzy plainly thought it was a perfect place for politics. But the momentum of the crowd swept him down the pier. He was bound for the deprocessing center whether he wanted to go there or not.

Hearing what the bigger soldier called him made a light go on in Diana's head. "Oh," she said. "I should've known."

Several of the New York–based activists nodded wisely. "You can't expect those people to be reasonable," a man said. The New Yorkers nodded again, almost in unison.

"Well," Diana said, and then, a beat later, "Most regular Americans appreciate what we're doing, anyway."

"I should hope so!" the man agreed. He waved his flag. More and more soldiers coming home from Germany clumped by them.

HANS KLEIN HAD SET THE *INTERNATIONAL HERALD-TRIBUNE* RIGHT IN the middle of Reinhard Heydrich's desk. The picture on the front page was plenty to seize the *Reichsprotektor*'s attention. There was a long file of marching U.S. soldiers, photographed with New York City's skyscrapers in the background. GIs LEAVING OCCUPATION DUTY, the headline read. Heydrich stared and stared. A picture of a beautiful woman was nothing next to this. He hadn't felt so splendid since . . . when?

Since that Czech's gun jammed. *More than five years ago now,* he thought, wonder filling him. So much had happened since, so very much. Not all of it was what he'd expected. Not much of it was what he'd wanted. And so many things had yet to happen. The *Reich* and the Party *would* be redeemed.

Klein came in. Had he been skulking in the corridor, waiting for Heydrich to pick up the marvelous newspaper? His grin said he had. "How about that?" he said.

"How about that?" Heydrich echoed, and his thin lips also shaped a smile. "Like so many whipped dogs, they're running. Running!"

"That was the idea all along," the *Oberscharführer* reminded him.

"*Aber natürlich,*" Heydrich said. "But getting them to do it—! I thought we would have to keep going longer than this. But the Americans pulled as much as we pushed. More! We never came close to hurting them enough to make them go."

"And the American government didn't shoot those people marching and squawking," Klein said. "I'm damned if I understand why not."

Since Heydrich didn't, either, he only shrugged. "You use your enemy's weaknesses against him. That's the whole idea in war. That's how we beat France. We made a big, showy threat in Holland and

Belgium, and the French and English couldn't run fast enough to fight there. Then the real thrust came through the Ardennes, where France was weak, and the *Wehrmacht* paraded under the *Arc de Triomphe*."

"The French won't want to get out of their zone now," Hans Klein predicted.

"Yes, I know." That France had an occupation zone in Germany still infuriated Heydrich. The USA, the UK, the USSR—they'd earned the right to try to hold down the *Reich,* anyhow. But what had the French done? Ridden on other people's coattails, and damn all else. The *Reichsprotektor* pulled his thoughts back to what needed doing next. "Now that the Amis are going, I don't think the Tommies will stick around much longer. England isn't what it used to be. When America spits, the English go swimming."

"I like that." Klein grinned again.

"And if we hold two zones"—Heydrich pursued his own train of thought—"we have enough of the *Reich* to do something worthwhile with. Not the *Grossdeutsches Reich,* maybe, but a *Deutsches Reich* again."

"I like that, too." But Hans Klein hadn't finished, for he asked, "How much will the Russians like it, though?"

Automatically, Heydrich's head swung toward the east. Here deep underground, directions should have been meaningless. For all practical purposes, they were. All the same, Heydrich might have had a compass implanted behind his eyes. He knew from which direction the Red Army would come if it came.

"They won't like it," he admitted. "Even so, I don't think they'll invade as long as we walk soft for a while once we get in."

"They'd better not—that's all I've got to say," Klein replied. "We sure as hell can't stop 'em if they do."

Heydrich grunted. "I know," he said gruffly. "Believe me, trading the Amis for the Ivans is the last thing I want." And wasn't that the sad and sorry truth? The German freedom fighters had probably hurt the Russians worse than they'd hurt the Americans. But the Red Army wasn't going away, dammit. The Russians hunkered down in their occupation zone and fought back.

"Well, *Herr Reichsprotektor,* what do we do about it, then?" Klein turned Heydrich's title into a sour joke. What good was a *Reichsprotektor* who couldn't protect the *Reich*?

"My bet is, the Americans won't let Stalin move all the way to the Rhine," Heydrich answered. "They look weak leaving Germany themselves. They won't be able to afford to look weak twice in a row here, especially not when the Reds in China are kicking the crap out of the Nationalists. All we have to do is make sure we look like the lesser of two evils."

Hitler never had figured that out. Right up to the end, he'd expected the Anglo-Americans to join him in the crusade against Bolshevism. But he'd scared them even worse than Stalin did. And so . . . Heydrich led the resistance from a hidden mineshaft God only knew how many meters underground.

Klein threw back his head and laughed like a loon. "Sweet suffering Jesus, sir, but that's funny! We make the Americans run away, and then we use them to keep the Russians from coming in? Oh, my!" He laughed some more.

"It is strange, I know. It should work, though, if we play our cards right. Or do you see it differently?" Heydrich asked. A couple of Foreign Ministry staffers were down here to advise him on such things. He'd talked with them. But he also respected Klein's judgment. The Foreign Ministry people had brains and education. Klein thought with his gut and the plain good sense that made him win money whenever he sat down to play skat or poker. You needed the whole bunch if you were going to get anywhere.

The *Oberscharführer* considered. "Yeah, we might bring that off if we're careful. The Ivans are scared of the atom bomb."

"Hell, so am I," Heydrich said. "As soon as we're able to, we get our own. And we have to get to work on our rockets again, too. Once we can blow Moscow and Washington off the map—"

"We're back in business," Klein finished for him.

"Damn right we are," Heydrich agreed.

VLADIMIR BOKOV NEITHER SPOKE NOR UNDERSTOOD ENGLISH. HE had no trouble at all with German, though. All the Berlin papers, those from the Russian zone and the ones printed in the zones the other Allies held, were full of news and pictures of the American pullout. He wouldn't have believed it if he weren't seeing it with his own eyes. Even seeing, he had trouble believing.

"They're going, Comrade Colonel!" he mourned. "The stupid motherfuckers are really going. Is that why we handed them the DP?"

"We handed them the DP so General Vlasov could bust our balls with it for the rest of our lives," Moisei Shteinberg answered. "He'll do it, too—he's just the type."

"Too right he is!" Bokov was gloomily aware he was the one who'd pushed hardest for working with the Americans. He wouldn't be the only one who remembered, either. Everybody who wanted to get ahead of him and everybody who wanted to hold him down would throw it in his face. After a while, nobody would have to. The whole world—the whole world of the NKVD, anyhow, which was the only world that mattered to him—would know he was a fuckup.

"Both the officers who took Birnbaum were Jews, you said. If anything gives me hope, that does," Shteinberg said. "They'll push things."

"I'm sure they want Heydrich's scalp, Comrade Colonel. But how much will they be able to do when everything's going to pieces around them? *Bozhemoi!* You can't even be sure they're still on this side of the ocean," Bokov said.

"Don't remind me." Shteinberg scowled. "I just wish I could know we'd take care of things ourselves once the Americans all disappear."

"What's to stop us?" Bokov demanded. "If the Fascists grab power in the western zones, of course we'll run them out and kill as many of them as we can. They can't even slow us down—we'd be on the Rhine in a week."

"Of course we would, if we were only fighting the Heydrichites," Moisei Shteinberg said. "But the Americans don't want us on the Rhine. Neither do the French."

"Fuck the French! Fuck the Americans, too." The first part of what Bokov said came out fiercely. His voice faltered when he tried the second curse.

Colonel Shteinberg gave back a sad nod. "You begin to see what I mean. The French are nothing . . . by themselves. But the Americans are a different story. You can despise them, but you can't ignore them. They have those damned bombs, and they have the big bombers that can carry them into the motherland. If they say, 'No, you can't do this,' then we can't, not till we have atom bombs of our own."

"Fuck the Americans!" Bokov said again, this time as savagely as he wanted to. "Fuck them in the ass! If they walk away from their worry when it's our worry, too, and then they don't let us clean it up—"

"Yes? What then? What can we do about it?" Shteinberg asked.

"Those bastards," Bokov whispered, in lieu of admitting the Soviet Union couldn't do a damn thing. "Those cocksucking bastards. They have to want to see the Fascists reestablish themselves. If they walk out and they don't let us walk in . . . What other explanation is there?" Bokov had made a career out of looking for plots against the USSR. He didn't need to look very hard to see one here.

"Do you know what the really mad thing is, Volodya?" Shteinberg said.

"Everything!" Bokov raged.

"No. The really mad thing is that every intelligence report I've seen says the American officers here in Germany don't want to leave. The soldiers do, but who cares what soldiers think? The officers are all furious. *They* don't want to see the Nazi monster come back to life. Neither does Truman. He fought against the Germans in the last war."

Bokov figured Truman had basically the same powers as Stalin's. "Then he should arrest the fools who are screwing up his policies. Do they *want* to fight three German wars?"

"They don't think they'll have to. They've got the bomb, and they've got those planes, and they think that's all they'll ever need," Shteinberg answered.

"Truman should drop the bomb on them, then," Bokov said. "Why doesn't he put them all behind barbed wire, or else two meters down in the ground?"

"Americans are soft. Would they be walking away from Germany if they weren't?" Shteinberg said. "Not always—they fought well enough before the surrender."

"Took them long enough to do it," Bokov said scornfully. He'd heard that the Americans lost only 400,000 dead against Germany and Japan combined. For the Red Army, that was a campaign, not a war.

"Yes, it did. Almost took them too long—although the Anglo-American attack on Sicily and Italy helped us a lot after Kursk, because Hitler took troops away from the east to fight them."

Shteinberg looked annoyed at himself. "But that's not what I was talking about. They're soft with one another, too. They don't have a strong secret police force, and they don't clean out their troublemakers with purges."

"They'll live to regret it," Bokov said, and then, "No. Some of them *won't* live to regret it, and they'll regret it while they're dying."

"I understood you," Shteinberg said.

Bokov would have been surprised if his superior hadn't. He had little use for Jews, but nobody could say they weren't a brainy bunch. That was how they got by. So many of the Old Bolsheviks had been Jews—but, however brainy they were, the purges nailed almost all of them sooner or later.

"Are you sure the Americans won't let us go in and clean up their mess?" Bokov asked, hoping against hope (and painfully aware the USSR hadn't cleaned up its own Heydrichite mess).

"Sure? I'm not sure of anything." Colonel Shteinberg tapped a shoulder board, which showed the two colored stripes and three small stars of his rank. "These don't turn me into a prophet. I'm just telling you how things look to me. I'll tell you something else, too: I hope I'm wrong."

"So do I, sir!" Bokov said. But Shteinberg was a brainy Jew. Maybe not a prophet, but his take on the shape of things to come felt as real to Bokov as if he'd already read it in *Red Star* or *Pravda*.

ANOTHER GODDAMN ALPINE VALLEY, LOU WEISSBERG THOUGHT AS THE jeep chugged to the top of another goddamn Alpine pass. Then the driver amazed him by waving at the vista ahead and saying, "Wow! That's mighty goddamn pretty, y'know?"

Lou looked at it with new eyes. All of a sudden, it wasn't just a place he had to get into, get through, and get out of in one piece. It wasn't a part of work he was doing. It wasn't one more place much like too many other places he'd visited lately, and too much like too many more he'd probably visit soon.

"You're right," he said, and listened to the surprise in his own voice. "That is mighty goddamn pretty."

A village lay far below. The steep-roofed houses and the church spire looked like toys. A stream ran by the village, silvery as mercury in the sunlight. The fields were a vibrant green. The meadows above them were a different vibrant green. Specks of gray and brown moved slowly across the meadows: not lice and fleas but sheep and cattle and maybe horses.

Above the meadows were fir forests. They too were green, but another green altogether, a green that knew what cold and death were and yet a green that would stay green after fields and meadows went gold and then gray. And above the firs? Black jagged rock streaked with snow and ice and a sky as blue as a bruise on God's cheek.

"*Mighty* goddamn pretty," Lou repeated, sounding even more surprised the second time he said it.

Shmuel Birnbaum stirred beside him. "*Vus?*" the DP asked, more than a little irritably. He didn't speak English, so he didn't know the vista was mighty goddamn pretty. Lou told him. Birnbaum looked down the valley. He looked back at Lou, as if wondering about the size of his brainpan. "Pretty? It's got Germans in it, right?"

"Well, yeah. But—" This time, Lou listened to himself floundering. "I mean, it didn't get bombed or anything."

True, no craters marred the meadows' complexions. What bomber pilot in his right mind would have wasted high explosives on Fusswaschendorf, or whatever the village was called?

Birnbaum delivered his own two-word verdict: "Too bad."

American Jews, seeing what the Nazis had done to their European kinsfolk, were shocked and appalled and grimly determined no such catastrophe should ever befall Jewry again. Eastern European Jews, or the relict of them remaining after Hitler's blood-drenched tide rolled back, often made their American cousins seem paragons of meekness and mercy. They hadn't just seen what the Nazis were up to; they'd gone through it. As with so many things, experience made all the difference.

The convoy of jeeps and armored cars drove down into the valley. Lou's heart thumped harder as the kid behind the machine gun swung the muzzle back and forth through a long arc. Nobody'd fired on them yet. Lou approved of that. He wanted it to continue for, oh, the next six or eight million years.

"This place look familiar?" he asked.

Shmuel Birnbaum shook his head. "Nah. Just another fucking valley. Where I come from, it's flat. Never imagined there were so many mountains and valleys in the whole world, let alone one corner of one shitty country."

"Uh-huh," Lou said. The Alps stretched over way more than a corner of one country. Giving Birnbaum geography lessons struck him as a waste of time. It might turn out to matter, though. If they had to cross into the American zone in Austria, he'd need to try and deal with a whole new military bureaucracy. The prospect did not delight his heart, or even his descending colon.

They stopped in the village for lunch. The locals stared at them as if they'd fallen from the moon. Some of the stares were because they wore American uniforms, which likely weren't much seen in these parts. Others were aimed more specifically at Lou and Birnbaum. "Aren't those a couple of . . . ?" one villager said to another, not realizing the strangers could follow his language.

"Don't be silly," his friend answered. "We got rid of *them.*"

Lou's laugh came straight out of a horror movie. "Don't believe everything you hear, fool," he said in German in a voice from beyond the grave. A moment later, he wished he hadn't thought of it like that. Countless Jews in the grave, or dead and denied even the last scrap of dignity.

But he scared hell out of the krauts. They edged around him and Shmuel Birnbaum as if they were seeing ghosts. He and the DP were heavily armed ghosts, too. Mess with them and you might end up talking from the back side of beyond yourself.

Out of the village. Through the valley. Some of the Germans up on the meadows were bound to be herdsmen. Others were more likely bandits, whether on Heydrich's team or not. The convoy moved fast enough and had enough weaponry to keep them from causing trouble.

Up the next pass. The jeeps climbed like mountain goats. The armored cars labored but managed. Once past the crest, they got another mighty goddamn pretty view.

Beside Lou, Shmuel Birnbaum gasped and stiffened. "This one," he choked out.

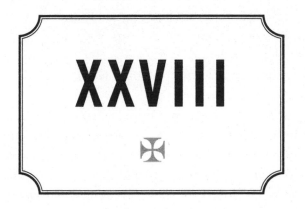

XXVIII

California again. Diana McGraw had never gone to the West Coast before poor Pat got killed. Now she'd lost track of how many times she'd come out here. It wasn't surprising. She sometimes lost track of where she was. She'd get off a train or wake up in a hotel bed and think, *Wait! This is* . . . Then it would come to her. But she still got those weird moments of dissociation. She got them more often as she traveled more, in fact.

No danger of that here, though. She hadn't taken the train to San Francisco. She'd flown in a big, droning DC-4 (from St. Louis, anyhow; she'd taken the train to get that far). The plane didn't give her as much room as a Pullman berth would have, but it got where it was going much faster. And the ride was surprisingly smooth, except for some turbulence climbing over the Rockies.

"We'll be fine, folks," the pilot said over the intercom as the airliner bumped through air pockets. "I flew the Hump during the war. Next to that, this is a piece of cake." People sheepishly smiled at one another. Diana felt embarrassed about her jitters. The DC-4 went right on flying.

So here she was, talking to a sea of people in Golden Gate Park, about as far west as she could go if she didn't want to start swimming. She could smell the Pacific Ocean. It smelled different from the Atlantic . . . cleaner, somehow. She didn't think that was her imagination, not when she'd been in New York City not long before. The breeze that blew off the ocean tugged at her hair and pulled wisps loose in spite of everything bobby pins could do.

"This fight started two years ago now," she said. "When we set out, nobody thought we had a prayer. The government was going to do whatever it was going to do. Listen to people who thought it was doing things wrong? Fat chance!"

Applause rolled up from the crowd like rising surf. The sun came out from behind a cloud. The day got warmer. The breeze from the Pacific felt friendlier. It was somewhere in the sixties. Tonight, it would be somewhere in the fifties. Diana knew she was in San Francisco, all right. But she couldn't tell by the weather if it was March or May, August or October or December.

"We *made* Harry Truman listen! He didn't want to, but he had to," she said, and the crowd's cheers got louder. "He said he knew best. We showed him he didn't. He said he wanted to go on wasting lives in Germany. We told him he couldn't. He said he'd do it anyway. We elected a Congress that wouldn't let him."

"That's right!" Several people in the front rows shouted the same thing at the same time. Diana couldn't make out all the other cries of approval, but she had no doubt that was what they were.

She remembered the big slug of gin that kindly neighbor'd given her the day she got the War Department telegram. It had done a lot for her. But the noise that meant a lot of people agreed with her about something important—no, that a lot of people *followed* her over something important—had a kick gin couldn't come close to. (It had kick enough to let her forget—part of the time—that some people who didn't follow her had guns. She got nervous whenever she thought about Gus van Slyke. Had that bullet been aimed at *her*?)

"And we did it! We, the people of the United States! We did it!" Diana didn't show her nerves. She liked to quote the Constitution whenever she could. It made the blockheads who still called her anti-American have a harder time. "Our boys *are* coming home. Before too much longer, we'll be out of Germany for good. No other family will have to go through what too many families have gone through already. And that will be good for the whole country."

"It sure will!" The cry rose up from the thousands out there on the grass.

"But we aren't finished yet," Diana went on. "We've only started. That stubborn man in the White House still wants to do all the things the Eightieth Congress won't let him do. He's started to show his cards. He's going to campaign against Congress next year. He's going to try to bring back enough people who think like him so he can do all the foolish things he wants to. Folks, he's going to campaign against the little people. He's going to campaign against us! Will we let him get away with it?"

"*Nooo!*" This time, the crowd's reply was a long wolf howl. Diana wished it would carry all the way to Washington. Maybe not now. Come November next year, it would.

"*No* is right. We know what we want, and we know how to get it," Diana said. "After we send Harry Truman home—and Bess, and Margaret, and Margaret's piano—we'll go right on forming our more perfect union. We can do it. We will do it. We *are* the people."

"*We* are *the people!*" the crowd roared as Diana stepped away from the microphone. She waved to them. They shouted louder than ever. Some of them cried out her name. If she'd grinned any wider, the top of her head would have fallen off. Who needed gin—who needed anything else—when you could have . . . this?

"I don't know whether I want to go on after that," said the San Francisco politico who followed her to the mike. The sympathetic laugh he got was enough to let him launch into his speech. He ripped into the Truman administration even harder than Diana had. The crowd loved it.

Policemen prowled the edge of the crowd to keep pro-administration hotheads from starting trouble. Diana hoped they'd do more good than they had in Indianapolis. Pickets who followed the Truman line did march beyond the cops' perimeter. They shouted and heckled, but they were a long way from the speakers' platform. And there weren't very many of them. Diana marveled at that. When she was first starting out, opponents outnumbered and outshouted allies as often as not. No more. The country had swung her way. She shook her head, standing up there in the cool breeze off the Pacific. She'd made the country swing her way.

The sun was going down toward the sea when the rally broke up. Diana went to dinner with some of the locals who'd spoken in the park. The Cliff House looked out over the sea. You could watch the sun set, have a couple of drinks, and eat fish and clams and scallops that had been doing whatever they did in the ocean only a few hours before.

You could also watch the sea lions and water birds on Seal Rocks. Diana didn't think she'd ever seen wild seals before. These beasts weren't real wild; they hardly moved at all. A big white bird lit on one sea lion's back. The animal just sat there on the rock. Maybe it was asleep, and the bird didn't wake it up.

"Can I drive you back to your hotel?" the politico who'd come on after Diana asked when dinner was done. His name was Marvin Something; she couldn't remember what. She also couldn't remember if he was a city councilman or a county supervisor. She wasn't sure it made any difference. The city of San Francisco filled all of San Francisco County.

"Thanks. That's nice of you," she said.

And it was. The Palace Hotel was way over on the other side of town, near the Bay. San Francisco was a compact city, but even so. . . .

Marvin drove a Packard. Diana tried not to hold it against him; she was still biased in favor of General Motors cars. Traffic had started to thin out. He didn't take long to get to the hotel at the corner of New Montgomery and Market. The Palace was famous for, among other things, endings. Before the big earthquake of 1906, a King of Hawaii had died there. Afterwards, and after a rebuilding, it was the place where President Harding breathed his last.

"Funny," Diana said. "I wasn't anywhere near so sorry when Harding passed away as I was when FDR died. I don't think anybody was."

"I know I wasn't," Marvin said. "But Roosevelt was special, and Harding was just kinda there, if you know what I mean. You didn't feel like your father'd just died."

"That's what it was, all right. Except Roosevelt was everybody's father," Diana said. She'd had so much land on her in a few months in 1945—the President's death (which really did feel like a family member's), and then poor Pat's. She wondered how she'd got through it.

Marvin found a parking space right by the hotel. If that wasn't a miracle, it came close. He jumped out, hurried around the hood, and held her door open so she could get out. "Can I buy you a drink?" he asked as she did.

"I'm kind of tired . . . but sure. Why not?" she said. Sometimes you needed an extra one—maybe an extra two—to come down from the excitement a good rally stirred up. "Help me sleep tonight."

"There you go," Marvin agreed.

After that drink, Diana said, "I'm getting tight." Because it wasn't just *a* drink. How many had she had at the Cliff House? She couldn't remember, which probably wasn't a good sign.

But Marvin said, "Bird can't fly on one wing," and waved to the bartender again. Diana snickered. It wouldn't have seemed so funny if she hadn't had a good deal already, but she had, so it did. Following that train of logic—if it was a train, and if it was logic—seemed pretty funny, too.

She wobbled when she got up and headed for her room. Somehow, she wasn't surprised when Marvin came with her. They walked right past the house dick—he couldn't have been anything else—on the way back to the elevators. He nodded and touched the brim of his fedora and didn't stir from the chair where he lounged. His job was to keep out-of-town businessmen from bringing hookers up to their rooms. A respected local civic leader? A dignitary who'd led a rally? He didn't think twice about letting them by.

Diana didn't think twice about it, either, not till she found that Marvin had walked into the room with her. That turned out to be a little too late. He was nuzzling her neck and nibbling her ear, and then he was kissing her.

She could have yelled. She could have clouted him. Maybe she would have if she'd been sober. And maybe she would have, if Ed had left her happier the last few times they'd slept together. *Don't I deserve something better than that?* she thought. Even though she wasn't sure whether Marvin was it, she lay down with him to find out.

He surprised her. Well, of course he did—she didn't know what he was going to do before he did it, the way she had with Ed the past umpteen years. And he did some things Ed would never have dreamt of doing. Diana discovered she enjoyed them, and wondered why the devil Ed hadn't thought of them.

Then she stopped thinking about Ed. She stopped thinking at all, as she discovered that *enjoyed* was much too mild a word.

In due course, Marvin grunted and quivered. Then he grinned. "How about that?" he said as he slid away. He sounded indecently pleased with himself, and that was exactly the right word.

"How about that?" Diana echoed. She was delighted at what had just happened—she was too honest with herself to have any doubts on that score. But she was also angry at herself for being so delighted. And which counted for more . . . she was damned if she could say.

Marvin, fortunately, didn't hang around afterwards. Why should he? He'd got what he wanted. He quickly dressed, knotted his tie with fussy precision, slipped on his jacket, grinned one more time as he blew her a kiss, and he was gone.

Which left Diana all alone in the fading afterglow. "I didn't come here for this," she told the hotel room. It didn't say anything. It wasn't that it didn't believe her. It flat didn't care. How many times, from how many people, had it heard the same thing before?

She jumped off the bed. The stories it could have told . . . She didn't want to hear them. But she'd have to sleep in it tonight unless she curled up on the floor. And just because she hadn't come there for that didn't mean it hadn't happened. Now she had to try to figure out what it meant and what she was supposed to do about it.

VLADIMIR BOKOV DIDN'T LOVE PAPERWORK, BUT HE WAS GOOD AT IT. Interrogation reports, intelligence estimates, disposition reports, all the minutiae of totalitarianism in action . . . How could you know what you'd done to people, or how many of them you'd done it to, unless you kept careful records?

Someone, somewhere, someday, would pay attention to all the paperwork he turned out. It might be Colonel Shteinberg, who had to subsume Bokov's reports into his own. Or it might be someone back in Moscow, someone who would decide whether Bokov rose or fell because of the documents he produced. He intended to rise. Good paperwork and good connections were the road to higher ground in the Soviet Union.

He was detailing the lies a captured Heydrichite tried to palm off as gospel truth when an explosion almost lifted him out of his chair and dropped him on the floor. His first, automatic, response was annoyance. How was he going to get anything done if people kept blowing things up around him?

Only afterwards did he wonder *what* the Fascist bandits had blown up this time. If that wasn't a truck exploding, he'd never heard one. Maybe NKVD and Red Army security had made the hapless driver touch off his all-wheel-drive bomb far from its intended target.

Maybe. It had happened before. But it hadn't happened very often. Bokov had his doubts.

A telephone rang in an office down the hall. Somebody answered it, listened, and let fly with an impassioned stream of *mat*. The phone slammed down. Hard enough to break it? If not, it wasn't from lack of effort. A roar of pure rage followed: "Fuck their mothers—the cunts got the Red Army monument!"

Bokov sprang to his feet with a foul-mouthed, furious shout of his own. Someone's head would roll in the dust for that. The monument had been unveiled on November 7, 1945, to commemorate the anniversary of the October Revolution (a name that showed how the Julian calendar had complicated life in prerevolutionary Russia). It was made of marble from the wreckage of the *Reichs* Chancellery, and topped with a bronze of a Soviet soldier with bayoneted rifle flanked by what were supposed to have been the first two Red Army tanks into Berlin.

Colonel Shteinberg burst into Bokov's office. "You heard?" the senior NKVD man asked.

"I heard," Bokov agreed grimly. "Shall we go find out just what they did to it?"

"Not till we're ordered to," Shteinberg answered. "They've got that trick of using one blast to draw more people in, then touching off another one. Why run into a trap?"

"Well, you're right," Bokov said—the Heydrichites would try that whenever they thought they could get away with it. Something else occurred to him: "Would even two and a half tonnes of explosives blow up that monument?"

"Beats me," Shteinberg said. "They wouldn't do it any good, though." He paused, his face suddenly thoughtful rather than angry or resigned. "Wait a minute. Didn't you write the memo about alertness last year to make sure we protected that monument?"

"I did, Comrade Colonel," Bokov said. Nobody would be able to claim he hadn't done his part. Paperwork wasn't just for giving enemies of the state what they deserved. If you'd served the Soviet Union the way you should have, and if you had the papers to prove it, you were bulletproof.

"But of course that *was* last year. No one could expect a unit to stay alert for a whole year." Sarcasm dripped from Shteinberg's voice like juice from a ripe peach after you took a bite. Then he paused again. "Of course, I don't know if the same unit still has the duty. All the same, though, that memo went everywhere in the Soviet zone, didn't it?"

"That's what I heard, sir." Bokov didn't have the paperwork to prove it had, not at his beck and call. Somebody would. People could find out exactly where it had gone. If it was supposed to have gone everywhere and hadn't, people could find out who'd dropped the ball.

A sergeant stuck his head into Bokov's office. He looked relieved when he saw Moisei Shteinberg. "A telephone call for you, Comrade Colonel."

"I'm coming." Shteinberg hurried away. He came back about ten minutes later. Bokov couldn't read his expression. The colonel asked, "Do you know—did you know—a lieutenant colonel named Surkov? A tanks officer?"

"Surkov . . ." Bokov had to think before he answered, "Wasn't he one of the men with the armored regiment in the division that guarded the monument last year? I talked to him about . . . about tricks the Heydrichites might try." It came back to him now. "Why, sir?"

"Because as soon as the monument went up, he took his service pistol out of the holster, stuck it in his mouth, and blew off the top of his head."

"Oh . . . damnation," Bokov muttered. Poor Surkov must have decided killing himself looked like a better bet than whatever the Red Army and the NKVD would do to him. He might not have been wrong, either. Remembering what he'd talked about with the newly dead officer, Bokov said, "Don't tell me the Heydrichites used one of our tanks to get the explosives to the monument."

Colonel Shteinberg jerked in surprise, then froze into catlike immobility. "How did you know that, Volodya, when I only found out about it myself just now?" he asked, his voice ominously quiet.

"I didn't *know*, sir. But Surkov and I talked about that kind of trick. He knew it was a possibility. Or he knew a year ago. But he and his men must have slacked off and stopped worrying about it when nothing happened. Then something did—and he would've remembered he should've been on his toes. And since he wasn't . . ." Bokov mimed shooting himself.

"I see. Yes, that makes good sense." Colonel Shteinberg lifted his cap in salute. Mockingly? Bokov was damned if he could tell. Shteinberg went on, "Your deduction is fine indeed. You should be Sherlock Bokov, not Vladimir."

Bokov had read his share of Sherlock Holmes stories in translation. Many Russians had; unlike so many English and American authors, Arthur Conan Doyle was ideologically inoffensive. All the same, he said, "How much good does it do to know who the criminal is when you can't catch him because he's blown himself to smithereens?"

"A point," the senior NKVD officer admitted. "But only some of a point. These Fascist jackals run in packs. Sometimes the trail of one will lead you to the next."

"Sometimes it will, yes, sir. Only sometimes it won't." Bokov hesitated, then hurried on so that what he said came from his mouth and not Shteinberg's: "Doesn't look like the Americans have done anything with that damned DP we gave them, for instance." Shteinberg couldn't blame him for that if he'd already blamed himself. He hoped Shteinberg couldn't, anyhow.

The Jew stayed silent so long, Bokov started to worry. At last, though, Shteinberg said, "Don't lose any sleep over that one, Volodya. If it doesn't work out, then it doesn't. But the world won't end if one single solitary cat happens to land by a bowl of cream."

Would he have said the same thing had the man they let go been an anti-Fascist German, not another Jew? Vladimir Bokov had his doubts. By the nature of things, he had to keep them to himself.

"And besides—" Shteinberg added, and not another word. But

when he puffed out his cheeks, narrowed his eyes, and glowered, he did a remarkable impression of Lieutenant General Yuri Vlasov. Maybe there was a mike hidden in Bokov's office, maybe not. There was no cinema camera. Nobody but the two of them would ever know he'd just wordlessly said they'd given the evil-tempered general a finger in the eye. And Bokov couldn't prove a thing.

"If they stole a tank, they couldn't have done it with one lone man," Bokov said. "Did we know where they did it yet? Do we know how?"

"We may. I don't." Moisei Shteinberg sighed. "Something went wrong somewhere—you can count on that. We forgot about a machine, or we figured the Germans couldn't make it start because we couldn't, or a guard got drunk and passed out, or the Heydrichites knocked somebody over the head, or somebody who spoke Russian had forged papers, or . . ." He spread his hands as if to say he could go on.

Some of the schemes he proposed struck Bokov as more likely than others, but any one of them was possible. "Why do we fuck up like this all the time?" Bokov burst out.

"It's not as though the rest of the Allies haven't got bitten, too." The other NKVD man gave such consolation as he could. "And the Germans lost the big war, so they aren't immune, either."

"What does that mean?" Bokov answered his own question: "The whole human race is fucked up, that's what!"

One of Shteinberg's dark eyebrows rose a few millimeters: "And this surprises you because . . . ?"

Joe Martin nodded to Jerry Duncan. "The chair recognizes the gentleman from Indiana," the Speaker of the House said.

"Thank you, Mr. Speaker," Jerry said. "I rise to discuss the administration's flawed—no, I should say failed—policy in Germany."

"You've got no right to do that," Sam Rayburn growled from the other side of the aisle. "The administration can't carry out its policy in Germany, because you people won't let it. Running away and giving the place back to the Nazis is your policy, not the President's."

Bang! Speaker Martin brought down his gavel with obvious relish.

"The gentleman from Texas is out of order, as I am sure he knows perfectly well."

"I'll tell you what's out of order," Rayburn said. "This idiotic retreat you're ramming down everybody's throat is out of order, that's what."

Bang! Bang! "That will be quite enough of that, Mr. Rayburn. Quite enough." Martin often repeated himself for emphasis. *Diana McGraw does the same thing,* Jerry thought. Then he wondered if he did it himself without noticing. The Speaker of the House went on, "Mr. Duncan has the floor. You may continue, Mr. Duncan."

"Thank you again, Mr. Speaker," Jerry said. "It's nice to have somebody on my side up there. I'm still getting used to that."

A ripple of laughter ran through the not especially crowded House chamber. Even Sam Rayburn smiled gruffly. While he was up on the dais, he hadn't been on Jerry's side, and he didn't give two whoops in hell who knew it.

"We had the wrong troops in the wrong places, and they were trying to accomplish the wrong mission," Jerry went on. "Other than that, everything was fine with President Truman's policy."

Most Republicans in the chamber applauded, along with the growing number of anti-occupation Democrats. Catcalls and boos rose from the pro-administration Democrats, and from the Republicans, mostly in the Northeast, who couldn't see their way clear to agreeing with the majority in their own party.

"We tried everything we knew how to do. Did we manage to stop the German partisans, or even slow them down very much? We did not," Jerry said. "No one's been able to slow them down very much The way they blew up the Russians' monument in Berlin proves that. If the Russians can't keep them from doing things like that, nobody's going to be able to."

The Russians are tough, evil bastards. They can do all the stuff we haven't got the stomach to do ourselves. Jerry didn't come right out and put that in his speech, but it lay below and behind his words. By the way several Congressmen nodded, they heard what he wasn't saying—heard it loud and clear.

"Isn't it time we deal with what we've got instead of what we wish we had?" he asked. "Let the damned Nazis come out in the open—not because we love them, because we know they're there. Once they are out in the open, they won't be able to cause nearly so much trouble."

"Tell it to Frankfurt," Sam Rayburn said. "How many years before it'll be fit for human beings to live there again?"

"Mr. Duncan has the floor," the Speaker said, and used the gavel again.

"Thank you, Mr. Speaker. The partisans weren't out in the open when they attacked our poorly guarded compound in Frankfurt," Jerry said. "When they come out of hiding, we'll know who they are and where their strength lies. And we will sit over them with our planes and our bombs, and we will make sure they stay inside their own borders."

"Till one of their rockets lands on New York City—or Washington," Rayburn said.

"Oh, come off it!" Jerry rolled his eyes. "I do believe the distinguished gentleman from Texas has been pawing through too many of those magazines with the bug-eyed monsters on the cover."

He got a laugh, but it was a more nervous laugh than he would have liked. And Rayburn said, "The gentleman from Indiana had better tell that to London and Antwerp. Anybody who hit London yesterday will be able to hit New York—and Moscow—tomorrow."

Jerry was saved not by the bell but by the gavel. "The gentleman from Texas is out of order, as I've reminded him before," Joe Martin said. "It's also my opinion that his argument forgets all about where we are today."

Martin got a much bigger, much deeper laugh than Jerry Duncan had. When the Speaker of the House cracked a joke, Congressmen who knew what was good for them found it funny. Some Speakers had long memories for slights of any kind. Sam Rayburn had, when he was on the rostrum in front of the House. You crossed him at your professional peril. Joe Martin seemed more easygoing than the dour Texan, but he might yet find he needed to toughen up one of these days.

Now he nodded to Jerry. "You may continue, Mr. Duncan. Hopefully, you may continue without further interruptions from the peanut gallery." He glanced in Sam Rayburn's direction. Rayburn looked back, unrepentant.

"Thank you, Mr. Speaker. I was almost done," Jerry said. "I did

want to add for the record that I'm proud the person who first pub-
licly pointed out that the President's German policy has no clothes on
is from my district. The whole country owes Mrs. Diana McGraw a
vote of thanks."

"She has a lot to answer for, all right, but that's not the same
thing," Rayburn said. Speaker Martin gaveled him into silence—
about a dozen words too late to suit Jerry.

By now, Bernie Cobb had seen too goddamn many German
Alpine valleys. The most excitement he'd ever got was when the blast
that sealed one mineshaft touched off an underground collapse.

When they stuck him in the back of a truck and hauled him off on
what he figured was another wild-goose chase, he just shrugged. Most
of the other soldiers under the canvas roof pissed and moaned right
from the start. One of them even asked him, "Why aren't you bitching like the rest of us?"

"What's the use?" Bernie answered. "We're going where they tell
us to, and we'll do what they say once we get there."

"That's what's wrong," the other GI said.

"It's the fuckin' Army. This is how it works," Bernie said, more
patiently than he'd expected. "Besides, would you rather be back in
Nuremberg or Munich or somewhere like that? Out in the open, at
least you've got a chance of seeing the fanatics before they start shooting at you."

"I don't want to be here at all," the other soldier said. Several
more men nodded. The guy doing the talking went on, "Damn war
was supposed to be over almost two and a half years ago. Only reason we're still fucking around in this miserable country is that Harry
Truman's a goddamn jerk." His friends nodded some more.

The sentiment had its points. Bernie had said things not very different himself. Hearing it from a punk who plainly hadn't seen Germany before V-E Day only pissed him off, though. "You better
remember, the Jerries don't know you don't wanna be here," he said.
"You don't keep your eyes open, they'll punch your ticket for you
toot sweet. Or else you'll be the star in one of their movies, and then
we'll find what's left of you by the side of the road. So keep your eyes
open and your mouth shut, huh?"

"Sorry, General!" the new draftee said. His friends snickered. They would all have edged away from Bernie, except the truck was too tightly packed to make edging away possible, let alone practical.

Bernie barely had room to snake a pack of cigarettes out of his jacket pocket. After he lit up, one of the guys who'd made it plainest that he thought Bernie was an idiot tried to cadge a smoke from him. Bernie was tempted to tell him to shove it. The other guy likely would have done that to him. But he'd learned you always shared in the field—if you ran out of this or that, somebody else would share with you.

He couldn't help saying, "I don't look like such a jerk now that I've got something you want, huh?"

"Yeah, well—" The fellow did manage to seem faintly embarrassed. He held the Chesterfield out to Bernie. "Can you give me a light, too?"

"Jeez Louise!" Bernie said, but he did.

After a while, the truck stopped at a checkpoint. An MP with a grease gun eyed the soldiers in the back with a look that said he thought they were all SS men in disguise. "Who won the American League pennant in '44?" he demanded fiercely.

"The Browns. Only time they've ever done it," Bernie answered before anybody else could. "I was already over here by then, but I know that."

He figured the MP would shut up, but the guy didn't. "Did they win the Series?" the snowdrop asked. "One of you other clowns—not him."

"No," said the soldier who didn't want to be in Germany at all. "The Cards beat 'em in . . . was it seven games?"

"Six," Bernie said.

"Okay." Now the MP was satisfied. "You guys are Americans, all right. You can go on."

"What the hell are we getting into?" Bernie asked.

"You think they tell me what's going on?" the MP said. The PFC driving the truck put it back in gear. It rolled down into the valley.

"Wonder what they woulda done if we didn't know baseball," said one of the GIs in the back.

"Fucked us over and wasted a bunch of everybody's time," Bernie said. "Then when it finally did get straightened out they would've acted like it was our fault for being such a dumb bunch of cock-suckers."

"You don't like MPs, do you?" the soldier asked him.

"Gee, how'd you figure that out?" Bernie said, deadpan. Almost everybody back there laughed.

It got warmer as the truck went down into the valley—not warm, but warmer. Bernie munched on part of a D-ration bar. The damn thing tasted the way he'd always thought a chocolate-flavored candle would. It was too waxy to be enjoyable, but a whole bar would keep you running all day. D-rats were supposed to have all the vitamins and stuff you needed. Bernie didn't know about that. He did know they were the perfect antidote for prunes; if you had to live on them for two or three days, the memory, among other things, lingered for quite a while afterwards. But it was what he had on him. Unlike these new guys, he didn't feel like scrounging from people he didn't know.

After a while, the truck stopped. "Ritz Hotel!" the driver shouted. "All ashore that's going ashore!"

"Funny guy—a fuckin' comedian," Bernie said. "He should take it on the radio . . . and then stuff it."

"There you go, man," said the kid who didn't want to be there. They agreed about something, anyhow.

One by one, the GIs hopped out. It wasn't the Ritz. It was a bunch of olive-drab tents set down in the middle of the valley. A barbed-wire perimeter and machine-gun nests protected by thick layers of sand-bags protected the camp from direct assault.

"What the fuck is all this?" said one of the soldiers who'd got out of the truck with Bernie.

"Whatever it is, I don't like it. It feels like a trap," Bernie said. The other soldier gave him a funny look, but he set his jaw, nodded, and waved to the mountains reaching up to the sky on either side. "Fuck-ing fanatics want to throw stuff down on us, who's gonna stop 'em? High ground counts for a lot." He spoke from experience, which was something the other guy probably didn't have.

A captain came out of a tent, followed by an older guy in black-dyed fatigues without any insignia—some kind of civilian attached to the Army. "It's not a trap, on account of we hold the heights," the captain said. By the way he talked, he came from New York or New Jersey or somewhere around there. "We hold this whole goddamn valley, matter of fact. And somewhere under it, I hope like hell, is Reinhard Heydrich. We're gonna dig the son of a bitch out."

"How many other Nazis has he got with him?" asked one of the other fellows just off the deuce-and-a-half. "They gonna shoot it out with us?" He didn't sound delighted at the prospect.

"However many pals he has, that's their tough luck. We've got what we need to blast 'em all," the captain answered. He was skinny and sharp-nosed. *A Jew*, Bernie judged. So was the fellow in black fatigues, unless he missed his guess. No wonder the officer'd stayed so gung-ho, then. Bernie wasn't sure he had himself. Then the captain said, "There's a million bucks on Heydrich's head, remember. A cool million, and you'll never hear from the IRS. Think about that, guys."

They thought about it. They liked it . . . better than they had before, anyhow. Bernie looked down the valley. Other encampments were in place. And . . . He started laughing.

"What's funny?" the captain snapped.

"Sorry, sir," he said, "but I been here before—patrol last year." He remembered the farmhouse with the dirty pictures. "Maybe I walked on Heydrich's grave."

The captain's grin made him look years younger. "Yeah," he said. "Maybe you did."

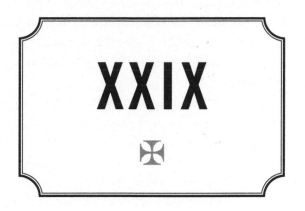

XXIX

There was a graveyard up on the mountainside. The Americans in the valley paid it no attention. Why should they? By the tumbled headstones and leaning crosses over the graves, it had been there a long, long time. No one shot at the Amis from the position. No one down on the valley floor seemed to remember it was around.

All of which suited Reinhard Heydrich fine. One of those leaning crosses was a dummy. It concealed a periscope, from which an observer surveyed the scene below. Heydrich admired the conceit. He'd filched it from a Russian field fortification the *Waffen*-SS somehow smoked out. This was an improved version. The observer had a field telephone. He wasn't actually in a grave, but in a passage that led down to the main mine. If he saw trouble coming, he could get away. Explosives in the passage would make sure nobody followed him.

"They keep bringing in more troops and more digging equipment, *Herr Reichsprotektor,*" he said now, his voice tinny in Heydrich's ear. "It sure looks like they know something. What are we going to do?"

Heydrich didn't want to believe the Amis could know where his hideout lay. They'd come through here before, done some superficial damage, and gone on their way. They'd treated this valley no differently from two dozen others in the Alps.

They were treating it differently now, dammit. *How?* Heydrich wondered. *Why?* Had they found one of the drops where his people communicated with the outside world? He couldn't believe it. The drops were well sited, and everybody who knew about them had the discipline to use them discreetly.

A traitor? Heydrich was sure that would have been Hans Klein's guess. And it wasn't unlikely, worse luck. Somebody who decided a million dollars would set him up for life could cause a lot of trouble. But everyone who was supposed to be underground here was accounted for. Some men in Jochen Peiper's underground center knew where this one was. They would have betrayed both of them, though. And there was no sign Peiper's center was in trouble. One of the outside connections, then? Even if the worst happened here, Heydrich hoped the pigdog wouldn't live to enjoy his foul loot.

Or—a new thought—could one of the laborers who'd dug most of this place out of the living rock have survived in spite of everything? Could he have figured out what he'd been working on? Could he have gone to the Amis with the story? Would they have believed somebody like that?

Heydrich shook his head. "Impossible," he muttered. The extermination camps were most efficient. He knew that. He damn well should have. Hadn't he set the *Einsatzgruppen* in motion against the Jews of Eastern Europe? Hadn't he organized the Wannsee Conference, which got all the antisemitic forces in the *Reich* moving on parallel tracks against the Jewish enemy? So, no, surviving laborers were anything but likely.

But the observer in the graveyard heard him, which he hadn't intended. "It's not impossible, *Herr Reichsprotektor*. I only wish it were. But they're really here," the man said. "What will we do? What can we do?"

That was a better question than Heydrich wished it were. He and his men had escape routes. They would have sufficed to let the Germans give most bands of attackers the slip. But the American net was cast wider than Heydrich had ever dreamt it could be.

Decision crystallized in the *Reichsprotektor*'s mind. "For now, we sit tight," he answered. "They may have a good notion we're here, but they can't be sure. Finding us won't be easy. Neither will digging us out."

"I sure hope you're right, sir," the observer said, and rang off.

Heydrich hoped he was right, too. The generators would run out of fuel before too long—or maybe he'd have to turn them off to keep their noise from betraying itself to listening devices. The mines had good natural ventilation, but even so. . . . Heydrich tried to imagine running the war for the liberation of the *Reich* by candle- and lantern light.

Napoleon had fought his wars that way. So had Clausewitz, and even Moltke. None of them, though, had tried to do it from hundreds of meters underground. The sun rose every day for them. It never rose for Heydrich. When the candles and lanterns ran low . . .

"Klein!" he called.

"Yes, sir?" The *Oberscharführer* wasn't far away. Heydrich hadn't thought he would be.

The decision that had crystallized broke up and re-formed. "Looks to me like we'll have to try to break out," the *Reichsprotektor* said. "We have . . . some people who won't be able to fight or to keep up. You know who I'm talking about?" He waited for Klein to nod, then went on, "Good. I want you to see that's taken care of, all right?"

Hans Klein nodded again. "I'll make sure of it. Too bad, *nicht wahr?* Such a waste, after we went to all the trouble to grab them."

"It is, isn't it?" Heydrich sighed. He wanted an atom bomb as fast as he could get one after the *Reich* was free again. Germany needed that weapon. "Why don't you leave Wirtz and Diebner for now? We can always tend to them later if we have to. The others . . . It *is* too bad, but they'd better disappear."

"Right you are, *Herr Reichsprotektor.*" Klein sketched a salute and hurried away.

Reinhard Heydrich sighed once more. He didn't know how or why things had gone wrong in the valley, but they had. Not everything worked out the way you wished it would. He patted his tunic. He had a cyanide capsule in his breast pocket, and others in other places about his person. Everybody down here did. Even if the Amis caught him, they wouldn't question him or make sport of him or try him. He just had to bite down. If Himmler had done it, Heydrich was sure he could, too.

"THERE, CAPTAIN." SHMUEL BIRNBAUM POINTED TO WHAT HAD BEEN a mineshaft till an explosive charge closed up the front of it. "That one heads straight down. You could do like the people in the Jules Verne story and go straight to the center of the earth."

"I read that book when I was a kid," Lou Weissberg said. He'd read it in English, of course. Birnbaum would have seen it in Russian, or maybe Yiddish, or possibly even German. And it was really written in French. Ideas bounced across the world like rubber balls.

The main idea in Lou's head now was seeing Heydrich dead. Maybe, if you chopped off the German Freedom Front's head, the body would flop like a chicken that met the hatchet and then fall over and die. Maybe. *Alevai.* Lou muttered to himself. *Please, God. Don't You owe us a little something, anyway?* It wasn't exactly a prayer— more a bitter question. When the Nazis efficiently went about the business of murdering Jews by the million, God showed He'd got out of the habit of listening to prayers.

If God wouldn't take care of things (or if God wasn't there to take care of things, which Lou found much too likely), mere mortals would have to do their goddamnedest. Lou waved to the crews of the waiting bulldozers and steam shovels. "Come and get 'em!" he yelled, as if he were calling them to dinner.

They rumbled forward on their tracks, filling the pure mountain air with the stink of diesel exhaust. Dozer blades and the steam shovels' buckets dug into the mountainside. Earth and stones went into piles off to either side of the closed shaft. This place wouldn't be nearly so scenic after the excavators got through. Maybe that bothered the Germans who lived here. Lou was no tourist. He hadn't come for the view.

Along with the dirt and boulders, the earth-moving equipment also dislodged timbers that had helped support the sides and roof of the shaft. Over the *blat!* of his engine, a dozer jockey shouted, "Damn things look like they've been here since B.C. You sure we're in the right place, Captain?"

Lou wasn't sure of anything. The people working under him needed to know that like they needed a hole in the head, though. He didn't even look back at Shmuel Birnbaum as he nodded. "This is all camouflage," he declared. "C'mon—you know the Germans do shit like that."

"Hope you're right, sir," the dozer driver said, and plunged forward again.

So do I, Lou thought. If this didn't work out the way he hoped it would, if he didn't come up with a big burrow full of Nazis if not with the *Reichsprotektor*'s head on a platter, the Army would be only too happy to separate him from the service and boot his butt back to New Jersey. Chances were it would throw Howard Frank out, too. They would get exactly what eighty percent of the soldiers in Germany craved most: a ride home. It was, naturally, the last thing either of them wanted. If that wasn't the Army way of doing things, Lou couldn't imagine what would be.

The earth-movers were tearing the living crap out of the opening to the mineshaft. Lou wondered if they would just peel back the whole mountainside to get at whatever it concealed. Wouldn't they fill the valley floor below with rocks and dirt if they did?

But the guys who ran the growling, farting, grinding machinery were more purposeful than that. They stayed on the old mine's trail. Before long, the dozer blades and the steam shovels' steel jaws clanged off some serious boulders. Here and there, they had to back out so demolition crews could make big ones into, well, littler ones, anyhow.

That dozer driver said, "Big old honking landslide, I bet. This woulda closed the place down better than our charge of dynamite."

"Just keep going, goddammit." Lou had the courage of his convictions. Of course, Hitler had also had the courage of his. *Now, am I right, or nothing but a stubborn jackass? Is it the good turtle soup, or merely the mock?* Lou wondered. *One way or the other, I'll find out.*

Bulldozers and steam shovels kept banging through rocks. The drivers shouted to one another. Lou couldn't always make out what they said. That was bound to be just as well. When one of them jerked a thumb in his direction and then spun an index finger in a circle next to his temple, Lou couldn't stay in much doubt about what the GI meant.

Neither could Shmuel Birnbaum. "They think you're crazy," the DP said. "So they think I'm crazy, too."

"Yeah, well, fuck 'em all," Lou answered. "Long as they do what I tell 'em to, who gives a rat's ass what they think?" Birnbaum gave him a look. Lou had no trouble translating it—something like *You're the champion of democracy?* And, in a weird way, Lou was. But democracy and Army life mixed like water and sodium—they caught fire when they touched. What did democracy give rise to in the Army? *We want to go home!* and damn all else. The system might stink, but it worked.

The sun sank lower and lower, toward the pass in the west. Shadows stretched. A chilly breeze started moaning. Then one of the dozer drivers urgently waved to the rest. That had to mean *Hang on!* His cry of amazement pierced the diesel roar: "Fuck me up the asshole!" He pointed to something Lou couldn't make out.

After scuttling like a pair of ragged claws to position himself better, Lou did see what had astonished him: a black hole driven straight into the side of the mountain. Sure as shit, the mine went on after the supposed cave-in. Which meant . . . well, they'd have to see what it meant. One thing it meant was that Shmuel Birnbaum wasn't crazy—or not on account of that, anyway.

Lou was about to send men into that hole when explosive charges went off somewhere deep inside. The black opening fell in on itself. A great cloud of dust and more than a few rocks—some up to fist-sized and beyond—flew out. They clattered off the olive-drab machinery. One smashed a steam shovel's windshield. Another caught a bulldozer driver in the shoulder. His howl said it sure didn't do him any good.

But what those mine blasts said . . . Lou put it into plain, everyday English: "We've got the motherfuckers!"

NIGHT. BLACK NIGHT. BLACK AS THE INSIDE OF AN ELEPHANT. COLD, too. Bernie Cobb wished he had an overcoat, not just his thin, crappy Eisenhower jacket. He laughed at himself. *Why don't you wish for a hotel room and a bottle of bourbon and a naked blonde with legs up to there?* If you were gonna wish, you should *wish*.

It might be dark, but it wasn't quiet. Way down the mountainside from where he crouched in the gloom, Army engineers tore away at the blocked mineshaft. *Something* was sure as hell going on down there. Bernie still thought that was funny as hell. He'd been there when the demolitions guy closed that hole in the first place. If it turned out to be important now, the krauts had done a fuck of a job of disguising it. Well, they were good at that stuff. He'd seen as much since the minute he got to Europe.

Generators grunted down there, powering spotlights that bathed the work scene in harsh white light. Bernie looked every which way but that one. When he watched what was going on down there, his eyes lost their dark adaptation. He wondered how many of the guys scattered over the mountainside with him would think of that. Odds were most of 'em were rubbernecking for all they were worth.

He thought about passing the word to be careful about it. Only one thing stopped him—the likelihood the other GIs would tell him to fuck off. They knew everything there was to know about soldiering. Or if they didn't, they didn't want to hear about it. Chances were it wouldn't matter. If the Germans were trapped down there, they wouldn't be coming out.

Then again, even critters knew better than to dig a burrow with only one opening. Didn't Jerry? He could be an arrogant bastard. Maybe he'd figured nobody would ever find his perfect hidey-hole. Or maybe . . . Maybe the American troops who'd combed this territory had missed some escape hatches. That might not be so good.

Here and there, soldiers on the mountainside were smoking. Bernie could see the glowing coal at the end of a cigarette for a surprising distance. And when somebody lit a match or flicked a Zippo, the yellow flare drew the eye like a magnet. Most of the other guys didn't believe anything bad could happen. Bernie'd been through the mill. He was a confirmed pessimist.

He shivered and wished for an overcoat again. The blonde, the booze, and the bed might be more fun, but the coat was more practical.

His watch—GI issue—had glowing hands. Those wouldn't give him away—you couldn't see them from farther than about six inches. He held the watch up to his face. 0230. "Shit," he muttered. Another hour and a half before somebody came to relieve him.

He undid his fly and relieved himself. That, sadly, didn't get him out of being stuck here. He tramped along. Once he tripped over a rock he never saw. He flailed frantically, and almost dropped his grease gun. Only his Army boots saved him from a twisted ankle.

Any kraut in the neighborhood could have plugged him. So could any soldier allegedly on his side. He'd made enough noise to let them all know right where he was. If any of them had been as jittery as he was . . . But nobody fired at him. All the Americans assumed he was only a clumsy GI. Which he was, but they shouldn't have thought that way.

And then, on the slopes across the valley from him, the balloon really did go up. Mortars and machine guns and rifles all opened up at the same time. The incoming fire was aimed at the tiny area the spotlights lit up. Almost in slow motion, a driver tumbled off his seat atop a bulldozer. He started to clutch at himself as he fell, but never finished the motion—he must have been hit as bad as anyone could be. When he hit the ground, he didn't move.

"Fuck!" Bernie said. The krauts were way the hell up the mountains over there—he could see where their muzzle flashes were coming from. His submachine gun was as useless as a bow and arrow. It didn't have a fraction of the range he needed. All he could do up here was watch the fur fly.

The Germans were out and fighting in at least company strength. Bernie did some more swearing. They hadn't come out in those numbers since the surrender. And where the devil did they come out from? *From up out of the ground, dumbshit:* he answered his own question. Sure as hell, the American patrols that came through here hadn't found anywhere near all the hidden doorways Jerry'd dug for himself.

Somebody at the opening to the mineshaft had his head on straight. No more than thirty seconds after the Americans there started taking fire, the spotlights went out, plunging the whole valley into blackness. The mortars and MG42s would still have the range, but they couldn't see what they were shooting at any more. That had to make a big difference.

"Let's go help 'em!" a guy not far from Bernie yelled. He knew which way to run, anyhow. Bernie was all set to go stumbling down the side of the mountain, too.

But somebody else farther away said, "No! Sit tight!" with an officer's snap to his voice. The man went on, "If they popped up over there, they can pop up here, too. That attack may be a diversion. Hold your ground and see what happens next—that's an order."

Maybe it was a smart order. Maybe it was stupid, or even cowardly. No way to know till things played out.

The Americans had more than just bulldozers and steam shovels down closer to the valley floor. Armored cars started shooting at the German mortar and machine-gun positions. A 37mm gun wasn't much, but it was a hell of a lot better than nothing. And how could the krauts hurt the armored cars unless they dropped a mortar bomb right on top of one?

"C'mon, guys!" Bernie said, as if his team were trying to rally in the late innings.

Then he found out what the krauts could do. A streak of rocket fire lit up the night and slammed into one of those armored cars. *Panzerschreck* or *Panzerfaust*? Bernie couldn't tell from up here. It hardly mattered, anyhow. Both weapons were designed to pierce the frontal armor on a main battle tank. No wonder the armored car went up in a fireball.

"Jesus! Where'd that asshole come from?" Bernie said. How many secret holes did the Germans have? He had the bad feeling his side was liable to find out.

LOU WEISSBERG BARELY NOTICED WHEN THE FIRST COUPLE OF MORTAR bombs came in. The earth-movers made so much noise, the only thing that told him what was up was a graceful fountain of earth rising into the air—and a sharp steel fragment whining past his ear and clanking off a truck's fender.

A split second later, machine-gun bullets cracked by him. When they hit metal, they sounded like pebbles banging on a tin roof. When they hit flesh . . . A man tumbled from a bulldozer, thumped down onto the ground, and never moved again. The bullet that got him in the head might have been a baseball bat smacking into a clay jug full of water. Lou knew he would remember that sound the rest of his days, however much he tried to forget it.

"Holy shit! They're shooting at us!" someone yelled.

"Get down!" somebody else added.

That struck Lou as some of the best advice he'd ever heard. He flattened out on the ground and wriggled toward the closest vehicle. If he could put it between him and the deadly spray of bullets . . . it might not matter much, since the truck wasn't armored.

Halfway there, though, he had a rush of brains to the head. "Douse the lights!" he sang out, as loud as he could. For a wonder, somebody who could do something about it heard him. Blackness thudded down.

That didn't stop the machine-gun bullets from snarling by or the mortar bombs from hissing in and going *bam!,* the way he'd hoped it would. But then, what he knew about real combat would have fit in a K-ration can, if not on the head of a pin. That was, or had been, the advantage of CIC work. It was real soldiering: you tried to find out what the bad guys were up to, and to stop them from doing it. You mostly didn't go out there to shoot and get shot yourself. Except now Lou did.

He hadn't shit himself. He was moderately proud of that. Lying there with bullets and pieces of jagged metal flying every which way all around him, he didn't have much else to be proud of.

"Hey, Birnbaum! You there?" he shouted—in English, because he knew damn well his own side would figure Yiddish was German, and would try to liquidate him if he used it.

"Here," the DP answered. The word was as near identical as made no difference in all three languages.

"Good," Lou said: another cognate, though in the Yiddish dialect he and Shmuel Birnbaum shared, it came out more like *geet.* Birnbaum must have been through more combat than he had himself—a lot more, odds were. The DP knew what to do to try to stay alive. His reply hadn't come from more than three inches off the ground.

When the American armored cars started shooting back at the Germans on the mountainside, Lou let out a war whoop Sitting Bull would have been proud of. Shell bursts stalked the machine guns' malignant muzzle flashes. He whooped again when two MG42s fell silent in quick succession.

Then an armored car blew up. By the light of the fireball—and by the flame trail from the antitank rocket that had killed it—Lou spotted a kraut trying to slide back into the night. He opened up with his carbine. He couldn't do anything to the Germans farther away. This son of a bitch . . . Lou wasn't the only guy spraying lead at him. The Jerry went down. Whether he was hit or trying to avoid fire, Lou couldn't have said. He also had no idea whether he'd personally shot the German. He knew he never would.

Somebody running forward tripped over Lou and fell headlong. "Shit!" Lou said, at the same time as the other guy was going, "Motherfuck!" The heartfelt profanity convinced each of them the other was a Yank, so neither opened up.

The light from the blazing car let the other guy recognize Lou. "Well, you got it right, Captain," he said—he was the driver who'd thought this whole exercise was a waste of time. "Goddamn krauts were down there."

"Oh, maybe a few," Lou said dryly, which startled a laugh out of the driver.

Another German let fly with *Panzerfaust* or *Panzerschreck*. This one missed the armored car it was aimed at. It blew up when it hit something else a hundred yards beyond. Shrieks said it hurt people, too. But the armored car kept blasting away at the enemy on the mountainside, which counted for more.

"How long till the cavalry gets here?" the driver asked.

That made Lou think of Sitting Bull again. It also made him cuss some more. The first thing he should have done—well, maybe the second, after killing the lights—was to tell the radioman to scream for help. Dammit, he *wasn't* a front-line officer. He didn't think that way. He could hope the radioman had done it on his own. For that matter, he could hope the radioman had stayed alive to do it. But he should have made sure of it himself.

Combat was an unforgiving place. How many lives would one small mistake cost? And the more immediately crowding question: *will one of them be mine?*

REINHARD HEYDRICH SPOKE INTO A MICROPHONE: "GERMAN FREE-dom Front Radio. Code Four. German Freedom Front Radio. Code Four. German Freedom Front Radio. Code Four." He pushed the mike away. "All right. They know it's an emergency. If we get away, we get away. If we don't . . ." He made himself shrug. "Peiper's a solid man. He'll carry on."

"Hell with him," Hans Klein said. "I don't plan on dying now, any more than I did when those Czech bastards tried to bump you off."

"Good." Heydrich didn't plan on dying, either. That might have nothing to do with the price of beer, worse luck.

Faintly echoing down the corridors and shafts from very far away, gunfire said the diversionary force was punishing the Americans. In the short run, that would make them stop excavating. In the very slightly longer run, it would show them they needed to tear everything in this valley to pieces, the mountainsides included.

The move, then, was to take advantage of the short run and not to stick around for the very slightly longer run. Now, to bring it off. Heydrich pulled a panel off the wall. Behind the panel was a red button. Heydrich pushed it. "Let's go," he said, a certain amount of urgency in his voice.

"Right you are, sir." Klein grabbed a different microphone, one hooked up to the PA system. *"Achtung!"* His voice echoed through the mine. "Get your lanterns and torches. Lights going out—now!"

Logically, they didn't have to do that. As long as the last few hundred meters of the escape passage were dark, nothing else made any difference. But sometimes logic had nothing to do with anything. If you were leaving forever a place that had served you well for a long time, it was dead to you after that. And, being dead, it should be seen to die.

The generators sighed into silence. The lights went out. For a split second, the blackness was the deepest Heydrich had ever known. Then good old reliable Klein flicked on his torch. The beam speared through the inky air. When God said "Let there be light!" He must have seen a contrast as absolute as this. Reinhard Heydrich never had, not till now.

He turned on his own torch. That was better. Somebody not too far away let out a horrible yell. Probably a poor claustrophobic bastard who thought the darkness was swallowing him whole. If he didn't cut that out quick, they'd have to knock him over the head and leave him here. One way or another, he shut up. Heydrich was glad he didn't have to find out how.

When he went out into the corridor, more torch beams flashed up and down it. He wondered if all the men gathering there recognized him. He'd left his usual uniform and *Ritterkreuz* behind. His outfit said he was a *Sturmmann*—a lance-corporal. So did his papers.

But his voice . . . Everyone down here knew his voice. "We will use

Tunnel Three," he said crisply. "As some of you will know, the diversion on the far side of the valley is going well. The undisciplined Americans will surely rush every man they have into the fight against such a large, obvious enemy grouping. And that will clear the escape area for us. Any questions?"

No one said a word. Kurt Diebner stared owlishly through his thick glasses. He wore a sergeant's uniform, though no one could have made a less convincing soldier. Wirtz played another lance-corporal, and seemed slightly better suited to the role. They'd been told the other physicists were evacuated earlier. Maybe they believed that, maybe not. What they believed counted for little now.

"Some of you don't have greatcoats," Klein said. "Go get 'em. It'll be cold on the mountainside." Diebner was one of the men who needed a coat. Heydrich might have known he would be. A real SS noncom went with him as he got it, to make sure he didn't try to disappear.

"When we get over the mountains, there will be people to take us in," Heydrich promised. "We'll split up, we'll stay hidden, and before too long we'll be with our friends again. Once we are, we'll give the Amis the horse-laugh. For now—let's move!"

They moved. The only ones who seemed uncertain of the way were the physicists. The others had been down here longer than Wirtz and Diebner. And, unlike the slide-rule boys, the SS personnel were encouraged to explore their underground world. They might have needed to try an escape far more desperate than this one. Heydrich thought he could have done it in absolute darkness, without even a match to light the way. If you knew where to run your hand, shallow direction markers on the walls would guide you along. He was glad he didn't have to try it, though.

Like the other escape tunnels, Three was carved out of the living rock. It wasn't prettied up the way the main body of the command center was. It didn't resemble barracks and offices. Heydrich's boots thunked off stone as he hurried along. He led from the front. He might be dressed as a *Sturmmann,* but he didn't act like one.

Heydrich grunted in satisfaction when his torch showed the stairs ahead. They led to the camouflaged mountainside doorway that would let him slide out of this trap as he'd slid out of the one the Amis set when he rescued the German physicists.

He climbed the stairs. There it was: the underside of the stainless-steel escape hatch. It would have dirt and grass on top of it. It also had a periscope beside it. If someone needed to come out here by daylight, he could make sure it was safe. Heydrich pushed up the periscope now, too, but he couldn't see a goddamn thing. Either the diversionary party's attack had knocked out the Americans' lights or the Amis had had the sense to turn them off themselves.

Well, it wouldn't matter. "Kill your torches," he said. When the others had, he undogged the escape hatch and pushed up. It was heavy. He felt and heard roots and shoots tearing as he shoved. Then the hatchway swung open. Cold, grass-scented outside air poured into the tunnel.

"Come on!" he said. "North and west once we're out!"

"How will we know which way that is?" Diebner asked plaintively.

"I can steer by the stars, if there are stars. And if there aren't, I have a compass." Heydrich didn't bother hiding his scorn. "Now up! Move it!" He might have been a drill sergeant at physical training—except a drill sergeant wouldn't murder a man who couldn't keep up, while Heydrich intended to.

One by one, the Germans emerged. Heydrich looked around. No moon, but some stars. Once his eyes got used to nearly full dark again, he'd be fine.

BERNIE COBB SAT ON A BOULDER, WATCHING THE FIREFIGHT DOWN below. He wished like hell he were on his way down there to give the guys on his side a hand. He could slip off in the darkness, and that officer would never be the wiser. . . . How many other GIs had already done just that? More than a few, unless he missed his guess.

For the moment, discipline held Bernie here. For the moment. When they asked him why he hadn't helped out, what would he say? *I was only following orders,* maybe? That didn't cut it. Bernie knew it didn't. They'd already hanged plenty of death-camp guards who tried singing that song.

"Shit," he muttered, and then "Fuck," and then "Motherfucking son of a bitch." None of which helped. He stood up and took a couple of steps down the mountainside, drawn by the racket of automatic weapons and bursting shells.

Then he heard a much smaller noise behind him. There weren't supposed to be any noises back there. It might have been another American soldier heading down toward the fight. It might have been, yeah, but it didn't quite sound like that. Next thing Bernie knew, he was flat behind that boulder, the grease gun cradled in his hands, his index finger on the trigger. He didn't know what was going on up there, and he didn't want to find out the hard way.

The noise went on. It got louder. It sounded like somebody or something trying to push up through the grass from below. Unless it was the world's biggest fucking gopher (did they even have gophers over here?), that should have been impossible outside of a horror movie. It should have been, unless. . . .

Abruptly, the noise cut off. What followed was a perfectly human grunt of satisfaction, and what sounded like footsteps on stone or concrete. Then the footsteps were on dirt instead. And then somebody spoke in a low voice—but, unmistakably, in German.

Even as Bernie grabbed for a grenade, more people came up out of, well, whatever the hell that place was. An escape tunnel, he supposed. He waited. He'd only get one chance at this. He had to do it right the first time. How many of those assholes were there, anyway? Was it the whole fucking *Reichstag*? No—the other house was over on the far slope of the valley, making life miserable for the Americans down below.

At last, after what seemed like twenty minutes longer than forever, he didn't hear any more footfalls on stone. The krauts milled around on the grassy mountainside, muttering in soft voices. *Sorting out what to do before they do it,* Bernie thought. *Yeah, they're Germans, all right.*

Any second now, though, they'd go do it instead of talking about it. If he was gonna get 'em, best to do it while they were still bunched up. As quietly as he could, he pulled the grenade's pin. Then he rose up onto his knees and flung it into their midst. He heard a thump, a startled exclamation, a *blam!,* and all the screams he could've hoped for.

He fired a short burst from his grease gun. More screams! "Jerries!" he yelled at the top of his lungs. "Whole buncha fuckin' Jerries!" He squeezed off another burst and bellyflopped down behind the boulder again.

Just in time, too. Quite a few of the Germans had to be hurt. They all had to be discombobulated. All the same, some of them were pros. Bullets from one of their nasty assault rifles spanged off the boulder in front of Bernie and snarled by overhead. He slid to the left and returned fire again, more to give the krauts something new to worry about than in the serious expectation of hitting them.

If too many GIs had ignored the officer's orders, he was screwed. The Germans would flank him out and slaughter him like a fat hog on barbecue day. Sure as shit, here came urgent running footsteps, around toward the right side of the boulder. Hardly even looking, Bernie twisted and fired. His magazine ran dry, but not before he won himself a screech and a moan from the Jerries.

And then fire started coming in on the krauts from both sides. M-1s and grease guns could put a lot of lead in the air. "Thank you, Jesus!" Bernie murmured—he did still have friends in the neighborhood, after all. With those friends raking the Germans, they had too much on their plate to care about finishing him off.

He stuck another magazine on his submachine gun and banged away at them again. It wasn't aimed fire, but it didn't have to be. If you spat out enough bullets, some of them were bound to bite. And even the ones that didn't scared the crap out of people they just missed.

"Surrender!" somebody shouted in English, following it with *"Hände hoch!"*

Damned if that wasn't the officer who'd told everybody to sit tight. He'd turned out to be 112 percent right—probably right enough to win himself a medal.

Bernie wasn't sure any Germans were left *to* surrender. But someone called, *"Waffenstillstand! Bitte, Waffenstillstand!"* They wanted a truce. They even said please. No matter what they wanted or how polite they were, Bernie didn't stand up.

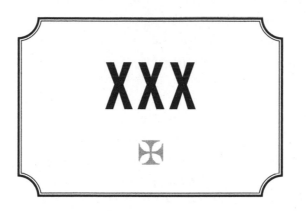

XXX

When Lou Weissberg heard the shooting start on the mountainside above him, he thought he was really and truly screwed. How many troops had the Nazis hidden in this stinking subterranean fortress of theirs? A division's worth? That had to be impossible . . . didn't it?

But the shooting up there didn't last long. As soon as it stopped, he forgot about it, because the diehards on the far slope were still doing their goddamnedest to murder him. And then, off in the distance, he saw the headlights of a truck convoy coming down from the head of the pass. He breathed a long heartfelt sigh of relief. As soon as the reinforcements arrived, his ass was saved.

And a great burden slid off his shoulders. He might have fucked up, but the radioman hadn't. As long as *somebody'd* kept his head, the story would probably have a happy ending.

Not right away, though. "They better kill those lights, or the krauts'll knock the shit out of 'em when they get a little closer," said a GI not far from him.

Sure as hell, mortar bombs did start dropping near the oncoming trucks. One of them took a direct hit, caught fire, and slewed off the road. The other drivers suddenly got smart. Almost in unison, their headlights went out.

The trucks stopped close enough to let Lou hear the order the officer in charge gave his men: "We're going up that hill, and we're gonna clean those assholes out!" Then he said one more thing: "Come on!"

They went. Every so often, one of them would shoot at something. That let the diehards know they were on the way. Machine-gun tracers stabbed through the night toward them. Other tracers replied—the new guys had machine guns of their own. And they had a mortar crew. Lou cheered when red sparks rose steeply into the air. But the American bombs burst short of the enemy positions. The Germans, damn them, had more range because they were shooting downhill.

Even so, they could see the writing on the wall. They quit pounding the men by the mineshaft. A couple of MG42s—*Hitler's saws,* the Russians called the vicious German machine guns—kept spraying death at the Americans advancing upslope. What were the fanatics not manning those machine guns doing? Trying to get away, unless Lou had lost his marbles.

He hardly cared. "Jesus," he said. "I think I lived through it." He realized how much he wanted a cigarette. He also realized a sniper still might ventilate his brainpan if he lit up. Regretfully, he didn't. He discovered he had a hunk of D-ration bar in the same pocket as his Luckies. Gnawing on the hard chocolate wasn't the same, but it was better than nothing.

He knew the Jerries' jig was up when the MG42s stopped ripping the air apart. Maybe their crews were dead, or maybe those men were trying to escape, too. Again, he had trouble caring. Nobody was trying to shoot him right this minute. That, he cared about. A few spatters of gunfire went on, up there on the mountainside, when Germans and Americans got too close to one another. But the main event was done.

Part of Lou wanted to sleep for a week. The rest wondered whether he'd ever sleep again with so much adrenaline zinging through him. Shaking his head, he stood up and started trying to think like an officer once more. "Do what you can for the wounded," he told the men who'd gone through the fight with him. "We should have medics here real soon now—docs, too, I hope."

"Some of these guys are bleeding bad, sir," a GI said out of the night. "They don't get plasma or something pretty damn quick, they ain't gonna make it."

"Yeah," Lou said unhappily. He didn't know what else to say, because he couldn't do one single thing about it.

Then he heard footsteps coming down from above. "Don't shoot, nobody!" someone called in accents surely American. "I gotta talk to the guy in charge of diggin' out this mine."

"That's me," Lou called. "What's up?"

The Yank thumped closer. Or was he an English-speaking German with an explosive vest, intent on vengeance? *Dr. Freud would call that paranoia,* Lou thought. *But you're not paranoid when they're really after you,* he retorted to himself. And then all that silly fluff blew out of his head, because the guy said, "We've got Heydrich's body up there. Somebody's one rich motherfucker."

"Heydrich?" Lou said dazedly. "For sure? No shit?"

"Looks just like him—we've all seen enough posters to know. His face ain't hardly tore up at all," the GI answered. "Papers on the body say he's some horseshit noncom, but you know what that kinda crap's gonna be worth. And there's another German noncom still breathin' who says it's him."

"Heydrich," Lou said again. He could hardly believe it, even if it was exactly what he'd been trying to accomplish. "Take me to him. This I gotta see."

He stumped uphill after the soldier. He stumbled in the darkness a couple of times, but he didn't fall. Before long, he was breathing hard. A desk job with the CIC didn't keep him in great shape. But he would have walked up the side of Mt. Everest on his hands to see Reinhard Heydrich dead.

No more shooting on this slope. Up ahead, a couple of flashlight beams marked the place where the GI was taking him. He saw American soldiers and guys in *Feldgrau* milling around. All the Germans kept hands above head.

"Here comes the captain," his escort called so nobody would get jumpy. "He wants to see the body."

Lots of German corpses in uniform lay in a compact knot, with others out around the fringes. "Looks like a bunch of 'em got taken by surprise," Lou remarked.

"Yes, sir," the soldier agreed. "They came out right behind one of our guys. He chucked a grenade into 'em, and then he started shooting 'em up."

"Good for him," Lou said. The air stank of blood and shit and smokeless powder. One of the GIs shone a flashlight at him. He waved. The beam swerved away: he was judged all right. He raised his voice a little: "Show me Heydrich."

"Over here, sir," another man called. He had a flashlight, too, and pointed it at a pale, still face on the ground. "This bastard."

Lou bent down. The dead man's pale, narrow eyes were still open, but he wasn't seeing anything. The face was long and thin. So was the nose, which had a slight kink in it. "Son of a gun," Lou whispered. "I think it really is him." He undid the corpse's tunic. Whoever this guy was, he'd taken grenade fragments and bullets in the chest and belly. "Shine it under his arm," Lou told the GI with the light. "I want to check his blood group."

He had to wipe away blood before he could make out the tattoo. It was an A—just what he wanted to see. "Well?" the soldier asked.

"Yeah." Lou felt as if he'd swallowed a big slug of straight bourbon. "It matches." He paused, remembering. "The guy who brought me up here said you'd captured another Jerry in noncom's clothes who could ID him."

"That's right, sir." The other American turned away for a moment. "Hey, Manny! Bring that cocksucker over here. The captain wants him."

"Sure," said somebody—presumably Manny. He spoke a couple of words of rudimentary German: *"Du! Komm!"*

Unlike Heydrich, the man who came over to Lou blinked when the GI shone a flashlight in his eyes. He looked like a guy who'd been a noncom for a long time—put a different uniform on him and he would have made a perfect American tech sergeant. "Who are you?" Lou asked. He pointed to the dead man. "How do you know this is Heydrich?"

"I am *Oberscharführer* Johannes Klein," the noncom answered. "I was the *Reichsprotektor*'s driver, and then his aide when we went underground."

"Wow," Lou said. Klein's name was on his list, too—on all kinds of CIC lists. Nobody seemed to know what he looked like. Well, here he was, in the flesh. Quite a bit of flesh, too. Whatever the diehards had been doing underground, they hadn't been starving. Lou dragged his attention back to the business at hand. "So what happened here? What went wrong for you?"

"He made a mistake," Klein answered matter-of-factly. He sounded like an American noncom giving an officer the back of his hand, too. "He thought the diversionary attack would pull your men off this side of the mountain. He turned out to be wrong. We had just come out when. . . ." He spread his hands. One of them had blood on it, but it wasn't his.

Another German came over. He stared down at Heydrich's body for a long time. "So he is truly dead," he muttered, more to himself than to Lou.

"What difference does it make to you? Who are you, anyway?" Lou asked him *auf Deutsch.*

"I am Karl Wirtz," the man answered in fluent British English.

For a second, the name didn't mean anything to Lou. Then it did. "The physicist!" he exclaimed. Wirtz nodded. Lou tried to ask something that wasn't too dumb. The best he could come up with was, "Where are your, uh, colleagues?"

"Poor Professor Diebner lies over there. Sadly, he is dead," Wirtz said. "The others . . . I do not know what has happened to the others." He nodded toward Klein. "But I believe the *Oberscharführer* may."

"How about it?" Lou said. Johannes Klein only shrugged. Wirtz's grimace told what he thought of that. Lou thought the same thing. "So—you disposed of them, did you?"

Klein shrugged again. "At the *Reichsprotektor's* order. They could never have kept up during the escape." His shoulders went up and down one more time. "Fat lot of good it turned out to do."

Do you always kill people on your own side? Lou didn't ask it, however much he wanted to. He was too sure Klein would look at him and say something like *Of course I do, if my superior tells me to.* He'd already been down that road with too many other Germans. So he stuck to what might be immediately useful: "Where were you going to go after you came out of your tunnel?"

"We were to split up and head for safe houses in the next valley," Klein said. "The only one I know of is the one I was to go to. And then—" He stopped.

"Then what? Come on—talk," Lou said. He didn't believe Klein knew about only one safe house, either. If he was Heydrich's aide, wouldn't he have found out about plenty of them?

"Well, you will have heard this by now, I'm sure." The *Oberschar-führer* seemed to be talking himself into talking, so to speak. After a moment, he went on, "Sooner or later, Jochen Peiper's people would pick us up and take us to his headquarters."

"Ah?" Lou's ears quivered and came to attention. "And where's that?"

"I have no idea. I never tried to find out. I suppose the *Reichspro-tektor* must have known, but I don't think anyone else down below"—Klein stamped his foot on the mountainside—"had any idea. What we weren't told, we couldn't give away if we got caught."

"Huh," Lou said. "We'll see about that." The kraut gave a much more elaborate denial here than he had about the safe houses. Maybe that meant he was bullshitting. On the other hand, maybe it meant he was telling the exact truth. Some remorseless squeezing of everybody left alive who'd come up out of the ground would tell the tale. Lou tried another question: "What do you know about Peiper?"

"Only that the *Reichsprotektor* thought he was an able man," Klein said.

Lou grunted. He didn't know as much about Jochen Peiper as he wished he did. Nobody outside the fanatics' shadowy network did. Peiper had been a promising and rapidly rising young panzer officer in the *Waffen*-SS till he dropped out of sight late in 1943. Since V-E Day, Heydrich had been the German Freedom Front's visible face. Could Peiper step out of the shadows and keep the enemy fighting? Lou hoped like hell the answer was no.

The ground under his feet rumbled and jerked. "What was that?" Professor Wirtz yipped.

"Explosives and incendiaries," Klein said calmly. "The *Reichspro-tektor* started the timer before we left. No one will learn anything from what we could not bring." Even now, he sounded proud of Heydrich.

"Aw, shit," Lou said wearily. Germanic thoroughness could drive you nuts. It could also screw you to the wall. Not wanting to think about that, he switched to English and asked, "Where's the guy who jumped on the Jerries after they came out of their hole in the ground?"

" 'At's me." The dogface who came up looked like . . . a dogface. "Name's Bernie Cobb. Watcha need, sir?"

"Well, Cobb, there's a Jewish DP down by the mineshaft"—Lou hoped like anything that Birnbaum was still in one piece—"who's got a pretty fair claim to part of the reward for Heydrich. I'd say you're odds-on for the rest."

"Holy fuck." Cobb started to laugh. "Wasn't so long ago I told a buddy I'd never catch the asshole on my own. Shows what I know, don't it?"

"Sure does," Lou sad. "But you were on the ball, and it paid off."

"When the shooting started, we wanted to go down and give you guys a hand," Cobb said. "But one of our officers held us in position. That's why I was at where I was at. He oughta get a chunk."

"Maybe he will," Lou said.

Cobb pointed at him. "And what about you, Captain? Weren't you the guy in charge of digging these fuckers out? That's who Jonesy went to get. Sounds like you have a claim on some yourself."

"Me?" Lou's voice hadn't broken like this since he was seventeen. "You gotta be kidding!"

"They're gonna give it to somebody," Bernie Cobb said. "If you flushed out dickhead here"—he nodded toward Heydrich's corpse— "you deserve a chunk."

Do I want any? Lou wondered. *How many Jews, how many Americans, did that son of a bitch murder? Can I take money because of a man like that? But can I turn down a big part of a million bucks? Wouldn't my wife murder me if I did? Wouldn't any jury in the world acquit her if she did?*

"Fuck it. We'll sort it out later," he said. Dawn was starting to lighten the eastern sky. A new day was coming.

Tom Schmidt hadn't seen President Truman so chipper since— when? He couldn't remember ever seeing Truman so chipper. The President beamed at the reporters filing into the White House press room.

"We killed the black-hearted son of a bitch," Truman announced without preamble. "Reinhard Heydrich, who earned the lovely nick-names of Butcher, Hangman, and Man with the Iron Heart, got what he deserved in the Bavarian Alps last night. The head of the lie called the German Freedom Front died trying to escape his underground headquarters as American troops were digging him out. Most of the other people in that hole in the ground—maybe all of them—were also captured or killed." He grinned out at the assembled reporters. "How about *that,* boys?"

They all tried to shout questions at once. "Who got him?" seemed to be the one that came most often.

Truman glanced down at his notes. "The man who seems likeliest to have done it is Private Bernard Cobb. He comes from New Mex-ico, a little town near Albuquerque."

"Are they sure it's Heydrich?" Tom asked before anybody else could get in a different question. "How do they know?"

"It's really him, Tom, no matter how much that disappoints you and the *Tribune,*" the President jabbed, and his grin got even wider. "An officer who knows what he looks like identified him at the scene. German prisoners confirmed his identity. His blood-group tattoo matches Heydrich's group—his blood type, we'd say here. And his fingerprints match, too. The Nazis could pull a lot of stunts, but I don't see how they could manage that."

Tom didn't see how they could, either. No matter what Harry Tru-man thought, he wasn't sorry Heydrich was dead. Anybody who'd spent any time at all in post-surrender Germany knew Reinhard Hey-drich was indeed a black-hearted son of a bitch. Whether he was sorry the Truman administration was taking credit for Heydrich's long-overdue demise might be a different story.

"How'd we finally catch him?" another reporter asked.

Truman beamed at him. "Because the bastard's own past came back to bite him, that's how. The Nazis used slave laborers to dig their hideouts. Then they killed them—dead men tell no tales. But this man lived through Auschwitz. Eventually, Soviet intelligence learned he had important information. The Russians passed him on to us, because Heydrich's hole was in our zone. We found it, and Hey-drich was in it, and now we don't have to worry about him any more."

"We worked with the Russians?" the reporters yelled—except for the ones who yelled, "The Russians worked with us?"

"That's right." Truman nodded happily. "We sure did. They sure did. When it comes to the damn Nazis, everybody works together against them. Everybody in the whole world, near as I can see, except the Republicans in Congress and some chuckleheads who've started a silly movement that means well but can't see what's important in the long run—oh, and some reporters who want us to fail in Germany because they think writing snotty stories sells papers."

To Tom and at least half a dozen other people in the press room, that was waving a red flag in front of a bull. "Well, we got him even though we're bringing our troops home, right?" another reporter said.

"We didn't catch him *because* we're bringing them home. We caught him *in spite of* that," the President snapped. "If we'd learned of this a few months from now, we wouldn't have had the manpower to do anything about it. Heydrich would still be down there thumbing his nose at us."

"Now that he's dead, you expect the German Freedom Front to fold up and die with him, right?" somebody else called before Tom could.

"We hope it will." All of a sudden, Truman turned cagey. "We don't know that for a fact. We ought to leave men in Germany in case it doesn't."

"Wait a minute!" Tom said. "A minute ago, getting rid of Heydrich was the greatest thing ever. Now it may not mean anything? Don't you want it both ways?"

"I want to make sure Americans can stay safe and secure. Why do you have trouble seeing that?" Truman said.

"Because lots of Americans keep getting killed in Germany? Because the German Freedom Front hasn't gone away?" Tom suggested. "How does that make us safe and secure?"

The President let out an exasperated sniff. "Because we aren't getting ready to fight the Third World War against the Germans, that's how. Shall we declare victory and then pull out? I couldn't look the American people in the eye if we pulled a stunt like that."

"But if the fanatics quiet down now that Heydrich's dead, doesn't that mean we don't need to stay any more?"

"Not if they're playing possum till we're gone," Truman answered. "They aren't fools, unlike some people I could name." He stared hard in Tom's direction.

"Love you, too, sir," Tom said, and got a chuckle from Truman. HEYDRICH'S GONE—SO WHAT? Tom scribbled in his notebook. If he couldn't build a column around that, he wasn't half trying.

"FUCK ME IN THE MOUTH! THEY GOT HIM!" VLADIMIR BOKOV exulted.

"They did," Colonel Shteinberg agreed. "I wouldn't have bet on it when you gave them that Birnbaum, but they did. Now we find out how much difference it ends up making."

"It's got to make some," Bokov said. "We haven't been the same here since the Nazis poisoned so many officers at the New Year's Eve celebration. Only stands to reason that losing their top leader will hurt them, too."

"Well, yes, when you put it like that. They're bound to be less efficient for a while—maybe less dangerous, too." Shteinberg paused to light a cigarette before adding, "But that's not the point."

"Comrade Colonel?" Bokov said, in lieu of *Well, what* is *the point, dammit?* He knew how much rope the Jew gave him, and the answer here was *not enough for that.*

Moisei Shteinberg inhaled, blew out smoke, inhaled again, and finally said, "After the Heydrichites pulled off the New Year's Eve massacre, what did we do?"

"We went after them. What else?" Bokov knew he'd never forget the benzedrine buzz—or the grippe it battled. He also knew he'd never forget how flattened he'd been getting over both of them at once.

"There you go, Volodya." If Shteinberg's nod said Bokov was slower than he might have been, it also said he'd got where he needed to go. Shteinberg continued, "*That's* the point. We didn't give up. We didn't figure we'd lost and run away like a litter of scared puppies."

"The way the Americans are now," Bokov put in.

"Yes." But Colonel Shteinberg brushed that aside: "So now we have to see what the Heydrichites do without Heydrich. If they say,

'We can't go on without the *Reichsprotektor*,' and they forget about their weapons and go back to being farmers and shopkeepers and factory workers, we've won. But if they have the spirit to keep fighting under a new commander—in that case, we didn't do as much as we would have wanted to."

Reluctantly, Bokov nodded back. "Well, you're right, Comrade Colonel," he allowed. Part of his reluctance involved admitting to himself that Shteinberg really was a clever Jew—more clever than he was himself, dammit. And part involved acknowledging that the Fascist bandits really might regroup and keep harassing Soviet authorities—and, incidentally, the Anglo-Americans. "*Bozhemoi,* but I want them to fold up like a concertina!"

"Oh, so do I, Volodya. If I prayed, that's what I would pray for." Colonel Shteinberg blew out a long stream of smoke and ground out the cigarette. "But we're men now, yes? Not children, I mean. You don't get what you wish for, and you'd better remember it. You get what you get, and you have to make the best of it, whatever it turns out to be. That's what a man does. Am I right or am I wrong?"

Bokov couldn't very well say he was wrong. It might be a cold-blooded—no, a cold-hearted—way to look at the world, but if you looked at it any other way you'd end up dead or in a camp in short order. What Bokov did say was, "Let's see General Vlasov make the best of this!"

"Oh, he will," Shteinberg said, but the way he smiled said how little he loved Yuri Vlasov himself. Bokov doubted whether Vlasov's mother could have loved him. If she had, wouldn't the son of a bitch have come out better? Colonel Shteinberg said, "He'll show his superiors that he authorized the transfer of Prisoner Birnbaum to the Americans, and that it turned out well. He doesn't need any more than that to cover his own worthless ass."

"*Da,*" Bokov said resignedly. They'd both known from the beginning that Vlasov would do something like that if handing Birnbaum over gave good results. Bokov's anger flared anyhow. "He should have done it sooner, the pigheaded son of a bitch!"

"Of course he should. But saying no is always easier. So is doing nothing. If you do nothing, you can't very well do anything wrong. All you have to say is, you were exercising due caution." Shteinberg made the words—which Bokov himself had used more often than he suddenly cared to remember—sound faintly, or perhaps not so faintly, obscene.

Bokov lit a cigarette of his own—a good Russian Belomor, not an American brand. He needed it. The White Sea tasted the way a cigarette ought to. You took a drag on one of these, you knew you were smoking something! The name of the brand commemorated the opening of the White Sea canal before the war. Most Soviet citizens knew it had opened, and were proud of that. They knew no more. Bokov did. But not even the NKVD captain knew how many tens of thousands of *zeks* had given up the ghost digging the canal with picks and shovels in weather that made Leningrad's look tropical. Well, none of them would trouble the state's security again.

Which led to another security question: "Comrade Colonel, what do we do when the Americans finish clearing out? The English won't be far behind them, either."

"That damned atom bomb," Moisei Shteinberg said, as he had the last time Bokov asked the same question. It was more urgent, less hypothetical, than it had been then. But *that damned atom bomb* remained a complete and depressing answer. Till the Soviet Union had its own—which would, of course, be used only in the cause of peace—Marshal Stalin's hands were tied.

"How long?" Bokov demanded, as if security would let an ordinary NKVD colonel learn such things.

And, naturally, Shteinberg just shrugged. "When we do—that's all I can tell you. No, wait." He caught himself. "There's one thing more. Heydrich was hiding the German physicists he kidnapped in his headquarters. They're all supposed to be dead or captured. So that will slow the fanatics down even if worse comes to worst." He shrugged again, this time in a very Jewish way, as if to say, *It's not so good, but maybe it could be worse.*

Bokov knew what *if worse comes to worst meant,* too. It meant a revived Fascist state in western Germany, and damn all the USSR could do about it. That was about as bad as things could get, all right. "Let's hope they do give up now that Heydrich's dead and gone," he said.

"Yes," Shteinberg said. "Let's."

JOCHEN PEIPER HADN'T WANTED TO GO DOWN INTO A HOLE IN THE ground and pull it in after him. That was putting it mildly. The *Waffen*-SS hadn't had many better panzer officers. He'd scared the shit out of the Ivans, and well he might have. The last thing he'd looked for was a peremptory order from Reinhard Heydrich. He'd taken his career—maybe his life—in his hands and gone over Heydrich's head to Heinrich Himmler. All that got him was an even more peremptory order to shut up and do what Heydrich told him to.

So he did. As the *Reich* crumbled into ruin, he slowly realized he was doing something worthwhile, even if it wasn't what he'd had in mind when he signed up for the SS. If Germany was going to rebuild itself, if it wasn't going to get slammed into an American or Russian mold, it had to hold on to its own spirit and do its best to drive the occupiers nuts.

Fighting the long underground war was less exciting than a panzer battle. It turned out to be more intricate, more exacting. Was it more interesting? Peiper didn't want to admit that, even to himself. He did what he could to help the cause of German liberty. He did what the *Reichsprotektor* told him to do. He quit complaining. No one would have listened to him any which way.

He didn't even complain about being a spare tire. Like any good commander, Heydrich had run the resistance movement his own way. As there had been only one *Führer* before him, there was only one *Reichsprotektor*.

And now I'm it, Peiper thought. The radio, the newspapers, and the magazines in American-occupied Germany were full of gloating glee because Heydrich had fallen in service of the cause. He'd been photographed dead more often than he ever was alive. THE GERMAN FREEDOM FRONT'S FRONT MAN IS NO MORE, a typical headline proclaimed proudly.

Jochen Peiper assembled the men who shared the underground secondary headquarters with him. "We're fighting a war, and when you fight a war you go on even if you lose your general," he said. "The man who's next in line steps up, and you go on. The *Reichsprotektor* was a great German. We'll miss him. He gave us hope for freedom even in the blackest days. He inspired the Werewolves to remind the enemy Germany wasn't altogether beaten. The best way to honor his memory is to go on and free our country from the invaders' yoke."

He eyed them. A few of the fighters didn't want to meet his gaze. They feared—or else they hoped, which would be worse—the struggle had died with the *Reichsprotektor.* But most of the SS men and soldiers seemed ready to keep on soldiering. That was what Peiper most wanted to see. He had to hope he wasn't seeing it regardless of whether it was there or not.

"We can do this. We can, dammit!" he insisted. "We've already got the Americans on the run. We have to show them they haven't cut the heart out of us. Reinhard Heydrich *was* a great man, a great German, a great National Socialist. No one would say anything different. But when great men fall, the ones they leave behind have to keep up the battle. And the *Reichsprotektor* had some ideas he didn't live to use. We'll see how wild they can drive the enemy."

"What kind of ideas?" a man inquired.

"Well, for instance . . ." Peiper talked for some little while. He could have kissed the noncom who'd asked the question. If the troops were interested in what to try next, they wouldn't brood because they'd lost their longtime commander. Or Peiper could hope they wouldn't, anyhow.

But then another man asked, "Can the Americans sniff us out now?"

After a moment's hesitation, Peiper answered, "Anything that can happen can happen to you, Heinz. They were supposed to use up all the workers who dug out the *Reichsprotektor*'s headquarters, but it sounds like somebody got through in spite of everything. That's just bad luck. I don't think it's likely that that kind of thing could crop up here, too, but it's possible."

Unlike Heydrich, he'd had no direct role in eliminating *Untermenschen.* He'd been a combat soldier before his superiors tapped him for this slot. But he wasn't naïve about what the *Reich* had been up to. He talked about it in the same allusive, elusive, oddly dispassionate way someone who'd served in an extermination camp might have. If you talked about it that way, you didn't dwell on what you were actually doing. Workers got used up, not killed. The survivor got through; he didn't live. Jochen wished to God the bastard hadn't lived.

Heinz had another awkward question: "What will we do without the physicists the *Reichsprotektor* liberated?"

"The best we can." Peiper spread his hands. "I don't know what else to tell you. We'll be able to find other scientists who know some of what they knew, and we'll find more people who can learn. We're Germans. Other people would come here to study before the war. There are bound to be men who can do what we need. Remember, we know it's possible now, and we didn't during the war."

Heinz nodded, apparently satisfied. Peiper wasn't satisfied himself—not even close. He knew too well that losing those physicists meant Germany would take longer to build atom bombs. And he knew the resurgent *Reich* would need those bombs to keep it safe from the Americans and the Russians.

But, as he'd told the junior officer, all you could do was all you could do. He wasn't even sure the fighters outside this headquarters would obey his orders. He had to nail that down first. If they wouldn't follow him, the Amis and Tommies and Ivans had won after all. After keeping up the fight for so long despite the surrender of *Wehrmacht* and government, giving up now would be tragic.

He went back to his office to draft a proclamation. *The struggle continues,* he wrote. *The hope for National Socialism, the hope for a revived German folkish state, does not lie in any one man. A man may fall. Adolf Hitler did; now Reinhard Heydrich has as well. But the cause goes on. The cause will always go on, because it is right and just. We shall not rest until we free our Fatherland.* Sieg heil!

He looked it over, then nodded to himself. Yes, it would definitely do. He signed his name. After another moment's hesitation, he added *Reichsprotektor* below the signature. Even though Heydrich had originally had the title because he governed the protectorate of Bohemia and Moravia, it also suited a partisan leader trying to shield Germany from the foes who oppressed her.

The headquarters had a small print shop, with a hand press not much different from the ones Martin Luther's printers would have used. That would be plenty to get out a few hundred copies of the proclamation. Sympathetic printers in the U.S. and British zones could make thousands more once it reached them. Word would spread.

Which raised another question. Peiper wondered whether his fighters ought to stay quiet for a while. It might lull the enemy into a false sense of security. It would let Peiper consolidate his own authority within the German Freedom Front. Everybody'd known, and known of—and feared—Heydrich. By the nature of things, the number two man in any outfit was far more anonymous.

Peiper drummed his fingers on the desk. *"Nein,"* he muttered. Heydrich hadn't made the Americans start bailing out of their zone by acting meek and mild. He'd harried them so harshly that they were glad to go. The best way to keep them on the run was to keep goosing them.

And the Russians . . . ! No Russian ever born had ever admired meekness and mildness. The only way to get Ivan's attention was to hit him in the face, and to keep on hitting him till he had to notice you. Peiper had fought the Red Army out in the open till he was recruited for the twilight struggle. Running it out of the Soviet zone wouldn't be easy. He knew that. But not fighting, against the Russians, meant giving up.

He'd found his answers. He knew what kind of orders to give. Whether anyone would listen to them . . . He shook his head and said *"Nein"* again, louder this time. Some people would always follow a superior's commands. He could use them to eliminate the fainthearts. No, to eliminate a few of them. That should scare the rest back into obedience. Fear was as much a weapon as an assault rifle.

It all seemed simple and straightforward. Peiper laughed at himself. If everything were as simple and straightforward as it seemed, the *Reich* would never have got itself into this mess. Well, the job of getting it out had landed on his shoulders. He'd do his damnedest.

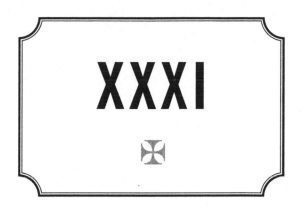

XXXI

When the phone rang, it was the Mothers Against the Madness in Germany line. It usually was, these days. "Diana McGraw," Diana said in her crisp public voice.

"Hi, Mrs. McGraw. E. A. Stuart here, from the *Times,*" the reporter replied in her ear.

"Hello, E.A. How are you?" Diana said. Only the *Indianapolis Times,* not the one from Los Angeles, let alone New York's. Well, she lived next door to Indianapolis. And other papers would pick up whatever she said to Stuart. She'd got used to having people all over the world pay attention to what she thought. She liked it, in fact.

"I'm fine, thanks. Yourself?" Unlike reporters from far away, E.A. knew her well enough to chitchat for a bit before he got down to business. He might have thought it would soften her up. And he might have been right.

"Doing all right." Diana wasn't lying . . . too much. Her conscience still gnawed at her for that San Francisco night. She did feel bad about it—and she felt worse because she'd felt so good while it was going on. *I was drunk,* she told herself. *I didn't know what I was doing.* The first part of that was true. The rest? She'd known what she was doing, all right. And she'd gone and done it. And she'd enjoyed it like anything—then. Afterwards was a different story. Afterwards commonly was. She ducked away from the worries: "What can I do for you this morning?"

"Well, I was wondering if you wanted to comment on the death of Reinhard Heydrich."

"I'm glad the miserable skunk is dead," Diana said at once. "So many people have called me a Nazi, and it's a filthy lie. You know it's a lie, E.A. The maniacs that evil so-and-so led murdered my Pat. If we'd caught him alive, I'd've been glad to string him up myself."

"To hang the Hangman?" Stuart asked.

Diana nodded, which the reporter couldn't see. "That's right," she said. "That's just right."

"Okay." By the pause, E. A. Stuart was likely nodding, too. "How do you think his death changes the situation in Germany?"

Since Diana'd been thinking about that ever since the news broke, she could answer without the least hesitation: "It just gives us one more reason to keep bringing our troops back to America. We've been saying all along that we wanted him dead, that we needed him dead, that he was the most dangerous man in the world, and I don't know what all else. Fine. Now he's dead. Now the fanatics can't cause anywhere near as much trouble as they could before. That means we've got even less excuse for sticking around. The sooner all the soldiers come home, the better."

"Hang on," Stuart said. She could hear him scribbling notes. Even though he took shorthand, she'd got ahead of him. Then he asked, "What would have happened if all the American soldiers were out of Germany before we found out where Heydrich was hiding out?"

Diana scowled at the telephone. *Doggone it, E.A., you're supposed to be on my side.* But she didn't say it out loud. He would have to deny it, and he might have to go out of his way to show it wasn't true. That wouldn't be so good.

"Maybe we would have gone back after him. I've never said we shouldn't get rid of him," she answered. "Or maybe the German police could have dug him out on their own."

"Mm. Maybe." Stuart didn't sound as if he believed it. He tried a different kind of question: "How do you feel about President Truman taking credit for bumping him off?"

"If we'd caught Heydrich right after V-E day, he would've been entitled to some," Diana said tartly. "Now we're only a couple of months away from 1948. It's not just about time Heydrich's dead—it's way past time."

"Hang on," E. A. Stuart said once more, and then, "Okey-doke. Got it. Thanks a lot, Mrs. McGraw. 'Bye." He hung up.

"So long." Diana set the phone down, too. She heated up the coffee, took the pot off the stove, and poured herself a cup. It wasn't as good as it had been when she made it right after she and Ed got up, but it wasn't too much like battery acid yet. And she was too lazy to fix a fresh pot.

Battery acid. She shook her head. Would the comparison even have occurred to her if Ed hadn't worked at the Delco-Remy plant since the Year One? How many car and truck batteries did they turn out there every year? Zillions—that was all she knew.

The phone rang again. This time, it was a reporter from the *St. Louis Post-Dispatch*. He wanted to find out what she thought of Heydrich's untimely demise, too. She was still all for it. He asked almost the same questions as E. A. Stuart had. Later on, she got a call from the *Boston Globe*, and one from the *Los Angeles Mirror-News*.

"Do you feel like you've got revenge for your son now?" the reporter from the *Mirror-News* asked.

That was a more . . . interesting question than she usually got. "I don't know," she said slowly. "When it's your own flesh and blood . . . No, it's not revenge, or not enough revenge. I don't think there can be enough revenge for your own child. I'm still glad Heydrich's dead, though."

"You and everybody else. Well, thanks." The reporter didn't even say good-bye. He just went off to write up his piece.

In between phone calls, life went on. Diana sliced potatoes and carrots and chopped onions and put them into a pan with a pot roast. If a few tears fell, she could blame them on the onions. Supper went into the oven.

Ed got home about twenty to six, the way he always did. He took a Burgie out of the icebox, drank it faster than he was in the habit of doing, and then opened another one. "You all right?" Diana asked. "You don't do that very often." Ever since she got back from San Francisco, she'd watched him more closely than usual.

He let out a wordless grunt and got to work on the second beer. That alarmed her. Everything alarmed her these days—a sure sign of her guilty conscience. That same guilty conscience had made her extra accommodating in the bedroom since coming home. If only it had made her take more pleasure in what went on there.

Doggedly, she tried again: "Everything all right at the plant?"

"Fine," Ed said. He poured down the Burgermeister.

He opened another one to go with supper. "You'll get snockered," Diana warned. She remembered too well what had happened when she got snockered. Ed just shrugged. He killed the beer, and killed one more while she was doing the dishes.

That seemed to get him where he needed to go. While she dried the last fork and put away the dish towel, he sat there waiting. "It's a mess, isn't it?" he said, sounding sad and resigned at the same time.

"What is?" Her voice, by contrast, was a thin, nervous squeak.

"Us," he said, and then, as if that weren't comprehensive enough, "Everything."

"What? We're fine! I love you!" *The lady doth protest too much, methinks.* Diana hadn't read any Shakespeare since high school. Why did that particular line have to come back to her right now? Why? Because she was protesting too goddamn much—why else?

"Yeah, well . . ." Ed turned toward the icebox, as if to get one more Burgie. But he didn't. His smile was sad, too, sad and sweet at the same time. "You've got your head turned, babe. It took a while, but you do."

"What are you talking about?" Diana wouldn't have sounded so scared if she hadn't known precisely what he was talking about.

He spelled it out for her anyhow: "You go here, you go there, you go all over the darn place. Reporters call you all the time. How many calls you get today on account of Heydrich's kicked the bucket?"

"Four." Automatically, she answered with the truth.

"Uh-huh." Ed nodded. "And you hang around with big shots when you go traveling. Congressmen and mayors and Lord knows who all. And they figure you're a big shot, too, 'cause you've got all this clout you made for yourself, and that's great. And I bet they hit on you, too—you're a darn good-lookin' gal. I oughta know, huh? And then you come home."

"I'm glad to come home," Diana said. And she always had been, till this last trip.

Ed went on as if she hadn't spoken: "You come home, and waddaya got? Me. Foreman at Delco-Remy. Ain't gonna be anything more than foreman at Delco-Remy if I get as old as Methuselah. And it isn't enough any more. I can tell."

"How?" she whispered. Did she have a scarlet A on her chest? Did she remember high-school lit classes better than she'd ever thought she could? She sure did, but why, for God's sake?

"How?" Her husband snorted. "I've known you for thirty years, that's how. I'm not smart like a big shot, but I'm not blind, either."

Diana started to cry. "I didn't want this to happen. I didn't want any of this to happen—not any of it. If Pat was alive—" She cried harder. Ed hadn't really guessed. She hadn't really admitted anything, either. But how much difference did that make? He'd nailed everything else down tight. Hadn't he just! "What are we going to do?" she wailed.

His shoulder went up and down in a tired shrug. "I dunno, babe. What *are* we gonna do?"

When it came to American foreign policy, she found answers with the greatest of ease, and she was always sure they were right. Here? Here she had no answers at all. She started crying again.

"HE'S DEAD. GOOD RIDDANCE TO HIM," JERRY DUNCAN SAID ON THE House floor. "And now, God willing, the fanatics in Germany will see that their cause is hopeless. And, I note, this is all happening even though our troops are coming home from Europe. The world hasn't fallen to pieces. And it won't fall to pieces, in spite of the doomsayers' croakings in this very House."

Congressmen who agreed with him clapped and cheered. Congressmen who didn't were much less polite. Boos, catcalls, shaken fists . . . Jerry didn't seen any upraised middle fingers this time, which was progress of a sort. He did hear several insistent shouts: "Mr. Speaker! Mr. Speaker! *Mr. Speaker!*"

Joe Martin pointed. "The chair recognizes the Representative from California."

"Thank you, Mr. Speaker," Helen Gahagan Douglas said.

Maybe Martin had recognized her because her voice stood out among those of the Democrats clamoring for his notice (and well it might—not only was she a woman, but she'd also sung opera, so she had impressive volume when she needed it). Or maybe he'd thought she would be milder than most of her colleagues. If he had, he was unduly optimistic. Now that the wartime consensus lay dead, nobody saw much point to mildness any more.

And Congresswoman Douglas proved as much, saying, "Many years ago, Chancellor Bismarck remarked that God loved children, drunkards, and the United States of America. The way things are these days, I hesitate to speak well of any German, but it seems to me that Bismarck knew what he was talking about. The distinguished gentleman from Indiana wouldn't be celebrating Reinhard Heydrich's death today if he'd got his own heart's desire a few months earlier. If we didn't have any men on the ground to dig him out once we learned where he hid, he'd still be down there sneering at us."

People on her side applauded. People on Jerry's side were at least as rude to Helen Gahagan Douglas as people who agreed with her had been to him. The first thing that ran through his mind was *Well, fuck you, bitch*. He didn't say it. Consensus might have expired, but civility, though hospitalized, still breathed.

And she *wasn't* a bitch, and Jerry knew it perfectly well when he wasn't pissed off himself. She was a highly capable Congresswoman who disagreed with him on the President's German policy. The way things went these days, the distinction seemed ever more academic.

"Mr. Speaker!" Jerry said.

"You have the floor, Mr. Duncan," Joe Martin replied.

"Thanks, Mr. Speaker. How many of our young men did the fanatics murder and torture while we lingered in Germany because President Truman couldn't see we didn't belong there? Are they a fair trade for Heydrich?" Jerry asked. Attacking the President was easier and more likely to be profitable than swinging directly at Helen Gahagan Douglas.

She didn't mind swinging right at him. "If someone makes a habit of murdering and torturing our young men—and that's what the

Nazis do, no doubt about it—isn't it better to make sure he can't do it any more than to run away from him?" she demanded.

"I would say yes, except the Army has made it much too plain they can't do that, either," Jerry answered.

"How do you expect it to, when you've been doing everything you could to hamstring it since V-E Day?" Helen Gahagan Douglas said. "You've been blaming the administration for Chiang Kai-shek's losses in China. But when the administration tries to blame this Congress for our losses in Germany, you don't think that's fair."

"It isn't fair," Jerry snapped. "Our losses in Germany started long before Republicans gained the majority. We gained it not least because of American losses in Germany. And those losses started almost before the ink dried on the so-called surrender. The Army in Germany had full wartime appropriations in 1945, as I am sure the distinguished Representative from California recalls." His tone declared he was sure of no such thing. "Even with those full appropriations, even with that flood of manpower, the U.S. Army had no better luck against partisan warfare than the *Wehrmacht* did in France or Russia or Yugoslavia."

"Mr. Speaker!" Congresswoman Douglas exclaimed. "It's outrageous to compare the United States Army to Hitler's murder machine! Outrageous!"

"I wasn't comparing them, except to point out that even the *Wehrmacht* couldn't stamp out partisans. The Red Army isn't having much fun trying it, either. And if you can't hope to win a fight like that, why keep flushing blood down the toilet trying?" Jerry said.

Neither Helen Gahagan Douglas nor any of the other pro-administration Representatives wanted to listen to him. They yelled and fussed and carried on. So did the Congressmen on Jerry's side. Up on the rostrum, Joe Martin banged his gavel and, not for the first time, looked as if he had no idea why he'd ever wanted to become Speaker of the House.

FLASHBULBS BURST LIKE ARTILLERY SHELLS. BLINKING, LOU WEISSberg tried to hide a shiver. He knew more about bursting shells—or at least mortar bombs—than he'd ever wanted to find out. Up there on the platform with him stood Bernie Cobb, Shmuel Birnbaum in black fatigues with "DP" armband, and Second Lieutenant Mark Davenport, the young officer who'd stopped Cobb and his buddies from leaving their position, so they'd been there when Heydrich and company came out.

Also on the platform stood General Lucius D. Clay. Lou had figured the only way he'd get to meet the commander of American forces in Germany was by monumentally screwing up. He'd never dreamt he could do something right enough to draw a four-star general's notice. Life was full of surprises.

Clay stepped over to the microphone. More flashbulbs went off. Reporters got out notebooks and poised themselves to report. A movie camera recorded the event for posterity—and for the newsreel before next week's two-reeler, or maybe week after next's.

Looking straight into the camera, General Clay said, "These four brave men with me today are most responsible for ridding the world of Reinhard Heydrich, would-be *Führer* of the Nazi diehards and war criminal beyond compare. The U.S. Army and the government of the United States take pride in honoring them and rewarding them for their courage."

Lou translated Clay's remarks into low-voiced Yiddish for Shmuel Birnbaum. Then Clay called the DP's name. Lou stepped up to the mike with him to go on interpreting. Clay said, "We offered a million dollars for help leading to Heydrich's capture or death. Mr. Birnbaum, who was forced to help excavate the Nazi leader's headquarters and who later narrowly escaped the murder that would have silenced him forever, gave information that led us to him. His share of the reward will be $250,000."

Reporters and soldiers gave Birnbaum a hand. Shyly, his head bobbed up and down as he acknowledged the applause. "What will you do with the money?" somebody called. Lou translated the question.

"I want to go to Palestine," the DP answered without hesitation. "Everybody else has a homeland. Jews should have one, too." After Lou also translated that, the mostly American crowd nodded. Englishmen wouldn't have; the UK wasn't having much fun trying to keep its old League of Nations mandate from exploding into civil war. An ordinary Jewish DP would have had a devil of a time even getting British permission to enter Palestine. For the man who'd fingered

Reinhard Heydrich, though—and for a man with a quarter of a million smackers in his pocket—many more things were possible.

Birnbaum and Lou stepped back. "Lieutenant Mark Davenport!" Lucius Clay said.

Davenport strode forward and delivered a parade-ground salute. "Sir!" he said. He was skinny and blond, and looked about seventeen.

"For your cool head, for your gallantry on the mountainside, and for your vital role in ensuring that Heydrich could not escape after coming out of his shelter, I am pleased to promote you to first lieutenant, to present you with a Silver Star in recognition of your courage, and to reward you with $250,000. Congratulations!"

"Thank you very much, sir!" Davenport sounded as if he couldn't believe what was happening to him. Well, if he didn't, who could blame him? As if to compound the surreal atmosphere, Clay personally pinned the Silver Star on his chest.

"Private Bernard Cobb!" Before Cobb could even salute him, General Clay corrected himself: "*Sergeant* Bernard Cobb!"

"Thanks, sir." Bernie Cobb did salute then. Lou had got to know him a little the past few hectic days. Cobb had had as much of the Army as he wanted, and then some. Three stripes on his sleeve wouldn't impress him. Neither would a Silver Star, even if Lucius Clay presented it with his own hands. A quarter of a million dollars were bound to be a different story.

"What will you do next?" a reporter asked.

"Soon as I get out of the Army, I'm going back to New Mexico," Cobb answered. "I'll buy me a house, buy a car, maybe go to school, find a girl, find a job, settle down. No offense to anybody, but I've worn a uniform as long as I want to."

"The Army needs men like you, but I have to admit I understand— and I sympathize," General Clay said. Then he turned to Lou. "Captain—no, Major—Louis Weissberg!"

"Sir!" Lou blinked—he hadn't expected the promotion. Down in the crowd, Howard Frank grinned and waved and gave him a thumbs-up.

Lou wasn't sure he deserved a Silver Star, either. Unlike Bernie Cobb or Lieutenant Davenport, he'd spent a hell of a lot more time in Heydrich's valley getting shot at than shooting. Then Lucius Clay said, "You earned your share of the reward for ending Reinhard Heydrich's career not just in the valley last week but also in your relent-less pursuit of him and of other war criminals since V-E Day. As I told Sergeant Cobb, the Army needs more men like you. Well done!"

"Thank you, sir!" Lou's salute was as snappy as he could make it. He felt about ready to bust his buttons with pride. If America wasn't the greatest country in the world . . . No, it damn well was, and that was all there was to it. His folks had come through Ellis Island with nothing but the clothes on their backs. He wished they could see him now, college-educated and exchanging salutes with a four-star gen-eral. If something like this wasn't the dream of every hard-working immigrant's son, what would be?

"Hey, Captain—uh, Major!" a reporter called. "You're in the Counter-Intelligence Corps, right?"

"Well, yeah," Lou said uncomfortably. The one thing wrong with getting your name in the paper was that you weren't so useful to the CIC after you did. *A well-known spy* was your basic contradiction in terms.

The reporter didn't care—or, more likely, didn't even think about it. "Those Nazi so-and-so's gonna dry up and blow away now that Heydrich's dead and gone?" he asked, poising pencil above notebook to wait for Lou's reply. A good story . . . That, he cared about.

Lucius Clay leaned toward Lou, too, anxious to hear his answer. It wasn't an enormous, showy lean: only an inch or so, two at the most. But any lean at all from the straight-spined general seemed remark-able. With Clay leaning, Lou picked his words with even more care than he would have otherwise. "Nobody *knows* what's coming up— I figure that's how come everybody spends so much time guessing and hoping about it," he said. "So the most I can give you now is a guess and a hope. My guess is, we've got a decent chance that they'll quit. And you can bet I hope like anything I'm right."

What was *a decent chance*? Thirty percent? Eighty percent? Lou didn't say, because he had no idea. The reporter didn't notice, and wrote down what he did say. General Clay, on the other hand, recog-nized bullshit when he heard it. He made a point of straightening up again: Lou showed he didn't have any better notion than Clay did himself. Lou wished he could have sounded surer. Hell, he wished he could have been surer. Too bad life didn't work that way.

BERNIE COBB WAS DRUNK. HE WAS DRUNK AS A LORD, IN FACT—OR HE thought so, even if no lords were around for comparison. He couldn't remember ever buying drinks for so many other guys before, either. Of course, he'd also never had a quarter of a million bucks burning a hole in his pocket before.

He didn't exactly have a quarter of a million bucks now. In spite of the fancy ceremony with General Clay, the money was going into a Stateside bank account for him. The idea was to keep him from blowing the wad before the Army shipped him home. Whoever'd decided on that knew what he was doing—and knew Bernie much too well.

So what he was spending was back pay and poker winnings and whatever other cash he could scrape together. You had to throw some kind of bash when $250,000 came your way, didn't you? Bernie thought so. And the Silver Star didn't hurt.

"So when do they turn you loose and send you back?" asked one of his many new-found close friends.

That set Bernie laughing. Right now, almost anything would, but this was really funny. "Y'know the medal they pinned on me? Even with the way they're bumping up points, that gave me enough for my Ruptured Duck. So as soon as they find me a ship or a plane, I am fucking gone!"

People laughed and cheered and pounded him on the back. Why not? He was still slapping money down on the bar. Somebody else asked him, "Did you know it was Heydrich when you opened up on those Jerries?"

"Shit, no," Bernie answered. "All I knew was, they were Germans and they weren't supposed to be there. I figured I better get 'em while they were still all bunched up, like, so I did."

"Sometimes you'd rather be lucky than good." The other GI sounded jealous. And he had a quarter of a million reasons to sound that way. No, a quarter of a million and one, because Bernie had a ticket home, too. Well, the way things were going, everybody'd be heading back from Germany soon. Bernie didn't know if he liked that. But he liked going home himself just fine.

ENGINES ROARING, THE BIG TRIPLE-TAILED CONSTELLATION ROLLED
down the runway outside of Amsterdam. The TWA airliner took off
smooth as you please. It would stop at Paris to let passengers off and
take on new ones, and to top up its fuel tanks. Then it would cross the
Atlantic—eight or ten times as fast as the fastest ocean liner—and
land at New York City.

Over the intercom, the pilot explained all that in English and
French and Dutch. Before the war, he surely would have used German, too. He didn't think he needed to now. Konrad could follow
English, and Dutch after a fashion, but it didn't matter. Regardless
of what the pilot thought the flight would be doing, Konrad and his
friends had other plans.

Konrad and Max carried Dutch passports—or excellent forgeries
of Dutch passports, anyhow. A couple of rows farther back, Arnold
and Hermann flew on Belgian passports—or equally excellent forgeries. Along with the false documents, all four men had also brought
cut-down Schmeissers onto the plane. But the submachine guns
weren't on display, not yet.

A steward came down the aisle with a tray of drinks. It was almost
empty by the time it got to Konrad and Max. Plenty of people needed
help forgetting they were three or four kilometers up in the air. Max
took a cocktail. Konrad didn't.

They landed at Orly Airport. Like the rest of the people going on
to New York, Konrad and Max and Arnold and Hermann sat tight
while other stylish men and women got off and on. If you couldn't
afford stylish clothes, odds were you couldn't afford a plane ticket,
either.

After the layover, the L-049 took off again. The pilot came on the
intercom to brag in his three languages about the meals TWA would
be serving. Then he explained how to fold the seats down into reasonable approximations of beds. No matter how much faster than a ship
it was, the airliner would still take a long time to get to New York
City.

It would take far longer than the pilot expected, but he didn't
know that yet. Time he found out.

"Ready?" Konrad asked quietly. Max nodded. Konrad twisted and looked back over his shoulder. He caught Arnold's eye, and Hermann's. They nodded, too. All four Germans took their Schmeissers out of their travel cases. No one had searched them before they boarded. Except for a few panicky editorial writers, no one had seen the need, even after the German Freedom Front flew that captured C-47 into the Russians' Berlin courthouse.

A stewardess—quite a pretty girl, really—was drawing near when Konrad and Max, Arnold and Hermann, all stood up at the same time. "What's going on?" she asked, sounding more curious than alarmed.

Then she saw the Schmeissers. Her eyes—green as jade—opened so wide, Konrad could see white all around the irises, as he might have with a spooked horse on the Eastern Front. *Crash!* The tray of drinks hit the floor.

"Don't do anything dumb," Konrad said—he was lead man in this operation not least because he knew English. "Take us to the cockpit."

"What—What will you do?" The girl's voice quavered, which was hardly a surprise.

"Nobody will get hurt if people do what we say," Konrad answered, which committed him to nothing. He gestured sharply with the Schmeisser's muzzle. "Now go on! Move!"

When the cockpit door opened, the pilot grinned at the stewardess. "Hey, beautiful! What's going on?" Then he saw the four men with submachine guns behind her. His jaw dropped. "What the hell?"

"I will shoot you if you do not do everything I tell you," Konrad said. "The plane will crash. Everyone will die. If you do what I tell you, I think everyone can live. Is it a bargain?"

"Who the hell are you?" the pilot demanded.

That was a fair question. He meant *Are you a pack of crazy people?* If he decided Konrad and his friends were, he wouldn't see any point to dealing with them. He might think crashing the plane now would be the best thing he could do, so they wouldn't try to make him fly it into a building or something. Since Konrad didn't want to die, he spoke quickly: "We belong to the German Freedom Front. We were soldiers in the war. We still fight to liberate the Fatherland."

Pilot and copilot looked at each other. Neither seemed to like the answer very much. "What do you want us to do?" the pilot asked after a considerable pause.

"Fly this airplane to Madrid. Land there," Konrad replied. "We will—how do you say it?—use the airplane and the passengers as poker chips to move our cause forward. We will not shoot unless you try to overpower us. Everyone in that case will be very unhappy."

"When we go off course, the radar will see it," the pilot said. "They'll call us up and ask us what's wrong. What are we supposed to tell 'em?"

"Tell them the truth. Tell them you have men from the German Freedom Front on your airplane. Tell them these men require you to fly to Spain," Konrad answered.

The pilot eyed him. "You son of a bitch! You want everybody to know!"

"*Aber natürlich,*" Konrad said. "The world must learn we are still fighting for a free Germany, and we are serious in what we do." As he had with the stewardess, he let a twitch of the Schmeisser's muzzle make his point for him. "Now—to Madrid."

"Right. To fucking Madrid," the pilot muttered. The L-049 swung from west to south.

Not five minutes later, a voice on the radio said, "TWA flight 57, this is Paris Control. Why have you changed course? Over."

The pilot grabbed the microphone. "Paris Control, this is TWA 57. We have four men from the German Freedom Front aboard. They are all armed, and they have directed us to fly to Madrid. To keep our passengers and crew safe, we are obeying. Over." He clicked off the mike and looked back over his shoulder at Konrad. "There. Happy now?"

"You did what was needed. That is good," Konrad answered. The pilot's eyebrows said he didn't think so.

"Jesus Christ!" Paris Control burst out. "Say that again, TWA 57." At Konrad's nod, the pilot did. "Jesus!" Paris Control repeated. Then he asked, "Have the assholes hurt anybody?"

"Negative. They say they won't if we play along with 'em. You might watch what you call 'em, since they're in the cockpit with us."

"Er—roger that," Paris Control said. A different voice came over the air: "Shall we scramble fighters?"

"Negative! Say again, negative!" the pilot replied. "Not unless you aim to shoot us down. What else can fighters do?"

A long silence followed. At last, Paris Control said, "You may proceed. We will inform Spanish air officials of the situation."

"Thank you," the pilot said. He looked disgusted. Paris Control had sounded disgusted. Some of the Anglo-Americans had wanted to clean out Franco's Spain after the *Wehrmacht* surrendered. They hadn't done it, though, even if Spain sheltered more than a few German refugees and other Europeans who'd supported the *Reich*'s crusade against Bolshevism. Maybe they remembered that Franco hadn't let the *Führer* come in and run the English out of Gibraltar. All by itself, that had gone a long way toward costing Germany the war.

"Can we tell the passengers what's going on?" the copilot asked. "They're bound to be wondering by now."

"Go ahead," Konrad said, and then, in German, to his comrades, "If anybody back there makes trouble, kill him."

Word went out over the airliner's intercom. The copilot warned people not to do anything silly, and nobody did. The Constellation flew on, almost at right angles to its planned course.

After a while, Konrad saw the peaks of the Pyrenees ahead. The L-049 flew high above them. The land on the other side was Spain. He and his fellow hijackers grinned at one another. Everything was going according to plan. The Spanish ground-control man who came on the radio hardly spoke English. He and the pilot went back and forth in French. Konrad didn't know any, but Max and Hermann did. They nodded to show nothing was wrong.

Spanish planes came up to look the airliner over. "Son of a bitch!" the pilot exclaimed. "Thought I'd never seen another goddamn Messerschmitt again!"

To Konrad, the German design carried happier associations. "We sold many of them to Spain," he said. "The Spaniards must use them yet."

"I guess." The pilot still sounded shaken.

He wasn't too shaken to land smoothly, though. Tanks rolled toward the Constellation. They were also German—outdated Panzer IIIs—which did nothing to reassure Konrad. "Tell them to go away, or the passengers will answer for it," he said sharply. The American relayed the message. The tanks pulled back.

"People are hungry. May I serve a meal?" the stewardess asked.

"*Ja.* Go ahead. Hermann, keep an eye on things," Konrad said. Hermann smiled and nodded. Plainly, he was happy to keep an eye on the cute stewardess. That wasn't what Konrad had meant, but. . . . The lead hijacker turned back to the pilot. "You can talk to the control tower, yes?"

"Yes," the man said. "They finally found a guy who really knows some English, too."

"Good. Very good. Get in touch with him." When the pilot had, Konrad took a folded sheet of paper out of his inside jacket pocket. "Send to the tower the just demands of the German Freedom Front. Tell the tower to send these demands on to the troops unlawfully and improperly occupying Germany. Have you got it?"

"Take it easy. Let me give 'em that much before I start forgetting," the pilot said. Konrad waved agreement. The pilot spoke into the microphone. Then he looked back to the hijacker to find out what came next.

Konrad was only too happy to oblige him. "First, all demands must be met within seventy-two hours. After that, we cannot answer for the safety of the passengers."

"You'll start shooting people, you mean," the pilot observed bleakly.

"*Ja,*" Konrad said. "If we do not do this, no one pays attention to us. Send the warning." After the pilot had, Konrad resumed: "We demand the immediate liberation of all prisoners captured while resisting the unlawful occupation. We demand also an end to the unlawful ban against National Socialist participation in German political life. And we demand—"

"Maybe you should start shooting now," the pilot said. "They won't give you any of that stuff."

Konrad hefted his Schmeisser. "You had better hope they do."

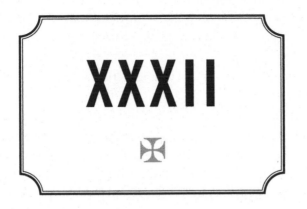

XXXII

Had Lou Weissberg tried for a year, he would have had trouble coming up with a photo he less wanted to see on the front page of the *International Herald-Tribune*. There was the big four-engined airliner parked at the edge of a runway in Madrid. There was the doorway, open. There was a faint view of a Nazi bastard with a submachine gun standing in the doorway. And there on the tarmac below the doorway lay a crumpled corpse in a spreading pool of blood.

"Motherfuckers even picked a Jew to murder first," Lou snarled in helpless, frustrated fury—the story beside the photo said the dead man's name was David Levinsky. "Probably the only Jew on the plane, but they found him, all right."

"Sure they did," Howard Frank agreed. "After everything you've seen since you got here, how come you're surprised now?"

Lou sighed and lit a cigarette. "Maybe 'cause they're still exactly the same assholes they were before, even though Heydrich's dead. Why did Clay bother giving me a medal and all that cash if killing the bastard didn't change anything?"

"He must have hoped it would, too," Major Frank said. "And if you don't want the money, I'll take it off your hands. I bet I can figure out something to do with it."

"You know what you can do with it—sideways," Lou said. Chuckling, Frank lit up, too. Lou went on, "And the goddamn Spaniards just stand around watching with their thumbs up their asses."

"Portuguese, too," Major Frank said. A DC-4 had been hijacked to Lisbon. The Nazis aboard that plane hadn't started shooting hostages yet.

"Yeah, the Portuguese, too. We shoulda gone into both countries after V-E Day. Then the krauts wouldn't have anywhere to hide—I don't think you can fly nonstop from Europe to Buenos Aires," Lou said. "But you know the real pisser?"

Howard Frank suddenly seemed fascinated by the glowing coal on his cigarette. At last, without much wanting to, he said, *"Nu?"*

"The real pisser is, we're still loading GIs onto troopships and taking them home," Lou said. "That hasn't slowed down one goddamn bit. I mean, why should it? We knocked the crap out of the Nazis, so they aren't dangerous any more. Sure makes sense to me! Must make sense to you, too, right?"

"Riiight." Frank stretched out the word like a train whistle fading in the distance. "Go close the door to my office, willya?"

"Huh? How come?" Lou said. Major Frank just looked at him. "Okay, okay. All right, already." Lou walked over and shut it.

By the time he got back, Frank had produced an almost-full pint of bourbon from nowhere—more likely, from a desk drawer. He took a knock and handed Lou the bottle. "Here. Get the taste out of your mouth."

"Thanks!" Lou was glad to drink. It wouldn't help the poor SOBs in Madrid or Lisbon, but it made him feel better. "Ahh! You're a *mensh.*"

"Well, I try." Major Frank tilted the pint back again, not so far this time. "Russians have the same worry we do—just before you came in with the paper, I heard on the radio that there's a hijacked plane in Prague."

"Fuck!" Lou said. That made him want more bourbon himself, so he took some. "Fanatics have a new toy, don't they?"

Howard Frank nodded. "Looks that way."

"But what can they accomplish?" Lou asked. "No matter how many hostages they kill, we won't do what they say. That'd be asking for even more trouble, if such a thing is possible. And they've gotta know the Russians'll tell 'em to piss up a rope."

"Sure." Frank nodded again. "The kind of publicity they're getting, though—you can't buy headlines like that. And if they're pulling this crap on regular airline flights, they'll make us start patting people down and going through everybody's luggage and stuff like that. It'll cost millions of dollars and flush even more millions of man-hours down the shitter."

"Lord, will it ever!" Lou exclaimed, picturing the mess in his mind. "Millions and millions of dollars."

"Uh-huh." Major Frank eyed the bourbon longingly. This time, though, he didn't pick it up. "And I guess that's why nobody's stormed the planes in Madrid and Lisbon. If a bunch of hostages get shot, who do we blame? Franco and Salazar, right? That's how they're bound to see it, anyway."

Lou grunted. He also wanted another snort, and also hung back. "Makes sense. I almost wish it didn't, but it does. But if the fucking SS men are shooting hostages anyway . . ."

"Hey, it's happening in Europe. A bunch of the people on those planes are bound to be foreigners. So it's nothing anybody in the United States needs to worry about, is it?" Frank said.

"Of course not." But Lou reached for the bourbon after all.

VLADIMIR BOKOV HAD ALL KINDS OF REASONS NOT TO WANT TO GO TO the Prague airport. He'd had plenty of work on his plate back in Berlin—important work, too, not just stuff to make time go by. Dealing with Czechoslovakian officials was still tricky. Too many of them thought they could restore the bourgeois republic they'd had before the war. They didn't see that, with Soviet troops occupying their country, it had to accommodate itself to the USSR. And dealing with the Nazi terrorists who'd hijacked this Li-2 and ordered it flown here might be even trickier.

None of which had anything to do with anything. When Bokov and Colonel Shteinberg got orders to drop everything, to go to Prague, and to recapture the passenger plane without making concessions, they went. What other choice did they have? None, and Bokov knew it.

Which didn't keep him from complaining. "Why us?" he groused, peering at the Li-2 through captured German binoculars (better than any the Soviet Union made).

"Why us, Volodya?" Moisei Shteinberg's chuckle said he was amused to find such naïveté in a fellow NKVD officer. "You mean you don't know?"

"If I did, would I be pissing and moaning like this?" Bokov answered irritably.

"I'll tell you why, then." And Shteinberg proceeded to do just that: "Lieutenant General Vlasov, that's why. We did well giving Birnbaum to the Americans after he didn't want us to. So now he gives us this mess. If we don't make a hash of it, we solve his problem for him. And if we do, he's even with us, and he writes something good and foul on our fitness report."

"Well, fuck me!" Bokov said, and not another word. He thumped his forehead with the heel of his hand, as if to admit he should have seen that for himself. And he should have. As soon as Shteinberg pointed it out to him, he knew it was true. In Yuri Vlasov's shoes, Bokov would have done the same thing.

All the troops ringing the Li-2 belonged to the Red Army. The Czechoslovakians had grumbled about that, which did them no good whatever. The plane was Russian. That gave the Soviet commandant in Prague all the excuse he needed to use his own men. If some pimp of a Czech colonel who'd probably get purged once the other shoe here dropped didn't like it, too goddamn bad.

The radio crackled to life. "Do you read me, Prague airport?" one of the Nazi hijackers asked.

"We hear you, yes," Bokov answered in German.

"You'd better get cracking on our demands, then," the fanatic said. "Time's running short. If we don't know for sure that you're freeing prisoners and moving soldiers out of the *Vaterland*, it's too bad for the people on this plane."

"We are doing what you told us to do," Bokov lied. Not even the Americans were stupid enough to yield to the hijackers' demands. If you did that even once, you set yourself up for endless trouble down the line.

"We'd better see some sign of it, or we start shooting," the German warned.

"There's no hope for you if you do," Bokov said. That was true, but there'd been no hope for the fanatics once they commandeered the airplane.

"Maybe not, but there's no hope for your important people, either," the Nazi said. The passengers *were* important: officers, engineers, agricultural officials, a prominent violinist. No one but important people flew, not in Soviet airspace. But that also had nothing to do with anything.

A Red Army lieutenant handed Colonel Shteinberg a note. He read it and nodded to Bokov. "Don't do anything hasty," Bokov told the fanatic. "We'll do what you want, and we'll get you the evidence you need. Out." He made sure he'd switched off before asking Shteinberg, "Everything's ready?" The Jew nodded again. Bokov switched frequencies on the radio and said one word in Russian: *"Now!"*

Three 105mm shells slammed into the Li-2's cockpit. They blew off most of the plane's nose. A truck with a scaling ladder—taken from a Prague fire engine—sped down the runway. The ladder went up. Red Army men with submachine guns swarmed into what was left of the cockpit.

Another truck raced over to the Li-2's right-side doorway. This one needed a shorter ladder. The first soldier up it sprayed the lock with bullets from his PPSh. Then he threw the door open and sprang into the plane. The rest of his squad followed.

It was all over in less time than it took to tell. The Russians threw two hijackers' bodies out of the Li-2's shattered nose. One more corpse came out through the side door. They were bound to be dead already, but men on the ground filled them full of lead anyway, just to stay safe.

Then live soldiers and passengers started coming out. Another lieutenant hurried back to the tower to report to Shteinberg and Bokov. "Your plan worked very well," he said, saluting the NKVD men. "The sons of bitches only had time to shoot three men, and one of them isn't badly hurt. Oh, and shell fragments killed the pilot and wounded the copilot and one passenger."

"Too bad, but it's the cost of doing business," Bokov said.

Colonel Shteinberg nodded. "Cheaper than dealing with hijackers any day."

A moment later, the Li-2 caught fire. Blasting the cockpit had pretty much wrecked it anyway. The Red Army soldiers and the surviving people who'd been aboard pulled away in a hurry. Vladimir Bokov impassively watched the fat column of black smoke rise into the sky. The plane was part of the cost of doing business, too.

And as for Lieutenant General Yuri Pavlovich Vlasov . . . *Go fuck yourself, Yuri Pavlovich,* Bokov thought happily. The senior NKVD man had given Bokov and Shteinberg this assignment hoping they would botch it: Shteinberg was bound to be right about that. But they hadn't. They'd done as well with it as anyone could reasonably hope to do. They'd given no concessions, the hijackers were dead, and most of the passengers were alive. If Vlasov didn't like it . . . *Drop dead, cuntface.* Bokov grinned. Maybe he'd said it out loud, because Moisei Shteinberg smiled, too. Or maybe the Jew was just thinking along with him. After what they'd managed here together, that wouldn't surprise him at all.

SEEING WHAT HIS HIJACKINGS HAD WROUGHT, JOCHEN PEIPER WAS more happy than not. One thing was clear: taking over a Russian plane didn't yield enough to make it worthwhile. The Russians, as he already had painful reason to understand, proved at least as remorseless and relentless as his own people. To them, the hijacked aircraft and the people aboard it were expendable. As long as they got rid of the hijackers, they didn't care about anything else.

"All right," Peiper muttered. "We won't mess with them again. Not like that, anyhow."

But the plane that landed in Madrid, and the one that came down in Lisbon . . . Both of those were successes, no two ways about it. The German fighting men aboard had killed a few fat, rich fools. They'd got wonderful publicity. Every airline that flew anywhere in Western Europe was frantically revamping security procedures. That would cost piles of dollars or pounds or francs or whatever currency they used. It would also cost them endless wasted time and uncountable passenger goodwill.

The team in Madrid had even managed to torch their Constellation as they walked out. They were in jail now, as were the hijackers who'd gone to Lisbon. The USA, and UK, and France were all screaming for their heads. Jochen Peiper didn't think they'd get them. The *Reich* still had friends in high places in Spain and Portugal, even if those friends had to work quietly and discreetly these days. His best guess was that the hijacking teams would stay locked up till the foofaraw died down, and then, without any fuss, someone would open the door, shove them out through it, and do his goddamnedest to pretend the whole thing never happened.

That suited Peiper fine. He didn't think he would have any trouble recruiting people for more hijackings.

And the rest of the German Freedom Front's business seemed to be going well enough. Most important, the Amis hadn't brought bulldozers and steam shovels into this valley to dig out Peiper's headquarters. Nobody the enemy had caught when they dug out Heydrich must have known where this place was. Peiper had hoped that would prove true, but he'd known too well there was no guarantee. Either Heydrich had paid proper attention to security, or luck meant no one who knew what he shouldn't had survived. Peiper didn't—couldn't—know which, but either would do.

Roadside bombs, sabotaged vehicles and railroad lines, poisoned liquor, brave men in explosive vests who could take out a platoon of Amis or Tommies or Ivans if they pressed the button at the right time . . . All that was the small change of partisan warfare—unless you had to try to stop it. Peiper's side had had to do that in Russia and Poland . . . and Yugoslavia, and Greece, and France, and the Low Countries, and Norway. Unfortunately, the *Reich* hadn't made a popular overlord.

Now the Germans got to jump up and down on the other pan in the scale. If the Anglo-Americans and the Russians (oh, yes—and the French, too) didn't like it, let them have the joy of figuring out what to do about it. The Americans had already decided they didn't know. The English weren't likely to be far behind. And then . . .

Then what? Peiper wondered. But he knew. *Then we take over, that's what.* The Anglo-Americans would leave behind political parties and policemen to try to keep the National Socialists from reclaiming the power that was rightly theirs. Peiper chuckled. How long would that last? Not bloody long!

In the German-occupied East, how many Russian policemen had also served the Red Army or the NKVD? Way too goddamn many—

Jochen Peiper knew that for sure. And how many German policemen in the occupied *Reich* also served the German Freedom Front? Quite a few—Peiper also knew that for sure.

"The fight goes on," he murmured, and nodded to himself. "Whoever has the most patience—he wins." He nodded again. The Americans and the English had already seen more trouble than they'd ever wanted. Before too long, the French would, too. Without the Anglo-Americans to prop them up, they weren't much. The Russians . . . Jochen Peiper grimaced. The Russians were a different story. Against the Russians, you had to look a lifetime down the line if you were going to accomplish anything. But a free and independent and National Socialist *Deutsches Reich* in western Germany would do for a start. Peiper thought they could win that much pretty soon.

ANYBODY COULD GO TO NEW YORK CITY TO INTERVIEW TROOPS COMing home. Since Tom Schmidt couldn't go to Germany, he didn't want to go to New York. Yes, lots of people—and lots of reporters—did, but wasn't that the point? What were your chances of finding an interesting story if you did the same thing as everybody else? Pretty goddamn slim, that's what.

And so Tom went to Baltimore instead. It was a major port, nobody else except people from there gave two whoops in hell about it, and it was only a little more than an hour by train from Washington. How could you not like the combination?

It was chilly and rainy there, as it had been when he set out from Union Station. Winter wasn't on the calendar yet, but it sure was in the air. He stood under an umbrella a few paces beyond the tent that called itself a deprocessing center and waited for demobilized soldiers to come by. Out at the end of the pier squatted the *Peter Gray*, as unlovely a rustbucket as shipfitters had ever slapped together. Tom wondered who the Liberty ship was named for. Not the one-armed outfielder on the 1945 Browns, surely? But what other even slightly famous Pete Gray had there been?

MPs discouraged him from getting to the returning soldiers before they went through the deprocessing center. That irked him. "I happen to know other people have been able to talk to them beforehand," he fumed.

All he got back from the sergeant in charge of the MPs was a shrug and a dismissive, "Sorry, sir." The three-striper didn't sound one bit sorry. Tacking insult on to injury, he added, "You understand—we've got our orders."

So did the guards at Dachau and Belsen. Tom almost said it. He would have if he'd figured it would do him any good. But the boss MP's dull eyes and blunt features argued that he would have made a pretty good concentration-camp guard himself. That being so, hearing himself compared to one would have pissed him off all the more. He had no real reason to run Tom in, which might not stop him from inventing one. Sometimes the smartest thing you could do was keep your mouth shut.

Here came a soldier proudly wearing a shiny new Ruptured Duck on his lapel. "Talk to you a minute?" Tom asked. "Tom Schmidt, from the *Chicago Tribune*." Taking notes, he realized, would be a bitch. It was like driving the hills of San Francisco, where you needed one foot on the gas, one on the brake, and one on the clutch. Here he needed one hand for the umbrella, one for the pencil, and one for the notebook.

As things turned out, he didn't need pencil or notebook this time. The GI shook his head and kept walking. "Sorry, Mac. All I wanna do is haul ass for the train station, get aboard, and head for home."

"Where is home?" Tom was nothing if not persistent. It did him no good this time. The soldier or ex-soldier or whatever he was shook his head again. He splashed every time his Army boots came down on the concrete. That had to be better than slopping through mud, though. Slowly, as if in a Hollywood dissolve, the curtain of rain made him disappear.

Here came another tired-looking GI. Tom took another shot at it: "Tom Schmidt, *Chicago Tribune*. Can I talk to you for a little bit?"

The GI—one stripe on his sleeve made him a PFC—paused. "Okay. Why not? You gonna put me in the paper?"

Tom nodded. "That's the idea. What's your name?"

"Atkins. Gil Atkins."

"Where you from, Gil?" If Tom held both the notebook and the umbrella in his left hand, he could take notes . . . after a fashion.

"Sioux City, Iowa."

"How about that?" Tom said: one of the rare phrases you could use with almost anything. He'd been to Sioux City. It was a place where nobody died of excess excitement. "What did you do there?"

"Short-order cook."

"Were you a cook in the Army, too?"

"Not fuckin' likely. I lugged a BAR."

"Did you get to Germany before V-E Day or after?"

"After, not that it made much difference. Krauts may have said they gave up, but that didn't mean shit, and everybody knew it. I'm just glad I made it home in one piece." The kid's face clouded over. "Bunch of my buddies didn't."

"I'm sorry," Tom said. Gil Atkins only shrugged; maybe he recognized purely polite sympathy when he heard it. Tom tried again: "So you're glad to come home from Germany, then?"

"Oh, hell, yes!" Nothing wrong with Atkins' sincerity.

"What's the best thing about being back in the States?"

"Lord! Where do I start?" Quite seriously, the returning PFC ticked off points on his fingers: "Let's see. When I get on the train, I won't have to worry that the fanatics have planted a block of TNT on the tracks. When I get into a jeep—sorry, I mean a car—I won't have to watch the bushes by the side of the road to make sure no cocksucker with a rocket or a machine gun can blow it up. When I walk down the street, I won't have to worry somebody'll chuck a grenade under my feet and run away. I won't have to wonder if the guy coming past me has dynamite and nails on under his coat. I won't have to think the pretty gal pushing the baby carriage has maybe got a big old mine in there instead of a baby. I won't have to be scared somebody's gonna bomb the place where I'm sleeping. If I buy myself a shot, I won't have to wonder whether some asshole poisoned it. I won't . . . Shit, buddy, I could go on a lot longer, but you've got the message, doncha?"

"I just might, yeah." Tom mimed writer's cramp, which made Atkins chuckle. "What do you think about the people who don't think we ought to be pulling out of Germany?"

"Well, that depends. There were some of those guys over there, and you gotta respect them. I mean, hell, they were laying it on the line like everybody else, y'know? So that was okay. But the people back here, the safe, fat, happy people who wouldn't be in any danger regardless of what goes on in Germany—fuck them and the horse they rode in on. Those clowns are ready to fight to the last drop of my blood. That's how it looks to me, anyways." Gil Atkins chuckled again, this time in mild embarrassment. "You're gonna have to take out some words before you can put this in your paper, huh?"

"That's part of the business," Tom said. "Thanks for taking the time to talk to me. You helped a lot."

"Only time I ever got in the paper before was on account of a car crash," Atkins said. "And that one wasn't even my fault—other guy was drunk, and he sideswiped me." He bobbed his head and tramped off. Before long, no doubt, he'd find the station. He'd ride back to Sioux City and start scrambling eggs and frying bacon and flipping hamburgers. He'd have a regular job again. Hell, he'd have his life back again. Try as Tom might, he couldn't see what was so bad about that.

Tom had his own job, too. "Hi. I'm Tom Schmidt, from the *Chicago Tribune*. Can I talk to you for a minute?" This guy with his shiny Ruptured Duck walked past him as if he didn't exist. Try again—what else could you do? "Hello. My name's Tom Schmidt. I'm from the *Chicago Tribune*. . . ."

"AULD LANG SYNE" CAME OUT OF THE RADIO. GUY LOMBARDO'S orchestra was playing in the New Year, the same as usual. Over the music, the announcer said, "In less than a minute now, the lighted ball in Times Square will drop. It will usher out 1947 and bring in 1948. Another year to look forward to . . ."

Ed McGraw looked down at his wristwatch. "Boy, I'm a whole year fast," he said.

Buster Neft laughed. So did Betsy. Stan looked around, wide-eyed. He'd stayed up way past his bedtime, but New Year's Eve was special. He would be three pretty soon, which seemed impossible to his grandmother.

Diana McGraw only smiled at Ed's joke. He made it about every other New Year. And when he wasn't a year fast, he was a year slow. Yeah, Diana had heard it before, too many times. She'd heard just about everything from him too many times.

"The ball is dropping!" the announcer said. "Happy New Year!"

"Happy New Year!" Ed lifted his beer. All the grownups had

drinks of one kind or another. Even Stan had a glass of grape juice. If he wanted to pretend it was wine—well, why not?

Betsy raised her highball in Diana's direction. "Here's to you, Mom! If anybody made 1947 what it was, you're the one."

"Thanks," Diana said. Along with the rest of her family, she drank the toast. It was true enough. American soldiers were coming home from Germany. Most of them were already back, and the ones who weren't would be before long. Diana had had a lot to do with that.

And now it was—literally was, this past minute or so—last year's news. The second phone line here didn't ring as often as it had even a couple of months earlier. The withdrawal wasn't controversial any more; it was an accomplished fact. By the nature of things, accomplished facts weren't news. The world was starting to forget about Diana McGraw and Mothers Against the War in Germany. Why not? They'd won.

Pretty soon, she'd go back to being just another housewife from Anderson, Indiana. Up till Pat got killed, she hadn't thought about being anything else. She still wished she'd never had any reason— well, never had *that* reason, anyhow—to think about anything else.

But she'd got used to going all over the country for the cause. She'd got used to fielding phone calls from reporters and Congressmen and other important people. She'd got used to being an important person herself. And she could watch that fade like a cheap blouse the first time it met bleach. Once you'd been famous—even a little bit famous—how did you get used to ordinary life?

Baseball players had to deal with it. So did actors who had one or two hit movies and then saw their careers fizzle out. Some managed gracefully. Others grabbed the limelight a little while longer by doing something disgraceful.

Diana might have managed that if news of her tryst with Marvin (she still couldn't remember his last name) had made the papers. Everybody on the other side would have been delighted to see her exposed as a woman without any morals to call her own.

But nobody knew about that little encounter except the parties involved. She had no idea whether Marvin's conscience bothered him. She would have bet against it. He was a man, after all. Men took what they could get, and tried to get it even when they couldn't.

Women weren't supposed to do things like that. Which didn't mean they didn't, only that they weren't supposed to. What bothered Diana most about ending up in bed with Marvin Whoozis was how much fun she'd had while it was going on. Marvin had casually shown her more varieties of delight in half an hour than Ed had since the end of World War I. Darn it, when Ed went Over There, couldn't a Mademoiselle from Amentières have taught him a little something? Evidently not.

And having a better idea of what she was missing only left Diana more frustrated when Ed wanted to lay her down. He still hadn't figured out exactly what was wrong, even if he knew something was. She had no idea how to tell him, either. If she suddenly wanted him to start doing this and that when he'd never done—probably never even imagined doing—this and that before, what would he think? Most likely, that some other guy had done this and that with her while she was on one of her junkets.

He'd be right, too.

If only this and that—especially that—didn't feel so good! If only she hadn't got smashed with Marvin! If only . . . fame weren't rolling away like the afternoon train bound for Indianapolis.

Which brought her back to where she'd started, full circle.

She realized Betsy'd just said something. She also realized she had no idea what. "I'm sorry, dear," she said. "Your old mother was woolgathering there, I'm afraid. Must be second childhood coming on."

"Oh, sure," her daughter said with a snort. "What I said was, Buster and I'd better head for home. Stan won't last much longer, and—"

"*Not* sleepy," Stan declared, but he spoiled it with a tonsil-showing yawn.

"We know you're not, Killer, but we're going home anyway," Buster said. Stan yawned again. He was too "not sleepy" to put up much of an argument. Buster went on, "Maybe I'll show up for my shift tomorrow, and maybe I won't."

"Yeah, me, too," Ed agreed. "Hey, tomorrow's Friday. Who wants to work a one-day week right after New Year's?"

Their daughter and son-in-law and grandson headed out into the cold. Stan dozed off on Buster's shoulder before the Nefts even made it out the door. It closed behind them. That left Diana and Ed all alone.

"Happy New Year, babe," he said.

"You, too," she replied automatically, even as she wondered, *How?*

"Want to—you know—celebrate, like?"

Her answering yawn was pretty much authentic. "Can we hold off a day? I'm really sleepy, and I don't have to pretend I'm not, the way Stan does."

Ed chuckled. "He's a corker, all right. Yeah, it'll keep a day. Sure."

He was accommodating, which meant she'd have to be accommodating tomorrow night. And she'd lie there thinking about what Marvin knew and he didn't, and. . . . *Stop that!* she told herself firmly. But herself didn't want to listen.

"Hey, babe," he said, more anxiety than he usually showed in his voice. "It'll be okay, right?"

"Sure, Ed." She might have been soothing little Stan. *How?* she wondered again.

"You did what you set out to do. I'm proud of you," Ed said.

"I just wish I'd never set out to do it. I wish I'd never had to," Diana said. And that was nothing but the truth. If Pat were alive . . . But he wasn't, and he never would be. She started to cry. She'd been doing that a lot lately. Ed took her in his arms. He thought he knew all the reasons he was soothing her.

LOU WEISSBERG WAS TAKING PAPERS OUT OF FILING CABINETS AND stuffing then into boxes when Howard Frank came in to see how he was doing. Lou was glad for the chance to stop for a couple of minutes. "Last man out of Germany—is me, or maybe you," he said.

Major Frank winced. "It's not quite *that* bad," he said.

"Close enough, goddammit," Lou said. "A garrison in Berlin. A few air bases and a little bit of armor—just enough to make the Red Army think twice about marching in . . . if we're very, very lucky. Not enough to hold down the goddamn fanatics, and fat chance we'll ever bring any guys back to take care of that."

"The Christian Democrats and the Social Democrats say they can whip the Nazis in any halfway honest election. The German police say they can fight the bastards off. They get a lot of the equipment we're leaving behind," Frank insisted.

"Yeah, all the other parties were so wonderful at stopping Hitler in 1933, too," Lou said, which made his friend flinch again. "And how many German cops still get up on their hind legs and whinny every time they hear the *'Horst Wessel Lied'*?"

"Some, sure. Not too many. I hope." Major Frank spread his hands. "We've done the best we could, considering. . . ."

"Yeah. Considering." Lou made an ordinary word sound extraordinarily foul.

"Unless you want to stay here as a civilian, we're heading for home day after tomorrow," Frank said. "In its infinite wisdom, Congress has decided that's the best thing—the very best thing—the United States can do."

"Oh, yeah. Every fucking American Jew ever born is dying to be a civilian in Germany. *Dying* is just what I'd do here, you bet." Lou's loud opinion of Congress and its infinite wisdom would have got him shot for treason in any totalitarian country—and in about half the democracies currently in business, too.

All Howard Frank did was sadly wag an index finger and say, "Naughty, naughty." A moment later, he added, "You must be slipping, man. I've called those assholes way worse than that."

"Well, goody for you," Lou said. "You gonna resign your commission after we get back to the States?"

This time, Major Frank looked genuinely sorrowful. He nodded anyway. "Yeah. After we go and do this, I don't see any point to staying in. You?"

"Same here," Lou said. "Back to my family, back to teaching English, back to being a civilian. And I'll spend the rest of my days hoping I can live out the rest of my days before things blow up again, know what I mean?"

"Don't I wish I didn't!" Frank exclaimed. "Now that you've cheered me up, I'll go back and cram more of my crap into boxes. The records will all be on file—if anybody ever bothers to look at 'em."

"Yeah," Lou said. "If."

Two days later, trucks and halftracks pulled up in front of the commandeered Nuremberg hotel to take departing soldiers and the paperwork of an occupation gone bad north to the sea, and to the ships waiting to carry them across the Atlantic. Outside the building, Lou smoked a last cigarette and shot the shit with one of the German gendarmes who'd be taking over the place once the Americans were gone. Rolf was a pretty good guy. He'd been a corporal during the war—but *Wehrmacht,* not *Waffen*-SS. In his dyed-black U.S. fatigues and American helmet, he looked nothing like a German soldier. So Lou tried to tell himself, anyhow.

"We will miss you when you go," the gendarme said. "You are the only thing standing between us and chaos."

"You guys will do fine on your own," Lou answered. You always reassured a sickroom patient, even—especially—when you didn't think he'd make it.

"I fear the new parties will not have the moral authority they need to oppose the old order," Rolf said. "I fear we—the police—will not have the weapons to hold back the fanatics."

"Sure you will," said Lou, who feared the very same things. Somebody yelled at him from a halftrack. He cussed under his breath, then handed Rolf what was left of the pack of Chesterfields. "Good luck to you, my friend."

"*Danke schön!*" The gendarme happily pocketed the smokes. Lou trotted over to the halftrack and clambered up and in. The CIC convoy, protected not only by armored cars but also by Sherman tanks, rumbled away from the hotel, away from Nuremberg—and, soon, away from Germany.

ROLF HALBRITTER COUGHED FROM THE DUST THE RETREATING CONvoy kicked up. He shook his head in wonder not far from awe. The Amis were really and truly going—no, really and truly gone.

Which meant . . . He had a badge pinned on the underside of his collar, where it didn't show. Now he could wear it openly again. It was round, with a red outer ring that carried a legend in bronze letters: NATIONALSOZIALISTISCHE DEUTSCHE ARBEITERPARTEI. The white inner circle held a black swastika. Every Party member had one just like it. Pretty soon, they'd all be showing it, too.

HISTORICAL NOTE

There really was a German resistance movement after V-E Day. It was never very effective; it got off to a very late start, as the Nazis took much longer than they might have to realize they weren't going to win the straight-up war. And it was hamstrung because the *Wehrmacht,* the SS, the Hitler Youth, the *Luftwaffe,* and the Nazi Party all tried to take charge of it—which often meant that, for all practical purposes, no one took charge of it. By 1947, it had mostly petered out. Perry Biddiscombe's two important books, *Werewolf!: The History of the National Socialist Guerrilla Movement 1944–1946* (Toronto: 1998) and *The Last Nazis: SS Werewolf Guerrilla Resistance in Europe 1944–1947* (Stroud, Gloucestershire and Charleston, S.C.: 2000) document what it did and failed to do in the real world.

I have tried to imagine circumstances under which the German resistance might have been much more effective. *The Man with the Iron Heart* is the result. In the real world, of course, the attack on Reinhard Heydrich that failed in this novel succeeded. Jozef Gabcik and Jan Kubis were the assassins. They both killed themselves under attack by the SS on 18 June 1942. The SS also wiped the Czech village of Lidice off the map in revenge for Heydrich's murder. A good recent biography of Heydrich is Mario R. Dederichs (Geoffrey Brooks, translator), *Heydrich: The Face of Evil* (London and St. Paul: 2006).

How would we have dealt with asymmetrical warfare had we met it in the 1940s in Europe rather than in the 1960s in Vietnam or in the present decade in Iraq? Conversely, how would the Soviets have dealt with it? I have no certain answers—by the nature of this kind of speculation, one can't come up with certain answers. Sometimes—as here, I hope—posing the questions is interesting and instructive all by itself.

German nuclear physicists really were brought to England for interrogation and then returned to Germany as described here. And the Germans really did leave ten grams of radium behind in Hechingen. Jeremy Bernstein, *Hitler's Uranium Club: The Secret Recordings at Farm Hall* (Woodbury, N.Y.: 1996) is the indispensable source for the episode. To this day, no one seems to know what became of the radium.

Unwary readers may suppose that no Congressman would say a President wanted to send troops anywhere to get their heads blown off for his amusement: words I've put in a Republican Congressman's mouth aimed at President Truman. But, as reported in the October 24, 2007, *Los Angeles Times,* California Democratic Representative Pete Stark did say that, aiming the charge at President Bush. Truth really can be stranger than fiction. A motion to censure Congressman Stark failed, but he did subsequently apologize.

ABOUT THE AUTHOR

HARRY TURTLEDOVE is an award-winning author of science fiction and fantasy. His alternate-history works include *The Guns of the South*; *How Few Remain* (winner of the Sidewise Award for Best Novel); the Worldwar saga: *In the Balance, Tilting the Balance, Upsetting the Balance,* and *Striking the Balance;* the Colonization books: *Second Contact, Down to Earth,* and *Aftershocks;* the Great War epics: *American Front, Walk in Hell,* and *Breakthroughs;* the American Empire novels: *Blood & Iron, The Center Cannot Hold,* and *Victorious Opposition;* and the Settling Accounts series: *Return Engagement, Drive to the East, The Grapple,* and *In at the Death.* Turtledove is married to fellow novelist Laura Frankos. They have three daughters: Alison, Rachel, and Rebecca.

ABOUT THE TYPE

This book was set in Sabon, a typeface designed by the well-known German typographer Jan Tschichold (1902–74). Sabon's design is based upon the original letter forms of Claude Garamond and was created specifically to be used for three sources: foundry type for hand composition, Linotype, and Monotype. Tschichold named his typeface for the famous Frankfurt typefounder Jacques Sabon, who died in 1580.